The Glass Kitchen

The Glass Kitchen

❖

Linda Francis Lee

St. Martin's Press
New York

THE GLASS KITCHEN. Copyright © 2014 by Linda Francis Lee. All rights reserved. Printed in the United States of America. For information, address St. Martin's Press, 175 Fifth Avenue, New York, N.Y. 10010.

www.stmartins.com

Design by Kathryn Parise

LIBRARY OF CONGRESS CATALOGING-IN-PUBLICATION DATA

Lee, Linda Francis.
   The Glass Kitchen / Linda Francis Lee. — First edition.
      p. cm
ISBN 978-0-312-38227-8 (hardcover)
ISBN 978-1-4668-5061-3 (e-book)
   1. Divorced women—Fiction.   2. Women cooks—Fiction.
3. Clairvoyance—Fiction.   4. Cooking—Psychological aspects.
5. Widowers—Fiction.   6. Manhattan (New York, N.Y.)—Fiction.
7. Texas—Fiction.   I. Title.
   PS3612.E225G53 2014
   813'.6—dc23

                                        2014000125

St. Martin's Press books may be purchased for educational, business, or promotional use. For information on bulk purchases, please contact Macmillan Corporate and Premium Sales Department at 1-800-221-7945, extension 5442, or write specialmarkets@macmillan.com.

First Edition: June 2014

10 9 8 7 6 5 4 3 2 1

Acknowledgments

❖

W HAT WOULD I HAVE DONE without great friends and family who helped in so many ways while I wrote this book? To all of them, I raise a glass in thanks.

Amelia Grey, Lisa Kleypas, M. J. Rose, Sarah MacLean, Alana Sanko, Jill and Regi Brack, Julie Blattberg, Lisa Chambers, and Liz Brack— good friends who were always ready with book talk and/or impromptu dinners.

Stella Brack and Anna Vettori—for a peek into today's Manhattan school world.

Joseph Bell, Peter Longo, Kevin Lynch, and Ron Smith—for lovely, long meals filled with amazing food and laughter. To Peter, for The Explorers Club, and Kevin, who who should have been a knight. To Joe, for teaching me the magic of ices. And it's hard to quantify how many times Ron saved one of my recipes.

Alessandro Vettori and his beautiful wife, Mary—for family dinners and elegant parties.

Jennifer Enderlin—a writer's dream, editor extraordinaire—for believing in this book and going above and beyond to make it the best it could be.

The amazing team at St. Martin's Press, who cares a great deal about books, most especially Sally Richardson, the late and greatly missed Matthew Shear, Lisa Senz, Alison Lazarus, John Murphy, John Karle, Dori Weintraub, and Jeff Dodes.

Carilyn Francis Johnson—for being the best sister, amazing best friend, and, as much as it pains me to admit it, still the best cook in the family.

And to Michael, as always, who is there during my cooking triumphs, but more important—given my predilection for adventures in the kitchen—is there to step in during my cooking catastrophes, ready to roll up his sleeves and help, or . . . eat whatever I put in front of him, with a smile on his face. What is that if not true love?

Cheers!

First Course

❖

Appetizer

Chile Cheese and Bacon-Stuffed
Cherry Tomatoes

One

❖

ON THE MORNING her sister went missing, Portia Cuthcart woke up to thoughts of blueberries and peaches.

The taste of fruit filled her mouth, so sweet, so real, as if she'd been eating in her dreams. With a groggy yawn, she scooted out of bed. She pulled on her favorite fluffy slippers and big-girl's robe, then shuffled into the tiny kitchen of the double-wide trailer on the outskirts of Willow Creek, Texas. Without thinking about what she was doing, she pulled blueberries from the icebox and peaches from the fruit bin.

She might have been only seven years old, but she was smart enough to know that her mother would have a fit if she pulled out knives, or did anything near the two-burner hot plate. Instead, Portia pulled the peaches apart, catching the sticky-sweet juice on her tongue as it ran down her fingers. She found a slice of angel food cake wrapped in plastic and plopped the fruit on top.

Just as she stood back, satisfied with what she had made, her parents tumbled into the trailer like apples poured out of a bushel basket, disorderly, frantic.

Portia's oldest sister, Cordelia, followed. "Olivia's missing," Cordelia stated with all the jaundiced arrogance of a thirteen-year-old convinced she had the answers to everyone's ills. "Disappeared," she clarified with a snap of her fingers, "just like that."

Portia knitted her brow, her hair a cloud of whipped-butter curls dancing around her face. Olivia was always in trouble, but she usually did bad stuff right in front of their eyes. "Nobody disappears just like that, Cordie. You're exaggerating."

Her mother didn't seem to hear. Mama stared at the fruit and cake.

"Don't be mad," Portia blurted. "I didn't use any knives."

Her mother dropped to her knees in front of Portia. "Peaches and blueberries. Olivia's favorites. Why did you make this?"

Portia blinked, pushing a curl out of her eye. "I don't know. I woke up thinking about them."

For a second, her mother looked stricken; then she pressed her lips together. "Earl," she said, turning to Daddy, "Olivia's down by the far horse pasture, near the peach tree and blueberry patch."

Her parents' eyes met before they glanced back at Portia. Then her mother stood and pushed Daddy out the door. Even though the emergency was over, Mama's face was still tense, her eyes dark.

Twenty minutes later, the missing eleven-year-old Olivia pranced up the three metal steps of the trailer in front of Daddy, her lips stained with blueberries, her dress splotched with peach juice, flowers tangled in her hair.

It was the first time food gave Portia an answer before a question had been asked.

Not an hour after Olivia was found, Portia and her mother were in the family's ancient pickup truck, bumping along the dirt roads of backwater Texas until they came to her grandmother's café, a place that had been handed down through generations of Gram's ancestors. The Glass Kitchen. Portia loved how its whitewashed clapboard walls and green tin roof, giant yawning windows, and lattice entwined with purple wisteria made her think of doll houses and thatch-roofed cottages.

Excited to see Gram, Portia jumped out of the old truck and followed her mother in through the front door. The melting-brown-sugar and buttery-cinnamon smells reminded her that The Glass Kitchen was not for play. It was real, a place where people came from miles around to eat and talk with Portia's grandmother.

Portia smiled at all the regulars, but her mother didn't seem to notice anyone, which was odd because Mama always used her best company manners wherever they went. But today she walked straight toward Gram, who sat at her usual table off to the side. Gram always sat in the same place, watching the goings-on, doling out advice, and making food recommendations for all those who asked. And everyone asked. Portia had a faint memory of a time when Gram actually did the cooking, but now she left it to others, to hired help who stayed hidden behind swinging doors.

"She has it," was all Mama said.

Gram sat back, the sun streaming through the windows, catching in the long gray hair she pulled back in a simple braid. "I suspected as much."

Portia didn't understand what was happening, then was surprised when Gram turned to her and beckoned her close. "You have a gift, Portia. A *knowing,* just like me, just like generations of your ancestors. Now it's my job to teach you how to use it."

Mama pressed her eyes closed, steepling her hands in front of her face.

Despite her mama's frown, Portia was excited about this knowing thing. It made her feel special, chosen, and as each day passed, she began to walk around with a new sense of purpose, pulling apart more peaches and making creations in a way that set her older sisters' teeth on edge. Cordelia and Olivia weren't nearly as happy about the special gift Portia supposedly had.

But four months later, the thick Texas air was sucked dry when the girls' daddy was shot dead in a hunting accident. Four months after that, their mama died, too. The official report cited cause of death as severe cardiac arrhythmia, but everyone in town said she'd died of a broken heart.

Stunned and silenced, Portia and her sisters moved in with Gram above the restaurant. Cordelia found comfort in books, Olivia in flowers. Portia found comfort when Gram started bringing her into the kitchen in earnest. But strangely, Gram didn't mention one thing about the knowing, much less teach her anything about it. Mostly Gram taught her the simple mechanics of cooking and baking.

Still, that worked. The Glass Kitchen was known to heal people with its slow-cooked meals and layered confections, and it healed Portia, too. Gradually, like sugar brought to a slow boil, Portia began to ease out of a brittle state and find a place for herself among the painted-wood tables and pitted silverware in a way Cordelia and Olivia never did.

And then it began to happen in earnest, like the dream of peaches and blueberries, but more real, more frequent.

Without a single one of those promised lessons from her grandmother, Portia began to see and taste food without having it in front of her, the images coming to her like instincts, automatic and without thought. She found that she knew things without having to be taught. Rich dark chocolate would calm a person who was hiding their anxiety. Hot red chili mixed with eggs first thing in the morning relieved symptoms of someone about to succumb to a terrible cold. Suddenly her world made sense, as if she had found a hidden switch, the meaning of what she was supposed to do blazing to life like a Christmas tree lighting up in a burst of color.

During that first school year, and the ones that followed, without her parents, Portia spent her days studying and her nights and weekends in the kitchen. During the summers, Portia and her sisters traveled to New York City to stay with Gram's sister. Great-aunt Evie had moved away forty years earlier, escaping a prescribed life that boxed her in. Once in New York, Evie became an actress on Broadway, famous enough to buy a town house on the Upper West Side.

"This place will be yours one day," Evie told the girls.

All three sisters loved the old town house that rose up from the city sidewalk like a five-layer wedding cake decorated with perfect fondant icing. Cordelia and Olivia promised each other that as soon as they could, they would move to New York City for good. Portia didn't believe for a second that either of them would do it.

But ten years after their parents' deaths, three years after Cordelia married, Portia woke up knowing she had to bake a five-layer cake with perfect fondant icing. Once the cake was finished, Portia stood back, her heart twisting, and knew Cordelia was leaving Texas. No one was surprised when Olivia followed her to New York six months later.

Portia missed her sisters, but her days were full. She became the main cook at The Glass Kitchen while Gram sat out front doling out advice and food choices. And still no lessons on the knowing.

One day Portia whipped up a mixed-up mess of sweet potatoes and asparagus, two items that never went together. But somehow, the way she made it, had people ordering more. Just as she served up the last portion, in walked the young lawyer and up-and-coming Texas state senator Robert Baleau, and her world shifted. Despite being born and raised in Willow Creek, he was as foreign to Portia as if he'd moved there from Greece. He was from the opposite side of town, from a world of debutante balls and heirloom pearls. With his sandy blond hair and laughing blue eyes, he charmed her, moved her with his devotion to serving the people, not to mention her.

Soon he began taking her with him as he traveled around the county to political functions. People all over the region loved Portia and said that she made a pretty boy more real. All she cared about was that she adored Robert.

The day he proposed, she threw her arms around him before she could think twice. "Yes, yes, yes!" she said as he laughed and twirled her around.

Surprisingly, Robert's wealthy parents approved. It was Gram who didn't.

"They'll hurt you," Gram said, scowling. "You're not part of their world, and you never will be."

But with every day that passed, more and more of Robert's world embraced Portia Cuthcart, the girl who grew up in a double-wide—even if the fancier people weren't particularly comfortable talking about The Glass Kitchen or the legendary Gram.

As the wedding grew near, another shift began, as slow as thyme breaking through the earth in spring. Robert began to notice that Portia knew things. At first, he laughed them off. But soon he began to tense every time she knew she needed to bake or cook something—like his mother's favorite lemon bars just before she invited Portia over for tea. Or tuna casserole in a tinfoil pan, the kind perfect for freezing and giving to someone in need—just before a neighbor's wife died.

One morning Portia woke knowing she had to make long, thick strands of pulled taffy that she wove into thin lengths of rope. Robert walked into the kitchen and came to a surprised stop when he saw the braided candy spread across the kitchen counter along with everything else she had known she needed. "This is unnatural," he said quietly.

Confused, Portia blinked. "What's unnatural about whipped cream, Saran Wrap, and ropes of taffy?"

She was almost certain Robert blushed and looked uncomfortable. "Portia, sweet, normal women don't know things that other people are thinking."

"My grandmother knows." Portia kept her hands moving, twisting the taffy before it could stiffen.

"I rest my case. If anyone isn't normal, it's your grandmother."

Her hands stilled. "Robert. There is nothing wrong with Gram. And there is nothing wrong with me."

He blinked, then blurted, "You're telling me that after I had sexual thoughts this afternoon, and you went out and put together the very things I fantasized about, that that's normal?"

As soon as the words were out of his mouth, his eyes widened. Portia was shocked, too, but then she laughed. "You were fantasizing about me? Me and ropes of taffy and whipped cream?"

She let her laughter turn into a sexy smile; then she wiped her hands and walked over to him. For half a second, the good Christian politician started to succumb, but then he took her hands and gave them a reassuring little squeeze, placing them against his heart. "I want to marry you, Portia. But I need you to be like other women. I need you to . . . not bake pies before the church announces a bake sale. I need you to be *normal*. Can you do that for me?"

Portia was stunned into silence.

Robert kissed her on the brow and refused to discuss it any further. She knew to his mind it was a simple yes-or-no question.

Since it was Monday, The Glass Kitchen was closed. As soon as Robert left, Portia went in search of her grandmother, needing to talk. Something had been off with Gram recently. Great-aunt Evie had died only a month before, leaving the town house to the girls. They all missed her, but with Gram it was as if a piece of her had died along with her sister.

Portia walked into the kitchen and realized that Gram wasn't there in the same second that another bout of knowing buckled her over at the waist.

Heart pounding, she started to prepare the meal that hit her so hard. Her famous cherry tomatoes stuffed with chile, cheese, and bacon, along with pulled pork, endive slaw, and potato pancakes with homemade catsup. She cooked, knowing she could do nothing else, though she was surprised when she realized she needed to set the table for only one.

Gram must have gone out for the day without telling her. But ten minutes after Portia sat down to eat, Gram walked into the kitchen from the back parking lot. At the sight of the meal and single place setting, Gram had to steady herself on the counter's edge.

Portia leaped up and started gathering another plate and silverware.

"No need," Gram said, setting her handbag down, then headed out of the kitchen.

Portia raced after her, but at the doorway to her grandmother's bedroom, Gram turned and pressed her dry hand to Portia's cheek. "It's time. I should have known you'd learn the knowing whether I taught you or not."

"What are you talking about?"

Gram smiled then, a resigned smile. But she didn't answer. She shut the bedroom door.

Portia returned to the kitchen and paced, hating that she didn't know what the meal meant. An eerie sense of dread rushed through her. She decided that if Gram wanted to go somewhere, she wouldn't let her take the car. She wouldn't allow her near the stove or the knives. She would keep her safe from whatever might be coming, anything that could have been predicted by the single place setting.

It was summer and hot, the painfully blue afternoon sky parched by heat and humidity. Gram didn't return to the kitchen until nearly four o'clock.

Portia jumped and ran across the hard-tile floor. "What's wrong?"

"It's time for you to take over The Glass Kitchen for good."

"What? No!"

Portia kept trying to solve whatever was wrong. But that ended when Gram stepped around her and headed for the back door of The Glass Kitchen.

"Where are you going?"

Gram didn't retrieve her handbag or keys. There was nothing Portia could take away to keep her from leaving.

"Gram, you can't leave!"

Gram didn't listen. She walked out the door, Portia following, pleading, "Gram, where are you going?"

But what Portia hadn't expected was that her grandmother would stop abruptly underneath the suddenly stormy Texas sky and raise her hands high. Lightning came down like the crack of God's hand, quick and reaching, striking Gram.

Shock, along with electricity, surged through Portia, knocking her off her feet like a rag doll thrown to the dirt by an angry child. Her blouse ripped at the shoulder, blood marking the white material like a brand.

The rest was a blur—people hurrying to them, the ambulance screaming into the yard. What stood out was that Portia knew she was responsible. If only she hadn't cooked the meal. If only she had set the table for two instead of one. If only she hadn't allowed her grandmother to walk out the door. If only she had never had even a glimpse of the knowing.

But *if onlys* didn't change anything. Gram was gone, all because of a meal Portia hadn't even begun to understand but had prepared.

Standing in the dirt lot, The Glass Kitchen behind her, Portia promised herself she wouldn't cook again.

A month later, she married Robert, then began shaping herself into the perfect Texas politician's wife, erasing everything she could of herself until she was a blank slate of polite smiles and innocuous conversation. She slammed the lid shut on the knowing.

And became normal.

Second Course

❖

Soup

Crab and Sweet Corn Chowder

Two

❖

THE SOUND OF TRAFFIC woke Portia.

Minutes ticked by before she realized where she was. New York City, on the Upper West Side, in the garden apartment of Great-aunt Evie's old town house, three years after her wedding, a month after her divorce from Robert Baleau.

Portia rolled over, covering her head with the pillow.

For the last three years, she had closed the door on visions of food until she had practically forgotten her unnerving ability was there. She'd worked hard to be like everyone else.

To be normal.

She groaned into the pillow. The only way she could be called normal was if normal meant stupid, not to mention naive. Why hadn't she realized that her husband didn't want her anymore? Why hadn't she figured out that the only real reason he wanted her at all was to make him seem more appealing to voters? More than that, why hadn't she known he would be so callous in getting rid of her after he'd come home and told her he wanted a divorce?

Not long after Robert had secured his place in politics, the supposedly good Christian politican developed a wandering eye, or maybe just gave in to it. Naturally, she had been the last to hear the whispers. But what she definitely hadn't heard until after the divorce papers were set in front of her was that the real reason he needed a divorce was because he had gotten one of his aides pregnant.

When the surprisingly quick divorce came through, she had fled Texas in a storm of devastation and betrayal, finding herself shipwrecked on the island of Manhattan, with nothing more than the two hastily packed suitcases and her grandmother's cherished Glass Kitchen cookbooks— thrown in even though she didn't want them.

Rolling back over, she tossed the pillow aside. She had arrived in New York City a month ago, but she had been in Great-aunt Evie's town house only since late last night, using an old key she had kept on her key chain. Before Evie had died, she had divided the town house up into three apartments, two of which she had rented out for income. Upon her death, one apartment had gone to each of the sisters.

Cordelia and Olivia had sold their floors. Before the divorce, Robert had wanted to sell her floor, too, with the garden out back, but she had never signed the contract. Thank God. While she was having a hard time imagining herself living in New York City, she wasn't crazy. Staying in Texas, where Robert and his pregnant new wife had already started to rule her world, was an awful thought. Here in New York, she had some-thing of her own. Everything was going as well as could be expected, given that her bank account was nearly as bare as Great-aunt Evie's kitchen cupboards.

The early morning air in New York was far cooler than it would have been in Texas, especially in the ancient bathroom, where the windows barely shut out the chilly gusts. Portia braced her hands on the old-fashioned sink, looked at herself in the mirror. Her eyes were still a deep violet blue, but the circles beneath them hinted at the stress that kept her awake at night. A year ago, she'd had sensibly cut, shoulder-length blond hair—perfect for a Texas politician's wife—tamed by a blow-dryer, hair spray, and a velvet headband. She scoffed. She'd been a cliché of big hair, sure, but what was she now? An even bigger cliché of the wronged wife kicked out of her own bed by her husband and the ex–best friend whom she herself had convinced Robert to hire as an aide. As her life spiraled out of control, so had her hair, growing and curling as it had when she was a child.

She turned on the old-fashioned spigot, the pipes clanging before spitting out a gush of water that she splashed on her face. Then she froze when her head filled with images of cake, thick swirls of buttercream frosting between chocolate layers. Her breath caught, her fingers curling around the sink edge. It had been three whole years since she'd been hit by images of food. But she knew the images were real—or would be if she allowed the *knowing* to take over.

She shook her head hard. She was normal now. The knowing was in the past. She hadn't done so much as toast a slice of bread in the last three years.

But the feeling wouldn't leave her alone, and with a groan she realized that the knowing was back, as if her move to New York, to this town house, had chiseled away every inch of normalcy she had cobbled together.

The images swirled through her. She needed to bake. Cake. A layered chocolate cake. With vanilla buttercream frosting.

The images were as clear as four-color photos from a coffee table book on baking. She could taste the mix of vanilla, butter, and cream whipped into a sugar frosting as if she had spooned it into her mouth. The chocolate smelled so real that a chill of awareness ran along her skin, pooling in her fingertips. She itched to bake.

But the last thing she needed in her life right now was to contend with something else she couldn't control.

She fought harder, but another bit of knowing hit. It wasn't just baking. She needed to cook, too. A roast.

She pressed one of her great-aunt's threadbare white towels to her face, resisting the urge. She had devoted the last three years to being the perfect wife. She had let her grandmother's Glass Kitchen go, closing the doors for good and selling the property for next to nothing to a developer who only wanted the land, splitting the money with her sisters. Her job had been to be at her husband's side at any function. Given that she had signed a pre-nuptial agreement, and with the meager settlement Robert had yet to pay her, she barely had two pennies to rub together. The last thing she needed to do was to waste money preparing a big meal. But the need wouldn't let go, and with a shudder gasp she gave in completely, the last of her crumbling walls coming down. Flowers, she realized. She needed flowers, too.

The knowing was rusty, coming at her in fits and starts, much like the water sluicing unevenly out of the faucet. Groaning, Portia dressed in jeans instead of a conservative skirt, and a big sweater instead of a silk blouse. She found flowered Keds in her great-aunt's closet, which she dusted off to wear rather than sensible heels. She wasn't Mrs. Robert Baleau anymore. She was Portia Cuthcart again, having taken back her maiden name.

The goal, her grandmother always said in the few times she actually said anything about the knowing, was to give in to the simple act of doing and have faith that eventually everything would make sense.

"Great," Portia muttered.

Once dressed, she went to her still-packed suitcases. A tiny bead of sweat broke out on her forehead when her fingers brushed against the spine of a Glass Kitchen cookbook. The handmade books had been passed down just as the knowing had, though just as with lessons on the knowing, Gram had never shared the books, either. Portia never knew they existed until after her grandmother's death.

Now she cracked the spine on the first of three volumes, her pulse beating in her temples. She recognized Gram's writing, notes scribbled between the crudely typed lines, new details learned and added, old ingredients scratched out. She turned the pages, her breath high in her chest, short bursts. Each generation of Cuthcart women had written in the margins, filling in newly learned wisdom along with the recipes. But even the recipes held gems of magic.

For perfectly boiled water, let it jump with enthusiasm, but not so energetically that it becomes exhausted, tiring the food it will boil.

And:

Never prepare a meal in anger, for the end result will fill the recipients with bile.

An hour later, when she came to the end of the volume, Portia jerked up, the book falling to the ground. Enough!

She scrambled out of the apartment, the cool morning air hitting her like a gasp of relief. With the Keds dangling in her fingers, she just stood there for a second, breathing, in, out, before she finally sat down to pull on the flowered sneakers.

She had just finished tying the last shoelace when she saw him.

He was tall, lean, with broad shoulders, dark brown hair. He looked primal, with a firm jaw and hard brow, walking toward her with a fluidity that seemed physically impossible, given his size. He had none of Robert's pretty-boy good looks, and there didn't seem to be anything practiced or politically correct about him. From the look of him, she imagined he was one of those New York businessmen she had heard about who traded stocks like third-world countries trade rulers, easily and ruthlessly.

Of course he wasn't dressed like a businessman. He wore a black T-shirt, long athletic shorts, and sweat-slicked hair. He had the smooth, tight muscles of someone who was athletic but didn't spend his days as an athlete. It wasn't hard to imagine him showering and then heading out of this tree-lined neighborhood on his way to some glass-and-steel office building in the concrete jungle of Midtown Manhattan.

She knew the minute he saw her, the way his eyes narrowed as if trying to understand something. She felt the same thing, as if she knew him, or should.

Images of food rushed through her head, surprising her. Fried chicken. Sweet jalapeño mustard. Mashed potatoes. Biscuits. And a pie. Big and sweet, strawberries with whipped cream—so Texan, so opposite this fierce New Yorker.

Good news or bad? she wondered before she could stop herself.

"No, no, no," she whispered. The images of food meant nothing at all. She wanted nothing to do with him, with any guy, at this point in her life. And she definitely didn't want anything to do with the kind she felt certain wielded power like a club. Robert charmed his way into control, but she knew on sight that this man would take it by force.

When he reached the steps, he stopped, looking at her with an intensity that felt both assessing and oddly possessive. It might have been an hour, or a second; no smile, no awkwardness, and her breathing settled low. She became acutely aware of herself, and him. Everything about this man pulled her in, which was ridiculous. He could be a serial killer. He could be demented, insane. With a body like that, he probably didn't eat sugar. A deal killer, for sure.

His head cocked to the side. "Do I know you?"

Portia smiled—she was Texan, after all, and had learned manners at a young age, even if it was out of a library book her mother "accidentally" forgot to return—and his expression turned to something deeper, richer like a salted hot fudge.

"No," she answered, the word nearly sticking in her throat. "Should you?"

Desire had caused the storm that left her shipwrecked in Manhattan— the desire her husband felt for another woman. But there had been her own desire, too, the desire for intensity and excitement in her own life, which she had suppressed when she married Robert. Sitting there, she felt that desire stir inside her like the first bubble rising in a pot of caramelizing sugar.

"I guess not," he said. "But you seem familiar." He put his foot on the bottom step, his hand on the railing, bringing him into her space with a confidence likely born of always getting what he wanted. "Do you run in the park?"

She glanced down at her flowered sneakers and wrinkled her nose.

"Okay, so I haven't seen you running," he said, his voice still rich and creamy but sliding into humor. Peppermint, she thought, the corner of his mouth hitching at one corner.

Portia laughed outright with the sort of ease she hadn't felt in months. Somehow this man who looked like he knew his way around darkness had chased hers away. "You don't approve of my shoes?"

"Is that what those are?" His lips hitched higher, a curl of his slowly drying hair falling forward and making him look more approachable.

"What are you, the fashion police?"

That caught him off guard. "Me? Hardly."

Portia stood up, skipped down, and stopped. Two steps still separated them, but given the difference in height, they stood nearly face-to-face. His laughter fled, and his eyes narrowed as he looked at her mouth. Her breathing slowed, and everything around her disappeared. She could make out the sparks of cognac in what she had thought were solid brown eyes. His nose was large, but somehow went perfectly with his strong face and jaw. His mouth was full, sensual. No one would call this man pretty, but something about the way his features came together drew her in. She felt a need, an urge to reach out, touch him. Which was crazy.

A truck turned the corner, hitting a crack in the asphalt with a loud bang, and she blinked. The man straightened.

Portia glanced around, took in the back side of the Dakota apartment building with its Gothic façade, antiquated moat, and wrought-iron balustrade around the perimeter, as if everything in her world hadn't shifted at the sight of this man.

He straightened abruptly, that sense of control settling back around him. "Can I help you with something?"

"No. No. I was just tying my shoelaces."

"Ah, then, fine."

He started up the stairs. She went stiff.

He stopped and raised his hands. "I live here."

"You live here? As in, you live in this place? Right here?"

His brow furrowed. "Yes."

This was her upstairs neighbor. More specifically, this was Gabriel Kane, the owner of the rest of the town house, the man she—or rather, Robert—had agreed to sell her apartment to before she refused at the last minute.

"Then these are your steps. Wow! Great place," Portia managed inanely.

Initially, she had sent word that she wasn't prepared to sell, at least not yet. No contracts had been signed. She had needed time to get her thoughts together. That was a month ago. Then, the minute she made the final decision that she was keeping the property, she had left a message with Gabriel Kane's lawyer herself, explaining the unexpected changes in her life.

She had apologized up and down but hadn't heard back. Granted, she had only left the message the day before, but she had assumed she'd hear right away. She had slipped into the apartment late last night, using the old key in hopes of avoiding Kane for as long as possible.

She didn't doubt for a second that the man was furious with her for backing out of the contract after he'd already bought the rest of the building from her sisters. There was no question in her mind that he would try forcing her to sell. Chicken that she was, she was counting on his lawyer to convince him otherwise. Even she knew a deal wasn't a deal until documents were signed.

"Have a great day!"

She practically leaped to the sidewalk, catching sight of an old man who was sitting in the window next door, peering out at her as she dashed toward Columbus Avenue.

Three

✦

"Some things are true whether you believe them or not."

Gram's favorite saying. She had repeated it to Portia and her sisters more times than any of the three cared to count.

The minute Portia turned onto Columbus she fell against the nearest wall. Her knees were weak, her breath coming out in uneven jerks. Whether she wanted to believe it or not, Gabriel Kane had made her think of food. A meal. A meal at odds with everything he appeared to be and made her acutely aware of being a stranger in a strange land.

Thankfully, once her breathing started to ease, so did images of fried chicken and sweet jalapeño mustard. She remained against the wall for a bit longer as the images faded even more until they were gone, and she pushed away on a ragged breath and spaghetti legs. Seeing the man mixed in with thoughts of a meal was a fluke, she reassured herself. The images of food had nothing to do with the man or her apartment. And she felt certain she was right when her thoughts and tingling fingertips circled back to chocolate cake.

Next thing she knew, Portia hurried into the Fairway Market on

Broadway. The grocery store was unlike anything she had seen in Texas. Bins of fruit and vegetables lined the sidewalk, forming narrow entrances into the market. Inside, the aisles were crowded, no inch of space wasted. In the fresh vegetables and fruit section she was surrounded by piles of romaine and red-leaf lettuce, velvety thick green kale that gave away to fuzzy kiwi and mounds of apples. Standing with her eyes closed, Portia waited a second, trying not to panic. Then, realizing there was no help for it, she gave in to the knowing, not to the fluke meal inspired by Gabriel Kane, but to the chocolate cake and roast that had hit her earlier.

She started picking out vegetables. Cauliflower that she would top with Gruyère and cheddar cheeses; spinach she would flash fry with garlic and olive oil.

In the meat department, she asked for a standing rib roast to serve eight. Then she stopped. "No," she said to the butcher, her eyes half-closed in concentration, "just give me enough for four."

Portia made it through the store in record time. Herbs, spices. Eggs, flour. Baking soda. A laundry list of staples. At the last second, she realized she needed to make a chowder. Crab and corn with a dash of cayenne pepper. Hot, spicy.

Within the hour, she was back at the apartment and had the vegetables cleaned and set aside, the roast ready to go into the old oven that thankfully worked. The chowder done. Now it was time to start the cake.

The lower cabinet creaked when she pulled it open. Inside, she found an old Dormeyer Mix-Well stand mixer, plus several mixing bowls that had been washed so many times, the once bold red was a splotchy pink. The simple act of sifting flour soothed her, like meeting up with a once-cherished old friend. She closed her eyes as she mixed in the salt and baking powder.

She had to rinse the scuffed Revere Ware pots and pans before she started melting the Baker's Chocolate in a makeshift double boiler. Once that was done she moved on to the sugar, butter, and eggs until the rich chocolate layers of cake were baked and cooled. When she finally swirled the last bit of vanilla buttercream into place, Portia stood back with a sense that all was as it should have been. But she still had no sense of why she'd made the meal.

Good news or bad?

Frustration flashed though her. But she pushed it aside and focused on placing tall wooden stools around the old kitchen island. Four place settings. Four seats.

With her sisters living in New York, it stood to reason they would come over. But including Portia, that made only three. Who was the fourth?

The man upstairs?

Portia instantly shook the thought away. A completely different meal had sprung into her head when she saw him.

She glanced at the table. She still needed flowers.

The small corner market had rows of fresh flowers in white plastic buckets. Standing, the early fall sun on her shoulders, she opened her mind. She assessed the fuchsia roses and violet freesias, vibrant orange and pink gerbera daisies. Willowy white snapdragons.

It took a second before she realized what she needed. Daisies. Bright yellow daisies.

Looking down at the bucket of cheerful flowers, Portia felt light-headed. If she had to create a meal to cheer people up, then whatever lay ahead had to be bad.

Anxiety rose through her like dough rising in a towel-covered bowl. The image of the pulled-pork meal and her grandmother stepping into the lightning flashed through her. She hated the anxiety involved with the knowing and food. She hated not understanding, hated waiting for something bad to happen.

Portia cursed herself for taking a glimpse inside the Pandora's box of knowing. For three years she had kept the lid shut. If nothing else, she'd had peace. She needed to keep it that way. End of story.

She wanted to chuck the roast and cake in the garbage. But at this point, whatever was coming couldn't be stopped.

Or could it? Had there been a way she could have stopped her grandmother from being struck down by lightning?

Portia still didn't know why the sight of the meal had sent her grandmother out into the lightning. She only knew that if she hadn't made that meal and set the table for one, Gram never would have gone out into that storm.

Nothing had changed.

"No, Gram," Portia whispered. "Nothing about the Cuthcart knowing is a gift. Not to you. Not to me."

Taking a deep breath, she pushed the memory away, pulled out her cell phone, and called Cordelia, then Olivia, to find out if they were okay. Anxiety circled in her stomach, trepidation tapping behind her eyes. She was forced to leave messages.

She raced through a mental list of what else it could be. Robert?

Portia felt a shiver of hope, but guilt quickly followed. If something had happened to Robert, the knowing would surely have had her buying champagne.

Back at the apartment, she put the flowers on the table and started to pace. Finally, hoping for a distraction, she turned on Evie's ancient television. It was tuned to a news program and still working.

"The investment firm Atlantica General has confirmed the loss of two billion dollars of investor money. It is being reported that the loss was due to fraudulent trades by the firm's Low Risk group. If allegations of malfeasance are true, no doubt people will go to jail over this."

Portia's heartbeat flared, slowed, and then flared again. Cordelia's husband, James, worked for Atlantica General. Worse, James worked in the Low Risk group. Since starting at Atlantica ten years earlier, he had been a rising star, becoming one of the most successful young bankers at the giant.

She sat down hard, only to jump up again when someone knocked at the door.

Portia raced over and yanked the door open to find her other sister, Olivia.

"Did you hear?" Olivia said.

"About James?"

"Yes," her middle sister said without so much as a hello or hug as she walked in the door.

Back in Texas, Portia knew that the three Cuthcart sisters had been considered three kinds of blondes. Cordelia, the oldest, was pretty with her straightened hair and patrician nose. If Cordelia had been born to resemble a queen, middle-sister Olivia had been born to be the nymph. With her Cupid's-bow mouth and violet eyes, she lured men in to the rocky shores of her world. Portia knew that while her sisters were queens and nymphs, she was considered cute, the girl next door. There were worse things to be, sure, but just once she would have liked to be the beautiful one or the exotic one.

Today, Olivia wore olive-colored cargo pants that hung low on her hips, a multicolored yoga top that showed off her beautifully sculpted arms, and some sort of shoe that looked equal parts comfort and fashion. Olivia was the wild child of the family, living in a walk-up apartment on the Lower East Side, a serial dater who had broken more than a few men's hearts. Why she refused to settle down was a mystery to her sisters, a mystery that Cordelia and Portia had dissected from every angle but still didn't understand. Though Portia was starting to think that Olivia was just smarter than they were. Than she was, anyway.

Olivia glanced at the table and raised a brow, but didn't say anything.

Portia knew that look. Olivia didn't particularly care one way or the other about the knowing. As far as she was concerned, it had nothing to do with her. But that didn't mean she liked it.

"God, I hope that fourth setting isn't for James," Olivia stated, turning from the table. "Though you'd have to think he's probably surrounded by lawyers. Or cops."

Portia shivered.

Despite the crispness of her words, Portia knew why her sister was there. Long ago their mother had made her daughters promise that no matter where they were or how angry they were at each other at the time, if one of them needed the other, they would be there. No questions asked.

Which meant Portia knew what would happen next.

Cordelia sailed into the apartment like a perfectly dressed mother duck, not a hair out of place on her head, her subtle hints of makeup perfectly done, her blue eyes alert, determined as she set her expensive handbag on a chair.

At thirteen, Cordelia had perfected the jaundiced arrogance of a girl who believed she had all the answers. At thirty-five, Cordelia still felt she had all the answers. Where Olivia had always been considered the passionate sister, the oldest Cuthcart girl never showed any sort of emotion at all.

"We saw the news," Portia said. "Is everything okay with James?"

Cordelia's always stiff upper lip trembled.

"Jesus, Cordie," Olivia stated with all the calm certainty that there was no problem too big to be solved. "Is James getting arrested?"

"Olivia," Portia barked, just as Cordelia blurted, "No!"

Portia sagged. "What a relief."

"Not a relief," Cordelia stated. "He wasn't a party to the bad deals, but part of the two billion dollars was every penny of our life savings."

Cordelia stood there in her cashmere and pearls, her standard uniform for all the charity work she did in the city, tears in her eyes.

Portia wrapped her arms around Cordelia. Olivia just stood there. Portia gave her a look, after which Olivia gave a silent sigh, then came over and joined the hug.

"I am not crying," Cordelia stated, even as tears rolled.

"Of course not," Portia said.

"Nope, not you," Olivia added.

They stood that way for a few seconds, their hearts beating nearly as one until Portia broke the spell. "Stop stepping on my toes, Olivia."

Olivia burst out laughing. "I knew you couldn't take more than a few seconds of hugging."

"I can take hugging, Olivia. You're the one who can't take it. That's why you stepped on my toes."

But then they turned back to Cordelia.

"You're going to be okay," Portia said.

"Absolutely," Olivia added.

Cordelia stepped away, smoothed her bob, straightened her blouse, and drew a deep breath. "I love you guys," she whispered, and quickly cleared her throat. "It really is okay. But I'm stressed and I can't show it in front of James."

If Olivia was like a decadent chocolate-covered strawberry, and Portia a pineapple-and-spice hummingbird cupcake, then Cordelia was peanut brittle, still sweet, though with something more substantial added by way of peanuts, but unbendable.

"James says it'll be fine. So it will be." She raised her chin. "I'm sure it's not every cent of our life's savings. I'm overreacting, which is childish." Tears welled once more; Cordelia drew a deep breath and shook them away. "I just needed to let it out, then see that it isn't so dire. I couldn't do that at home."

Portia shot Olivia a quick glance, but she didn't say what she was thinking—that Cordelia always put a good face on a bad situation.

Cordelia caught sight of the food in the little kitchen, then turned and stared at the wooden stools around the island, the plates, the flowers. But when Olivia caught Cordelia's eye and raised a brow, Cordelia looked away. Portia had asked her oldest sister once why she hated the knowing so much that she generally pretended it didn't exist. Cordelia had dismissed the question out of hand. But Portia still wondered.

The three of them pulled up around the makeshift table and served each other plates piled high with Portia's feast. No one mentioned the unspoken question hanging in the air. Who was the last seat for? Instead, Portia and Olivia caught up on every bit of Texas gossip until Cordelia was able to breathe again, quickly turning back into the oldest sister.

"It's time to talk. I'm not the only one with problems," Cordelia said, breaking in. "You've moved in here, Portia. But have you figured out how you're going to support yourself?"

Olivia shook her head and sat back. "Sheez, Cordie, give her a break. She's barely divorced."

"*Barely* doesn't have any influence on a bank balance."

"She's right, Olivia. But I'm working on it."

"Really?" Cordelia got one of her know-it-all looks. "What are you thinking about doing?"

"Okay, so I don't know yet, Cord. But something will come to me."

"Let's make a list of possibilities."

Olivia groaned. "You and your lists."

Portia agreed. More than that, she knew this wasn't headed anywhere good. "Maybe later."

"There's no time like the present," Cordelia stated, her cheer exaggerated and fake.

If Portia hadn't known that her sister mainly wanted to distract herself from her own problems, she would have fought harder. As it was, she didn't know how to say no when her sister said, "Let's brainstorm."

"Cordelia—"

"It'll be fun!" Even more fake. "Just us girls, letting dreams run wild."

Olivia all but rolled her eyes. "You know she's not letting this go."

"Fine. I could be an assistant," Portia stated.

"Assistant to whom?"

Only Cordelia, and grammar zealots, would use *whom* in a casual conversation. Portia considered. "To an executive."

"You don't type." This from Olivia.

Portia glared at her one supporter. "Fine." She glanced back at Cordelia. "Then maybe I could be an editor."

"As if they don't type? Besides, an editor of what?"

Portia shot Cordelia a look. "Books."

"You barely graduated from high school—"

"I graduated!"

"But the only class you liked was Home Economics. I can't believe any school still offers those classes. Definitely don't tell anyone in New York about it."

"Why not?"

Cordelia didn't bother to answer. "I know what you could do. If anyone asks, tell them you went to cooking school. They teach cooking in Home Ec, right? They'll eat that up. New Yorkers are all about food." Cordelia hesitated, then said, "You know that."

Portia eyed her. "I don't cook."

Her sisters glanced at the meal in front of them.

"This was an aberration," she said. "I do not cook. Not anymore. You know that."

Cordelia and Olivia exchanged a glance.

Portia knew they were going to say something, something she wouldn't want to discuss. "Stop. Really. Don't worry about me. I'll get a job. First thing tomorrow I'll start working on my résumé."

Finally Cordelia stood. "I take it the bathroom in this place works?"

"No, but there's a Porta-Potty in the garden."

Cordelia's eyes went wide.

"Just joking."

This time, everyone laughed, even Cordelia, the tension in the room easing.

Cordelia headed out of the kitchen, and Olivia cupped her hands around a mug of hot mint tea laced with honey. Portia started to clear the table. But when she reached for the unused place setting, she heard Cordelia in the tiny foyer.

"Who are you?" the oldest sister was asking.

Portia glanced out of the kitchen and saw a young girl, eleven, maybe twelve, standing just inside the front door. Her curly light brown hair puffed like a cloud around creamy white skin, making her big brown eyes look even bigger. Freckles stood out on her nose, perfect and contained, like crayon dots drawn by a child. While the dots were meticulous, the girl was not. She wore a navy blue sweater over a white blouse that was mostly untucked from a navy blue plaid skirt. Her headband was askew, one kneesock up, the other down, spilling into black flats, finishing off what was clearly one of the private school uniforms that children wore in Manhattan.

"I'm Ariel, from upstairs." She looked around. "I heard all the noise. The door was open." Her pursed mouth dared them to contradict her. "Are you squatters or something?"

Olivia laughed out loud.

"No," Portia said. "We're not squatters. I live here."

The girl studied them, as if trying to get her head around anyone living in this run-down apartment. "But you weren't here yesterday."

"I moved in last night."

Cordelia scowled. "I still can't believe you moved here. You should have kept staying with me."

When Portia first arrived in New York, she had gone straight to Cordelia, not sure what to do about the apartment. But as with so many things with Portia, she had woken up yesterday morning knowing what she had to do. Next thing she knew, she made the call to the lawyer, then moved in here.

"And the rest of you are, what . . . friends?" the girl asked.

"Sisters."

"You must be Gabriel Kane's child," Cordelia said.

"You know my dad?"

"Olivia and I sold our apartments to your father."

The girl wasn't paying attention. She eyed the food.

Cordelia shifted into mother mode. "Are you hungry?"

"Starving. The new housekeeper-slash-cook made dinner, but it was really weird, like scary weird, and seriously, who wants to eat scary food?"

"Have a seat." Cordelia retrieved a plate as if it were her own home and loaded it with food. Just before she set it down at the extra place setting, she froze.

Her eyes narrowed, and her mouth pinched. Portia hated the battle she sensed going on in her sister. But she didn't repeat Gram's words.

Some things are true whether you believe them or not.

"Sit," Cordelia finally said, setting down the plate. "Eat, before it gets cold."

Four

⁙

THEY SAT BACK DOWN on the stools while Ariel gobbled up her food and Portia, Cordelia, and Olivia stared at her.

"What?" Ariel said, glancing up through a curtain of wispy bangs, the fork halting halfway to her mouth. "You've never seen a girl eat before?"

Cordelia smiled in the condescendingly maternal way she had perfected by age ten. "Perhaps we've never seen a young girl eat so fast."

Ariel shrugged, unbothered by the implied reprimand. "Like I said, I'm starved."

Cordelia started to speak, but Portia cut her off. "Let her eat in peace, Cord."

Olivia laughed. "Yes, eat. Though tell us," she added, studying the girl, "who all lives in your apartment?"

Ariel looked confused. "*Who all*? What kind of word is that?"

"It's a Texas thing," Portia clarified. "You know, like *y'all* for *you all.*"

"I don't get it. Who adds *all* to *you*?"

"It doesn't matter," Olivia interjected, waving the words away. "I just wondered who lives with you upstairs."

Olivia said the words casually, but Portia knew better. She knew her sister. Olivia was always interested in the possibility of a new man.

"Just me, my dad, and Miranda."

Olivia scowled. "Miranda?"

"My sister."

"Oh, really." Olivia's smile returned, slow, delicious. "So, your dad's single?"

"Olivia," Portia and Cordelia both snapped.

Cordelia no doubt said that because Olivia was being rude. Portia wanted to think she did it for the same reason, but the truth was that at the mention of the man upstairs, she felt, well, possessive. The thought of Olivia's lack of inhibition and beautifully sculpted body in relation to Gabriel Kane didn't sit well—which was ridiculous, since Portia was barely divorced and certainly not interested in Gabriel herself. But there it was.

"What?" Olivia asked, her tone defensive. "What did I say?"

Cordelia sighed. "One, it's inappropriate to ask a man's child if he's single."

"And two," Portia picked up the thread, "you only like guys who are . . ." She hesitated, glanced at Ariel, and then leaned closer. "T-A-K-E-N."

Ariel narrowed her eyes.

Olivia scoffed. "Now who is being inappropriate in front of the K-I-D?"

"Hello," Ariel said. "I can S-P-E-L-L."

Olivia pushed more food in front of her. "Keep eating." She turned back to her sisters. "I do *not* like guys who are taken."

Portia and Cordelia rolled their eyes.

"I don't," Olivia persisted, reaching up to twist her mass of curls into a loose knot on her head. When she let go, her hair fell in a tumble around her shoulders. "Martin wasn't taken. Neither was Daniel. And what about George?"

"True. But let's see. Martin, you broke up with because he had a cat."

"Sue me. I'm a dog person."

"Well then, Daniel should have been perfect for you: He had a dog," Cordelia said. "I can't remember why you broke up with him, just that you did via text message."

"Does anyone under the age of fifty use the word *via*?" Olivia shot back. "How old are you really?"

"You know very well I am"—she glanced at Ariel—"twenty-eight."

"Not!" Olivia and Portia laughed. "Thirty-five if you're a day!"

"Don't change the subject," Cordelia snipped. "We're not finished. You mentioned George."

Olivia shrugged and looked away.

Cordelia tsked. "Poor George. He would have been better off with a text. He only found out about your change of heart when he came home to your all's apartment and saw you'd thrown his clothes out the window."

Ariel gaped, fork forgotten in her hand.

"He deserved it," Olivia stated with calm certainty. "Besides, the apartment was a fifth-floor walk-up. I wasn't going to spend hours walking up and down those stairs taking everything down to the street. That's a rite of passage. Every woman should throw a guy's clothes out a window once in her life."

Cordelia scoffed. "A rite of passage is a sorority hazing or a bat mitzvah."

"Maybe for you, Miss Marry-the-first-guy-you-date."

"I dated!"

Portia groaned. "Please stop."

Olivia and Cordelia ignored her.

"You only dated one other guy, Cordelia, and that didn't turn out so well."

"What happened?" Ariel asked.

Without Portia noticing, the girl had dumped everything out of her backpack and had retrieved a notebook. She sat now, poised with pen in hand over an empty page, like a reporter, or overeager detective. Next to her plate, a smorgasbord of paraphernalia littered the table. Several pens of assorted colors, a calculator covered in $E = mc^2$ stickers, a wild-haired rendering of Einstein painted in fluorescent-green nail polish on an inhaler, a half-eaten KitKat bar, a mini-bottle of antibacterial gel, and multicolored knit socks with separate coverings for each toe, like gloves for feet. Portia loved the socks.

"What happened to the only other guy you dated?" Ariel persisted, ready to write.

"Nothing," the three sisters said in unison, which brought them back together, the energy between them shifting.

Olivia touched Cordelia's hand. That was the way with Olivia. Wild and carefree, blazing through anything bad with a bold fearlessness, but underneath a caring that Portia sometimes thought her sister worked hard to hide.

"Dating practically only one guy has served you well," Olivia said. "You and James are great together, and you'll survive whatever is going on now."

Cordelia gave her a determined smile. "Thank you, sweetie."

They shared a comfortable moment, Portia just barely realizing that Ariel studied them like a scientist scrutinizing a foreign species.

Olivia didn't seem to notice at all, lost in her own thoughts, until she wrinkled her nose, then leaned closer. Portia could see the sparkle in her eyes that she knew meant trouble.

"So it goes without saying that you and James are perfect, yada yada," Olivia said with another wave of her hand. "But let's just pretend. If you *had* dated anyone else before you left Texas, who would it have been? Brody, right? You were madly in love with Brody. You would have slept with—"

"Olivia!" Portia barked, nodding toward Ariel. "Inappropriate. On so many levels."

Olivia just shrugged innocently, though she didn't look innocent at all, and squeezed Cordelia's hand.

Ariel shook her head and rose, wandering out of the kitchen, surprising them when music suddenly blared. "Oops," she called out from the living room. "Sorry."

"It's Evie's old radio," Olivia said.

The three of them pushed up from the stools and walked through the arch that led to the rest of the apartment. "Remember how Evie would turn it on and make us dance with her?" Portia said.

"Yeah, and not to classical music."

"Swing."

"And rock."

"Punk!" Olivia cried out with a laugh.

Portia couldn't help herself: She twirled the dial, and the minute an old eighties punk song came on, she started dancing. "Come on! Let's dance!"

The others stared at her. But then Portia pulled Olivia in. Once Olivia got going, they turned to Cordelia.

"Oh, no. I'm too old for this."

"You're never too old for dancing. Besides, just a minute ago you swore you were twenty-eight."

Portia dragged her onto the floor, and she felt her sister's stress start melting away. All three of them danced and flailed. They turned in hops and sweeps toward Ariel, who looked half-wistful, half-disdainful, and they extended their hands.

"No way. I don't know how to dance."

"Knowing how doesn't matter," Olivia bellowed.

Then suddenly Ariel was in their midst, gyrating and waving her arms, shouting out random words from the chorus.

"Dance, baby!"

At the end of the number, Olivia swirled the dial, then smiled. "I love this one." She turned it up louder, then sang along to a crooning Brad Paisley ballad. She hooked her arm through Cordelia's, and Portia saw their older sister shake her head, but she smiled. And soon they all were singing. Even Ariel got into the act. Until the music snapped off mid-verse.

"What's going on here?"

Portia nearly tripped at the sight of Gabriel Kane.

He appeared every bit as powerful as he had earlier in the day, though now there was no trace of a smile. If possible, everything dark about his eyes grew darker as he took her in, his gaze sliding over her in a heated sear. She could have sworn he seemed confused, as if he couldn't reconcile the woman on the steps with the woman standing in the apartment.

"Dad!" Ariel laughed. If she was aware of the darkness, she didn't show it. "Come dance it out with us!"

Dad didn't look amused.

"Ariel, go upstairs."

Ariel's smile turned to a gape. "What did I do?"

"Upstairs."

"Dad!"

"Up. Stairs."

Portia watched Ariel march to the kitchen, stuff all her belongings back into her backpack, then sulk off. Cordelia, she noticed, quickly smoothed her already smooth hair, looking surprisingly uncomfortable. Olivia, on the other hand, definitely wasn't put off by Gabriel's tone. She looked him up and down. "Hi, I'm Olivia," she said, stepping closer.

Portia felt an instant flash of irritation.

"Good God, Olivia," Cordelia groaned, walking forward and extending her hand. "I'm Cordelia Callahan. Olivia and I sold you our portions of the town house."

"Gabriel Kane." He shook her hand.

He nodded briefly to Olivia, polite, but that was all, before turning back to Portia. She felt that same sense of vertigo she had experienced on the front steps, the world reeling a bit at the sight of him.

"This is our sister Portia," Cordelia put in.

Gabriel didn't look away from Portia. "We met. This morning."

Cordelia gaped for one silent second before saying, "You've met?"

Olivia only considered her.

"Sort of," Portia conceded.

Gabriel's eyes narrowed. "I didn't realized she was the woman who—"

The words broke off, and Portia filled in the gap: "*who backed out of selling me the apartment.*"

He brow creased, his voice growing hard. "Why didn't you tell me who you were earlier?"

She grimaced and shrugged; the best answer she could come up with without having to admit she had hoped to avoid him like a girl in grade school.

His frown deepened, but Cordelia stepped forward, wearing a determinedly cheerful Texas welcome. "Would you like something to eat, Mr. Kane? Portia made more than enough food."

He glanced back into the kitchen, looking at the four used place settings. Then he turned to Portia. "You fed my daughter?"

"I hope that's okay," she said, forcing a smile. "She was hungry. As Cordelia said, we had plenty. I can make you a plate, too." *Please say no,* she prayed.

He looked like he wanted to say something, though something that had nothing to do with food. But after what looked like a frustrated second, he shook his head. "No, but thank you. And thank you for feeding Ariel." He started to leave, then turned back. "We need to discuss the apartment."

Portia smiled big. "Of course! We'll discuss tomorrow."

Though she knew she would do everything in her power to avoid him like the plague. The last thing she wanted was to discuss anything with Gabriel Kane.

Five

❖

ARIEL KANE WAS ALMOST entirely certain she was disappearing. Using every millimeter of her massively smart brain, she was trying to figure out if it was even possible for a person to disappear. So far she hadn't come up with any sort of quantifiable answer despite the fact that she wrote everything she could down in her journal. Anything that seemed important, she took notes on. The only thing that was definite, however, was that she was definitely starving, even though barely an hour ago the ladies downstairs had shoveled heaping piles of really good food onto her plate. But not even the roast or cake made her feel less hungry.

Hungry or not, Ariel had liked sitting there while they gabbed away. Portia, the one who seemed to live there, with her sandy blond hair and giant blue eyes, was pretty but tired looking, like a favorite doll who had been played with too much. Then there was Olivia, the middle sister, Ariel had learned, the same kind of pretty as Portia, those blue-blue eyes and long curly hair, only wilder, alive, like if you touched her you'd feel a zap. And last, Cordelia, the only one who seemed like an adult, again with the blue-blue eyes and really blond hair, only hers was straight, perfect, not one thing about her out of place. Ariel had seen tons of women like that, mothers of other girls, both in New Jersey and now here in New York.

Whatever. There had been something nice about the way the sisters yakked away, like everything in the world was normal, a world where people didn't disappear. Ariel liked that best. Then they started dancing, which was really embarrassing because they were so bad.

At first she had felt bad seeing the three sisters dancing together, leaving her out. Then they had turned to her, pulling her into their circle. They didn't even notice that her dancing was as bad as theirs. Even worse, maybe. Her throat swelled like a big baby's just thinking about it. Only then her dad had shown up and ruined it.

He was pretty good at that, given that he had pretty much ruined her life. If things were different, she'd be back in her old room in New Jersey instead of sitting on the fourth floor of this town house. Her dad just up and moved them here six months ago, never bothering to ask if she wanted a new room, or a new bed, or even a new life.

The only good news was that she knew for a fact that her dad hadn't sold their old house. It still had all their old furniture in it. With any luck, he'd give up this New York City nonsense and move them back where they belonged.

She pulled out her journal and started to write, this time because she was supposed to. More specifically, the Shrink her dad had hired said she had to write out her feelings about her mom.

Ariel hated this kind of journal writing. It made her think about Mom, which made her feel like a bee buzzing in a jar, banging around trying to get out. Sure, her mom had died. And sure, she could hardly breathe whenever she thought about it. But Ariel was not some below-average preteen who needed help, which was exactly what she had told her dad. He had carted her and her sister, Miranda, off to an idiot therapist anyway. So she mainly used her journal to write down her observations about the world.

During her first visit with the Shrink, Ariel had sat in the guy's office on a creepy black leather sofa. When he started by asking her how she was feeling, she refused to give in to the tears that burned in her throat, and responded by asking him what self-respecting medical professional had black leather anything, especially in his office. He had looked at her, didn't bother to answer, and scribbled something on his notepad.

After that, she had simply said "No Comment" to everything else he asked, interjecting observations about the weather every once in a while to shake things up, until finally the guy realized she wasn't going to start talking away all of a sudden. He said fine. Since she wouldn't talk to him, she should write down her feelings in a journal.

Next thing she knew, her dad had gone out and bought her a pink diary with a miniature key. Hello, she was almost thirteen, not eight. When she mentioned this, directly after asking her dad if he'd like to join her for a cocktail before dinner—which he either didn't hear or intentionally ignored—he brought home a fancy journal with a leather cover. Like she was some sort of self-help freak. Again, nearly thirteen. Not thirty.

On the bright side, it did give her an idea for a title for her journal. *Musings of a Freak*. Intelligent, a little off-center. In a word, her. Ariel Kane.

So, anyway, she was supposed to write down her feelings. Truthfully, if she managed to get beyond the sick feeling that she constantly had about her mom, what she felt was cramped. Her dad, who never used to be at home when her mom was alive, suddenly went all *I'm going to be the perfect father* on them, pulling up stakes in Montclair, New Jersey, moving Ariel and her sister to the Upper West Side, into a town house that was like a hundred years old.

Since they'd moved here, all her dad did was work on the place (or should she say, boss other people around while they worked on the place), sit at the big desk in the downstairs office, reading *The Financial Times*, studying computer screens—basically making sure his empire stayed, well, empirick—and meddle in her life. Correction: *ruin* her life.

But the fact was, there was something about her dad that made people do what he told them. When he walked into a room, people quieted. When he asked a question, people embarrassed themselves trying to come up with the answer. He wasn't handsome, not like her uncle Anthony, whom everyone said was totally beautiful. But still, her dad didn't have to say much to have people jumping through hoops to do his bidding. At least that was the case with everyone but her older sister, Miranda.

Miranda was sixteen and had been forced to leave her boyfriend behind when they moved into the city. Ariel had seen the guy once only even back in New Jersey, since Miranda did a really great job of keeping him out of their dad's sight. Dad would combust if he found out Miranda had a boyfriend. While Ariel couldn't say the guy was anything to write home about, clearly Miranda thought he was, since now she spent most of her time slamming doors and throwing herself across her bed, going on and on about how unfair life was.

No question Dad needed more to do with his time.

For a while after Mom died, all three of them had walked around like zombies in a movie. For six months they had barely put one foot in front of the other. Then, out of nowhere, just as the school year ended and summer was starting, Dad came home and told them it was time to move on.

Move on?

Like people could do that?

Though really, moving to New York had made it possible to turn the whole dead-mom thing into a secret. Ariel had learned the hard way that people completely freaked if they heard.

So, in June they had moved into the city. In July, she and her sister had started with the Shrink. In September, she and Miranda had started new schools. Now it was nearly October and there was no sign that her dad was going to stop being in charge of all of their day-to-day stuff. She had pretty much given up on him going back to his old ways of distractedly asking them how their day was while reading the newspaper.

Previous scenario before everything went to hell in a hand-basket went something like this. . . .

Father Reading *The Wall Street Journal*: "How was your day, Ariel?"

Extremely Intelligent and Witty Daughter: "Great, just finished watching a bunch of porn online and I need ten dollars for lunch."

FRWSJ: "Ten dollars for what?" Said while turning page.

EIAWD: "Lunch."

FRWSJ: "Fine."

Conversations like that were totally things of the past (she didn't think it appropriate to put in writing her dad's new, not-improved-as-far-as-she-was-concerned reaction to the most recent time she had used her Internet porn wit), and Ariel figured she had no choice but to take matters into her own hands and find her father a distraction.

Since Gabriel Kane was nothing if not a poster boy for perfect behavior, he couldn't be tempted with the normal things like partying, poker nights, strippers, or even taking massively smart classes in the quest to be the next Renaissance man. Never mind. Ariel had put together a plan, one that would produce something/someone to take his mind off her and Miranda. She had tried to run the idea by her sister, but Miranda just rolled her eyes, announced that the Stupid Shrink should give refunds, and left Ariel standing alone on the stairs.

Seriously, if it weren't for her snooping, Ariel wouldn't know anything at all about what Miranda was up to. Thank goodness the Shrink had made Miranda write in a journal, too. And Miranda wasn't as good at hiding hers as Ariel was.

It was after reading Miranda's latest lovesick entry about the left-behind boyfriend and wanting to get back at dad *"for ruining my life!!!"* that Ariel decided to find a new woman to keep their dad busy. Not a wife. No way would he ever marry again. He totally loved her mom. But a nice lady, someone to date, was the best Ariel had come up with.

Granted, for the last few months, Dad had dated plenty, but he hadn't met anyone who held his attention for more than a nanosecond. And it was going to take more than a nanosecond to get him out of their hair.

In her original plan, she had considered taking out an online dating ad.

Wanted: Girlfriend

Nice man seeks really nice lady. There's a kid involved (a little lanky, but cute in her own extremely intelligent way), though she won't be any trouble, and I swear you'll like her. Interested parties call: 212-555-0654.

Perfect wording, like a commercial for a made-for-TV movie, and that was bound to interest somebody. She figured there was zero reason to mention Miranda. At this point, a full-fledged high school–variety teenager would probably be a deal breaker for any sane woman.

But in the end, she couldn't go through with it. If she spent her lunch money on an ad, one, it would take more than a few lunches' worth to afford it; and two, what was she going to eat in the meantime? Contrary to popular belief, not all newly pubescent girls had dreams of anorexia. Beyond that, how did you screen out all the skanks, gold diggers, and weirdos when you ran an ad to the masses?

Of course, now there was Portia, from downstairs. She was interesting, if you could overlook the awful apartment. Was it possible to like living in a place with cracked windows and uneven floors? And what was up with the sink? Big and deep, with the pipes showing underneath. Ariel could have sworn she had seen pictures in her social studies book of places like that from New York City in the Dark Ages.

Not a big plus, but the lady seemed to be available, and she didn't have that gold digger look in her eye. No self-respecting gold digger would get anywhere near that run-down apartment.

But she was kind of cool, even though she was a horrible dancer. Her hair was a nice sort of curly, which Ariel liked. And boy, could she cook. Didn't they say that the way to a man's heart was through his stomach?

Whatever, Ariel had to get this taken care of.

Miranda's journal entries were getting weirder. She had gone from just drawing big teardrops all over a blank page to writing *Life Sucks!* And now she had moved on to *I Hate Dad.* No exclamation mark. Strangely, an exclamation mark would have made Ariel feel better about it. An exclamation mark meant emotion. Miranda's journal didn't seem to have an ounce of emotion in it anymore.

Ariel knew from experience that the clock was ticking before her sister did something stupid.

She wasn't sure how she would hold on if another bad thing happened.

She was done with bad things. Seriously done.

Now she just needed the universe to listen to her.

Six

❖

I F ANYONE HAD TOLD Portia a year ago that the only job she could get in New York City would be as a "hamburger," she would have laughed and rolled her eyes. Not that she was much of an eye roller. But really? A hamburger? Could anyone with half a brain believe that a woman as smart as her could go from highly regarded Texas political wife to, well, hamburger?

But after two weeks of unsuccessful job hunting, that was exactly what she had done. Or rather, what she had become.

"Shoo!" Portia hissed, waddling down West Seventy-third Street as fast as the hamburger suit allowed, attempting to outpace the pack of little dogs that had escaped their dog walker.

It wasn't as if she hadn't thrown her heart into looking for a job. She had. She'd made calls and sent out résumés, but not a single person had been willing to so much as interview her. Sure, two weeks wasn't that long in the scheme of things, but her bank account told a different tale. She needed money, sooner rather than later. Robert still hadn't deposited the settlement in her account, and her savings were evaporating like a reservoir in the middle of a Texas dry spell.

As a result, she had jumped for joy when she received the e-mail from Angus Industries offering her a job in public relations. In hindsight, she should have wondered why they offered her employment without so much as an interview or a phone call. It turned out that *Food Industries PR* for Angus Industries hadn't entailed any actual public relations work. Instead, when Portia arrived at the address provided, only a block away from her apartment, she found herself at Burger Boy, where she was handed a rubber hamburger suit and told to direct the public to the fast-food hellhole.

When Portia realized what the job entailed, she wanted to say no. A thousand different ways she *should* say no flashed through her mind. But her pride had to balance the staggering expense of living in New York. Was it possible that a two-dollar box of cereal in Texas cost five dollars in NYC?

End result?

She had pulled on the burger suit, though no sooner had the manager zipped her up than Portia thought it smelled strange. Mr. Burger Boy had assured her she was imagining things. But as she stood on Columbus Avenue trying to entice passersby with discount coupons, the unseasonably hot fall day beating down on her, the suit began to waft the aroma of charcoal-grilled burgers. Not long after that, the dogs that had been sitting clustered around their dog walker as he talked on his cell phone made a break for it and came after her, leashes flying in the wind, like buzzards sensing fresh kill.

The manager emerged from Burger Boy just long enough to threaten her miserable life if she let one of those dogs take a chunk out of his costume. She had tried to wiggle out of the suit, but the zipper was stuck. When the manager disappeared back inside the shop, she had fled.

Now she waddled down the long block toward home, going as fast as she could. Her hair had gotten loose, curls falling all over her face.

One thing was for sure: This was all her ex-husband's fault. Well, her husband and her ex-friend Sissy LePlante. Portia swung along as fast as she could, her mind full of revenge fantasies—all of them involving skewering, grilling, or butchering. Hamburger related.

She was only two town houses away from her apartment when she realized that one dog was still following her. "Damnation!" she yelped, swatting at the pesky Jack Russell terrier leaping at her side, vibrating with excitement as he tried to get a piece of one of the two faux meat patties circling her waist. The only thing that kept the terrier from true success was that it kept getting tangled in its trailing leash.

Her husband thought she was a pushover? *Right.* Portia swung around and met the dog's eye. "Go home!" she thundered.

He squeaked, tucked his leg between his legs, and tore off.

"Ha!" she chirped, swinging back around.

Straight ahead, she could see the thick green trees of Central Park at the end of the long tunnel formed by apartment buildings. Pedestrians, locals and tourists alike, got out of her way. No one, not even the hardcore New Yorkers who had given her nothing but grief since she'd moved to town, were going to mess with Portia Cuthcart in a burger suit, a murderous light in her eyes.

Finally, she made it to the town house. All she had to do was get inside her apartment, find a knife, and cut the burger right off her body before she suffocated or melted.

She barreled up the front steps and through the thankfully, if surprisingly, open front door into the building's small vestibule. Momentum and velocity squeezed her through the opening, the sound of thick rubber against the door seal like a beach ball being rubbed to a squeal.

But if bad things come in threes—one, the burger suit, two, the dogs—then number three had to be the cherry on top . . . or the garnish on the burger. The very neighbor she had been working to avoid was in the vestibule, now crowded into a corner, his daughter on the opposite side.

Even plastered against the wall, Gabriel Kane made awareness slide along her skin.

"Oh, hello, Ariel," she stated, her smile forced. "Mr. Kane." What wouldn't she have given to be dressed in a fabulous little dress rather than ten pounds of rubber.

"This is a surprise," he replied, not looking one bit happy. "Though it explains where you've been every time I've stopped by to meet with you."

Awareness, indeed. Sheez. How many times did she have to remind herself that he was an arrogant New Yorker who wanted something from her, though not anything that had to do with shivers of awareness. "That's me. A regular busy beaver."

His eyes widened fractionally. It didn't take a genius to guess he wasn't a man used to people snapping at him. But after a second, a smile tugged at the corner of his lips. "You mean, a busy *burger*."

Portia glared at him. "Ha-ha."

His reluctant half smile ticked up a notch. Heat rushed through her, the kind of heat that had nothing to do with the layers of the thick rubber suit, which just made her all the angrier.

The man wasn't good looking in any classical sense, and never mind his broad shoulders, dark hair, and darker eyes. His features were rough-hewn in contrast to the quality of the suit he wore.

Portia hated his perfect suit.

On the other hand . . . that imperfect face? Lust. Even wrapped in a hamburger suit, she couldn't miss the flash of non-rubber-induced heat rushing down her body. Yep, pure lust.

I'm attracted to men who are kind and quietly intelligent, she told herself. Men who had sandy blond hair and light blue eyes, who held doors for ladies, and made liberal use of words like *please* and *thank you.*

The type of men who were stupid enough to run off with their wife's best friend.

"Do you work for Five Guys?" Ariel asked. "That's my favorite. If I was going to be a burger, I'd totally work for them."

Gabriel raised one of those dark brows. "How is it in the competitive world of burgers?"

The book about courtesy her mother stole from the library was hard to set aside, even north of the Mason-Dixon Line. Portia drew a deep breath, fought for a polite smile, and said, "I was hired as a . . . representative of Burger Boy, not Five Guys. Now, if you'll excuse me, I'll just get out of your way."

But when she tried to move to the smaller door leading down to her apartment, she realized she wasn't going to fit. Momentum had gotten her through the wider door. Nothing short of a good hard shove was going to get her through the other one.

Gabriel's raised brow raised a little bit more.

Damn, damn, damn.

"Need some help?" he asked.

What Portia would have given to be able to say *"No need to bother your little ol' self,"* flip her hair, and sashay off. But just as she had never been much of an eye roller, she had never been good at hair flipping or sashaying either. That was Olivia's department.

"Bless your heart. Maybe a tiny push," she conceded.

"'Bless your heart'?"

"Just give me a push," she practically growled at him.

It took more than a tiny push to get her levered down the stairs without pitching headfirst like an overlarge bowling ball. While Gabriel angled her down the steps, Ariel called out if he started to make a move that would have her tumbling. But then they came to a grinding halt with Portia only halfway down the steps.

"We're stuck," Gabriel ground out.

"Hold on!" Ariel said, shoving her shoulder into the burger suit and flailing around underneath, trying to get a better look. "Found it! The lettuce is caught on the banister."

It wasn't bad enough that her husband had come home and announced out of the blue that he was divorcing her. Or that her former friend Sissy was now living in the house Portia had worked so hard to make a home. No, she had to get stuck in a burger suit and be manhandled down a stairwell by the kind of man who made her want to forget she was a lady. She really was going to kill her ex-husband, right along with the Burger Boy manager.

Gabriel and Ariel managed to get Portia to her apartment door, but then she came to a halt again. She stood on her toes, trying to see over the burger suit, then didn't bother to swallow back a curse. Not even a good Texas woman should have to live through this humiliation.

"A problem?" Gabriel asked, his tone utterly even. But he was grinning. She could just imagine him having a wonderful time telling all his sophisticated New York friends about the hamburger who lived downstairs. Though it hit her with surprising certainty that this wasn't a man who told tales out of school. In fact, she felt equally certain he was a man who didn't surround himself with friends at all, or even confidants.

Never having imagined she'd be wearing a burger suit, she had forgotten all about how she planned to get back inside. "Thankfully, I keep a key under the mat."

His grin flatlined and his brows slammed together. "You keep a key under the mat? In New York City?"

Portia's eyes narrowed. She'd had it. With him. With life. With this whole damned employment disaster. "Last I heard, burgers don't carry handbags."

Ariel gave a snort of laughter, which earned her a glare as well. "Go upstairs," he snapped.

"What did I do this time?"

"Upstairs."

It took a second, but Ariel stamped her way back up the stairs into the vestibule, then slammed the door to their apartment.

When Gabriel finally got Portia through her door, she waddled with determination over to the kitchen and managed to pluck the sharpest knife out of the drawer. With the grace of a sumo wrestler, she lifted the blade high like a samurai on the verge of seppuku. But before Portia could plunge the knife deep into the rubber bun, Gabriel was on her, grabbing her wrist and twisting it so that the knife skittered across the cracked linoleum floor. "Are you insane?" he demanded.

Her mouth fell open, then closed, then open again as if mimicking the very pedestrians who had gaped at her when she barreled down the sidewalk, a pack of yapping minidogs behind her.

"I'm not trying to kill myself, you, you . . . you!"

Quick comebacks had never been her strong suit.

"I am not trying to hurt myself," she said, enunciating each syllable. "The zipper's stuck. I have to cut myself out of this thing."

Gabriel fell back a step, and started to say something.

"No more sarcastic comments or weird assumptions," she snapped icily. "Just get me the knife." She wasn't feeling icy, though. Gabriel's eyes had changed. He wasn't looking at her waist—or her lack of one, given the suit—he was looking at her mouth.

Portia's heart sped up.

He didn't retrieve the knife. He turned her around, his hands impersonal. But when he jerked the zipper, it wouldn't budge. "Bend over and hold on," he said, pointing to the counter.

Portia turned slightly to look at him over her shoulder and glowered.

"Please?" he added as an afterthought.

Murder, she decided, was too good for Robert after putting her in this situation.

With a low growl, she shook her hair back, trying to get her curls out of her face again. Then she bent over.

But nothing happened.

She tried to glance behind her again. "The zipper? You? Working it?" She gave a scoffing laugh.

"You know, Ms. Cuthcart," Gabriel said, surprising her because suddenly he was so close his lips nearly touched her ear. "Once I get you out of this contraption, if I ever lean you over anything again, you won't be laughing."

Even in this damned burger suit a pulse of awareness shot between them that could have set all that rubber on fire.

Portia swallowed, then forced herself to roll her eyes, not that he could see. It was that or beg him to throw her over whatever he pleased the minute he managed to get her burger-free.

"Men always think that women never laugh at their technique," she managed. "I can assure you that you're all wrong."

She felt him stiffen, and then he burst out laughing. "God, you're a piece of work."

Before she could come up with a fitting response, Gabriel gave a good hard yank and the zipper came free.

The ceiling fan whirled above, and as soon as the burger fell open into two parts, she drew in a ragged breath, turning around. "Oh, my Lord, that feels good," she breathed.

She tugged at the suit, but he had to help before her arms popped out. Her little white tank top was damp with sweat and clung to every curve she had.

Glancing up, she saw his eyes had darkened again, as if he wanted to peel the rest of the burger right off of her. And not in a helpful Boy Scout kind of way.

Portia had been divorced only a little over a month, but she couldn't remember the last time she'd had sex. Not that her ex-husband suffered a similar fate. He'd had plenty of sex, with Sissy. The only person not having sex in her marriage was her.

Everything around them evaporated. The sounds of traffic. The thoughts of outrageously expensive groceries she couldn't afford. Even her ex-husband and ex–best friend's betrayal seemed distant.

Gabriel reached out, but he dropped his hand just before touching her. "What kind of a woman goes around in a burger suit?" he asked, his tone quiet.

She told herself to step away, but couldn't. "The kind who's looking for gainful employment."

"So you'll stoop to anything tossed your way?"

She stiffened, the mood sharp again. "No, not just anything. I turned down the position of Hot Dog, complete with an 'Eat Me' sign."

His features hardened before suddenly he shook his head and the side of his mouth quirked up. "You're impossible." He reached for her again. "Come on, let's get you out of this."

"I can do it."

He stepped back and raised a brow.

She struggled with the rubber before he pushed her hands aside, gently this time. She looked at him for a second, the air around them charged; then she gave in. As he started tugging the suit away, his gaze held hers, until finally he focused. In seconds he had sprung her free.

Thankfully, she was wearing some of Evie's old leggings. She wilted back against the counter, his eyes traveling down her body and then back up to her face.

"You need water," he said finally.

"I'm fine."

He went to the cabinet anyway, found a glass, and filled it from the tap. "Drink."

She felt too exhausted to do anything. "I'm fine, really."

"Portia." Just that, his tone warning.

She didn't know if it was the way he said her name or the way his voice settled deep in his chest, but suddenly she felt emotional. Suddenly everything was too much. She took the water and sipped.

"All of it," he stated, but softly.

The words ran along her senses, and he didn't take his eyes off her until she did as she was told. As soon as she was done, he took the glass from her hands, his fingers brushing against hers, and put it on the counter. Then he looked at her as if searching for something, just as he had that first day she saw him when she was sitting on the front steps. After a second, not seeming to find the answer, or maybe just not liking the one he found, he reached out and tucked an errant strand of hair behind her ear. "You should eat something, then take a cool shower."

He stood close, and with her back against the counter, there was nowhere for her to go. She realized she wanted to sink into this man, and probably would have. There were moments in life, she had heard about, when a person finds where they are meant to be. She had thought that was the case with the knowing. Then again with Robert. And both times the feeling had been proven wrong. But there was something about this man, in this place, that made her feel like a parched traveler stumbling out of the desert and finding a cool sea.

"Who are you really?" she asked without thinking.

But just then his cell phone buzzed and he glanced at the screen.

"I've got to take this." He ran his gaze over her, yet again assessing. "Then we need to talk."

He retucked that same errant curl behind her ear that had sprung free again, and smiled, seeming amused, then headed for the door.

"You with the talking," she managed, a bit of her old self returning. "Next you'll be asking to do facials and braid my hair."

He gave a surprised laugh before he shook his head and kept going.

"Just so you know, there's nothing to talk about!" she called after him. "Especially not the apartment. The only thing I'm prepared to sell is this burger suit, but it's seen better days."

His rumbling laughter was shut off by the closing door.

Seven

❖

A RIEL'S SOCIAL STUDIES teacher droned on.

Mr. Wickman was old—ancient, really. Probably forty. He was tall, thin as a rail, and had one eye that drooped. The kids called him Wink. Ariel hated that, hated how mean the kids could be. But she hated Mr. Wickman's assignment even more.

A report on ancestry.

Ariel got it. No sense belaboring a topic that had been massively boring the first time around. The last thing she wanted to do, on top of writing in a journal, was poke around in her family history. Yeah, right, she could see that.

Hey, Dad, tell me about Mom and her family.

When pigs flew, maybe.

A better topic was Portia downstairs. Ariel still laughed every time she thought of her barreling into the building dressed as a hamburger and practically squeezing the life out of them. Even more amazing, it was the first time Ariel had seen her dad smile in, like, forever. Granted, he swallowed it back before it took hold. But she'd seen it.

Whatever. It was a good sign. The only way to tell for sure if Portia could distract Dad was to have her over for dinner. Ariel had read on the Internet that you could tell a lot about a person by the way they ate. Did they throw salt over their shoulder if they spilled something? Did they chew with their mouth open? Did they tuck their napkin under their chin instead of putting them in their lap?

She was pretty sure Portia would pass the test, because she was smart and funny. Plus there was the whole *she can cook* thing. If she invited Portia to dinner and asked her to bring a cake, even if the dinner turned out to be a train wreck, they'd at least get a dessert out of the deal.

The only problem was that Ariel knew if she mentioned dinner to her dad, he'd never say yes. So really, why ask? On top of that, she had to do something, and fast. That morning she'd found a new guy's name written all over Miranda's journal.

Dustin
Dustin Ferris
Mrs. Dustin Ferris

Miranda was kind of young to be thinking Mrs. Anything. Hadn't she heard about being a feminist, breaking glass ceilings, and keeping her own name? But it didn't take a genius to figure out that Miranda liked some new guy named Dustin. Which explained why her mood was getting better. Though if their dad found out about it, things would get a whole lot worse.

That was an even better reason to haul Portia upstairs and make her join them for dinner. Miss Potentially Bonkers Burger couldn't be worse than another Family Night of Miranda ignoring Dad, and Dad pointedly *not* ignoring Miranda.

Ariel bolted out of class feeling better despite the fact that she had to find a way to dig around in her family tree without anyone in her family knowing. She had a plan to distract her dad.

As soon as Ariel got home, she wrote out the invitation.

Dear Portia,
	You are totally invited to dinner.
	Tomorrow night with the Kane Family.
	7 P.M.
	Don't be late.

							Your upstairs neighbor,
							Ariel Kane

P.S. Feel free to bring a cake.

Eight

❖❖❖

PORTIA STOPPED DEAD with the urge to bake a cake.

The need hit her hard and strong, surprising her. She hadn't woken to, or felt a single stab of knowing since she'd made the meal that first day in the apartment. But the image of that same chocolate cake she had woken to that day circled through her, making it difficult to breathe.

"Control, Portia," she whispered. "You're in control of your life now. Not Robert. And certainly not the knowing."

Despite the hamburger debacle, not to mention her dwindling bank account, she felt freer than she had in years. For the first time ever, she was living her own life. For the first time, she wasn't at the mercy of things she couldn't control. The money situation had to be solved, sure, but that didn't negate the fact that she felt alive.

Her walks through the streets of New York amazed her that she lived here. She didn't care that she made solemn-faced neighbors scurry away from her wide Texas smiles. *"I am here!"* she wanted to shout. She was making a new and fabulous life! Or would! Hope made her buoyant.

She had managed to avoid Gabriel for another two days, but obviously it wasn't going to last. Based on his repeated comments about the conversation they needed to have, she figured the man's lawyer hadn't given a good enough explanation as to why she had backed out of the sale.

But she should have known that no explanation left on an answering machine would be good enough. Gabriel Kane wasn't the sort of man who ever gave up. If he wanted something, he would take it. She had figured that out the day she saw him from the front steps.

Just as with the other aspects of her life, she had to take control of this, too, and make it clear why she couldn't sell. So when the dinner invitation slid under her door, she decided it was time to address the situation head-on.

She reread the invitation, then felt a surge of surprised worry when she noticed the mention of cake. But she pushed that aside, too.

Instead, she focused on what she had been meaning to do since she had slipped through the front door. Clean.

Before fleeing to New York, she hadn't seen the apartment in years. During the first month she had been in Manhattan, she had stayed with Cordelia in her fancy Central Park West duplex apartment and had been too consumed with loss to give any thought to what she would do next or where she would live long-term. But after that month of staying with her sister, she had been hit with the certainty that she couldn't stay with Cordelia and her husband any longer. With that thought she knew exactly where she would go. Great-aunt Evie's garden apartment.

Standing in the apartment now, Portia took in the dark draperies and grime. The apartment flowed back to French doors that opened onto the garden, which sat a few steps up in the rear. The kitchen was rustic, with a cast-iron stove, a sink, an ancient refrigerator, and an old stone fireplace that Portia couldn't imagine had been used in years, if not decades. The slate floor in the entry and the hardwood throughout the rest of the apartment were murky and scuffed, uneven in places. The bathroom was dingy, but had a beautiful antique ball-and-claw tub. Portia felt sure there was potential.

She unearthed cleaning supplies from the kitchen cabinet and got to work. She pulled every stick of furniture out into the back garden. She rolled up all the rugs and dragged them out, too. Once the apartment was empty, she tied a scarf over her nose and took down the dusty curtains she planned to wash. She swept down the exposed-brick walls and hardwood floors, and even found a hand broom to tackle the fireplace.

When she finished and looked around, sweat rolling down her back and streaking her face, nothing looked any cleaner than when she had started.

So she started over, this time with hot water, Clorox, rags, and a mop. She scrubbed everything in sight until her hands were raw and red. By the end of the day, she was covered in grime and soot, her hair a tangle. But when she drifted off to sleep, the apartment was clean, and she had a deep sense that for whatever reason, she had come home.

The next morning, she woke with a groan. Every bone in her body ached. But when she glanced around and saw what she had accomplished, excitement drummed through her. She also thought of the dinner invitation. Though she shouldn't have been, she was excited about that, too.

She gave a thought to giving in and making the cake herself, then pushed it away. She hurried out to purchase the least-expensive dessert she could find. Once she had that taken care of, she resorted to her great-aunt's closet again. She found a fabulous pair of long, flowing, gray flannel, pinstriped pants with wide cuffs by Yves Saint Laurent, and a simple cotton blouse made in Paris as well. Then at five minutes before seven that evening, Portia headed upstairs with the cake.

Inside the vestibule, next to the front door, a series of work permits had been posted. Portia hadn't been in New York City long, but it didn't take a genius to figure out that her neighbor was in the process of renovating the rest of the town house.

Out of habit, she knocked. In all the years she and her sisters had spent summers with Aunt Evie, the doorbell had never worked. When no one answered, she knocked again, this time more loudly. Eventually

Ariel peeked out the curtain over the side window. "What are you doing just standing there?" Ariel asked, pulling open the door.

"I knocked."

"Haven't you heard of a doorbell?"

The girl looked at Portia like she was crazy, popping out and pressing the button like a game show hostess demonstrating how to spin the wheel. Bells sounded, a sign that the new owner wasn't content with broken stuff.

Portia felt an odd feeling of displacement at the thought, as if the work permits and new doorbell meant her old life was really gone. Which was ridiculous. Her husband divorcing her had put that particular pony to bed, not a stranger remodeling her great-aunt's former home.

"My great-aunt used to live here," Portia said, distracted. "Back then, the doorbell was broken."

"Seriously? Someone you know used to live here?"

"Yes, my great-aunt," Portia repeated, walking farther into the town house.

The structure was the same, but nothing else. The entire inside had been gutted and refurbished. The old Victorian wallpaper was gone, stripped, the walls redone with a bright white textured plaster. Portia shouldn't have missed the water stains shaped like butterflies and dragons, but she did.

The carpet had been pulled up, the wood underneath refinished and covered with Oriental rugs. Expensive art hung above expensive furniture. Everything was perfectly done, and in the back of Portia's head she knew it was beautiful. But that was *way* back in her head, pushed aside by the fact that the work she had done in her own apartment suddenly felt inadequate compared to this. Glumly, she noted that one of the man's rugs could no doubt have paid for an entire year's worth of property taxes that Portia now had to figure out how to pay.

"Where's your aunt now?" Ariel asked.

"She died. A few years back." The words came out more abruptly than Portia intended. She thought for a second that Ariel flinched, but then the girl rolled her eyes.

"Was she old?"

"Yes, but very lively and dear. She left the building to my sisters and me. My sisters sold the upper floors to your dad."

"So that's why you're in the basement. I take it she didn't like you as much as the others."

Portia laughed. "She left me the garden apartment, not a basement. She knew I love gardens."

"My mom's dead," Ariel said. "Like your aunt. But my mom wasn't old." She turned away as if she hadn't said anything all that important.

It took Portia a second to absorb the words. Was that why she felt a connection to Ariel when she barely knew her? Did girls who had lost mothers have a hidden bond?

"That looks like a store-bought cake," Ariel said, shifting gears before Portia could respond.

"It is."

"You were supposed to bring one of those amazing cakes you make yourself."

Ariel gaped. "You did both the other night."

"Sorry. That was then. This is now."

Ariel's shoulders slumped. But then she drew an exaggerated breath. She shrugged. "I can only do so much."

Portia followed the girl toward the back of the house. Unless there had been major structural changes, Portia knew they were coming to the sunroom, her favorite part of the house.

But it wasn't the room that she saw. It was Gabriel.

"Damn it, Dan, that isn't acceptable," he said into a cell phone. "I've told you, I'm not going to relent. Make them pay."

He stood with his back to them, looking out the tall windows, phone pressed to his ear. Everything about him felt barely controlled, hardly contained. Without warning, he turned and saw her.

The dark of his eyes grew intense as his gaze met hers before it slowly drifted over her.

"You remember our neighbor, Daddy," Ariel said, sweet as pie, emphasis on the word *Daddy*.

Portia hadn't seen him since the burger incident three days ago, and he seemed to take her in, assessing to determine if she was fine.

She scowled at the memory of the incident, which made him raise a brow, his lips quirking.

A voice squawked anxiously from the phone he was holding. "I'm here," he said smoothly, seeming reluctant to turn away. But eventually he did, concentrating on the call.

Ariel leaned close. "I use the whole Daddy thing to soften him up. For some reason, he likes it. Go figure." She cocked her head. "Come on. Let's put that *store-bought* cake in the kitchen."

Portia followed Ariel through a swinging door and into the kitchen. The heat of the oven hit her along with the bright yellow and white walls, white trim and crown molding. The kitchen had been redone as well, but instead of making it into something different, it had become a newer version of its old self. She had to concede she loved it.

An older woman stood at the wide granite counter, making a salad. She didn't say hello or glance up.

"Come on," Ariel said, taking the cake and setting it on the counter, then herding Portia through another swinging door into the dining room. "That's Gerta, and she hates being interrupted. Dad hasn't had very good luck finding housekeepers. We should wait in here."

But before Portia could do anything like question, sit, or bolt for the front door, Gabriel walked into the room. Heat filled her like milk and honey coming to a slow boil. Truth to tell, she felt nervous, what with her promising herself to deal head-on with this man regarding the apartment, and nervous was bad.

He leaned his shoulder against the doorjamb, arms crossed on his chest. "So," he said.

"So?" she countered.

"What's with the outfit?"

She looked him up and down. "People don't really call clothes *outfits* anymore, at least not guys." She considered him for a moment. "Take that, combined with the whole obsession-with-talking thing, and I have to ask: Is your favorite color pink? Have you ever worn tight jeans and cuffed them at the hem with loafers and no socks? No, wait; have you ever worn man clogs?"

His lips twitched. "Hardly. Never. And no. But you, on the other hand, look like you just stepped out of *Saturday Night Fever.*"

"I was going more for *Annie Hall.* Same year. Smarter movie."

Ariel looked traumatized, as if she couldn't imagine how or where this type of conversation was coming from. Portia shook the sarcasm free. She drummed up a good, if strained, Texas smile. And Ariel grew visibly relieved. Gabriel just looked like he was trying not to laugh.

"What's going on?" An older, more put-together version of Ariel walked in. She had to be the older daughter Ariel had mentioned.

Unlike her younger sister, this one's light brown hair was long and straight, and she had grown into her eyes and mouth. She wore a lime green T-shirt tucked into a short, fitted denim skirt that flared around her thighs, and multicolored tennis shoes with a wedged heel. "Nana's here," she said. She looked Portia up and down. "Who are you?"

"She's our new neighbor," Ariel supplied dejectedly.

Miranda gave her a once-over, then shrugged. "Cool clothes."

Portia shot Gabriel a triumphant smile.

Footsteps resounded from behind Miranda's shoulder. "Where is everyone?"

A woman of about sixty-five walked into the kitchen. Beautiful and elegantly put together, she seemed like a woman who was used to commanding attention. "There you are. Miranda, I saw you walk by without opening the door, which was astonishingly rude. I had to use my key. Gabriel, if I've told you once, I've told you a thousand times, don't let these girls run roughshod over you."

"As if that were possible," Miranda muttered.

The woman shot a pointed look at Gabriel, but a clatter of pots and pans in the kitchen interrupted.

The woman started to say something, but then she saw Portia. "Oh, I didn't realize we had company." As if she weren't a guest. "I'm Helen Kane. Gabriel's mother."

"Hi, I'm Portia Cuthcart. I live downstairs."

"Downstairs?" Yet another person who gave Portia a once-over. "I thought the apartment was empty," Helen continued. "Have you lived there long?"

"No, not long. My great-aunt used to own the building and left it to me and my sisters." Portia knew she was babbling, but she couldn't seem to stop.

Helen turned to her son. "I thought you were buying it for Anthony."

"Mother, I'm handling this."

"Gabriel, don't tell me you didn't go through with the deal. I know you don't want Anthony here, but I won't forgive you if you decided against buying the garden level just to keep him away."

"Mother, enough."

The woman composed herself with effort, turning back to Portia, who felt more uncomfortable than ever.

"Do you have people here, dear?" the woman finally asked. "Friends. Family. I'm sure there are plenty of places you'd rather live than downstairs in the godforsaken apartment."

Portia didn't know what to think or do. Clearly it wasn't going to be as easy to explain not selling as she had hoped. "My sisters are here."

"How lovely. Family really is the most important thing." Helen said the words with more emphasis than necessary, turning back to Gabriel. "Where is your brother?"

If possible, Gabriel's expression grew even more guarded. "I told you, Mother, he isn't coming. We both know that Anthony only shows up when he needs money. Another reason why he doesn't need me to buy him an apartment that he won't spend time in."

"That's not true. He's coming." Her voice rose. "He promised."

Miranda's head shot up, fingers stilling on her iPhone, eyes brightening with excitement. "Uncle Anthony is coming?"

Gabriel opened his mouth, but his mother cut him off. "Yes, he is. He's coming to town and he promised he'd arrive by dinner." The grandmother shot Gabriel a glare. "When he arrives, he'll be staying with me, for obvious reasons."

"Dinner," the cook announced.

"We need to wait," Helen Kane said, rummaging around in her Chanel bag until she found a cell phone.

"Mother, how many times has Anthony said he's coming to town, then failed to show up?" Gabriel refocused on Portia. "Thank you for stopping by," he said. "Ariel, show Ms. Cuthcart to the door?"

Portia blinked.

"Dad," Ariel interjected, "I told you, we invited her to dinner."

Gabriel stared at his younger daughter, irritation riding across his face. "No, you didn't tell me."

"I didn't? Oops, bad me."

"Ariel, doesn't your father know that you invited me to dinner?"

Ariel wrinkled her nose. "Not exactly."

Just great. "I'll go."

"You can't! You brought a cake. Dad, you can't kick her out after she brought us a cake."

"Way to be polite, Dad," Miranda said.

Was that a hint of desperation in his eyes?

Gabriel ran his hand through his hair. "Sorry for the confusion. Please. Join us."

"Really, I—"

Ariel grabbed Portia's arm and pulled her toward a chair. Without jerking away, there wasn't much she could do.

The dining room had been transformed into a breezy space. Billowing lightweight curtains framed French doors leading to a Juliet balcony. It was beautiful, in a picture-perfect magazine sort of way. But there was nothing personal about it.

"Nice, huh?" Ariel said.

"Absolutely lovely!" She might have added too much enthusiasm in an attempt to cover up a real lack of it.

Gabriel raised a brow, but didn't comment.

Helen Kane managed to delay the meal for another ten minutes waiting for her other son, but finally gave in when Gabriel pointed out that Anthony was already forty-five minutes late. The family sat in silence as they were served a meal of tough beef tenderloin, overdone asparagus, underdone potatoes, wilted salad, and slices of plain white bread.

Portia thought of her own grandmother, of the cookbooks, of the knowledge that charred beef would fill a person with heated anger. The last thing this family needed was more anger.

Miranda's phone rang, and she started to answer.

"What did I tell you about phone calls at dinner?"

"But, Dad!"

"No buts."

Miranda glared.

Gabriel pretended not to notice. Ariel sighed. The grandmother kept looking toward the door.

This family was unhappy. This family needed food—light, nutritious meals. Happy food. Menus rushed unbidden through Portia's head. A fluffy quiche. Arugula salad with a light balsamic dressing.

The thought surprised Portia, and she pushed this one away, too.

Miranda glared. "You're a terrible dad, you know? Nobody I know has to put up with this stupid stuff at home."

Portia opened her mouth, and closed it again. Gabriel's face closed, his eyes expressionless. Helen raised a brow much like her son did so often.

"Hey, Dad?" Ariel said, breaking the silence. "I think you're doing a great job."

Apparently the task of peacemaking had fallen to Ariel.

The tense silence was interrupted when the doorbell rang.

"That's him!" Helen lit up like a Christmas tree.

Miranda bolted from the table and dashed to the door.

"Uncle Anthony!" rang through the town house.

Portia heard a deep voice laugh and footsteps headed their way. Helen stood. For his part, Gabriel remained seated at the head of the table, his jaw visibly tight. But as his brother entered the room, he rose to greet him as if ingrained manners took over.

The man who entered couldn't have been more different from his brother. It wasn't that they didn't look alike; they did. They had the same dark hair and dark eyes, the same set to their jaw. But something about the way Anthony Kane's features came together made him seem like light to Gabriel's dark—Beauty to the Beast.

Gabriel extended his hand. Anthony smiled and pulled his brother in for a bear hug.

When they stepped apart, Portia saw that Gabriel's face hadn't eased.

Anthony just laughed, and turned to his mother. Helen Kane looked as if she was on the verge of tears.

"It's about time you noticed your mother," she said, opening her arms.

Portia watched as Anthony pulled his mother into another fierce hug, then set her at arm's length. "God, you are the best-looking woman I've seen in a long time." He actually twirled her around, like two dancers on a stage.

Then, suddenly, the force of Anthony's attention turned to her.

"Hello there, beautiful. Who are you?"

Portia felt Ariel's surprised glance, Helen's narrowed-eye glare, even something decidedly tense coming from Gabriel. But no one introduced her.

"I'm Portia Cuthcart," she offered. "I live downstairs."

Anthony took Portia's hand and lifted it dramatically in the air. "Oh, to have a neighbor like you," he said, his eyes laughing. He leaned down to kiss the backs of her fingers.

"Good Lord, Anthony," Helen said. "I can see you haven't lost any charm while you were away." She sounded both jealous and proud.

"I wouldn't call it charm."

Gabriel hadn't moved, but Portia felt his tension settle into something deeper, more nuanced as he said the words.

Anthony dropped into a chair next to his mother. He snatched up the woman's hand and peppered kisses up to her wrist, making her scoff and bat him about the head.

What would it be like, Portia wondered, to be the less-favored child? She felt an instant desire to defend Gabriel. Then she shook the thought away. If anyone in this room needed protecting, it definitely wasn't Gabriel Kane.

"You can't believe how good it is to be back in the States, sitting at a real table, eating civilized food," Anthony said, his lightning-quick attention span shifting to the serving dishes in front of him. After a closer look, he made a face. "Two out of three isn't bad."

"Where've you been, Uncle Anthony?" Miranda asked.

"Here and there," he said, serving himself a plate. "Mostly there."

Miranda giggled, though Ariel's face stayed as expressionless as her father's.

Anthony glanced at his brother. "You'd hate the places I've been. We never know when we're going to get shot at. No showers for days. We spend weeks hiking to where we need to be. No cushy Easy Street for us."

If Portia hadn't met either man and she'd had to guess which one lived a less civilized life, it would have been Gabriel.

"What do you do?" Portia asked.

Gabriel glanced at his brother. "Yes, Anthony, what do you do?"

Anthony ignored his brother. "I'm a writer. I've done a bunch of work for newspapers."

"Yes, like *The Alliance Sun* and *The Waco Citizen*," Gabriel interjected.

Anthony glared, but then shrugged. "Right now I'm working on a book proposal."

Gabriel began sawing at the leathery meat on his plate. "Translation: He's out of a job."

Anthony's jaw set.

Ariel jumped in. "Speaking of jobs, Dad! Did you know that Portia is a cook?"

Anthony stabbed one of the rock-hard potatoes and waved it in the air. "Maybe you should hire her to cook for you, given the bang-up job you're doing as 'Mr. Mom.'"

Gabriel looked him in the eye. "Maybe you should worry about finding your own job."

"Me? I'll get a job. But, frankly, I'm in no hurry."

"Interesting. I assumed the only reason you showed up this time was because you were broke."

Anthony glared right back at his brother. "Turns out, I'm about to come into some money," he said coolly.

"Really?" Gabriel asked. "Then you signed the documents?"

"What documents?" Helen demanded.

Anthony's easy smile returned. "I haven't signed a thing yet, big brother. I've got to make sure I'm getting the best deal."

The tension that had wound around Gabriel like a rope pulled tight.

Anthony turned to his mother. "But let me tell you, I've lucked into the most amazing opportunity. It's a deal that helps the environment *and* promises to pay back investors tenfold. All I need is five grand."

The light in Helen's eyes visibly dimmed, and Portia knew with a sinking sense of certainty that Anthony had sprung many "deals" on his mother before.

Gabriel opened his mouth, but luckily his cell phone rang. He glanced at the screen. "If you'll excuse me. I have to take this." He directed a humorless smile at his brother. "It's about a real job." Then he stood up and left the room, saying, "Dan, is the Global deal done?"

Portia wanted nothing more than to hightail it out of Dodge. Apparently the rules regarding no cell phones at the dinner table applied only to adolescents. Which gave her the perfect way out.

"Oh dear, I forgot all about a call I have to take, too." She hopped to her feet. "This really was lovely, but I have to go. If you'll excuse me . . ."

Helen gave her a measured smile, and Anthony a lavish one. Miranda barely looked up from her own cell phone, which she had grabbed the minute Gabriel left the room.

Ariel looked miserable. "Sorry."

"There's nothing to apologize for," she said, keeping her tone bright. "You were sweet to invite me. Bye!"

Nine

✦

THE NEXT MORNING, Ariel stared at her open journal, her neat block writing, the consistent Bic pen–blue ink. She always used her blue pen for the journal. All those lines of static blue ink should have made her feel better, but didn't.

Her family was a mess. But unlike perfect block letters or math problems, there didn't seem to be any orderly solutions in sight.

She missed her mom in a way that was so big that it constantly wanted to burst out of her. Mom had been so smart, but in a different sort of way. Not math smart, like her, or even money smart, like her dad, but something way more useful really. She knew how to deal with problems. She wouldn't have come up with some lame plan of getting another woman to distract anyone.

Tears burned in the back of her throat. Not that crying would do any good. During the last year since Mom had died, Ariel had learned that over and over again.

She considered giving up on playing matchmaker between her dad and Portia. No question it was a ridiculous idea, and felt traitorous to her mom. Plus, Portia was weird. The only thing was that there was the whole *Portia had made her dad laugh* thing when she'd had on that burger suit. Which led Ariel right back to the fact that she didn't have a better plan.

A few minutes later, Ariel found her dad in the kitchen dressed for work, peering into one of the big pots Gerta normally used to make her awful soup. Bread was toasting in the toaster oven.

"Hey," Ariel said, coming up beside him. "You're cooking?" She looked over at the toaster oven, then into the pot, and wrinkled her nose. "What is it?"

"Oatmeal." He stirred it a few more times, like that would make it edible.

"Where's Gerta?"

"She quit."

"Quit?" She stepped back. "Ugh. Dad. That's totally burned. Can't you smell it?"

He jerked the pan off the stove, dumped it in the sink, and turned on the water. A sizzle and fog rose when the water hit the pan. Then he yanked the burned bread out of the toaster. By then, Ariel would have bet the whole house smelled liked a campfire cookout gone awry.

Grumbling, her dad opened the refrigerator and pulled out some milk. Then he stuck it on the table with three bowls and a box of cereal.

"Oh, joy, Wheaties."

Her father scowled at her.

"Miranda!" he bellowed in the general direction of the doorway.

Ariel sat down at the table. "You know, I was serious the other day," she said, deciding that if there was no other option than the Portia Plan, then there was no time like the present for a Portia Pitch, "about Portia cooking for us. But if you don't want to hire her outright, have you ever thought of, I don't know"—she made a show of considering—"dating her?"

He sliced her a look that she could only classify as irritated. "I'm not interested in dating Portia," he said, pouring milk on her cereal. "As for hiring her, didn't she say something about *not* cooking?"

Ariel tried to look serious and pensive. "I happen to know differently. But that's neither here nor there."

"Neither here nor there?"

"Dad, seriously? You sound like Miranda. Whatever, we're talking about Portia. It's probably good you don't want to date her." She nodded, just like the Shrink did whenever she bothered to say something, as if that would encourage her to start yakking away. "Now that she's had a chance to get to know you, she'd never go out with you, anyway." Didn't every man like a challenge?

Unfortunately, other than snort, her dad didn't take the bait. "I am not dating the woman downstairs."

"She's not just any woman. She's Portia, who can cook regardless of what she says." She shot him a broad, encouraging smile. "Portia, who could provide your growing daughters with much-needed food, even if she just bought it and brought it home to us." She dragged the last word out just a hair. "I mean, really, she *is* looking for a job."

"Are you suggesting I date a woman for convenience?"

"I've heard of worse reasons to ask someone out. In fact, I was watching *Jersey Shore*—"

"What were you doing watching *Jersey Shore*?"

"Stay with me, Dad; that isn't the point."

"The point is that you shouldn't be watching cr—" He cut himself off. "Trash. You shouldn't be watching trash."

"Does this fall into the category of kid blocks on computers and 'No, Ariel, you're too young for a cell phone'? Because, seriously, just think what would happen if I got lost and I didn't have a cell phone? If I had a cell phone, all I'd have to do is call you and say, 'Hey, Dad, guess where I am?'" She wrinkled her nose. "Hmm, I guess that wouldn't work since, given the whole lost thing, I wouldn't know where I was. Whatever—"

"Not 'whatever.'" Her dad glared even more. "No twelve-year-old needs a cell phone."

"You've forgotten that I'm almost thirteen, but I won't mention that since you're probably sensitive about forgetting things. And, really, Dad, you could do a lot worse than Portia. Her hair is great, for one thing."

Her dad just shook his head, though Ariel wasn't sure why. Maybe it was about the way Portia looked. Truthfully, who could blame him? He had seen Portia in all her flowered-Keds-and–strange-clothes glory. Maybe if Ariel figured out how to fix Portia up some, he'd take the bait. Hair, clothes, attitude. But how to make over an adult?

Great. Something else she had to figure out.

She picked up her bowl, set it in the sink, and headed for Trident Prep. But if managing the illogical workings of the standard American family was tricky, three and a half hours later she decided the whole middle-school hierarchy thing was preposterous when she sat at a back lunch table in the school cafeteria and her tiny world erupted in a battlefield of peer pressure and social awkwardness.

It wasn't like she had been popular in New Jersey or anything, but Ariel was her sister's sister and she had lived there forever, so people left her alone. But now she was the new girl, and no one had even heard of her sister—who went to a different school anyway. Ariel was on her own. Plus, Mindi Hansen thought she was the head of the world and— no surprise—she couldn't stand Ariel.

Ariel was sitting by herself doing homework when Mindi came over. "So, uh, Ariel, right?"

"Last I heard."

Mindi obviously couldn't take a joke. "What are you?" she demanded, tone biting. "A geek, a nerd, a moron?"

Mindi's friends all laughed as they walked away.

"Actually," Ariel muttered to the girls' backs, "I'm someone who doesn't need other people's approval to understand my self-worth."

Quite frankly, she blamed her dad for what happened next. If he hadn't made her go to the Shrink, she never would have known anything about self-worth and outside approval.

Mindi froze in her Tory Burch ballet flats. "What did you say?"

"Nothing." Her heart pounded like a fist on a drum. But because she just never learned, she opened her mouth and added, "There's no point in repeating it because you'd never understand."

It was that or give in to the knot of total sad-anger raging inside her—which she had no intention of doing. What would come out? Crying? Disappearing right then and there instead of the slow melting away it felt like she was doing every day?

Mindi leaned closer. "So, Ariel"—saying her name as three long, drawn-out syllables—"where's your *mom*?"

The question caught her by surprise.

Mindi tapped a pink nail on her cheek. "Let me see. Is your mom, like, dead?"

Ariel just stared at her.

"And not dead of, like, cancer or something. She wrecked her car driving like a maniac in New Jersey, right?"

Ariel's mother *had* died in a car accident, slowly disappearing as she bled out before the ambulance could get there. Ariel knew, because she had been in the car.

"That's not cool," one of Mindi's friends said, grabbing her by the arm. "You're putting the B in Bitch, girl. Let it go."

Mindi tossed her hair, smiled, and walked away.

Ten

✦

PORTIA GASPED AWAKE with the taste of apples in her mouth—crisp green apples smothered in brown sugar and spice. She needed to bake.

Lying tangled in the sheets, she tried to calm her racing heart. She tried to write off this urge, too. It was nothing more than a knee-jerk reaction to moving to the Big Apple. But no matter how forcefully she told herself she had stuffed the knowing back down, she realized that she hadn't. Not really. When she should have smelled bleach and sundried cotton, it was the scent of apples and buttery caramel that swirled in her mind.

The urges to bake and cook were getting stronger, the knowing coming back to life like simple syrup spun into cotton candy.

For those first couple of weeks she had managed to feel alive and carefree. But with every day that passed with her unable to find a real job, the images of food growing more persistent, panic started to grow. The only thing that kept her from a full-blown panic attack was the promise of Robert's settlement.

Groggy and disoriented, Portia made it out of the bedroom just when

Cordelia arrived. Maybe her sister knocked, maybe not, but whatever the case, Cordelia walked right in using her own key, holding her cell phone to her ear with her other hand.

"I'm here. I've got to go," Cordelia said, looking at Portia. "I promise," she added quickly. "I'll call as soon as I know anything." She dropped her phone into her handbag.

Cordelia wore a cream blouse with a camel cashmere sweater tied around her shoulders, camel pants, and brown suede Chanel ballet flats. Her hair was pulled back in a demure twist at the nape of her neck, pearls at her ears. She looked just like a politician's wife. No politician's wife would be caught dead in Aunt Evie's old dress, which Portia was now wearing regularly.

"Who was that?" she asked, trying to pull herself together. She had no interest in letting Cordelia know she was out of sorts.

"Oh, just Olivia."

"*Just* Olivia?" Portia sliced her a look. "What do you need to let her know?"

Cordelia waved the words away. "Nothing." Then she looked around. "My God, you must have worked around the clock." She brushed past Portia, walking into the kitchen. "The place is still hideous, but at least now it's clean."

Cordelia sat down at the table and pulled out a stack of books and two magazines from her shoulder bag. Portia sat down opposite her. Her oldest sister was infamous for the self-help articles and books she distributed like a librarian encouraging a reluctant reader.

"I thought you might like some company," Cordelia said, setting the assorted reading on the table.

"Did you think I'd be driving myself crazy by now?"

"Something like that." Cordelia didn't smile, didn't laugh. Instead, she pushed the stack across the table.

Portia's eyebrow flew up. "*Bon Appétit? Fine Cooking* magazine? *Restaurant Management for Dummies?*"

With a shrug that didn't match the determination in her eyes, Cordelia pulled a plastic shopping bag from the tote. "I stopped at the market."

"How sweet," Portia said, trying to sound sincere. "But I have more than enough groceries."

"What do you mean?" Cordelia scoffed. "I bet you hardly have anything in this place. Plus, I brought you a surprise. A present."

Portia stared as Cordelia began pulling items out of the bags with the efficiency of a nurse preparing an operating room for surgery.

"Remember that fresh apple cake you used to make?"

Portia's heart practically stilled in her chest.

Cordelia continued, laying out ingredients on the counter. She looked through the window, momentarily distracted. "It made me think about how much I miss The Glass Kitchen. For days now I've done nothing but think about that place."

Portia's heart surged into her throat. "You hated everything about The Glass Kitchen."

"I did not. I might have been too young to appreciate it, but I didn't hate it. But that's beside the point. I would be over the moon if you'd make me one of your famous apple cakes."

Portia stared at the ingredients her sister had lined up with perfect precision on the scratched countertop. Apples. Butter. Brown sugar.

Cordelia cocked her head. "What is it?"

"Nothing," Portia said, her voice weak. "It's just that I'm not in the mood to bake, is all."

That was a lie. Her fingers itched to dive in, peel, and core, sift the flour, fold in the softened butter and brown sugar. Again and again since moving into the apartment she'd had to ignore her tingling fingertips and the smells of chocolate and vanilla that didn't really exist. She had thrown every bit of food in the apartment away, and it still hadn't helped.

"I don't believe you," Cordelia said. "You want to bake like nobody's business. I can see it in your eyes."

"No."

It was panic that glittered in her eyes. It was her fingers that wanted to betray her.

But her brain knew the real cost of baking. She didn't want to be someone who knew things. She didn't want to sense that something was going to happen and have no idea what that was until it was too late.

The *knowing* spelled worry and stress and desperately trying to save people. Under no circumstances did she want the stress and uncertainty of the knowing back in her life. "No," she repeated, determined.

Cordelia sat there, quiet and watchful. After a second, she said, "Just hear me out."

"Cordelia—"

Cordelia raised her hand, stopping her. "Olivia and I were talking. We want to open a restaurant."

Portia felt the blood drain from her face.

Cordelia didn't let up. "A café, really. Something small. A quaint version of, well, The Glass Kitchen. We thought, maybe, you had brought Gram's cookbooks with you."

While Portia didn't want any part of the knowing, she *definitely* wanted nothing to do with another Glass Kitchen.

"It makes all the sense in the world," Cordelia continued, with more of that calm efficiency. "And, of course, you'll do it with us. Olivia and I agree."

"You and Olivia?" As if that decided everything. Apparently, nothing had changed after the loss of her grandmother, her home, her husband. She was still the little sister to be bossed around.

"Yes, and it will be fabulous—"

"No."

"Portia, it could be like old times."

"What has that got to do with old times? You and Olivia weren't there. You had nothing to do with The Glass Kitchen. You were *here*, in New York. You—" Portia cut herself off, forcing herself to be calm.

"No," she reiterated, and to make sure her point was understood, she walked to the front door and opened it. "I have a million things to do."

Like throw herself back in bed and never get up.

"Just listen." Cordelia stopped herself and drew a deep breath. After a second, she continued. "If you must know, I haven't been completely . . . forthcoming." She pursed her lips, lines showing age in a way Portia hadn't noticed before. "The truth is, Olivia and I need a Glass Kitchen."

Portia studied her. "What do you mean?"

"I need something." Cordelia said, looking away. "I'd be great running a restaurant with my sisters. I see it so clearly. I see you and me and Olivia creating the sort of place you can't find in New York. Magical food in a magical space. Gourmand Texas style. How can it not be a huge success?"

"Cordelia, opening a restaurant is a hugely iffy proposition under the best of circumstances, and it's not like any of us are in a strong position right now."

Cordelia blushed, surprising Portia even more. Cordelia had always been so sure of herself. But then she pulled her shoulders back and looked Portia in the eye.

"I want to open a Glass Kitchen because it's my legacy as much as yours. But more than that, James was wrong. Everything isn't going to be all right. It's one thing to lose our savings. But James took out a substantial loan against his next bonus—that would be the bonus he won't receive. Portia, I have to find a way to make money, make a living for my family. And Olivia is no better off than I am, teaching yoga, arranging flowers, or whatever it is she does between boyfriends. She's spent every dime she made when she sold her part of this place. We need this."

Portia felt light-headed with worry. Then anger. How many times had she saved her older sisters when they were growing up?

Portia closed her eyes, recalling the time Olivia took a job as a caterer with a mom-and-pop shop that was The Glass Kitchen's only real competition. As the middle sister, Olivia had been determined to be independent, to prove that she wasn't reliant upon Gram or Cordelia or even Portia. Portia had been planning the night's menu when she knew she had to make bouillabaisse—but not for dinner. The next afternoon, when the bouillabaisse was perfect, with loaves of French bread just done, Olivia flew in through the back door of the Kitchen.

"I promised the mayor's wife I could cater a French meal for her party tonight. I promised it would be great! But everything I've made is a disaster."

Portia stood silently as Olivia glanced over at the old cast-iron stove and took a deep breath. "I have to have it, Portia," she said. She didn't need to be told the answer to her dilemma was in the pot.

Now Portia stood in the small apartment in New York City, Cordelia in front of her again, tension thick in the room.

"Yes, but remember the strawberry preserves?" Cordelia said quietly, as if she were reading Portia's mind.

Of course she remembered. She couldn't forget any of it. The bad. The good. She remembered the strawberries, could smell them as if they were sitting in front of her on the counter. It had been a day when she and her sisters had argued. Afterward, all Portia could think about was making strawberry preserves. She had ended up making a huge vat of the preserves only to realize she didn't have anything to can them in. Cordelia and Olivia had shown up with boxes of Ball jars they'd gotten at a yard sale for a penny apiece. They had ladled in tense silence, filling jars, setting them aside to cool, much as their tempers cooled.

Once they were done, without a word of apology, Olivia had smiled with that impudent glint of hers, and pulled Portia and Cordelia into a dance. Then they took the preserves to an outdoor flea market and made enough money to pay for the dress Cordelia needed for her wedding to James.

The knowing had provided the bridge back to each other, a way for Olivia to keep her job, a way for Cordelia to pay for a dress she couldn't afford. Some of the few times the knowing worked for good, when it made Portia's world better, rather than signaling a loss to come.

"I love James," Cordelia said now. "I'll do whatever it takes to help him. But I need help. Olivia needs help. And, sweetie, so do you."

That had always been the way with the Cuthcart sisters. Fighting, furious, but unable to live without one another.

Portia hesitated. "Tell me this, Cord. Do you really want to open a café, or is it that you don't know what else to do?"

Cordelia answered. "Both. Did it ever occur to you that maybe, just maybe, you might not have been betrayed by your husband if you hadn't been suppressing who you really are? Did it ever occur to you that turning your back on the . . . that trait Gram swore by made you blind to what was really going on with Robert and Sissy?"

The words hurt more than they should have. It wasn't as if Portia hadn't wondered exactly that. But it didn't change anything.

"Just think about it," Cordelia said, then gathered her things and left.

Portia paced from room to room in her small apartment. Small, at least, compared to the Texas house she and Robert had lived in. Size was relative in New York City. A closet in Texas was a million-dollar bargain in the city.

An hour later, the chirp of her cell phone caught her off guard. She grabbed her phone only to be brought up short by the display.

Robert Baleau.

She grabbed the counter, ducking as if her ex-husband could see her.

"No, no, no," she whispered, letting the call go to voice mail.

As soon as the line was free, she dialed Cordelia.

"I'm at Saks; I can't talk."

Portia blinked. "You were just here. How can you be at Saks now, especially if your husband is out of work?"

"I'm just browsing. It's like . . . therapy."

"Tell me you didn't just say that."

"What do you want, Portia?" Cordelia shot back.

"Robert just called."

"Oh, my Lord! What did he say?"

"I don't know. I didn't answer." Her phone beeped. "He left a message."

"Listen to it and call me back."

Not a minute after she was done listening, her phone rang again and she answered to Cordelia, saying, "I've patched in Olivia."

"What did that rat say?" Olivia demanded.

Portia's hand shook as she held her phone. "He said he wants to talk to me. He wants to know where I am."

"He doesn't know?" Cordelia was surprised.

"No. And I don't want him to know. If he calls either of you, you know nothing."

"What about his lawyer?"

"Everything is going through *my* lawyer."

"Have you gotten your settlement yet?" Olivia asked.

"No. Not yet."

"Yep, typical male crap," Olivia added. "I swear, you should have told the world about how he treated you. Why you haven't told anyone who would listen what an ass he is makes zero sense."

"I've told you. I have no interest in being in the news, and me telling the world that the good Christian politician Robert Baleau divorced me so he could marry my ex–best friend puts me smack dab in the middle of the news as yet another pathetic wronged-politician's wife. I've already told you, no thanks."

Olivia scoffed. "Portia—"

"No. I am not going there. Listen, I've got to run."

She couldn't breathe. She had to get out.

She pressed end, then threw on one of Evie's old sweaters, grabbed her purse, and bolted. She didn't slow down until she came to Columbus Avenue and the same bakery where she'd bought the cake for the Kanes: Cutie's.

Before she thought it through, she was inside buying a baker's box full of every variety of cupcake they sold. She couldn't have explained the impulse if she had tried. She barely managed to cover the cost from the money she had in her wallet. Then she carried them home, nearly running all the way back, before slamming into her apartment. The minute she launched herself into the kitchen, she tore into the cupcakes like an alcoholic plunging into a binge.

Maybe thirty minutes later, maybe an hour, the door opened and Ariel walked in, finding Portia at the kitchen counter, half-eaten cupcakes spilling across the scarred linoleum.

"What are you doing?" Ariel said, gaping.

"These are terrible!"

"What do you mean, terrible?"

"Awful, hideous, dry. I tried one and couldn't believe it. So then I started testing more of them, and so far they've all failed!"

"You're testing cupcakes? Are they supposed to answer directly, or are you giving them a multiple-choice exam?"

"Ha-ha," Portia said, taking a bite of a bright pink cupcake. She swallowed with a gulp of water. "Gah, these are awful."

"They can't be awful." Ariel picked up the box. "Cutie's Bakery. These are, like, the most famous cupcakes around."

"So I've heard. Have one."

"No thanks. I had a bite of that cake you brought from them. It wasn't even close to as good as the one you made that first night. Hint hint."

The words hit Portia in the gut, swirling around like plump, juicy blueberries folded into the kind of thick, sweetened batter perfect for licking off a spoon. Abruptly she stood, her mind whirling, when a huge *bang* sounded outside.

She and Ariel ran up the stairs and out the open door.

Gabriel was already there, two steps down. He wore faded Levi's and a navy blue T-shirt that stretched across his chest. The sun hit his hair, the brown so dark it was nearly black. He looked great, Portia thought. Really great. No surprise there. What *was* a surprise was that he was howling with laughter, talking to a guy who was obviously a contractor.

His eyes crinkled at the sides when he grinned like that, making him look downright approachable. Who would have guessed the beast had it in him?

Portia forced herself to focus, noticing for the first time that the outer front door had been ripped out. She gasped. "You can't do that!"

Gabriel turned. "What's all over your forehead?"

Portia swiped her skin, coming away with frosting. "Don't think you can distract me with your, your . . . scowl."

"My scowl?" He looked amused.

"You cannot rip out my aunt's front door. I'm going to call someone, the historic society or something. I'm sure it's listed. You can't just rip out doors!"

"This is none of your business," Gabriel said, the laughter disappearing.

"This is my home—of course it's my business!"

He raised a brow.

"Okay, so it's both of our homes. You on the top, me on the bottom."

That got a different kind of raised brow.

"Errr!" Portia grumbled. "That door belongs to both of us!"

Gabriel's jaw set.

"Well?" she demanded. "I bet we're something like one of those insane apartment building co-ops they have in Manhattan, you know, giving everyone who lives there equal rights. I have rights to that front door, just as much as you do."

"The door was rotting. And if you don't like what I'm doing, you can always leave."

"Funny. But I can't. I have nowhere else to go." Belatedly, she realized that after all her ranting, he just might ask her for half the price of the rotting door.

It flashed through her mind that maybe she should just sell him the apartment and be done with it. She had been scouring *the New York Times* real estate section, and she knew she could make a small fortune by selling.

Gabriel clearly saw her moment of vulnerability because he suddenly looked like a shark circling a floundering cruise ship tourist. He sensed blood. "Ariel," he said, "can you give me a second to talk to Ms. Cuthcart?"

Ariel glanced between the two of them, shrugged, and trotted back inside.

Gabriel took two steps up. There was an intent look to his face that . . . well, Portia had the distinct idea that he was going to reach out and kiss her, never mind the work crew milling down below on the sidewalk.

But at the last second Gabriel's eyes cleared and he said, "Why are you here?"

Portia blinked—then blinked again, hating the implication that she didn't belong.

That was the thing. She *did* belong. Ever since that first morning she woke up in the garden apartment, she had felt as if her whole life had been bringing her to this place. Texas wasn't home anymore. New York City was.

"I belong here," she said. Then found herself blurting out, "You don't like me, do you?"

That threw him. He gave her a look as if to say, *"You are such a girl."* And who could blame him?

Aloud, he said, "I don't even know you."

Unbidden, the image of the way he had looked at her after peeling her out of the burger suit came to mind. He had wanted to know her that day, at least on some level.

"This is not about liking or not liking you," he stated firmly.

"Dad!" Miranda marched out the front door. "There isn't a thing to eat in the whole house! Are you trying to starve us? Huh? Is that what you really want?"

Gabriel took a deep breath. "Give me a second, Miranda. I'll fix it."

"Yeah, right. Sure, you will."

She wheeled back inside.

"Listen," Gabriel said, dragging his hands through his hair. "You need a job, right? Given the demise of the burger suit, I mean."

"And?" Portia said carefully.

"The girls need someone to make meals for them. Breakfast and dinner, on school days."

Portia felt her blood begin to boil. "Are you offering me a job as your cook?"

He eyed her. "I guess I am."

"Either you are or you aren't."

"Fine, yes. I am offering you a job." He told her an amount he would pay, and her stomach actually rumbled at the thought of all the boxes of cereal, not to mention fabulous food, she could buy with the amount. But then she remembered.

"What is the matter with everyone? How many times do I have to say that I don't cook? Not anymore!"

Though she wanted to. God help her, she did.

Portia reminded herself of things that were normal. White picket fences. Food that didn't come in visions. She took a deep, steadying breath.

"Ariel says you do. And you couldn't be worse than me. Just give it some thought. In the meantime, I suggest you get out of the way before the workmen run you over."

He left her standing on the steps. When Portia gathered herself and glanced around, she noticed the old man next door. Despite the closed window, the man raised a challenging eyebrow, as if he'd heard every word.

Her great-aunt Evie had followed her dream and moved to New York when it became clear that her future didn't lie in Willow Creek, Texas.

"The measure of a person isn't the bumps you hit in the road," Gram had always said. *"It's how you pick yourself up and move forward."*

She could almost hear Gram asking a question: *"Who are you, Portia?"*

Every direction she turned, she was hit with images and urges, thoughts and knowing. Then something else hit her, harder than it had before.

If she had been true to who she really was, would Robert have been able to deceive her, as Cordelia had said?

And suddenly she lost the fight. Before she could think better of it, she dialed Cordelia, who answered on the first ring.

"Get me the names of some investment bankers."

A beat passed before her sister spoke. "What for?"

"We're going to open The Glass Kitchen in New York."

Third Course

❖

Salad

Grapefruit and Avocado Salad
with Poppy Seed Dressing

Eleven

❖

PORTIA GROANED over what she had done.

But there was no turning back, and as night fell later that day she managed to nurture a flicker of hope. She was giving in to cooking. She would bake. She would open a Glass Kitchen with her sisters. But she would do both like a normal person.

That was the key. It would be three normal sisters opening a normal restaurant in New York, serving the kind of normal food that was the opposite of the tiny portions so often served in Manhattan. None of that fancy food that was better to look at than to eat.

But Portia knew there was something else she had to do.

Stepping out into the dark garden, she noted the metal fire escape that zigzagged up the back of the town house.

The maze of metal ladders and landings used to be a dangerous wreck, but she'd bet anything that Gabriel would have had it fixed. She had no doubt he was a man who took care of his own. He was a man her grand-mother would have respected.

The thought surprised her, left her off-balance.

She glanced up to the higher floors of the town house and found that the third-floor light was on. Back in the day, the room had been her great-aunt's library. Gabriel Kane must have left it as a library, because through the sheer curtains she could just make out his large shape as he stood in front of the tall windows.

Without thinking, she started climbing the fire escape, just as she'd done as a girl. She didn't want to go to the front door and ring the newly working bell. She didn't want to call—not that she had his number. She didn't want to wait until morning. If she waited a second longer, she would change her mind.

Her handholds were firm as she climbed, the years slipping away until she was just a girl with her sisters in New York for the summer. She had loved climbing the fire escape. Cordelia had not.

"Portia! Get down here," Cordelia had always demanded, her voice bouncing against the tall buildings surrounding them.

Olivia had always laughed, egging Portia on. "Keep going, Portia!"

But even Olivia had never followed Portia up the narrow ladders and landings. Portia was the only one who scaled the metal stairs like a cat, slipping into one of their bedrooms or Evie's library. Cordelia and Olivia would fly into the house, then dash upstairs to find Portia already curled up in Evie's favorite chair with one of their aunt's magazines.

All these years later, with each handhold and step up the stairs, she came to the third floor once again, but this time Gabriel Kane stood inside.

Gossamer-thin draperies covered the library windows. Portia knocked and nearly fell backward when Gabriel whipped aside the curtains, something dangerous in his face.

"Oh," she squeaked.

Before she could fall, flee, or figure out how to get back down without killing herself, Gabriel's face shifted from dangerous to fierce. She felt like kindling in front of a flame. It wasn't nearly as comforting as a welcome mat, but Portia would take what she could get, given a plunge to the earth made his harsh expression seem appealing.

At least that's what she thought until he wrenched open the window, grabbed her arms, and pulled her inside.

She wasn't a big woman, but still. Gabriel lifted her with the ease of a bodybuilder lifting a can of peas. "What the hell are you doing out there?"

He was angry, she realized. Really angry.

"You could have killed yourself on that thing."

She remembered him giving her that glass of water and making her drink. Now this. The man seemed oddly protective for a guy who clearly wanted nothing to do with her.

The fire in his eyes made Portia feel alive and reckless. "But I didn't!" She gave him a sunny Texas smile. "More than that, I thought about your offer. Of a job."

She watched as he visibly reined in his anger. "That was fast."

She cocked her head. "That's me. Fast, decisive." In her dreams, sure, but he didn't have to know that. "Are you impressed?"

"I'm impressed you didn't fall and break your neck."

She scoffed. "I've been climbing that fire escape since I was in grade school."

"You're certainly acting like you're in grade school."

"Sheesh, Portia," she said out loud. "You handed him that one."

He looked at her as if he hadn't a clue what to make of her. "Who are you?"

She laughed, delighted. "Have you noticed that every time you see me, you wonder who I am?"

Gabriel ground his teeth.

"But that isn't what you meant."

His narrowed eyes showed he still wasn't amused.

"All right. If you want the truth of it, then I've come to tell you that I officially accept the position as the Kane Family Cook."

It all made sense. It would give her an income while she and her sisters got the business going. The job wasn't full-time, and there wasn't much in the way of commuting, so she'd have plenty of time to work on The Glass Kitchen.

Gabriel stared at her long and hard, not uttering a word.

Portia glanced around the room and noticed that everything about her aunt's library was gone. The books, the bookshelves, the paintings. "You've ruined this room, too!"

"I didn't ruin it."

Her head shot around. "You did too—"

He didn't let her finish. "You make me forget I'm a man who doesn't do things without knowing every possible consequence," he said, then pulled her to him, his mouth coming down on hers.

Of all the responses Portia had expected, kissing wasn't one of them. She tensed, her hands coming up to his chest to push him away, though she didn't do it. Instead, her body melted and she opened her mouth to him.

"God, you drive me insane," he said raggedly.

"Same page," she answered, her arms circling his neck as she leaned into him. His muffled groan sent heat through her. She wanted him, even though nothing good could come from getting involved with a neighbor—a neighbor who had offered her a job. Would he take back his offer?

Right then, she didn't care.

Gabriel's hands ran down either side of her spine. Her breath caught when he cupped her hips, pressing her to him. The kiss wasn't soft. It was demanding, his tongue tangling with hers, and she gave up all hope of breaking away.

He backed her against the wall, his hands flattened on either side of her head. In the past, with Robert, she had always wanted more, wanted some deeper connection, but she had contented herself with a white-picket-fence sense of normalcy. Nothing about the way Gabriel Kane made her feel had anything to do with white-picket fences.

"You have driven me mad since the day I walked up to the steps and found you sitting there," Gabriel said, his lips trailing down her neck.

"You with the compliments."

"It wasn't meant to be."

Her head fell back, her eyes closed. "Of course not," she breathed.

Portia felt the strength of his muscles beneath his button-down shirt. At his waist, she hardly believed it when she tugged up the material. She wanted to feel skin, feel heat. When his shirttail came free, she slipped her hands underneath to his abdomen, her palms sliding up over warm, taut skin, the single line of hair from his navel to his chest.

She felt his breath shudder before he reclaimed control of her body, and she did nothing to stop him. Portia wanted more, moaning as he gave it to her, his hand slipping beneath her shirt, his thumb dipping into her navel. Their kiss grew wilder, a kind of craving that she'd never experienced, and certainly never succumbed to. But right then, she would have given him anything.

The tips of his fingers brushed against her hip, then slid back, cupping her hips and pulling her to him.

"God, you taste good," he murmured against her lips. "Like honey."

He tasted like nothing so tame as honey. He was a decadent, caramelized brandy that made her press against him like a madwoman. Those clever fingers found her lacy boy-short panties, sliding his palm under the elastic, his foot nudging her legs wider.

She trembled, her breath catching in her throat. He deepened their kiss, turning it fierce, just as he brought his hand around and his fingers slid low.

"*Dad?*"

A paralyzed moment passed before Portia realized Ariel was headed their way.

"Fuck!" Gabriel ground out.

Right this second, she wished.

Instead, she sagged against the wall, trying to steady herself.

"*Dad? Where are you?*"

Portia could hear footsteps coming down the hall now, and she pushed him away so she could straighten her clothes. Gabriel shoved in his shirt-tail, turning to the closed door, ready to face his daughter. Portia, on the other hand, chose the coward's way out and slipped back out onto the fire escape.

He pivoted back to her. "Don't leave," he commanded, his voice low and fierce.

"I'll start work in the morning," she said, throwing herself down the stairs, her heart pounding.

Back in her own kitchen, she looked around, as if the room would have changed. But everything looked the same, despite the fact that her world had just been rocked.

Twelve

✦

ARIEL WAS ALMOST CERTAIN that her dad had been messing around on the fire escape.

That, of course, was totally impossible, since he had forbidden her and Miranda from going anywhere near the escape, even after he'd had workmen practically rebuild the thing.

Ariel had no problem obeying. While she wasn't about to admit it, even the thought of having to go up or down the narrow metal stairs and landings terrified her. But Dad's laying down the law had sent Miranda into one of her fits.

"*So, what are we supposed to do if there's, like, a fire?*" Miranda had snapped in the tone of voice that never failed to get a rise out of their dad.

Tit for tat, Ariel thought.

Whatever. There was no reason why her dad would have been doing anything anywhere near the fire escape.

"What are you doing?" she asked, coming over to look past him. The garden below was dark. "Is Portia down there?"

She glanced sideways at him, thinking he would scoff at her, but there was a strange look on his face. Almost a guilty look. "You've been peeking!" She went right up to the glass and peered out. "You know, Dad, that's, like, a crime or something."

"I was not peeking out the window."

It wasn't hard to imagine Portia out in that garden dancing or something.

"I read *Harriet the Spy*," she said, craning her neck. "I know what people get up to in New York. Next thing I know, you'll get yourself a pair of binoculars. I'd better warn Portia."

"*Ariel*." Even she knew better than to keep going when he had that tone. It meant business.

"Good night!" she said cheerily, running back out of the room before he could launch into some sort of lecture.

But the next morning, if the possibility of her dad doing something on the fire escape was a surprise, breakfast was a real Lollapalooza of surprises.

"Good morning!"

Ariel blinked at the sight of Portia standing in their kitchen, wearing another pair of her whackjob high-waisted, wide-bottomed pants, a white T-shirt, and an old-fashioned apron tied around her waist.

"What are you doing here?" Ariel asked, still frozen in the doorway.

"Believe me," Portia said, "I'm as surprised as you by this turn of events."

"What do you mean?"

"I'm your new head cook and chief bottle washer."

"Seriously? Dad hired you?"

"He did." Portia got a weird look on her face, then shook it away.

Ariel came over and peered inside the pot on the stove. "Sheez, what are you making?"

"Doughnuts."

"Dad actually took my advice, amazing. And does anyone other than Dunkin' make doughnuts?"

"Your advice? Then thank you. I guess. And funny."

"I thought you didn't cook anymore."

"I wasn't." Portia gave the big spoon a swirl around the pot of boiling oil. "But sometimes we have to be brave in order to dig deep and find answers. Even if we're not sure we're going to like the answers."

"I don't want to be mean, but you sound like a really bad infomercial."

Portia laughed, and started extracting golden-brown fried balls. After placing them on a paper towel–covered plate, she tossed them into a brown paper bag and started shaking.

Ariel's mouth started watering. "Powdered-sugar doughnuts!"

Footsteps stopped in the doorway. "My favorite."

Ariel and Portia turned; Ariel blinked. "Uncle Anthony."

"None other." He sauntered into the kitchen. "And look who else is here," he added, winking at Ariel, then smiling big and wide at Portia.

Ariel liked her uncle well enough, though she probably would have liked him better if Miranda didn't act like an airheaded nitwit whenever he showed up. It was the same with their grandmother. Nana was totally mean to Ariel's dad, but she gushed like a demented schoolgirl when her younger son came to town. Ariel figured Nana was in hog's heaven now that Uncle Anthony was staying with her.

Thankfully, Dad wasn't like Nana. Ariel was pretty sure he loved both her and Miranda the same. And if she was ever a mom—not that she was going to be, because it was a seriously awful job, as far as she could tell—she'd love all her kids the same. Even if one of them was as mean as Miranda.

Uncle Anthony walked over the stove, never taking his eyes off their neighbor. "Portia, right?" he asked.

"Yes, Portia Cuthcart."

"From downstairs," he added.

"Right again."

Just in case Portia and her dad were getting something going, the last thing Ariel needed was her uncle getting in the way. You only had to be around Anthony for five minutes to realize that grown ladies turned into mush the minute they saw him. Which made no sense since he was like a math equation with only one answer: He never committed. So how come she, twelve-nearly-thirteen-year-old Ariel Kane, had figured this out when full-grown women hadn't?

Anthony picked up a doughnut and popped it into his mouth. "Amazing," he said, licking his fingers. He actually sounded surprised. "So amazing that I'd like to take you out to dinner to show my appreciation."

Portia laughed, swatting his fingers away. "No thanks. Hands off my doughnuts."

He stole another, anyway.

"You're like a ten-year-old who's used to getting his way."

"You've pegged my little brother so quickly."

Dad to the rescue! Ariel gave him a big grin.

"Gabriel," Anthony said, minus the big grin. He looked at Portia. "Even as a kid, he was a wet blanket."

"Not everyone can make it through life on the largess of others."

If Ariel wasn't mistaken, something weird was happening with Uncle Anthony's jaw, sort of like a spasm. A definite sign that he was mad. But then her uncle just laughed, making her think she'd imagined it.

"Ms. Cuthcart," her dad said in clipped tones.

The two of them exchanged a massively weird glance, and for half a second Ariel thought her dad was going to fire Portia on the spot. That, or Portia was going to up and quit.

Instead, Dad glanced at the doughnuts on the counter. "This is what you've chosen to feed my children for breakfast?"

"No." Portia opened the oven door and pulled out a platter. "For the girls, eggs, turkey bacon, whole wheat toast." From another pot on the stove, she whipped off the lid. "Oatmeal." Then, like some crazed hostess on a game show, she walked over to the refrigerator, from which she produced a bowl of cut-up fruit and some orange juice.

"Covering all bases, I see," Dad said.

"Yep, that's me." She threw him a look, kind of sideways under her lashes. "Though now that I think about it, not so unlike you last night covering a few of your own."

Dad's jaw dropped, then snapped closed. There was that weird look in his eyes again, though.

Portia turned away, like she had surprised herself.

"Isn't this interesting," Uncle Anthony said in a kind of sour voice. Which was even weirder.

Miranda walked in just then. She scowled at their dad, for whatever reason, this time. Then she saw Uncle Anthony. "Hi!" she said with a big smile.

"Hi, yourself," Anthony said, grinning back.

Her dad got that frustrated look about him, but instead of saying something mean, he just asked, "Anthony, what are you doing here?"

Ariel could feel tension in the room like she felt heat coming from the oven. It made her stomach clench and worry come up in her throat, a worry that was always there these days.

She didn't dare tell the Shrink about the worry, because he would tell her dad, and then there would be hell to pay. Dad would watch her like a hawk, just like he watched Miranda. As it stood now, Ariel knew her dad felt pretty certain she was under control with the whole journal and Shrink thing. She wanted to keep it that way.

Miranda glanced at Portia, seemed surprised, though not in a good away, then sat down.

Ariel focused on serving a plate. She really hated all this weird family mess that, even as smart as she was, she hardly understood.

It took a second before something occurred to her. "How did you know what our favorite stuff was?"

Portia bit her lip. "Really? I mean, I figured I'd just make a little bit of everything."

"I have to get to work," Dad said.

"But you haven't eaten!" Portia blurted.

Dad gave her a look, grabbed a piece of toast, and then he was gone.

"Are you staying for breakfast?" Miranda asked Anthony.

Anthony was frowning after Dad, but he looked back and his smile returned. "I wouldn't miss it."

They all sat around the kitchen table. Portia was still cooking and didn't sit down, but Uncle Anthony yakked at her the whole time anyway. "So, are you going to go out with me?" he asked again.

She just laughed and said, "No."

"We got an assignment at school," Ariel said, breaking in. "We have to write about our family tree. Uncle Anthony, can you tell me something about Mom that you think I don't already know. Like, when was the first time you met her? Did Dad do the *bring his date home to meet the family* sort of thing and there she was?"

Uncle Anthony looked totally weird. "Your mom?" But then he got a faraway look in his eyes and a kind of dreamy smile. "The first time I met your mom I thought she was the prettiest girl I'd ever seen." He focused on Miranda. "You're the spitting image of Victoria."

"Really?"

Ariel scowled. She wished she looked like their mom. But no, she looked like some mongrel dog.

"So when did you meet her?" Ariel asked.

Anthony sat back. "Actually, I met your mom before your dad did."

"No way!" Miranda breathed.

Great, more unstable ground. Sheesh.

Miranda came over and sat next to Uncle Anthony. "What was she like when you met her?"

"Well, like I said, she was beautiful. She walked into this place I used to go with a bunch of friends. Downtown. You know, music, dancing. We were young. Or younger," he added with a twist of his mouth. "Vic walked in like she owned the place. She gave off so much wattage that you saw nothing but her." Uncle Anthony gave sort of a half laugh. "Victoria

Polanski. God, was she a handful." He cleared his throat. "Like I said, she was just as gorgeous as Miranda here."

Ariel ignored that and persisted. "Where was she from? New Jersey? Long Island? Did she grow up by Nana on the Upper East Side?"

Anthony blinked, coming back to himself, then leaned over and chucked Ariel on the chin. "Ask your dad that, A. I'm sure he'd love to talk about the old days."

Yeah, right. She'd jump all over that. Not.

Her uncle glanced at the clock. "Gotta go." He stood and walked over to the stove, where Portia was taking another batch of doughnuts out of the pot.

"You're sure you can't spare a few hours to keep a guy company?"

"I'm sure."

"I guess I'll have to settle for another of your doughnuts." He grabbed one up. Just before he popped it in his mouth, he added, "At least for now."

Thirteen

⋄⋄⋄

PORTIA FIRED UP THE LAPTOP she had borrowed from Cordelia and spent the next hour figuring out what a business plan looked like. She knew all about the practical elements of running a café, having learned the ropes at her grandmother's side, so it wasn't too hard. Plus, Cordelia and Olivia were coming over later to help.

Quite frankly, her intent was as much about work as it was about filling her head with something besides the memory of that kiss. She hardly knew how to square it away in her brain other than to chalk it up to the greatest kiss known to man. Which was melodramatic and completely absurd, especially given the fact that she hadn't much to compare it to. She snorted. She didn't need anything to compare it to. The man could kiss.

By the middle of the afternoon, her head was ready to explode with numbers and business details. She told herself that what really mattered was her ability to create food that wowed people. Which made her think of those Cutie's cupcakes. And she knew with certainty that she could fix them.

The doorbell buzzed just as she was starting to put everything together, and Ariel walked in. "Are you baking?"

"Yes."

"Something good."

"One can only hope."

"Interesting. You don't strike me as the sarcastic type."

Portia rolled her eyes, which she noticed Ariel ignored as she started rooting around in her backpack. The girl pulled out notebooks and magazines and set them on the table. Portia went back to her I Can Do Better Than Cutie's cupcake. She had all the bowls and utensils out by the time Ariel was ready, her own project set up. Poster boards, magazines marked with Post-its, and some sort of list.

"What's that?" Portia asked.

"Think of me as your fairy godmother."

"You're on the young side. Shouldn't I be the fairy godmother?"

"My clothes are fine. Yours? Not so much. I'm going to fix you up. You can thank me with one of those cupcakes."

"Fix me up?"

"So you can catch a, well, guy."

Portia's mouth fell open.

"I know you're divorced and all. Still, you're not so old that you can give up dating for the rest of your life. Right?"

"Are you sure you're a child?" Portia asked faintly.

"I prefer preadult female. Now, stop talking and listen."

Two minutes into Ariel's "presentation," Portia decided to ignore her and focus on the hideous Cutie's cupcakes. If she wanted a makeover, she could ask one of her sisters. Well, not Cordelia.

Of course, Ariel just kept talking. She had ripped out a load of "perfect outfits" from *Teen Vogue*. But if Portia ever had money again, she wouldn't be buying short, pleated skirts and platform tennis shoes.

The Cutie's cupcakes were missing something. The more Ariel talked, the more Portia craved the cupcake fix. She mixed the dry ingredients in a bowl, stirring slowly, feeling a sense of peace come over her. Ariel battled on, talking about how tights could be coordinated with a short skirt.

Portia finished her first "fix" on the cupcakes, writing down what she had done, just as her grandmother had taught her.

Ariel peered at her. "Are you sure you're listening to me?"

Portia put the batch in the preheated oven. "You bet," she answered.

"I don't believe you."

"Don't you have homework to do?"

"I spent a lot of time on this. The least you could do is listen."

"I am! Think of me as a multitasker. I can bake and listen. Tell me more about stockings."

"Not stockings," Ariel said with disgust. "Tights! There's a big difference, you know."

"Sorry. Of course."

Ariel's eagle eye stayed on her as Portia went back to the mixing bowl and started on a second batch. An hour or so passed with Ariel talking and Portia baking.

Oddly, it felt good to have Ariel's high voice providing a counterpoint to the sounds of baking. But by the time cupcakes covered every inch of counter space, Ariel was running out of steam. "Looks" from *Teen Vogue* and *Tiger Beat* battled with the cupcakes for space on the counter and kitchen island.

"I just can't believe that *Tiger Beat* is still in business," Portia said. "And you know I'll never wear pants like that, don't you? I'm not seventeen."

"These are totally swaggy pants," Ariel said indignantly. "Justin Bieber—not that I'm a Belieber or anything, but still—he wore them on his last tour. In leather."

"Do I really look like a woman who would wear *swaggy* leather pants?"

"Well, the other things, then. I got these magazines out of Miranda's room. She totally knows how to dress and she marked the pages, so everything I told you about is like picked by an expert."

"Picked by a teenager," Portia said, pushing the cupcakes on the table closer together so she could put out another tray. "*For* a teenager."

"My dad says she dresses like she's sixteen going on twenty-six. You can't be much older than twenty-six. Right?"

"I'm twenty-nine, and fashion isn't a priority for me right now."

"Like I didn't already know that."

Portia just laughed and kept working.

"You know, you're not really like other adults. Just saying."

"Why not?"

"You don't get worked up like the teachers at school. They always look mortally wounded or bear-woken-in-winter mad whenever I start talking without thinking my words through, which is pretty much all the time."

Portia just laughed again, concentrating on the elaborate designs she was swirling into the cupcake frosting.

Everything was nearly done when the doorbell rang.

"I'll get it," Ariel said, as though she lived there.

Miranda followed Ariel back into the kitchen, which was unexpected.

"Hi, Miranda," Portia said.

The girl stood there scowling, not looking even a bit happy to be there. "Yeah, hi—" The words froze in the air, and she stared at the table. "Oh, my gosh! How did you know?"

Portia took a deep breath. "Know what?"

"The cupcakes! How did you know I needed cupcakes? We're having a sophomore class bake sale and everyone has to bring something."

Portia couldn't speak. She hated this feeling, hated that she couldn't just bake like a normal person. In the morning she'd had the Kanes' favorite breakfast without knowing a single thing about what they liked to eat. Now this.

"Awesome!" Miranda exclaimed.

Gabriel chose that moment to walk into the apartment. "I rang the bell, but no one heard," he said.

When he saw Miranda laughing, the hard planes of his face eased, if only slightly. "I got your text that you needed cupcakes," he said to Miranda. "There's that cupcake place on Columbus." His eyes shifted to the kitchen counters. "What's this?"

"Cupcakes," Ariel said.

Portia tried to ignore the way Ariel eyed her.

"Can you believe it! Portia already made them," Miranda crowed. But then she seemed to realize what she was doing and stopped, the glower firmly back in place.

"How did you know?" he asked Portia.

"I didn't. I was experimenting." She refused to give in to the queasy emotions she felt. Maybe she just made the cupcakes because of Cutie's. And maybe she was going stark raving mad. She turned to the girls. "Can you find some boxes to put them in? How many do you need, Miranda?"

"A lot. Like six dozen," Miranda said.

Portia didn't need to count. She knew on a sigh that if she did, there would be exactly six dozen sitting on the counter.

The girls went out to find boxes, which left Portia and Gabriel standing alone.

"You have batter on your face. Again."

"Last time it was frosting."

She would have sworn he swallowed back a smile.

She wiped her cheek and found a swipe of strawberry shortcake cupcake mix.

"How did you know about the cupcakes? Really."

"I didn't. I was trying to come up with a way to make Cutie's cupcakes better. And I did." She took a mock little bow. "The German chocolate cake was easy. So was the vanilla buttercream. But the strawberry shortcake gave me fits. Turns out, the final fix came when I baked a fresh strawberry in the middle of a vanilla sour-cream batter instead of strawberry batter with chunks of strawberries. Here, try one."

"No, thanks."

"What, you're watching your boyish figure?"

Gabriel gave a surprised bark of laughter, snagged the cupcake, and took a bite. The amazement on his face made her smile. He stared at her concoction almost suspiciously before looking at her.

"And?" Portia prompted.

"And what?"

"What do you think?"

"I think you can bake."

"I'll take that as your way of saying you think it's good. Thank you." She shot him a saucy look, to which he raised a brow, his eyes intent on her.

The memory of him dragging her through the window and pulling her close made her light-headed, and she wondered if he was thinking about the same thing.

After a second he focused and saw the books. He picked up one with his free hand. "'*Hospitality and Restaurant Practices*'?" He cocked his head. "What's this for?"

"My sisters and I are going to open a restaurant."

Saying it out loud thrilled her and terrified her in turn.

For a second she thought he was going to laugh. She just held his gaze.

"You're serious."

"As serious as an accountant at an IRS audit."

His face closed off, reminding her of the ruthlessness she had first noticed about him on the front steps. "You have no business opening a restaurant."

"Says who?"

"Says the guy who watched you try to extricate yourself from a burger suit with a knife."

Her mouth fell open. "Burger suits and restaurants are two different kettles of fish."

"Kettles of fish? Now there's great business terminology."

"Yep, Texas style."

"You're in New York, sweetheart."

"I am not your sweetheart, thank my lucky stars."

"Another of your quaint Texas sayings? What was the last one I heard you use? 'Bless your heart'?"

She sliced him a tooth-grinding smile. "While you might not like them, you can bet your backside that a café that serves the kind of fare we create in Texas would have people lined up around the corner. Or, as we say in Texas, till the cows come home."

He raised a brow as he eyed her. "Did you know that sixty percent of all restaurants fail?"

"Really, I thought the number would be higher."

"Eighty percent in New York City."

She refused to gulp. "Wow, I thought the number was more like ninety-five percent."

"Some statistics put the number that high."

Double non-gulp.

"Is it possible that something has left Portia Cuthcart speechless?"

She glared at him. "Okay, funny guy."

His head cocked, but she kept going.

"I stand by my belief that a Glass Kitchen in New York will work."

"Then tell me, if you're such a prodigious businesswoman, what's your cost-to-baked-goods ratio?"

"What?"

"Don't know? How about margins? What kind of margins do you expect to achieve?"

She stammered.

The way he looked at her liquefied her insides, and she felt sorry for anyone who went up against him.

"Nope?" he said. "Then how much does a bushel of flour cost? Or how about the cost of small-business insurance?"

Her eyes narrowed.

"There's more to running a café," he finished, holding up her cupcake for demonstration, "than being good in the kitchen."

Finally she broke free of her shocked stupor and walked over to him. "One, bakers don't buy bushels of flour. We buy it by the pound, and last I checked—namely, this morning—a five-pound bag was going for $4.95; ten pounds, $8.95; twenty-five, $20.50. As to *two* on your rapid-fire list of insulting questions, small-business insurance varies, depending on the size of the small business, how many employees, what the business is, not to mention the city and state in which said small business is run. Having been a *prodigious* part of my grandmother's restaurant, The Glass Kitchen, back in Texas, I'm well aware that there's more to running a café than being a good cook."

She stopped directly in front of him. "My sister Cordelia has plenty of access to investors, all of whom will be interested to hear how I took a famous but hideous tasting Cutie's cupcake and turned it into the mouthwatering delight you now hold in your hand." She snatched the partially eaten cake away from him. "Or should I say, held in your hand."

She expected him to be embarrassed or, short of that, at least contrite. But no, not Gabriel Kane. He just looked at her, assessing, and she had to remind herself she wasn't intimidated by him.

"Good-bye," she said pointedly.

Gabriel raised a brow, then surprised her when he licked the frosting from his fingers. "Insulting. Rapid-fire. You're cute when you get feisty."

"Ack!" It was all she could do not to launch the cupcake at his head.

"Before you get carried away," he went on, smooth as butter, "I have something for you."

She eyed him. He pulled a key from his pocket and handed it over. "For my place. This way you can come and go when you need to, from the job that actually pays you money."

She reconsidered launching the cupcake.

"I'll leave money on the kitchen table to buy food. Later, I'll show you how I order online, if you want to do that instead."

Then he reached out, surprising her yet again, and wiped a smudge of frosting from the corner of her mouth. His gaze locked with hers as he sucked the sugar from his finger. "How is it that again and again, you make me forget the type of man I am?"

Portia felt heat rising in her cheeks. This was ridiculous. She didn't like aggravating men. In all the years she had known Robert, he had never once aggravated her, at least not before he divorced her. And then he had devastated her, which wasn't the same.

Truth to tell, for the first time since Robert had come home with his big announcement, Portia felt that maybe he had done her a favor.

When she dragged her gaze from Gabriel's lips, their eyes met. For a second she thought he would kiss her again. But then his mouth went hard, his eyes shuttering, and she was certain irritation ran along his body like an electric current.

There will be no more of that, his expression told her.

Relief mixed with disappointment.

I couldn't agree more, she shot back wordlessly.

He nodded and disappeared through the doorway.

Fourteen

⬩⬩⬩

Three days later, Portia forgot to set her alarm and ended up dashing up the stairs at ten minutes after seven, having barely thrown on cargo pants and a white cotton tee, and hastily brushed her teeth.

Gabriel leaned against the kitchen counter, reading the newspaper, a cup of coffee in his hand. His hair was still wet from the shower, a little long and raked back. He looked better than her cupcakes. Damn, damn, damn.

She had hoped to get breakfast done early; she had a lunch meeting a block away on Columbus Avenue with a potential investor. Cordelia had made the arrangements, and her sisters were supposed to meet her there. But Olivia had already e-mailed that she couldn't make it; she had been asked to sub for an advanced yoga class.

"*Since Olivia's bailing, you have to be there, Cordelia,*" Portia wrote back. "*When you made it a lunch meeting, you promised to pay.*"

"*Stop worrying, P! It's lunch; it won't cost much. And I'll be there.*"

"Late?" Gabriel asked, breaking into her thoughts. "Only three days in?"

"It's seven o'clock," Portia stated. "Okay, seven-ish."

"I didn't realize that in a professional workplace seven sharp was more of a loose term."

"God, you're funny."

He gave her a strange look.

"What? No one's called you funny before?"

"No," Gabriel said, the word quiet.

She looked at him, but before she could probe, he folded the newspaper and tossed it on the counter. "The girls should be down any minute. I have a meeting at eight. Though maybe the Civic Board really meant eight-ish. And at two I'm meeting the contractor here. Or maybe it's two-ish."

She shot him a look. "That probably *is* what they meant."

His shout of laughter surprised them both.

She smiled at him then. "I won't be late tomorrow, promise."

A remnant of his smile seemed to fight with his standard glower. "Good girl."

The words caught her off guard. *Good girl.* She had always been just that. Fun, maybe, but not much more than that. Always good.

She realized she was tired of being the good girl. What would happen if she wasn't, if she gave in and lost herself in Gabriel Kane?

The girls entered, though it was a second before she realized Gabriel had already left. So much for losing herself in him.

"Good morning!" Portia said.

"What are you? A cheerleader?" Miranda grumbled.

"Hey, I made you cupcakes. Seems like you'd be in a better mood."

"Yeah, okay, thanks."

"Now, now, Little Miss Sunshine," Portia teased, setting her own concerns aside.

Ariel grimaced. "You're kidding, right?"

Miranda went over to a cabinet and pulled out a box of sugar cereal. "Maybe she thinks she'll get paid more if we give her a good report."

"Aren't you the cynic?" Portia said, swiping the box away.

"Hey! That's my breakfast."

"Not as long as I'm in charge of feeding you." Portia rummaged in the refrigerator. "Who's up for eggs, bacon, and toast?"

Miranda and Ariel exchanged a glance. "Ah, no one."

Portia made them eggs, bacon, and toast anyway, which Ariel ate and Miranda picked at, but picked at enough that Portia gave her a thumbs-up.

"Surely she'll take it down a notch after she's been here a while," Miranda said to Ariel as the girls headed out the door.

"I heard that," Portia called after them.

"You were supposed to."

⁎

Once Portia finished up in the kitchen, she returned downstairs to get ready for the lunch meeting. After a quick bath, she dressed with care. Ariel wasn't wrong about Portia needing a different look. Vintage clothes weren't going to win her any prizes for business professionalism. So she did what she could with the clothes she had. Texas politician's–wife clothes. Navy blue St. John Knits. Not a staple on the Upper West Side of Manhattan, but sure to instill more confidence than Annie Hall one-offs.

Ready to go, Portia fired up her computer to check her e-mail. The headline of Google News caught her attention.

Gabriel Kane Brings Global Inc. Down

Gabriel Kane? Her Gabriel Kane? Or, rather, her neighbor Gabriel Kane? Portia quickly amended.

The article was definitely about her neighbor, who, it turned out, wasn't your Average Joe. His primary concern wasn't going into one of those dime-a-dozen glass-and-steel office towers by day and bossing around a stream of people redoing his apartment by . . . well, the rest of the time. If the article was to be believed, his raison d'être appeared to be very publicly destroying some company named Global Inc. The reporter further went on to say that once Gabriel's investment in the company went sour, he vindictively went after Global Inc., driving their stock price into the ground.

Portia headed out, her mind spinning. Yikes. While Gabriel looked ruthless, she couldn't help but remember the way he had made her drink water after spilling out of the hamburger suit, or how he had seemed fierce about the danger on the fire escape. Not to mention the way he was trying to do right by his girls. She had to believe he was fair. That he wasn't a man to bring people down ruthlessly. The article had to be an exaggeration. But on top of that, she realized that her neighbor was an investor.

With the thought tumbling around, she walked into La Maison five minutes early and was seated outside. Five minutes passed and Cordelia still hadn't shown up. Portia checked her phone; nothing. After ten minutes, Portia dialed her older sister, but the call went straight to voice mail.

"You better be just about here, Cordelia," she muttered into the phone.

Russell Bertram showed up by himself after a few minutes. "Portia?" he said, coming up to her and extending his hand.

According to Cordelia, he was the most promising of the investors on their list. He was handsome, with fair skin and coppery brown hair longer than a Texas banker would have allowed. He wore a brown sports jacket with blue pinstripes over a white button-down shirt and jeans. He didn't seem anything like an investment guy. He definitely seemed too young to have enough money to invest in a café. But before more than a few words had left his mouth, Portia realized he was utterly charming.

"Sorry I'm late. I volunteer at my old school. They have a young-entrepreneur's group." He gave her a lopsided grin. "Once a month I spill out words of wisdom. If only they knew what a lousy student I was back then."

Portia laughed. "Maybe you should tell them. It would be inspirational."

"So tell me, how's Cordelia? And James? I don't know either of them well, but James helped me a lot when I put together my own fund."

"They're both doing great. James has a lot of amazing stuff going on." She prayed it was true.

"That's good. I was worried when I heard he got caught in the Atlantica General blowup. But if anyone could land on his feet, it's James."

Portia liked Russell more with each minute that passed. He ordered a surprisingly big meal, and when he suggested wine, she thought about how tired she was of being a good girl. She laughed and agreed.

They talked about the best restaurants in the city—ones he had been to, ones she had only read about, given her whole no-money problem. They even delved into Manhattan real estate, if only because no meal in New York was complete without mention of a street address or a co-op. There wasn't a single mention of why they were actually there.

When Russell ordered a second glass of wine for each of them, Portia didn't refuse. He leaned forward and looked her in the eye. "So, tell me, I hear you work with Gabriel Kane."

The wine must have muddled her brain. "Pardon?"

"Don't go coy on me." He grinned, his blue eyes shining with schoolboy charm. "When I asked Cordelia about your experience, she said you work with Gabriel Kane."

Portia's head jerked back. Why would Cordelia say anything about her cooking for Gabriel?

But a second later, it hit her. Cordelia had known Gabriel was an investment guy all along. She had used his name as bait to get the meeting. No wonder her sister hadn't shown up.

She ground her teeth. "You know him?" She tried to smile, trying to figure out how to salvage the lunch. She wouldn't out and out lie, but she saw no reason to tell this guy that she not only didn't work for Gabriel in any investment capacity, but that Gabriel had made it clear what he thought of her opening a Glass Kitchen.

Russell gave a modest shrug. "I know *of* him. Who doesn't? But I've never met him." He leaned forward, his elbows on the table, his forearms encircling his wine. "I have the greatest investment opportunity, one I know will blow Kane away. I've tried to get in to see him, but no luck. When you invited me to lunch, I figured you must have heard about it. I take it you do legwork for Kane."

Portia blinked. "Legwork?"

"You know, get the lay of the land. See if something is worthwhile to show Kane?"

"You're here because you have an investment opportunity you want to present to Gabriel?"

He smiled, excited. "Yes! This is awesome."

Suddenly he seemed exactly as young as he looked. This was a man who thought he was getting the chance of a lifetime. He had no money to invest. He needed investors.

Disappointment seeped through her, every ounce of wine making itself known.

"Not so awesome," she replied wearily.

Russell's blue eyes stopped sparkling. "What do you mean?"

"I'm not here about your project."

"Kane didn't send you?"

"No."

Freckles she hadn't noticed before popped out on his pale skin as he hunched forward.

For a half a second he just sat there. Then he glanced at her expensive St. John suit and managed a guileless smile. "So," he said, "even if you're not scouting for Kane, are you looking for your own investment opportunities?"

He looked so dejected and sweet with those freckles and tousled red-brown hair, not to mention so fruitlessly hopeful, that she felt a nearly maternal need to comfort him, despite her own stinging disappointment. She reached across the table and squeezed his hand. "I wish I was."

"Then why did you want to meet . . ." His voice trailed off as he looked at her hand on his. "I'm being stupid, aren't I? Now I'm embarrassed. Your sister told me you were divorced and had just moved to New York."

A heartbeat passed as she tried to make sense of what he was saying. Then it hit her, blood searing through her cheeks, and she jerked her hand way. To her horror, Russell blushed, too.

"Look," he said awkwardly, "lunch was nice and all. I mean, I enjoyed meeting you. But, well, I'm not—I have a girlfriend."

Her mouth opened, then closed, then opened again.

But before she could think of what to say, he jumped to his feet.

"Listen, I've got to go. But I'm glad you invited me to lunch." His blush deepened. "I mean, you're great. And if I was the kind of guy to have a fling, I would love having a fling with you." If possible, he blushed even more. "Sorry, that came out wrong. Okay, anyway, gotta go. Thanks for lunch!"

Then he was gone.

She was mortified, aghast. But seconds later, she was frantic. Forget that he thought she was trying to have a fling with him. He'd left her with the check.

She scrambled into her purse, praying she'd find more than she knew was actually there. Sure, she expected that she, or rather Cordelia, would pay for lunch when it was meant to be their pitch to him, sans wine and steak. But steak! For lunch! The minute he'd ordered wine, Portia had assumed he would pay.

And it was all Cordelia's fault. What had her sister been thinking, giving him the impression that she could help him gain access to Gabriel Kane?

Portia really was going to kill her sister.

Her hands trembled, a trickle of sweat forming beneath her fancy suit as she pulled out her credit card and handed it over. Not more than a few minutes later, the waitress returned. "Ma'am, I'm afraid your card was rejected."

She cringed. "You're sure?"

"Sometimes the machine just doesn't like the card. Do you have another?"

"Well, no." Part of Portia's alimony deal with Robert was that he would pay her expenses for six months while she got settled—but she had only the one credit card, which he obviously wasn't paying. Why was she surprised?

"Then it'll have to be cash."

Portia rummaged through her wallet again, but no wad of bills miraculously appeared. She started counting out what she had, but didn't come close to the $150 bill.

All she could do was call Cordelia. But Cordelia still didn't answer. Neither did Olivia. Not that Olivia had more money than she did.

Portia counted her money again.

In the end, she left her driver's license with the manager and ran across the street to the ATM.

As soon as she paid, she went straight home. With every step she took, her anger grew. *I can't believe Cordelia did this to me*, she raged as she took the steps to the town house. *I am absolutely, positively going to kill Cordelia*, she promised herself as she slammed into her apartment.

She came to a dead stop when she heard the noise, and a smell biting at her nose.

"Portia, is that you?"

"Cordelia?"

Portia marched into the kitchen to find Cordelia there, an apron tied over her perfect clothes. The counters and stove were covered with pots and pans. Fingerprints and swipes marked the thin coating of flour that covered the surfaces like a child's watercolor painting project.

"What in the world are you doing?" she gasped.

Cordelia laughed, delighted, though there was something off about the look in her eyes. "What does it look like I'm doing?"

"Making a mess! And where were you at lunch?"

Cordelia paused mid-stir. "Oh my Lord! Lunch! Sorry. But just look at this. I'm cooking and baking! I woke up this morning," she rushed on, "thinking of food. Just like how it happens to you. I have the *knowing!*"

"What?" Portia tried to make sense of the scene. After a second, she noticed that Cordelia's clothes weren't so perfect, after all. In fact, for the first time she could remember, her sister wore wrinkled pants, the blouse not coordinating with the rest of the outfit. And her hair. Cordelia usually spent a great deal of time at the salon having her tresses professionally done. Portia speculated that Cordelia hadn't been to the hairdresser in a while.

"Cord, are you okay?"

Cordelia whipped around, spoon in hand, some sort of liquid flying across the room. "I'm fine! Don't I look fine? Of course I look fine. You're just saying that because I forgot about lunch. I am sorry, Portia."

"Okay, sweetie," Portia said carefully, coming closer. "Not to worry about the lunch."

Behind her, she heard the front door open and close.

"Hey!" Olivia called out, then stopped in the kitchen doorway. Her long, curly blond hair was pulled up in a messy twist, her full lips shiny with a nude gloss, her standard yoga attire fitting like a second skin. "What happened in here?"

Portia and Olivia exchanged a glance. Portia shrugged carefully. "I came home to this."

"Why isn't she cooking at her own place?"

"I wondered the same thing."

"She looks off."

"Don't mention it to her. She's sensitive."

"I'm standing right here, and I am not one bit sensitive. I'm cooking! It's perfect. And it's a sign that opening a Glass Kitchen in New York is going to be even more perfect! I'll be able to cook, too!"

Portia and Olivia exchanged another glance. "Everything is burned," Olivia mouthed.

"I know," Portia mouthed in return, picking up a bowl filled with wilted lettuce swimming in dressing. She sniffed and tasted. Butter lettuce with, perhaps, a raspberry vinaigrette.

Olivia walked up to Cordelia, as if approaching a wild animal. "Sweetie, give me the spoon. I'll keep stirring, then you can tell us all about waking up with the knowing."

It looked like Cordelia would protest, but then her fake cheer and shoulders sank, like a rock in water. She relinquished the spoon, then walked over to one of the stools and sat.

Olivia set the utensil aside, then sat next to her.

Cordelia looked around, seeming to notice the mess for the first time. "I don't have the knowing, do I?"

Olivia took her hands and squeezed. "Probably not." She leaned forward and pressed her forehead to Cordelia's. "Which you didn't want anyway, remember?"

Portia turned away from them, wishing not for the first time that she had the same confidence with people that seemed to come to Olivia as easily as breathing. Portia focused on the pot on the stove and tasted whatever it was in the pot. She grimaced. "It's not the worst stew I've ever tasted."

"It's supposed to be cream sauce. I was going to make creamed beef on toast."

Portia turned off the heat, set the spoon aside, and walked over to sit next to her sisters. "Creamed beef?"

"Daddy's favorite," Cordelia said, the words quiet.

"Oh my God!" Olivia laughed. "That awful stuff?"

"You didn't love it?" Cordelia asked.

"Seriously? Toasted bread slathered in creamed beef? No one loved that meal. Not even Daddy."

Portia joined in, smiling as she remembered. "No, Daddy didn't love anything about creamed beef on toast. But he loved Mama, and I swear she never knew that he barely choked every bite down." She looked at the scratched linoleum. "What I'd give to have even half the love that Daddy felt for Mama."

The sisters were quiet then. Portia knew they were lost in their own thoughts, their own memories of their parents. Then all of a sudden, Olivia leaped up.

"No dancing!" Portia said automatically. "And no singing!"

"Ha! Do I look that predictable? No. Let's play Spit!"

Another of Daddy's favorites.

Olivia raced into living room, and Portia heard her rummaging around in one of Aunt Evie's cabinets.

"I am not playing Spit," Cordelia stated.

Portia felt a trickle of relief. Cordelia was sounding more like her normal self again.

"Don't be a stick in the mud," Olivia teased with a wry twist of lips when she returned with a deck of ancient playing cards.

When they were growing up, their father had loved teaching his girls the rough-and-oh-so-impolite game called Spit, a game completely at odds with their mother's book on manners. How many times had Daddy teased Mama about turning his girls into sissies, making Mama laugh until they ended up in the back of the trailer, the laughter shifting into something that pushed the girls out the door into the hardscrabble yard?

"You only want to play because you always won," Portia said, smiling, grabbing up cards the minute Olivia handed her a pack.

Olivia and Portia played a quick hand, Cordelia looking on with a jaundiced eye.

"I win! And I'm starving!" Olivia said, as she started separating the cards.

Portia whipped up a quick meal for her sisters to eat from the few things left in the refrigerator. Sandwiches and a grapefruit and avocado salad topped with poppy seed dressing. The two sisters played and ate, while Cordelia only ate.

"You might win," Cordelia said, finally picking up her deck of cards "but only because you always cheat." With a put-upon sigh, she set up to play without having to be reminded how.

"I did not cheat," Olivia said, then cried out, "Spit!" to start the game just before Cordelia was ready.

"See! Cheating," Cordelia yelped, her fingers stumbling as Portia and Olivia started working their cards.

Portia lost herself in the game, worry fading away, laughing, as she slid a 2 onto a 3 just before Olivia got her own card there.

"Rats!" Olivia cried, slapping down a King, Queen, Jack, and a 10 with rapid-fire quickness, then threw up her hands. "I win!"

Portia was just a few cards behind. But Olivia leaped up and cheered. "I won! I won! You guys are turtles!"

Cordelia took a deep breath, then set her cards down. "Sorry about the mess, Portia. And sorry about lunch. But I better get home." She ate her last bite of poppy seed–covered avocado, took off the apron, and smoothed back her hair before gathering her handbag. She walked to the kitchen doorway, then abruptly turned back. "Oh, and I probably should mention, it looks like James is going to be indicted."

Fifteen

❖❖❖

T HE NEXT DAY, Ariel walked into the town house after school.

She loved asking questions, though she wasn't big on answering them, as the Shrink had learned. But what was weird was that the Shrink didn't even seem to know what the right questions were, much less know to ask them. Her mom died over a year ago now, but he kept asking her to tell him what she felt. Hello, lousy.

She wanted him to tell her something massively smart that would make her feel better, like: "*Given the trajectory of matter over time, the miasma of your mind will not stay stagnant, therefore your sorrow will morph and change, making you feel more hopeful soon.*" Or: "*Given how incredibly smart you are, Ariel—a genius, really—your astounding brain is sifting through the data and soon it will make sense out of the senseless occasion of your mother's death, and then you'll start feeling better.*" Even a lame: "*Everything is going to be okay*" would do in a pinch. But nope, he never spoke a word that made her feel anything other than that he really was a quack.

Whatever. Plus, what did it matter? Her mom was dead. Dead. She wasn't coming back. How did that ever get better?

It didn't.

But right then, Ariel had other problems. The report on her dysfunctional family, or what was left of it.

Yesterday she had roughed out a few pages, mainly in her journal. But that just made her realize she didn't know anything about her family. It was like some sort of twisted nursery rhyme. Her mom was dead. Her dad made money. Her uncle was sort of sleazy. And her grandmother . . . Ariel hardly knew what to say about her. Nana was bizarre. The woman didn't seem anything like a grandmother, or even a mother.

And then there was Miranda, who could be summed up as completely nuts. Or, maybe, nympho.

Just that morning she was muttering in her cell phone the way she always did, but Ariel managed to overhear her anyway. She was talking about a dare. With a boy.

Which meant it was time to raid the journal again, because someone had to look out for the family, now that Mom was gone. And poor Dad was just too clueless when it came to Miranda.

Ariel dropped her bag in the foyer, checked around the house, then snuck into Miranda's room and found her journal.

A big, boldly written **DARE** blazed on top of a new page.

"Bingo," Ariel whispered.

Tuesday, October 1

I don't totally hate school anymore. I met some girls who are pretty nice. Not as nice as my old friends back in Jersey, but they'll have to do. One way or another, I am going to get back to NJ. God, I miss our old house and Kasey just down the block. My new friend Becky lives on the Upper East Side, and her mom is a total stay-at-home type who is always there, or at least someone is always there. I'm the only girl I've met so far who doesn't go home to someone. Actually, though, I'm lucky because I can do stuff and they can't. Becky dared me to

ask Dustin Bradford over after school. DARE. No question Dad
would go Dark Side if he found out.

The sound of the front door opening took a second to register. Ariel slapped the journal shut and shoved it under the mattress. She was just shutting the door when Miranda rounded the bend in the staircase.

Her sister stopped short. "Were you in my room?"

Ariel scoffed. "No."

"Then why are you standing in front of my door?"

"I heard you coming up the stairs."

Miranda's eyes narrowed; then she waved Ariel away like she wasn't important enough to spend another second dealing with. "You are *never* allowed in my room."

"Like there is anything in there that I'd want." *Nympho*, she added silently.

She ran down the stairs and surprised Portia in the kitchen, unpacking groceries. "Hey, Ariel."

"Hey? Is that a Texas thing, too?"

Portia laughed. "I take it you don't say *hey*."

"Nah. I pretty much stick to *hi* or the occasional *how do you do*—you know, when I want to throw off an adult."

"Throw off an adult, huh?" Portia pulled a chicken from the bag. Next came onions and celery, carrots and brown rice.

"Most adults are clueless."

"I'm an adult."

"The jury's still out on you."

Portia laughed. "Tell me something I don't already know."

The woman definitely wasn't easy to peg.

Ariel stood there a bit longer until Portia glanced over at her. "What?"

"I've been at school. All day. I'm a kid."

"And?"

"Aren't you going to ask me whether I have homework to do? Or whether I was bullied in gym? Or whether I threw up?"

"You don't really look like the throw-up type."

She had her there.

Miranda practically danced into the kitchen.

Portia glanced over her shoulder. "Hey, you."

Miranda didn't say a word. She walked over to the refrigerator and pulled out a bottle of VitaminWater, then circled back to lean against the stainless-steel door and sighed, a weird smile on her face.

"What's wrong with you?" Ariel asked.

"Nothing's wrong. Everything's great."

Portia turned back to the sink. "She's in love."

Miranda's eyes went wide. Then she did an even bigger sigh, tons of dreamy slathered on. It made Ariel want to gag.

"Maybe a little." She giggled.

Portia kept working on dinner, washing the chicken, putting it in a pot.

"So who is it?" Ariel asked.

"Like you'd know him," Miranda scoffed.

Portia still didn't say a word, but then Miranda went off like a race-horse.

"His name is Dustin. He's the cutest boy in school. Becky says so."

Uh-oh. Dustin was coming to fruition.

"He's in my algebra class." Miranda said. "I hate algebra. Sooooo, I asked him to come over and help me! Not that he's any better at it than I am, but he's going to come over." She glared at Ariel just as Portia walked into the pantry. "No telling Dad," she hissed. "I told an adult I have someone coming over. I told *her*." She nodded toward the pantry.

Who would have guessed Miranda was smart enough to come up with a way to win a dare without breaking the letter of the law? Dad's law, that is.

"Me? Do I look like a snitch?"

Of course Ariel had already thought of several ways she could use this information to her advantage. But she really didn't tattle.

Portia returned to the sink, and Miranda walked over to stand next to her.

"What are you making?"

What? The girl who hardly ever came out of her room except to barely eat and fight with Dad was making conversation?

"A cross between chicken and rice and chicken soup," Portia said.

"Cool."

Cool? Who was this girl? First, a non-adult adult, now a non-glowering teenager?

"My mom never cooked," Miranda said. "But she loved my dad. And he loved her. A lot." Miranda's smiled shifted and changed. "In fact, just because you cook for us doesn't mean you can take her place."

"Miranda!" Ariel gasped.

Portia turned her head, didn't look one bit ruffled. More like she looked determined, like she had been reminded of something totally true.

"Not to worry, Miranda," she said. "I'm not trying to take her place. I'm just working for your dad. Your mom is your mom, and always will be."

Hello, *our* mom.

But Ariel didn't say that, either. She didn't care to go into Miranda's story about how their mom and dad brought home the wrong baby when they picked up Ariel, but then the hospital wouldn't take her back. Sure, Ariel was smart enough to know that this was in no way possible. But Miranda said it with such authority that Ariel was half convinced there was some truth to the story. Maybe just that her parents hadn't believed someone who looked like Ariel could be their child. Thank God Ariel had their mom's weird green eyes, so no one could pretend she wasn't their kid.

Miranda took a carrot and chomped down on it, turning away from Portia so she could glower at Ariel. "She might not have cooked, but she was fun."

"Mom? Fun?"

The words were out of Ariel's mouth before she could swallow them back.

Miranda glanced at her. "Of course." Like Ariel was a moron. "You heard what Uncle Anthony said. She was the life of the party. And she was totally fun when . . ."

The words trailed off.

Portia glanced over at Miranda, but still didn't say a word.

"Mom wasn't fun," Ariel said, "she was, like, beautiful. Always the perfect clothes and hair, always had her nails done. Totally beautiful."

Miranda eyed Ariel, seemed on the verge of rolling her eyes, but relented. "She was all that. But she was fun, too. At least she was totally fun before you landed on our doorstep looking like a troll."

Ariel felt the blood rise in her face. As always in circumstances like this, words eluded her. Her quick brain slowed; her heart hurt.

"Miranda." This from Portia.

"What?" Miranda snapped back.

"You know what."

Now Portia was being an adult. She had that steady gaze thing down pat. And Miranda backed down.

"Whatever. Mom was fun even after you arr—"

Another look.

"Fine. After you came home and weren't a total troll." She drew a breath. "She really was fun. When you were a baby, she could make you laugh and laugh."

Ariel's throat went tight, the same way it did whenever the Shrink asked her to talk about their mom. Then a memory hit her. "I remember a time, once, when Mom dragged me into the backyard to plant violets and watermelon. She laughed and said it would be fun." The kitchen grew comfortably quiet. Finally, like giving in or something, Portia asked, "Do you have a photo of your mom?"

Miranda shrugged, then pushed up. "I do." She went upstairs, then returned in a flash. "This is her. It's the only one I have since Dad packed all the others away. But it's a great one."

The photo made Ariel's throat tighten even more. It showed Miranda, Mom, Dad, and Ariel, all laughing, Mom leaning up against Dad.

But the photo had been taken when Ariel was little. Other than in this picture, she had never seen her mother laugh or lean against Dad.

"You should put it out," Portia said.

Miranda gave her a look. "Yeah, so Dad can bite my head off? No thanks."

Ariel explained. "He doesn't like being reminded of Mom. Which makes it really hard to do the report I'm working on."

"What report?"

"The one on our family. We have to write a paper on our family tree, without it just being a family tree. I ask, what does that even mean?"

"I had to do one of those when I was in middle school," Miranda said. "I just asked Mom a bunch of questions. She told me stories about herself as a kid."

"Really? What did she say?" Ariel asked, the words kind of breathy.

"Not much. I just wrote about her wanting to be a princess when she was young, and how it was special to me since I wanted the same thing when I was her age. I got an A." Miranda looked at Ariel wryly. "You could hand in the same report, but I don't think anyone would believe that you ever wanted to be a princess."

Ariel's heart twisted even more. Her mom had wanted to be a princess?

Miranda's cell rang. One glance at the screen and she dashed from the kitchen, then out the front door.

Ariel and Portia watched her go. After a second, Portia poured a glass of coconut water with ice and handed it to Ariel. "I bet you have your own stories to tell about your mom, stories that are completely yours."

"How do you know?"

"I'm a sister, just like you. And I'm a younger sister, just like you. All you have to do is dig around, find the memories. They'll be there."

"Dig around?"

"You know, ask questions, search out answers?"

"Like a detective?"

Portia laughed. "Exactly. Ariel, the Twelve-Year-Old Detective."

"I'm nearly thirteen!"

"All the better."

Portia turned back to the pile of food on the counter. Ariel took the glass and then headed out of the room to her dad's office.

She felt a little better. She could look for some memories, like Portia said. She could get her own A, and not with some idiotic story about a princess, either. She would do an Internet search.

In the office, she fired up her dad's computer, the one that didn't have any kid blocks. She opened her backpack and rummaged around, looking for a pen and some paper. She really needed to clean out her backpack now. Before she knew it, she'd be thirteen. And, seriously, what self-respecting teenager carried around a calculator covered in stickers; a painted inhaler; or crazy socks with individual toes, like gloves for feet. She had outgrown them all.

But then there was the whole thing she couldn't get out of her head. Her mom had given her the stickers. Her mom had whipped out the nail polish and painted Einstein on the inhaler after Ariel had refused to carry it around because it was stupid.

And the socks? She'd found those after her mom died, like some sort of weird relic from the past. Her mom had been super fancy. How many times had Ariel wondered how a girl who owned those socks could grow up to be a woman who always wore boring clothes and tons of pearls?

As usual, there were more questions than answers.

Ariel went to Google and typed in her mom's name. Photos popped up. Ariel had seen them before. After all, she'd Googled her mom a zillion other times. No new photos. No new news, either. Just the same articles, the ones about all the good works Mom did, and all the variations on "Social Scion Dies in Crash."

Pressure built up behind Ariel's eyes.

Quickly, she moved on. This time, she typed in the name her uncle had used, Victoria Polanski. The computer spun for a second, and up popped a whole new batch of images. Mom way younger than Ariel had ever seen her. Mom with a group of girls glammed up like that old group the Spice Girls, arms linked, drinks in hand. The caption read: *Beauty Times Four.*

The article went on about Mom and a whole bunch of other people attending a big bash at a bar opening in Union Square.

Ariel couldn't have been more shocked if she'd read that her mother was a vampire. This image, and the one that was lodged in her head, didn't match. At all.

She kept scrolling down until she came to a photo of her dad. Actually it was of her dad and uncle, standing on either side of her mom. This time, the caption read: *Two Beauties and a Beast.* It said that her mom was a beauty, sure, but it was mainly about how her uncle was the beauty to his older brother's beast. The thought made her hurt a little bit more.

Quickly, she clicked on another link, anything to distract herself. But what popped up made her flinch. An obituary. She hated obituaries. Avoided them like the plague.

On second glance, she breathed a little easier when she realized it wasn't for her mother. Instead, it was for a man named Bohater Polanski. *Bohater Polanski?*

Ariel scanned the notice. The man was born in Poland; immigrated to the United States when he was a teenager; married, then lost his young wife; was a longtime maintenance engineer at the Amsterdam Houses, the same complex where he raised his only daughter, Wisia "Victoria" Polanski.

Her pulse slowed.

The photo included with the notice showed an old man with no smile but clearly proud of the teenage girl standing next to him, as if it were the only photo of the man to be found. Even Ariel couldn't deny that the girl was her mother.

With her heart in her throat, she Googled "Amsterdam Houses."

Ariel stared at the screen. Her la-di-da mother, who refused to socialize with anyone who wasn't from the "right" family, was raised by a man she had never bothered to mention, in a housing project in an iffy section of the Upper West Side.

That was the woman who could paint Einstein in lime green nail polish and who owned crazy gloves made for feet.

Sixteen

✦

A CRASH STARTLED PORTIA and she dashed out of the Kanes' kitchen.

"Ariel?"

"Everything's fine! No need—"

Portia came to a stop in the doorway to what looked like Gabriel's office. The room had heavier furniture than the study one floor up. Ariel stood at a mahogany desk with a drinking glass at her feet, a spray of coconut water and ice cubes splashed across the floor.

"Ah, clumsy me." Ariel closed the computer window, then turned off the machine. "I guess I made a mess."

Portia eyed the computer. "What are you doing?"

"Homework."

"That didn't look like homework."

"Portia, seriously, you're showing your age. This is how we do homework now. On computers. We do research on the Internet, then write intelligent reports suffused with impressive detail." Ariel stepped high over the water and drinking glass. "I'll get some towels." She walked across the hall and retrieved two hand towels from the half bath. "But don't worry, I don't think less of you for not knowing that." Her smile widened, and she dropped down and mopped up the mess. Portia dropped down next to her, and they had it all cleaned up in seconds.

"Ariel, seriously," Portia said in a perfect version of a teenage accent, if she said so herself. "Do I look like I just fell off the turnip truck?"

Ariel eyed her. "You probably don't want me to answer that."

Then she surprised Portia when she leaped up, tossed the towels back in the bath, and grabbed her hand. "I'm starved."

Portia was still worried about Cordelia. After her announcement about the possible indictment, she had later explained that the authorities had started probing not just the bank, but James as well. James had not left the apartment in days.

Portia's unease grew when she and Ariel returned to the Kanes' kitchen and found that Miranda was back, this time with a boy.

Ariel stopped so fast that Portia bumped into her.

"Ariel," Miranda snapped. "Shouldn't you be upstairs or something, doing homework?" She eyed Portia. "And aren't you, like, finished playing maid for the day?"

The boy actually laughed, though he also gave Portia a once-over like a bad imitation of a lech in a seedy bar. He looked older than Miranda, though he wore the same school uniform. His blond hair was shaggy, but somehow seemed professionally cut that way, as if he—or his mom—had paid two hundred dollars for the trim.

"This is your maid?" he asked. "My mom needs to fire whoever finds our housekeepers. Ours are always old and major ugly."

Portia wrinkled her nose. "Do kids in New York really talk like that?"

"Huh?" the boy said.

"Ignore her," Miranda said. "Come on, Dustin, let's go upstairs to my room."

Ariel's eyes went wide. "You can't take a boy to your bedroom! Dad will kill you!"

"Well, he won't be home for hours, so he won't ever know. Right?"

"I guess," Ariel muttered.

"Right, Portia?"

"Don't get me involved in this. I'm just the *maid*, remember?"

"Whatever. Come on, Dustin."

Portia cursed under her breath. "Miranda, I don't think it's such a good idea to go upstairs. Stay down here, in the garden room."

Miranda jerked around and gave her a look. "Dad hired you as a cook, I get it. But guess what? That doesn't make you my babysitter!"

The boy laughed. "Dude," he said with a nod.

"Your dad won't be happy if he finds out you took a guy to your room. He might well decide that you *need* a babysitter."

Portia didn't register the sound of the front door opening until Miranda's eyes went wide.

"What's up?" Dustin asked.

"It's Dad," Ariel said. "He's going to kill you. *Dude.*"

"You have to go," Miranda added. "Shit, how do we get you out of here? What is Dad doing home so early?"

Before Portia could intervene, Miranda pushed the boy out the window and shooed him down the fire escape.

"Portia's door is always open. I'll take him out through there once Dad's inside," Ariel said as if Portia weren't standing there.

Miranda nodded. "Great."

"Hello, Dad!" Ariel sang frantically, blowing by him as he walked into the kitchen. "Back in a flash."

Gabriel stood, taking in the retreating form of Ariel, and then turned to take in Miranda and Portia. "Did I miss something?"

"No," Miranda blurted. "Not a thing. Right, Portia?"

Gabriel glanced between Miranda and her. What would she do if he asked her what was going on?

Just a few minutes later, Ariel burst back in.

Finally, he asked, "What's for dinner?"

"It's only five o'clock," Portia said.

"I thought I'd come home early. See how my girls were doing."

"Ah, yeah. Great," Miranda stated. She tucked her hair behind her ear and strode past him.

"I'm glad you're home, Dad," Ariel said, as if trying to reassure him that he was loved.

Gabriel smiled. "Thanks, sweetheart."

Then his cell phone rang, and he disappeared into his study. Portia was left alone again to finish dinner and was on the verge of leaving when Gabriel, Miranda, and Ariel reappeared.

"Dinner's ready," Portia said.

"Why don't you stay?" Gabriel said.

Portia glanced around to see whom he was talking to. "Me?"

"Yes, you."

"Thanks, but I can't."

"Come on," Ariel chimed in. "Stay."

Miranda glared.

Portia shook her head. "Nope. But thanks." No way was she getting roped into another dinner with this crew, despite the fact that she was starving.

At six, she found a can of tuna in her cabinet downstairs. At seven, she had eaten and cleaned, then started to pace. At eight, she called Olivia to get away from her thoughts. At nine, she called to check in on Cordelia, though her call went to voice mail. At ten, she went out, hoping to stop her circling thoughts. She was worried and irritable over one unavoidable fact. She was running out of money.

She walked for nearly an hour, but didn't feel one bit better. When she returned to the apartment, Gabriel was sitting on the front steps, his forearms on his knees.

He didn't say a word as she approached.

He always took her breath away, the mix of power and brutality, stirred together with an ache that was only visible if you looked closely.

She didn't need to be with any man right then; she had enough complications as it was. Not to mention the fact that this man had his own set of problems, the biggest of which being that he had lost his wife—the mother of his daughters—the one who didn't cook but was fun, at least according to Miranda. More than that—if she needed more than that—was the fact that she worked for him. To top things off, if . . . no, *when* things fell apart, they would be stuck in the same building, coming and going through the same cramped vestibule.

She hated that he made her want to forget everything and dive into him.

"I want a raise."

He cocked a brow, leaning back, planting his elbows on the step behind him, a grin sliding across his face. "Last I heard, *Hello* was the accepted form of greeting in the U.S."

She slapped her thigh. "God, you with the jokes. But I'm serious. And as you just pointed out, this is the U.S. Haven't you heard of redistribution of wealth? You appear to have lots. I need some. Hence the raise."

His grin hitched into a smile. "You've barely made half a dozen meals."

"A half dozen of the best meals you've had in a long time."

"It's pretty hard to get breakfast wrong."

"You'd think. But I have a nose, Mr. Kane, and the smell of burned oatmeal wafted from your kitchen the other morning."

"Wafted?"

"Don't change the subject."

His dark hair looked black as night in the sun, the waves reflecting the light, his matching eyes so dark that she couldn't tell where the pupils ended and the irises began.

"You're a good cook. I'll give you that."

"And then there were the cupcakes."

"True."

"Then you'll give me the raise?"

"No."

She heaved a melodramatic sigh, somehow feeling better already. "This really isn't funny," she said.

"Actually, it sort of is. You look like you're sucking on a lemon."

She shook her head with a jerk. "Untrue!"

"Nope, true."

"Do men your age say words like 'nope'?"

"This from the woman who just used the word 'wafting.'"

For a second, she thought he was going to laugh outright. Again. This man who people said was ruthless. But then the lightness dissolved, his face shifting back into hard, unyielding edges, and he stood. "Haven't you heard how intimidating I am?"

She rolled her eyes. "Who could have missed Big Bad You on the front of *The New York Times*?" She patted his shirt. "Go scare those poor guys at Global Guppy, or whatever company you're trouncing. I'm not afraid of you."

He actually looked a little insulted.

"One article does not a ruthless magnate make, Gabriel. What're you doing? Warming up to doing a Donald Trump 'You're Fired'?"

"Me channeling Donald Trump is about as likely as me giving you a raise."

"Well, you do have better hair."

His head fell back, and he looked up to the sky. "Three females in one suddenly small town house, not a one of them who listens to a word I say."

"Ariel listens."

He glanced back at her. "When she wants to."

They walked up the stairs and into the vestibule, but when she reached the entry to her apartment, she turned back. He was watching her, hands jammed into his pockets.

"For the record, I don't believe a word of that article," she told him.

He studied her. "You should. Every word of it's true. I get what I want, Portia. And I crush anyone who gets in my way."

She blinked, then broke into laughter. "If you're not careful, someone's going to ask you to star in your own reality-TV show."

His eyes narrowed in a way that gave her a flutter of alarm.

"Were you sitting out there for a reason?" she hurried on.

He appeared to debate letting her change the subject. "I rang your bell and you weren't home."

"I was out."

"What, no business plans to refine?"

"Ha-ha. You with the joking."

He stood there for a second. "I'm guessing Miranda had a boy here this afternoon."

Portia stiffened.

"I'm not an idiot, Portia. I assume he went out the kitchen window after I came in the door."

She debated. "Yeah, he did."

They stood in silence for a moment or two longer.

"I didn't know much about the girls before my wife died," he said, surprising her. "Now it's just me taking care of them. And I know what those boys are thinking. That's one thing I know about, being a kid lusting after a girl. You don't think about the fact that one day you'll probably have your own daughter."

"You know what they say about karma," she said delicately.

"I say it's a pain in the ass," Gabriel muttered.

Portia smiled at him. "There's more to raising girls than protecting them. You need to figure out how to have fun with them. Let them see that you *can* have fun. Make them feel at ease so they'll open up to you."

Gabriel's jaw set. "I know how to have fun."

"Really?" she challenged.

"Really."

"Prove it."

He glanced at her. "I don't have to prove anything."

"Maybe that's true in business. But with your daughters? Do you really believe you don't have to prove anything, especially when you admit that you weren't a big part of their life before their mother passed away?"

"What am I supposed to do?"

The noise of New York felt distant, as if just the two of them existed in this city of millions.

"Make something up," she suggested.

"What?" The word came out as a snap.

"I don't mean lie. I'm talking about simple kid things. Like looking up in the sky and finding shapes in clouds."

"I am not a child."

"No, you're a dad who's trying to connect with two daughters. You need to remember what it's like to be young, Gabriel."

He grumbled something, and then said, "There are no clouds."

"You can't see them because of the streetlight. But I bet if we go up on the roof," she said, her tone teasing and singsong, "we could see some."

"It's night."

"There's a full moon."

"We are not going up to the roof."

She ignored his glower, then headed for the front door. "Come on. It'll be fun."

"Ms. Cuthcart—"

"Don't go all 'Ms. Cuthcart' on me. I've wanted to see the roof again ever since I got here."

She stood in the vestibule, waiting expectantly at his front door, his hard gaze locking with hers. She caught her lower lip in her teeth, trying to look sweet and innocent.

"That would work better if I didn't know you're only sweet around me when it suits you."

She gave a surprised burst of laughter. "Touché."

After a second, he relented and put his key in the lock. Before he could change his mind, she slipped inside and started tiptoeing up the stairs.

Amazingly, Gabriel followed, floor after floor, quiet so the girls wouldn't hear them. When they came to the doorway that led to the roof, Gabriel reached out and opened it for her.

The minute she stepped outside, Portia smelled the cool evening air. She felt like the clock had been turned back, Gram still alive, Great-aunt Evie still here, the summers filled with promise of a very different kind of adventure. Portia had loved New York when she was younger, but in a way that was so different from what she felt for Texas, with its giant blue sky and easygoing charm, like sweet tea over ice on a hot day. In New York, nothing was easy; everything was dense, nothing fluffy about it, like bagels slathered with thick cream cheese.

Of course, Gabriel had renovated the space. Latticework provided privacy from the town house next door, a cabana-like structure creating a private space. The long swathes of roofing had been covered with a wooden deck. A table perfect for rooftop picnics stood to one side, with two chaise lounges perched at the far end.

The sky was a dark blue, almost black, the buildings like silhouettes. Only a hint of clouds could be seen.

"It's too dark," Gabriel stated, then turned back as if either this space, or the night sky, or maybe Portia, made him feel too much.

"Not so fast." Without thinking, she grabbed his hand.

He glanced down, and Portia felt the shock of his skin on hers. He didn't tug away when he dragged his gaze back to hers, but the expression on his face was unfathomable. "Are you intimidated by anything?" he asked softly.

Portia let go and walked away from him, with the same overwhelming awareness that he made her feel sliding through her like a warm sip of brandy. "Of course I am," she called back.

"Like what?

The future. A life derailed. Twice. Not understanding what I did wrong, or what I could have done different to make things turn out right.

But she didn't say any of that.

"Hmmm, like what?" She studied the wide black sky. "Like sports metaphors, navigating the Thirty-fourth Street subway station—I mean, seriously, how many subway lines do they have down there?—and SquareBob SpongePants. Or is it SpongeBob SquarePants? Whatever, I don't get him or his underwater bikini world."

She heard what sounded like a reluctant snort of laughter as she went over to one of the chaise lounges that sat side by side at the edge of the roof. After a second, she said, "Up here I feel completely alone, despite all the windows, the lights burning. Or maybe it's because I know that even if someone does see me, here, in New York, no one cares. It's freeing." She lay down and looked up at the sky. Finally she looked over at him.

"Come on, Gabriel. The girls are asleep. They'll never know you were up here instead down in front of your computer, slogging away like a efficient hamster on a wheel."

She was almost certain he muttered a few curse words and that he would storm back downstairs. Instead, he stood there for a second before he strode across the roof, those broad hands of his shoved in his pants pockets. After a moment more, he lay down on the chaise next to hers, so close that they nearly touched.

"What do you see?" she asked finally.

When he didn't answer, she rolled her head to glance over at him. He was looking at her, and this time his eyes held unmistakable heat.

The night air drifted between them, something charged. She told herself that she hadn't had sex in well over a year and that of course a guy like Gabriel with all his barely contained control would make her think of just that. Sex. It made sense that he intrigued her despite the fact that she knew nothing good could come out of getting involved with her neighbor. Besides, he had kissed her. Sue her, she wanted another taste. Which, despite all her bravado about him not intimidating her, was about as sane as thinking it was safe to pet a cuddly-looking grizzly bear.

"The clouds. What do you see?" she asked.

He stared at her. "I see a woman who is tilting at windmills."

Her eyes narrowed, thoughts of kissing and sex gone. "What does that mean?"

"Not a fan of Don Quixote?"

"Stop showing off and explain."

His shout of laughter seemed to surprise him. "'Showing off.' You are priceless."

She scowled.

"Fine, Don Quixote went around—"

"With Sancho Panza, trying to rekindle chivalry. Got that, but really don't know how it applies to me."

"So you know more than you're letting on."

"And you don't do the same thing?"

She made out his smile in the dark.

"Don Quixote kept fighting battles that he couldn't win."

She sucked in her breath.

"As when he tried to battle windmills that he thought were giants that could be beaten."

"I take it in your oh-so-*not* subtle way you're telling me I'm fighting a losing battle," she said.

"You sound like Ariel."

"You should sound more like Ariel."

He shook his head, but he still smiled.

"Just so we're clear, which battle am I losing?" she asked.

"The Glass Kitchen."

Portia bristled. "The Glass Kitchen is not a losing battle." It couldn't be.

"The way you're going about it certainly is."

"What does that mean?"

"You're not asking enough questions."

"I ask plenty of questions."

She forced herself not to cringe at the memory of her disastrous investor lunch.

"What questions should I be asking?" she asked, her tone completely even.

"According to Henry Ravel, you didn't ask him anything other than where did he prefer to meet. Midtown or Upper West Side."

"Ack! How do you know about Henry Ravel?"

Henry Ravel had been at her second ill-fated investor meeting. The second meeting that had ended abruptly when he learned she wasn't associated with Gabriel Kane, at least in terms of investing.

"He called me."

"About what?" Though she was afraid she knew.

"Somehow he got the impression that you're working with me."

Portia groaned. "Sorry about that. He's the second person my sister has done that to. But Cordelia's out of sorts, and I haven't found a good time to scream at her."

"I'm not worried about the calls," he said. "But here's the thing: Even if I thought you should open a Glass Kitchen—which I don't—you're going about it all wrong. As I said, you're not asking enough questions."

Portia looked up at the sky. The clouds were riding high and fast, like horsemen chasing across the sky. As much as she knew she should jump all over his advice, she just didn't want it. "Okay, you want questions, how about this: If you can't see or hear a tree fall in the forest, has it really fallen?"

"You're impossible," he muttered, and before she knew what was happening, he reached over and dragged her into his arms, her legs sliding between his as they lay together on his chaise.

"Oh," Portia whispered, their mouths only inches apart.

"Yes, oh," he whispered.

Her heart beat hard. She wanted to feel his lips on hers again. She wanted him to wrap her in his arms and make her feel all the things that she hadn't felt in years, if ever.

But just when he ran his hands up into her hair, she couldn't help herself. "I do have one important question. Why have you erased all traces of the girls' mother . . . your wife?"

They were so close that she could just make out the way his pupils contracted, the only sign of anger.

He didn't respond. He just looked at her. After a long second, he put her aside as if she didn't weigh anything at all and got up. He didn't help her to her feet. He didn't wait for her as he headed for the door.

"See," she called after him. "No one likes the important questions. Not even you."

He didn't respond, and the door shut closed firmly behind him.

Seventeen

❖

W HAT'S WRONG?"
Portia found Ariel at the table, head on forearms, a loaf of bread and a jar of peanut butter by her side, a knife sticking out of the peanut butter like a metal pole planted in a pot. "Ariel?"

The girl stirred and groaned. "What's going on?"

"You tell me," Portia said, pulling out a chair next to Ariel and sitting down.

It was four in the afternoon. She planned to make breaded veal cutlets, mashed potatoes, and green beans, then leave it for the Kanes to eat. Between the cupcakes and the cooking, not to mention the trip up to the roof with Gabriel, Portia felt she was getting pulled into this family despite her best efforts to resist them.

With a silent sigh, she pressed the back of her hand to Ariel's forehead to see if she had a fever.

"What's going on?" Ariel repeated groggily, then winced at the sight of the peanut butter. "Oh, yeah. I was hungry. But I never got around to making the sandwich."

"Didn't you eat lunch at school?"

"Not really."

"Why not?"

"The lunch room is not the best environment for eating."

"What is that supposed to mean?"

Ariel rolled her head and looked at her. "It means that it's not a five-star restaurant, okay?"

Portia studied her for a second. "Not feeling well?"

But Ariel wasn't hot. She didn't sound sick either. She sounded more dismayed than ill.

Stop getting involved with this family, Portia warned herself. *Remain detached. You are the cook. The* maid, *as Miranda said.*

"So, do you want to talk about whatever's bothering you?" she asked instead, cursing herself even as the words came out of her mouth.

Ariel eyed her for a second and then shook her head. "Nothing to talk about."

Portia debated, then shrugged. "Okay, then I'll get started on dinner."

She could feel Ariel's eyes on her back.

"Portia?" she said after a few minutes.

"Yes?"

"Did you mean it when you said that if you want answers, you need to dig, even if it makes you uncomfortable?"

Had she said that?

"You totally said that," Ariel said, yet again reading her mind.

"We were talking about your report."

"That's what I'm doing. Trying to write a good report."

Portia stopped working for a second and thought about it. "Yeah, I guess I meant it. We all have to dig sometimes. We all have to ask questions. Even if we don't really want to hear the answers."

Ariel grabbed the peanut butter, pushed up, and headed for the door. "Thanks."

Portia eyed her. "Are you sure you're okay?"

"I'm fine," Ariel answered. "Really."

An hour later, dinner prepared, Portia thought she heard the outer front door open and close. But she didn't hear the bell ring.

A few minutes after that, she heard a door again. This time, the bell rang.

Curious, she made her way to the foyer and opened the front door. In the vestibule she found Anthony Kane and her sister.

"Olivia?"

"There you are." Her sister smiled that particular brand of smile she had, like a single-malt scotch mixed with honey, both sophisticated and sultry sweet. Her long curly hair was loose, her long-sleeved white T-shirt tucked into jeans, a gossamer scarf twisted artfully around her neck. Of all the sisters, Olivia was the most comfortable in her own skin, throwing clothes together with an easy flair that made other women try to emulate her. On Olivia, the clothes made her look like a muse in an artist's painting. And no doubt Olivia had served as an artist's muse. Clothed, unclothed. Olivia had never been shy.

"I went downstairs, but no one was home," Olivia said. "Lucky me, when I was leaving," she added, her Texas accent stronger than usual, "I ran into this gorgeous man."

Portia rolled her eyes. Anthony laughed appreciatively.

"Nothing better than a female who speaks her mind," he said to Olivia.

The outer door opened and Gabriel walked in. He stopped at the sight of Anthony.

The four of them stood in the entry foyer of the Kanes' house as Gabriel curtly acknowledged Olivia, glanced at Portia, and then gave his brother a particularly forbidding smile. "You're here," he said.

His younger brother put out his hands, palms held up. "In the flesh," he said, his smile wide and charming. "You said you'd have a check for me. Of course I'd be here."

Gabriel's jaw ticked. More than ever, he looked the part of the beast. "My study. Now. We'll discuss."

"Discuss? I know what that means." He took Olivia's arm instead of following. "Maybe you should take a second to think about just what there is to discuss, Gabriel. In the meantime, I think this is as good a time as any to get to know Portia's beautiful sister."

"Anthony," Gabriel stated.

"Just give me a few minutes, big brother. I have no plans for the rest of the night." He looked at Olivia. "At least not yet."

Olivia laughed and let him guide her out the door.

Portia glanced at Gabriel. He gave her a hard look.

"Hey, he's your brother," she said.

"And she's your sister." He turned on his heel and headed for his study.

A few minutes later, Portia found Anthony and Olivia sitting at her kitchen table downstairs, each of them with a glass of fresh-squeezed lemonade.

"I came by to make sure we are still on for tonight," Olivia said. "The Bandana Ball, remember?"

Portia grimaced.

"Portia." Olivia eyed her. "Tell me you didn't forget."

"What's a 'bandana ball'?" Anthony asked.

"It's the best party in all of Manhattan," Olivia said. "Every year Texans in New York put on a huge gala event to raise money for Texas charities. This year is a push for Texas literacy. And every year Portia and her—" She cursed. "Well, Portia came to town to join us. This year she's already here." She sliced Portia a look. "Here and going."

"Do you dress up in ballgowns made of bandanas?" Anthony asked with a laugh.

"Actually, no. You dress up in Western wear. Boots, hats, jewels. We bought four tickets, but Cordelia is . . . well, a bit out of sorts these days, which means we have two extra." Olivia turned to Portia. "You can't back out on me, too."

"I'm sure you have plenty of friends to take."

"No way. You're going with me if I have to dress you myself and drag you to the Mandarin Oriental Hotel."

"I'll go." Anthony said.

Olivia gave him the once-over. "Perfect." She paused. "In fact, I have an idea. I think we need to get your brother to come as well. How can Portia say no if her *boss* is going?"

"He's not my boss."

Olivia gave her a look. "Do you work for him?"

"Sort of."

"How do you *sort of* work for someone?"

The *boss* chose that moment to walk in, without so much as a knock.

"If there is anyone who can *sort of* work for someone, Olivia, it's your sister."

Olivia laughed appreciatively. Portia scowled. But it was Anthony whose expression shifted the most when Gabriel turned to him.

"I'm running out of patience, Anthony. I have the papers ready upstairs," Gabriel said.

Olivia interrupted without an apparent thought for the tension that crackled through the room. "Come to the Bandana Ball with us, Gabriel Kane." She turned to Anthony. "Convince him to join us. Two Kane guys, two Cuthcart girls."

"Olivia," Portia snapped. "Stop."

"I think it's a great idea," Anthony said. "We'll go together. Dance up a storm." He glanced at the clock. "Gotta go if I'm going to have time to pretty up! I'll sign tomorrow, Gabriel."

Olivia grabbed Portia's hands and leaned close. "And don't you dare wear something boring."

⁘

"I can't believe I got talked into this," Gabriel stated.

Portia sat at a table underneath the vaulted ceiling of the Mandarin's ballroom on Columbus Circle, looking out over Central Park, hardly believing she was there either. But Olivia had pointed out that by not go-ing, she was letting her ex-husband take away something else from her that she loved.

Country-western music filled the hall, the strings and crooning at odds with the elegance of the modern hotel. Bales of hay and old-fashioned wagon wheels decorated a room full of men dressed in tux jackets, bow ties, jeans, and cowboy boots. The women wore diamonds the size of Texas, denim skirts of varying lengths, and stiletto heels straight off the runways of Paris.

Texas women might like their hair styled and their diamonds big, but you wouldn't find a single self-respecting Texas female in a pair of cowboy boots.

Gabriel looked as if someone had picked him up and landed him on the moon.

"Having a touch of culture shock?" she asked.

He gave her a wry look.

He wore a black suit and a silver-gray tie. Hot, yes. Texas Bandana Ball? No.

She glanced out at the dance floor. Anthony and Olivia were al-ready there, laughing, having fun. Gabriel hadn't moved since they had arrived.

"Hey, I know," she said, her tone needling, "why don't we do some-thing no one would expect us to do and, say, dance."

"I don't dance."

"That's how the whole *unexpected* thing works—doing something you wouldn't normally do."

"I've already exceeded my quota of the unexpected for the night."

"How's that?"

"I'm here."

She laughed at that. "Fine, don't dance. But could you go sit some-place else then?"

"What?"

"Someone else might ask me to dance," she explained, "but not if you're sitting here with me. And as long as I'm here, I plan to dance."

"I'm not leaving you at this table alone."

She wrinkled her nose. "It's hardly a dangerous street corner in the Bronx. And I'm hardly alone. We're surrounded with hundreds of people. Oh! There's a guy I know. I bet he'll dance with me."

She jumped up, but she hadn't gotten a step away when a woman came toward the man and led him onto the dance floor. When she glanced back, Gabriel looked exasperated but amused, too.

"If you'd worn running shoes, you could have gotten there faster."

She shot him a sharp look.

The music coming from the speakers stopped, and a band appeared onstage. At the sight of the country-western band Asleep at the Wheel, the crowd erupted in wild applause; minutes later, the dance floor filled to overflowing.

"What are they doing?" Gabriel asked, his face a mask of disbelief.

Portia laughed. "It's the Cotton-Eyed Joe."

Lines of dancers formed spokes, looking like a wheel turning as they danced side by side, shouting out the words. Namely, "Bullshit!"

No surprise, Anthony was at the center, Olivia next to him, her head tossed back in the sort of abandon that drew men in.

Portia watched, wishing she were out there, wishing she possessed her sister's ease, if not her abandoned behavior. Portia had been in Manhattan for only a few months, but already Texas felt distant. The women with their diamonds flashing in the glittering lights, heels high, fabulous attire, be it short skirts or long. The men with their wide, friendly smiles. But as much as she missed the only place she had ever called home, more and more she was finding that she felt as though she belonged here in New York. She wasn't even exactly sure why.

She was startled out of her thoughts when two women stopped abruptly on the opposite side of her table.

"Portia? Is that you?"

Portia blinked, then felt her heart squeeze to a halt in her chest. "Hi, Meryl. Hi, Betsy."

The two women gasped and hurried around to her. "Oh, my Lord! I never in a million years thought I'd see you again, much less here! How are you, honey?"

"Yes, how are you?" Betsy added with her own gasp.

Meryl Swindon and Betsy Baker had been a part of Portia's world since elementary school. And, like Portia, they had married into the better part of Willow Creek. But unlike Portia, they had moved easily in the new world of heirloom pearls and Francis 1st silver. The only event Portia had truly loved was once a year when she and her husband had traveled to New York to attend the Bandana Ball. Here, in New York, these proper Texans let down their hair. They were more at ease, feeling a camaraderie in a foreign place that they didn't share at similar events in their hometown.

"I'm doing great!" she replied with that thick cheerfulness she had nearly forgotten about in the few months she had been in Manhattan. "You both look fabulous!"

She felt more than saw Gabriel's raised brow at her exaggerated cheer.

"You do, too!" Meryl and Betsy said.

"You look, . . . different," Meryl added.

"Truly fabulous," Betsy said. "I swear, after Robert divorced you, I thought the next time I saw you, you'd be a wreck. I mean, who wouldn't be after Robert made it so public that you weren't the woman for him."

By then, Gabriel had stood, every inch the gentleman. Portia felt a sizzle of tension coming from him, filling her with a disconcerting rush of embarrassment. Meryl and Betsy looked at Gabriel, and seemed to assess him with a Texas woman's eye.

"You're obviously doing better than we possibly could have imagined," Betsy continued on, then introduced herself.

The women wouldn't ever have known that he wasn't perfectly happy to make small talk with them. But Portia could feel tension run through him, a tension she didn't understand as he turned to look at her, studying her while Meryl and Betsy went on about something else.

Finally, they walked away and Portia looked up at Gabriel. "Come on," she all but begged, not wanting him to ask a single question. "This is a party. Dance with me!"

The song ended, the next starting up, and Anthony returned to the table. "I can't believe you two are just sitting here."

Olivia came up beside him. "Once upon a time, Portia used to be a great dancer. That is, until she married that ass—"

"Olivia!"

"Don't you give me that look, Portia," Olivia said, undaunted. Instead, she came over to Portia, sitting down next to her and forcing her to turn, her always languid eyes fierce. She took Portia's hands and gave her a little shake. "I saw Meryl and Betsy come over to you. I know how they are, no doubt going on about Robert. But let me tell you, you are better than all the Meryls and Betsys put together. And you certainly deserved better than that philandering prick. If I could, I'd castrate him myself."

Portia felt the sting of embarrassment at Olivia's words, the brutal honesty that she was never uncomfortable with. But mostly she was embarrassed that Gabriel heard the truth about her marriage.

A man Olivia had promised a dance to came up. Olivia didn't look at him. "Are you okay?" she asked Portia.

"I'm fine. Really. Go dance."

Olivia appeared conflicted.

Portia would have stood, wanting to get away from Gabriel's questioning gaze, but Anthony caught her arm while she was still sitting down. "Come dance with me."

He ran his hand down to her fingers, trying to pull her away from the table. She sensed more than felt the tension that flared through Gabriel. She saw the two men look at each other, Gabriel like a dangerous jaguar, Anthony like a spoiled Abyssinian cat.

"Thank you, Anthony, but I can't dance with you," she said.

She wanted to dance, but not with Gabriel's brother.

Just then another man walked up to them.

"Gabriel. Anthony," the newcomer said by way of hello.

He was tall and good looking, with blond hair and blue eyes. The quintessential all-American boy.

"William," the brothers said in unison. The man extended his hand to Portia. "William Langford," he said.

"Hello, I'm Portia Cuthcart."

"Portia. A fan of Shakespeare?"

"That would have been my mother. First Cordelia, then Olivia, and finally me, Portia."

William laughed easily. He had charm, but not the bad-boy variety. His was more the elegant man about town. "Would you like to dance?" he asked.

"Forget it, Langford," Anthony said with a proprietary smile. "She's dancing with me."

"Actually, she's dancing with me."

Gabriel stepped closer.

Anthony cocked his head, eyes narrowed. Portia could only look at Gabriel, take in the harsh angles of his face.

But as he took Portia's elbow, to help her from her seat, she jerked to a stop.

Anthony laughed. "Second thoughts about dancing with my big brother?"

Portia gave Anthony a look, one learned at the knee of her grandmother, a woman who didn't put up with anything.

"Hard to go anywhere when I'm pinned down." She nodded toward Anthony's foot. "You're standing on my shawl."

The group looked down to see Anthony's fancy boot on the tail end of Portia's gossamer-thin, golden scarf, which had partially unwound and drifted to the floor. Tiny translucent sequins glittered in the ballroom lights.

"Though I guess I don't need it," she added.

She stood, letting the wisp of fabric unwind completely, slipping from her shoulders, leaving them bare.

Every ounce of darkness in Gabriel shifted to heat.

When the scarf had been draped elegantly, no one had noticed that Portia wore a strapless gold brocade bustier she'd found in her aunt's trunks. Instead of the traditional blue denim skirt, she wore a gold denim she suspected Evie had worn to some Texan event of her own, back in the day.

Olivia's eyes sparkled with a sister's pride.

Portia focused on Gabriel, who stood next to her, his expression indecipherable.

"Our dance, Mr. Kane," she said, taking his hand and allowing him to guide her onto the floor. But once there, he held her stiffly as they stepped into a country waltz.

He was a good head taller than her, despite her heels. Portia felt tiny, delicate—and definitely undesirable, despite the flash of heat she had seen in his eyes seconds before.

"You're maddening, you know. One minute you step forward like some warrior staking your claim for the dance. The next you're holding me like I haven't had a bath in a week. You could at least try to pretend you're enjoying this dance."

"I'm not."

"Then you shouldn't have asked!"

"I didn't. You asked. More like you begged. Twice. It was pathetic." He smiled at her then, his body easing. "I felt obligated. I don't usually do pity, but there you have it."

"I bet you make girls swoon regularly with speeches like that."

"You got what you wanted, didn't you?"

The country waltz was beautiful, reminiscent of an earlier life spent in Texas, her parents dancing under the stars outside the trailer, and Gabriel's steps settled. They made their way around the floor, each turn easier as they learned each other's rhythm.

"True, I did."

Portia felt her tension ease and they circled the floor in earnest, his hand at her waist, her palm resting on the hard muscles of his shoulder. After a few minutes, she said, "Admit it. You're enjoying yourself."

"Not true." But she caught a glimpse of his smile.

The music shifted, changing without stopping, to a soulful country three-step, still basically a waltz. Gabriel didn't miss a beat. He shifted his step with the song, pulling her even closer. He smelled like Texas on a summer morning, the heat simmering, but the harshness lost in the overnight cool. Portia thought of long grasses and wild plains. She itched to press even closer.

"I can see how happy you are," he said, his voice lower. "Your eyes shine when you're happy, Portia. Did anyone ever tell you that?"

She tripped, but he caught her easily.

They made another circle of the floor.

"I miss this," she said finally.

"Dancing?"

"Yes. Dancing, and country music."

"What else?" he prompted softly.

"Kissing," she said.

She felt the sudden surge of tension in his shoulder.

"I miss being carefree, driving along two-lane country roads, stopping at Willow Creek Lake, walking along the sandy edge in bare feet."

"Kissing and . . . ?"

"Just kissing. Sweet, innocent kisses from teenage boys with more hormones than they knew what to do with."

"Was one of them your husband?" he asked.

"No. No sweet kisses from my husband. Or ex-husband."

The music came to an end, and Gabriel cupped her chin and tilted her face until she met his gaze. "Your husband's an ass," he said. The intensity of his expression melted her heart, melted her dark thoughts.

"Ex-husband," she repeated.

"Come on," he said, taking her hand. "I saw some games."

"The carnival booths!"

Portia had never been good with beanbags or horseshoes. But when they came to a baseball booth, she stopped.

Gabriel eyed her. "A woman who wants to throw?"

"You'd rather I just bat my eyelashes and drink sweet tea?"

"Do you even know how to bat your eyelashes?"

She tucked her chin and gazed up at him, her eyes sultry, then did just that.

He laughed out loud.

"I used to watch Olivia practice in the mirror when we were growing up."

He shook his head, his smile easing the harshness of his features. "All right." He handed over a set of tickets.

"You go first," Portia offered. "I want to watch, see how it's done."

"Fine."

Gabriel took up one of the six baseballs set in front of him, aimed, threw, and sent the ball through the small round opening with ease.

"Not bad," she conceded.

Standing tall, his expression intent, Gabriel sent three more through the opening in quick succession with the ease of a major-league baseball player. A small crowd formed around him. By the time he had made five of the six, the crowd was bigger and more raucous.

"Do you think I can make the last one?" he asked her, his smile challenging her.

"You've made five of six easily. I'm guessing you'll make the last."

He turned back with a grin on his face. Taking aim, he pulled his arm back, then threw, but not before the group of men whooped—then groaned—when he jerked slightly and missed.

"Oops," Portia said, walking forward with a deliberate sway to her hips, her gown glittering in the lights as she held out a hand. "My turn."

Gabriel handed over the three necessary tickets. He smiled at her, playful, wicked.

She felt a shiver of joy at the sight of this man. "Thank you," she told him as the vendor set out six baseballs, the crowd quieting.

"Ready?" the vendor asked.

Portia nodded, focusing. She threw once, twice, not stopping as the crowd started to go wild. *Thwack, thwack, thwack,* until she'd made five of the six throws. Tossing the sixth ball in her hand, one corner of her mouth turned up, she said, "Not bad for a girl, huh?"

Gabriel laughed out loud. "I take it you've played baseball."

"My daddy made a diamond in a field not far from our trailer."

She noticed the way Gabriel's brow twitched at the mention of their trailer. But by then, the crowd of men cheered and stomped in their tux jackets, bow ties, and jeans. Gabriel looked at her with an amused smile, and for half a second, she would have sworn he was proud.

Turning back, her heart slammed against her ribs. She had indeed thrown a baseball since she was big enough to hold a ball, then played this exact game at carnivals since she was six. She could throw in her sleep. But with Gabriel looking on, not taunting her as she had expected, yet somehow looking at her in a whole new way, her nerves flared. But then she forced herself to stop thinking, aimed, threw, and sent the ball dead center through the opening.

The crowd erupted, and Gabriel tipped his head back and laughed again. He took her elbow.

"Hey, mister. Don't you want the stuffed animal?"

"No, thanks."

Portia tugged away and dashed back. "Of course we want it!" She grabbed all two feet of the plush giraffe and hugged it close.

Gabriel laughed and guided her through the crowd, back toward their table, but the last thing she wanted was to spend another second inside.

"I've had the perfect night. But now it's time for me to turn into a pumpkin."

"I'll take you home," he said.

"You don't have to. Stay. Enjoy yourself."

He gave her a look. "You can't be serious."

Which made her laugh. "Good point."

Gabriel guided her out into the night, barely stopping at their table to gather her shawl. It was late, but Portia started to walk.

"We're not walking home dressed like this. Not to mention the hour."

"You're forgetting how safe New York is now."

"I'm not forgetting. It could be three in the afternoon and I still wouldn't let you walk in that dress."

Normally she would have bristled at his tone, but she refused to let him ruin her perfect night.

"All right. How about a bus?" She hurried across Broadway, then Central Park West, to the opposite side of Columbus Circle.

"No way am I taking a bus," Gabriel said, still beside her.

"Then you'd better find yourself a cab!"

She came to the M10 bus stop on the north side of the circle just as a lumbering bus pulled to a stop. She dashed inside. Gabriel stood at the bottom of the steps for half a second before muttering a curse and leaping up beside her just as the doors closed.

"Does everything have to be your way, Portia?"

"You're just used to everything being *your* way. I know how to compromise."

Given the hour, the bus was empty expect for the driver and a man clearly getting off from the night shift, half asleep at the back. Portia slid onto a hard-plastic two-seater. Gabriel hung his head and sat down beside her.

They headed north on Central Park West, her knee brushing against his as the bus swayed like a boat on a gentle sea. The sky was dark but crystal clear; the sidewalks were crowded even at midnight. To the right beyond the sidewalk, the old stone wall of Central Park surrounded the giant rectangle of trees, lakes, and winding paths. To the left, mostly prewar apartment buildings lined the way like a wall of ancient stone and brick. This new world was nothing like Portia's old one back in Texas, but the longer she was in Manhattan, the more she fell in love.

"Thank you for coming with me tonight."

He was silent for a moment. "You're welcome."

When they reached the Seventy-second Street stop, Gabriel took her hand and pulled her off of the bus.

"Let's take a carriage through the park," Portia said.

"It's late."

"You go on." She started to walk toward the carriages lined up at the entrance to the park, but he caught her around the waist.

They looked at each other before he glanced at her mouth. "I thought you were open to compromise," he said.

"Ha!"

He didn't say anything else. When he grabbed her hand and started walking up Central Park West, she followed. And when they came to the town house, a thrill ran down her spine when he guided her down the steps to her apartment.

Eighteen

✦

PORTIA FELT NERVOUS. "Well, thanks again for going with me."

Gabriel had leaned back against the wall.

"You have an amazing throwing arm," she offered, her voice clattering. "Almost as good as mine."

He just studied her.

She kept chattering. "It was fun. Lots of fun."

His lips quirked up as she rambled. And really, she did have pride.

"So then, good night." She raised her chin and squatted as gracefully as she could to retrieve the key she kept under the mat.

That wiped the quirk off his mouth. "I told you not to keep a key there."

"You tell me a lot of things."

He pushed away from the wall, dragging his hands through his hair. She saw the flash of frustration she made him feel on a fairly regular basis. And right alongside all that pride she'd just had was a wide swath of sympathy, for him. She cocked her head and gave him a sympathetic smile.

"Don't you dare look at me like that," he bit out.

"Like what?"

"Like I'm some sort of lost . . . puppy."

"You? Hardly. More like a wounded beast."

That surprised him. And she certainly hadn't intended to say any such thing. The words had just slipped out.

His frustration turned to something darker.

"I'm sorry," she said. "Really."

The frustration shifted again and he drew a deep breath. He nodded, and she realized that he was going to leave. Without thinking yet again, she caught his hand.

He stilled, and looked at their fingers, his expression wary. Then slowly he looked up at her. He was fighting, she could see it, and he had no intention of giving in to her.

"Good night," he said, pulling away.

She should have been embarrassed. Instead, she reached up on tiptoes, slipping her hands on either side of his head, and pulled him down to her. She had dreamed of his kiss since the night he had dragged her through the window. After an evening of carefree baseball throwing and dancing, she felt lovely and alive. Careless. She didn't want it to end.

They were close, she looking into his eyes. Then she pressed her lips to his. Soft. Barely a kiss. And he groaned into her mouth.

She could feel the way he dragged in a breath, the way he worked to marshal control. Then he gave in with a groan, or maybe a curse, and he crushed her body to his.

Portia closed her eyes and inhaled the scent of him. There was nothing sweet or chaste about their kiss now. It was hot and consuming. She tasted the smoky sweetness of bourbon on his tongue. She melted into him when he ran his hand down her spine, pressing her even closer.

"Give me that damned key."

He unlocked the door and they crashed into her apartment, hands tugging at clothes, searching out skin. The kiss turned desperate. He tangled his tongue with hers, gentleness gone. He cupped the side of her face, tilting her head back, forcing her to look at him. Her breath shuddered as he ran his thumb across her lips. "I want you," he said.

More proof that Gabriel wasn't a man who asked. He demanded. And this demanding man wanted her. The feeling was heady and emotional.

He swept her up into his arms and headed unerringly for her bedroom. It was the only room she'd had time to paint. Small even by New York standards, it was painted a pearly blue that reminded her of a Texas sky—not on a hot day, but a cool one by Southern standards.

She saw the room through his eyes. Upstairs, everything was decorated with exquisite, refined taste that was paid for. She'd lived that life, albeit with Texas rather than New York style. This room was all *hers*. She'd stenciled the moldings with cream fleur-de-lis and hung luscious silk drapes in her tall windows. No need for anyone to know that the silk had once been a ball gown of her aunt's. In the dim light it gave the room an unmistakable luster, a touch of what she believed Paris would be like on a moonlit night.

He set her down, letting go of her legs but holding her close, bringing her body into line with his. He dipped his head, kissing the bare skin of her shoulder. "What's this?" he asked.

It took a second before she realized what he was talking about. "A scar," she said, her stomach twisting at the memory of running into that sudden storm, crying, as she fought to reach her grandmother—and then the lightning throwing her to the ground in a tangle beside Gram, both of them like rag dolls in the dirt.

She began to push away.

"Stop," he said, kissing the scar in a way that made her shiver with something more than desire.

She forgot about scars, her grandmother, the past.

The kiss in his library had been amazing, but this was different. He backed her up until her thighs hit the side of the mattress, his hands cupping her face.

"I've been trying to get you out of my head, but you keep creeping back in. You distract me, make me lose focus." His hands drifted lower, his thumbs brushing her lips, then even lower until they brushed against her collarbone. "But I can't stay away."

She closed her eyes as he swept her up and put her on the bed.

He came over her. The scent of him filled her, like spice and wild grasses. He slid his knee between her legs, nudging one to the side before he sank down into her, and she could feel every inch of his erection through her skirt. With his arms on either side of her head, he kissed her, coaxing her mouth open, his tongue slipping inside.

Portia ran her hands up his arms, her fingers touching his face. Reality unraveled around them like thread from a spool. Nothing in the world existed but the two of them, touching, kissing, his body pressing into hers. Just when it seemed he couldn't get enough, he broke the kiss and pulled back to look at her. She could see restraint trying to seep back to the surface. But then it was gone.

With one twist, he had the ties on her bustier falling to the sides. She gasped as cool air hit her skin. His palm came to her breast, pushing it high, his thumb brushing against her skin, an inarticulate sound breaking from her throat.

She arched to him, felt his hand skimming up her leg, gathering the hem of the skirt. Then with a quick jerk, he dragged the skirt off her body and tossed it on the floor.

He slid his hand down her stomach, slipping beneath the thin silk of her panties. The more he took, the more he seemed to need as he reclaimed her mouth.

She moaned, couldn't help it when she thrust against his hand.

"Yes," he murmured.

He was slow and sensual, caressing her, kissing her until she couldn't take it anymore. She bit his lip, groaning against him. But just when he tangled his hand in her hair and entered her, hard, her senses suddenly jangled. She jolted as the images of fried chicken, sweet jalapeño

mustard, mashed potatoes, cole slaw, buttermilk biscuits, and strawberry pie flashed through her mind. It was the meal that had first come
to her when she was sitting on the front steps and Gabriel had appeared
like a promise.

But a promise of what?

Nineteen

❖

ARIEL STILL DIDN'T KNOW much of anything about her mom's family, other than that they had lived in a housing project only blocks from her dad's town house, and her granddad was named Bohater. Bohater? Seriously?

Not that she knew much more about her dad's family that wasn't the standard brown-haired, brown-eyed sort of stuff. Not the ingredients of an A-plus social studies report.

Determined to find something that fell between boring and the whole "My really fancy, rich mom used to be a wild partier and never bothered to tell anyone that she grew up in a really bad part of town" that would get her killed by her dad, she went back to the Internet. Googling her parents still didn't bring up anything she hadn't already learned.

Then it occurred to her: She had never heard a peep about her mom and dad getting married. Didn't that stuff show up someplace? And if her parents had been in the news for parties they attended, didn't it make sense they'd be in the news when they got married? Didn't weddings make for great stories? A wedding report had to get her something decent, right?

She Googled that, too, but found nothing. If only she knew the date they got married. Didn't there have to be some kind of record?

After more searching, all she came up with to find records was the City Clerk's Web site. She'd have to go downtown, which was practically like going to New Jersey. No way.

The house was super quiet; Ariel was home only because her school was off a half day for teacher training. She hadn't bothered to tell her dad, since she had a key to the house and could take care of herself. Besides, she had wanted time alone at home. All the better to exercise her detective skills.

Well, no time like the present. Her dad was at work; Miranda's school didn't have a half day; Portia was probably down in the basement cooking her brains out, or whatever she did in her spare time. Even if Ariel couldn't make it to the City Clerk's, she had time for a house search.

She bolted up the steps to the top floor that her dad used more for storage than for anything else. There were cedar closets and cabinets filled with drawers that lined the walls. There was a TV and a sound system in there, not set up, sort of like extra. And her old bike was there, too.

She ignored the stairs that continued on to the roof and started going through every nook and cranny. Surely there had to be more stuff about her family. A wedding date. Birthdays.

Looking in drawer after drawer at all the stuff the movers had unpacked and put away, Ariel found nothing. She grew more frantic with each cabinet she finished.

She had nearly given up when she found a box marked MIRANDA in the back of a closet. Not exactly what she was looking for, but she'd take what she could get.

Inside was a baby book. Date of birth. Footprints. A hospital bracelet. A photo. Miranda's first curl. First tooth. But then the book went blank.

It was as if their mom had gotten tired of documenting her first child's existence.

No matter how much she dug, Ariel couldn't find a corresponding book for herself.

"Figures," she muttered to the empty room. Maybe she'd always been a little bit invisible.

When she'd searched every corner, Ariel stopped and looked around the room, mystified. She knew that the only stuff her dad had brought with them from the old house was important stuff like papers and files. But even with that, it was like her mom had disappeared, too. Her mom, her parents' marriage. Her stomach churned.

Returning to the kitchen, she realized what she had to do. It was already after one, but if she took a cab, she could be down at the records office, get her parents' wedding record, and hightail it home before her dad even thought about leaving his office.

Yanking on a light jacket, counting out a wad of ones and fives, and even a ten-dollar bill, Ariel flew out the front door. A cab was driving by, and she waved her arm.

When she barreled inside, the cabbie barely glanced at her.

"The City Clerk's office," she said in a tone of voice that meant business.

He craned his neck. "Where?" His accent was thick, and he looked like he ate little girls for breakfast.

"One forty-one Worth Street. It's downtown."

"I know where Worth Street is."

"Okay then, good."

He snorted, turned, and threw the car into gear. They were off.

Panic set in as soon as they turned left onto Columbus Avenue. "Be brave, be brave, be brave," Ariel whispered to herself.

She hadn't given much thought to the fact that she was going to be in a car. The kind of car that wrecked. Just like when she was with her mom. She had barely been in a car since.

Ariel reached up, wrapped herself securely in the seat belt, and prayed.

The cabbie careened through traffic, clutching the steering wheel with both hands and talking the whole time into his cell phone headset. She couldn't understand a word. There was a ton of traffic, but that didn't faze him.

Ariel closed her eyes, concentrating. "If you take one yellow cab," she whispered to herself, "moving at one hundred miles per hour for five-second intervals, how long will it take the cab to go three miles?"

But word problems didn't calm her.

"You say something?" the cabbie called back to her, their eyes meeting in the rearview mirror.

"No. Not a word. No reason to look back here. Best to look up ahead." *Where the traffic and cars are,* Ariel added to herself.

They took rights, then lefts, and swooped under a bridge. By the time they arrived in front of a building made of huge rectangular bricks, Ariel's legs were rubbery. On the backside of a heinous cab ride, she wasn't sure she was up to the task of sleuthing out any information.

But which was worse? Stay in the cab and ask to be taken home, or get her sea legs back and continue her mission? The decision was made for her when the driver barked out the fare.

"Eighteen?" Ariel squeaked. "You mean eighteen dollars?"

He jerked around, eyes murderous. "Eighteen! If you don't have money, you should no get in my cab!"

"Oh, no, it's fine. I have the money."

Keeping her hands from shaking by sheer force of will, Ariel counted out eighteen dollars. She knew she was supposed to tip, so she added some more. The cabbie grabbed it, waved her out of his car, and raced off, leaving her standing on the curb with only three dollars.

As much as she couldn't imagine getting back in a cab, the thought of taking the subway home paralyzed her. She didn't have a clue how to take the train home from downtown.

She started to panic.

"Buck up, Ariel," she chided herself. "It's a subway. You take it on the Upper West Side all the time."

She turned to face the imposing heights of the City Clerk's office. "You are fine," she whispered to herself.

Inside she was confronted by intense security. She made it through, though not without a few raised eyebrows, and stopped at the information desk. "I'm here for the records department."

A gruff woman with steel-gray hair looked down at her. "What kind of records?"

"Marriage."

"You seem kinda young to be getting married."

A man behind the desk glanced up from whatever he was doing and chuckled. "A mite young, indeed."

Great. A couple of jokesters. "I'm doing a report for school." Ariel tried to look young and smart and like she had a really good reason for them to let her in. "We have to document a city record's search. I'm going to write about my experience working with New York City and the kind of treatment one gets while pursuing their rights within the law."

"Whoo-whee," the man said with a chuckle.

The woman got serious. "Are you some kid reporter?"

"Well no. Just doing a report for Miss Thompson's social studies."

The woman glanced at her watch for the first time, probably noting that as it was early afternoon, Ariel should have been in school.

"It's a teachers' training day. I'm using the time to finalize the details of my research."

God, she was good.

"Whoo-whee," the man said again. "A smart one."

The woman debated, and then nodded toward a hallway. "Third door on your left."

"Thank you," Ariel said. "I appreciate how helpful you've been."

Maybe that was a little much, she conceded. But she was glad she had thought of the whole research angle. She was even gladder after waiting in line for nearly an hour only to learn that she had to be one of the spouses to get the record.

"But, ma'am, I'm just doing a report. I don't want the actual record. I'm just reporting on how it's done." Ariel trotted out the whole social studies angle, eyes wide and earnest. "So if I could just look up a record and explain how the process is handled, you know, how easy it really is for New Yorkers to get the things they need from the government, I would appreciate it."

This woman gave her a strange look, half disbelief, half worry. No one wanted to be shown up by some kid publishing a tell-all blog.

And her dad said the Internet was a bad thing.

"Fine," the woman said. "Go to that door over there and tell Ida I said to help you."

Thankfully, Ida couldn't have cared less who Ariel was, why she was there, or what she wanted. Ariel blurted out her mother's maiden name and father's name, and with a few keystrokes, Ida came back with a date. "June 27, 1998."

Ariel wrote it down so she wouldn't forget it. Something seemed wrong, but she couldn't place what. She gave her parents' names again. "That's definitely the date for them, right?"

"Yes."

Ida clearly wasn't one to waste words. "Is that all you want?" she said. "It's 3:15. We close at 3:45."

"Really?" That seemed really early to close an office. But then Ariel realized she had to get home before anyone found out she was gone. And she still had to figure out the subway route. She slapped her notebook shut. "I mean, no problem."

But outside, her heart raced. Spotting a policeman, she raced over to him. "Where is the subway? Ah, sir."

The guy gave her a crooked smile and pointed. "At that brown building, take a right. The subway is a few blocks up on Canal Street."

She followed his directions. Sure enough, when she came to Canal

Street she saw the station. But it was for the N and R trains. She had never even heard of the N or R train.

Fear started to creep up, the kind of fear Ariel rarely allowed herself to feel. "You are not a panicker, Ariel," she muttered.

Shaking herself, she found one of the posted subway maps. The spider's web of multicolored lines wasn't for the faint of heart, but Ariel wasn't faint of heart, she reminded herself.

With her remaining three dollars, she purchased a single-ride Metro-Card and made it to the uptown platform just as a train arrived. She hopped on. The bell rang, the doors slid shut, and Ariel offered up another prayer that this train would get her somewhere close to the Upper West Side.

"Excuse me," she said to a lady standing next to her.

The woman narrowed her eyes at her.

"Does this go to Seventy-second Street on the Upper West Side?"

The woman hesitated, and in the silence, another woman answered. "No, sweetie, it doesn't. You'll need to get off at Thirty-fourth and change to a B. Or, if you need a 1, 2, or 3, you'll have to go to Forty-Second and change there."

Ariel's head spun with a plethora of numbers and an alphabet soup of letters. She concentrated with every ounce of her ability as they came into each station. Prince. Eighth Street. Fourteenth Street. Stop after stop, the train getting more and more crowded, making it harder and harder to see station signs. Finally Ariel caught a glimpse of a sign when they pulled into the Thirty-fourth Street station. She squirmed out, relieved, only to find that she didn't have a clue what to do next.

"Excuse me, I'm looking for the B train."

She made it to a B just as it arrived in the station. On board, her heart pounded at stop after stop until she recognized Seventy-second Street.

When she came up onto street level across from Central Park, she was only a block from home. Ariel had never been so glad to see the horse-drawn carriages and masses of people taking photos of the building where some singer named John Lennon had been shot. And when she blew into her house, falling back against the closed door with a gasp, she nearly broke down in tears.

"What's wrong with you?"

Her head jerked up. Miranda stood at the top of the stairs, scowling.

Ariel blinked furiously. She had no idea what to say. She had been fixated on the maze of subway tunnels and platforms, and hadn't yet thought about the information she had found: Their mom and dad's wedding was on June 27, 1998.

Miranda was born on November 19, 1998. Five months after their parents were married.

Twenty

❖

A T FIVE, Portia bolted upstairs to make dinner. From the sunroom, she was surprised when she heard Gabriel's and Anthony's heated voices. She hadn't seen or talked to Gabriel since he'd slipped out of her bedroom that morning. She felt her body in a way that she hadn't in years, if ever. He had allowed her no modesty. He had taken what he wanted. But, if she was completely fair, he had given as well. Her body shuddered and sighed at the thought. "Bad, bad, bad," she muttered to herself.

There was no denying that the whole fried chicken–meal thing had thrown her.

The other issue that threw her was that Robert had called three times during the day, but without leaving much by way of messages. Then her lawyer had called, saying that her ex was contesting the small amount he was supposed to pay her.

Her stomach twisted at the thought. She had to breathe through her nose to try to stay calm, releasing her breath slowly into the quiet kitchen. She didn't have the money to fight him. Very soon, even with the money she was making from working for Gabriel, she wasn't going to be able to survive in New York.

For the first time she was having to admit to herself that she might have to sell the garden apartment. No question the clock was ticking on her dream of building a new life in the city.

She left lasagna and garlic bread warming in the oven and a salad in the refrigerator and tiptoed out of the house. Once she was outside, the beads of panic didn't lessen. Nothing was going as planned in New York. She felt as if she was trying to start over, transform her life, remake herself in quicksand. The harder she tried to get free, the deeper she sank. Trying to cook without embracing the knowing wasn't working; it popped up constantly without warning. Trying not to fall for Gabriel? Also not working. Creating a viable way to support herself and help her sisters? Going the way of women wearing hats.

With no answer in sight, she began to walk. Traffic was heavy on Central Park West before she crossed into the park, veering onto the bridle path. Trees overarched like a canopy of green, runners passing her, generally in pairs, followed by two mounted policemen on giant horses. Portia walked fast, trying to outpace her thoughts. But even when she came to the Reservoir, she couldn't slow her brain.

She headed out of the park, then turned south. She walked forever, hooking over to Broadway and the crush of tiny shops.

It was right outside of the Sabon bath shop that it hit her, the scent of luscious soaps drifting out into the street. Inside, the space was filled with soap and lotions, bath washes and candles. Her senses were filled, surrounded. Teased.

In an instant, after hours of walking and trying to stay out of her brain, a glimmer of an answer came to her like disparate ingredients coming together to make an unexpectedly perfect whole.

She couldn't get home fast enough. Banging into the apartment, Portia went straight to the cabinet where she had stored the Glass Kitchen cookbooks. She pulled out volumes one and two, skimming through the first. Then she took up the second book, leaving the third volume where it was stored. Holding the second in her arms, close to her chest, she drew a deep breath.

The answer was here, she realized, in this cookbook. She just had to find it.

She cracked open the old spine and started flipping through the pages, taking notes. Once she had five pages of hurried scribbles, she condensed things down into one single shopping list. Then she began to turn the vision into reality, and a week later, a week of barely managing to avoid Gabriel with an odd assortment of excuses and meal preparation at even odder times, Portia was ready. She had finally put into place exactly what she needed to prove that a Glass Kitchen would work in New York City.

Fourth Course

✦

Palate Cleanser

Blood Orange Ice

Twenty-one

"WHAT IS GOING ON here?"

Gabriel stood in the doorway of her apartment, dark tension carved into his features, and for a heartbeat Portia forgot all about what she was doing. She just stared at the man.

He wore a simple black T-shirt that showed off his chest and arms, his dark hair raked back. He looked rugged and sexy, and memories of his hands and mouth on her body made every inch of her thrum to life.

Bad, bad, bad, she reminded herself.

His dark gaze narrowed.

"We've created a version of The Glass Kitchen," she hurriedly explained, giving him a sunny smile.

Olivia and Cordelia came out of the kitchen to stand behind her. Cordelia glanced from Portia to Gabriel, then back. "Portia, didn't you clear this with him?"

Cordelia still wasn't herself, her husband's problem growing deeper. Portia and Olivia did everything they could to keep her mind occupied, and Portia still hadn't had the heart to question Cordelia about implying to people that somehow Gabriel was involved with The Glass Kitchen.

"Actually, it's more a venture where I'm cooking the food of The Glass Kitchen, and people can come to try it."

After reading the second Glass Kitchen cookbook, she had taken its advice to heart. Losing herself in the words, she had put them into action.

For a meal to work truly, it must be an experience. From the moment a guest arrives in The Glass Kitchen to the moment they set their napkin down, they must be enchanted. More importantly, the giver of food must believe that they have the power to enchant. No person, whether she is a scientist or a cook, can find success if she doesn't first believe that she holds power in her hands—not to use over people, but to use for the good of another. Food, especially, is about giving. A cook must find a way to make the recipient a believer, for what is a person who sits down to a beautiful meal but someone who wants to believe?

As she read the words, Portia had finally set aside her own misgivings and opened herself up to what might come. It had been then that solutions appeared. Her sisters had shown up without her having to ask, the three of them working day after day in a way that gave each hope that a Glass Kitchen really could happen. For a week they had pulled down Aunt Evie's dark draperies, replacing them with a cheerful gingham Cordelia found in the huge sale bins in the Garment District. Olivia filled the space with flowers. The sisters had bought white paper bags and pink baker boxes, then sat around the kitchen island drinking wine, laughing, and hand-decorating them.

Once the apartment was ready, Portia had begun to plan out what foods they would showcase in this little glimpse into a Glass Kitchen world. Her sisters couldn't help her with this part. Portia had let go, and dishes had come to her, all of which she wrote down and prepared to make. Then, at eight that morning, she got to work. Olivia and Cordelia served as *sous*-chefs; they started by making a decadent beef bourguignon. Olivia and Cordelia washed and chopped as Portia browned layer after layer of beef, bacon, carrots, and onion, folding in the beef stock and wine, then putting it in to slow bake as they dove into the remaining dishes. They opened all the windows and ran four swiveling fans Portia had bought and found that pushed the scent of the baking and cooking out onto the sidewalk. Then they had put up a fairly discreet sign in the window, hand-painted by Olivia: THE GLASS KITCHEN.

Portia had gotten the idea while walking down Broadway and passing the French soap store. Scents had spilled into the street from the shop— lavender and primrose, musk and sandalwood—luring passersby inside. Portia had realized that the best way to get investors interested was to show them a version of The Glass Kitchen. The food. The aromas. She had realized, standing there on Broadway, that she needed to create a mini version of her grandmother's restaurant to lure people in. This way, they'd have no monthly rent as they would if they tried to lease out space somewhere else. No extra utility bills. It was perfect. Standing there now with her sisters flanking her, she explained as much to Gabriel. "Ta-da!" she finished. "What do you think?"

Gabriel's jaw hung slack for a second before he snapped it shut. "You can't open a restaurant here."

"But that's the thing! It's not a restaurant."

"Definitely not a restaurant," Olivia confirmed, then raised a brow at Gabriel's pointed glower.

"It's just an example of a restaurant," Portia hurried on. "At best, it's more like counter service to go!"

He narrowed his eyes.

She gulped and persevered. "We're showcasing the fabulous food we'll be making at the *real* Glass Kitchen when we open it somewhere else.

This way, people can get a taste, get the feel of what our café will be like, get excited."

She spread her arms wide to encompass the old pine table they had painted robin's egg blue, lightly sanding it in places so the white primer showed through. She had pulled out Aunt Evie's moss green platters and bowls, filling enough of them with everything from cheesy quiches to creamy chocolate pies, butterscotch cupcakes to the beef bourguignon to cover every inch of counter space. The place smelled heavenly.

"Admit it, you're drooling."

"You can't open anything here. Not a restaurant. Not even an example of a restaurant." Each word enunciated.

"Says who?"

"Says the zoning laws," he bit out.

Portia felt his exacting gaze all the way down to her bones, and not in a good way. She ignored it. All they were doing was giving people a taste of her food. Granted, they would be charging for those tastes. But they weren't doing anything close to opening a real retail establishment.

"Olivia and I will let you two talk," Cordelia said, gathering her bag.

"Seriously?" Oliva protested. "This is just getting interesting."

Gabriel turned to Olivia with an expression that made her shrug; then she strolled out the front door after Cordelia.

Portia swallowed as Gabriel stepped closer. Then she squared her shoulders. "Has anyone pointed out how moody you are? One minute you're all—" She searched for the right word.

"*I'm all* what?" The words were deep, sensual, but still exacting.

"One minute you're, well, nice. Then the next you go all Sybil on me and out comes the big bad beast."

The words flew out, yet again, before she thought them through, and emotion shot through Gabriel's eyes. But a second later that implacable façade was back in place.

"This is just an experiment, Gabriel," she hurried on. "We're going to show investors how much people love my grandmother's food. That's it."

Portia felt a flash of panic. She had spent the rest of her meager savings pulling it together. "This is just temporary, and only a way to show investors how great our food is," she pointed out.

"You can't run a restaurant out of my home!"

"My home. And it's not a restaurant!"

His gaze slammed into hers, then took a deep breath, dragging his hands through his hair.

The doorbell rang.

"Now what?" he snapped.

Footsteps clattered down the steps before Cordelia and Olivia dragged a woman inside.

"Our first customer!"

"Seriously?" Portia squeaked. "I mean, yay!"

"Ah, well," the woman looked a little frightened by the sisters' enthusiastic welcome. "I was just walking by, smelled the heavenly aroma, and noticed your sign tucked in the window. I thought . . . well, I thought this was a restaurant, not a home."

"Actually, it's just three sisters cooking!" Portia emphasized for Gabriel. "Cooking and baking very real food! Think of it as a kid's lemonade stand. Come in!"

"I don't know."

"Don't worry, we're from Texas, which might mean crazy, but definitely not dangerous. Just look at all the wonderful things we have."

Hesitantly, the woman came farther inside—though one glare from Gabriel made her stop dead in her tracks.

"Don't mind him," Portia said. "He's not as ornery as he looks."

The woman saw the fragrant dishes on the counter, and every bit of hesitation evaporated. "This is wonderful!" she said, walking straight past Gabriel. "Quiche? And pie? Is this a tart?"

Portia explained the dishes while Cordelia offered samples. By the time the woman headed out, she was loaded with food Olivia had wrapped up. At the door, the woman stopped and shook her head. "I just have to tell you, you saved me."

"What do you mean?" Portia asked cautiously.

"I'm having a book party for a friend tonight, and the caterer canceled. Last minute, said she had an emergency and no backup plan. I had no idea what I was going to do. I turned down Seventy-third by accident." She beamed at all three of them. "At least I thought it was an accident."

The woman left in a rustle of white bags and pink boxes. Cordelia and Olivia started talking. When Portia turned, Gabriel was still there. Their eyes met and held. Despite herself, a slow pulse of heat went through her body. He was like the darkest, richest hot chocolate she could have imagined. She remembered the way he had stared at her, hard, his jaw ticking, then the ruthless control that seemed to shatter when she had reached up on tiptoes and kissed him. Barely a kiss, tentative, before he crushed her to him with a groan.

A breath sighed out of her at the memory, and his gaze drifted to her mouth. But then the buzzer rang again, making her blink, and he seemed to remember that they weren't alone.

"This isn't over," he said, his voice curt.

He left before she could respond. She drew a breath, pushed worry from her mind, before all three sisters squealed in delight and danced it out in the seconds before their next customer arrived.

‧❖‧

For the next two days, Portia cooked and baked like a dervish while Cordelia sold The Glass Kitchen's fare to a growing line of people who had heard about their amazing food. She still cooked breakfast and supper upstairs as well, though there were no more cheeky conversations in the kitchen with her employer. Actually, she didn't see Gabriel at all, as if he stayed away intentionally.

But after the third day of sales, with every minute of her last three days filled to overflowing, she was lying in her bed, still damp from a shower, completely exhausted, when there was a knock on the garden door. She opened it to find Gabriel. Surprised, she glanced from him to the fire escape.

He stood there and looked at her, just looked, his jaw working, his eyes narrowed in frustration. "Even with strangers traipsing in and out, I can't stay away from you."

His voice was hungry, and he reached for her even as the words left his mouth.

They fell back into her apartment, he kicking the door closed. He made love to her with an intensity that made her arch and cry out, his hands and mouth possessively taking her body. There was a near desperation in the way they came together, both of them knowing it was a bad idea, but neither able to fight it. He lost himself in her body until early dawn, when he rolled over, kissed her shoulder, and said, "I have to get back upstairs before the girls wake up."

Portia felt drugged, her limbs deliciously weak, her body sore and aching in a wonderfully used way. "Be up soon," she murmured, burrowing into the sheets and covers. "Making huevos rancheros for you guys this morning."

⁛

A few days later, she finished another breakfast upstairs—after Gabriel had pulled her behind a door, slammed her against the wall, and kissed her until her head spun—then she came down to her apartment to start cooking for The Glass Kitchen. She decided to make salmon baked in a touch of olive oil, topped with pine nuts, and served over spinach flash-fried in the salmon-and-olive-oil drippings. She added brown rice that she had slow-boiled with the herb hawthorn. Just as she finished, Cordelia arrived with a woman she had found standing on the sidewalk out front.

"My husband has high blood pressure," she explained, negotiating the stairs down into Portia's apartment with care. "He's never happy with anything I make for supper, so I should tell you that you probably don't have anything that will work for me."

Cordelia took a look at the meal, raised an eyebrow at Portia, and then turned to the woman. "This is the perfect meal for your husband's high blood pressure. Fish oil, nuts, hawthorn, whole grains."

Next, a pumpkin pie went to a woman who couldn't sleep.

"Pie?" she asked in a doubtful tone.

"Pumpkin," Portia clarified, "is good for insomnia."

An apricot crumble spiced with cloves and topped with oats and brown sugar went to a woman drawn with stress. Then a man walked through the door, shoulders slumped. Cordelia and Olivia eyed him for a second.

"I know the feeling," Olivia said, and fetched him a half gallon of the celery and cabbage soup Portia had found herself preparing earlier.

The man peered into the container, grew a tad queasier, and said, "No thanks."

"Do you or don't you have a hangover?" Olivia demanded, then drew a breath. "Really," she added more kindly. "Eat this and you'll feel better."

He came back the next day for more.

"Cabbage is no cure for drinking too much," Cordelia told him.

He just shrugged and slapped down his money for two quarts of soup instead of one.

The knowing was steering Portia with a force and intensity that she had never experienced before. She tried to be happy about it, but it was hard not to worry. Yes, the knowing had brought good into her life, but the good was far outweighed by the bad. So she worked all day, and then when Gabriel came down the fire escape to her, they made love half the night. She didn't tell her sisters. He was her secret. They behaved with circumspection when they met in the kitchen (most of the time); they never went on dates; they never talked about anything serious. When it came to The Glass Kitchen, they existed in a sort of wary standoff, too busy losing themselves in each other to talk about it.

Ariel started wandering into The Glass Kitchen after school and doing her homework at a space she had carved out for herself in a corner. It was easy to forget she was there. One afternoon about two weeks into their new endeavor, Olivia jumped when Ariel spoke.

"Sweetie, you scared me." Olivia laughed. "When you scrunch up like that, doing homework like a mad little scientist, it's like you're practically invisible."

After that, Ariel planted herself at the end of the kitchen counter, where no one could help but see her.

A few days later Portia was upstairs completing the Kanes' meal of grilled lamb chops, sliced potatoes roasted in olive oil, and sautéed broccoli rabe. After having found a stack of blood oranges at a street cart on Columbus, she planned to surprise her charges with a blood orange ice she had thrown together, minus the orange liqueur Gram had always included.

Miranda walked into the kitchen, ignoring Portia and Ariel. She pulled out some green tea in a tiny bag, threw it in a cup of water, then slammed it into the microwave.

Miranda's phone beeped with a text. Her fingers flew over the keyboard as she responded, forgetting as the tea circled. Portia wasn't paying close attention when Miranda pulled the cup out and immediately took a drink.

"Ahg!" the girl cried, dropping the cup to the counter with a splash.

Portia had just finished chopping the flavored ice. She instantly put a scoopful into a glass. "Put this in your mouth!"

The girl gasped and gagged, closing her eyes, and she sucked on the shards of ice. After long seconds, she sagged back against the counter and swallowed, then just stared at Portia.

"It's weird, you know," Ariel said, looking at them.

"What's weird?"

They turned and saw Gabriel walking into the kitchen, going through the mail.

"Hey," Portia said softly.

He shot her a look under those thick lashes of his that made her remember the way he had shuddered the night before when she had kissed a path down his abdomen.

After a second, he shifted his gaze to his daughters.

"What's weird, A?"

The girl shrugged. "Portia makes stuff downstairs, and then random people show up who need whatever she makes. Or even here. She made some strange ice just before Miranda burned the cra—I mean, crud—out of her mouth. It's, well, weird. Like magic."

"Ariel," Gabriel stated, his voice crisp. "There's no such thing as magic. It's a fact of life that people see what they want to see. They adjust their expectations to what they see in front of them." He turned to Miranda. "Are you okay?"

"I'm fine," she snapped.

"See, you're fine *now*, after the ice," Ariel persisted. "I've seen it happen, lots of times."

Portia felt a shiver of unease. "I wish I had a magic wand," she said with a laugh she didn't feel. "But the truth is that I make whatever I feel like, and hungry people want it. End of story." She displayed their dinner. "Just like you all want to eat tonight."

Ariel rolled her eyes. "There's that *you all* thing again."

"Yep, *you all* better eat before it gets cold." Portia walked over to the door as casually as she could.

"See ya!"

She waved, bolting when Gabriel gave her a curious look and started to say something.

Twenty-two

❖

ARIEL HAD BEEN SITTING at her spot in Portia's kitchen for days, brewing over how she could get more info on her mom and dad, while the sisters cooked. She did her best to keep the whole invisible thing to herself. If she hadn't already been going to the Shrink, mentioning the invisible thing would definitely have gotten her carted off to one.

Somewhere between a batch of cheese tarts and custard-filled cream puffs, Ariel realized that with some careful questioning, surely her grandmother would spill some info on Mom and Dad that would help with the report. Which left Ariel figuring out a way to get to Nana's house that didn't involve a taxi. Subways, Ariel had learned, didn't go across town north of Fifty-ninth Street.

It was a few days later when she finally managed to sneak her old bike out of the town house. Of the few things from the old house they had brought with them, she wasn't sure how a bicycle had made the cut. But, yay, it had.

She hopped on the bike without bothering to change out of her school uniform. She had a good three hours, maybe four, before her dad came home—plenty of time to get to her grandmother's, then back.

She went straight into Central Park at Seventy-second Street because obviously that was way safer than riding around with all the taxis at her back. She hadn't ridden the bike in years. But now that she was wheeling down the curving road into the park, streamers on the handlebars fluttering in the wind, remembering just how much she used to love riding Ethel.

She named her bike that because of watching reruns of *I Love Lucy* with her mom. As much as Ariel would have liked to be Lucy, she knew she was more the sidekick. She was Ethel. Mom never agreed with her, but Ariel went ahead and named her bike that, to mark the truth of it. Moms always think their kids are lead actors, even when it's obvious to the whole world that they aren't.

All she had to do was cross at the Seventy-second Street transverse, then take the walking path to the pedestrian exit at Seventy-seventh Street on the east side. Bikes weren't allowed on the walking path, but still she decided it was better to risk getting chased down by a park ranger than to ride on the park road because of all the cabs.

It didn't take Ariel more than fifteen minutes to make it from her house to her grandmother's. After chaining the bike to a pole on the sidewalk, she rang the bell on the towering stone town house. Ariel's town house was nice and all, redbrick with a fancy green tin mansard roof, but her grandmother's was like a mansion. Big blocks of stone, curlicues carved everywhere, and a massively imposing door. Even after her dad managed to buy the basement of their town house from Portia, it would never be this fancy.

Ariel buzzed a second time before the intercom crackled and the housekeeper's voice floated out.

"Hi, Carmen. It's Ariel. I came to see my grandmother."

"Oh, *chica*. Does your *abuela* know you are coming?"

"No. But I wanted to surprise her."

True. She didn't want her grandmother to put her off.

"So sweet. Such a good *nieta*." The door lock buzzed. Ariel grabbed the handle and pushed inside. Her grandmother was coming downstairs with a confused look on her face when Ariel walked into the living room.

"Ariel?"

Helen Kane didn't look happy. Not that it was a surprise. She wasn't exactly the milk-and-cookies type of grandmother.

"Hi, Grandma!"

Helen shuddered.

"Oh, sorry," Ariel said, adding, "Nana."

Helen drew a deep breath, as if Ariel tried every last ounce of her patience. Ariel had always assumed that it was her mom who made Helen crazy. But Mom was dead, and her grandmother hadn't changed.

"Why are you here, dear?"

At least she got a *dear* out of the deal.

"I thought I'd stop by and say hello." Hopefully put some of her weird worries to rest. "Now that we live so close, it seems like a shame not to see you more!"

She could tell from Helen's hard gaze that she wasn't buying that fib.

"Is Uncle Anthony here?"

Helen hesitated. "No, he's out."

"Oh, darn." Not.

"You're here to see your uncle?"

"I'm mainly here to see you. But I was just thinking about all the amazing things he's done in his life."

Her grandmother's hard gaze softened. "Yes, he has done a lot."

Forget the fact that the man didn't work—or so her dad said—but whatever. Ariel knew that complimenting the golden boy would soften Helen Kane right up.

"Yeah, I was thinking about Uncle Anthony's trip to Africa. It sounded really awesome."

Her grandmother raised an eyebrow. "Anthony told you about his trip?"

Actually, no. Ages ago, Ariel had heard about the Africa trip when her mom and dad were fighting. Dad had used Africa as an example of her uncle's irresponsibility. Mom said it showed he was adventurous. But Nana didn't need to know that.

"Actually, my dad talked about it."

"Well, I suppose it was a long time ago."

"Totally. But I don't remember when exactly he went. Ages and ages ago, right?"

"It was nineteen ninety-eight."

Helen walked through the living room and went into the kitchen. Despite the lack of invitation, Ariel followed.

"Carmen, I'd like my tea now," Helen said.

"*Si, señora.*" The housekeeper gave her employer a meaningful look and nodded toward Ariel.

Helen sighed. "Ariel, would you like some tea?"

"Sure. Tea would be great."

She followed her grandmother into a back sitting room that overlooked the gardens one level below. The gardens at Ariel's house were a mess, though she had seen Portia out there a time or two digging around.

"Oh, yeah, I remember now. Uncle Anthony went in nineteen ninety-eight. I wasn't even born then."

Carmen brought a tray filled with fancy china stuff and made a big to-do about serving, like Nana was a queen or something.

"So, you were telling me about Uncle Anthony going to Africa," Ariel prompted, taking a sip, trying her best not to spill anything.

"Was I?"

"Yes, you said he went in nineteen ninety-eight? Did he go in the spring or summer?"

"Why do you want to know?"

Ariel wasn't about to answer that question, at least not truthfully. "I just can't quite get it in my head. You see, I'm writing a social studies report." That was true. "About our family." Also true. "About cool things our family does." Sort of true. "And Uncle Anthony is the King of Cool Stuff."

Nana smiled, but it was a sad smile. "Yes, he is. Always has been." She sat back and looked out into the garden. "You should have seen him as a little boy. The most beautiful child anyone had ever seen. Everyone said so. I couldn't go anywhere without people stopping me—on the street, mind you—and commenting on what a beautiful child he was."

Ariel refrained from asking where Dad had been in all this walking-the-beautiful-baby-around business. She wanted answers and while she didn't completely have her head wrapped around the thoughts bubbling to the surface, she figured it was better to avoid bringing her dad into it.

"When he was young," Helen continued, "Anthony went on any adventure his father and I allowed. When he was six, he asked to go to sleepaway camp in Vermont. Sleepaway camp at six!" Helen chuckled. "At ten, it was camp in Colorado. Then Montana. I couldn't believe it. At seventeen, he wanted to travel to Costa Rica on summer break to build houses for the less fortunate."

In some recess of her mind, Ariel remembered another conversation she'd overheard. Her dad and uncle going at it, yet again.

You had to go everywhere I did, her dad had shouted.

I looked up to my older brother. What of it?

You didn't go because you admired me. You went to show that everyone, everywhere, loved you better.

Ariel had expected her uncle to deny it.

And they did, didn't they?

Silence, followed by her dad's cold voice.

Yes. They always loved you more.

Ariel hadn't understood at the time, and she hadn't thought of it again until now. Sitting with her grandmother, a sick feeling started to build in her stomach.

"Yeah," she said with a laugh she didn't feel. "Uncle Anthony is amazing. Costa Rica at seventeen. And you said he went to Africa in nineteen ninety-eight?"

"Yes. May nineteen ninety-eight. He hasn't lived in New York full-time since."

Ariel's heart pounded so hard that she bumped the teacup, the china clattering. Helen jerked her gaze away from the window, her normal smooth beauty pinched as she took in Ariel. "It's your father's fault that he left, you know," Helen said, as if trying to gain supporters to her cause.

"What do you mean?"

"It's a very sad thing when one brother is jealous of another," Nana said, her mouth sort of pinching together. "I'll tell you for your own good, since you have a sibling as well. And so you can understand that your father is just plain being unfair to your uncle. Your father has always hated the attention Anthony received. So when Anthony wanted to go to camp, Gabriel made us send him, too. Vermont. Colorado. Costa Rica."

Ariel wasn't quite sure how to respond to this. *I believe it was the other way around* didn't seem to be what Helen had in mind.

"And then Anthony met Victoria." The pinched look turned bitter. "Even more than your father, Victoria was responsible for everything falling apart. As much as I'm not one to speak ill of the dead, the first time I met her, she looked like—" She cut herself off and focused on Ariel, her lips pursed hard. "Like a girl raised in a housing project. But your mother was smart. The next time I saw her, she was wearing a sweater set and pearls. She played Gabriel against my Anthony. In the end, she ran Anthony off to Africa, heartbroken, when she chose Gabriel over him. I've always wondered what Gabriel did to win her. He'd never won against Anthony. Ever."

By then, her grandmother was leaning forward, intent, lost to her own words. Then she sat back abruptly and eyed Ariel warily.

Ariel sat, stunned. She couldn't believe what her grandmother was saying. Uncle Anthony had said he met her mom first—but he'd dated her? More than that, how could Nana say this stuff about her dad?

She sat up straight. "A mom shouldn't love one kid more than the other."

Helen glanced out the window. "Mother or not, there are some people who simply pull everyone to them. Anthony is like that." She looked back, directly at Ariel. "Your father always made it hard to love him."

Ariel's chest was burning so much that she couldn't even think of what to say. So she jerked up from her seat and dashed to the front door, slamming out into the street. As soon as she managed to free her bike she pedaled as fast as she could back across the park to the Upper West Side, tears flying in the wind along with the streamers.

Twenty-three

✥

PORTIA LOVED THE SMELLS of cooking and baking. It turned a house into a home.

It was October, barely two weeks after she and her sisters had opened up the test version of The Glass Kitchen. Standing at the sink, she washed her hands, getting ready to start cooking for the day. Ariel had been quiet lately, sitting at the end of the counter, busy doing homework and writing in her journal. But sometimes she just sat there, lost in thought, her brow creased. Portia had asked if anything was wrong. Ariel had blinked, then scoffed, diving back into homework.

And then last night Portia had dreamed of apples again. When her mind swirled with images of her grandmother's moist apple cake, she had gasped awake, her heart pounding. Between Ariel, Gabriel, and her rapidly dwindling money, Portia felt as if a noose were gradually slipping tighter around her neck. And with every day that had passed, the knowing grew a little bit more. Part of her reveled in it. But the other part still held out against it, worried about what it meant to give in to the knowing completely.

Given the dream, she shouldn't have been surprised a few hours later, as she stood at the counter making a fresh batch of sweet tea, when Cordelia arrived.

She looked tired and disheveled, distracted as she walked in carrying a bag of groceries. "I thought we could give that cake a second try."

"What cake?" Portia asked carefully.

"The apple cake."

The only thing that surprised Portia was the pure, unadulterated spark of excitement that flared inside her, as if finally she could let go of any remnants of worry.

Cordelia looked at her, though her eyes were dull. "I knew it. I knew that today was apple cake day. Just like I know that my life is over."

Portia stiffened. "What?"

Olivia walked in next. "What do you mean your life is over? What's wrong now?"

Cordelia looked her sisters in the eye, seeming to come to a decision. "You mean what's wrong besides lying to people and telling them that Portia works with Gabriel Kane in order to get meetings?"

Portia's head snapped back. "You really did it?" She had hoped there would be some explanation, some misunderstanding.

Cordelia pressed her eyes closed, then sighed. "Yes, I did it. I started out doing it the right way when I first tried to get appointments with investors. But I never got past the receptionists. Then I sort of casually mentioned that you knew Gabriel Kane, which morphed into you worked for Gabriel Kane, which morphed even more into you worked *with* Gabriel Kane." She cringed. "That had people lining up to take a meeting with you." Her face was red with strained emotion. "I shouldn't have done it, I know. But with all this mess with James, I felt desperate. It was like getting the appointments was proof that I could make something happen in my life."

Portia came over and took the bag away, setting it down. Olivia joined them.

"Hey, sweetie," Olivia said, wrapping her arms around Cordelia. "It's okay. It will all work out. Things always do. Just like it will all work out with James."

"But it won't. It turns out there's an e-mail trail a mile long."

Olivia couldn't seem to help herself when she snorted. "Who, in this day and age, leaves an e-mail trail?"

"Obviously my husband." Cordelia drew a shaky breath, and when she spoke, her voice cracked. "Me. Dirt poor. Again."

Portia took her sister by the shoulders. "Not a single one of us wants to go back to our trailer-park roots. But whatever happens, I know you'll get through this. Daddy taught us to be fighters. And I just realized that not one of us has been fighting for ourselves. Not really. Not well enough. We've been hanging in the wind, at the mercy of what comes our way. Daddy would hate that."

She saw the shift in Cordelia's eyes; she even saw it come into Olivia's eyes, as if the mention of their father brought his strength into the room.

"You've been dealt a bad hand, Cord," Portia continued. "But it's time you started taking control in the right way. You've got to pull your head out of the sand, start fixing your life."

Cordelia pressed her eyes closed. "But how?"

"I don't know," Portia said honestly. "But we'll figure something out, just like we figured out how to open a version of The Glass Kitchen without money, and it's working."

She prayed she wasn't lying.

"Now," she said, stepping away with a decisive nod, "we are going to drink to that." She retrieved three glasses and poured lemonade into each.

Portia and her sisters raised their glasses. "To Earl Cuthcart," she said.

"May his daughters do him proud," Olivia continued.

Cordelia drew a deep breath. "To taking charge . . . and responsibility."

The three of them clinked, then drank, and more of what Portia thought of as her father's strength swirled through the room like a warm Texas breeze.

Just then, someone knocked. A second later, Gabriel walked in.

As always, everything about him spoke of a man who took his power for granted. Portia watched as he surveyed the scene.

Cordelia didn't bother with so much as a hello. Her chin rose, the glass still in her hand. "I've been using your name to get appointments for us with investors. I'm sorry. I knew it was wrong, but I did it anyway."

Olivia gave a snort of surprised laughter. "Way to jump into it, Cord."

Gabriel's expression grew scary. Portia held her breath. But at the same time, she couldn't have been prouder of Cordelia.

"Gabriel," Portia started to say as he strode over to them with a slow, predatory gait. This was a man who crushed people, happily, for less than using his name without his consent.

Portia's heart all but stopped when he halted in front of Cordelia. Portia scuttled closer to her sister protectively as Gabriel looked at Cordelia hard.

"I appreciate your honesty," he said finally, surprising Portia. "I appreciate you telling me face-to-face. There are more than a few men who don't have it in them to do the same."

Cordelia's squared shoulders started to round, relief putting out the fire.

"Hey," Gabriel said, this time softly. "Things have a way of working out like they should." Surprisingly, a smile eased his face.

The smile he gave her sister made Portia's knees weak with gratitude. And when he turned to look at her, she nearly threw her arms around his shoulders. As if he understood, one side of his mouth crooked up in a smile as he took her glass, drinking a long, slow pull.

Somehow the gesture felt intimate, as if they had kissed rather than shared a glass, and Portia blushed.

Thankfully, Cordelia was too caught up in being let off the hook to notice.

Flustered, Portia swiped the glass back. "Would you like me to get you some lemonade?"

"No need." He took hers again, turning back to Cordelia as he leaned against the counter. "If there's anything I can do to help, I will."

If Cordelia had been anyone else, and Gabriel a less formidable man, Portia was sure her sister would have flung her arms around him. Instead, Cordelia steadied her trembling lip and said, "Thank you. I appreciate it."

Gabriel nodded, took one last pull on Portia's lemonade, then handed it back. "I have a meeting and won't be here for dinner. It'll just be the girls." He focused on her. "I won't be home until late."

Up went Olivia's radar and eyebrow, and Portia felt another blush coming on. But still, Cordelia was too caught up in anything but her own misery as Gabriel said his good-byes and was out the door.

Portia was doing a little shaking of her own as she began cooking. Olivia started to say something, but Portia jerked her head in Cordelia's direction. Olivia relented and got on the computer. Cordelia managed to find a smile and chat up the customers who trickled steadily through the door.

But just as Portia finished the regular items on their menu and was about to start on the apple cake, she froze, having to brace her hands on the counter.

"Portia? What's wrong?"

She couldn't answer. Her head spun; her heart pounded. The knowing was getting stronger. It had never felt like this before. It had never *demanded*. "I need figs," she said, her eyes closed, the words labored. "And chocolate. And chili."

"What?"

When Portia opened her eyes, she saw that Cordelia's face radiated concern.

"I need it. Now."

They left the place a mess, and she and Cordelia dashed to the store, leaving Olivia to man the counter.

"I spoke too soon about the knowing. I hate this part of it," Cordelia muttered as they flew through the small Pioneer market just a block from the town house. "The sudden bursts? The way everything used to come to a standstill, our lives, everything on hold while Gram went off on a cooking tangent? That was when we were little. Later, she'd have you doing the cooking." Cordelia grabbed a packet of chili powder and tossed it into their basket with more force than necessary.

"You're the one who pushed me to get back into this. Do you think I like being at the mercy of a bunch of figs, for pity's sake?"

Cordelia gave a shout of wry laughter.

They made it through the market in record time, returning to the apartment just as the timer went off for a small potato casserole. Cordelia's phone buzzed with a call from James, so she had to go. Olivia took off for the yoga class she was now teaching regularly, and Portia dove back into the kitchen as if the very thing she had been running from for the last three years could save her.

After twenty minutes, her nerves started to calm. Not a single customer found their way to the front door to disrupt her. After forty minutes, her breathing had slowed. And after another hour, she was lost in the rhythm, following the knowing as if it were steps to a dance she'd learned as a child.

She brought port wine, sugar, and chili powder to a boil and let the mix simmer until she had a fragrant syrup. At the last minute, she added cinnamon. Setting it aside, she melted bittersweet chocolate, stirring until the mixture was smooth.

With every stir of the wooden spoon, images danced in Portia's head. Of happiness, of love, of forbidden fruit that promised sex. She thought of Gabriel's chest as he reared over her at night, his gaze locked with hers, and felt a shiver that went down her fingers and made the spoon shake.

For some reason, she didn't dip the figs whole, but decided to chop them into bite-sized morsels, then dipped the pieces in the chocolate and set them on a waxed paper–covered baking sheet to cool.

When that was done, she realized she had plenty of the chocolate-chili-cinnamon concoction left over—along with a bag of unsalted peanuts. Refusing to question it, she dipped the peanuts and set those out, too.

That afternoon, after the candies were cooled and wrapped in cellophane bags, she escaped the apartment and perched on the front steps outside. The day had gotten surprisingly cold.

The old man next door, whom Portia had only seen sitting in the window, emerged from a cab. He looked dapper in an ancient but immaculately kept sports jacket with equally ancient pants, perfectly polished cordovan loafers, and steel-wool gray hair.

"Hello," Portia called out.

The man nodded, walked toward the curb in front of his town house, his posture severely stooped. When he got to the curb he took a step toward it, but his cane stuck on a crack in the sidewalk.

Portia dashed over and offered a hand.

The man gave Portia a wry little smile and took her hand. Together they managed the steps one at a time. Halfway up, the man had to stop to catch his breath. "It's awful getting old," he told Portia. "Just in case you're wondering."

"It's not for sissies," Portia answered. "That's what my grandmother always said."

The old man snorted. "Not for sissies, indeed. It's this blasted chest cold I can't get rid of that makes me so weak. Congestion, I suppose."

"Really? You have congestion?"

He peered at her. "You don't have to look pleased about it."

"No, no! Not pleased that you're congested. It's just that this morning I made chocolate-and-cinnamon-chili-coated peanuts. The cinnamon and chili are perfect for cold congestion, the peanuts provide protein for strength, and the chocolate, well, chocolate gets your endorphins going so you'll feel better." She laughed, delighted and relieved. The demanding sense of needing to make the candies hadn't meant anything bad was going to happen. "Can I give you some for your cold?"

"That's the most absurd thing I've ever heard. Chocolate peanuts for colds."

"Chocolate *cinnamon-chili* peanuts! Just try some. They certainly aren't going to make you feel worse."

Before she could say anything else, another man came down the stairs to meet them. He was equally old, dressed equally well, but was more mobile. Where the man on Portia's arm had wiry gray hair, this man had dyed his red. His skin was smoother, his carriage erect.

"Well, look what we have here—the woman from next door." He stopped in front of her, beaming. "Even prettier up close."

Portia smiled back, charmed.

"I'm Marcus, my dear. And while this old grump bucket probably hasn't mentioned a word about it, he's Stanley."

"Hi, Marcus. I'm—"

"Portia, from next door. We know. Stanley has been giving me regular reports on his sightings."

Of course she'd seen him at the window, but . . . "You've been watching me?"

"*I* haven't," Marcus said. "But Stanley here has done little else." He smiled wickedly and leaned forward. "Very *Rear Window*, don't you think? And, rest assured, you've provided more entertainment than we've had around this place in ages."

The whole thing was a little weird, but Stanley's complete lack of guilt and Marcus's smiling charm made it difficult to do anything but laugh a little herself. "But how do you know my name?"

Marcus hooked his arm through Portia's free elbow. "Didn't you know that the postman knows everything? And he's about the only company we get these days."

Stanley coughed.

"The peanuts!" Portia said. "I have to get them."

"I'm not eating anything you make. How do I know they aren't poisoned?"

"Ha! Do you think I'd get you all this way into your apartment only to poison you?"

"Portia, love, go get whatever it is you're talking about," Marcus said. "We could use some new nuts around here."

Portia laughed, dashed out of the men's apartment and into hers. Grabbing two bags of peanuts, she wheeled back next door, flipping the OPEN sign to CLOSED. When she returned, Marcus was helping Stanley back into his favorite spot by the window with a caring devotion.

Embarrassed to be walking in on such a sweet scene, Portia set the bags down quietly and started to leave.

"We knew your great-aunt," Stanley said, his eyes still closed, his head back.

"You knew Evie?"

"She bought her town house around the same time Marcus and I bought ours. And let me tell you, this wasn't considered a good neighborhood back then. We didn't spend time together, really. She was an actress," he said, tone at once disdainful and amused. "I was a Broadway producer, and Marcus here was an agent. Actresses always tried to befriend us, and we learned to keep our distance."

He sat up a bit straighter and opened his eyes. "Evie was different. She didn't want any favors from anyone. Swore she would make it on her own, and she did. Even after she found success, we didn't socialize, but we watched out for each other. How could we not, all of us living in these giant town houses? Just me and Marcus, and Evie by herself. Plus, there was the Texas thing. I was born in Texas to a Southern mother who loved to cook. Evie's sister loved to cook—well, you must know that if you're her niece." Stanley gave Portia that wry little smile of his. "I remember you, too," he continued, "along with the rest of Evie's wild Texas nieces: Running up and down the fire escape at all hours. I was sure one of you was going to fall to your death."

Portia smiled back. "It was just me on the fire escape. And I survived."

"Yes, you did. And now that man and his daughters have moved in. Are you living with him?"

"No!"

Stanley snorted.

Marcus wiggled his eyebrows at her. "I still haven't managed to catch a glimpse of him. Though Stanley says he's something to be seen. All rugged and manly."

"Good God, man, you can't let the neighbors know that I'm ogling them!" Stanley said.

Marcus laughed, and Stanley began slowly eating his nuts. A few minutes later, Portia found herself in their kitchen, making a cup of hot chamomile tea. She brought it back out to Stanley, who sipped it, and soon his breathing grew easier. A tension in Marcus's face, which she hadn't realized was there until it was gone, also eased.

"I'd better go." Portia wrote down her cell number. "If you need anything, I'm right next door."

"Evie always said you were like her own children. She loved it when you came to visit."

"We loved visiting." Portia squeezed Stanley's hand, hugged Marcus, and headed home. That was one of the things she had made herself forget when she pushed the knowing away: It always brought about unexpected interactions with strangers. Food had a way of bringing people together.

But every peaceful thought evaporated when she walked into her kitchen and found that someone had taken all the candied figs and nuts. The question circled in her head. Why? And, more important, who?

Twenty-four

⬩⬩⬩

ARIEL USED HER KEY to get in the town house. The muted sound of rock music drifted down to her through the walls. She dropped her backpack in the foyer, tilting her chin up to look at the ceiling, trying to understand where the noise was coming from. "Dad?"

But Dad wouldn't be home. It was barely three. And he sure as heck wouldn't be listening to any sort of music that thumped and buzzed.

"Miranda?" No answer.

"Portia?" No way Portia would be playing loud music in their house.

She headed up the stairs to the second floor, then on to the third, the music getting louder the higher she went. The whole thing made Ariel feel nervous. But she was pretty sure Miranda was up in the attic doing who knew what.

When she got all the way up, the door was closed, but the music was impossibly loud now, thumping through the wood door. Ariel hesitated, her hand on the knob, then opened the door.

If she thought the music couldn't get louder, she was wrong. The beat pounded through the room, making her body buzz and her eardrums hurt. No one noticed her, not any of the three guys who lounged around the floor, or the two girls, plus Miranda, who sat Indian style next to them. Ariel only recognized the creep Dustin.

All of them were laughing hysterically. Not that Ariel could hear the sound of their laughter over the music, but she could see how their faces contorted and moved, like watching a silent movie where everyone on-screen was laughing.

It took another second before the smell hit her. A weird sweet smoke smell. And wine. Like her mother used to drink in their house in New Jersey with its big formal living room and dining room, the giant kitchen and den. Ariel still held out hope that her dad would see the light and take them back to Montclair. Weird stuff like Miranda smoking pot and drinking alcohol didn't happen back in New Jersey.

Ariel stood there frozen, smoke wrapping around her stinging her nose and eyes, as she wondered what to do.

The teenagers still didn't know she was there. They kept laughing and throwing little chocolate-covered balls, trying to get them into each other's mouths. As if this were really funny.

The creep noticed her first. He reached over and turned down the sound system. "Hey." Dustin laughed. "Dude."

Seriously?

"What's up?" he added.

Miranda jerked around, her hair flying around her shoulders. When she saw Ariel, her eyes narrowed to mean, thin slits. "Are you spying again?"

"I am not spying!"

"I am not spying!" Miranda mimicked cruelly, making the other kids laugh.

Ariel felt a burn, thinking it was embarrassment, but even that didn't deter her. "You're smoking pot. And drinking. Dad could come home any minute."

"Yep," one of the girls said, still laughing. "She's spying. Little sisters are a pain in the ass."

Miranda glared. "Dad isn't home. And he's not coming home anytime soon. So just go and mind your own business, freak."

The name hurt worse than it should have. Ariel knew people thought she was a freak. Even she had put the description in the title of her journal. But Miranda had never called her that. Since their mom died, Miranda hadn't been that nice to her, but she hadn't been outright cruel like she was being now.

Ariel pushed back the tears in her throat, dashing at her eyes that burned and teared, and not for the first time she wished she were a tougher sort of sister, one who would put shaving cream in her sister's bed, or pour ice-cold water on her feet when she was sleeping. "You're going to get in trouble, Miranda," was all she managed, the words sticking in her throat. "Big trouble. You're smoking *pot*."

All of a sudden, the creep leaped at her. Ariel felt her eyes pop open like some sort of cartoon character and she started to back up.

He grabbed her around the shoulders and spun her around. "She isn't a spy! She's cool! Right, dude?"

Everything around her rushed by. It was beyond insanity, she knew, but she felt something. Noticed. Which was ridiculous. Appalled at herself, she pushed at his arm. "Put me down, you Neanderthal!"

He did, then offered her a chocolate ball. "For the lady," he said, sweeping a bow. "In fact, you can have all of mine." He pushed a little bag filled with chocolate at her.

Ariel scowled at him. But his smile, his bow, his offer of perfect chocolate candy drew her in and she took the bag.

"You have the coolest hair," the other girl said, as if she were her greatest friend, then turned a pointed look at the girl who had called her a spy.

"Oh, yeah, majorly cool," that girl added.

They all started talking to her then, each of them offering her chocolate. Miranda rolled her eyes.

Ariel didn't need Miranda to tell her that the kids didn't really think anything about her was cool; they just wanted to make sure she didn't tell on them. But the whole not being invisible thing seduced her even if it wasn't real.

"Don't you dare tell Dad," Miranda said, dragging a deep pull of the joint into her lungs before blowing it out in a rush.

Ariel just stood there, holding tight to the bag of chocolate, smoke wrapping around her as she tried to figure out what she should do. She had just decided that it was her dad's problem, not hers, when she realized that the burning in her throat and lungs had gotten worse. It happened fast then. Her throat started to close off in a way it hadn't in years, teasing her into believing that she had outgrown stupid reactions to weird things in the air.

In a flash, she could hardly breathe.

Miranda and the other kids had fired up the sound system again, and the walls throbbed and swelled. Trying her hardest not to panic, Ariel dropped the chocolate and pivoted toward the door. She half ran, half tripped down the stairs to her room, frantically digging around in her backpack as she tried to suck in gasps of breath. Calculator. Antibacterial gel. Socks. Pen after pen. Her head started to throb and swell like the walls upstairs, the music growing fainter even as some part of her realized the music was really getting louder. But just as a massively tired feeling swelled through her body, her fingers clamped around the inhaler, and she jerked it out. The nail-polish picture her mother had painted on it fluttered in front of her eyes. Without thinking, she jammed Einstein into her mouth, squeezing as hard as she could, praying he was smart enough to save her.

Twenty-five

❖

PORTIA WALKED INTO the Kanes' house at five that evening. As she was walking in, a small crew of what she knew were Miranda's friends came out. The boy Dustin wagged an eyebrow at her. She glowered back in what she hoped was a stern schoolteacher sort of way. The boy only laughed.

Portia had been spending her days doing exactly three things: cooking, baking, and telling herself to stop thinking about Gabriel Kane. Actually, that made it four things, the fourth being the time she spent thinking about Gabriel. Which was a lot.

Then there had been the nights. But she really tried not to think too much about those. She still found it hard to believe that she was having utterly passionate, completely uncommitted sex with her upstairs neighbor. Her, Portia Cuthcart. Always safe. Always careful. Always proper. She still hadn't even been out on a date with him. The Bandana Ball didn't count. Olivia had all but forced him to go.

Sure, something in her old Texas soul whispered unhelpful things about cows and milk for free. But everything in this newer New York soul had her reveling in being someone so unlike the woman she had become in Texas—soft, a ghost of her former self.

Her thoughts were interrupted just as she was finishing up dinner for the Kanes when Ariel walked into the kitchen looking a bit gray. She sat down without saying more than a listless hi.

Miranda followed a few second later. "What is Ariel telling you?" she demanded, more belligerent than usual.

Portia considered. "What's going on with you two now?"

"Nothing," they said in tandem.

Miranda shot her sister a sharp scowl, then wheeled around and left. A moment later Ariel got up and walked out, too. Portia heard first one bedroom door slam, then another.

Don't get involved, she told herself. *A smart woman doesn't get involved with her secret lover's children.*

Which just got her mind circling back to the same thing she wasn't supposed to be thinking about. Gabriel.

Last night he had come down the fire escape in that way he did. When she had opened the door, she found him standing there, his hair still damp from a shower, raked back with his hands. He wore a T-shirt instead of a button-down, old jeans that hung low on his hips, and a pair of Converse with no socks. He stepped inside without asking, as if he couldn't do anything else, a strong man giving in to her in a way that made her feel heady with a foreign sort of power. This strong man wanted her. This powerful man couldn't stay away from her. A thrill ran through her at the thought.

Standing at the door, he showed no trace of the civilized businessman who stepped out of his town car every evening. He walked into the room as if he owned it and pulled his T-shirt over his head, throwing it to the side.

The twist in Portia's stomach at the sight of him was so raw and primal that she couldn't shape words.

"Portia," he said finally, the word dragged out on a breath, then just stood there.

"Gabriel, are you okay?"

He pressed his eyes closed, blowing a hard breath out his nose. "No."

Then he dragged her into his arms and took her over to the old wrought-iron bed. They made love with a kind of ferocity that made the bed slam against the wall. But even that wasn't enough, and five minutes after, they started over, sweaty bodies turning over each other, the only sounds ragged gasps and moans. At some point, he flipped her on her back and pinned her down, his face wild as they gave in to sensation without words, he never taking his eyes off her.

Finally, later, when they were lying next to each other, gasping, it was Gabriel who broke the silence, the edge in him eased, if only slightly. Lying in the semidarkness, he came up on one elbow, demanding to know everything about her, pinning her down when she was elusive.

So she told him about her parents, her grandmother, the stories all whitewashed and pretty. Evie and the town house, the way it had looked in its prime, the way she had loved it. The way she and her sisters used to play dress-up with their aunts' old costumes.

He listened intently, his fingers running along her arm and shoulders, circling slowly across her collarbone, as if drawing her words along her skin.

But at some point he captured her hands with his and rolled over on top of her, breaking off her sentence. "Portia," he groaned against her mouth, his free hand sliding down her body, no longer lazy, rather intent.

She lost herself to his touch. But at the back of her mind she worried. What they shared was sweaty and complicated. Despite all her talk of uncommitted sex, he refused to let her keep her boundaries. With the exception of that one earlier kiss, he maintained control of her, her body, of his. But she also knew that he let down his guard with her. Gabriel was a man who was used to control. What would he do if he lost what he no doubt felt defined him?

The bang of the kitchen cabinet yanked her out of her thoughts.

"Dinner still isn't ready?" Miranda demanded. "Hello, I'm starving."

Portia blushed as if the teenager could possibly know what she had been thinking. Miranda made a strangled scoffing sound. "Dinner. In this century."

By the time Ariel and Miranda were seated at the table and Portia was neatening up from preparing the meal of juicy pork chops, green beans with almonds, and creamy cheese-filled grits before she left, she heard the front door open, and her knees went weak.

She glanced up and saw Gabriel coming down the hallway. He stopped in the doorway and just looked at her.

"Jeez, what's up with you, Dad?" Miranda sneered.

Portia jerked her head down and focused on the stove. Instead of snapping at his daughter's tone, Gabriel walked over and kissed the top of Miranda's head. "Sorry, honey. It's been a good day."

For a second, Portia was certain Miranda was about to cry. But then she jerked up from her chair.

"A good day?" she bit out. "Have you looked outside? It's, like, totally cloudy."

She slammed her chair back and stomped off, leaving her nearly full dinner plate behind.

"Miranda!" Gabriel snapped, all that ease disappearing from his eyes as he started after her.

Ariel dropped her head and concentrated on the food Portia had set in front of her.

Later, after the girls had gone to bed and Portia was sound asleep, he came down the fire escape.

"This is New York," Gabriel said, his tone sharp, waking her. "You need to keep your windows locked."

"I do," Portia murmured. "You came in through the glass door. Using a key you shouldn't have. There has to be a law against that."

She was dimly aware that he carried the cardboard sign she had posted earlier. "I take it that among your plethora of skills, reading isn't one of them?"

"I read." He tossed the sign aside, then slid between the sheets, pulling her close.

She rolled over onto her stomach, burrowing deeper into the sheets and blankets, hugging the pillow. Gabriel lifted up her hair and ran his lips along the nape of her neck. Then other kisses, his hands leaving her hair. "You think I'm sexy," he said.

She groaned. "Of course that's what you took away from the sign."

"'All Sexy Cat Burglars Keep Out.'"

"I should have just written 'Keep Out.' Simple. To the point." It had just seemed too mean. But she wanted him to stay away. The more he came down the fire escape, the harder it was to remain in the frame of mind of being okay with an arrangement where they were nothing more than two single adults having casual sex. She was turning into a pathetic, old-fashioned cliché. The more she had sex with him, the less casual it felt. Given the man she realized he was, there was no way this could end well. She had come to understand that he wanted something from her that he hated needing. Hated that he gave in to repeatedly.

"That isn't fair," she gasped when he pulled the sheet low.

"What isn't fair?" he asked, running his tongue along the shell of her ear.

"I'm exhausted. I've been cooking all day."

"I'm the one who's exhausted," he countered, sitting up briefly to rip off his shirt and kick his shorts away. Falling back to her, he rolled her over, her arms above her head, loosely pinning her wrists with one of his large hands. His eyes flared as he took her in, her breasts high through the old T-shirt she wore. "I haven't slept since I met you."

"At all? Not one second of sleep."

He grinned down at her. "Barely." His free hand slipped beneath the soft cotton of her tee, his thigh sliding over her hips. Portia moaned into his mouth, tasting him.

"You're like a demented cat burglar," she murmured, gasping as his thumb brushed the peak of her breast.

"A *sexy* cat burglar," he reminded her, running his tongue along the same path his thumb had just grazed.

"You're also my boss," she managed. "My upstairs neighbor. A man, need I remind you, who is trying to kick me out of my apartment."

He had the good grace to tense at that.

"Basically," she continued, trying her hardest to stay focused as he resumed his attention to her body, "this all adds up to a really bad idea. Beyond that—if you need a *beyond that*—one of these days someone is going to figure out what is going on here. My money is on Ariel. And as much as she likes me, I'm not sure she's going to like *you* and me. I know Miranda won't."

"Let me worry about my daughters. Besides, at one point, Ariel was trying to get me to ask you out."

"Really?"

"Really. She thought it a small price to pay for a decent meal."

Portia snorted.

He tugged her shirt over her head and left it tangled around her wrists, his hand holding her wrists secure. There it was again. Gabriel maintaining control. "You're beautiful, you know."

This time, she scoffed. "I'm cute, at best."

He met Portia's eyes with an intensity that made her breath catch. "You are beautiful," he said in a way that dared her to contradict him.

She loved the sound of the words, the fact that she could tell he believed it. He dipped his head, making love to her with his mouth, going slowly, never rushing. She felt the electric pull between her legs.

"Oh, to hell with the sign," she whispered, and stopped thinking altogether.

He still held her captive, but she turned as best she could to press up against him. He laughed when she cursed at him, his palm sliding over her stomach, then lower to her hip. Portia felt as if she had stopped breathing when he brought one of her knees up, nudging her legs apart, the palm of his hand skimming down the inside of her thigh. But he avoided her center.

"Gabriel, please," she pleaded, twisting again to free her hands, but he held her secure. She wanted more.

"I know," he murmured against her skin. "But not yet."

He dipped his head back to her. Her breath came in pants as he refused to allow her to move.

He stroked and kissed, then surprised her when he dropped his hand from her wrists and slipped down her body, pressing her knees farther apart.

Reality flashed into her head like lights flipped on with a switch. She had never done anything like this. She sat up and tried to pull free. "Gabriel!" she said, pushing at him.

But he was far too strong for her. "Shhh," he said, nipping the skin of her inner thigh.

"I just don't do that," Portia said, even as her body shook. "I'm not comfortable with that. It's private."

"Not private," he stated against her skin. "Mine," he said so softly that she felt certain he was saying it to himself rather than to her.

She fell back at the first touch of his tongue to her core, and when he pressed her legs even farther apart, she allowed that, too. Sensation rode through her, the kind that lust lends to a girl who isn't used to being wild. She let go, she opened to him, and when she gave in so freely, she felt a shift in him.

With a groan he reared over her like he could do nothing else, entering her hard, his careful control lost. He didn't say anything else, just moved, fast and sure, needing something, reaching, bringing her to another orgasm. Only when she cried out did he let go completely, his body tensing and shuddering.

He collapsed on top of her and they lay that way for minutes, or maybe longer, connected, her eyes closed. She could feel his warm breath on her neck, his breathing ragged. When she opened her eyes, he pushed up on his elbows and stared at her. "What are you doing to me?" he whispered.

"Gabriel—"

He pressed his forehead to hers, then rolled away. She expected him to keep going and get off the bed. Instead, he dragged her to him, wrapping her in his arms.

"Go to sleep, Portia."

"But—"

"Portia, sleep."

She debated. But then he tucked her close, his chest to her back, the tension finally easing out of him completely, and she drifted off to sleep.

Twenty-six

✦

D AD, REALLY, I don't need to go to the Shrink anymore. I'm fine.
You're fine. Miranda's fine." Ariel plastered a big fat smile on her
face. "We're all fine, remember?"

Which was far from true, but Ariel was tired of figuring out ways to
avoid talking to the Shrink. It was exhausting to come up with new and
increasingly inventive ways not to talk about anything that mattered.

Her dad sat at the desk in his study, looking out the window instead
of at all sorts of business stuff spread out in front of him. Just sitting. Just
looking. So not like her dad.

She felt a flicker of worry. No way her dad could die on her, too, surely.

He turned back and studied her. She studied him right back. Something was definitely different about him, though thankfully as best she
could tell, he looked perfectly healthy.

An image of her mom popped into her head, dancing around her dad,
laughing. *"What can I do to wipe that scowl away?"*

Her dad would look back at her mom in that way of his, massively
intense.

Her dad was scary, but he was really great, too. Like, she remembered that when he got home late from his office, he would come sit on the edge of her mattress even though she pretended to be asleep. He wouldn't say anything; he'd just have a look and then lean down and kiss her forehead. She knew he did the same thing to Miranda. Miranda had told her once. Of course he hadn't sat on the edge of either of their mattresses since their mom had died. As far as she knew, anyway.

"First off, Ariel," he said, "I don't appreciate you calling Dr. Parson the Shrink."

Ariel swallowed back the retort that no amount of lipstick on a pig was going to make that pig anything but. Calling the Shrink Dr. Parson wasn't going to make him less of a quack.

"Second, Dr. Parson said that when you're in his office, you refuse to speak to him."

"I talk."

"About the weather. Or you grill him on his credentials."

"I ask: Does a man who lives and works in the twenty-first century seriously wear a goatee and round tortoise-shell glasses? I have two words for you: Fake Freud."

"Ariel."

"Okay, so maybe I shouldn't judge him based on his Freud facial hair, but come on, he has a black leather sofa. Seriously, Dad, I know everyone says you're a genius, but maybe money smarts don't translate into regular street smarts. I tell you, the guy isn't for real."

Her dad looked amused for a nanosecond before he wiped the humor from his face as fast as good old Wink swiped his big block letters from the dry board at school.

"As much as I appreciate your assessment of my intellect, I assure you that Dr. Parson is for real. And *for real* you have to go tomorrow."

Sure enough, at 3:30 the next afternoon, Ariel found herself on that black sofa.

"Have you ever considered getting one of those Victorian-type couches, or whatever they're called? Chesterfields. I Googled that for you. I think Freud must have had a Chesterfield in his office." Ariel made a production of considering the idea. "Tell me, Dr. Parson, do you think Freud would have had a leather sofa in his office if they'd been available back then? Because, really, I don't think yours is working."

Ariel could have sworn that the guy actually blushed—at least as much as a guy with a beard could blush. No matter how hard she tried, she never managed to flummox her dad. She had to give him that.

"Ariel," Dr. Parson finally stated, "we are here to discuss the unfortunate things that have happened to you, not my furniture choices—"

"Maybe you *should* talk to someone about your unfortunate furn—"

"Ariel." He barked her name before pulling himself together. Ariel's personal diagnosis? The guy was losing it.

He leaned forward. "We've been talking for three months. I've been patient. I've let you discuss whatever you want. I've asked you to write your feelings down in a journal. And I've done this in the hopes that you'd learn to trust me."

She barely held back a snort.

Dr. Parson narrowed his eyes. "Ariel," he said. "There's one question I haven't asked you directly, the one question that matters, the one question that I shouldn't have to ask because you should want to talk to me about it on your own. Since that hasn't happened, tell me: What happened in the car?"

Her heart came to a full-blown stop.

Ariel had to force herself to breathe, air in, air out. She felt the sweat on the palms of her hands. It took a second to drum up a smile.

"I don't know what you're talking about."

"I think you do."

Life had been so simple before. One dad, one mom, one sister—all of them living in a house in Montclair, New Jersey.

"You're only hurting yourself by bottling it up."

He leaned even closer, his elbows on his knees, his tablet and pen set aside.

"Why won't you talk about it, Ariel? Are you protecting someone?"

The words were like a kick to the stomach. She searched for something to say, something sarcastic, something to distract him. But she couldn't find anything. The facts were just facts. Life could change in an instant.

She turned her head and focused on all those degrees framed and lined up on the plain white walls. One frame was slightly off. She had told him several times. Once he had stood up all of a sudden and strode over, straightened it, and then turned back. *"There,"* he had stated.

Ariel had seen that he regretted his show of temper. It was the only time she had liked him. It was the only time she had thought about showing him what was inside her. But then he had come back to his chair, drawn a deep breath, and settled back into his Fake Freud persona.

Now the frame was crooked again.

"I'm not keeping a secret," she said finally. "There's no one to protect."

"Tell me about the accident, Ariel." He hesitated. "Please."

A sigh escaped her lips. "Fine. My mom was driving me to a Mathlete competition in Paramus. I was in the backseat; she was in the front." Her leg betrayed her, swinging too fast and hitting the coffee table. She made it stop. "She was driving really fast on the Garden State Parkway. We were late. We swerved. We wrecked. The car flew over the rail. Mom died. I didn't."

The guy sat there for something like a full minute. Ariel knew, because she was counting, not to see how long it would take before he talked again, but to keep her mind focused on something besides the accident.

Finally he found words again. "How did that make you feel?"

How did it make her feel? How did he think it made her feel?

She glanced at the clock and stood. "Oops, look at that. Time's up."

Startled, the Shrink glanced over at the clock and blinked. "Ariel," he said.

But she was already banging out the door.

Twenty-seven

✥

FOR THE LAST THREE WEEKS Portia had done little more than cook for The Glass Kitchen. Now she stood in the middle of her apartment, the day's assortment of menu items already sold and out the door, and her head swam with images of cake. But not just any cake: a festive concoction loaded with candles. She closed her eyes and knew she needed to plan a birthday party.

But for whom?

She'd have to make the cake later because she needed to get upstairs to make dinner for the Kanes. When she walked into their kitchen, Miranda and Ariel were sitting at the table. Ariel was pretending to do homework; Miranda was staring at her silent cell phone.

"Hey," Portia said.

"Hey," Ariel replied with little enthusiasm. Miranda just rolled her eyes.

"What's up?"

"Nothing," Miranda snapped.

"She's waiting for the creep . . . I mean, Dustin . . . to call," Ariel explained hastily.

Miranda shot her little sister a glare. "You didn't think he was a creep the other day when you—"

She stopped abruptly, glancing at Portia. Both girls jerked back to what they had been doing.

Miranda looked back down at her cell phone, her jaw set, but a moment later her lips started to tremble. "He's not going to call. He broke up with me. He says I'm not mature enough for him."

Portia sighed. "Boys can be real jerks," she said, leaning her hip against the kitchen counter. "Let me guess: You wouldn't . . . sleep with him, right?"

Ariel gasped.

Miranda scowled. "It wasn't like that."

Portia just waited.

"Okay, maybe it was like that. Don't you dare tell Dad!" She dropped her head to her arms. "I hate New York! I miss New Jersey!"

With a mental sigh, Portia walked over to Miranda and, after only a brief hesitation, stroked her hair. "Oh, sweetie."

Miranda drew a shaky breath. "My mom used to call me that." She started to cry. "It's her birthday today. Or it would have been."

A shiver ran down Portia's spine. The birthday cake. Not for some unknown someone who would show up at the apartment.

Once again, her first instinct was to run, but she sat down and hugged Miranda instead. Ariel looked on with that same expression she'd had when Portia and her sisters were dancing it out. Portia extended her other arm, and Ariel tucked under it like a baby bird. With another sigh, Portia realized she was getting pulled in closer and closer to this family.

"I miss her," Miranda choked out, sobs racking her body.

Ariel didn't say anything. She just squeezed in closer.

"When my sisters and I were your ages," Portia finally said, "our parents died. So I know how awful it is."

"B-b-both of them?" Miranda asked.

"Yep. We went to live with our grandmother." Portia hesitated one last second, then plunged ahead. "And every year on our mom's birthday, we celebrated with a party. What do you say we make a cake and have a birthday party for your mom?"

Miranda sniffled and straightened up. "I guess so."

Ariel peered across from under Portia's arm at her sister. "But what if it makes Dad too sad?"

Miranda's features hardened. "Erasing her is the wrong way to miss her."

That's all it took. Instead of making dinner, Portia showed the girls how to make a birthday cake. And then she let them do it by themselves, trusting that the act of making something for their mother would be healing.

Portia started on party sandwiches, little small square bites of cucumber and cream cheese, smoked turkey with gouda, ham and cheddar nestled inside bread with the crusts cut off while the girls worked together as a pair. When Ariel saw what she was doing, she laughed, the clear, bright laughter of a child rather than the mini adult she so often sounded like. "It's going to be a real party!" Ariel cheered.

The three worked together in a surprising harmony, and soon the cake was done. When Portia finished making the sandwiches and putting them in the refrigerator, she went downstairs and found streamers and an old HAPPY BIRTHDAY sign in Aunt Evie's boxes.

By the time they heard the front door open and close, they had the dining room set with birthday paraphernalia, party sandwiches covering the table, and a cake at the center of it all.

"I smell something good," Gabriel called out when he came in the front door.

Portia held her breath. She had simply followed the knowing without a thought for the consequences.

"What's this?" Gabriel asked as he came around the corner. He took in the balloons and the banner. "Whose birthday is it?"

No one spoke. Portia watched as understanding dawned, and she went cold. The hard planes of Gabriel's face crumpled, sharp edges going weak.

He didn't look like he was on the verge of crying. It was more that some aching part of his soul had escaped the carefully controlled façade.

Miranda must have been watching his face, too, because when she spoke her voice was harsh. "It's a birthday party. For Mom."

Gabriel couldn't seem to find words, but he looked every inch a wounded beast.

"All you want to do is forget her!" Miranda accused him when he didn't say anything. "You want us to forget her! You made us come to this awful place and be with these awful people who break up with us and don't like us and tell us we don't fit in—all because you don't want to think about Mom. Well, guess what, *we* loved her! We miss her!"

"Miranda, that's enough," Gabriel said, the words catching in his throat.

"No, it's not! I hate you! I hate you for moving us here!" She bolted from the room, her steps rapping a staccato beat up the stairs.

Ariel's small face looked so thin and fragile that Portia was shocked. The girl was obviously taking in everyone's pain, with no idea what to do about it.

"I'm sorry if we hurt you with the party," Ariel choked out, and ran from the room before Gabriel could speak.

He looked at Portia. The hard planes were back in place. "What in the hell is going on?"

Portia took a deep breath. "The girls were upset when I got here. Miranda's boyfriend broke up with her."

He narrowed his eyes at the boyfriend mention.

"But the real problem, Gabriel, is that they feel they can't talk about their mother."

"I'm paying a fortune to a shrink so they have someone to talk to!"

"They need to talk to you."

He plowed his hands through his hair. "So you got it in your head to throw a party for a dead woman."

"Exactly," Portia shot back. "My grandmother did the same thing for me and my sisters after our mother died. It made us feel as if she was still with us, somehow."

He strode to the table and stared at the cake.

"Of course you miss her, Gabriel, but your daughters are still here. They need to celebrate their mother. If they're at all like me, they're terrified that they'll forget her, that at some point a whole day will pass and they won't even remember it was her birthday." Idiotically, tears pricked Portia's eyes.

Gabriel turned to leave, but stopped at the door, his back to her. "Things are fine, Portia. Just leave it alone."

Her mouth dropped open when he left. "Things aren't fine," she called after him. "You're smart enough to know that."

He disappeared up the stairs without replying. Stunned, Portia stared after him. Was he going to leave it at that?

She had promised herself that she wouldn't get involved, wouldn't open herself up to this family. While she had opened herself to the knowing, she had promised herself that she wouldn't use the knowing with Gabriel and the girls. Look what had happened when she had. She'd made a cake for the man's dead wife, wrecking all three of them.

Go back downstairs, she told herself.

Instead, she followed Gabriel, taking the stairs two at a time up to the office level. He wasn't there, so she kept going, hearing noise from the floor above. She tiptoed up the last flight and stopped in the doorway of a room that she had barely noticed the night they had gone to the roof. She saw now that it was being used for storage. There was an old bike and boxes, though there was also a sound system and television, even though there were no sofas or chairs.

Gabriel stood inside a closet, pulling a box that seemed to have been hidden in the very back on a high shelf. He strode over and set it down with a thump, wrenched off the top, and pulled out several framed photographs.

Something aching and painful twisted inside her: jealousy. Every time

Gabriel came into her arms, she conveniently forgot about his wife. But watching Gabriel stare at the photos of the woman, she had a blinding reminder of why she had told herself to stay away from this man. She started to turn away.

"I'm selfish."

His voice stopped her.

"You asked weeks ago why I didn't have photos out, why I wasn't keeping the memory of my wife alive for the girls. Miranda's right. I didn't want to remember."

Portia's heart twisted a little more. "You loved her, and now she's gone," she said, her voice coming out a near whisper. "It's okay to want to avoid the pain."

He hesitated. "It's not that." He ran his hands over his face. "How am I supposed to know what's right or wrong? For the girls? They don't come with an instruction manual."

Portia gave him a faint smile. "You just have to keep trying. That's all they want."

He swallowed, nodded at her. "Get the girls, will you? I have an idea."

Portia found Miranda lying on her bed, curled on her side, eyes squeezed shut, earbuds in her ears. Portia knocked, then knocked more loudly, but there was no answer. With no help for it, Portia walked through the open door and sat on the bed. In for a penny, in for a pound. "Hey, kiddo."

Miranda rolled her eyes. "Who calls people 'kiddo'?" Her voice rasped a little from all the tears.

Portia knew Miranda was lashing out because she was hurting. "Your dad wants you and Ariel to go upstairs."

"What's he going to do, lock us in the attic?"

"Oh, honey, he's figuring things out as he goes. He's bound to make some mistakes along the way."

The girl snorted. "You think?"

"He's trying right now. Give him a chance."

"What? You're telling me that he's planning to sing Happy Birthday? Dive into the cake?" But Miranda sat up and scooted off the bed.

Portia didn't have the faintest idea what Gabriel had in mind, so she just said, "Let's get Ariel."

They walked down the hall. Ariel's bedroom was empty.

"Where is she?" Portia asked, frowning.

Miranda gave her a funny look, walked into the room, and knocked on the closet. "Hey, A, you in there?"

"No," came the muffled reply.

Miranda pulled open the door. Portia could just make out Ariel sitting cross-legged in the corner, writing in a journal.

"What part of *no* didn't you understand?" she snapped.

"The part where Dad doesn't take *no* for an answer when he wants us upstairs."

Ariel scowled.

"Supposedly, he sent Portia down for us," Miranda added.

Ariel glanced between Miranda and Portia, then closed the journal and started to put it away, only to stop. "Turn around," she instructed them.

Once the book was hidden, Portia, Miranda, and Ariel headed up the stairs to the top floor and found Gabriel standing in front of a television set.

Miranda glared at him, not making it easy.

"I thought we could watch some DVDs."

"You made us come up here to watch TV?" Miranda demanded.

Gabriel didn't let the sarcasm deter him. "Not TV. Home movies. Ones of you girls and . . . Mom."

Ariel flew forward. Miranda just stayed by Portia in the doorway, visibly tense.

Gabriel looked at her. "There's that great one of you and Mom dressed in matching clothes for Easter."

Miranda bit her lip, and then came forward reluctantly. As she got close, Gabriel pulled her into a hug and then pulled Ariel in with them. "I'm sorry," he said.

Portia felt tears backing up in her throat. She began to turn away.

"Where're you going?" Gabriel blurted.

"It's time for me to get home," Portia said, summoning a smile.

"No!" Gabriel and Ariel said. Even Miranda gave Portia a half smile. Ariel raced over and pulled her into the room.

In addition to the DVDs, Gabriel had gotten four slices of cake and a tray full of the party sandwiches. The four of them sank down onto the floor to eat and watch.

Victoria Kane had been a beauty. Dark hair, deep blue eyes, and the sort of rosebud mouth that made men go wild. She seemed about twenty-five in the first DVD. She danced for the camera and winked before pulling Gabriel close and kissing him. The kiss was deeply intimate, like a movie kiss between two characters in love. Portia had to swallow hard.

But both girls were smiling. "Mom was beautiful," Miranda breathed.

Gabriel took a deep breath as he stared at the screen.

They watched Miranda's third birthday, an elegant Christmas party, and Ariel's sixth birthday before they were finally done. At the end, Ariel threw her arms around her dad's neck, and he hugged her fiercely. Miranda conceded a nod, and he nodded back, though Portia could see that he wanted more.

The girls trooped downstairs to go to bed. Gabriel sat quietly, staring without seeing. Portia went over and slipped down next to him on the floor, their backs against the wall.

"That was a lovely thing to do for the girls. But obviously painful for you."

"Painful?"

"It's not just the girls who are grieving," Portia said, stumbling over what to say. "You have to remember that you're in pain, too. I could see how much you loved her."

Gabriel reached over and took Portia's hand, running his thumb over her knuckles. Then he said, in an absolutely even tone, "I never loved her at all."

She barely understood the words. "What?"

He heaved a sigh, dropping his head back against the wall. "We never should have married. She loved partying, just like Anthony. We wouldn't have gotten married, but she got pregnant."

Portia was stunned. Gabriel didn't seem like the kind of man who got anyone pregnant by accident. "So you married her?"

"I figured I wouldn't be the greatest father, but I couldn't allow a child of mine to be raised by a woman who liked partying as much as Victoria did. The only way I could make sure that my child was taken care of was if I married the mother." He sat quietly for a moment, then added, "Victoria wasn't very maternal, but she did her best. And she loved the girls. You can see that."

Portia leaned her head on his shoulder. Gabriel had intrigued her, maddened her, filled her with desire. But now all that swirled together into something stronger. She thought of how he had handled Cordelia's confession. How he struggled to be a good father. "You're a good man, Gabriel Kane."

There was a long pause. "Tell that to Miranda."

"She'll come around."

He sighed, then stood, taking her hand and drawing her to her feet. "Will she?"

He looked exhausted and ravaged, as if his young daughters could bring him down in a way that multinational conglomerates couldn't. He might have been ruthless when it came to business, but this man was anything but when it came to Miranda and Ariel. This man loved his girls, but he didn't know the first thing about how to manage his way through their lives.

Portia reached up and wrapped her arms around him. He leaned over, pulling her into him, burying his face in the crook of her neck. Seconds ticked by before she felt his body ease.

"Thank you," he whispered into her hair. "Thank you for tonight."

Finally, he let her go, and together they cleaned up the mess. Downstairs in his kitchen, they worked like two cogs in a wheel. When they finished up in there, she realized that finger sandwiches and cake couldn't possibly be enough for him to eat.

"Sit," she told him softly, gently pulling him over to the table. When he tried to pull her to him, take control, she spun away.

He watched her with greedy eyes, greedy for her, greedy for the food, as she made an omelet gooey with melted cheese, bacon on the side, along with thick slices of homemade bread slathered in butter and jam. It was the kind of meal her mother used to make for Daddy when he came home late and exhausted from one of the manual jobs he had managed to drum up. Food that comforted as much as it sustained.

Portia set the plate in front of Gabriel. He looked from the food to her, something deep and nearly overwhelming in his eyes.

"Thank you," he whispered to her again.

When he picked up the fork and took a bite, she knew that the emotion in his face was about a great deal more than how delicious it tasted. And she realized then that with his mother, his brother, and even his wife, this was a man who had always taken care of everyone else. No one had ever taken care of him.

She remembered the way he had taken her the night before, holding her down, kissing her so intimately. She had expected to feel awkward afterward. Instead, she felt only a flare of slow carnal desire at the memory. And rightness.

She realized something that had been there for a while, but she had been reluctant to admit it, even to herself. She wanted more from him than a secret love affair.

At the thought, she sucked in her breath when images of food hit her. The fried chicken, the sweet jalapeño mustard—the same images that had hit her the first time when he walked toward her on the sidewalk, then again after the first time they made love. Gabriel's Meal.

Every day it had shimmered just beyond her thoughts, like a heavy pan of sauce simmering on a back burner. The more they made love, she realized, the stronger the image of the meal became. That was what she had been trying so hard not to think about.

Was it a gift? Or a warning? Good news or bad?

She didn't know.

But if she wanted more from him, more for them, then she would have to find out. She would have to make Gabriel's Meal.

Twenty-eight

✦

L IFE, ARIEL KNEW, often made no sense, a fact that could make even a smart girl want to trade in her brain for an obsession with acne cures and makeup tips. Almost.

Life didn't hand out easy equations with perfect answers. Instead, there were things like one minute your mom was there, and the next she was gone. One minute your sister was awful, and the next she was nice. But how long before Miranda turned mean again?

The second Ariel figured her dad was asleep, she snuck back upstairs and retrieved the DVDs. Back inside her room, she curled up in her closet and popped one of the discs into her laptop, fast-forwarding to all the scenes with her mom.

There were days when she could hardly remember what her mom looked like—at least, how Mom looked before the accident. What she mostly remembered was the way Mom looked in the car.

Ariel's stomach hurt at the memory, which never did anyone any good. What's more, a real shrink should have gotten that. Shouldn't he know that talking about the accident was massively screwed up and totally a waste of time?

Of course, in all her trying to convince her dad that the guy was a quack, she couldn't talk about the accident because she had zero interest in letting him or anyone else know that she had to watch her mom die in the car. If Dad knew she had been conscious while it happened, he'd have her locked up for good, figuring she was about to go all *Girl, Interrupted* or something. So she kept quiet. Besides, it would just make him feel worse. That was something she'd figured out since the accident: Why say the stuff that hurt other people? No point.

Sitting in the closet, Ariel started to fall asleep to footage of her own birthday party the year before. But she jolted fully awake when she heard a crash in the entry hall. Sharp voices sounded, coming all the way up the stairs and into her closet. Miranda and her dad.

Ariel focused on the computer screen. "Everything is fine," she whispered, tracing the lines of her mother's image as she brought a store-bought cake from the kitchen, birthday candles flickering.

But her father's voice boomed, making it hard to stay focused on the screen. "Where the hell do you think you're going, young lady?"

"Out, Dad. I'm going out!"

"Like hell you are!"

Miranda sounded as angry as their father, the truce from earlier swept away like store-bought or even homemade cake scraped from a plate into the trash.

Ariel started to hum. She found another DVD, one they hadn't watched, and popped it in the computer. She could ignore the fight if she tried hard enough. She would pretend that everything was fine.

She clicked on play and Mom and Miranda flared to life, laughing as they chased each other around the den. Mom was dressed up in a tight red dress that stopped just above her knees, her hair teased and puffy, and her lips painted a darker shade of red. Ariel's own voice from behind the camera asked where she was going.

Her mom laughed. *"Where am I going?"* She made a big production of considering the question. *"A book party, darling. Yes, one of those book groups where people talk about characters who are happy and lead exciting lives."*

"Is Dad going, too?" Ariel heard herself ask.

For a second, her mom's smile tightened. *"Dad is busy."*

Mom had put makeup on Miranda, who was in seventh grade back then, and her sister strutted into the frame, primping for the camera. *"I'm fabulous,"* she cooed into the lens. *"Simply fabulous."*

Ariel heard herself snort in the background.

Miranda stuck out her tongue and twirled away.

Pulling the computer closer, Ariel focused on the screen, remembering the details of their old house. The dark hardwood floors, the huge rugs, the fancy furniture. Her mother had liked fancy. Her dad never had.

"All you have to do is pay for it, Gabriel. It's not like you live in it all that much."

The memory leaped out from somewhere, jarring Ariel back into watching the DVD. Their old doorbell rang and Ariel watched her mother's expression change, her laughter gone as she smoothed her dress.

"How do I look, sweetie?"

"Perfect," Ariel heard herself say.

In the background of the spinning footage, Miranda raced to the door while her mother stood, waiting.

"Turn that thing off, A."

But she hadn't, and Mom had forgotten she was there. Miranda ran back into the room, excited, and suddenly Ariel remembered what had happened next.

Her heart started to pound as Uncle Anthony walked onto the screen, dressed in a sports jacket, blue shirt, and jeans. He stopped when he saw her mom, smiling at her.

"Anthony!" her mother cried.

Then the footage snapped off. She could remember hitting the power button and going over to say hi.

Uncle Anthony had come in and out of their lives for as long as she could remember. And for as long as she could remember, he made her mom smile and made her dad really mad.

The difficult thing about life was that once you learned things, you couldn't unlearn them. Like remembering her uncle walking into their house in Montclair. Her uncle loving her mom first, before her dad came along. The date of her parents' marriage and Miranda's birthday. It was like her parents had done everything they could to hide the date they got married. Ugh. Her heart thumped in a way that made the back of her eyes hurt and her throat swell.

Suddenly, she heard Miranda flying up the stairs.

"Your acting out stops now, do you hear me?" Dad roared, his voice thrumming through the walls as he followed after her.

"Up yours!" Miranda shrieked back.

"You do not sneak out of this house," he ground out.

Ariel shut the laptop and pressed her hands to her ears.

"No, no, no," she whispered. Whispering *no* never did any good, but she did it anyway. Same as she had in the car, lying there with her mom.

The memory made her get to her feet, unsteady at first, before she threw open the door. This time she wasn't locked down by a seat belt and crumpled metal. This time she could do something. Help, maybe.

She opened the door to her bedroom just in time to see Dad walk by, gripping Miranda by the arm, propelling her toward her bedroom. For a second, she barely recognized her sister. Miranda wore a tight dress that she definitely didn't buy with Dad in tow, and she held a pair of those super-high heels. The five-inch ones that Miranda would never have been able to walk in. Not that she was going to get a chance to try since Ariel was pretty sure their dad would kill her first. Or lock her away until she was twenty-one.

"You can't do this! My friends are waiting for me! It's hard enough to make friends around here without you making it impossible!" Miranda screamed.

Not that Dad listened. He forced Miranda to her room. "What kind of friends are you meeting?" he demanded. "Dressed like that?"

Ariel backed up and closed her door, then ran over to her window that led out to the fire escape. When she pulled it open, cool air struck her face, bringing the sound of the city with it. Ariel clenched her teeth as she stepped out onto the thin metal landing. She hated heights, hated the fire escape, had loved it when her dad had forbidden both her and Miranda from going anywhere near the fire escape. In her nearly thirteen years, Ariel had never completely defied her father. She had left that to Miranda. But the only way she knew how to help was to distract her dad from how mad he was at Miranda. She would make him mad at her.

Clasping her fingers tightly around the railing, ignoring the fear that the metal would disintegrate under her feet, letting her crash into the garden below, making her disappear, Ariel crawled over to her sister's window. By then, her dad stood inside Miranda's room lecturing, Miranda screaming back.

Just then the wind gusted and the fire escape swayed, the metal groaning in protest. Ariel's stomach heaved, and she realized she was acting like an idiot. She leaped up, but her sneaker caught in the metal grating and she fell against her sister's window.

Faster than she would have thought possible, her dad was across the room. He had never been pretty, not like Uncle Anthony. But now the look on his face was terrifying. For one thing, he didn't recognize her at first. The minute he did, he wrenched open the window and hauled her inside.

"Oops," she managed, a smile faltering on her lips. "I guess I'm in trouble now."

Ariel watched the gears in his head churn, emotion flashing across his face. Miranda was staring at her like she was crazy. Which she probably was.

"Go to your room, Ariel," her father said. The words seemed to stick in his throat.

"You know how you always think I should talk?" she said instead. "Well, guess what, I'm ready."

"Go to your room!" he shouted.

He didn't wait for her to leave. He turned around and went down the stairs without another word.

Ariel stood frozen, hoping he wouldn't leave the house, leave them. Instead, he slammed the door of his study.

"Are you crazy?" Miranda hissed.

Ariel forced a smile she didn't feel. "Me? Nah?"

"You did that on purpose."

"Get caught on the fire escape on purpose? Now *you're* crazy."

Miranda looked at her, and suddenly Ariel couldn't stop herself. "Mir?"

"What?"

"Couldn't you be a little bit nicer to Dad?"

Miranda's lips pursed. "Why would I do that? Dad's an ass."

"So—so he doesn't get, like, so mad that he leaves us," Ariel whispered. "He could just hire someone to deal with us, you know, and go back to work all the time."

For a second, Miranda looked shocked. Then the hardness returned. "No. I cannot be one bit nicer to Dad, and frankly, if he hired someone to be here with us, all the better. My friends talk all the time how they just have to pay their nannies or help or whoever twenty bucks every time they want to sneak out." She flopped on her bed, grabbed a pillow, and hugged it tight. "I'm going to pray he hires someone. Anyone's better than him."

Ariel bolted out of the room before Miranda could say another hateful word. She didn't know how to explain that while Miranda might not be a perfect sister, and their family was massively broken, they were all she had left. It was like a punch in the gut to think that Miranda didn't care one bit what happened to what was left of their sorry family.

Ariel waited an hour past the Vesuvius blowup before she tiptoed downstairs. She was starving. Drama did that. If this family stuff didn't get fixed soon she'd probably get as fat as a beach ball. Whatever, she told herself. Again.

She had pretty much repeated that word over and over in the last hour. Wasn't there some sort of three-strikes rule? Crawling out onto the fire escape was her first offense. Two more to go before her dad did something like send her off to boarding school.

After eating a sandwich, she saw a dim light coming from her dad's study, so she peeked inside. At first she didn't understand what he was doing. He was sort of lying in his big leather chair, the one with oversized padded arms. Sound asleep. She couldn't remember a time when she'd seen her dad sleeping. Lying there, he looked almost peaceful.

It was a strange thought, and Ariel felt stupid tears well up. She, the non-crier.

Just like with the fire escape, before she could think better of it, she slid carefully down into the big chair right next to him. They used to sit that way sometimes, back when he would read aloud to her. She was still skinny, so she fit next to him, like a cork in a bottle. He didn't wake up.

"Sorry I climbed the fire escape," she whispered.

He didn't move.

He had one of those clocks that actually ticked, and Ariel's eyelids started to get heavy. She wondered if the Shrink had told her dad about their last session. If he had, her dad hadn't mentioned it.

Just as her eyelids were fluttering closed, she whispered, "What would you do if I told you why I was really in the car with Mom? Why we were going so fast?"

He didn't answer, his breathing still deep.

Ariel didn't remember drifting off, but when she woke the next morning she was tucked into her bed.

Twenty-nine

❖

NOT EVEN A MONTH after Portia and her sisters opened the doors, so to speak, word of mouth about The Glass Kitchen rippled through New York City like a YouTube video going viral. Sure, the food was great, but it didn't hurt that Portia was able to provide everyone who came to her door with just what they needed, and Cordelia made sure they knew it. It also didn't hurt that Olivia was a natural with social media on the Internet. The Cuthcart sisters had become a perfect team.

But what Portia was really thinking about was that it had been two days since she had made Gabriel the plate of eggs and realized she wanted more from him. But as it happened, since that realization he hadn't come down the fire escape once. He hadn't so much as stopped by. It was odd, not to mention disconcerting, since she'd been trying to drum up the nerve to make the Gabriel Meal.

She was on the verge of finding some schoolgirl way to run into him when he walked through her front door.

Her heart squeezed with a mix of disappointment and relief when he didn't rush toward her with a kiss. Not that he was the rush-toward-her sort. But still.

Instead, he had that dangerous look of his, and his greeting consisted of precisely seven words. "You are not meeting with Richard Zaslow."

Portia stiffened. "How do you know I'm meeting with Richard Zaslow?"

"Did you really think I wouldn't hear about it?"

Portia's eyes narrowed.

"Don't get that look," he said, his expression guarded. "He's not for you."

"Not for me? He has billions of dollars, is famous for turning food businesses into huge successes, and he called us. How's that not for me?"

"Let me guess. He called you after he saw the photo in *The New York Observer*."

"So?"

"The three of you looked great, kind of like Charlie's Angels in aprons. Richard likes women. And he's especially good at making things happen for business owners he sleeps with."

Portia gasped. "I don't believe for a second he was sleeping with Bartalow Bing when he turned him into the Fat Chef."

"Bing was an exception."

"I think his ex-wife is the exception." Everybody knew the story of how struggling cookie baker Rachel Turnbell met Richard Zaslow. Pretty soon they were rumored to be sleeping together, then they married, and all the while he poured millions into making her business a success. Not long after she was dubbed the Cookie Queen, Rachel had filed for divorce, but not before her business had started selling about 35 percent of all cookies sold nationwide. "My guess is he learned his lesson about mixing business with pleasure."

She finished setting out the day's fare with a little more energy than was needed. *Bang!* went the brussels sprouts and pancetta. *Slap!* went the flour tortillas next to the fajita meat.

He came up next to her and turned her back to him, his hands surprisingly gentle. "Look at me, Portia."

Reluctantly, she did.

"He's not for you."

"Really?" Portia sliced him a wry expression, stepping away. "Do you have someone better in mind? Are *you* offering up the money?"

She had tossed out the words without thinking, but he looked at her long and hard.

She held up her hand. "Don't bother answering with that 'Restaurants in New York City have an eighty percent failure rate.'"

He still stared at her.

The doorbell buzzed. Gabriel went to the door before Portia could. "Dick," he stated, pulling open the door.

Richard Zaslow looked surprised. "Gabriel, what are you doing here?"

"Actually, I'm here trying to convince Portia that you're not a great investor match for her."

"Gabriel!"

Both men looked at her, and then Gabriel swung back to Richard. Richard gave Gabriel an appraising grin that Portia didn't like one bit. She realized belatedly that these two men were friends.

"She has you by the short hairs, doesn't she?" Richard said.

Gabriel grunted, not so much a threat as a primal acknowledgment between two men who were man enough to admit how things really were.

Richard slapped Gabriel on the back. "Good luck with that," he said, then turned to Portia. "Take him for everything he's worth," he teased, then left.

Portia's mouth fell open. "What was that all about?"

Gabriel looked dangerously pleased, a full-watt smile that made Portia want to laugh despite the fact that she was furious.

"I guess he wasn't all that interested," Gabriel said with an innocent shrug.

Portia's answer involved the kind of profanity that would have made her ex-husband faint. But not Gabriel. He grinned at her, and then hooked his arm around her waist and pulled her to him, kissing her in that way that made her knees weak.

❖

That night he came to her with no words, just strode up behind her as she sat brushing her hair at her great-aunt's vanity. He took the brush and began slowly pulling the bristles through her thick hair. It had grown out and bore no resemblance to a blown-out pageboy perfectly contained by a velvet headband.

Their eyes held in the mirror.

"I'm giving you the money," he said softly.

She blinked, then stared back at him.

"I'll take care of you. You don't need to worry about money anymore."

Portia jerked around to face him. "What are you talking about?"

"You want to open a Glass Kitchen. I'll provide the money." To prove his point, he pulled a check from his pocket.

She gasped at the amount, followed by a slow burn starting under her breastbone.

"You can stop wearing your aunt's castoffs—"

She cut him off. "Are you giving me this money because you believe in The Glass Kitchen?"

He stared at her. "Does it matter why I'm giving it to you?"

"Of course it does! I don't want you giving me money just because you're sleeping with me!"

Gabriel's expression darkened. "This has nothing to do with us sleeping together. You need money. I have money. And before you rip up that check, if I were you, I'd ask your sisters what they think of the offer. I'm not so sure they'd be as quick to turn my money away."

She ground her teeth. She knew he was right, but still. He believed she would fail. Could she take money from a man who didn't believe in her? Part of her cheered with a resounding *yes*. But another part of her, this newer part that was trying hard to prove she could make it on her own merit, cringed.

Finding an investor who genuinely believed in The Glass Kitchen held more meaning to her than simply being provided with the money. It was symbolic. Gaining an impartial investor would prove that someone truly believed in what she was doing. Finding an impartial investor struck her as a powerful step toward proving that she wasn't dependent on a man in her life. Her husband had supported her, given her a home, provided her with a life. But the minute he got tired of her and wanted to move on, all of that had been swept from underneath her like feet giving way under a wave.

She felt her chin set.

His eyes narrowed, but there was a glint of laughter in them, too. "Stubborn females will be the death of me."

⁙

During the next week, despite Gabriel's frustration at her refusal to deposit his check, Portia cooked and baked for potential investors. Every night when she was alone, she pulled the check out of The Glass Kitchen cookbook, where she had hidden it. With each day that passed, her bank balance ticked lower, and she knew she couldn't afford not to take his money. But every night she ended up tucking the check back into the book.

Cordelia set the table again and again with the pitted silverware and stoneware dishes. Olivia arranged everything until the setting was a worthy tableaux for an elegant country-style magazine. Portia fed them food that made them melt, made them happy. And then it began to happen. The food began to work. By the end of the week they had offers from four different investor groups, as if the food combined with Gabriel's check in the cookbook had worked like a magician conjuring up a rabbit in a hat.

Cordelia, Olivia, and Portia sat around the table on Friday evening going over each offer, as stunned as they were thrilled.

"Can you believe it?" Olivia laughed.

"I'm amazed," Portia said.

"I am not," Cordelia said, shaking her head. "I've said it all along. In this age of cooking madness, who wouldn't want to invest in three sisters from Texas cooking food to die for?"

Portia's mind froze, memories of her grandmother springing to her mind. The storm. The meal of pulled pork and the lightning.

Cordelia reached across the table. "Sorry, sweetie. I wasn't thinking."

Olivia jumped up from her seat. "Let's celebrate!"

After no more than one circle around the living room to Toby Keith, Ariel must have heard and poked her head in the door, dancing her way inside without waiting for an invitation.

Two songs in, Olivia headed back to the kitchen. "This calls for margaritas!" She glanced at Ariel. "And a virgin margarita for the kid."

Cordelia went in search of chips. Portia made a batch of fresh guacamole. Ariel threw herself onto a stool, grinning madly.

"You guys are the weirdest adults ever. You know that, right?" She took a sip of the sweet drink. "So what are you celebrating?"

"Great investor meetings, and"—Olivia dragged out the word—"a newspaper interview with *The New York Post* coming up!"

"That's good, huh?"

"It's fabulous," Cordelia confirmed.

"Dad'll be happy, too."

"No need to tell your dad," Portia said instantly.

"But he'll want to know!"

"Of course, he will. But could I surprise him?" Portia wanted to tell him herself. Return his check. She felt certain that he would grumble at her, but that deep down he would be proud of her.

She also hoped that it would be the beginning of a shift between them. If she felt she was making her life work, she could breathe again, she could believe things were supposed to work out. She could make Gabriel's Meal without fear.

Ariel blinked, but then she nodded. "Okay, you tell him." She glanced at the clock. "I've got to go."

Portia, Cordelia, and Olivia lifted their glasses as she left. "To The Glass Kitchen!"

"To three sexy sisters in New York City!" Olivia cheered.

Cordelia made a face. "You'll have to carry that flag by yourself. I'm too old, and Portia hasn't had sex in months."

Portia choked on her margarita.

Cordelia and Olivia stopped and studied her. "Portia?" they said in unison.

"What?" She tried to look nonchalant. Innocent.

"Hell," Olivia snapped. "Who are you sleeping with?"

"No one!"

"Liar! You're blushing!"

"Stop!"

"We are not stopping," Cordelia persisted. "Who in the world are you having sex with?" She blinked in confusion. "One of the investors?"

"Of course not!" Portia exclaimed.

Olivia laughed as she sat back. "Then who?"

"That's private."

Olivia raised a brow, glanced at Cordelia, then back. "How very un-Portia like. Our little sister has a secret lover."

But when Portia looked closer, she was sure Olivia knew just who that secret lover really was.

Fifth Course

❖

The Entrée

Fried Chicken with
Sweet Jalapeño Mustard

Thirty

❖

Portia's life was falling into place. The money was coming in for
The Glass Kitchen. The sisters were working together in a way that
gave her hope that it was a good idea. And she wanted to believe there
could be more between her and Gabriel Kane.

Which meant she couldn't put off making Gabriel's Meal any longer.

She remembered her grandmother's meal. She remembered what
turned out to be Cordelia's meal, which she'd had to make when she woke
up with the knowing after moving to Manhattan. Both had foretold bad
news.

But there had been good meals, too, she reminded herself. Meals that
had saved her sisters. Meals that had helped people since she had been
cooking these last several weeks. Though, really, each of those instances
had been the result of single items. A pie. A pot of French stew. A soup.
A bag of spicy chocolates.

A tremor of nerves raced along her skin. Entire meals coming to mind
had been few and far between.

She wrote out the menu she had seen in her head. Fried chicken, sweet jalapeño mustard, mashed potatoes, slaw, biscuits, and pie—strawberry pie with fresh whipped cream piled high. Her hands shook as she started to prepare. Once she opened the floodgates to the meal, a relentless, nearly strangling need filled her.

What scared her most was the pie. It was her grandmother's decadent concoction—a definite sign. But, again, of what?

Next, Portia started a list—not of ingredients, but of people whom she felt certain she needed to invite. Powering up her computer, she composed a short e-mail.

> Dear Friends and Family,
>   I'm preparing a meal tonight at 7:30. No need to bring anything. I hope you all can join me. Love, Portia

Just that.

She sent the e-mail to Cordelia, Olivia, Gabriel, Miranda, and Ariel. However reluctant she was, she also knew she had to send it to Gabriel's mother and brother.

The last two guests made her the most nervous. Why would she need to invite them? Was this meal a way to start building a connection between Gabriel's family and hers? Or proof that there was too much distance between their two worlds to cross?

As she always did, Portia went to Fairway to pick up the ingredients she didn't have. The chicken, the cabbage, the potatoes. Milk and butter.

The strawberry pie again gave her pause; strawberries weren't in season. Was she setting out to fail before she ever got started? But then she remembered she was in New York City, a place where anything could be found at any time. Strawberries were in season somewhere, and they made their way without fail to the city that had everything.

As soon as Portia returned home, she got to work. She didn't check the answering machine. She didn't check e-mail for responses. If she had learned anything about the knowing, it was that whatever was to come was beyond her control. Guests would come or not. Once the invitation was issued, nothing she could say would make a difference.

Before she started cooking, she raced out and got flowers, though her instinct to buy freesia, delphinium, and hydrangea didn't offer any insight to what was coming.

She took great care in setting the table, pulling two smaller tables together in the living room. She added an antique linen tablecloth that had belonged to her aunt, candles, and the flowers in the center. By the time she had shopped and done the prep work, she had only three hours before the guests were due to arrive. The apartment was ready.

Now for the food.

The sense of peace came first. A smile broke out on her face, and she even laughed. She felt better and better by the minute.

First, the chicken, filling a brown paper bag with flour and seasoning. Then the potatoes, peeling and cutting, putting them on to boil. The apartment grew hot, and she wiped her hands on her apron, then raced into the living room to open the back French doors.

She mixed up the biscuit dough and set it aside in one of Evie's old mixing bowls. The pie came next. She cut up brilliant red strawberries and sugared them, a feather-light crust, whipped the cream, and put it in the refrigerator. She would have to fry the chicken after she bathed, but that couldn't be helped if she wanted the crispy outside to be perfect.

Then she took a bath, soaking in lavender, and dressed with care. A crisp white cotton blouse and floral skirt, with low heels. At the last minute, she found a pair of old pearls that had been Evie's. "This is the right thing to do," she told her reflection.

By the time she returned to the kitchen, she had only thirty minutes left. She mashed the potatoes, mixing in more butter than was good for a person.

Her front door opened, startling her. How had the time gone so fast?

"What's going on?" Olivia called out.

Her sister wore workout clothes, hair pulled back in a messy ponytail.

She took one look at Portia and stopped in her tracks. "Really, what's going on? Nice clothes. Your hair. And you're wearing makeup." She narrowed her eyes. "Your e-mail only said dinner. Who all is coming?"

The bell rang, and Cordelia walked in, dressed in a casual way that wasn't Cordelia at all.

"Why didn't you answer my e-mail?" Cordelia said. Then, like Olivia, she took in Portia's attire. "What's going on?"

Cordelia glanced back into the living room and saw the table settings. The two older sisters exchanged a wary glance.

"You had to make a meal," Olivia said, her voice hard.

"I hate this!" Cordelia said.

Olivia scoffed. "How is it possible that you, who pushed Portia back into the knowing, are acting like this is a surprise? You know the weird meals you get with the knowing. It's not her fault."

"Look at me!" Cordelia exclaimed, gesturing to her clothes. "Based on that table, this is a dinner for more than just the three of us. I look like a bag lady." She glared at Portia. "Why didn't you warn me?"

"You should have known," Olivia said. "The e-mail said 'Dear Friends and Family.' When was the last time Portia had us over for dinner with that kind of an invitation? *I* should have known."

Portia's smile flatlined, her heart leaping into her throat.

The bell rang again and Ariel burst in. "Miranda can't come. She got Dad to let her stay with a friend."

More bad news. Miranda was supposed to be there.

Ariel didn't look any happier than Portia felt. But before Portia could ask about Miranda, the smell of burning potatoes hit her.

"Oh, no!"

She was barely aware that Helen Kane and Anthony were at the door before she dashed into the kitchen. She couldn't think of anything right then, other than saving the meal.

Thirty-one

⬩⬩⬩

A RIEL SLIPPED OUT of Portia's living room, escaping the suddenly crowded apartment, the smell of weird, burned potatoes stinging her nose. She snuck out the back door, then up three brick steps leading to the town house's garden. She curled up in an oversized sweater she'd found up on the storage floor, one that must have been her dad's. She tucked herself out of sight, huddling against the growing cold, her thick wool, multicolored socks with toes shoved into a wild pair of boots that she had been certain Portia would love. Except Portia had been too worried about her cooking to notice.

She tucked her chin against her knees. She was starting to feel as if she was really losing it. Sure, she had beaten back the Shrink's questions and not spilled her guts. But it didn't mean she'd stopped *thinking*. In fact, she couldn't stop thinking, and all her thoughts were weird. Like why was her sister being so awful.

"Miranda," she said to the empty garden, "why can't you just give Dad a break?"

Like that would work. Miranda would just slam the bedroom door in her face.

Plus, she didn't even feel like talking to Miranda, because she felt a little guilty about reading her journal. Which she was now mostly doing to learn anything she could about her family. The problem with that was that every time she dug Miranda's diary out from underneath the mattress, she found out that her sister was getting deeper and deeper into trouble. Miranda was determined to be friends with the popular kids, and that meant doing whatever the creep Dustin wanted her to do. But it wasn't as if Ariel could *do* anything with that information. She wasn't a snitch. She wasn't a spy.

But, seriously, how was it possible Miranda could be so stupid?

Voices coming from inside Portia's apartment caught her attention.

"Mother, just tell Gabriel to give me the money!"

"What, so you can leave?"

Ariel peeked back in through the door and saw her uncle and grandmother standing not two feet inside the living room. No one else was in sight. The sisters had have been in the kitchen. Ugh. The last person Ariel wanted to talk to was her uncle, but still, her grandmother's question made her curious. Uncle Anthony wanted to leave? Already?

"You've been gone for over a year, Anthony. Why can't you stay and get a job here in the city?"

"I don't need my mother or brother to take care of me, or make decisions for me. I'm a grown man!"

"Then act like one!"

Ariel couldn't see Uncle Anthony's face because his back was to her, but he must have been really mad, because suddenly Nana was hanging on his arm in a massively pathetic way.

"I'm sorry, Anthony. I didn't mean it. I just wish you wouldn't stay away so long."

Nana made a sad weepy sound that almost—almost—made Ariel feel sorry for her, except the woman was so completely awful to Dad and not to Anthony. It wasn't fair.

"I feel that the only reason you come back is to get money from Gabriel."

"He owes me!"

Nana sighed. "Fine. Then sign his papers and he'll pay you."

"A pittance. No thanks. I'm not leaving until he pays up, big-time. And not until he hands this apartment over to me. That was the deal. The money and the apartment. It was supposed to be mine! I saw the papers, for God's sake. He's already bought the damned place. All he has to do is sign it over to me!"

"Keep your voice down! You promised to stay quiet until he got it worked out with Portia."

Ariel frowned. The apartment was supposed to be Anthony's?

"What are you talking about?"

But it wasn't Nana or Uncle Anthony who spoke this time. Ariel practically fell into the apartment as she swung her head toward the kitchen. Portia stood there, frozen, holding a smoking pan of burned chicken with two oven mitts, her brow furrowed as she looked back and forth between Nana and Anthony.

"What are you talking about?" Portia repeated. "The apartment is mine, not Gabriel's, and certainly not yours, Anthony."

Only then did Ariel notice that Portia wasn't the only person who had shown up unexpectedly in the living room. Her dad stood just inside the front door, looking totally like he was going to kill someone.

Thirty-two

✦

THE MEAL was ruined.

The chicken had burned; the mashed potatoes were a sea of soupy lumps; the biscuits were charred rocks of hardened dough.

Portia held the pan of burned chicken and tried to understand what Anthony was saying. She took in the fury on Gabriel's face and the guilty delight on his brother's as they both looked at her.

"That's right, Portia," Anthony said, swiveling his head to smile at his older brother. "When Gabriel bought the apartment, he promised it to me."

"Damn it, Anthony," Gabriel bit out.

Portia blinked as she tried to make sense of it. She looked at Gabriel. "But the apartment isn't yours. I didn't go through with the sale."

Gabriel dragged a hand through his hair, and suddenly the pieces came together like a Rubik's Cube settling into place.

Her mouth fell open. "That's impossible! I never signed the documents."

He stared at her, and she could see the way he willed things to be different. "The papers were signed, Portia. And notarized."

Her knees went weak, recognizing the truth. Suddenly, a lot of things made sense. Gabriel demanding to know what she was doing in the apartment. All the times he had started to say something, only to cut himself off.

Robert must have gone through with the sale by forging her signature.

Portia felt sick, angry, and betrayed. What's more, with each piece of the puzzle that fell into place, this meal made more and more sense.

Burned chicken for betrayal by Robert, who had not only sold the only thing she owned, but had also kept the money.

Soupy potatoes for a relationship with Gabriel that had no true bond.

Coleslaw she had mixed with dressing that went bad for a Glass Kitchen in New York, a sour idea from the start.

Rock-hard rolls for a stubborn woman who had repeatedly refused to make a meal that would have led her much earlier to a greater truth—the reality that when she had seen Gabriel, and the shimmering images of fried chicken and sweet jalapeño mustard had come to her, it had foretold disaster between her and Gabriel Kane.

"Welcome to my world, babe," Anthony said with a laugh. "My brother does what he wants, when he wants, regardless of how many people he hurts in the process."

"Fuck," Gabriel ground out.

"Is that why you let her stay here, big brother? So you could fuck her?"

Portia's head jerked up just in time to see Gabriel fly across the room. Anthony's eyes went wide.

"Gabriel, no!" their mother shouted.

Gabriel ignored her, jerking Anthony up and throwing him against the wall. "Damn you!" he roared.

Anthony lunged back at Gabriel, screaming. But he was no match for the bigger man. Gabriel had him pinned to the wall in a moment. "You leave Portia out of this."

"What in the world is going on here?"

Portia jerked around. A man she had never seen before stood at the open front door.

The newcomer's face was wrinkled with distaste. "I'm a New York City inspector conducting an unannounced property visit. Our office was notified that someone is illegally running a retail establishment out of a ground-floor residential building." He glanced around. "Based on the sign in the window and the posted hours, I'd say the report is correct." His mouth twisted. "A restaurant and, what, a fight club?"

The inspector walked straight in and began snapping photos—of The Glass Kitchen sign, the daily menu. He also snapped the shocked faces and Anthony's bloody nose. He had an unobstructed view straight into the kitchen, the pots and pans lined up on the counter like ship-wrecks on a worn linoleum sea.

"I can explain," Portia said hurriedly, stumbling over to the table and dropping the pan of chicken down.

"Don't bother. Save your explanations for zoning court."

Thirty-three

❖

ARIEL SAT ON the edge of her bed, shoes hooked over the side bed-rail, her feet jiggling as she tried her hardest to calm down. After the disaster downstairs, she had flown to her room to get away. She hadn't left since.

Things were getting worse. Anthony and Dad fighting. Some inspector guy showing up. Portia getting in trouble.

But the worst was seeing the look on Portia's face when she learned that she didn't own her apartment. Talk about surprise. Ariel had been as surprised as Portia. How come none of them had known? And why hadn't her dad said something sooner?

Just then there was a strange noise outside her bedroom door. Miranda giggled, tiptoeing down the hallway toward her own bedroom, even though she was supposed to be spending the night with a friend. Ariel started to confront her, but then she heard someone else laugh, the sound deeper, and she knew it was a boy.

"Shhh!" Miranda whispered, with another giggle.

"I'm being quiet. You're the one making all the noise."

Dustin. Ariel realized that Miranda was giving in to the guy. She was going to have sex, right there in their house, their dad somewhere downstairs, probably in his study.

Her legs started jiggling again as she heard Miranda's door click shut, then louder, muffled giggling. She fell back on the mattress and planted the pillow over her head.

Minutes ticked by. A muffled quiet. Slowly, Ariel started to breathe again and she pulled the pillow away. She hated to think what the silence meant.

But then something worse happened.

"Miranda?"

Ariel gasped, and leaped off the bed and raced to her door, flinging it open. But it was too late.

Her dad stood in front of her sister's closed door. "Miranda, open this door right now."

"*Go away!*"

Dad grabbed the door handle, but it was locked. He pounded on the hard wood. "Open this door," he demanded, banging on the door.

"*No! I hate you! You ruin everything!*"

Dad didn't wait another second. He was a big guy, strong. So it shouldn't have been a surprise when he rammed his shoulder into the door and it crashed open.

It looked like the movies, the sound awful, like a huge, splintering crack that went straight to Ariel's gut. She could hardly believe what she was watching. What had happened to her normal family?

"What in the hell is going on here?"

"Whoa, dude!"

"Don't you *fucking* 'dude' me, you degenerate. Get the hell away from my daughter."

"Dad! This is my room! You can't just barge in here!"

"I am your father. You will do what I say!"

Ariel figured her dad must be looking way scary, because the next thing she knew, Dustin was dashing down the hall, pulling on his shirt, his belt unbuckled. She felt even sicker now.

"I hate you!" Miranda shouted the words so loud that Ariel could practically hear her spit.

"So you said!" Dad bellowed back.

Then he pulled a deep breath. "Damn it, Miranda. What do you think you're doing? You're barely sixteen years old."

"Dustin loves me! And I love him!"

"*Dustin* is a hormonal asshole who just wants to get laid!"

Ariel squeezed her eyes shut. Who was the man shouting like that? How could that guy be her dad?

"Oh, really?" Miranda spat. "You know that from experience?"

"I am trying," their father stated, his voice cold and angry. "I have put up with your antics. I have put up with your sarcasm. I have put up with you talking back. But I've had it."

"Have you?" Miranda sneered. "Well, guess what? I've had it, too! If Mom were here, she'd want me to have a boyfriend."

"Your mother isn't here! And you sneaking a boy into this house to . . . to . . . do—"

"Do what, Dad?" Miranda scoffed. "Fuck? Like you and Portia?"

Silence. A great big painful silence.

Dad and Portia? Ariel felt light-headed. She remembered what Uncle Anthony had said. She didn't know why, but she thought she was going to throw up.

"Like I didn't know," Miranda spat.

It seemed like forever before her dad said, "You are grounded."

"Great, there's an original response, *Dad*. But I'd think you'd have a bigger bag of tricks than that. You think grounding me will keep me away from Dustin? I love him! You wouldn't understand love. I know more than you think about you and love!"

Ariel jumped back as their dad slammed out of the room, then hammered his way downstairs.

The only thing left in the hall was part of the door panel and the shiny brass doorknob that had rolled out of Miranda's room like Humpty Dumpty after the fall.

Thirty-four

❖

PORTIA WAS VAGUELY AWARE that morning had finally come. She had spent the whole night cleaning up the disarray of pots and pans. The city inspector was long gone. But he'd left her with a general citation. Plus, he reeled off the list of things he could and would cite her for if she didn't cease and desist immediately—everything from improper sanitation to a ten-thousand-dollar fine for illegal posting of a sign. After her head stopped reeling, with tears streaming down her face, she had ripped The Glass Kitchen sign out of the window.

No matter how she looked at it, the testing version of The Glass Kitchen was over.

Portia dropped into one of the ancient living room chairs and thought of the last meal she had made for her grandmother, a meal for just one person. When Gram had seen it, she'd been shocked. But after long minutes she had pulled a deep breath.

"It's your time now, Portia," *Gram had said*. "It's your legacy."

"Gram, I just cook! You're the one people come to see. You give them advice. You tell them the kinds of food that will restore them. You are *The Glass Kitchen*."

Gram had looked at her for an eternity, seeming to consider. Then finally: "My sweet Portia. I lost the knowing years ago. I woke up one morning and it was gone. I didn't want to believe it, and I kept cooking, trying to pretend it wasn't true. But the Kitchen began to fail. Nothing I cooked was right. When I still had the knowing, no one gave a thought as to why they were drawn here, because they always left sated, with answers, with calm.

"Even after the food started to fail, they continued to come since by then I was famous. But once they started leaving unsatisfied, they had to find a way to explain why they were drawn to me, to my food, in the first place. Suddenly answers mattered. As people do, they found excuses. That's when people started calling me crazy.

"Ever since the day your knowing found Olivia, the day your mother brought you to me, I told myself I needed to teach you the ways. But," she hesitated, "I couldn't do it. I told myself that it was because I wanted you to have a normal life. Truth to tell, I didn't want to share the spotlight. That's why I didn't help you develop the knowing. Only when I realized that I had lost mine did I accept that I needed you to save The Glass Kitchen. To save me. If you knew what to cook and bake, I'd know what the people needed to be told to find their calm. So I brought you into the kitchen in earnest then, but to cook, only to cook. Still not teaching you. But you developed the knowing anyway, more powerfully even than me.

"But none of that matters now. It's your time to do it all, Portia. I know you're tired of not being set free to explore. And you've shown me by making this meal. Making it for one."

"Gram, I don't want to do this without you! That's not why I made the meal for one."

Then why had she made the meal for one? Why had she known what to prepare, how to set the table? Deep down, she had wanted to fly.

"*Hush, child,*" Gram had said.

Then she had walked out into that Texas storm, shocking Portia.

She had married Robert and suppressed the knowing, as if that could keep her guilt at bay.

But marriage to Robert had failed. If she was truthful, deep down she had wanted more. She had wanted a Glass Kitchen. She had wanted passion. She had wanted to fly, just as Gram had said.

Portia's head fell back, and a word escaped her mouth that was, frankly, blasphemous. After her failed marriage, she had thought she had found passion and a Glass Kitchen in New York. But that had all been a lie as well.

She went to the closet and pulled out the two suitcases she had put away, throwing the few things she had brought with her from Texas back inside. This wasn't her home. She should have understood that the moment Gabriel Kane had first seen her in the apartment and demanded to know why she was there.

But the most humiliating thing of all? He must not have told her because he had wanted her. She had seen the way he looked at her from the very first time. The heat. The desire. And he was nothing if not a man who got what he wanted.

She had slept her way into free rent.

She bit her lip savagely for a moment before she had the tears under control. She refused, absolutely refused, to cry. If she started, she might never stop—not with the gut-wrenching pain of Robert's betrayal mixed together with that of Gabriel, whom she had thought was different.

Her cell phone rang, and Cordelia's number popped up. Portia had to figure out what to do next, but she couldn't do that at either sister's apartment.

Thoughts of chocolate drifted through her head. She tasted it, smelled it. She pressed ignore on the phone as it occurred to her where she might go.

❖

Twenty-four hours later, her cell phone was still ringing every time she turned around. Cordelia, Olivia. Gabriel. Everyone wanted to know where she had gone.

This time, it was Cordelia, her fifth call in an hour. Portia turned back to the TV.

"How can you watch that garbage?"

She ignored the question, though she shot her hosts a half smile. "You know," she said, "Texas hair gets a bad rap for being big. But it has nothing on New Jersey hair." Portia took a particularly unladylike bite of a Little Debbie cake, her words muffled by the premade pastry. "Not a thing."

"I guess they didn't teach you manners in Texas when they were teaching you how to do hair?"

Portia swallowed and glanced over. "Seriously, Stan, have you tasted these things? They're amazing."

Stanley rolled his eyes, shuffled over, and sat in the chair next to her. "How long do you plan on staying here?"

"You said I could stay as long as I liked."

"No, Marcus said you could stay as long as you like. The only reason I didn't slam the door in your face when you showed up like a half-drowned cat in a storm was because I felt indebted after those chocolate nuts you gave me." He sniffed. "Lucky for you, you showed up when I was experiencing a moment of weakness."

Portia shot him a dark grin. "You better work on your gruff thing. A person only has to know you for more than a minute to realize you're a softie."

Marcus strode into the room. "He's a mean old man, don't let him fool you." But he leaned down and kissed Stanley on the top of his head.

A twist of yearning hit Portia's gut at the sight of two people committed to each other for so many years. That was what she had wanted out of life: a partner who knew all her traits, good and bad, and loved her anyway.

She unwrapped another cake in a crackle of clear plastic, then took a giant bite.

Stanley scoffed. "Where's the woman who made all those chocolate nuts and figs? The one who cooked and baked, the one who went on and on with all her talk about the joy to be found in food."

Portia raised the half-eaten prefabricated cake in the air. "Don't know her, never met her. But if I did, I'd tell her to stuff a Little Debbie cake in her obnoxiously cheerful face. And, really, you can't be tired of me yet."

"I'm hiding the Hostess Sno Balls," Stanley grumbled.

Marcus laughed.

After Stanley and Marcus went back to the kitchen, Portia slouched lower in her seat. Stanley was right. She had hardly moved from her spot in front of the television. For all her pull-herself-up-by-the-bootstraps pep talk about fixing her life, she didn't have the first clue how to do it. So she hadn't. For the first time ever, Portia was just sitting around and feeling sorry for herself.

Even in Texas, when everything had gone to hell in a handbasket, she had been proactive. Sure, she had fled. But she had actively fled.

Right now, all she wanted to do was flip through cable stations until she found yet another show filled with people who probably couldn't spell *kitchen* much less know what to do in one.

And she refused to feel one bit guilty about it.

Thirty-five

✦

PORTIA WAS GONE. Vanished.

For three whole days, Ariel listened and watched as her dad tramped up and down the stairs to Portia's apartment. Every time he returned back upstairs he still didn't have any idea where she was. For all three of those days, Ariel tucked in her shirt, folded her ankle socks neatly around her ankles, brushed her hair, and even wore a headband she thought her dad would like. Like that would help.

He only looked at her oddly, and didn't say a word. He also didn't say a word about their missing neighbor.

She even tried to get him to talk about it, doing her best Shrink Speak, but finally he snapped, "That's enough, Ariel. She's gone."

Anyone who didn't know him would have sworn he couldn't have cared less. But Ariel knew better. She knew he was hurting. Her dad dealt with stuff just like she did, swallowing it back, not letting on. It was one of the ways that she and her dad were exactly alike.

Plus, every night he went down the fire escape like a lovesick burglar.

Of course he didn't stay down there long, because really, what was there to find?

The problem was that unless her dad went out and found her, Portia wasn't coming back. And there was no sign that he was planning to do that.

It was getting her worried. What if he didn't get the Portia Problem fixed? She'd have to do it for him.

But she had promised to be a good daughter and let him fix things. So she continued to tuck in her shirt and worked hard to smile and be polite. Being a perfect daughter was proving even more difficult than her genealogy report.

But on the fourth day, she'd had it. She woke up knowing that her dad wasn't going to get the job done. Here she was being, like, so perfect, and what good was that doing?

She started thinking, taking notes in her journal, figured things out. With a start she realized that she was doing perfect wrong! She needed to do the kind of perfect Mother Teresa did, and based on every photo she had seen, Mother Teresa didn't worry about tucking in her blouse. She was out there doing, helping, mucking around doing the dirty work. If it had been up to Mother Teresa, she would be out helping Dad right along with the lepers! She wouldn't sit on the sidelines!

As quietly she could, Ariel sneaked downstairs to Portia's apartment, using the key Portia kept hidden under the mat, regardless of the fact that Dad always did the whole growling thing whenever something came up about it. Once inside, she walked from room to room, looking for a clue.

"Where are you, Portia?" she said aloud, feeling like an idiot, especially since the walls didn't talk back. "Where did you go?"

Finally she ended up in the kitchen. She was about to leave when she saw a slip of paper on the floor. She read it a couple of times before dashing upstairs, bursting into her dad's study, and handing over the sheet of paper.

He gave it a quick look, then eyed her. "What's this?"

"A recipe!"

"I know that, Ariel. But why are you showing me?"

"Dad," she said as nicely as she could, since she was still sort of trying to be the perfect daughter, even if it was the Mother Teresa version, "it's a *recipe*. For chocolate-covered peanuts and figs."

Her dad sat back in the leather chair and stared at the piece of paper. Ariel saw the resistance on his face. But she wasn't completely sure what he was resisting.

"Dad," Ariel repeated. "Like Portia always said, some things are true whether we believe them or not."

She watched as he looked back at her, his eyes narrowing.

"She left us, Ariel. Even if I were inclined to look for her, I don't know where to find her, and a fig recipe isn't going to tell me."

Ariel's mouth gaped. Finally, she gave in and rolled her eyes. "Seriously? You can't figure it out based on the chocolate chili recipe? The one Portia made. The one she told you about because all the extra bags disappeared."

The chocolates that had drawn her in like a pathetic puppy to her sister's soiree. Not that her dad knew that part of it.

"You can't figure it out based on that?" She enunciated each syllable, unable to hold back the sarcasm any longer.

Her dad's eyes narrowed even more, but then he drew a breath and his face kind of softened. "I'm glad to see my old Ariel is back."

She peered at him across the massive desk. "What do you mean, the 'old Ariel'?"

"The one who doesn't measure her words." Then he stood. "What you're telling me is that Portia's been right next door all this time."

"There's hope for you yet," she cheered, racing around the desk and throwing her arms around him.

Thirty-six

❖

PORTIA JERKED IN SURPRISE when she heard Stanley and Marcus's buzzer.

"Well, well, well," Stanley said, glimpsing out the window. "Look who's here?"

"Who?"

"Our neighbor."

"Ariel? Miranda?"

"Nope. Their father."

"I'm not here!"

Marcus tsked. "You're here. You're sitting right there."

"No way! He lied to me! He . . . he . . ." She cut herself off. There was nothing to explain. "I am not here."

Finally, Marcus conceded, and told Gabriel she wasn't available.

"That's not the same as I'm not here!"

"True, but it also isn't a lie."

He had her there.

Portia stayed in front of the TV. In fact, she sat there for the whole next day, too. A *Top Model* marathon kept her glued to the screen. Stanley threw up his hands and grumbled. Marcus *tsked*, but was utterly kind. Finally, after a total of five days, Marcus said, "Portia, sweetie, don't you want to go outside? Get some fresh air?"

Portia sat in front of the television, wearing a pair of old Adidas sweat pants Marcus had donated to the cause, and a misshapen *Chorus Line* T-shirt he had given her outright when she had run through the few clothes she had of her own. But she couldn't leave. She couldn't talk to Gabriel. What would she say? *How could you not have told me that you owned the apartment? How did you make love to me over and over again, all the while you knew that you owned the only thing I thought I could call my own?* How could she ever trust him?

Or even, to herself: *What in the world am I going to do with my life?*

"How about we take a walk in the park?" Marcus suggested. "Or, say, you change up your clothes?"

"I changed. I wore a *Cats* T-shirt yesterday. And before that, I wore the one I found in the bag headed for the thrift store: *Ain't Misbehavin'*."

"Of course. How could I forget the black Magic Marker you used to cross out *Ain't*?"

She glanced over, eyeballing him to see if sweet Marcus was being sarcastic. "You're sounding an awful lot like Ariel."

As soon as the words were out of her mouth, Portia felt even worse. She missed Gabriel more than she knew how to say. But she also missed Ariel. Even Miranda, a bit. Still, she couldn't bear thinking about Gabriel making love to her while knowing he owned her apartment and not telling her.

She groaned, then slid down even farther front of the TV. Obviously, she should feel guilty about camping out on Marcus and Stanley's over-stuffed chair, not facing her problems head-on—especially after that whole *don't be a chicken* speech she had given Cordelia. She was starting to feel guilty. But just a little.

"I'm fine," she said.

She heard Stanley shuffle in; the two men whispered for several moments. Portia heard phrases like: *Not natural for a woman to let herself go, Too much TV isn't good for her psyche,* and, *Ain't Misbehavin, really was one of the most overrated musicals of the 70s.*

"I can hear you two."

"We just think you're a bit, well, discombobulated." This from Marcus.

"Pshaw. She's a wreck. And she looks like one, too." Stanley.

Portia jerked up. "Fine. I'll go take a bath, wash my hair."

"Sweetie," Marcus said, his grimace apologetic. "We weren't talking about your hair, which, by the bye, is hideous. But we aren't ones to judge."

Portia scowled.

"We're referring to your mental state. *You* are a wreck. We discussed it after breakfast and decided we had no choice but to take matters into our own hands."

Portia narrowed her eyes. "What did you do?"

The door buzzer sounded.

"Seriously, what have you done?"

"It's for your own good," Marcus said.

Stanley scoffed as he shuffled to the door. Next thing she knew, they had guests.

Portia jumped to her feet. "Traitor!" Portia glared at Marcus and Stanley. "You know I'm not in the mood for family!"

Marcus grimaced. Stanley shuffled back to his seat by the window, not one bit apologetic.

"You are the traitor!" Cordelia shouted. "Not taking our calls. Going MIA without a single word to let us know you were okay and not dead in a ditch."

"I don't do worry!" Olivia stated.

"Good God, look at you," Cordelia went on. "You *do* look like you've been in a ditch."

Stanley snorted in agreement.

"You need to stop with this nonsense." Cordelia walked over to Portia, took her hand, and pulled her toward the staircase. "It's time you rejoin the living." She glanced over at Marcus. "I take it there's a bathroom upstairs with a sink, running water?"

"Up the stairs, second door on the right," Marcus supplied. "Her meager stash of belongings is in the bedroom one door beyond that."

Portia didn't know if she wanted to scream or cry as Cordelia and Olivia herded her up the stairs.

"I don't need the two of you marching in here thinking you can boss me around!"

"We aren't bossing you around," Olivia said. "We're taking charge while you're mentally incapacitated."

"I'm tired of this!" Portia snapped. "I'm tired of both of you always in my business. I'm tired of trying to live the kind of life I want, only to get upended every time I turn around!" Lord, it felt good to let it out. "And I'm tried of always having to save—"

She cut herself off. It only felt good for so long. She was angry at her sisters. But, really, she knew she was angry at the world. She had never been one to intentionally hurt anyone.

"Tired of having to save us," Cordelia supplied for her.

"Of course that's what she thinks," Olivia said to Cordelia. "Poor little Portia is sure she wouldn't be in this mess if the two of us hadn't browbeaten her into this whole Glass Kitchen fiasco. And if she hadn't been busy trying to get the café started, then she would've been able to find a real job and not have to take one cooking for Gabriel, which is the only reason she got involved with him and HAD SEX!"

"Olivia!" Portia snapped.

"Of course she knew," Cordelia said. "She's Olivia. And of course she told me."

"It sucks being you," Olivia added with more than a little sarcasm.

Portia ground her teeth as her sisters pushed and prodded her down the hallway of Stanley and Marcus's old town house. "You don't know the first thing about what it's like to be me."

Olivia held up her hand, seesawing her thumb and forefinger, much as she used to do when they were children. "The world's smallest violin is playing for you, baby sister."

Cordelia rolled her eyes. "The fact is, Portia Desdemona, you have a gift or talent or maybe even a curse, which is really nothing more than a wildly in-tune intuition that freaks you out. For that matter, it freaks me out. But so what?"

Olivia nodded like a member of the choir. "So what!" she echoed.

Portia's frustration bubbled up. "You don't understand!"

"Stop feeling sorry for yourself!" Cordelia barked. "Did it ever occur to you that I would love to have a gift? Any gift? That I'd give my eyeteeth to feel special, to feel like I'm someone other than a woman who just tries to get by in a regular life in a regular world that falls apart for no good reason?"

Olivia and Portia stopped and gaped at Cordelia.

"Who knew?" Olivia said. "At least about feeling regular. How come you forgot to act regular, if you're feeling that way?"

Tears suddenly welled up in Cordelia's eyes.

"Olivia!" Portia snapped, and turned to her older sister. "Cordelia, honey, your world isn't falling apart. James is going to be fine. You all are going to be fine."

Yet again, it was always this way with them. Sniping, fighting, arguing, taking sides as alliances ebbed and flowed through each encounter. Now the sisters stopped and stared at one another, then did what they always did best: They sighed—half a laugh, half resignation—then hugged.

"We don't care what you do, Portia," Cordelia said, choked up. "Just do something. Stop hiding. You can't keep living a half life, not embracing the knowing, but not embracing anything else, either. You've got to find a way to live your life, sweetie. Not Gram's, not Robert's, not ours. Yours. And that takes being strong enough to stand up to whoever is trying to sway you. Even if it's us." Cordelia gave Portia a little shake. "Now, clean up. Olivia and I are here to help. But you have to let us know what you want help with."

The sisters left Portia standing in the bathroom. She looked in the mirror, giving herself a hard glare. "You are not this person," she said to her reflection.

Thirty minutes later, Portia was bathed, dressed, and sitting cross-legged on the floor in her borrowed bedroom. Cordelia and Olivia had left, but not before she promised to call them tomorrow with a plan.

Portia took a deep breath, unzipped her suitcase. She sat there for long minutes more, then nodded her head and pulled out all three Glass Kitchen cookbooks. Whether she liked it or not, the knowing was her legacy. It had led her in so many ways, giving her answers, even if she didn't like the answers it had given. But she couldn't deny that the answers were true.

She didn't bother with the first two books. She went straight to the third volume. The one Gram had always said wasn't for novices. The one she hadn't read until now.

She cracked the old spine and found spidery handwriting on the first page.

Every kitchen should be filled with glass—to drink from, to see through, to reflect the light of a wonderful meal prepared with love. To ensure that the light is not lost, I have filled these pages with everything that has been passed down to me from earlier generations of Cuthcart women. I hope each generation to come will do the same.

Imogen Cuthcart
The Republic of Texas, 1839

Portia started to read the fragile pages, first tentatively, then greedily. Images swirled as she read. Stews and roasts, herbs and spices, broth and gravy, cookies and pies. Sweet and sour. Joy and laughter, pain and sorrow. No life could be without these.

The language was stilted, the meals old-fashioned, but the advice was progressive, considering how old the book must have been. Each time Portia came to a notation, she recognized the ones that her grandmother had made, modern takes on antiquated forms of cooking, be it the update of a gas oven from coal-stoked, or a mixer to replace beating a cake by hand.

There were as many recipes for folk medicine as for meals. Obviously food had been the main source of healing for her forebearers. Gram had traded in her own version of food as a great healer, both physically and mentally. What surprised Portia was how each of these older, more complicated entries made so much sense to her, as if she already knew the wisdom she found copied down so carefully over the years, as if she had been born with a knowing that was far deeper than her ancestors', truly deeper than her grandmother's, as Gram had said.

Portia turned the last page and the breath rushed out of her. Gram had written this page herself, years after the book was originally compiled.

I dreamed a meal. A big meal. A final meal. I keep telling myself that it's impossible to know for sure. My knowing is coming in fits and starts these days. But the images of food in this meal are strong, and I've been at this long enough to know, to feel certain, that when I see this meal, it will be time for me to stop. What I don't know is what I will do when my turn is over, when it is time for me to pass the baton. How will I be able to bear it when my whole life has been the knowing?

Though that shouldn't be my worry. I should worry that I haven't taught Portia what she needs to know. Why is it so hard for me to let go? Why is it so hard for me to teach her? Why won't I let her read any of these books, and most especially this one?

Because I'm jealous that she has always had more power than me, and if she reads it, she'll realize that she doesn't need me at all.

The Meal

Chile cheese and bacon-
stuffed cherry tomatoes
Pulled pork
Endive slaw
Potato pancakes
Homemade catsup

Portia stared at the entry. Her chest constricted.

It wasn't *her* selfishness coming to fruition through the food and the single place setting that had pushed Gram into the lightning. It had been Gram's meal, Gram's knowing, that had been realized in Portia's cooking.

She felt weak with relief, freed—a feeling followed quickly by a burst of frustrated anger.

"It didn't have to be that way, Gram," she whispered to the empty room.

If Portia had known her grandmother had lost the knowing, she would have worked with her to find a way forward for both of them. If she had known, she wouldn't have fallen into the trap of living a half life with Robert. Trapped in a half life of guilt thinking she had made a meal that had killed her grandmother.

But it also meant that now she finally knew how to move forward.

Thirty-seven

✦

ARIEL CRAWLED OUT her window to the fire escape. She still hated the fire escape, but crawling out onto the thin metal stairs moved all her worry away from her disintegrating family and onto the fact that at any second, she could plunge to her death. Okay, so maybe that was an exaggeration, but try telling that to her brain. Three stories above ground seemed really high when she was standing on two-foot-wide thin slates of metal.

But tonight even the precariousness of her perch on the fire escape wasn't helping. It had been a week since Portia had left them, and she needed someone to talk to. Not the Shrink. Not her dad. And definitely not Miranda, since Miranda was the person she needed to talk about. Which left Portia, and Portia was gone.

Not that her dad was doing anything about it. Hello! He should have been dragging Portia back where she belonged—downstairs in the garden apartment that should have been hers.

The thought of that made her smile, since Ariel had spent the whole first few weeks Portia had lived there calling it a basement. But just like Portia, Ariel had fallen in love with the old place.

With her legs dangling off the sides, she rested her forearms and chin on the metal side slat and looked out at the big buildings all around her. It was so different here in New York from their house in New Jersey. There, the house nestled into the cliff, gardens built up the back side, with stone steps taking you higher and higher. Her mom had loved those gardens. It felt weird to think that if Portia ever saw them, she'd love them, too.

Would Portia ever see their house? Maybe they would move back now that things were getting so awful with Miranda.

The sound of the door opening to the garden broke the quiet.

"Yep, I could easily live here."

Ariel scooted back against the wall. Peering through the floor slats, she watched as her uncle walked out into the garden. She couldn't in a million years imagine her dad buying the place for Anthony to live in. The two guys practically hated each other. So it didn't make sense.

"Anthony, you don't want to live here any more than Gabriel wants you here."

Her grandmother.

Anthony laughed, a sound that didn't seem very happy. "No, he doesn't, does he? I can't think of a better reason to move in. That should up the ante for what he's willing to pay me. Or if he gives it to me, like he promised, I'll sell the damn thing, take the money and run."

Her grandmother made a disgruntled noise, then walked back inside.

This whole thing was about money. Ariel took a deep breath. If she could figure out a way to convince her dad to give his brother what he wanted, then Anthony would be gone. It made so much sense. It was perfect. It would make everyone happy. Well, not Miranda, but she couldn't solve everything. But wasn't she good at talking to her dad, getting him to see her point of view?

Leaping up, she staggered, then grabbed the railing as she hurried as fast as she could down the zigzag of fire escape steps.

Her uncle looked up. "Ariel, what the f—"

She made it to the ground, safe, almost breathless, and gasped, "I'll get you the money, Uncle Anthony!"

"What?"

"I can tell you don't really want to live here! And Dad would hate it."

At the mention of his brother, Anthony's face creased hard.

"Don't you see, it's the perfect solution? I can make Dad see it. How much money do you want?"

As the words hurtled out of her mouth, she felt all the pieces of her world finally coming together.

"Why?" he said carefully. "Why would you do that?"

"Because!" she blurted out, "I know you're Miranda's dad!"

The words tumbled out before she could think them through, as if they had been dammed up and finally broken free. "I know you're her real dad. And I think she knows it, too, which is why she's acting worse and worse and getting in more and more trouble. It's because you're here and not being her dad, don't you see? But you don't want to be her dad, and if you stay, you make my dad mad. If you do stay, eventually something is going to explode and everything will come out, then everyone will know your secret, including my dad. Then what're you going to do?"

"Miranda's dad?" Uncle Anthony said. "What are you talking about? Jesus, I'm not Miranda's dad. Have you lost your mind?"

Ariel didn't believe him for a second. "Just tell me, Uncle Anthony. Tell me how much it will take to make you go away?"

His expression hardened, anger filling his eyes.

She drew a sharp breath. "Sorry! That came out wrong, I swear. It's just that we both know you'd be way happier not hanging out in New York. You love all that great mountain-climbing stuff, and wrestling with lions, or whatever it is you do."

"I do not wrestle lions."

He spaced the words in a really furious way. In fact, she'd never seen him so angry. "Sorry!" she repeated, thinking fast. "I swear, cross my heart, I won't tell a soul about you being Miranda's dad."

"I am *not* Miranda's father."

"Okay, seriously. You're forgetting who you're talking to. Me. The smart one. Of course you are. I saw when my mom and dad got married. I know Miranda's birthday. And your mom said you and my mom were in love before you left for Africa." She was on a roll, every last bit of what she'd learned spilling out. "Don't you see? If you stay, all you'll do is make things worse. For yourself!" she added quickly. "I swear, I can find a way to convince him to give you more money."

"Ariel—"

She had no idea she was crying until she felt the tears streaming down her face. "You have to *go*, Uncle Anthony. You can't let anyone know you're Miranda's dad!"

"Damn it, Ariel. I am not Miranda's dad! I'm yours!"

Thirty-eight

❖

A SOUND LIKE ocean waves rushed in Ariel's ears and the world jerked.

"What? No," she breathed. "No, no, no."

Her head spun, images of her mother dancing through her mind, like the home movies running in slow motion. Mom laughing. Mom dancing. Mom and Anthony. Always Anthony coming back into their lives.

Her mom had loved Anthony Kane, not his brother, Gabriel.

And, worst of all, awful Uncle Anthony was . . . was *her* father.

Ariel dashed back up the fire escape, Anthony muttering and cursing just behind her. But she didn't stop, didn't look back. She bolted up to Miranda's window instead of hers before Anthony could get her, and banged.

"What are you doing?" her sister demanded when she opened her window, Anthony flattened back into the shadows.

Coward.

The word rippled through her. The man who said he was her father was a coward. The one who was strong and great wasn't her real dad. How could that be true?

Ariel threw herself inside Miranda's room. She wanted her to do something, make the awful words go away. She wanted her sister to look at her like she loved her, like she cared. She wanted someone in this wacky world to see her, not let her disappear any more.

"Seriously, Ariel, what is your problem? You're not allowed out there."

"Uncle Anthony says he's my dad," she whispered, realizing that her hands shook. "You don't think it's true, do you?"

For half a second, Miranda's eyes widened. Then her cell phone rang. "Look, if it's true, it totally sucks. But I don't believe it. As much as I like him, we both know he'd do just about anything to get up in Dad's face." Her phone rang again. "Seriously, forget him." She flipped open her phone. "Hey, Dustin."

Her tone changed completely, her whole body going soft as she listened to whatever the Creep was saying.

"I'm totally ready," she said. "I'll meet you at Port Authority. The De-Camp bus to New Jersey."

Ariel gaped. "You're going to New Jersey?"

"Shit, I've gotta go. I'll meet you there." She glared at Ariel. "Don't you dare say a word. I'm already totally late. I'm going to the old house."

"What? Why?" Ariel gasped.

"We're going to . . . hang out."

"You're going out there to have sex with him!"

"What if I am? Are you going to be a total baby and tell Dad?"

At the mention of their dad, Ariel felt her lip tremble.

Miranda sighed, impatient. "Listen. We'll deal with the whole dad thing tomorrow. I mean seriously, what are the chances that it's true? Uncle Anthony can be so lame, and everyone knows he hates Dad. He probably said it just to be mean."

Ariel felt a sickening mix of gratitude that her sister said something nice and a sizzling worry about what Miranda was getting ready to do.

"Why do you have to go all the way out there to . . . do it?"

"Dustin thinks it will be fun. I shouldn't even tell you this, but the first time is supposed to be special. He has a surprise for me."

"But he broke up with you! Now he's saying you've got to go out to New Jersey to have special sex with him? That just seems weird."

"It is not weird! Kids go out to New Jersey all the time."

"Really?"

"Yes, really. We're taking the bus. Totally easy."

"But what will Dad say when he finds out?"

"He won't find out. He thinks I'm spending the night with Becky."

"This is a really bad idea, Mir."

"Tell Dad, and you're not my sister anymore." Miranda said it flat and mean; then she grabbed her bag and slammed the door on the way out.

❖

Ariel paced her bedroom. She felt sick and weird and terrified at the possibility that her dad wasn't her dad. Panic stuck in her throat, making it hard to breathe.

A lump swelled in her throat. What would she do if was true? What if Anthony took her away? What would she do if she had to go live with him? She couldn't imagine her dad not being her dad. She couldn't imagine him not coming in and checking on her in the middle of the night. After a whole life of him being Mr. Busy Working Guy, it seemed unfair that he'd get taken away now, when he was staying at home so much of the time.

Her uncle had to be lying. Just like Miranda had said.

The thoughts went round and round in her head until she felt as if she was going to throw up. But there was something else. Miranda had gone to New Jersey. To their old house.

Ariel buckled over, clutching her stomach, other memories pressing in on her. The fact was, their old house held something she hadn't wanted to face.

"*Do you remember my memory chest, Ariel?*"

The words hit Ariel hard, words she had refused to think about. They were her mother's words as she lay trapped in the car, blood streaking down her face.

"*Mom,*" Ariel had cried. She hadn't cared about any chest. "*You have to be okay!*"

Ariel had watched, terrified, as a tear rolled down her mom's temple, into her hair. "*You're a big girl now, A.*"

"*I'm only eleven!*"

"*Nearly twelve,*" her mother breathed.

Ariel still hadn't understood how she could be unhurt while her mom was such a broken mess. Plus, it was Ariel who had made her mom so angry that she had driven fast, too fast.

"*Ariel, pay attention.*" Her mother had struggled to speak. Ariel had experienced the awful feeling that she was watching her mother disappear.

"*Listen to me, Ariel. I was an idiot. I didn't think. But now you've got to find the box. It's in my study. Upstairs. In a little cabinet behind my memory chest. You have to get the box.*" She had tried to move and moaned. "*Find it. Make sure you give it to Gabriel.*"

Ariel was crying by then, hard and loud. "*What do you mean?*"

But her mom hadn't answered, her eyes fluttering closed, and Ariel watched her mother disappear.

"*Mom! Mommy!*"

Police and firefighters had arrived on the scene, pulling Ariel out of the car. But they hadn't been able to free her mom.

Over a year had passed since then, and Ariel hadn't done what her mom had asked. She hadn't wanted anything to do with the chest, or the box her mother must have hidden behind the chest. She had tried to pretend that her mother hadn't even said the words. She had resented the Shrink for wanting her to remember. But Portia had said that sometimes you had to dig deep to find answers. Ariel had hated when Portia said that. But now she knew she had to do it.

She flew to her stash of money, hoping she could catch up to Miranda. She'd have to sneak out of the house. So she wouldn't run into her dad. Or non-dad.

She swallowed back tears, shoved the money into her backpack, and made it out the front door without being caught.

⋙

It wasn't nearly as hard to get out of Manhattan as Ariel had thought it would be. She'd been saving money since the whole city clerk-cab fiasco. Every chance she got she asked her dad for money for this and that. Her dad never asked to see the birthday presents she supposedly bought for her nonexistent friends. She wasn't ever going to get caught in some random place again without enough money to get home.

Who knew that the next "home" she would need to get back to would be her old one in New Jersey? That was weird.

Of course she had always known that she'd have to go back someday.

She took a taxi to the Port Authority Bus Terminal and made it on to a DeCamp bus without anyone questioning her. By then, she'd missed Miranda, probably by a couple of buses, but she managed it herself. Pretty soon she was looking out the window of the bus as it hurtled through the Lincoln Tunnel, focusing on the way her ears popped as they drove deeper under the Hudson River. Better than focusing on what she'd find when she got to Montclair.

What would she do if she walked in on Miranda in bed with Dustin?

A few tears escaped, but she used her sleeve to swipe them away and kept staring out the window so no one could see.

When they came out of the tunnel, she saw the giant buildings of Manhattan standing like a wall of cement and glass just across the Hudson River. Twenty minutes later, the bus pulled into the parking lot by the Upper Montclair train stop. Everything looked the same as when they'd lived there before the accident. But of course it wasn't. It felt like some weird awful song.

She hitched the backpack over her shoulders and got off the bus. She went to the line of cabs, then asked the front driver to take her to the house.

He looked at her in the rearview mirror, then shrugged. "Sure."

They turned right out of the parking lot, drove over the railroad tracks, followed by another right, a left, then one more right on to a road tucked into a hill, exactly as she and her mom had done a hundred times, even down to Ariel sitting in the backseat.

The house stood on the left, giant with the long green lawn—all lit up like a Christmas tree, teenage kids going in and out of the front door.

Ariel pressed back against the seat.

Miranda wasn't out here having sex.

She was having a massive party.

Thirty-nine

✦

PORTIA SAT DOWN in Stanley and Marcus's living room, ready to get on with her life. Finally. She hadn't so much as turned on the TV since her sisters left. She had made a list. A bunch of lists, actually.

She had cleaned up, put away the last of the prepackaged food, cooked Stanley and Marcus a big, early dinner before her hosts took off for Lincoln Center and the opera, leaving her alone. But the moment she turned to the first of her lists, the doorbell rang, surprising her.

Portia peeked out the window. Gabriel stood on the steps, looking out at the street rather than at the door. He looked typically Gabriel—tall, fit, ruggedly beautiful in his own beastly way. The very sight of him sent a stab of ridiculous lust through her, followed by a wave of panic.

Like a criminal, she dropped to the floor, not wanting him to see her. He had proven to be an addiction, and there was no better way to cure the need than going cold turkey.

Not that he was making it easy. He called her cell phone practically every hour. The messages had started simple. *"Portia, we need to talk."* Gruff, impersonal, so very like Gabriel. From there, they had escalated.

"Portia, call me. We need to talk about the apartment." Before he moved on to a tightly controlled anger. *"Damn it, Portia. Let's deal with this like adults."* Then a sigh, as if giving in. *"Please."*

Which only pissed her off more.

After a few minutes, she heard Gabriel going back down the front steps. She rolled to the side, sitting up on the floor with her back against the wall. And thought about violets. Watermelon.

The images surged in her head. She could taste the sweet juicy meat of watermelon crunching in her teeth. She smelled the gentle scent of violets. And something else, sharp and pungent. Burning. Like fire.

She leaped up and yanked open the front door. "Where's Ariel?"

It came out in a bark.

Gabriel stopped halfway up his steps next door. The fierceness of his face softened, barely, but enough that she noticed.

"Portia." Nothing else. Just a note of relief.

She looked at him, just looked, frozen for a tiny second as if she could do nothing more than memorize all that beautiful harshness of him, the strong jaw, the dark eyes, the dark hair winging back, the obstinacy, imprinting him on her mind.

But then the relief was gone, and the man in control returned. "We need to talk."

"Gabriel, where is Ariel?" She ran down the stairs, then up his.

He scowled at her. "In her room."

"Are you sure?"

"Of course I am."

"Have you seen her?"

"What? Why should I? She's been in her room for hours doing homework."

"You know that for a fact? You haven't left?"

He frowned at her again. "I went downstairs once, to talk to Anthony."

"Anthony was here?"

"Now that it's vacant, he wants your apartment." He said it flatly, unforgiving, as if it were *her* fault that the apartment was free.

Her jaw went tight. "You might as well give it to him. It obviously isn't mine."

He hesitated, his tension palpable. "I should have told you about owning the apartment." As if this was all he had to say.

"Yes, you should have," she snapped. "Though obviously I've been an idiot about everything regarding the apartment." She laughed bitterly. "I should make a list of how rock-bottom stupid I've been. Let's see: I married the kind of man who would forge my signature to betray me. I moved into the place and set up shop, all the while not realizing I didn't own it. You did! But, hey, it gets better! The whole time I was staying there, I didn't realize that the guy I was stupidly falling in love with was giving me free rent to pay for all the free sex he was getting!"

"Fuck," he breathed.

"Yep, fuck," she snapped. "Convenient, huh? You didn't even have to pay cab fare to get me home. God, could I be any more stupid!" she practically shouted into the air. "I fell for the same kind of guy! Twice! For once, why can't I meet a man who'll be honest with me?"

She marched past him to the front door, hating him, hating that she still wanted him, hating that he wasn't the man she had believed him to be. And the minute she made sure everything was all right with Ariel, she would move farther away and cut Gabriel utterly and completely out of her life. She would not be stupid any longer. "We're going to check on your daughter."

The outer door was locked and she didn't have a key anymore. She had set it on the counter when she left. She turned back. Gabriel just stood there, staring at her. As always, she had no idea what he was thinking, but his jaw was rigid.

"I know you don't believe me," she stated, "but humor me. Open the door, Gabriel."

He pulled out his key, came up next to her, and turned the lock. But his arm blocked her way when she tried to enter.

"Now what?"

He touched her cheek barely, softly. She tried to jerk away, but she was trapped by his other arm. Gabriel stared at her forever, not allowing her to look away. She could see the emotion in his eyes. "We are going to talk about this, Portia. As I said, I should have told you. At some point you have to forgive me."

Her jaw dropped as she stared at him.

"Say something," he stated, his voice strangely rough.

Just forgive him? Like all he had to do was command her and she'd do his bidding?

"I think," she said deliberately, "that there is absolutely nothing to be gained from us talking. Now *move aside*."

His mouth went tight, but he moved.

Portia raced up the stairs, fighting back the burn in her eyes.

"Ariel?" she called, knocking on her bedroom door, Gabriel coming up behind her.

He knocked, louder than she had. "Ariel?" He turned the knob and pushed in. "Ariel!"

The room was empty, books lying out on the desk, the window to the fire escape open. A piece of paper was lying on Ariel's desk.

Portia says that sometimes you have to be brave and dig deep for answers.

Gabriel's jaw leaped, fury in his eyes. "What the hell is she talking about?"

Portia's head spun with images of food and flowers. "Violets," she whispered. She shut her eyes and concentrated. "And watermelons. Lots of watermelons."

"What are you talking about?"

"At your old house. In New Jersey. Ariel told me she and her mother planted violets. Then watermelons, and the watermelons went wild and took over the entire patch."

Gabriel's eyes narrowed, as if he were trying to remember. Something snagged. "What does that have to do with Ariel and this note?"

"She's gone home."

"Home is here."

"She thinks New Jersey is home, and she's gone there."

His face was a mask of disbelief mixed with denial, like grapefruit mixed with cayenne pepper. "You're telling me that my twelve-year-old daughter fled to New Jersey to return to our old house?"

"She's nearly thirteen," Portia said. She almost laughed but it turned to a strangled cry. "I think so."

"You *think?*"

"Yes. She's been searching for answers for a while."

"Answers to what?"

"I don't know. But whenever Anthony was around, she was asking questions."

His jaw worked. "About what?"

"Her mother."

"Why the hell didn't you tell me?" He leaned close, his expression harsh, his voice clipped. "Why the hell did you encourage her to ask questions?"

She refused to let his anger scare her. "A better question might be, is there something for her to find?"

He rocked back. "Damn it!"

She saw anguish in his eyes and she almost reached out—but managed to snatch back her hand. "I'll take that as a yes. You need to find Ariel. And I would start at your old house."

"Just like that. Because you thought of watermelons."

"And violets," Portia added.

"That's crazy," he snapped. "Hell, *you* are crazy. Ridiculous."

Crazy. Like her grandmother.

In yet another way, this man was no different from Robert. He wanted her to be normal. Not that any of it mattered anymore.

He pulled out his phone.

"Who are you calling?"

"Miranda. She's at a friend's house." He pressed a number, put the phone to his ear, then waited. He cursed. "Voice mail."

He strode out of the room and downstairs. He found a phone number scribbled on a piece of paper, then dialed.

"This is Gabriel Kane, Miranda's father. May I speak to my daughter?"

Portia watched as tension rose through his body.

"She's not there? She told me that she was spending the night."

More listening, fury building.

"Please ask your daughter if she knows where Miranda is."

The words were polite, but the tone was not. She could imagine that whoever was on the other end scrambled to do his bidding.

"What the—" He cut himself off. "Thank you."

He disconnected and looked at her. "Miranda and her friend aren't there. According to a brother, the girls are in New Jersey. Throwing a party."

"Ariel must have followed her." She met his hard gaze. "Some things are true, whether you believe them or not. Now, go. Find Ariel and Miranda."

He muttered a curse, then took her arm.

"What are you doing?"

"Like you said, I'm going to New Jersey. And you're going with me."

Forty

⬩⬩⬩

ARIEL WALKED UP the front path, the gentle curve of flagstone winding through the lawn, blue-black against the deep green grass. The weather was almost cold, much cooler than it had been just thirty minutes away in the city. She shivered and pulled her backpack tighter to her body.

The oversized front door was still painted red with giant black hinges, the mullioned glass inset like a portal to the way life used to be—as if her mom would be waiting on the other side. But if her mom was home, there wouldn't be teenagers drinking beer on the lawn.

Her entire body deflated, those stupid tears burning again. She made herself stop thinking about her mom. Miranda was in so much trouble if anyone found out about this party. With the drinking and everything, she'd probably be grounded for life.

As soon as Ariel walked through the front door, music hit her along with the smell of alcohol and smoke. No one gave her so much as a second glance. She walked through the entry and then three steps up into the main foyer. To the left, kids sprawled on sofas and chairs in the giant living room, white dust covers ripped off and tossed aside, lying around on the floor like melting ghosts. Two guys laughed as they tried to build a fire in the fireplace. Bags of marshmallows, a box of graham crackers, and a stack of Hershey's chocolate bars sat on the hearth.

They were going to make s'mores? In the fireplace? Did they think they were at summer camp or something? Idiots.

Ariel jerked away and crossed into the dining room. Two teens sat at the long dining table, beers in front of them. Ariel ignored them and walked on into the kitchen. But Miranda wasn't there either, or in the den just beyond that.

Retracing her path to the foyer, she weaved through a knot of teenagers as she started up the stairs. Halfway up was a small landing with a window seat. From the large, multipaned window Ariel could see the lights of Manhattan in the distance. For a second she just stood there, looking.

Growing up in New Jersey, she hadn't given any thought to the city. She knew her mother thought it was the greatest thing ever to have the view. Looking at it now, it made Ariel feel all the lonelier. A year or so ago, she would never have believed that she wouldn't still be living in this house. That her mom would be gone. That she would have moved to the city that had always seemed like a whole other planet, regardless of the fact that she could see it out the window.

A year ago, she never would have believed that her uncle would claim he was her father. Maybe she could ignore it? Would her uncle regret having said the words, maybe pretend he hadn't said them at all?

But Ariel wasn't going to take any chance that things could go haywire, catching her unaware. If the truth was here in this house, she was going to find it.

"I am not a baby," she told herself, climbing the rest of the stairs to the second floor, music thrumming up the walls, smoke following her. "I am not afraid of what I'm going to find."

Though the truth was, she was scared out of her wits. She could hardly believe she'd gotten herself down to the Port Authority, on a bus, then a taxi, and was now getting ready to dig around in her mom's study. Dad was going to kill her.

Which brought her back to the fact that Dad wasn't her dad. Or so Uncle Anthony said.

She felt another one of those disconcerting surges, like she disappeared just a little bit more. Shaking it off, she slipped into the study, closing the door behind her with a *click*. The music faded away as she walked to the big wooden chest that sat low on the floor, the hinged top covered by a thick cushion that matched the curtains.

Carefully, Ariel pried open the top, images flashing through her memory of the last time she had snuck into the room. She had been home sick from school, just a month before her mom died, and had woken from one of those feverish naps. The house felt so different in the middle of the day, during the week, the neighborhood weirdly quiet. She had woken up and went to find her mother, discovering her kneeling in front of the chest.

"*Mom?*"

Her mother had jerked up. At the sight of Ariel, she had dragged in a deep breath. "*Damn it, Ariel!*"

Ariel had flinched. Her totally proper mother cursing, her mother who always said anyone who cursed was white trash. Of course, now it turned out that Mom had grown up eating out of tin cans instead of with silver spoons.

Back then she'd been confused by her mother's anger. But now, Ariel thought about her mom growing up in the Amsterdam Houses, and wondered if the outburst had been from guilt. She'd probably been hiding that box . . . or whatever it was.

Ariel tucked her hair behind her ears, then rummaged around inside the chest, but found nothing. Not that she had expected to find anything there. Her mother had been specific about Ariel finding something behind it.

She lowered the top, then grabbed the edge of the chest and pulled hard, tugging it away from the wall. There wasn't any box she could see. The wallpaper was just barely darker, not faded, but other than that, she didn't notice anything different. She dropped to her knees and ran her hand down the pattern of vines and roses, slowly, feeling. Her heart pounded. The wall felt normal.

She sat back on her heels, trying to figure out what she had gotten wrong. Her mother had said the memory chest, she was sure of it. Leaning forward, she ran her hand down the wall again, this time even slower. Then she felt it. A seam, a break in the wallpaper over a tiny door.

She broke out in a sweat. A burst of laughter from downstairs startled her. She glanced back, but the door to the study was still closed.

She ran her hand along the seams, but didn't find a handle. Frustrated, she banged and it popped open. She squeaked in surprise, then peered inside. Her heart squeezed again when she saw a box at the very back of the space.

"*The box*," her mother had said to her. It had just been the two of them in the car, blood all over, Ariel staring in shock.

She pulled the box out with shaking hands. Her fingers shook as her thumb pulled back the metal clasp. The lock was stiff, and at first the lid wouldn't give.

When Ariel finally pried it open, she found a big manila envelope. It wasn't sealed and inside she found a to-do list, a key, and two smaller envelopes, one with *Gabriel* scrawled across the front. The other was addressed to *Mr. Carter Davis*. Underneath that, her mom had written *Bell, Longo, Lynch and Smith, LLC*. Lawyers.

Do not read, Ariel told herself. None of it was addressed to her. Her mom had said to give it to her dad. And no question, just like everything else, she knew she totally didn't want to know what was written inside either one of these letters. But she also knew she couldn't hide anymore from the stuff she didn't want to know. If she turned the letters over without reading them herself, her father would never let her in on whatever secret her mother had hidden.

Wasn't learning the truth the whole reason for coming all the way out to Montclair in the first place? Hadn't Miranda coming out here for whatever stupid reason given her the courage to follow? To find out? It seemed like a sign that it was time.

She read the to-do list first.

1. Get copy of the will
2. Make copy of Anthony's document
3. Call C. Davis

Since it looked like everything was still here, and there was no sign of a will, Ariel assumed her mom hadn't finished whatever she had been doing. Swallowing, she opened the letter to the lawyer first.

Dear Mr. Davis,

I got your name from a friend I used to know when my father was still living. He said you were discreet, and could help me. This is something I have needed to deal with for some time now, but haven't had the first clue how to do it. I am getting a copy of my will. I would like you to add an addendum based on documents I'm supplying. I've also included a letter to my husband. Once everything is completed, I would like you to hold on to the entire package. If something happens to me before I can deal with this situation in a better way, please give the letter, documents, keys, and amended will to my husband.

Thank you,
Victoria Polanski Kane

Ariel took a deep breath and then slid her fingers under the flap of the second envelope, her chipped and half-painted nails taunting her as she broke the seal. Her hands shook even more as she pulled out the letter and started to read.

Gabriel,

Not Dear Gabriel, or Dearest Gabriel. Just his name. Short. Harsh. Impersonal. She hated that.

> If you're reading this, something has happened to me, which
> hardly seems possible as I write these words. But that's not the point.
> Will it surprise you if I said I was never brave enough? I never
> was, not really. I'm still not, as writing this letter instead of telling you
> to your face proves. But here's the truth: I never meant to hurt you or
> the girls. In my own way, with this key and letter, I'm trying to fix
> things. Believe it or not, I really do try to be a better person, even if
> you would swear that I rarely succeed.

Ariel felt as if her mom's frustration and anger boiled from the page. All that stuff, that emotion between her parents that she had never let herself see.

> I know as I write this that eventually I'll have to fix things in a
> better way than this letter I'm going to give to a lawyer. But I haven't
> been able to bring myself to tell you what I've done. I've worked
> hard for years to keep my secret.
> Frankly, I plan to live a long life, so with any luck you'll never
> know that I was a fool. I always said "Fake it 'til you make it." I
> wonder if that ever works, or if we end up spending our lives trying to
> be someone we're not. Who knows? But I do know that when it came
> to the Kane brothers, Anthony believed in me. Your brother loved
> me for the drama of me. You never believed. You hated the drama.
> Why couldn't I have just wanted Anthony?

*The truth is, I wanted you all along, even though it was Anthony
who made me feel alive. Of course you never wanted me. I knew
that. But I wanted you anyway. I knew you'd give me the life
I wanted. So I got you the only way I knew how. I was young and
pretty, and had the sort of hunger that most hardscrabble, scared girls
have, which isn't so hard to understand, given where I came from.
I knew what I wanted and was determined to get it. That's all I could
see. I never considered who might get hurt in the process.*

*Of course you remember that drunken night when I seduced you
and ended up pregnant. You thought I was shallow, and you hated me
after that, but you married me anyway, as I was sure you would.
From the moment I met you, I knew you were a man who took his
responsibilities seriously. THAT is what I did love about you. And
I wanted that responsibility to be me. You would give me the life I
wanted. You would be my prince to my Cinderella. Foolish, I know.
But isn't that every poor girl's dream? Anthony would never be able to
do that for me. I thank my lucky stars every day for that night, for
Miranda. And I thank God you couldn't have loved Miranda more.
It's to your great credit that your resentment of me never spilled over
to our daughter.*

Proof that Miranda was Dad's real daughter.

Ariel's stomach lurched; she hated the truth, not that she really wanted
Miranda not to be legit. It was just that Miranda being legit proved that
Anthony hadn't lied about that part.

Her heart pounded, but she kept reading.

*That wasn't my only sin. I also knew you hated that Anthony
thought you seduced me to win me away from him. I'm still amazed
that you never told Anthony the truth: that I seduced you.*

If I'm really truthful, I loved that he was madly jealous that we

married. Do you understand the draw for a girl like me to have two
men seeming to fight for me, even if one of the men wasn't really
fighting for me, but for his unborn child? And when you never forgave
me—always made it clear that I had tricked you, even if it was
through your stoic silence—is it really a surprise that I would seek out
the only man who did make me feel beautiful and loved? When you
married me, I swore that I would never sleep with Anthony again,
and I swear I wouldn't have if you had ever tried to love me. Do you
get that part of this is your fault?

In the end, yes, I went back to your brother. Does it matter that it
wasn't right away? Does it matter that we both knew by then that
our marriage was falling apart?

Of course it doesn't. But even then, I was given a gift. This time,
it was Ariel.

Ariel moaned out loud, her fingers curling into the paper. She squeezed
her eyes closed, every inch of her growing hot and sick and hurting. But
she couldn't stop now.

Just as with Miranda, you loved Ariel from the moment she came
into the world. I saw the love in your eyes as you held Ariel for the
first time. I never had the heart to tell you Anthony was her father,
not even as a way to hurt you more when I still couldn't find a way to
make you want me. But Anthony knew, and I've paid dearly to keep
him quiet.

But that's the past.

Anthony Kane might love me in his own equally selfish way, but
he cares more about himself and money than anything else. Do not,
I repeat, do not ever let him convince you otherwise. If you are
reading this, then I'm no longer in a position to continue funneling
money to Anthony in order to keep Ariel safe. Please don't let him
hurt her. Please don't let him use her to hurt you. Hopefully by

the time you read this, I will have been able to pull it all together so
that you have everything you need to make sure he can't.

    I have done a lot of things I'm ashamed of. Despite how I got
them, the best thing I have produced in my life is our daughters. Ours.
Yours, Gabriel. Both of them. I can only hope my sins won't get in the
way of you keeping both of them safe.

Victoria

Ariel couldn't breathe. What did it mean? How could Anthony hurt
her? A scream pounded inside her, wanting to get out. Panic licked at her
as her greatest fear was realized, the one that she had been too afraid to
say out loud: Anthony really was her father, and Gabriel Kane didn't
know. Yet.

After he read this, would he turn her over to Anthony?

"No," she whispered.

Her fingers closed around the small key, deciding she should figure out
what the key opened before she told anyone about it. Inch by inch, she
went through her mom's study, biting her lip hard to keep the tears away.
Maybe her mom had a safe somewhere with money to pay off Anthony.
She picked up decorative boxes and frames filled with photos—photos
of her, Miranda, Dad—looking for something that needed a key.

There was nothing. Her mom would never have hidden the box or
whatever it was in the bedroom, not the one she shared with Dad. Ariel
stuffed the envelopes in her backpack and left the study. She peered
down the stairs. Most of the kids were in the living room playing weird
dare games. She could just make out a girl shoving marshmallows into her
mouth, one by one, the kids egging her on and then laughing when she
spit them out. Seriously, idiots. But there was no sign of Miranda or Dustin.

She ran down the stairs, through the dining room, through the swinging door into the kitchen, then into the den. A bunch of kids were in
there now, but still no Miranda. Ariel kept going to the stairway leading
to the basement.

Nerves made her slip and clatter down the thin wooden staircase, catching herself on the banister, stumbling into the dark space, but she managed to find the tiny chain that worked the lightbulb. The bulb cast a weak light, not much, but she managed to find a flashlight, then went through the basement. She was hardly breathing as she went through old metal lockers with no locks, cabinets, boxes. Nothing that needed a key.

"Damn, damn, *damn!*" she cried, slamming the lid on a trunk, dust puffing up in the dank air.

Crashing down onto a low work stool, she dropped her head into her hands. She was covered in dust and grime, her wild hair tangled, her clothes filthy. But she still didn't have what she needed.

She sat up all of a sudden. Would their mom have told Miranda something? Was that why Miranda had said they would talk later?

Ariel hurtled up the stairs from the basement, her backpack banging side to side on her shoulders like a pendulum as she ran. In the den, two kids were now making out on the couch, the TV blaring, beer cans lying about the tables like crumpled tin soldiers. She raced through the swinging door from the den to the kitchen and then to the dining room and found a girl crying at the table, a friend trying to console her. She didn't stop. In the foyer, another girl stood on the stairs sipping a beer, a guy leaning up against the banister, probably trying to convince her to go upstairs to one of the bedrooms.

Ariel ran past them. Her shoulders had started to ache, so she pulled off her backpack as she entered the living room. Just then a cheer erupted, startling her. Two boys were stuffing the fireplace with old newspapers and flicking burning matches onto the paper. Every time they got a leap of flames, they cheered.

These dopes were still trying to make s'mores. "You can't do that! You'll catch something on fire!"

They didn't even look at her.

Two girls sat on the hearth, pulling out the graham crackers and chocolate, shoving marshmallows onto a couple of pens. The fire was messy, ash getting everywhere. Just the sight of the chocolate made Ariel desperately wish she was back in New York, sitting at the counter island in Portia's kitchen, watching her work her magic with food. If only she'd never come out here.

If only she'd never gotten in the car with her mother.

Tears beat behind her eyes like prisoners trying to escape. Someone started retching and she jerked around. A kid was vomiting into one of her mom's decorative brass pots. Three boys circled around him, laughing hysterically. "Lightweight! Lightweight!"

One of them held a bottle of vodka. Probably her dad's. Already empty.

Just then, one of her mom's tasseled pillows flew by her head. "Who the fuck are you, little girl?" a boy shouted, from where he slouched on the sofa, beer can in hand. Another boy, somehow looking older, sat there, his brow furrowed.

She dropped her backpack and picked up the pillow, hugging it tight. "None of your business. Where's Miranda?"

A bunch of them whipped around to face her.

"Freakin' A. It's Miranda's sister."

Ariel hardly recognized Miranda's new friend Becky. She had on a ton of makeup. "What the hell are you doing here?" Becky demanded. "You're supposed to be in the city."

"Becks," another girl said. "Cool it." Then she smiled at Ariel, sweet, too sweet. "You want to play with us, Miranda's sister?"

"No. And you better get out of my house before I call the police."

The girl just laughed. "Seriously, you're not that uncool, are you? Come on, do shots with us."

Her face felt hot and sweaty, her heart pounding even harder. "Where's Miranda?"

"What a baby!" Becky said, turning away. She saw Ariel's backpack and yanked it up. "Do you have any money in here?"

Ariel grabbed for it, but Becky leaped out of the way and started pawing inside. Journal, pens, multicolored socks spilled out. "That's mine!" Ariel yelled.

"We need money for booze," Becky said, staying out of reach. "Your dad's a freaking millionaire, everyone knows that. But all he had in this place was a few stinking bottles of Ketel One."

Ariel grabbed for the pack again, but Becky smirked and tossed it to another girl.

Ariel pivoted and leaped for the other girl, who only laughed and threw the pack over her head to one of the guys, who tossed it to another kid in the foyer.

It was like a game playing out in slow motion, until she realized that Becky was laughing even harder. She turned around to find the girl was holding her journal.

"'Musings of a Freak,'" Becky read, giggling madly. "You *are* a freak."

The music swirled through Ariel's head like notes swimming through melting marshmallow. It took a moment to figure out that this awful girl was reading her thoughts out loud—her frustrations, her hopes, her fears—for everyone to hear. Part of her was mortified, and some other part pulsed with fury. But something else clawed at her and stung her nose.

Smoke still puffed out into the room instead of going up the chimney. The boys making s'mores didn't seem to care. One of them threw back a shot, then tossed his plastic cup into the fire, making the smoke smell so bitter she could taste it on her tongue.

"Hey, moron—" she heard someone say, but then a big *pop* sounded and the fire flared up, and still none of the smoke went up the chimney.

"Shit," one of the boys said, falling back a step.

"Yeah," another said. "Son of a bitch, you're a moron."

Somebody threw a glass of beer on the fire, but it didn't go out.

"Oh, no," Ariel cried, swiping her nose with her sleeve, as it only got worse. She grabbed a beer can from the table and ran forward, too, but the can was empty. The fire popped, a flying ember hitting her sleeve. She stared in shock as her shirt started to burn.

"Damn." The cool boy from the sofa pushed up, tore off his jacket, and wrapped her arm with his coat. Then he grabbed a full water bottle from his pack and threw the contents onto the flames, and the fire sizzled and hissed as it went out. "Seriously, morons," the guy muttered.

Ariel dropped the empty can, and still, she couldn't do anything but stare, her mouth open.

The guy leaned down and looked her in the eye. "You're okay, kid. Got it? Now go home. Get out of here. You're too young to get involved with this crazy shit."

Her lip trembled.

"You're fine, kid, really." He straightened and shook his head. "I'm out of here. If you want a ride, this is your chance."

She couldn't move. She wasn't fine. Nothing was fine.

He shrugged and headed for the door. "I'm out of here."

She lost it then. She started crying in big, gasping sobs as she staggered back from the hearth. She dashed at her eyes, swiping away soot and tears and a year of holding on by a thread.

She didn't care what any of them thought of her. She couldn't stop crying. It was all of it, the one tiny gesture of kindness from a stranger who walked out the door, the forgotten house, her mom, the dad who wasn't really her dad, the lies she hadn't known about, the life she didn't know how to fix.

Somebody put a hand on her shoulder and she twisted away, facing the fireplace, her body racked by tears, gasping as she tried to catch her breath. But all she managed to suck in was smoke.

With a gasp of surprise, she felt her lungs squeeze, her throat going tight. Her eyes burned, and she felt them start to bug out. She told herself not to panic. She wheeled back around, looking for her backpack. Looking for Einstein. But he wasn't there. Her backpack was gone.

She opened her mouth to cough, but it wouldn't come, just more smoke filled her mouth and nose.

The kids started to murmur, their faces distorting. But she couldn't move. Her legs felt wobbly, sounds overloud in her ears.

"What's wrong with her?" she barely heard.

"Stop being a freak!" Becky shouted.

"I think she's having some sort of fit. Crap."

"She's probably epileptic. She's gonna froth!"

"Damn, get me out of here."

The voices swelled in her head before growing distant. Then all of the sudden she saw Miranda run into the room. Ariel wanted to weep in relief when she felt her sister's hands grabbing for her, hands circling her arms, rough and frantic. But a second later she realized that it was too late. Her head swam, the prisoners behind her eyes finally going quiet, the world going black.

And she disappeared.

Forty-one

✦✦✦

As soon as Gabriel turned the Mercedes onto the narrow residential street, Portia knew for certain something was wrong. She felt it in the vibration of her thoughts, violets and watermelon flashing through her mind in a kaleidoscope of dread.

Gabriel must have felt it, too. He cursed beneath his breath and hit the gas, every ounce of civilized man falling away.

Portia had never been to New Jersey, much less to Montclair. The full moon cast silver light on the giant old houses that were set back from the road, built far apart, a gracious lawn rolling up to a sprawling Victorian with brilliant white latticework, followed by a stately redbrick Colonial, and finally a beautiful old Tudor, its slate roof shining like blue-black water in the bright night. The opposite side of the imposing street dropped off in a gentle cliff to even larger houses in the distance below.

Outside the Tudor, cars lined the road, lights blazing inside.

"The party," Gabriel bit out, slamming on the brake in front of the house.

Portia saw the teenagers coming and going. Gabriel double-parked in front of what she assumed was the Kanes' New Jersey house. Cars filled the long, narrow driveway that disappeared around back. Gabriel raced to the front door.

Portia was right behind him, unease filling her like hot water rising in a pan. It wasn't the idea that someone was throwing a party at Gabriel's house that concerned her. Something else quickened her pulse, a kind of horror that she couldn't name.

They were halfway across the lawn when kids started barreling out the front door, running and yelling at each other.

Gabriel pushed past them like a beast possessed, Portia at his heels. At some level the opulence of the house registered along with the dread, the sure knowledge that she didn't belong to this world, to this family. Robert's sprawling home was nothing compared to this stately mansion, her family's double-wide as foreign to this world as a mud hut on a Burmese hillside.

"Dad!"

Portia's heart stood still when she ran into the living room. Miranda was a mess of tears and wrecked hair, mascara streaming down her face, looking like a crying child playing dress-up.

"She's dead!"

Gabriel fell to his knees. When he did, Portia saw Ariel on the floor.

His roar filled the entire house as he pulled the girl into his arms. "What have you done?" he demanded.

"I didn't do anything!" Miranda cried, hugging herself.

Portia felt an odd calm come over her. She pulled out her cell phone. "Has anyone called 9-1-1?"

"I already did," Miranda managed, dropping down next to the girl and their father. "You have to fix her, Dad. Oh, God, it's my fault! Ariel! Wake up!"

Gabriel started CPR.

Kids were still running, a boy pounding down the stairs, towing a half-dressed girl. The music was nearly deafening, so Portia turned it off.

Then there was silence except for Miranda's sobs and Gabriel's measured counting as he blew air into Ariel's lungs and compressed her chest.

Portia sank onto her knees beside them. She took in the room, smelled the air. She turned back to Ariel. "Her lips are blue around the edges. It's an asthma attack. Where's her backpack?"

Gabriel and Miranda went stiff at the same time. Miranda leaped up. "It's got to be here somewhere!"

But the kids had evaporated. Ariel's backpack was nowhere in sight.

Gabriel raised his head, his hands compressing Ariel's chest with gentle force. "The yard," he ordered. "Someone dropped something in the yard."

Portia flew back out of the house and spotted Ariel's backpack lying in a forgotten heap in the dark. She careened back inside, ripping through its contents as she went until she found what she was looking for. She dropped down next to Gabriel, who grabbed the inhaler and put it into his daughter's mouth. He shot it once, then twice, then clamped his mouth over hers and resumed CPR.

Forty-two

❖

A RIEL SWAM in a murky place, where sound was muffled and light seemed overbright. But the worry, all the worry she had felt since the accident, was gone. She still felt the buzzing, but she was no longer a bee stuck in a jar.

She felt at peace.

This was where she wanted to be, a place where things were easier. This was what she had been moving toward ever since the accident, with all those horrible feelings slowly disappearing.

She had been right. She had disappeared, just like Mom.

For so long she had been afraid, but had refused to admit it. With the fear and worry suddenly gone, she felt herself expanding, as if she were flinging her arms wide and taking a deep breath.

But on the heels of that peace, she felt a tinge of panic trying to pry its way through the calm. Could she really leave her dad? Miranda? Even Portia? Would they be fine without her? Would they care?

"Ariel!"

The roar echoed in the quiet that surrounded her.

"No!"

She felt the vibration of the words against her body more than she heard them.

Dad?

"Ariel! Damn it, come back!"

For long seconds she felt the words, felt the way they surrounded her and pushed away the quiet. She felt torn between the peace and the wish to stop the pain she felt coming at her in a wave. The push, then the pull. The need to stay gone, the pull to go back.

Then all of a sudden, she saw her dad's face in her mind with that look he had at Mom's funeral when his mouth distorted and she knew he could have cried but wouldn't. Of Dad sitting at the breakfast table reading *The Wall Street Journal*, the way he had lowered the paper and raised a brow when she inquired if he was interested in having cocktails that evening, only to go back to reading without a word. Her dad, who didn't get ruffled by anything. Her dad, who she felt certain hovered over her now. Crying.

The world flooded back into her a startling gasp of breath, and she cried out in surprise. Air burned as it rushed into her lungs.

"Dad?" she managed, her tongue thick, her head light. She felt hot and cold all at once, and like she was going to be sick to her stomach.

Her father was leaning over her. "Ariel."

Not a question. A statement. But with the world coming back into focus, she remembered everything that was wrong, the peace gone.

He wasn't her dad at all.

Misery ripped through her as all the pieces jarred back into place. First her mom had been taken away. Now her dad. She wanted to go back to the quiet. She wanted to scream that it was all unfair. She wanted to tell him she would be the greatest daughter ever, that she'd do better this time at being perfect, that he'd be better off keeping her rather than giving her away.

But what if he didn't want her? What if he didn't want to deal with the trouble of always paying Anthony? How she wished he would never learn the truth.

She struggled to open her eyes. The minute she succeeded, her dad hugged her tight. "Oh, God," he whispered, making her feel safe for the first time since the accident.

"Dad?"

"God, Ariel," he said into her hair. "As soon as I get over the relief I feel right now, you're going to be in a mountain of trouble for running away."

"So you'll ground me?" she managed, wanting nothing more than her dad's infamous go-to form of punishment, anything to make her feel that their lives could be normal again.

He half laughed, half cursed, and held her tight.

Then Miranda came into view next to Dad's shoulder. "Ariel, I'm sorry!" she said, her voice warped by a sob. "I was so stupid to come out here. And it was stupid that I didn't come find you the minute I heard you were in the house. I—I almost killed you!"

Ariel shook her head, the effort making her senses spin. "No, you didn't."

Ambulance guys rushed in then, moving Miranda and her dad back.

That's when she saw Portia just looking at her, a strange mix of relief and sadness on her face. "Hey, kiddo. Welcome back."

As if Portia actually understood that she had gone, might not have returned.

Ariel smiled at her, feeling sort of shy, wanting to reach out, realizing that the one person she could have talked to all this time was Portia. She would have understood. Portia got all those things that weren't ordinary, like food that meant stuff, and how people could disappear.

But then her thoughts circled back to what she had found. As much as she didn't want to tell her dad about it, she couldn't be like her mother. No more secrets.

She pushed at the ambulance guy. "Dad?"

"What is it, Ariel?"

"I found a box Mom hid. It had a key and some letters in it."

Dad didn't seem to care. "Sweetheart, let the paramedics finish checking you over. We can talk about it later."

They started in on her—blood pressure, checking her eyes, temperature—then had her hooked up to an IV in record time.

"Quick onset, quick recovery. But to be on the safe side," one of them said, "she should be observed for twenty-four hours. We'll take her to Overlook."

"What?" Ariel said, her throat still burning. "Overlook, like the hospital? I can't go there. I have bigger problems. I found letters from Mom. And a key," she repeated.

The paramedics and Dad looked at one an other, and the paramedics fell back.

"What letters, Ariel? What key?"

"So," she began, hesitant, nervous, though her voice was getting stronger, the itch less intense, "you see, Mom told me I had to find the box."

Her dad got an even weirder look on his face.

"I don't mean she told me anything *after* she died. In the car, after we wrecked, before the police got there, she told me to find the box in her study."

"Why didn't you tell me?" he asked, his voice pained.

"I didn't want to know." Ariel tried to feel less stupid than she did right then. "But mostly, I guess, I didn't want Mom to be dead, and not finding the box made it less real."

"Who are the letters for, Ariel?"

She bit her lip, trying to push herself up to sit cross-legged, but her dad didn't let her.

"Fine," she exhaled. "Technically, one's for you. The other's for a lawyer." Then she rushed out the rest with a heave of breath. "But she told *me* to find the box, so I figured—"

"Ariel," he said, cutting her off, "let me have the letters."

As reluctantly as she had done anything in her life, she told him they were in her backpack. Once the pack was retrieved, he pulled the folded envelopes out. He read all of it. He swallowed hard, his throat working. Then he read the one to him again, and looked at her.

She told herself to have a little pride. Raising her chin, she said, "I guess I should call you Mr. Kane." She choked on the words, her voice clogged and raspy. "Too formal? How about Uncle Gabriel?"

"Oh, God," he whispered, pulling her back to him before setting her just far enough way that he could look her in the eye. "I'm your *dad*, Ariel. Always your dad."

Tears burned even hotter. "But the letter—"

"No buts. I raised you. I loved you from the second you were born."

"But Uncle Anthony—"

"Forget my brother, Ariel. You're my daughter, in every way that matters. And I keep what is mine. Always."

The words were fierce. "Really?"

"Really." He pulled her close. "You're mine, A."

It was sick possessive, but she had never liked her dad's whack-job bossy thing more than she did right then. She would have done her best to throw herself at him, despite the IV tube, but she couldn't. Not until the whole truth was out there. She couldn't leave it half done.

"Dad," Ariel whispered, not wanting to tell him the even bigger secret that she had tried to tuck away and forget, the last bit of poison she had refused to tell the Shrink, had refused to write in her journal. "Mom wrecked because of me."

His whole body went stiff. "What are you talking about, Ariel?"

She glanced over to where Portia was talking to Miranda, who was still crying. "I found Mom with, um, Anthony."

Her dad went completely still, and she felt the panic creep up again.

"Please explain." Short, clipped words, but her words spilled out in a rush.

"Miranda had gone into the city on a school trip. Mom forgot I only had a half day at school, then a Mathlete competition, so I walked home. And I, um, saw them, together."

His eyes narrowed. "I'm going to kill him."

"I waited outside for him to leave, so he wouldn't see me. When he left, I told Mom I knew. That I saw. That I was going to tell you."

Tears started streaming down her cheeks before she realized she was crying. "I was mad. I gave her the car keys and said—" The words stuck in her throat.

"What did you say, sweetheart?"

He looked at her with his craggy face, so fierce, but in that way he had that made her feel like he could do anything in the whole world.

"I told her if she was finished screwing Uncle Anthony"—she shuddered at the words—"that maybe she could find a few minutes to take me to the Mathlete competition." Ariel did her best to keep her voice steady, truthful. "Mom slammed into the car, mad."

Ariel had gotten in the backseat, just as angry. But her mom had acted like she wasn't even in the car, like she was invisible. Mom hadn't said a word about Anthony. No explanation, no promise that Ariel shouldn't worry, or that they would talk about it later. "She was really mad, her hands clenching on the wheel." She hesitated. "I might have been sort of mad, so . . . I asked her if she wanted me to tell you before I competed or after. Mom jerked her head back to look at me then. She turned away from the road, Dad, and started to say something to me." Ariel drew in a deep breath. "You know the rest."

Her dad's jaw worked, it seemed, like for a century. Finally he said, "Ariel, listen to me, and listen good. None of this, I mean none of it, is your fault. It's my fault, and your mother's fault. And Anthony's fault. But never yours. Do you understand me?"

Her eyes burned, relief washing through her, and she managed a nod, even if she wasn't entirely sure she believed it.

Portia must have thought they were finished talking, and she walked over. "You go with Ariel to the hospital," she said. "I'll drive Miranda back to the city and stay with her until you and Ariel are done."

Dad looked up. "Portia—"

"Gabriel, give me the keys," she said, stepping back.

Ariel watched as he stared at Portia, then nodded. "You're right. You and Miranda should go back. As soon as Ariel and I finish at the hospital, I'll call a car service."

He glanced at Miranda with a ferocious look, but at the same moment he stood and extended his arm. Miranda ran to him, and he pulled her into his chest.

"This isn't over," he said. "But we'll fix it. We'll fix whatever's wrong. Okay?"

Miranda hiccupped another sob, and nodded against his shirt.

Dad looked over her head at Portia and started to say something.

But Portia turned away, and Ariel saw a bunch of emotions race across his face. Anger? Frustration? Whatever it was, he definitely wasn't happy.

"Come on, Miranda," Portia said. "We'd better hurry." She took Dad's keys, then leaned over to Ariel. "Glad you're okay, kiddo."

Then she was out the door, Miranda in tow, Dad staring after her and looking like he wanted to punch the wall.

⋕

It took hours, but after another IV solution of some kind, and getting checked on every five seconds, eventually Ariel got the okay from the emergency room doctors to leave. But once they did, she and her dad didn't go home. It was somewhere around four in the morning. They went to a hotel near the hospital, just in case she had to go back in.

Which she wouldn't, but it made her feel better to have her dad fussing over her so much. Maybe he really did mean to keep her.

She took a long bath in a tub that was like a small pool while Dad went downstairs and managed to get someone to find them something to eat.

Finally, clean and fed, wrapped in one of the hotel's giant robes, Ariel curled into her dad's arms and looked up at him. He was sitting on the bed, his head back against the headboard. He seemed really tired, and it made her worry.

"Dad," she whispered.

He didn't open his eyes. "Hmmm?"

"I'm sorry I was the one who told you about the Uncle Anthony thing."

He didn't answer at first. "I already knew."

She jerked in his arms. "You already knew? For how long?"

"He told me six months after the funeral."

Exactly when they'd moved into the city. She took the information in, processing. "Is that why we left Montclair?"

"Yes. I wanted to be closer to you and Miranda."

"So he couldn't show up and take me while you were working in Manhattan?"

"Ariel, nothing like that is going to happen."

"But what if . . . what if Uncle Anthony fights for me? You know, because of money, or something."

He looked at her then, and that ferocious power thing he did so well was back. It didn't scare her at all, only made her feel weak with relief.

"There is no amount of money that will get in the way of you always being my daughter, Ariel."

"Is that what you two keep talking about? Is that what you want him to sign? Something that says I'm . . . not his?"

He pulled her closer. "Like I said, no matter what, you are my daughter. Don't ever forget that, Ariel. But, yes, I intend to make it legal."

"And that's how Uncle Anthony keeps getting money out of you? Like blackmail? Like he was doing to Mom?"

She felt him tense. "Let me worry about my brother. I will always take care of you. Can you trust me? Will you stop running around town trying to solve mysteries and let me do it for you?"

She blinked.

"Yep, I know all about your adventures."

"Are you mad?"

"I'm only angry at myself for not having gotten this dealt with sooner."

Ariel felt the vise around her chest ease. And just like the night she had fallen asleep in his study back in Manhattan, Ariel tucked herself even closer. She felt so tired, like all the energy she had used to keep things together had seeped out of her, in a good way, and she thought that finally she would really sleep.

"I bet you're going to rethink the whole no–cell phone thing now," she whispered as she drifted off.

She was almost sure she heard him laugh.

⋯

They headed out of the hotel in the morning and a car was waiting in the front drive. But instead of giving their address in Manhattan, her dad gave an address in Montclair.

"Where are we going?" she asked.

"To the bank." He held up the key she had found. "It's for a lockbox."

"How can you tell?"

"I used to have one just like it at a bank here in town. I never knew your mother had her own."

They walked into the bank and were ushered into a private area, a box pulled out and waiting on a table.

"Are you ready?" her dad asked.

Biting her lip, Ariel nodded.

Her dad took the key and opened the box. Ariel let out her breath in a rush.

"It's just papers!"

"Documents," he said as he began to read. When he finally set them down, he looked sort of angry, but also relieved.

"Your uncle Anthony signed over guardianship to me years ago. Though it cost Victoria to keep him quiet. She obviously intended to get it all to a lawyer so that if anything happened to her, there wouldn't be any confusion, but she didn't get it done in time." For half a second, intense anger flushed out everything else on her dad's face, but he swallowed it back. "After Victoria died, Anthony must have realized that no one knew about the documents, including me, so he started on me." He cut himself off after he seemed to remember Ariel was sitting there.

He leaned over and cupped her face. "All that matters," he stated, "is your mother made sure that legally, I'm still your dad."

Forty-three

◆◆◆

PORTIA HEARD A CAR pull up out front, then the outer door of the town house opened, and her heart surged into her throat.

Neither she nor Miranda had slept much in the hours since they'd returned to the city. Even though she was sure they would have said yes, Portia hadn't wanted to impose even further on Stanley and Marcus by asking that they put up both her and Miranda. Plus, Miranda would want to be at home so she could see that Ariel was okay the minute she returned. So Portia had stopped by next door to say good night, and then returned to the town house. She felt surrounded by memories in the house, the memory of her great-aunt and the memory of what she had thought she shared with Gabriel.

Miranda had fallen asleep on the sofa. Portia had hunkered down in an overstuffed chair, reminding herself that this house wasn't a home, not the kind where she belonged, with its perfect, expensive fabrics, sterile of emotion despite the rich materials and heavy silk.

After a few hours, she had realized she wasn't going to sleep at all, so she had gotten up and gone to the kitchen. Eventually Miranda had followed, and the two of them sat there, not saying much, until the front door opened.

Miranda leaped up and flew down the hall. Portia drew a deep breath, then followed.

When she came out into the hallway it was just in time to see Miranda throw herself at her dad and sister. "I'm sorry!" the teen cried.

Looking on, Portia's heart twisted. She loved the girls and would miss them. But after everything that had happened, she knew she had no future in this house.

As if sensing her thoughts, Gabriel glanced up. His eyes drifted over her, dark, assessing, as if trying to understand what she was thinking.

"Dad," Miranda said, drawing his attention.

Portia didn't wait to hear what the girl had to say. She used the distraction to make her escape.

She slipped past the three of them, heading for the front door.

"Portia," Gabriel stated, hard and clipped, like a demand he expected to be obeyed.

She went faster.

"Portia." This time softer, mixed with a sigh.

Portia didn't care. She raced out the front door, literally running over to Stanley and Marcus's.

Stanley raised a brow from his place by the window when she walked in, and Marcus bustled her over to the sofa, plopped down beside her, and said, "Tell me everything!"

Portia caught her breath. "Marcus!"

"You can't hold out on me, not after all the Little Debbie cakes I gave you! I am dying of curiosity. You didn't give us one single detail last night! Granted, it was late, but now, out with it!"

She sank back against the cushions, suddenly exhausted. "Miranda went to New Jersey. Ariel followed, had a bad asthma attack, and ended up in the hospital overnight. She's fine now. There."

"Glad to hear it, but now I want the good stuff," he demanded. "What happened with Gabriel? Tell me he groveled at your feet, apologizing up and down for not bothering to mention he owned your apartment!"

"No, no apology." She pursed her lips. "Not that an apology solves anything."

The words were barely out of her mouth when her cell phone rang. *Kane, Gabriel.*

She pressed ignore with relish. When she glanced up from the phone, Stanley and Marcus were looking at her. "What?" she said.

"You'll have to talk to him sometime."

"No, Marcus, I won't."

Marcus cringed.

Not two minutes later, someone was at the front door.

Stanley glanced out the window, then exchanged a glance with Marcus. This time it was Stanley who struggled up from the chair while Marcus gathered their coats.

"Where are you going?" she squeaked.

"No more hiding, Portia. Gabriel's a good man." Marcus paused and gave her one of the very few frowns she'd ever seen on his face. "True, he should have told you about owning the apartment. But he's still a good man. Deep down, you know that."

They hurried out the door, letting Gabriel in, but not before she heard Stanley growl, "You hurt her again, and you'll answer to us."

Once the door shut, Gabriel stepped forward. There was nothing soft and approachable about him. "We are going to talk, Portia."

"There's no point." She started to turn away, but he strode forward and took her arm. Not hard, not bruising; unrelenting, but oddly gentle. "You will listen to me. You owe me that."

All her careful calm evaporated. "I don't owe you anything! I'm not the one who lied and betrayed you."

"Damn it, I'm trying to apologize!"

She gasped her disbelief. "Last I heard, apologies don't start with barked-out orders!"

He visibly reined himself in, and let her go. With a few quick steps, she moved away.

He raked his hands through his hair. "I'm trying, Portia. I don't know the first thing about nice or simple. Charm. That's my brother's domain. I've always been hard." As if that made it better. "I know I've messed up at every turn. With you. With my daughters. Christ, I nearly lost one." The entire frame of his tall, hard-chiseled body shuddered, every bit of searing anger draining out of him. She felt his pain. She thought of the way he was when he made love to her, the control she knew he didn't believe he could afford to lose.

She wanted to reach out, but kept her hand at her side.

He stepped forward. She stepped back until she hit the wall. He didn't stop until he was inches from her. He took her in, assessing in that way he had, this time as if to determine if she was safe, as if he couldn't afford for someone else in his life to be hurt.

"Move away, Gabriel."

"That's not going to happen," he said softly. "We are going to talk. I am going to apologize. You need to stop running away from me and listen."

She met his gaze defiantly. "I don't *need* to do anything other than tell you to leave, because, apology or not, we're over."

He flinched, but didn't relent. "We haven't even begun, sweetheart."

"Don't 'sweetheart' me!" She tried to step sideways, but again he blocked her.

Then, as if he was giving in to something he fought, he ran one hand up her neck, his palm cupping her face, his thumb brushing over her cheek. She felt the tremor rush through his body, the heat that hit her. "If I could do it all over again," he said, his fingers sliding into her hair, "I would."

"But you can't," she snapped, forcing herself not to look at his mouth.

"I know that. I screwed up. I get that, too. And now I'm trying to explain. Something I haven't done a lot of in a long time."

"Ah, so the great Gabriel Kane, who doesn't answer to anyone, will deign to explain. And I'm supposed to be all excited about this big emotional breakthrough?"

His dark eyes went hard. "That isn't what I meant, Portia."

He looked at her, his jaw cemented before his eyes drifted to her lips. She knew he wanted to kiss her. Her heart sped up.

"I meant that it's not easy to explain because I hardly understand myself. I don't spend a lot of time thinking about what I feel, or why I couldn't bring myself to tell you I already owned the apartment. Not any of it. But from the first time I saw you sitting on the front steps, wearing those flowered shoes, something about you . . . spoke to me. Hell, I'd been dead for years, long before my wife died." He hesitated, as if searching for words, but clearly believing he had to. "Seeing you sitting there, I felt something . . . intense. Not long after, I recognized that if I let it happen, I would come to need you." His gaze hardened. "I don't *do* need."

"That's great," Portia said with a scoff, refusing to let up, unable to let up. She couldn't afford to. "You're just what every woman wants."

"Don't, Portia. Don't keep throwing this back at me." His face was ravaged. "I'm doing the best I can. I'm trying. At least give me that." He waited a breath, and when she remained silent, he continued. "I denied what you made me feel. Hell, I fought it tooth and nail. But every time I told myself to just tell you that I owned the apartment and kick you out, I couldn't. And that infuriated me. How had I become so weak? It's only been by not being weak that I've succeeded in life. Who the hell am I if I wasn't the strong guy? Look at this face, Portia."

Her breath caught in surprise.

"Is this the face of a man who can afford to be weak?" he demanded. "No, it's not. I learned that as a boy. But that's the thing: The minute you saw me, without having any idea who I was, or that I had money, you looked at me in a way I had never experienced before. You couldn't have been drawn to my money, because you had no idea who I was when you first saw me. You saw me walking toward you, I saw you see me. I saw the way you looked at me. Drawn in. You wanted *me*, Portia. I felt it. I saw it. And when you learned I had money, real money, the kind you needed, you wanted nothing to do with it. Do you know how amazing it was to me that you *didn't* want my money? Hell, you wouldn't even cash the check that I had to force you to take. Anyone else in your position would have snapped up my offer of financing—"

"Offered without believing in me," she interjected, holding on to her anger, hating that her heart was melting.

"But I gave you a check. It doesn't matter how it was offered, because you didn't want a penny of it anyway. Every day I have people who want a piece of me, but only for my money. Even my mother, my brother." He hesitated. "Even my wife. All they want or wanted from me was my money."

She swallowed back the ache she felt for him. She wanted to tell him there was beauty in every strong and harsh plane of his face. It got harder to hold out. Her fingers itched, not to bake, but to touch him. But on the heels of that thought came another. The reality of Gabriel's Meal, a reality that she wanted to run from, but couldn't. How could she after she had watched her grandmother being struck down by lightning based on a meal, the scar on her shoulder a reminder if she was ever inclined to forget?

Her heart slowed at the thought, a deep settling of resolve. As much as she loved him—and she knew she did—as much as she ached for him right then, despite what he had done to her, her grandmother's entry proved all the more that Cuthcart meals spoke truths.

The meal she had prepared for Gabriel had been followed by a very different kind of storm. Gabriel's Meal had been the beginning of a total unraveling of both their lives, starting with the fight between Gabriel and Anthony and ending with Ariel nearly dying, the arrival of the inspector squashing her dream sandwiched in between. Gabriel's Meal had spelled disaster.

"It's too late for us, Gabriel. You betrayed me. You lied to me." Emotion and pain swelled, pushing her on. "But the fact is," she stated, "you said I was ridiculous. Crazy."

"What are you talking about?"

"When I told you that Ariel was in New Jersey. You said, 'That's crazy. Hell, you are crazy. Ridiculous.'"

She could see by his expression that he remembered.

"And you didn't say it in some flip way. You looked me in the eye and I saw that you believed it. Admit it, Gabriel, you think I'm odd. Different. Ridiculous. Deep down, you don't believe in me. That makes you no different from my ex-husband. You both want me to be someone I'm not, someone who fits into a normal box, someone who doesn't know things because of food. My husband said I wasn't normal. You used different words, but you said the same thing." She had never felt so sad. "So no, despite the fact that all you have to do is touch me and I melt, despite the fact that I fell in love with you, madly, deeply, in a let-you-eat-crackers-in-my-bed, shouting-Stella-from-the-courtyard sort of way, there is no future for us." Her voice broke. "I deserve better than men who think of me as lesser than them, when they bother to think of me at all."

"Portia—"

She saw the pain in his eyes, but she didn't let up. "I deserve better than men who want me to fit whatever they think suits their particular life."

He stared at her hard, and she could see the truth sink in. And still, she didn't let up. "I thought you were a different kind of man, Gabriel."

He flinched.

She sucked in her breath, hating this, but held his gaze. "I fell I love with you, Gabriel. But you only thought of yourself. I deserve someone who will love me just the way I am. Now, please, move away. I want you to leave."

She saw the moment he realized she was serious, that she wasn't going to be convinced. After a long furious, aching second, he nodded.

He left her then, without looking back. And her heart broke a little bit more.

Forty-four

❖❖❖

"ROBERT BALEAU, please," Portia said into the phone, Stanley and Marcus standing on either side of her.

The woman who answered hesitated, then asked, "Who may I say is calling?"

Portia grimaced, glanced at Stanley, who scowled at her, then raised her chin. "His ex-wife."

The woman gasped. "Portia, is that you?"

Portia's stiffened. "Rayna?"

"I knew it! Portia, darlin', how are you?"

"I'm fine, how are you? What are you doing answering the phones?"

"Well, you know how you had to stay on top of everyone around here to get them to do their jobs. Now you're gone and that Sissy—" She cut herself off. "Let's just say that things aren't running too smoothly around here."

Portia had heard just that after a woman who used to work for Robert had tracked her down and offered her a bit of good fortune.

Rayna sighed over the phone. "He has me doing everything from answering the phones to dealing with the press. Lordy, do I miss you. And not just because without you things are a mess. Are you really okay?"

Portia searched for a cheerful voice to answer. "I'm great." She glanced at Stanley and Marcus. "And I'm about to be even better. Is Robert there?"

"Let me see—"

Suddenly Portia heard Rayna cover the receiver with her hand, but not before she heard Robert's familiar bark in the background.

Rayna came back, this time as proper as when she had first answered. "Yes, Mr. Baleau is in. I'll put you through." But just before she transferred the call, Rayna whispered into the phone, "Miss you."

Then the clicks before Robert bellowed into the phone. "Portia! It's about time you returned my calls."

As if she were a child reprimanded by an adult. It sank in that it had always been that way between the two of them, more so the longer they were married. She felt the sting of embarrassment.

Stanley must have sensed something, because he leaned forward and rasped, "We didn't spend the last twenty-four hours teaching you how to *not be* a nice girl to have you fall apart the minute you get on the phone with that guy!"

She squeezed her eyes closed. Their lessons didn't have one bit in common with the "ladylike behavior" her mother had drummed into her head. But even she had figured out that her mother's pilfered etiquette book was for the birds.

Every ounce of embarrassment and fury rose up, pushing every trace of devastation she felt over the loss of Gabriel aside. Never in her life had she wanted to kick someone's tail.

"It's time you pay what you owe me, Robert."

Stanley nodded.

Robert scoffed into the phone. "What are you talking about, Portia?"

"You owe me for the apartment!"

A surprised pause before, "Portia, you're upset—"

Stanley and Marcus waved their hands, shaking their heads. "Do not get upset!" they hissed.

"Me? Upset? Why would that be, Robert? You divorced me. Then you married the only friend I had in Willow Creek. Fine, that's your prerogative. But it's not your prerogative to withhold the money you owe me, both from our marriage settlement and the proceeds from the sale of *my* apartment—and let's not even discuss my forged signature."

"Portia, you need to calm down."

"Robert, I am calm, calm enough to tell you that I want the money you owe me wire-transferred into my bank account before the end of the day. I know exactly how much you got for my apartment, and I want every dime from the sale, as well as interest from the date of closing. *Capisce?*"

Stanley rolled his eyes. Marcus snickered. Sure, it was a little much. But she was on a roll.

Robert must have sensed that she was serious. Ever the consummate politician, he reined in the moral outrage and replaced it with something that had served him well in the past.

"Portia," he said, his tone aggrieved. "I feel terrible that you and I have come to this. But there is no reason for you to be going on so."

"Let me repeat myself: You must deposit every dollar you owe me in my bank account by the end of the day."

She could all but see him, nearly two thousand miles away, formulating yet another new move, a master playing chess. She was half certain he was enjoying himself.

"I don't have that kind of money readily available."

"Then you'd better find a way to get it. If you don't, I'll make sure your constituency learns you're a lying, cheating manipulator. I'm not so sure those same voters you say love you are going to be thrilled to reelect a man who swears he supports the sanctity of traditional marriage but got one of his employees—his wife's best friend, at that—pregnant while he was still married."

"I know you, Portia," he snapped, his patience spent. "You didn't fight me before. You won't fight me now. Nothing's changed. At heart, you're still a poor girl from a trailer park, raised by a crazy grandmother."

She laughed, which she knew he hadn't expected. "Maybe so. But what *has* changed is that I'm dead serious. Mark my words, I will tell the media about Sissy, but I'll tell the police about how you managed to sell my apartment. In case they don't teach basic law in that fancy law school you graduated from, forgery is illegal, Robert."

There was a moment of silence. "You wouldn't do that."

"Why on earth wouldn't I?"

She heard him draw a sharp breath. "You have no way to prove I spent a second alone with Sissy before I divorced you. Or how do you think you're going to prove I forged your signature. It's a perfect match."

"But that's the thing. Someone always knows the truth. You know that staffer you got to notarize my signature on the real estate documents? F. Don Whitting?"

The phone line crackled with a tense silence.

"Do you think for a second that if the district attorney's office starts poking around and asking questions, F. Don isn't going to cave and admit that you made him do it? I know you, Robert. I know how you operate. Plus, I just so happen to have all the proof I need to make a believer out of your constituency about Sissy."

She had obtained that proof of his infidelity from the fired employee.

"You can't do this!"

She nodded to Marcus, who pressed send on an ancient fax machine they still had attached to a second phone line, sending through a photograph showing a very naked Robert and Sissy, with a date stamp in the lower right corner.

"If I were you, Robert, I'd race to your fax machine and snag the proof before someone else sees it."

Robert cursed before the phone clattered on his desk. Portia waited,

Stanley looking smug, Marcus delighted, until her ex-husband came back on the line.

"You can't do this!" he railed.

"Granted, it's a little low-tech in this day and age of sex videos, but I'm guessing it will do the trick. Call your lawyer, Robert. Tell him to release my money or I'll start making some calls of my own. Police first, the Texas press second. You have until the end of the business day."

She hung up before he could respond, and Marcus and Portia danced. Even Stanley smiled.

Forty-five

❖

A S FAR AS Ariel could tell, her dad had really messed things up.
And the guy was supposed to be smart.

Once they got back from New Jersey, instead of solving things, her
dad had gone over to see Portia and obviously made things worse. He
had stormed back into the house and started ripping apart the basement
apartment like a man obsessed with erasing every little bit of the woman
who used to live there.

On top of that, he was erasing even more of their past by putting the
New Jersey house up for sale. She ached a little bit at the idea, because it
was like her mom had finally been put to rest. But she also didn't think she
would ever be able to walk back into that house anyway. So why not sell it?

Now, three days after the whole asthma debacle, she came home from
school to find piles of old linoleum on the front curb, waiting for the
garbage truck. One more piece of Portia ripped away.

She dropped her backpack in the vestibule, then found her dad in
Portia's apartment, the place a wreck. He wore a dust mask and seemed
to be taking the walls apart with a crowbar.

"What is it, Ariel?"

She stood there in the dust and wrecked surroundings, trying to decide the best way to proceed. "How's it going?"

She couldn't read his expression because of the mask, so she just shrugged and walked around the place, just like how she had walked around looking at things the first time she snuck in while Portia and her sisters were sitting around eating.

"Ariel? What do you need? Rosalie made some cake and left it out for you."

Rosalie had started yesterday, replacing Portia. Not to be mean or anything, but nobody could cook like Portia, and they all knew it.

"I'm fine." She shrugged again.

He jammed the crowbar into the top of a piece of molding.

"You know, I was wondering," she said, proud at how casual the words sounded.

He stopped what he was doing and shot her a narrow-eyed look. She refused to let it get to her. This was too important.

"How did you find me? In New Jersey?"

He got that odd look he was getting a lot lately. Ferocious mixed with determination.

"I mean, who would have guessed. New Jersey? Seriously? You found me in New Jersey all by yourself? Ha-ha."

"What are you getting at, Ariel?"

"Me? Getting at something?"

"Spit it out."

And she did. "It just seems to me that you must have had some help."

"Portia told me where to find you." He turned around and gave the molding another sharp jerk. Nails squealed.

Of course she knew that, or at least suspected it, and hadn't she proven she was a majorly great sleuth?

"Really?" She pretended surprise. "How'd she know where I was?"

"She said she knew because of food. And flowers."

He sounded weird, which was super insane since Portia had been doing bizarre things with food ever since she'd landed in their town house,
just as she herself had already told him.

"Portia's good at that, you know, doing uncanny stuff with food," she
reminded him.

He just grunted, attacking the wall again.

"You remember that, right?" Ariel said.

He just gave her a look and told her to go upstairs before he slammed
the crowbar back into another innocent-looking piece of molding.

"Men," she grumbled, marching out the door.

⁘

The weather started getting cold, and it looked like pretty soon it would
start snowing. Her dad just kept ripping away at the garden apartment.
While he'd had a whole crowd of people slaving away on their part of the
town house months earlier, he was using his own two hands to rip apart
the downstairs. Every day he worked down there, and every night he sat
at the kitchen table after she and Miranda had cleared away the food he
had cooked.

Yep, he was cooking again. Rosalie had lasted barely a week before
she had called them impossible and had departed. Ariel and Miranda
had made plans, or colluded, as a good detective would say, to run the
woman off. Sure, both of them felt bad about it, but someone had to do
something to make their dad see the light.

Instead of seeing the light, however, and clattering off to Portia and
convincing her to come back to them, he just added cooking back to his
list of duties. It was insanity, really, since even he admitted he was a horrible cook and they'd probably all keel over with food poisoning any day.
That, or starve.

Even more insane, Miranda had started helping him renovate the garden apartment. No sooner did Miranda get home from school than she
changed and headed downstairs like a regular Mini Me Construction Girl.

Ariel told herself it was ridiculous to be jealous. Dad had *chosen* her to be his daughter, even when he didn't have to.

The other surprise? Uncle Anthony.

"You know I love you, kid, right?" he said to her when he appeared one day in their kitchen, Dad looking like a ferocious, overprotective bear despite the apron he wore, since he was in the middle of making another awful dinner.

Ariel wasn't sure what to say to that. She looked at Anthony closely, trying to decide if he was the kind of guy who wanted the truth or a platitude. The thing was, she didn't have any idea what was in his mind.

"Sure, I know."

He gave her a wry look. "You're just saying that."

"Isn't that what you want to hear?"

"Nope. The fact is, I do love you, kid. Ariel." He glanced over at Dad, then bent down in front of her. "But I make a better uncle than a father. Do you understand that?"

Actually, she did, and she couldn't have agreed more. The tiny knot that had stayed inside her after having read one too many online articles about birth fathers wanting their kids back even after having signed them away eased.

She threw her arms around the guy's shoulders. "Thank you for letting me go, Uncle Anthony."

He held on tight for a long second, nodded at her dad, and left.

Later she had overheard her dad tell Nana that he'd given Anthony the money he wanted, even though all the new and better documents were already signed. Which made her heart buzz even more because her dad wanted her that much. Granted, it was not so buzzworthy that she obviously had a blackmailer's blood sloshing around in her veins. But she figured she was smart enough to beat it back if the need to con money out of people suddenly started rearing its ugly head.

After hanging up with Nana, her dad walked back into the study. He looked surprised to find her there. But she'd finally had it. He had fixed the Anthony thing. He was nearly done fixing the garden apartment. But, hello, why wasn't he taking all of her hints and fixing what was really wrong?

"You know, we've discussed how incredibly smart you are," she said without preamble.

"Why do I suspect I'm not going to like where this is going?" he said cautiously.

"I think you're stressed."

Up shot one of those eyebrows of his.

She hurried on. "Maybe with all that construction stress you're under downstairs, you haven't been totally able to figure out on your own that you need to do whatever it takes to get Portia back. Maybe it'd help if I made a suggestion."

"What kind of suggestion?"

"Groveling."

He skewered her with his eyes. "Groveling?"

"Yep, groveling, to Portia. And don't bother saying you don't grovel, Dad, because really, like I said, you've got to do whatever it takes. We need Portia. I do. Miranda sure as heck does. And, well"—she scrunched her shoulders—"I hate to break it to you, but you need her most of all."

Forty-six

❖

PORTIA STOOD ON Columbus Avenue, arms raised to the gently fall-ing snow, reveling in the mounting signs that her life was falling in place.

After growing up in Central Texas, she had virtually no experience with snow. She tilted her head back, feeling the brush of snowflakes against her skin.

Straightening, she looked into the windows of what used to be Cutie's Cupcakes. The awful pastries had finally taken their toll, and when they did, the place had closed down and the space had gone up for rent. Yet another sign.

First, Robert had actually paid her the money he owed her. Then, just when she was ready to make a move, this perfect space came up for rent.

The minute she saw it, Portia had pulled out her cell phone right there on the street and called Cordelia and Olivia.

Since that day, the three Cuthcart sisters had worked tirelessly around the clock getting The Glass Kitchen ready—the real one, not the illegal one in a residential building. They'd taken on not one but two investors, using Portia's money to hire a financial planner who made everything legal and set up an agreement that made sure Portia's money would be repaid out of the first profits. She planned to buy an apartment of her own as soon as she could.

They were starting out small, mostly baked goods and a few entrées. Hopefully, with a combination of Portia's knowing, Cordelia's chatty advice giving and constant supply of helpful books, and Olivia's ability to fill the space with the perfect assortment of flowers, not to mention network, they would soon be able to expand.

For the moment, Portia was living in a small rented apartment of her own, pretty close to The Glass Kitchen. Everything was going better than expected.

But still, she felt empty, even standing around in falling snow in front of a dream that had finally come true.

Of course, she knew why.

She hadn't heard a single word from Gabriel since he'd walked out of Stanley and Marcus's door a month ago. She should have been relieved. But all she felt was miserable.

Pulling her coat tight, she locked the doors of The Glass Kitchen and hurried the few blocks to her new apartment. Taking off her mittens, she checked her voice mail. The first message surprised her.

"*Portia, hi,*" the recording announced. "*It's Miranda. Miranda Kane.*"

As if Portia could forget.

"*I just thought you should know that Dad is using the kitchen. As in, he's cooking. I talked to Ariel about it, but she's being totally weird. She might have said something about how you, as a self-respecting adult, should be, like, trying to save me and her from Dad's cooking. Or something. All I know is that we are starving over here.*"

Portia heard the sound of Miranda unwrapping a piece of candy, as if her world was moving on and she needed to disconnect but didn't know how to break the tenuous connection. The thought tugged at Portia.

"I'm totally not into missing anyone, but Ariel misses you. I can tell. What-ever. I just thought you should know."

Portia didn't call back. What could she say? The girls had lost so much, and she felt guilty to be part of it. But calling them only prolonged the inevitable. She wouldn't ever be a part of their lives.

The next day she worked all day. The Glass Kitchen was packed. She should have felt joy, but by closing time, she felt a strange sensation, like she was getting sick. Worse, all she could think about was food. More specifically, Gabriel's Meal kept circling back into her head, like some cruel reminder of what she could never have.

The kitchen staff had already left, and Olivia and Cordelia had de-parted early, though not before Olivia had shaken her by the shoulders.

"Portia, you know I love you, but you have to stop moping around."

Portia could hardly argue, so she just gave her a lopsided smile.

"Yes, you do," Cordelia had added, gathering her things. "And may I point out that while the store is crowded, it's crowded with *widows*, Portia."

"What?"

Olivia bustled close. "You didn't notice? It's not just widows. There was that poor woman whose son just died after a heart operation."

Portia did remember—how could she not, when the woman had burst into tears at the sight of the cupcakes with little trains on them that she had made. They had both cried before the woman took away six cup-cakes so her family could celebrate her little boy's favorite treat.

"What are you saying?" Portia asked carefully.

"It's like all your buckets of sadness are bringing lines of mourners to The Glass Kitchen," Cordelia explained. "It's not bad, Portia. Lord knows, you're making them feel better. But I kind of miss a smile now and then, you know?"

Her sisters left her standing there speechless, until she finally turned around and started cleaning an already clean counter. A week's worth of customers started marching through her head—the eighty-year-old man with the exhausted eyes, the two women whose mother had just passed away . . .

"Crap," she said when she realized her sisters were mostly right. But the customers had all been grieving for someone they had lost. There was that man whose wife left him with a devastated five-year-old son, and that teenager who . . .

She snapped to attention when the bell rang and the door opened.

"We're not open—"

As she spoke, she turned and froze. Her hair was wild from a day of cooking and baking, and now cleaning. She looked awful and she knew it.

"Gabriel." She hated the breathy sound of her voice, the way her heart kicked up.

Of course he was still beautiful in that way she loved. Hard, craggy. Strong, as if with him she would always be safe. That was what had drawn her to him, right from the beginning. A beast would never let anyone hurt her.

Until he had.

"We're closed."

"Good," he said.

He made the point by turning over the little sign tacked to the door with yarn. "Now you really are closed."

"Which means you should be on the outside of the door. Not inside."

He flipped the lock.

Portia watched him, her eyes narrowing. "What do you think you're doing?"

"What I should have done weeks ago."

He had that way of seeming to catalog each part of her, as if reassuring himself that she was fine, that no harm had come to her in the weeks they had been apart. Portia stayed behind the counter, telling herself that she was above bolting for the side exit. She would deal with him as the adult she was.

"Gabriel," she said as he walked toward her, stopping on the opposite side of the narrow counter. "I really don't want to have another argument. Please."

"I messed up, Portia."

He'd already told her that, but this time, there was no anger in the words, only a commitment to truth.

"You said I didn't believe in you, that I didn't want you to be who you really are. I am going to prove that you're wrong. I do believe in you. I love you, Portia. I love you for every streak of frosting on your face. . . ." He bent over the gaily painted counter tiles and reached out to wipe her cheek, his thumb coming away with frosting. She was mortified until he licked the buttercream away, and her pulse leaped.

"I love you for each of the times you pushed me to see some truth I didn't want to face. For loving me just as I am. For taking care of my girls. For helping me save both of them."

His hand slid back into her hair and he leaned closer, his mouth hovering over hers. "I am going to prove to you that I listen. I am going to prove that I love you in that madly, deeply, let-you-eat-crackers-in-my-bed, shouting-Stella-from-the-courtyard sort of way."

Tears burned at the proof he had listened, at least to that.

"I love you for who you are. But I can't prove it to you here. Come to the town house, then I will prove it."

She managed to dash away the threat of tears. "You can't come in here and ask me to go to your house at the snap of your fingers." She raised her chin. "We are no longer friends with benefits, Gabriel. I'm sorry."

His features cemented, but not with anger. "We were never friends with benefits, Portia."

"Oh, that's right. We were fu—"

"Enough."

He said the word quietly, but with a strength that resonated through the café. "I love you, and the only thing that's *crazy* is if you think I'm going to let the best thing that ever happened to me walk out of my life."

He bent to her again and his hands ran down her arms. "Come home with me. Let me prove how much you mean to me."

When she started to resist, he shrugged. With one swift movement he lifted her over the counter as if she weighed nothing, putting her on her feet before him.

She shrieked with the surprise of it. At the same time, visions of the meal, Gabriel's Meal, danced through her head, taunting her.

"I can't," she breathed.

"Wrong answer," he told her, and actually smiled.

He bent down and had her over his shoulder before she realized what was happening.

"Put me down!"

"Sorry. Can't. If you won't walk on your own, I'll have to carry you."

"You can't carry me to your house like this," she snapped, bracing herself against his back and flailing her legs, trying to get down. "You'll get arrested!"

"If a cop stops me, I'll tell them what you've put me through and they'll drag you to the house for me."

"Ha-ha. If I tell them what you've put me through, they'd arrest *you* *and* throw away the key."

"Portia. I'm serious. One way or another, you're coming with me."

She made all sorts of outraged noises, but his grip only tightened, like a vise around her legs, and she realized she wasn't going to win this one.

"Are you going to walk?" he asked. "Or do I carry you?"

"Has anyone ever told you cavemen aren't attractive?"

"As a matter of fact, Ariel says pretty much the same thing all the time."

Instantly, she softened, her body easing on his shoulder. "How is she?"

"Missing you."

"Playing the guilt card?"

"Just telling the truth. Now, can I put you down so you can get your bag or whatever else you need? Or am I going to carry you home?"

He barely gave her a minute to get her coat and handbag.

"Front door's already locked," he said. "We'll go out the side door."

She glowered at him, but he remained unfazed, and all too soon they were walking up Columbus Avenue. He took her hand. She yanked it away, only to have him take it again.

"The caveman thing. Unattractive. Remember?"

He just laughed, pulled her hand up to his mouth, and kissed it. She hated that it felt good.

When they arrived on Seventy-third Street, the lights in the town house reminded her of how much she loved the place, standing tall like a wedding cake stacked up into the night sky, snow beginning to accumulate like icing on the window panes and eves.

Gabriel pulled her around to face him, his hand slipping into her hair and tugging her head back so he could see her eyes. "This is your home, Portia. You belong here. With me. With us."

She thought he was going to kiss her, but at the last minute, he pulled back. "First things first," he whispered.

They took the steps to the outer vestibule. She was surprised when he led her down to the garden apartment instead of straight inside to his apartment. The smell of fresh paint hit her first. Then she noticed the refinished hardwood floor on the stairs, the quaint welcome mat outside the open front door. Then she heard the sound of people.

"What's going on?" she demanded, her hand flying to her hair.

"You'll see."

"I'm a wreck!" she moaned, hanging back.

"Am I going to have to put you over my shoulder again?"

"You wouldn't dare."

He went for her, but she scampered back up a step. "Bossy."

"Stubborn."

It took a second for her mind to register all the people inside. Ariel, Miranda. Cordelia and Olivia. Even Stanley and Marcus.

Abruptly, the others became aware of her.

"Portia!"

She blinked, trying to take it in. Her friends and family were standing in the garden apartment . . . which had been completely redone.

"Don't you love it?" Ariel cried, flinging herself forward and winding her arms around Portia's waist. "Dad did it all himself."

Miranda nodded. "With his own hands."

Ariel stepped back. "Same thing, Mir."

"It's beautiful," Portia said, awed.

"It's your dream," Ariel explained, hands on her hips, looking bossy and worried, at the same time. "Not all perfect and professional like those people did upstairs. Dad took everything out, did it just like you wanted, then brought all the old junk back in, fixed up, cleaned up."

"Just as you described," Gabriel said, his voice deep with emotion. "I listened, Portia."

He had, that time they had lain together after making love, talking about her vision for the apartment.

"Oh, Gabriel, I don't know what to say."

Gabriel stepped forward and took her hands. "Portia, this is your home. The people here, we are your family. And in this town house, you have cooked or baked or done something for each person here. So I asked everyone to make something for you to show their thanks."

It was then that she noticed the table, set with the pitted silverware and mismatched dishes.

Stanley straightened, after placing a dish on the table. He took one look at her and grimaced. "Good Lord, woman, is that frosting in your hair?"

"Mind your manners, old man." This from Marcus, who was making room on the table for a platter.

"I can't tell you the last time I did anything in a kitchen," Stanley said, jutting out his chin. "But I did, for you. Because you're a dear," he added. "So I decided that I would make the one recipe I know. Sweet jalapeño mustard."

A jolt went through Portia.

"Can you believe it?" Marcus said. "A New Yorker who makes anything with jalapeños?"

"As you well know, I was born and raised in Texas. I might be old, but I still remember my mother's sweet jalapeño mustard."

Marcus wrapped a lanky arm around his partner's stooped shoulders. "Yes, once upon a time you were a good ol' boy from south of the Mason-Dixon Line. I made my fried chicken for you, Portia, to go with my beloved's mustard."

A chill ran down her spine.

"Miranda and I made biscuits!" Ariel cheered.

Portia couldn't move. She felt Olivia looking at her for a long beat, her brow furrowing. Then Olivia laughed and came forward, taking her hands, pulling her close, pressing her forehead to Portia's. "Some things are true whether you believe them or not," Olivia whispered just for her.

Portia's breath let out in a rush; then she threw her arms around her sister.

She then pivoted to face Gabriel. "But how did you know?"

His brow furrowed. "Know what?"

"The meal. You—this is the meal. It's *your* meal."

"What are you talking about? I just asked everyone to bring something for you, something they could make, something that meant something to them."

Portia swept her gaze over the table. The slaw was there, the buttery mashed potatoes. Each item from Gabriel's Meal sat on the table, just as she had seen it in her mind—this menu, in this garden apartment that she had loved since she was a child.

She didn't realize Gabriel had gone to the kitchen until she turned and found him reappearing. Before she could say anything, he held out a dish. "Strawberry pie—"

"With fresh whipped cream," Portia breathed.

"I made it," he said. "Can't swear to how good it is, but I know you love strawberries, and the girls say it's the only thing I've made in a month that was half edible."

"I can't believe it," Portia whispered. "*You* were the ones who were supposed to make the meal. Not me. That's why mine didn't work."

She looked at each person in turn, and then finally at Gabriel. "This is the meal that came to me when I first saw you on the steps. The meal I tried to make, but ruined."

She didn't wait another second. She ran to Gabriel, throwing her arms around him. "We're meant to be."

He tipped her head back. "It's the meal, the food, that's what convinced you?"

"Yes." Portia hesitated, holding her breath. "Do you understand?"

He looked into her eyes, really looked. Then he smiled. "What I understand is that the rest of my life will be filled with food, food that answers questions that haven't been asked yet, food that you know we need before we know why." He lowered his voice. "You're mine, Portia, and have been since the day I found you on the steps in your flowered shoes."

There was a universal groan, and Gabriel glanced over, as if he'd forgotten anyone else was there.

"What?" he demanded.

Ariel spoke up first. "Maybe think about asking her if she *wants* to be yours."

Portia only laughed. "The way I look at it," she said, "*he's* mine. The truth of a meal never lies. Seems only fair that I give back as good as I get."

Gabriel wrapped her in his arms then and kissed her, a deep claim mixed with an even deeper love and respect.

"Get a room," Olivia demanded with an amused smile.

"Seriously?" Miranda added.

"Sheez," Ariel chimed in.

"Come, sit, Portia," Cordelia said, taking charge. "Let's eat before it gets cold."

They gathered around the table and ate the meal, every last bite.

Later that night, Portia didn't return to the tiny rented apartment on Columbus Avenue. She stayed in the garden apartment and crawled into the old bed Gabriel had restored for her. Joy filled her for the first time in weeks when the man she was meant to be with climbed down the fire escape and into her room.

"Girls in bed?" she asked, sitting up.

He nodded and lay down next to her, pulling her to him. "I'm never letting you leave again," he whispered.

"No more secrets?"

"No more secrets."

"Can you really live with me knowing things are needed before we know why?"

He rolled on top of her, his hands framing her face. "I wouldn't have it any other way."

Then he kissed her, long and deep, and Portia knew she had truly found her home.

Sixth Course

❖

Dessert

Mountains of Wildly Sweet Watermelon
with Fresh Violet Garnish

Forty-seven

❖❖❖

T HE GLASS DOOR OPENED, ringing the old-fashioned bell over the entrance to The Glass Kitchen. But the café was closed, and the customer was told to come back the next day.

Miranda was doing homework, Portia frosting a cake. Cordelia was setting one of the long tables with old silver and mismatched earthenware, while Olivia was arranging flowers and playing around with some sort of new software.

Ariel sat hidden in a small area in the back that had yet to be organized. No one in The Glass Kitchen knew she was there. She hadn't meant to stay out of sight. But when she came in through the side door, everyone was so busy that no one noticed her.

She sighed at the thought, hating the possibility that she would always be disappearing, an adjunct to these people, not ever completely a part of them.

But the minute the thought flitted through her head, she realized what the cake Portia was frosting was for. Her birthday. Today she was thirteen.

Ariel had sat down on an overturned plastic bucket, shocked. All these people were throwing a surprise party for her. So she stayed out of sight while they finished preparing, even though the brand-new cell phone her dad had gotten her kept vibrating because Miranda was texting her over and over, wondering where she was. Ariel watched and listened as they talked about making all of her favorite things.

Her life had changed so much in the last few months. As the *New York Times* food critic had written, "The Glass Kitchen, owned and operated by three Texas sisters who create magical food in a world that sometimes spins too fast, is a must for demanding New Yorkers."

The original Glass Kitchen cookbooks were kept in a country cupboard near the old-fashioned register, and were going to be published next year. Portia might have hidden them away in a closet for the first months she was here, but now Ariel found her poring over them almost every day.

The bigger change had come when Portia married her dad and moved in with them. Slowly Portia was turning the whole place into what even Ariel could see was going to be a real home.

When she saw everything was ready, Ariel nearly chirped with excitement, pulling out her phone and finally answering one of her sister's texts.

"Ariel will be here any minute," Miranda shouted, excited in a way that was still hard to believe.

But Portia had pulled Miranda into her circle, which made Ariel wonder if all along Miranda hadn't felt a little bit invisible, too.

"Is everyone ready?" Portia asked. She was rubbing her stomach again, the way she'd started to now that she was carrying around a baby in there.

At first, Ariel had been jealous, afraid her dad and Portia having a baby would crowd her out. But watching everyone talk about Ariel's favorite things made her realize she wasn't being as incredibly smart as she really was to think that.

She saw her dad walk over and pull Portia close, putting his big hand over hers. "Ready," he said.

Ariel knew that was her cue.

She slipped out the side and started to run the short distance to the front door, but forced herself to calm down. Then, taking a deep breath, she walked the last few feet to the front of The Glass Kitchen and stepped inside.

The bell rang overhead. She watched as Dad and Portia, Cordelia and Olivia, Miranda, and Marcus and Stan, whipped around. Even her grandmother Helen was there, still sad that Uncle Anthony had moved to Spain, but sort of resigned. Dad, with Portia's help, or maybe her insistence, had been trying to include Nana in more of their family dinners. Good luck with that, Ariel had swallowed back more than once.

At the sight of her, the whole crew's eyes lit up.

"Surprise!" they cheered.

Ariel slapped her hand to her chest and gasped. "Oh, my gosh! For me?"

Portia raised an eyebrow, and Ariel knew that her new stepmom saw right through her. Ariel just smiled as everyone crowded around her, bellowing the Happy Birthday song, Marcus and Olivia doing a good job of hamming it up. As soon as they were done, Ariel's dad came over and picked her up, twirling her around. "Happy Birthday, sweetheart. You're now officially thirteen."

She held on tight, relishing the fact that he was her dad. No one could take her away from him. They had legal papers to prove it.

He set her down and guided her to the table. All of her favorite foods marched down the center like an ordered list of prime numbers. Or maybe not, she amended. Maybe the dishes were lined up like grilled cheese sandwiches and tomato soup, cupcakes, banana pudding. And watermelon. Mountains of wildly sweet watermelon littered with violet petals, and even a centerpiece made from those same purple flowers.

Watermelon and violets.

She felt her eyes get hot, because it was like Portia had made sure her mom was there, too. And then, proving the point, Portia's arms went around her from behind and she said, "I'm so happy that she led me to you, sweetie."

Ariel leaned back into her, holding on to her hands.

The day Portia and Dad got married, Portia told her that they were one big family now.

"We're like a big pot of vegetable stew," Portia told her that day. "All the better for the mix of different flavors, even if it's messy."

Everyone started talking to her at once then, asking her questions, handing her presents. In one way or another, all these people here in The Glass Kitchen, all of them mixed together, big and messy, looked at her, saw her. She realized then that Portia was right. This had been the solution to her problem all along, because a big, messy mix of family like this would never let her disappear.

THE GLASS KITCHEN MENU

◈

First Course
Appetizer
Chile Cheese and Bacon-Stuffed
Cherry Tomatoes

Second Course
Soup
Crab and Sweet Corn Chowder

Third Course
Salad
Grapefruit and Avocado Salad with
Poppy Seed Dressing

Fourth Course
Palate Cleanser
Blood Orange Ice

Fifth Course
The Entrée
Fried Chicken with Sweet Jalapeño Mustard

Sixth Course
Dessert
Mountains of Wildly Sweet Watermelon with
Fresh Violet Garnish

❖ *First Course* ❖

Appetizer

Chile Cheese and Bacon-Stuffed Cherry Tomatoes

INGREDIENTS

20 cherry tomatoes

½ lb. bacon, cooked and crumbled

⅓ cup chopped green chilies (Old El Paso canned works well)

½ cup grated mix of Asadero or Monterey Jack cheese with
   Cheddar cheese

DIRECTIONS

Preheat oven to 350°F. Carefully cut off a thin slice from the top of each tomato. Hollow out the pulp, leaving a thin layer inside, and discard the extra pulp. Turn the tomatoes upside down on a paper towel to drain. In a bowl, combine all the remaining ingredients. Mix well. Spoon the mixture into the tomatoes. Spray a cookie sheet with nonstick vegetable spray. Place the tomatoes on the cookie sheet. Bake approximately 15 minutes, or until the cheese is melty.

❖ *Second Course* ❖

Soup

Crab and Sweet Corn Chowder

INGREDIENTS

4 strips of bacon

2 tbsp. butter

½ cup yellow onion, chopped

½ cup carrot, chopped

½ cup celery, chopped

4 cups frozen yellow corn kernels, thawed

4 cups whole milk

3 cups low-salt chicken broth

1 medium potato, peeled and diced

Pinch of cayenne pepper

1 bay leaf

Salt and pepper to taste

6 tbsp. sour cream

½ lb. freshly cooked crab meat, cut into bite-sized pieces

DIRECTIONS

In a large saucepan, sauté the bacon until crisp. Place the bacon on a paper towel to drain. Pour off all but one tablespoon of bacon renderings. Add 1 tablespoon. butter, melt. Sauté the onion until soft. Add the carrots and celery; cook for 5 minutes. Set aside. Purée two cups of corn. Now, add all the corn to the onion, carrots, and celery. Mix thoroughly. Add the milk, broth, potatoes, cayenne pepper, and bay leaf, plus half of the crumbled, crisp bacon. Bring to a boil. Reduce the heat, cover, and simmer for 20 minutes. Remove the bay leaf. Add salt and pepper to taste.

Continue to simmer for an additional 10 minutes. Set the pan aside and let cool slightly. Stir in the sour cream.

Melt 1 tablespoon of butter in skillet. Sauté crab meat until heated.

Spoon the crab into bowls. Pour soup gently on top. Garnish with crumbled bacon.

Serves 6

Note: For a real Texas kick, season to taste with hot red pepper sauce.

❖ *Third Course* ❖

Salad

Grapefruit and Avocado Salad with Poppy Seed Dressing

INGREDIENTS

  3 ripe, sweet grapefruits
  3 ripe avocados
  6 leaves butter lettuce

DIRECTIONS

Cut the grapefruits in half crosswise. Use a knife to cut grapefruit sections from the membrane. Cut the avocados in half. Remove the seed. Peel off the skin. Slice avocados into long slices.

Poppy Seed Dressing

INGREDIENTS

⅓ cup sugar

½ cup vinegar

1 tsp. salt

1 tsp. ground dry mustard

1 cup olive oil

1 tbsp. poppy seeds

DIRECTIONS

Vigorously blend sugar, vinegar, salt, and mustard until the sugar dissolves. While still blending, slowly add the oil. When mixed, gently stir in the poppy seeds.

Makes approximately 1½ cups.

Place one butter lettuce leaf on individual plates. Place grapefruit sections and avocado slices on each lettuce leaf. Drizzle the poppy seeding dressing on top.

Serves 6

❖ Fourth Course ❖

Palate Cleanser

Blood Orange Ice

INGREDIENTS

   3 cups freshly squeezed blood orange juice (or use tangerines or
      oranges)
   ½ cup sugar
   Juice of 2 large limes—adjust based on sweetness of oranges—the
      sweeter the orange the more lime needed
   2 tbsp. orange liqueur
   1 tbsp. kirsch
   Vodka (optional)

DIRECTIONS

In a mixing bowl, stir together 1 cup blood orange juice and the sugar
until they are thoroughly dissolved. Stir in the remaining blood orange
juice, lime juice, orange liqueur, and kirsch. Mix thoroughly.

Pour the mixture into gallon-size plastic zip bags. Before zipping closed,
squeeze out as much air as possible. Freeze overnight.

Take the bags out of the freezer; manipulate the bags with your hands
just a bit to loosen up the ice. With a fork, break up then ice into small
chunks. (The consistency should be icy slush.) Spoon into glasses. Top
with splash of vodka if desired.

Serves 6

❖ *Fifth Course* ❖

The Entrée

Fried Chicken with Sweet Jalapeño Mustard

INGREDIENTS

2 cups panko

2 cups bread crumbs

Seasoned salt, salt and pepper to taste

2 to 3 eggs, scrambled (can use yogurt or buttermilk instead)

6 boneless, skinless chicken breasts (use kitchen mallet to pound
  into flat, even pieces)

6 boneless, skinless chicken thighs (use kitchen mallet to pound
  into flat, even pieces)

Vegetable oil for pan frying

DIRECTIONS:

Mix the panko, bread crumbs, and seasoning in a bowl for dipping, or
a bag for shaking.

Dip the pieces of chicken into the egg to coat; then dip in the bowl of
crumb mix. Coat the chicken in the mixture. (For extra-crispy chicken,
repeat the dipping steps.) Place the prepared chicken on a cookie sheet.

Cover the bottom of a large skillet with a thin layer of vegetable oil.
Heat on medium-high until hot. Carefully fill the bottom of the pan
with chicken pieces. Brown, approximately 4 to 6 minutes each side (de-
pending on the thickness of the chicken), until cooked thoroughly. Place
on a paper towel to drain.

Serves 6

Sweet Jalapeño Mustard

INGREDIENTS

  6 tbsp. mustard seeds

  ½ cup mustard powder

  3 tbsp. vinegar

  ½ cup white wine

  2 tsp. salt

  2 tbsp. honey

  2 tbsp. finely chopped jalapeños

DIRECTIONS

Stir together the mustard seeds and mustard powder. Mix with the vinegar and wine. Add the salt. Mix thoroughly. Mix in the honey and jalapeños. Pour the mixture into a jar. Refrigerate anywhere from 1 to 3 days to bring out flavors.

Makes approximately 1 cup

❖ *Sixth Course* ❖

Dessert

Mountains of Wildly Sweet Watermelon
with Fresh Violet Garnish

INGREDIENTS

  One whole, sweet watermelon

  Sprigs of violets, washed and stems removed

DIRECTIONS:

Lay the watermelon on the counter. Cut out two top sections, leaving a "handle" of the outer shell along the top length of the watermelon. Carefully hollow out the watermelon until left with a "watermelon basket." Cut the watermelon meat into bite-size pieces and return to the "basket." Place violets on top to garnish and serve.

❖

THE NOVELS OF
MRS APHRA BEHN

THE NOVELS OF
MRS APHRA BEHN

WITH AN INTRODUCTION BY

ERNEST A. BAKER, M.A.

40279
LONDON
GEORGE ROUTLEDGE AND SONS, LIMITED
NEW YORK: E. P. DUTTON & CO.

Printed in Great Britain at
The Mayflower Press, Plymouth.   William Brendon & Son, Ltd.

CONTENTS

CONTENTS

INTRODUCTION

To most people nowadays the name of Aphra Behn conveys nothing more intelligible than certain vague associations of license and impropriety. She is dimly remembered as the author of plays and novels, now unread, that embodied the immorality of Restoration times, and were all the more scandalous in that they were written by a woman. Her works are to be found in few libraries, and are rarely met with at the booksellers'. Although they were republished in an expensive form and in a limited edition in 1871, they have now been many years out of print. Nor is this much to be regretted. Her novels are worth reprinting now and again, not because they are more clever, but because they are less offensive to modern taste than her comedies; and in addition to their intrinsic merits, they have an interest for the student of literature. But a general reprint of the plays would hardly be justified, at least, in anything like a cheap and popular form. This is a case where, for many reasons, it is best to have one's reading done by proxy.

The obstacles which she herself has set to our appreciation have done her an injustice. In dismissing her merely as a purveyor of scandalous amusement in a profligate age, we are apt to give her none of the credit due to a long career of arduous work and of persevering struggle against adverse circumstances. Mrs. Behn was not only the first Englishwoman who became a novelist and a playwright, but the first of all those numerous women who have earned their livelihood by their pens.

We can form a better idea of the once popular Astrea from her works than from the scanty memorials that have come down to us; more is known of her personal character than about the events of her life. The so-called *History of the Life and Memoirs of Mrs. Aphra Behn, written by one of the Fair Sex*, and prefixed to the collection of her histories and novels published in 1735, is rather of the nature of a eulogium and of a vindication from certain aspersions on her conduct and originality than of any biographical value. The admiring writer, although she describes herself as an intimate friend, seems to have known less about her subject than the average journalist who is called upon to produce an obituary notice in a hurry, and to have pressed into her service a great deal of gossip, with letters, presumably written by Mrs. Behn, but undated, recounting tender episodes from Astrea's own history and that of her acquaintances, which read more like studies for her novels than authentic epistles. Astrea, probably, whilst she affected to pour out the secrets of her heart into the bosom of her friend, preferred to wrap the actual incidents of her life in romantic obscurity. Thus we are told that "She was a gentlewoman by birth, of a good family in the city of Canterbury in Kent; her father's name was Johnson, whose relation to the Lord Willoughby drew him for the advantageous post of Lieutenant-General of many isles, besides the continent of Surinam, from his quiet retreat at Canterbury, to run the hazardous voyage of the West-Indies. With him he took his chief riches, his wife and children, and in that number, Afra, his promising darling, our future heroine, and admired Astrea, who even in the first bud of infancy discovered such early hopes of her riper years, that she was equally her parents' joy and fears." But the recent discovery of Aphra's baptismal register has shown that she was born at Wye, and that her father was a barber; and, furthermore, whoever the friend or relative was with whom she went to Surinam, there is little reason to believe that he was her father. However that may be, this protector died on the voyage out; whilst the family did not return forthwith, but settled at St. John's Hill, the best house in Surinam—a house described very seductively in the pages of *Oroonoko*. Here befell the chapter of tragic events afterwards related, with a certain amount of idealisation, in the story of that famous negro prince. "One of the fair sex" makes it her business to defend Astrea from the scandalous gossip that arose about her friendship for Oroonoko—quite an unnecessary task. When the colony was ceded to the Dutch, Aphra, an attractive girl of eighteen, returned to England. As a matter of fact, this was before the Restoration, but her fair biographer states that she gave Charles II. "so pleasant and rational an account of his affairs there, and particularly of the misfortunes of Oroonoko, that he desired her to deliver them publicly to the world, and was satisfied of her abilities in the management of business, and the fidelity of our heroine to his interest." It was most likely through her marriage, later on, to Mr. Behn, a Dutchman who had become a wealthy merchant of the city of London, that she gained admittance to the Court. By the year 1666 he was dead, and Astrea was sent by the Government as a secret agent to the Low Countries, which were then at war with England.

Her memoirist gives a flowery account of her love adventures in Antwerp, with the letters of one of her suitors, Van Bruin—who was about twice the age and bulk of a more favoured lover, Van der Albert—and Astrea's replies. The episode and the letters, as they are given us, are like the burlesque of some tale of high-flown sentiment. "Most Transcendent Charmer," writes that elephantine euphuist, Van Bruin, "I have strove often to tell you the tempests of my heart, and with my own mouth scale the walls of your affections; but terrified with the strength of your fortifications, I concluded to make more regular approaches, and first attack you at a farther distance, and try first what a bombardment of letters would do; whether these carcasses of love, thrown into the sconces of your eyes, would break into the midst of your breast, beat down the court of guard of your aversion, and blow up the magazine of your cruelty, that you might be brought to a capitulation, and yield upon reasonable terms." This warlike language, perhaps, derives some appropriateness from the fact that the bulky Dutchman was addressing one of his country's foes. But Van Bruin was at no loss for metaphors, and he goes on to compare his inamorata, somewhat indelicately, with a ship, in a style that reminds one of a facetious dialogue in *Sam Slick*, clinching the simile with a rhetorical appeal: "Is it not a pity that so spruce a ship should be unmanned, should lie in the harbour for want of her crew?" Though she had the cruelty to encourage this "Most Magnificent Hero," as she addresses him in her reply, by answering him in the same rhapsodical vein, Mrs. Behn eventually dismissed him, and turned her attention to Albert. What follows is too like an incident repeatedly utilised in her comedies, and taxes credulity to the utmost. Albert, as wicked a young man as any of her favourite heroes, Willmore, Wilding, or the Rover, is already married, but has deserted his bride on the wedding day. To punish him Mrs. Behn contrives, like Isabella in *Measure for Measure*, to put the forsaken wife in her place, but, unfortunately, without succeeding in re-tying the marriage knot. Albert's subsequent stratagem for retaliating the affront in kind upon Astrea, is discomfited in a farcical manner by the substitution of a young gallant for the heroine.

The end of it was that Mrs. Behn promised to marry Albert, but before the union could be consummated he died; and soon after she returned to England, all but losing her life by shipwreck on the way. Her services as a spy had met with a severe snub from the Government. Through Van der Albert she had obtained early information of De Witt's intended raid upon the Thames. Though she sent instant intelligence of this to London, her warning was treated with ridicule; the Dutch fleet sailed, and she had the painful satisfaction of seeing her accuracy verified by the misfortunes of her country. She seems to have received no reward from the Government, and having been left by her husband without means, she now found herself obliged to write for a living. Henceforward tragedies, comedies, novels, and poems came in rapid succession from her pen. No literary task came amiss to her: she translated Van Dale's Latin *History of Oracles*, La Rochefoucauld's *Maxims*, and Fontenelle's *Plurality of Worlds*, prefixing to the last an able essay on translated prose. She collaborated in an English translation of Ovid's *Heroical Epistles* in 1683; and few occasions of public rejoicing passed uncelebrated by an ode from Astrea. The brief memoir already quoted contains a series of perfervid letters, signed Astrea, to one Lycidas, who appears to have treated her advances with indifference. Doubtless, her life was as free and unconventional for the seventeenth century as that of certain emancipated women of letters was for the nineteenth ; but we must not suppose her own conduct was as irregular as the life depicted in her comedies. Let the warm affection of her friend speak once more as to her personal character :—

She was of a generous and open temper, something passionate, very serviceable to her friends in all that was in her power ; and could sooner forgive an injury than do one. She was mistress of all the pleasing arts of conversation, but used 'em not to any but those who love plain-dealing. She was a woman of sense, and by consequence a lover of pleasure, as indeed all, both men and women, are ; but only some would be thought to be above the conditions of humanity, and place their chief pleasure in a proud vain hypocrisy. For my part, I knew her intimately, and never saw aught unbecoming the just modesty of our sex, tho' more gay and free than the folly of the precise will allow. She was, I'm satisfied, a greater honour to our sex than all the canting tribe of dissemblers that die with the false reputation of saints.

She died on the 16th of April, 1689, and was buried in Westminster Abbey, the marble slab that covered her being inscribed with "two wretched verses," made, so her friend relates, "by a very ingenious gentleman, tho' no poet— the very person whom the envious of our sex, and the malicious of the other, would needs have the author of most of hers." The person referred to is the playwright, Edward Ravenscroft, with whom she was on very intimate terms. There is no reason to believe that he was the author or part-author of any of her works, although he wrote a number of her epilogues.

It is usual to add a piquancy to reminiscences of ladies who write by giving particulars as to their earnings. All that we may be sure of in the case of Mrs. Aphra Behn is that she must have obtained a good deal more by her plays than by her novels. In her collected works, the latter are scarcely able to fill out two volumes of large print ; whereas the former occupy four thick and closely printed volumes, even with the omission of one or two inferior productions. Then, as now, there was a huge disproportion between the profits of fiction and of writing for the stage. Astrea's first attempt was a tragedy, written partly in rhyme and partly in prose, and entitled *The Young King; or, the Mistake*. It was adapted from a romance by La Calprenède. The scene is Dacia; the Dacians and the Scythians are at war; and the *dramatis personæ* consist of the hostile princes and their soldiers, with a crowd of shepherds and shepherdesses. No further description is necessary. The play failed to obtain either a manager or a publisher. Her next effort was more fortunate. This was *The Forc'd Marriage; or, the Jealous Bridegroom*, a tragi-comedy in blank verse, which was produced at the Duke's Theatre in 1671. Betterton and his wife took the part of the two lovers, and young Otway, a boy from college, appeared on the boards for the first and only time as the king. I need say no more about this work than that the scene is laid "within the Court of France," and the characters bear such names as Alcippus, Orgulius, Cleontius, Galatea. A very gross and immoral comedy, *The Amorous Prince*, was brought out the same year at the Duke's Theatre, and afterwards published.

An equally objectionable play, *The Dutch Lover*, was published in 1673. Here, though she drew upon her Dutch experiences in depicting the boorish Haunce van Ezel, a sort of gasconading Van Bruin, there is not much advance in realism. The plot is a series of errors of identity, blunders in the dark, mistaken relationships, with the ensuing complications. We have a man in love with his supposed sister, and engaged in mortal combat with his alleged brother; a gallant colonel impersonating the Dutch fop, in order to secure a bride with whom he falls in love by accident; stage tears, and conventional passion to excess. But if the incidents are far-fetched, they are brought about with exemplary skill. In spite of its intricacy, the plot is clearly developed; the dialogue is smooth and tripping, always lively, and sometimes witty. The play has, at all events, one excellence—that of workmanship. The blank verse, however, and the serious passages generally, are the most arrant bombast.

The next play was all in blank verse. *Abdelazar; or, the Moor's Revenge*, which was played at the Duke's Theatre in 1676, is an adaptation of the old tragedy, *Lust's Dominion*, erroneously ascribed to Marlowe; it reads like a travesty of *Macbeth*, ambition, however, playing in the long run a secondary part to sexual passion, as might be expected in a drama by Mrs. Behn. The usurper who murders his trusting sovereign, and puts to death all who oppose his way to the throne, is the Moorish chieftain, Abdelazar; and the woman who assists at his career of crime, and hopes to reign by his side, is the wife of the betrayed king. She helps on the death of her husband to pave the way for her paramour, and then by coquetting with another lover paralyses the opposition to Abdelazar. He meanwhile makes a handle of the new king's passion for his own wife, whom he loves, but sacrifices without a scruple to ambition. His rivals are overthrown, the crown of Spain is in his grasp, the infamous queen is no longer of use as an instrument of his villainy. He murders her. But, according to the ideas of Mrs. Behn and her public, what swayed most potently the greatest saint and the greatest sinner was sexual passion. The ferocious Abdelazar, who has slaughtered friend and foe without a qualm, now gives way to a fatal madness for the daughter of the royal house, throws the crown into her lap, and becomes the prey of his enemies.

This is a theme worthy of the early unchastened Elizabethans, Marlowe, Nash, and Kyd, who preceded Shakespeare, or of the school of Dryden, who succeeded him; it is what the age considered a pre-eminently tragic theme. As Mrs. Behn treated it, *Abdelazar* is merely rant and melodrama, masquerading as tragedy. Yet there are echoes of Elizabethan poetry in the distichs at the end of the scenes; and some of the lyrics are pure in feeling. Let me quote two, the second of them a favourite of Mr. Swinburne's, who justly styles it "that melodious and magnificent song."

I

Make haste, Amyntas, come away,
The sun is up and will not stay;
And oh ! how very short's a lover's day !
Make haste, Amyntas, to this grove,
Beneath whose shade so oft I've sat,
And heard my dear lov'd swain repeat
How much he Galatea lov'd;
Whilst all the list'ning birds around,
Sung to the music of the blessed sound.
Make haste, Amyntas, come away,
The sun is up and will not stay;
And oh ! how very short's a lover's day !

II

Love in fantastic triumph sat,
  Whilst bleeding hearts around him flow'd,
For whom fresh pains he did create,
  And strange tyrannic power he showed ;
From thy bright eyes he took his fires,
  Which round about in sport he hurl'd ;
But 'twas from mine he took desires,
  Enough t' undo the amorous world.

From me he took his sighs and tears,
  From thee his pride and cruelty ;
From me his languishments and fears,
  And every killing dart from thee ;
Thus thou and I the god have arm'd,
  And set him up a deity ;
But my poor heart alone is harm'd,
  Whilst thine the victor is, and free.

Often in reading *Abdelazar* one seems to recognise a suggestion from Shakespeare used or misused, travestied, yet not deprived entirely of dramatic force. Edmund, in *King Lear*, is brought to mind when we read :

> *Abd.* So I thank thee, Nature, that in making me
> Thou did'st design me villain,
> Hitting each faculty for active mischief :
> Thou skilful artist, thank thee for my face,
> It will discover nought that's hid within.
> Thus arm'd for ills,
> Darkness and Horror, I invoke your aid ;
> And thou dread Night, shade all your busy stars
> In blackest clouds,
> And let my dagger's brightness only serve
> To guide me to the mark, and guide it so,
> It may undo a kingdom at one blow.

Abdelazar's speech before the king's murder, on the other hand, is a crude parody of the famous prelude to Duncan's murder.

> 'Tis now dead time of night, when rapes, and murders
> Are hid beneath the horrid veil of darkness—
> I'll ring through all the court, with doleful sound,
> The sad alarms of murder—Murder—Zarrack—
> Take up thy standing yonder—Osmin, thou
> At the queen's apartment—cry out Murder—
> Whilst I, like his ill genius, do awake the king ;
> Perhaps in this disorder I may kill him.

But we get bombast surpassing this as we approach the climax.

> Prince Philip and the Cardinal now ride
> Like Jove in thunder ; we in storms must meet them.
> To arms ! to arms ! and then to victory,
> Resolv'd to conquer, or resolv'd to die.

This grandiloquence subsides into the most astounding bathos.

> *Sebast.* Advance, advance, my lord, with all your force,
> Or else the prince and victory is lost,
> Which now depends upon his single valour ;
> Who, like some ancient hero, or some god,
> Thunders amongst the thickest of his enemies,
> Destroying all before him in such numbers,
> That piles of dead obstruct his passage to the living—
> Relieve him straight, my lord, with our last cavalry and hopes.

Perhaps in this case, the faulty scansion and doubtful grammar are evidence of a corrupt text. Here is a sentimental passage, a description of night, intended to be poetical.

> *Queen.* Let all the chambers too be filled with lights :
> There's a solemnity, methinks, in night,
> That does insinuate love into the soul,
> And makes the bashful lover more assured.

> *Elvira.* Madam,
> You speak as if this were your first enjoyment.

> *Queen.* My first ! Oh, Elvira, his powers, like his charms,
> His wit, or bravery, every hour renews ;
> Love gathers sweets like flowers, which grow more fragrant
> The nearer they approach maturity.   [*Knock.*
> —Hark ! 'tis my Moor,—give him admittance straight.
> The thought comes o'er me like a gentle gale,
> Raising my blood into a thousand curls.

There are ranting passages, too long to quote, that merit the ridicule cast upon the Drydenian drama in *Chrononhotonthologos*, with its inimitable—

> *Bom.* A blow !—Shall Bombardinian take a blow ?
> Blush—blush, thou sun !—start back, thou rapid ocean !
> Hills ! vales ! seas ! mountains !—all commixing, crumble,
> And into chaos pulverise the world !
> For Bombardinian has received a blow,
> And Chrononhotonthologos shall die !

In her next play, *The Rover*, Mrs. Behn left these crude heroics for what was to be her most prolific comedy vein. It appeared anonymously, and was so successful that she followed it up immediately with another anonymous play, *The Debauchee*, which has been described as the worst and least original of all her dramatic works. *The Rover* was produced in 1677, and held the stage the longest of any of her plays. In 1681 she brought out a second part, changing the scene from Naples to Madrid; otherwise the sequel is almost a replica of the first.

What helped to make *The Rover* so popular was the subject. As she said in the Epilogue—

> The banished Cavaliers! a roving blade!
> A Popish carnival! a masquerade!
> The devil's in't if this will please the nation,
> In these our blessed times of reformation,
> When conventicling is so much in fashion,
> And yet——

Her argument is in the aposiopesis. This was the year before Titus Oates denounced the alleged Popish Plot; Shaftesbury was in opposition, the champion of Nonconformity, the idol of the populace, and the bugbear of the Court party, who believed him to be fomenting heresy and sedition. A year or two later, Mrs. Behn was to caricature him at full length in *The City Heiress; or, Sir Timothy Treat-all*. In *The Rover*, she was making the same political appeal to the party prejudices of the Tories. *Almighty rabble*, says the Prologue to the second part, "'tis to you this day our humble author dedicates the play."

A band of exiled Royalists are engaged in the chase of pleasure in a foreign capital. The most reckless and dissipated of the merry crew is Willmore, the Rover, one of those swaggering inconstants whom, according to Mrs. Behn, no woman can resist. A certain lady, nevertheless, observes, "I should as soon be enamoured on the north wind, a tempest, or a clap of thunder. Bless me from such a blast." The most prominent female character in each of the two plays bearing the name of "The Rover" is set down in the bill as "a famous curtezan'; so the indescribable nature of the incidents may be imagined. Willmore was born to dash the matrimonial schemes of soberer men;

he cuts the knot of all the intrigues, licit or illicit ; he is the impersonation of Astrea's code of sexual morality, of which the two most salient definitions are summed up as follows :—

"Conscience : a cheap pretence to cozen fools withal—"
"Constancy, that current coin for fools."

The dialogue is always full of life and vigour, often sparkling with wit, never quotable ; and it is the same with the highly diverting scenes of both these plays. One marvels at the state of society when such impudent things could be put on the stage, and an audience applaud them.

In *Sir Patient Fancy*, Mrs. Behn borrowed her plot from Molière's *Malade Imaginaire*. It is one of the most vivacious of her plays, and the most completely devoid of moral feeling. The valetudinarian is a rich old alderman, married to a beautiful young wife, who has a gallant. His suspicions being awakened, the jealous old man is persuaded, on what must be confessed very inadequate evidence, that Wittmore, the gallant, is really a suitor for his daughter. But the daughter has a lover already whom he dislikes, and so we have two intrigues going on—with divers others, be it understood—the lover and the gallant both in seeming rivalry courting the daughter of the house, whilst Wittmore and Lady Fancy are scheming to outwit the doubly deluded husband. The usual complications are provided in the usual way. There is a double assignation in the dark ; the gallant is mistaken for the lover, and the lover for the gallant ; and at the critical moment Sir Patient appears on the scene. Lady Fancy is one of the shameless and absolutely unscrupulous women Astrea loved to portray. She carries off the situation with unabashed address, continues to hoodwink her spouse, until, by a combination of accidents, her perfidy is revealed. But all the characters are so entirely absorbed in self that there is no bias in the reader's mind in favour either of the hypochondriacal knight the clever unfaithful wife, or the honest lovers; and the con fusion of the intriguers gives real satisfaction to nobody.

Betterton took the part of Wittmore, and Mrs. Gwyn that of the affected learned woman Lady Knowell, who must have been a very comic figure on the stage, well acted. She is one of those who think there is no learning but what

b

is comprised in the tongues of antiquity : she is a Mrs.
Malaprop in Latin.

O faugh ! Mr. Fancy, what have you said, mother tongue !
Can anything that's great or moving be expressed in filthy
English ?—I'll give you an energetic proof, Mr. Fancy ; observe
but divine Homer in the Grecian language—*Ton apamibomenos
prosiphe podas ochus Achilles !* ah, how it sounds ! which
English'd dwindles into the most grating stuff — Then the
swift-foot Achilles made reply ; oh faugh !

Her niece has very different views, and expresses the com-
moner opinion of her sex in the remark, " Sure he's too
much a gentleman to be a scholar."

Lady Knowell's excessive conversation bores Sir Patient
dreadfully, though he is no less a bore with his anxious
absorption in the progress of his imaginary ailments.   Says
one of the characters, " He has been on the point of going
off this twenty years."   He is continually setting his affairs
in order.   His favourite reading is furnished by prescriptions and apothecaries' bills, which provide him with a sort
of diary.   " By this rule, good Mr. Doctor," says he, " I am
sicker this month than I was the last."

Broader farce comes in with the daughter's clownish
suitor, Sir Credulous Easy, " a foolish Devonshire squire."

Sir Cred. Come, undo my portmantle, and equip me, that
I may look like some body before I see the ladies—Curry, thou
shalt e'en remove now from groom to footman ; for I'll ne'er
keep horse more, no, nor mare neither, since my poor Gillian's
departed this life.

Cur. Nay, to say truth, sir, 'twas a good-natur'd civil beast,
and so she remained to her last gasp, for she cou'd never have
left this world in a better time, as the saying is, so near her
journey's end.

Sir Cred. A civil beast !   Why was it civilly done of her,
thinkest thou, to die at Brentford, when had she liv'd till
to-morrow, she had been converted into money and have been
in my pocket ? for now I am to marry and live in town, I'll sell
off all my pads ; poor fool, I think she e'en died of grief I
wou'd have sold her.

Cur. Well, well, sir, her time was come you must think, and
we are all mortal as the saying is.

Sir Cred. Well, 'twas the loving'st tit — but grass and hay,
she's gone—where be her shoes, Curry ?

Cur. Here, sir, her skin went for good ale at Brentford.

[*Gives him the shoes.*

Sir Cred. Ah, how often has she carried me upon these shoes to Mother Jumbles. What pure ale she brewed!

At a later stage Sir Credulous enacts the part of Falstaff, taking refuge in a basket, in which he has to submit to various indignities without daring to move a muscle lest he betray himself. Mrs. Behn must have had indulgent audiences, who were satisfied with a very cheap kind of humour. In one scene, which has no more affectation of probability than a harlequinade, Sir Credulous is persuaded to feign dumbness, and to court his mistress by signs, whilst his pretended interpreter relieves him of his diamond ring, his cambric handkerchief, and his purse, as presents to the lady.

The *enfant terrible* is already a figure in low comedy. Sir Patient's seven-year-old daughter admonishes her father, when he tries to escape the loquacious Lady Knowell, in these terms :—

Fan. Shou'd I tell a lie, Sir Father, and to a lady of her quality?

Sir Pat. Her quality and she are a couple of impertinent things, which are very troublesome, and not to be endur'd I take it.

Fan. Sir, we shou'd bear with things we do not love sometimes, 'tis a sort of trial, sir, a kind of mortification fit for a good Christian.

Sir Pat. Why, what a notable talking baggage is this? How came you by this doctrine?

Fan. I remember, sir, you preached it once to my sister, when the old alderman was the text, whom you exhorted her to marry, but the wicked creature made ill use on't.

Unfortunately, Mrs. Behn's sense of propriety is so defective that she makes this precocious child the confidante of her elder sister's highly improper love affairs. 'For I have heard you say,' this budding coquette remarks, 'women were born to no other end than to love; and 'tis fit I should learn to live and die in my calling.' Such is the cynicism of one who has no faith in the virtue of her own sex, and less in that of men. Yet she could say, in her epilogue, to the coxcomb who cried 'Ah rot it—'tis a woman's comedy,'

> 'What has poor woman done, that she must be
> Debar'd from sense, and sacred poetry?'

Sacred poetry indeed!

In 1682, her most successful year, she brought out, besides *The False Count*, two political comedies, or at least, comedies that owed much of their popularity to their direct appeal to party feeling. *The Roundheads; or, the Good Old Cause* is a scurrilous lampoon on the Commonwealth. It represents the Parliamentarian generals, Fleetwood, Lambert, and Desborough, as sanctimonious hypocrites, each scheming to betray his comrades and raise himself to supreme office in the state, largely by the efforts of his wife. A traitor in the camp, Corporal Right, is described in the playbill as, 'An Oliverian commander, but honest and a cavalier in his heart.' This is an index to the character of the piece, which, if a man had written it, we should speak of as a cowardly attack on the fallen—a shameless appeal to the basest instincts of the mob. For the most part the abuse is too offensive to quote, but the following scene representing a meeting of the council of ladies will illustrate the spirit of Mrs. Behn's satire:—

Enter page with women, and Loveless dressed as a woman.

Lady Lambert. Gentlewomen, what's your business with us?

Lov. Gentlewomen! some of us are ladies.

L. Lam. Ladies, in good time; by what authority, and from whom do you derive your title of ladies?

Lov. From our husbands.

Gill. Husbands, who are they, and of what standing?

2 Lady. Of no long standing, I confess.

Gill. That's a common grievance indeed.

L. Desborough. And ought to be redressed.

L. Lam. And that shall be taken into consideration; write it down, Gilliflower, who made your husband a knight, woman?

Lov. Oliver the first, an't please ye.

L. Lam. Of horrid memory; write that down—who yours?

2 Lady. Richard the fourth, an't like your honour.

Gill. Of sottish memory; shall I write that down too?

L. Des. Most remarkably.

L. Cromwell. Heav'ns! can I hear this profanation of our Royal Family.

*   *   *   *   *   *

Lov. I petition for a pension; my husband, deceas'd, was a constant active man, in all the late rebellion, against the Man; he plundered my Lord Capel, he betray'd his dearest friend, Brown Bushel, who trusted his life in his hands, and several others; plundering their wives and children even to their smocks.

L. Lam. Most considerable service, and ought to be considered.

2 Lady. And most remarkably, at the trial of the late Man, I spit in's face, and betrayed the Earl of Holland to the Parliament.

L. Crom. In the king's face, you mean—it showed your zeal for the good cause.

2 Lady. And 'twas my husband that headed the rabble, to pull down Gog and Magog, the bishops, broke the idols in the windows, and turned the churches into stables and dens of thieves; robb'd the altar of the cathedral of the twelve pieces of plate called the twelve Apostles, turn'd eleven of 'em into money, and kept Judas for his own use at home.

L. Fleetwood. On my word, most wisely perform'd, note it down—

3 Lady. And my husband made libels on the Man from the first troubles to this day, defam'd and profaned the Woman and her children, printed all the Man's letters to the Woman with burlesque marginal notes, pull'd down the sumptuous shrines in churches, and with the golden and popish spoils adorn'd his house and chimney-pieces.

L. Lam. We shall consider these great services.

We must stop here; the rest of the scene is a more ribald kind of invective even than the foregoing.

In *The City Heiress* (1682), based on Middleton's *A Mad World, My Masters*, the satire is not so heavy, and has far more wit. There is no need to describe the plot, which has a family resemblance to most of the others. The hero is a certain Tom Wilding, the very counterpart of Wittmore and Willmore the Rover. He is the scapegrace nephew of Sir Timothy Treat-all, who is undisguisedly intended for Shaftesbury, Dryden's 'false Achitophel.' Sir Timothy is, of course, the general butt of the satire, being cozened of his property, tricked by his nephew into receiving him as an emissary from the Polish electors, and, to cap the whole, married to a supposed heiress, who turns out to be an impostor. In the scene where Wilding carries out his trickery the political meaning is very obvious.

Enter Wilding in disguise, Dresswell, footmen and pages.

Wild. Sir, by your reverend aspect, you shou'd be the renown'd Maitre de Hotel.

Sir Tim. Mater de Otell! I have not the honour to know any of that name, I am called Sir Timothy Treat-all. [*Bowing.*

Wild. The same, sir; I have been bred abroad, and thought all persons of quality had spoke French.

Sir Tim. Not City persons of quality, my lord.

Wild. I'm glad on't, sir; for 'tis a nation I hate, as indeed I do all monarchies.

Sir Tim. Hum! Hate monarchy! Your lordship is most welcome. [*Bows.*

Wild. Unless elective monarchies, which so resemble a commonwealth.

Sir Tim. Right, my lord; where every man may hope to take his turn—Your lordship is most singularly welcome.
[*Bows low.*

Wild. And though I am a stranger to your person, I am not to your fame, amongst the sober party of the Amsterdamians, all the French Hugonots throughout Geneva; even to Hungary and Poland, fame's trumpet sounds your praise, making the Pope to fear, the rest to admire you.

Sir Tim. I'm much obliged to the renowned mobile.

Wild. So you will say, when you shall hear my embassy. The Polanders by me salute you, sir, and have in the next new election pricked ye down for their succeeding king.

Sir Tim. How, my lord, pricked me down for their king! Why this is wonderful! pricked me, unworthy me down for a king! How cou'd I merit this amazing glory!

Wild. They know, he that can be so great a patriot to his native country, when but a private person, what must he be when power is on his side?

Sir Tim. Ay, my lord, my country, my bleeding country! there's the stop to all my rising greatness. Shall I be so ungrateful to disappoint this big expecting nation? defeat the sober party, and my neighbours, for any Polish crown? But yet, my lord, I will consider on't: meantime my house is yours.

Wild. I've brought you, sir, the measure of the crown: ha, it fits you to a hair. [*Pulls out a riband, measures his head.*] You were by heaven and nature fram'd that monarch.

When Sir Timothy finds out the trick that has been played upon him, he cries, 'Undone, undone! I shall never make Guildhall speech more: but he shall hang for't, if there be e'er a witness between this and Salamanca for money.' There are many more hits against false witnesses and credulous juries. When hard pressed, Sir Timothy is quite ready to protest himself a good friend even to the Pope.

Sir Tim. Nay, gentlemen, not but I love and honour his Holiness with all my soul ; and if his Grace did but know what I've done for him, d'ye see——

Fop. You done for the Pope, sirrah ! Why what have you done for the Pope ?

Sir Tim. Why, sir, an't like ye, I have done you very great service, very great service ; for I have been, d'ye see, in a small trial I had, the cause and occasion of invalidating the evidence to that degree, that I suppose no jury in Christendom will ever have the impudence to believe 'em hereafter, shou'd they swear against his Holiness and all the conclave of cardinals.

And when his house is found to be full of 'knavery, sedition, libels, rights and privileges, with a new fashion'd oath of abjuration, call'd the Association,' he shouts,

'Why I'll deny it, sir ; for what jury will believe so wise a magistrate as I cou'd communicate such secrets to such as you ? I'll say you forged 'em, and put 'em in—or print every one of 'em, and own 'em, as long as they were writ and published in London, sir. Come, come, the world is not so bad yet, but a man may speak treason within the walls of London, thanks be to God, and honest conscientious jurymen.'

Two later plays, *The Lucky Chance*, a comedy, and *The Emperor of the Moon*, a farce, were both failures. In *The Widow Ranter* Astrea tells the story of Bacon's rebellion in Virginia, and makes use of her own experiences of life in the American colonies.

It was the truth and power with which she recounted what she had herself witnessed in Surinam that has singled out for permanence the best of her novels, the story of the royal slave, Oroonoko. We need not give ear to the whispers of a liaison with the heroic black. A very different emotion inspires the tale, the same feeling of outraged humanity that in after days inflamed Mrs. Stowe. *Oroonoko* is the first emancipation novel. It is also the first glorification of the Natural Man. Mrs. Behn was, in a manner, the precursor of Bernardin de Saint-Pierre ; and in her attempts to depict the splendour of tropical scenery she foreshadows, though feebly, the prose-epics of Chateaubriand. There is fierce satire in *Oroonoko*. Who would think that Astrea, who entertained the depraved pit at the

Duke's Theatre, could have drawn those idyllic pictures of Oroonoko in his native Coromantien, of the truth and purity of the savage uncontaminated with the vices of Christian Europe, or have written such vehement invectives against the baseness and utter falsehood of the whites?

'These people represented to me,' she said, 'an absolute idea of the first state of innocence, before man knew how to sin: and 'tis most evident and plain that simple nature is the most harmless, inoffensive and virtuous mistress. 'Tis she alone, if she were permitted, that better instructs the world than all the inventions of man : religion would here but destroy that tranquillity they possess by ignorance ; and laws would teach 'em to know offences of which now they have no notion. They once made mourning and fasting for the death of the English governor, who had given his hand to come on such a day to 'em, and neither came nor sent ; believing when a man's word was past, nothing but death could or should prevent his keeping it : and when they saw he was not dead, they ask'd him what name they had for a man who promis'd a thing he did not do? The governor told them such a man was a lyar, which was a word of infamy to a gentleman. Then one of 'em replied, 'Governor, you are a lyar, and guilty of that infamy.'

It is said further on, 'Such ill morals are only practis'd in Christian countries, where they prefer the bare name of religion ; and, without virtue and morality, think that sufficient.'

Oroonoko is no savage, but the ideal man, as conceived by Mrs. Behn, the man out of Eden ; and in him she has an absolute criterion by which to judge and condemn the object of her satire—European civilisation. His bravery, wisdom, chastity, his high sense of honour, are the idealisations of a sentimental young lady, carried away by her admiration for a truly heroic figure, and disgusted by the vicious manners of the colonists, whom she describes as 'rogues and runagades, that have abandoned their own countries for rapine, murder, theft and villainies.' 'Do you not hear,' says Oroonoko, 'how they upbraid each other with infamy of life, below the wildest savages? And shall we render obedience to such a degenerate race, who have no one human virtue left, to distinguish them from the vilest creatures?'

The story has the natural elements of drama. Southern wrote a very bad tragedy on the theme of Mrs. Behn's narrative, altering it slightly, and adding a great deal of foulness that is, happily, not in the original. Oroonoko loves the beautiful Imoinda, a maiden of his own race, not the child of a European who has adopted a savage life, as in Southern's play. But when they are on the brink of happiness, the old king, Oroonoko's grandfather, demands her for his harem. Imoinda acts the part of Abishag the Shunamite, and her lover that of Adonijah. The vengeful monarch discovers their attachment, and sells her into slavery. Oroonoko, soon afterwards, is kidnapped, and finds himself in Surinam, where Imoinda is already famous as the beautiful slave, as chaste as she is beautiful. They recognise each other in a touching scene, and are suffered to be re-united. Oroonoko distinguishes himself by his virtue and prowess. But he quickly finds that his tyrants promise freedom to himself and Imoinda merely to delude them into good behaviour. He flies into the wilderness at the head of a body of slaves. The planters follow, the blacks fling down their arms, and Oroonoko surrenders on the assurance that they shall not be chastised. The white governor is a scoundrel. The magnanimous negro is put in irons and tortured. Imoinda is set apart for a worse fate. But she prefers to die at his beloved hands, rather than bear dishonour. Oroonoko, with Roman fortitude, slays his wife, and with the stoicism of the Indian smokes a pipe of tobacco while his captors execute him piecemeal.

The Fair Jilt; or, the Amours of Prince Tarquin and Miranda, also purports to be a recital of incidents Astrea herself had witnessed. 'As Love,' it begins, 'is the most noble and divine passion of the soul, so it is that to which we may justly attribute all the real satisfactions of life ; and without it man is unfinish'd and unhappy." She hardly succeeds in proving the divinity of the passion she portrays. Miranda is only a false name for a Beguine at Antwerp, who had many lovers ; Tarquin is the real name of a German prince, the most illustrious of her votaries. It is the story of a fair hypocrite, whose beauty drives men mad. Miranda, whose raging fever of desire reminds one of Phaedra, being repulsed by a handsome young friar, falls back on the device of Potiphar's wife, to secure revenge. This episode is full of force and vigour ; but Tarquin's subjugation to the enchantress, his complaisant obedience to her criminal

schemes, which is offered for our admiration as an example of the illimitable power of love, does not strike us so.
Passion, Mrs. Behn maintains, condones everything. There
is nothing too heinous, too flagitious, to attain a sort of
dignity if done in the cause of love. Tarquin attempts to
assassinate the Fair Jilt's sister, and is deservedly condemned
to death. The novelist depicts him as a martyr, and has
a tear to spare even for the more culpable Miranda.

> At last the bell toll'd, and he was to take leave of the princess,
> as his last work of life, and the most hard he had to accomplish.
> He threw himself at her feet, and gazing on her as she sat more
> dead than alive, overwhelm'd with silent grief, they both re-
> mained some moments speechless ; and then, as if one rising
> tide of tears had supplied both their eyes, it burst out in tears
> at the same instant: and when his sighs gave way, he utter'd
> a thousand farewells, so soft, so passionate, and moving, that
> all who were by were extremely touch'd with it, and said, 'That
> nothing could be seen more deplorable and melancholy.'

All that can be said in comment is, that there have been
novelists since Mrs. Behn who have written stuff that is
quite as false, lurid, and depraved, and readers who have
gushed over it. Only the sinners begotten of later romancers
do not sin with such abandon. Astrea has never lacked
successors, though the cut of her mantle has been altered
to suit the changes of the mode.

The omnipotence of love is again the theme in another
'true novel,' _The Nun ; or, the Perjured Beauty_, in which
a similar heroine is also the villain of the plot. Astrea
frankly accepted Charles the Second's well-known opinion
as to the frailty of woman. 'Virtue,' she makes one of her
characters say, 'is but a name kept from scandal, which the
most base of women best preserve.' But Ardelia does not
even trouble about appearances. She is one of those
passionate, insatiable, capricious women who play a leading
rôle in every one of Astrea's comedies, and are always
drawn with energy and truth because their author's heart
was in them. The plot is worked out with great ingenuity
in this story, and also in a later one, _The Lucky Mistake_, in
which the reader is kept in the titillations of suspense to the
final page. In the last-named, also, there is some attempt
at character-drawing.

Oroonoko was not the only novel in which Mrs. Behn

tried to portray ideal feelings and elevated morality. *Agnes de Castro* is a sweet, sentimental tragedy, which at least has the merit of being free from errors of taste. Agnes is maid-of-honour to Donna Constantia, wife of the Prince of Portugal, and has the misfortune to be loved by her mistress's husband. But there is no foul intrigue in the story. Don Pedro struggles honourably against his passion : 'his fault was not voluntary' : . . . 'a commanding power, a fatal star, had forc'd him to love in spite of himself.' The Princess is so high-minded—after the seventeenth-century pattern of high-mindedness—that she admits his innocence. 'I have no reproaches to make against you, knowing that 'tis inclination that disposes hearts, and not reason." Her complaisance goes so far that she even conjures Agnes not to deprive him of her society, since it is necessary to his happiness. But the truce is brought to a fatal ending by the malice of an envious woman, who persuades Constantia that the lovers are guilty, and so breaks her heart. The novel is painfully stilted, and reads like the discarded sketch for a tragedy, which had been worked up to suit another style.

It must be confessed that, apart from *Oroonoko*, Mrs. Behn's fiction is of very little importance in the history of our literature. Her best work was put into her comedies, which contain, not only much diversion, but also strong, and perhaps too highly coloured, pictures of the manners and morals of the pleasure-seekers of her time, in all classes. Unfortunately, it would be difficult indeed to compile even a book of elegant extracts that would give the modern reader any adequate idea of their merits, without either emasculating them altogether or nauseating him with their coarseness.

ERNEST A. BAKER

February, 1905.

THE HISTORY OF
THE ROYAL SLAVE

I DO not pretend, in giving you the history of this
ROYAL SLAVE, to entertain my Reader with the
adventures of a feigned hero, whose life and fortunes
fancy may manage at the poet's pleasure; nor, in
relating the truth, design to adorn it with any accidents, but such as arrived in earnest to him : and it
shall come simply into the world, recommended by
its own proper merits, and natural intrigues; there
being enough of reality to support it, and to render
it diverting, without the addition of invention.

I was myself an eye-witness to a great part of
what you will find here set down ; and what I could
not be witness of, I received from the mouth of the
chief actor in this history, the hero himself, who gave
us the whole transactions of his youth : and I shall
omit, for brevity's sake, a thousand little accidents
of his life, which, however pleasant to us, where history was scarce, and adventures very rare, yet might
prove tedious and heavy to my reader, in a world
where he finds diversions for every minute, new and
strange. But we who were perfectly charmed with
the character of this great man, were curious to
gather every circumstance of his life.

The scene of the last part of his adventures lies
in a colony in America, called Surinam, in the West
Indies.

But before I give you the story of this gallant slave,

it is fit I tell you the manner of bringing them to
these new colonies; those they make use of there,
not being natives of the place: for those we live with
in perfect amity, without daring to command them;
but, on the contrary, caress them with all the brotherly
and friendly affection in the world; trading with
them for their fish, venison, buffaloes' skins, and little
rarities; as marmosets, a sort of monkey, as big as
a rat or weasel, but of a marvellous and delicate
shape, having face and hands like a human creature;
and cousheries, a little beast in the form and fashion
of a lion, as big as a kitten, but so exactly made in
all parts like that noble beast, that it is it in
miniature: then for little parrakeets, great parrots,
mackaws and a thousand other birds and beasts of
wonderful and surprising forms, shapes, and colours:
for skins of prodigious snakes, of which there are
some three-score yards in length; as is the skin of
one that may be seen at his Majesty's Antiquary's;
where are also some rare flies, of amazing forms and
colours, presented to them by myself: some as big
as my fist, some less; and all of various excellences,
such as art cannot imitate. Then we trade for
feathers, which they order into all shapes, make
themselves little short habits of them, and glorious
wreaths for their heads, necks, arms and legs, whose
tinctures are inconceivable. I had a set of these
presented to me, and I gave them to the King's
Theatre; it was the dress of the Indian Queen,
infinitely admired by persons of quality; and was
inimitable. Besides these, a thousand little knacks,
and rarities in nature; and some of art, as their
baskets, weapons, aprons, etc. We dealt with them
with beads of all colours, knives, axes, pins, and
needles, which they used only as tools to drill holes
with in their ears, noses, and lips, where they hang
a great many little things; as long beads, bits of tin,
brass or silver beat thin, and any shining trinket.
The beads they weave into aprons about a quarter

of an ell long, and of the same breadth; working them very prettily in flowers of several colours; which apron they wear just before them, as Adam and Eve did the fig-leaves; the men wearing a long strip of linen, which they deal with us for. They thread these beads also on long cotton-threads, and make girdles to tie their aprons to, which come twenty times, or more, about the waist, and then cross, like a shoulder-belt, both ways, and round their necks, arms and legs. This adornment, with their long black hair, and the face painted in little specks or flowers here and there, makes them a wonderful figure to behold. Some of the beauties, which indeed are finely shaped, as almost all are, and who have pretty features, are charming and novel; for they have all that is called beauty, except the colour, which is a reddish yellow; or after a new oiling, which they often use to themselves, they are of the colour of a new brick, but smooth, soft and sleek. They are extreme modest and bashful, very shy, and nice of being touched. And though they are all thus naked, if one lives for ever among them, there is not to be seen an indecent action, or glance: and being continually used to see one another so unadorned, so like our first parents before the fall, it seems as if they had no wishes, there being nothing to heighten curiosity: but all you can see, you see at once, and every moment see; and where there is no novelty, there can be no curiosity. Not but I have seen a handsome young Indian, dying for love of a very beautiful young Indian maid; but all his court-ship was, to fold his arms, pursue her with his eyes, and sighs were all his language: whilst she, as if no such lover were present, or rather as if she desired none such, carefully guarded her eyes from beholding him; and never approached him, but she looked down with all the blushing modesty I have seen in the most severe and cautious of our world. And these people represented to me an absolute idea of the first state

of innocence, before man knew how to sin: And 'tis
most evident and plain, that simple Nature is the
most harmless, inoffensive and virtuous mistress.　It
is she alone, if she were permitted, that better instructs the world, than all the inventions of man:
religion would here but destroy that tranquillity they
possess by ignorance; and laws would but teach
them to know offences, of which now they have
no notion.　They once made mourning and fasting
for the death of the English Governor, who had given
his hand to come on such a day to them, and neither
came nor sent; believing when, a man's word was
past, nothing but death could or should prevent his
keeping it: and when they saw he was not dead,
they asked him what name they had for a man who
promised a thing he did not do?　The Governor
told them such a man was a liar, which was a word
of infamy to a gentleman.　Then one of them
replied, ' Governor, you are a liar, and guilty of that
infamy.'　They have a native justice, which knows
no fraud; and they understand no vice, or cunning,
but when they are taught by the white men.　They
have plurality of wives; which when they grow old,
serve those that succeed them, who are young, but
with a servitude easy and respected; and unless they
take slaves in war, they have no other attendants.

Those on that continent where I was, had no King;
but the oldest War-Captain was obeyed with great
resignation.

A War-Captain is a man who has led them on to
battle with conduct and success; of whom I shall
have occasion to speak more hereafter, and of some
other of their customs and manners, as they fall in
my way.

With these people, as I said, we live in perfect
tranquillity, and good understanding, as it behoves us
to do; they knowing all the places where to seek the
best food of the country, and the means of getting it;
and for very small and invaluable trifles, supplying

us with what it is almost impossible for us to get: for
they do not only in the woods, and over the Sevana's,
in hunting, supply the parts of hounds, by swiftly
scouring through those almost impassable places, and
by the mere activity of their feet, run down the
nimblest deer, and other eatable beasts; but in the
water, one would think they were gods of the rivers,
or fellow-citizens of the deep; so rare an art they
have in swimming, diving, and almost living in water;
by which they command the less swift inhabitants of
the floods.   And then for shooting, what they cannot
take, or reach with their hands, they do with arrows;
and have so admirable an aim, that they will split
almost a hair, and at any distance that an arrow can
reach: they will shoot down oranges, and other
fruit, and only touch the stalk with the dart's point,
that they may not hurt the fruit.   So that they being
on all occasions very useful to us, we find it absolutely
necessary to caress them as friends, and not to treat
them as slaves; nor dare we do otherwise, their
numbers so far surpassing ours in that continent.

Those then whom we make use of to work in our
plantations of sugar, are Negroes, black-slaves altogether, who are transported thither in this manner.

Those who want slaves, make a bargain with a
master, or a captain of a ship, and contract to pay
him so much apiece, a matter of twenty pound a head,
for as many as he agrees for, and to pay for them
when they shall be delivered on such a plantation: so
that when there arrives a ship laden with slaves, they
who have so contracted, go aboard, and receive their
number by lot; and perhaps in one lot that may be
for ten, there may happen to be three or four men,
the rest women and children.   Or be there more or
less of either sex, you are obliged to be contented
with your lot.

Coramantien, a country of blacks so called, was one
of those places in which they found the most advantageous trading for these slaves, and thither most of

our great traders in that merchandise traffic; for
that nation is very warlike and brave: and having a
continual campaign, being always in hostility with
one neighbouring Prince or other, they had the
fortune to take a great many captives: for all they
took in battle were sold as slaves; at least those
common men who could not ransom themselves. Of
these slaves so taken, the General only has all the
profit; and of these Generals our captains and masters of ships buy all their freights.

The King of Coramantien was of himself a man of
an hundred and odd years old, and had no son,
though he had many beautiful black wives: for most
certainly there are beauties that can charm of that
colour. In his younger years he had had many
gallant men to his sons, thirteen of whom died in
battle, conquering when they fell; and he had only
left him for his successor, one grandchild, son to one
of these dead victors, who, as soon as he could bear
a bow in his hand, and a quiver at his back, was sent
into the field, to be trained up by one of the oldest
Generals to war; where, from his natural inclination
to arms, and the occasions given him, with the good
conduct of the old General, he became, at the age of
seventeen, one of the most expert Captains, and
bravest soldiers that ever saw the field of Mars: so
that he was adored as the wonder of all that world,
and the darling of the soldiers. Besides, he was
adorned with a native beauty, so transcending all
those of his gloomy race, that he struck an awe and
reverence, even into those that knew not his quality;
as he did into me, who beheld him with surprise and
wonder, when afterwards he arrived in our world.

He had scarce arrived at his seventeenth year,
when, fighting by his side, the General was killed with
an arrow in his eye, which the Prince Oroonoko (for
so was this gallant Moor called) very narrowly
avoided; nor had he, if the General who saw the
arrow shot, and perceiving it aimed at the Prince,

had not bowed his head between, on purpose to receive it in his own body, rather than it should touch that of the Prince, and so saved him.

It was then, afflicted as Oroonoko was, that he was proclaimed General in the old man's place: and then it was, at the finishing of that war, which had continued for two years, that the Prince came to Court, where he had hardly been a month together, from the time of his fifth year to that of seventeen: and it was amazing to imagine where it was he learned so much humanity; or to give his accomplishments a juster name, where it was he got that real greatness of soul, those refined notions of true honour, that absolute generosity, and that softness that was capable of the highest passions of love and gallantry, whose objects were almost continually fighting men, or those mangled or dead, who heard no sounds but those of war and groans. Some part of it we may attribute to the care of a Frenchman of wit and learning, who finding it turn to a very good account to be a sort of royal tutor to this young black, and perceiving him very ready, apt, and quick of apprehension, took a great pleasure to teach him morals, language and science; and was for it extremely beloved and valued by him. Another reason was, he loved when he came from war, to see all the English gentlemen that traded thither; and did not only learn their language, but that of the Spaniard also, with whom he traded afterwards for slaves.

I have often seen and conversed with this great man, and been a witness to many of his mighty actions, and do assure my reader, the most illustrious Courts could not have produced a braver both for greatness of courage and mind, a judgment more solid, a wit more quick, and a conversation more sweet and diverting. He knew almost as much as if he had read much: he had heard of and admired the Romans: he had heard of the late Civil Wars in England, and the deplorable death of our great Monarch; and

would discourse of it with all the sense and abhorrence
of the injustice imaginable. He had an extreme
good and graceful mien, and all the civility of a well-
bred great man. He had nothing of barbarity in
his nature, but in all points addressed himself as if his
education had been in some European Court.

This great and just character of Oroonoko gave me
an extreme curiosity to see him, especially when
I knew he spoke French and English, and that I
could talk with him. But though I had heard so
much of him, I was as greatly surprised when I saw
him, as if I had heard nothing of him; so beyond all
report I found him. He came into the room, and
addressed himself to me, and some other women,
with the best grace in the world. He was pretty tall,
but of a shape the most exact that can be fancied:
the most famous statuary could not form the figure of
a man more admirably turned from head to foot. His
face was not of that brown rusty black which most of
that nation are, but a perfect ebony, or polished jet.
His eyes were the most awful that could be seen, and
very piercing; the white of them being like snow, as
were his teeth. His nose was rising and Roman,
instead of African and flat: his mouth the finest
shaped that could be seen; far from those great
turned lips, which are so natural to the rest of the
Negroes. The whole proportion and air of his face
was so nobly and exactly formed, that, bating his
colour, there could be nothing in nature more beautiful, agreeable and handsome. There was no one
grace wanting, that bears the standard of true beauty.
His hair came down to his shoulders, by the aids
of art, which was by pulling it out with a quill, and
keeping it combed; of which he took particular care.
Nor did the perfections of his mind come short
of those of his person; for his discourse was admirable upon almost any subject: and whoever had
heard him speak, would have been convinced of their
errors, that all fine wit is confined to the white men,

especially to those of Christendom; and would have confessed that Oroonoko was as capable even of reigning well, and of governing as wisely, had as great a soul, as politic maxims, and was as sensible of power, as any Prince civilised in the most refined schools of humanity and learning, or the most illustrious courts.

This Prince, such as I have described him, whose soul and body were so admirably adorned, was (while yet he was in the Court of his grandfather, as I said) as capable of love, as it was possible for a brave and gallant man to be; and in saying that, I have named the highest degree of love: for sure great souls are most capable of that passion.

I have already said, the old General was killed by the shot of an arrow, by the side of this Prince, in battle; and that Oroonoko was made General. This old dead hero had one only daughter left of his race, a beauty, that to describe her truly, one need say only, she was female to the noble male; the beautiful black Venus to our young Mars; as charming in her person as he, and of delicate virtues. I have seen a hundred white men sighing after her, and making a thousand vows at her feet, all in vain and unsuccessful. And she was indeed too great for any but a prince of her own nation to adore.

Oroonoko coming from the wars (which were now ended) after he had made his Court to his grandfather, he thought in honour he ought to make a visit to Imoinda, the daughter of his foster-father, the dead General; and to make some excuses to her, because his preservation was the occasion of her father's death; and to present her with those slaves that had been taken in this last battle, as the trophies of her father's victories. When he came, attended by all the young soldiers of any merit, he was infinitely surprised at the beauty of this fair Queen of Night, whose face and person were so exceeding all he had ever beheld, that lovely modesty with which she received him, that softness in her look and sighs, upon the melancholy occasion of this honour that was done by so great a man as Oroonoko, and a Prince of whom she had heard such admirable things; the awfulness wherewith she received him, and the sweetness of her words and behaviour while he stayed, gained a perfect conquest over his fierce heart, and made him feel, the victor could be subdued. So that having made his first compliments, and presented her an hundred and fifty slaves in fetters, he told her with his eyes, that he was not insensible of her charms; while Imoinda, who wished for nothing more than so glorious a conquest, was pleased to believe, she understood that silent language of new-born love; and, from that moment, put on all her additions to beauty.

The Prince returned to Court with quite another humour than before; and though he did not speak much of the fair Imoinda, he had the pleasure to hear all his followers speak of nothing but the charms of that maid, insomuch, that, even in the presence of the old King, they were extolling her, and heightening, if possible, the beauties they had found in her: so that nothing else was talked of, no other sound was heard in every corner where there were whisperers, but Imoinda! Imoinda!

It will be imagined Oroonoko stayed not long before he made his second visit; nor, considering his quality, not much longer before he told her, he adored her. I have often heard him say, that he admired by what strange inspiration he came to talk things so soft, and so passionate, who never knew love, nor was used to the conversation of women; but (to use his own words) he said, 'Most happily, some new, and, till then, unknown power instructed his heart and tongue in the language of love; and at the same time, in favour of him, inspired Imoinda with a sense of his passion.' She was touched with what he said, and returned it all in such answers as went to his very heart, with a pleasure unknown before. Nor did he use those obligations ill, that love had done him, but turned all his happy moments to the best advantage ; and as he knew no vice, his flame aimed at nothing but honour, if such a distinction may be made in love; and especially in that country, where men take to themselves as many as they can maintain; and where the only crime and sin against a woman, is, to turn her off, to abandon her to want, shame and misery; such ill morals are only practised in Christian countries, where they prefer the bare name of religion; and, without religion or morality, think that sufficient. But Oroonoko was none of these professors; but as he had right notions of honour, so he made her such propositions as were not only and barely such; but, contrary to the custom of his country, he made her, vows she should be the only woman he would possess while he lived ; that no age or wrinkles should incline him to change: for her soul would be always fine, and always young; and he should have an eternal idea in his mind of the charms she now bore; and should look into his heart for that idea, when he could find it no longer in her face.

After a thousand assurances of his lasting flame, and her eternal empire over him, she condescended to receive him for her husband; or rather, receive him, as the greatest honour the gods could do her.

There is a certain ceremony in these cases to be observed, which I forgot to ask how it was performed ; but it was concluded on both sides, that in obedience to him, the grandfather was to be first made acquainted with the design : for they pay a most absolute resignation to the monarch, especially when he is a parent also.

On the other side, the old King, who had many wives, and many concubines, wanted not court-flatterers to insinuate into his heart a thousand tender thoughts for this young beauty; and who represented her to his fancy, as the most charming he had ever

possessed in all the long race of his numerous years.
At this character, his old heart, like an extinguished
brand, most apt to take fire, felt new sparks of love,
and began to kindle; and now grown to his second
childhood, longed with impatience to behold this gay
thing, with whom, alas! he could but innocently play.
But how he should be confirmed she was this wonder,
before he used his power to call her to Court, (where
maidens never came, unless for the King's private
use) he was next to consider; and while he was so
doing, he had intelligence brought him, that Imoinda
was most certainly mistress to the Prince Oroonoko.
This gave him some chagrin: however, it gave him
also an opportunity, one day, when the Prince was
a hunting, to wait on a man of quality, as his slave
and attendant, who should go and make a present to
Imoinda, as from the Prince; he should then, unknown, see this fair maid, and have an opportunity to
hear what message she would return the Prince for
his present, and from thence gather the state of her
heart, and degree of her inclination. This was put in
execution, and the old monarch saw, and burned:
he found her all he had heard, and would not delay
his happiness, but found he should have some obstacle
to overcome her heart; for she expressed her sense
of the present the Prince had sent her, in terms so
sweet, so soft and pretty, with an air of love and joy
that could not be dissembled, insomuch that it was
past doubt whether she loved Oroonoko entirely.
This gave the old King some affliction; but he salved
it with this, that the obedience the people pay their
King, was not at all inferior to what they paid their
gods; and what love would not oblige Imoinda to do,
duty would compel her to.

He was therefore no sooner got into his apartment,
but he sent the Royal Veil to Imoinda; that is the
ceremony of invitation: he sends the lady he has a
mind to honour with his bed, a veil, with which she is
covered, and secured for the King's use; and it is

death to disobey ; besides, held a most impious disobedience.

It is not to be imagined the surprise and grief that
seized the lovely maid at this news and sight.   However, as delays in these cases are dangerous, and
pleading worse than treason ; trembling, and almost
fainting, she was obliged to suffer herself to be
covered, and led away.

They brought her thus to Court ; and the King,
who had caused a very rich bath to be prepared, was
led into it, where he sat under a canopy, in state, to
receive this longed-for virgin ; whom he having commanded to be brought to him, they (after disrobing
her) led her to the bath, and making fast the doors,
left her to descend.   The King, without more court-
ship, bade her throw off her mantle, and come to his
arms.   But Imoinda, all in tears, threw herself on the
marble, on the brink of the bath, and besought him to
hear her.   She told him, as she was a maid, how
proud of the divine glory she should have been of
having it in her power to oblige her King : but as by
the laws he could not, and from his Royal goodness
would not take from any man his wedded wife ; so she
believed she should be the occasion of making him
commit a great sin, if she did not reveal her state and
condition ; and tell him she was another's, and could
not be so happy to be his.

The King, enraged at this delay, hastily demanded
the name of the bold man, that had married a woman
of her degree, without his consent.   Imoinda seeing
his eyes fierce, and his hands tremble (whether with
age or anger, I know not, but she fancied the last)
almost repented she had said so much, for now she
feared the storm would fall on the Prince ; she therefore said a thousand things to appease the raging of
his flame, and to prepare him to hear who it was with
calmness : but before she spoke, he imagined who she
meant, but would not seem to do so, but commanded
her to lay aside her mantle, and suffer herself to receive

his caresses, or, by his gods he swore, that happy man
whom she was going to name should die, though
it were even Oroonoko himself. 'Therefore,' said he,
'deny this marriage, and swear thyself a maid.'
'That,' replied Imoinda, 'by all our powers I do;
for I am not yet known to my husband.' 'It is
enough,' said the King, 'it is enough both to satisfy
my conscience and my heart.' And rising from his
seat, he went and led her into the bath; it being in
vain for her to resist.

In this time, the Prince, who was returned from
hunting, went to visit his Imoinda, but found her
gone; and not only so, but heard she had received
the Royal Veil. This raised him to a storm; and in
his madness, they had much ado to save him from
laying violent hands on himself. Force first prevailed, and then reason: they urged all to him, that
might oppose his rage; but nothing weighed so
greatly with him as the King's old age, incapable of
injuring him with Imoinda. He would give way to
that hope, because it pleased him most, and flattered
best his heart. Yet this served not altogether to make
him cease his different passions, which sometimes
raged within him, and softened into showers. It was
not enough to appease him, to tell him, his grandfather was old, and could not that way injure him,
while he retained that awful duty which the young
men are used there to pay to their grave relations.
He could not be convinced he had no cause to sigh
and mourn for the loss of a mistress, he could not
with all his strength and courage retrieve, and he
would often cry, 'Oh, my friends! were she in walled
cities, or confined from me in fortifications of the
greatest strength; did enchantments or monsters
detain her from me; I would venture any hazard to
free her: but here, in the arms of a feeble old man,
my youth, my violent love, my trade in arms, and all
my vast desire of glory, avail me nothing. Imoinda
is as irrecoverably lost to me, as if she were snatched

by the cold arms of death. Oh! she is never to be retrieved. If I would wait tedious years; till fate should bow the old King to his grave, even that would not leave me Imoinda free; but still that custom that makes it so vile a crime for a son to marry his father's wives or mistresses, would hinder my happiness; unless I would either ignobly set an ill precedent to my successors, or abandon my country, and fly with her to some unknown world who never heard our story.'

But it was objected to him, that his case was not the same: for Imoinda being his lawful wife by solemn contract, it was he was the injured man, and might, if he so pleased, take Imoinda back, the breach of the law being on his grandfather's side; and that if he could circumvent him, and redeem her from the Otan, which is the Palace of the King's Women, a fort of Seraglio, it was both just and lawful for him so to do.

This reasoning had some force upon him, and he should have been entirely comforted, but for the thought that she was possessed by his grandfather. However, he loved her so well, that he was resolved to believe what most favoured his hope, and to endeavour to learn from Imoinda's own mouth, what only she could satisfy him in, whether she was robbed of that blessing which was only due to his faith and love. But as it was very hard to get a sight of the women (for no men ever entered into the Otan, but when the King went to entertain himself with some one of his wives or mistresses; and it was death, at any other time, for any other to go in) so he knew not how to contrive to get a sight of her.

While Oroonoko felt all the agonies of love, and suffered under a torment the most painful in the world, the old King was not exempted from his share of affliction. He was troubled, for having been forced, by an irresistible passion, to rob his son of a treasure, he knew, could not but be extremely dear to him;

since she was the most beautiful that ever had been seen, and had besides, all the sweetness and innocence of youth and modesty, with a charm of wit surpassing all. He found, that however she was forced to expose her lovely person to his withered arms, she could only sigh and weep there, and think of Oroonoko; and oftentimes could not forbear speaking of him, though her life were, by custom, forfeited by owning her passion. But she spoke not of a lover only, but of a Prince dear to him to whom she spoke; and of the praises of a man, who, till now, filled the old man's soul with joy at every recital of his bravery, or even his name. And it was this dotage on our young hero, that gave Imoinda a thousand privileges to speak of him without offending, and this condescension in the old King, that made her take the satisfaction of speaking of him so very often.

Besides, he many times inquired how the Prince bore himself: and those of whom he asked, being entirely slaves to the merits and virtues of the Prince, still answered what they thought conduced best to his service; which was, to make the old King fancy that the Prince had no more interest in Imoinda, and had resigned her willingly to the pleasure of the King; that he diverted himself with his mathematicians, his fortifications, his officers, and his hunting.

This pleased the old lover, who failed not to report these things again to Imoinda, that she might, by the example of her young lover, withdraw her heart, and rest better contented in his arms. But, however she was forced to receive this unwelcome news, in all appearance, with unconcern and content; her heart was bursting within, and she was only happy when she could get alone, to vent her griefs and moans with sighs and tears.

What reports of the Prince's conduct were made to the King, he thought good to justify, as far as possibly he could by his actions; and when he appeared in the presence of the King, he showed a face not at all betraying his heart: so that in a little time, the old man, being entirely convinced that he was no longer a lover of Imoinda, he carried him with him, in his train, to the Otan, often to banquet with his mistresses. But as soon as he entered, one day, into the apartment of Imoinda, with the King, at the first glance from her eyes, notwithstanding all his determined resolution, he was ready to sink in the place where he stood; and had certainly done so, but for the support of Aboan, a young man who was next to him; which, with his change of countenance, had betrayed him, had the King chanced to look that way. And I have observed, it is a very great error in those who laugh when one says, 'A Negro can change colour': for I have seen them as frequently blush, and look pale, and that as visibly as ever I saw in the most beautiful white. And it is certain, that both these changes were evident, this day, in both these lovers. And Imoinda, who saw with some joy the change in the Prince's face, and found it in her own, strove to divert the King from beholding either, by a forced caress, with which she met him; which was a new wound in the heart of the poor dying Prince. But as soon as the King was busied in looking on some fine thing of Imoinda's making, she had time to tell the Prince, with her angry, but love-darting eyes, that she resented his coldness, and bemoaned her own miserable captivity. Nor were his eyes silent, but answered hers again, as much as eyes could do, instructed by the most tender and most passionate heart that ever loved: and they spoke so well, and so effectually, as Imoinda no longer doubted but she was the only delight and darling of that soul she found pleading in them its right of love, which none was more willing to resign than she. And it was this powerful language alone that in an instant conveyed all the thoughts of their souls to each other; that they both found there wanted but oppor-

c

tunity to make them both entirely happy. But when
he saw another door opened by Onahal (a former old
wife of the King's, who now had charge of Imoinda)
and saw the prospect of a bed of state made ready,
with sweets and flowers for the dalliance of the King,
who immediately led the trembling victim from his
sight, into that prepared repose; what rage! what
wild frenzies seized his heart! which forcing to keep
within bounds, and to suffer without noise, it became
the more insupportable, and rent his soul with ten
thousand pains. He was forced to retire to vent his
groans, where he fell down on a carpet, and lay
struggling a long time, and only breathing now and
then—Oh Imoinda! When Onahal had finished her
necessary affair within, shutting the door, she came
forth, to wait till the King called; and hearing some
one sighing in the other room, she passed on, and
found the Prince in that deplorable condition, which
she thought needed her aid. She gave him cordials,
but all in vain; till finding the nature of his disease,
by his sighs, and naming Imoinda, she told him he
had not so much cause as he imagined to afflict himself: for if he knew the King so well as she did, he
would not lose a moment in jealousy; and that she
was confident that Imoinda bore, at this minute, part
in his affliction. Aboan was of the same opinion,
and both together persuaded him to re-assume his
courage; and all sitting down on the carpet, the
Prince said so many obliging things to Onahal, that
he half persuaded her to be of his party: and she
promised him, she would thus far comply with his
just desires, that she would let Imoinda know how
faithful he was, what he suffered, and what he said.

This discourse lasted till the King called, which
gave Oroonoko a certain satisfaction; and with the
hope Onahal had made him conceive, he assumed
a look as gay as it was possible a man in his circumstances could do: and presently after, he was called
in with the rest who waited without. The King com-

manded music to be brought, and several of his young wives and mistresses came all together by his command, to dance before him ; where Imoinda performed her part with an air and grace so surpassing all the rest, as her beauty was above them, and received the present ordained as a prize.   The Prince was every moment more charmed with the new beauties and graces he beheld in this fair one ; and while he gazed, and she danced, Onahal was retired to a window with Aboan.

This Onahal, as I said, was one of the Cast-Mistresses of the old King ; and it was these (now past their beauty) that were made guardians or governantes to the new and the young ones, and whose business it was to teach them all those wanton arts of love, with which they prevailed and charmed heretofore in their turn ; and who now treated the triumphing happy-ones with all the severity, as to liberty and freedom, that was possible, in revenge of the honours they rob them of ; envying them those satisfactions, those gallantries and presents, that were once made to themselves, while youth and beauty lasted, and which they now saw pass, as it were regardless by, and paid only to the bloomings.   And certainly, nothing is more afflicting to a decayed beauty, than to behold in itself declining charms, that were once adored ; and to find those caresses paid to new beauties, to which once she laid claim ; to hear them whisper, as she passes by, that once was a delicate woman.   Those abandoned ladies therefore endeavour to revenge all the despites and decays of time, on these flourishing happy-ones.   And it was this severity that gave Oroonoko a thousand fears he should never prevail with Onahal to see Imoinda. But, as I said, she was now retired to a window with Aboan.

This young man was not only one of the best quality, but a man extremely well made, and beautiful ; and coming often to attend the King to the Otan, he had subdued the heart of the antiquated Onahal, which had not forgot how pleasant it was to be in love. And though she had some decays in her face, she had none in her sense and wit; she was there agreeable still, even to Aboan's youth: so that he took pleasure in entertaining her with discourses of love. He knew also, that to make his court to these she-favourites, was the way to be great; these being the persons that do all affairs and business at Court. He had also observed that she had given him glances more tender and inviting than she had done to others of his quality. And now, when he saw that her favour could so absolutely oblige the Prince, he failed not to sigh in her ear, and look with eyes all soft upon her, and gave her hope that she had made some impressions on his heart. He found her pleased at this, and making a thousand advances to him: but the ceremony ending, and the King departing, broke up the company for that day, and his conversation.

Aboan failed not that night to tell the Prince of his success, and how advantageous the service of Onahal might be to his amour with Imoinda. The Prince was overjoyed with this good news, and besought him, if it were possible, to caress her so, as to engage her entirely, which he could not fail to do, if he complied with her desires: 'For then,' said the Prince, 'her life lying at your mercy, she must grant you the request you make in my behalf.' Aboan understood him, and assured him he would make love so effectually, that he would defy the most expert mistress of the art to find out whether he dissembled it, or had it really. And it was with impatience they waited the next opportunity of going to the Otan.

The wars came on, the time of taking the field approached; and it was impossible for the Prince to delay his going at the head of his Army to encounter the enemy; so that every day seemed a tedious year, till he saw his Imoinda: for he believed he could not live, if he were forced away without being so happy.

It was with impatience therefore that he expected the
next visit the King would make; and, according to
his wish, it was not long.

The parley of the eyes of these two lovers had not
passed so secretly, but an old jealous lover could spy
it; or rather, he wanted not flatterers who told him
they observed it: so that the Prince was hastened to
the camp, and this was the last visit he found he
should make to the Otan; he therefore urged Aboan
to make the best of this last effort, and to explain himself so to Onahal, that she deferring her enjoyment of
her young lover no longer, might make way for the
Prince to speak to Imoinda.

The whole affair being agreed on between the
Prince and Aboan, they attended the King, as the
custom was, to the Otan; where, while the whole
company was taken up in beholding the dancing and
antic postures the Women-Royal made to divert the
King, Onahal singled out Aboan, whom she found
most pliable to her wish. When she had him where
she believed she could not be heard, she sighed to him,
and softly cried, 'Ah, Aboan! when will you be
sensible of my passion? I confess it with my mouth,
because I would not give my eyes the lie; and you
have but too much already perceived they have confessed my flame: nor would I have you believe that
because I am the abandoned mistress of a King, I
esteem myself altogether divested of charms: No,
Aboan; I have still a rest of beauty enough engaging,
and have learned to please too well, not to be desirable. I can have lovers still, but will have none
but Aboan.' 'Madam,' replied the half-feigning
youth, 'you have already, by my eyes, found you can
still conquer; and I believe it is in pity of me you
condescend to this kind confession. But, Madam,
words are used to be so small a part of our country-
courtship, that it is rare one can get so happy an
opportunity as to tell one's heart; and those few
minutes we have, are forced to be snatched for more

certain proofs of love than speaking and sighing, and such I languish for.'

He spoke this with such a tone, that she hoped it true, and could not forbear believing it; and being wholly transported with joy for having subdued the finest of all the King's subjects to her desires, she took from her ears two large pearls, and commanded him to wear them in his. He would have refused them crying, 'Madam, these are not the proofs of your love that I expect; it is opportunity, it is a lone hour only that can make me happy." But forcing the pearls into his hand, she whispered softly to him, 'Oh! do not fear a woman's invention, when love sets her a thinking.' And pressing his hand, she cried, 'This night you shall be happy. Come to the gate of the orange-grove, behind the Otan, and I will be ready about midnight to receive you.' It was thus agreed, and she left him that no notice might be taken of their speaking together.

The ladies were still dancing, and the King, laid on a carpet, with a great deal of pleasure was beholding them, especially Imoinda, who that day appeared more lovely than ever, being enlivened with the good tidings Onahal had brought her, of the constant passion the Prince had for her. The Prince was laid on another carpet at the other end of the room, with his eyes fixed on the object of his soul; and as she turned or moved, so did they; and she alone gave his eyes and soul their motions. Nor did Imoinda employ her eyes to any other use, than in beholding with infinite pleasure the joy she produced in those of the Prince. But while she was more regarding him than the steps she took, she chanced to fall, and so near him, as that leaping with extreme force from the carpet, he caught her in his arms as she fell; and it was visible to the whole presence, the joy wherewith he received her. He clasped her close to his bosom, and quite forgot that reverence that was due to the mistress of a King, and that punishment that is the reward of a boldness of this nature. And had not the presence of mind of Imoinda (fonder of his safety than her own) befriended him, in making her spring from his arms, and fall into her dance again, he had at that instant met his death; for the old King, jealous to the last degree, rose up in rage, broke all the diversion, and led Imoinda to her apartment, and sent out word to the Prince, to go immediately to the camp; and that if he were found another night in Court, he should suffer the death ordained for disobedience to offenders.

You may imagine how welcome this news was to Oroonoko, whose unseasonable transport and caress of Imoinda was blamed by all men that loved him: and now he perceived his fault, yet cried, 'That for such another moment he would be content to die.'

All the Otan was in disorder about this accident; and Onahal was particularly concerned because on the Prince's stay depended her happiness; for she could no longer expect that of Aboan: so that ere they departed, they contrived it so that the Prince and he should both come that night to the grove of the Otan, which was all of oranges and citrons, and that there they would wait her orders.

They parted thus with grief enough till night, leaving the King in possession of the lovely maid. But nothing could appease the jealousy of the old lover; he would not be imposed on, but would have it that Imoinda made a false step on purpose to fall into Oroonoko's bosom, and that all things looked like a design on both sides; and it was in vain she protested her innocence; he was old and obstinate, and left her, more than half assured that his fear was true.

The King going to his apartment, sent to know where the Prince was, and if he intended to obey his command. The messenger returned, and told him, he found the Prince pensive, and altogether unprepared for the campaign; that he lay negligently on the ground, and answered very little. This confirmed the jealousy of the King, and he commanded that they should very narrowly and privately watch his motions; and that he should not stir from his apartment, but one spy or other should be employed to watch him: so that the hour approaching, wherein he was to go to the citron-grove; and taking only Aboan along with him, he leaves his apartment, and was watched to the very gate of the Otan; where he was seen to enter, and where they left him, to carry back the tidings to the King.

Oroonoko and Aboan were no sooner entered, but Onahal led the Prince to the apartment of Imoinda; who, not knowing any thing of her happiness, was laid in bed. But Onahal only left him in her chamber, to make the best of his opportunity, and took her dear Aboan to her own; where he showed the height of complaisance for his Prince, when, to give him an opportunity, he suffered himself to be caressed in bed by Onahal.

The Prince softly wakened Imoinda, who was not a little surprised with joy to find him there; and yet she trembled with a thousand fears. I believe he omitted saying nothing to this young maid, that might persuade her to suffer him to seize his own, and take the rights of love. And I believe she was not long resisting those arms where she so longed to be; and having opportunity, night, and silence, youth, love, and desire, he soon prevailed, and ravished in a moment what his old grandfather had been endeavouring for so many months.

It is not to be imagined the satisfaction of these two young lovers; nor the vows she made him, that she remained a spotless maid till that night, and that what she did with his grandfather had robbed him of no part of her virgin honour; the gods, in mercy and justice, having reserved that for her plighted lord, to whom of right it belonged. And it is impossible to express the transports he suffered, while he listened to a discourse so charming from her loved lips; and clasped that body in his arms, for whom he had so long languished; and nothing now afflicted him, but his sudden departure from her; for he told her the necessity, and his commands, but should depart satisfied in this, that since the old King had hitherto not been able to deprive him of those enjoyments which only belonged to him, he believed for the future he would be less able to injure him; so that, abating the scandal of the veil, which was no otherwise so, than that she was wife to another, he believed her safe, even in the arms of the King, and innocent; yet would he have ventured at the conquest of the world, and have given it all to have had her avoided that honour of receiving the Royal Veil. It was thus, between a thousand caresses, that both bemoaned the hard fate of youth and beauty, so liable to that cruel promotion : it was a glory that could well have been spared here, though desired and aimed at by all the young females of that kingdom.

But while they were thus fondly employed, forgetting how time ran on, and that the dawn must conduct him far away from his only happiness, they heard a great noise in the Otan, and unusual voices of men; at which the Prince, starting from the arms of the frighted Imoinda, ran to a little battle-axe he used to wear by his side; and having not so much leisure as to put on his habit, he opposed himself against some who were already opening the door : which they did with so much violence, that Oroonoko was not able to defend it; but was forced to cry out with a commanding voice, 'Whoever ye are that have the boldness to attempt to approach this apartment thus rudely; know, that I, the Prince Oroonoko, will revenge it with the certain death of him that first enters; therefore stand back, and know, this place is sacred to love and me this night; to-morrow 'tis the King's.'

This he spoke with a voice so resolved and assured,

that they soon retired from the door; but cried, ''Tis by the King's command we are come; and being satisfied by thy voice, O Prince, as much as if we had entered, we can report to the King the truth of all his fears, and leave thee to provide for thy own safety, as thou art advised by thy friends.'

At these words they departed, and left the Prince to take a short and sad leave of his Imoinda; who, trusting in the strength of her charms, believed she should appease the fury of a jealous King, by saying, she was surprised, and that it was by force of arms he got into her apartment. All her concern now was for his life, and therefore she hastened him to the camp, and with much ado prevailed on him to go. Nor was it she alone that prevailed; Aboan and Onahal both pleaded, and both assured him of a lie that should be well enough contrived to secure Imoinda. So that at last, with a heart sad as death, dying eyes, and sighing soul, Oroonoko departed, and took his way to the camp.

It was not long after, the King in person came to the Otan; where beholding Imoinda, with rage in his eyes, he upbraided her wickedness, and perfidy; and threatening her royal lover, she fell on her face at his feet, bedewing the floor with her tears, and imploring his pardon for a fault which she had not with her will committed; as Onahal, who was also prostrate with her, could testify: that, unknown to her, he had broken into her apartment, and ravished her. She spoke this much against her conscience; but to save her own life, it was absolutely necessary she should feign this falsity. She knew it could not injure the Prince, he being fled to an army that would stand by him, against any injuries that should assault him. However, this last thought of Imoinda's being ravished, changed the measures of his revenge; and whereas before he designed to be himself her executioner, he now resolved she should not die. But as it is the greatest crime in nature amongst them, to touch a woman after having been possessed by a son, a father, or a brother, so now he looked on Imoinda as a polluted thing wholly unfit for his embrace; nor would he resign her to his grandson, because she had received the Royal Veil: he therefore removes her from the Otan, with Onahal; whom he put into safe hands, with the order they should be both sold off as slaves to another country, either Christian or heathen, it was no matter where.

This cruel sentence, worse than death, they implored might be reversed; but their prayers were vain, and it was put in execution accordingly, and that with so much secrecy, that none, either without or within the Otan, knew anything of their absence, or their destiny.

The old King nevertheless executed this with a great deal of reluctancy; but he believed he had made a very great conquest over himself, when he had once resolved, and had performed what he resolved. He believed now, that his love had been unjust; and that he could not expect the gods, or Captain of the Clouds (as they call the unknown power) would suffer a better consequence from so ill a cause. He now begins to hold Oroonoko excused; and to say, he had reason for what he did. And now every body could assure the King how passionately Imoinda was beloved by the Prince; even those confessed it now, who said the contrary before his flame was not abated. So that the King being old, and not able to defend himself in war, and having no sons of all his race remaining alive, but only this to maintain him on his throne; and looking on this as a man disobliged, first by the rape of his mistress, or rather wife, and now by depriving him wholly of her, he feared, might make him desperate, and do some cruel thing, either to himself or his old grandfather the offender, he began to repent him extremely of the contempt he had, in his rage, put on Imoinda. Besides, he considered he ought in honour to have

killed her for this offence, if it had been one. He
ought to have had so much value and consideration
for a maid of her quality, as to have nobly put her to
death, and not to have sold her like a common slave;
the greatest revenge, and the most disgraceful of any,
and to which they a thousand times prefer death, and
implore it; as Imoinda did, but could not obtain that
honour. Seeing therefore it was certain that Oroonoko would highly resent this affront, he thought
good to make some excuse for his rashness to him;
and to that end, he sent a messenger to the camp,
with orders to treat with him about the matter, to
gain his pardon, and endeavour to mitigate his grief:
but that by no means he should tell him she was sold,
but secretly put to death; for he knew he should
never obtain his pardon for the other.

When the messenger came, he found the Prince
upon the point of engaging with the enemy; but as soon
as he heard of the arrival of the messenger, he commanded him to his tent, where he embraced him, and
received him with joy; which was soon abated by the
downcast looks of the messenger, who was instantly
demanded the cause by Oroonoko; who, impatient of
delay, asked a thousand questions in a breath, and all
concerning Imoinda. But there needed little return;
for he could almost answer himself of all he demanded, from his sight and eyes. At last the messenger casting himself at the Prince's feet, and kissing
them with all the submission of a man that had something to implore which he dreaded to utter, besought
him to hear with calmness what he had to deliver to
him, and to call up all his noble and heroic courage,
to encounter with his words, and defend himself
against the ungrateful things he had to relate. Oroonoko replied, with a deep sigh, and a languishing
voice, 'I am armed against their worst efforts, for I
know they will tell me, Imoinda is no more—— And
after that, you may spare the rest.' Then, commanding him to rise, he laid himself on a carpet, under a

rich pavilion, and remained a good while silent, and was hardly heard to sigh. When he was come a little to himself, the messenger asked him leave to deliver that part of his embassy which the Prince had not yet divined: and the Prince cried, 'I permit thee.' Then he told him the affliction the old King was in, for the rashness he had committed in his cruelty to Imoinda; and how he deigned to ask pardon for his offence, and to implore the Prince would not suffer that loss to touch his heart too sensibly, which now all the gods could not restore him, but might recompense him in glory, which he begged he would pursue; and that death, that common revenger of all injuries, would soon even the account between him and a feeble old man.

Oroonoko bad him return his duty to his lord and master; and to assure him, there was no account of revenge to be adjudged between them: if there was, he was the aggressor, and that death would be just, and, maugre his age, would see him righted; and he was contented to leave his share of glory to youths more fortunate and worthy of that favour from the gods: that henceforth he would never lift a weapon, or draw a bow, but abandon the small remains of his life to sighs and tears, and the continual thoughts of what his lord and grandfather had thought good to send out of the world, with all that youth, that innocence and beauty.

After having spoken this, whatever his greatest officers and men of the best rank could do, they could not raise him from the carpet, or persuade him to action, and resolutions of life; but commanding all to retire, he shut himself into his pavilion all that day, while the enemy was ready to engage: and wondering at the delay, the whole body of the chief of the army then addressed themselves to him, and to whom they had much ado to get admittance. They fell on their faces at the foot of his carpet, where they lay, and besought him with earnest prayers and tears

to lead them forth to battle, and not let the enemy
take advantages of them; and implored him to
have regard to his glory, and to the world, that depended on his courage and conduct. But he made no
other reply to all their supplications than this, that he
had now no more business for glory; and for the world,
it was a trifle not worth his care: 'Go,' continued he,
sighing, 'and divide it amongst you, and reap with
joy what you so vainly prize, and leave me to my
more welcome destiny.'

They then demanded what they should do, and
whom he would constitute in his room, that the confusion of ambitious youth and power might not ruin
their order, and make them a prey to the enemy. He
replied, he would not give himself that trouble, but
wished them to choose the bravest man amongst
them, let his quality or birth be what it would: 'For,
oh my friends!' says he, 'it is not titles make men
brave or good; or birth that bestows courage and
generosity, or makes the owner happy. Believe this,
when you behold Oroonoko the most wretched, and
abandoned by fortune, of all the creation of the
gods.' So turning himself about, he would make no
more reply to all they could urge or implore.

The army beholding their officers return unsuccessful, with sad faces and ominous looks, that presaged
no good luck, suffered a thousand fears to take possession of their hearts, and the enemy to come even
upon them before they could provide for their safety
by any defence: and though they were assured by
some who had a mind to animate them, that they
should be immediately headed by the Prince: and
that in the mean time Aboan had orders to command
as General; yet they were so dismayed for want of
that great example of bravery, that they could make
but a very feeble resistance; and, at last, downright
fled before the enemy, who pursued them to the very
tents, killing them: nor could all Aboan's courage,
which that day gained him immortal glory, shame

them into a manly defence of themselves. The
guards that were left behind about the Prince's tent,
seeing the soldiers flee before the enemy, and scatter
themselves over the plain, in great disorder, made
such outcries, as roused the Prince from his amorous
slumber, in which he had remained buried for two
days, without permitting any sustenance to approach
him.   But, in spite of all his resolutions, he had not
the constancy of grief to that degree, as to make
him insensible of the danger of his army; and in
that instant he leaped from his couch, and cried—
'Come, if we must die, let us meet death the noblest
way; and it will be more like Oroonoko to encounter
him at an army's head, opposing the torrent of a
conquering foe, than lazily on a couch, to wait his
lingering pleasure, and die every moment by a thousand racking thoughts; or be tamely taken by an
enemy, and led a whining, love-sick slave to adorn
the triumphs of Jamoan, that young victor, who already is entered beyond the limits I have prescribed
him.'

While he was speaking, he suffered his people to
dress him for the field; and sallying out of his
pavilion, with more life and vigour in his countenance
than ever he showed, he appeared like some Divine
Power descended to save his country from destruction :
and his people had purposely put him on all things
that might make him shine with most splendour, to
strike a reverend awe into the beholders.   He flew
into the thickest of those that were pursuing his men;
and being animated with despair, he fought as if he
came on purpose to die, and did such good things as
will not be believed that human strength could perform ; and such, as soon inspired all the rest with
new courage, and new ardour.   And now it was that
they began to fight indeed ; and so, as if they would
not be outdone even by their adored hero ; who
turning the tide of the victory, changing absolutely
the fate of the day, gained an entire conquest : and

Oroonoko having the good fortune to single out Jamoan, he took him prisoner with his own hand, having wounded him almost to death.

This Jamoan afterwards became very dear to him, being a man very gallant, and of excellent graces, and fine parts; so that he never put him amongst the rank of captives as they used to do, without distinction, for the common sale, or market, but kept him in his own court, where he retained nothing of the prisoner but the name, and returned no more into his own country; so great an affection he took for Oroonoko, and by a thousand tales and adventures of love and gallantry, flattered his disease of melancholy and languishment; which I have often heard him say had certainly killed him, but for the conversation of this prince and Aboan, and the French Governor he had from his childhood, of whom I have spoken before, and who was a man of admirable wit, great ingenuity and learning; all which he had infused into his young pupil. This Frenchman was banished out of his own country for some heretical notions he held; and though he was a man of very little religion, yet he had admirable morals, and a brave soul.

After the total defeat of Jamoan's army, which all fled, or were left dead upon the place, they spent some time in the camp; Oroonoko choosing rather to remain awhile there in his tents, than to enter into a Palace, or live in a Court where he had so lately suffered so great a loss; the officers therefore, who saw and knew his cause of discontent, invented all sorts of diversions and sports to entertain their Prince: so that what with those amusements abroad, and others at home, that is, within their tents, with the persuasions, arguments, and care of his friends and servants that he more peculiarly prized, he wore off in time a great part of that chagrin, and torture of despair, which the first efforts of Imoinda's death had given him; insomuch, as having received a thousand kind embassies from the King, and invitation to return to Court, he obeyed, though with no little reluctancy ; and when he did so, there was a visible change in him, and for a long time he was much more melancholy than before. But time lessens all extremes, and reduces them to mediums, and unconcern ; but no motives of beauties, though all endeavoured it, could engage him in any sort of amour, though he had all the invitations to it, both from his own youth, and other ambitions and designs.

Oroonoko was no sooner returned from this last conquest, and received at Court with all the joy and magnificence that could be expressed to a young victor, who was not only returned triumphant, but beloved like a deity, than there arrived in the port an English ship.

The master of it had often before been in these countries, and was very well known to Oroonoko, with whom he had trafficked for slaves, and had used to do the same with his predecessors.

This commander was a man of a finer sort of address and conversation, better bred, and more engaging, than most of that sort of men are ; so that he seemed rather never to have been bred out of a Court, than almost all his life at sea. This captain therefore was always better received at Court, than most of the traders to those countries were ; and especially by Oroonoko, who was more civilised, according to the European mode, than any other had been, and took more delight in the white nations ; and, above all, men of parts and wit. To this captain he sold abundance of his slaves ; and for the favour and esteem he had for him, made him many presents, and obliged him to stay at Court as long as possibly he could. Which the captain seemed to take as a very great honour done him, entertaining the Prince every day with globes and maps, and mathematical discourses and instruments ;

D

eating, drinking, hunting, and living with him with so much familiarity, that it was not to be doubted but he had gained very greatly upon the heart of this gallant young man. And the captain, in return of all these mighty favours, besought the Prince to honour his vessel with his presence some day or other at dinner, before he should set sail; which he condescended to accept, and appointed his day. The captain, on his part, failed not to have all things in a readiness, in the most magnificent order he could possibly; and the day being come, the captain, in his boat, richly adorned with carpets and velvet cushions, rowed to the shore to receive the Prince; with another long-boat, where was placed all his music and trumpets, with which Oroonoko was extremely delighted; who met him on the shore, attended by his French Governor, Jamoan, Aboan, and about a hundred of the noblest of the youths of the Court; and after they had first carried the Prince on board, the boats fetched the rest off; where they found a very splendid treat, with all sorts of fine wines; and were as well entertained, as it was possible in such a place to be.

The Prince having drunk hard of punch, and several sorts of wine, as did all the rest, (for great care was taken they should want nothing of that part of the entertainment) was very merry, and in great admiration of the ship, for he had never been in one before; so that he was curious of beholding every place where he decently might descend. The rest, no less curious, who were not quite overcome with drinking, rambled at their pleasure fore and aft, as their fancies guided them; so that the captain, who had well laid his design before, gave the word, and seized on all his guests; then, clapping great irons suddenly on the Prince, when he was leaped down into the hold, to view that part of the vessel, and locking him fast down, secured him. The same treachery was used to all the rest; and all in one

instant, in several places of the ship, were lashed
fast in irons, and betrayed to slavery. That great
design over, they set all hands at work to hoist sail;
and with as treacherous as fair a wind they made
from the shore with this innocent and glorious
prize, who thought of nothing less than such an
entertainment.

Some have commended this act, as brave in the
captain; but I will spare my sense of it, and leave
it to my reader to judge as he pleases. It may
be easily guessed, in what manner the Prince resented
this indignity, who may be best resembled to a lion
taken in a toil; so he raged, so he struggled for
liberty, but all in vain; and they had so wisely
managed his fetters, that he could not use a hand
in his defence, to quit himself of a life that would by
no means endure slavery; nor could he move from
the place where he was tied, to any solid part of the
ship, against which he might have beat his head, and
have finished his disgrace that way. So that being
deprived of all other means, he resolved to perish for
want of food; and pleased at last with that thought,
and toiled and tired by rage and indignation, he laid
himself down, and sullenly resolved upon dying, and
refused all things that were brought him.

This did not a little vex the captain, and the more
so, because he found almost all of them of the same
humour; so that the loss of so many brave slaves,
so tall and goodly to behold, would have been very
considerable; he therefore ordered one to go from
him (for he would not be seen himself) to Oroonoko,
and to assure him, he was afflicted for having rashly
done so inhospitable a deed, and which could not be
now remedied, since they were far from shore; but
since he resented it in so high a nature, he assured
him he would revoke his resolution, and set both him
and his friends ashore on the next land they should
touch at; and of this the messenger gave him his
oath, provided he would resolve to live. And

Oroonoko, whose honour was such, as he never had violated a word in his life himself, much less a solemn asseveration, believed in an instant what this man said; but replied, he expected, for a confirmation of this, to have his shameful fetters dismissed. This demand was carried to the captain; who returned him answer, that the offence had been so great which he had put upon the Prince, that he durst not trust him with liberty while he remained in the ship, for fear, lest by a valour natural to him, and a revenge that would animate that valour, he might commit some outrage fatal to himself, and the King his master, to whom the vessel did belong. To this Oroonoko replied, He would engage his honour to behave himself in all friendly order and manner, and obey the command of the captain, as he was lord of the King's vessel, and General of those men under his command.

This was delivered to the still doubting captain, who could not resolve to trust a heathen, he said, upon his parole, a man that had no sense or notion of the god that he worshipped. Oroonoko then replied, He was very sorry to hear that the captain pretended to the knowledge and worship of any gods, who had taught him no better principles, than not to credit as he would be credited. But they told him, the difference of their faith occasioned that distrust; for the captain had protested to him upon the word of a Christian, and sworn in the name of a great God; which if he should violate, he must expect eternal torments in the world to come. 'Is that all the obligations he has to be just to his oath?' replied Oroonoko. 'Let him know, I swear by my honour; which to violate, would not only render me contemptible and despised by all brave and honest men, and so give myself perpetual pain, but it would be eternally offending and displeasing to all mankind; harming, betraying, circumventing, and outraging all men. But punishments hereafter are

suffered by one's self; and the world takes no
cognizance whether this God has revenged them
or not, it is done so secretly, and deferred so long;
while the man of no honour suffers every moment
the scorn and contempt of the honester world, and
dies every day ignominiously in his fame, which is
more valuable than life. I speak not this to move
belief, but to show you how you mistake, when you
imagine, that he who will violate his honour, will
keep his word with his gods.' So, turning from him
with a disdainful smile, he refused to answer him,
when he urged him to know what answer he should
carry back to his captain; so that he departed without saying any more.

The captain pondering and consulting what to do,
it was concluded, that nothing but Oroonoko's liberty
would encourage any of the rest to eat, except the
Frenchman, whom the captain could not pretend
to keep prisoner, but only told him, he was secured,
because he might act something in favour of the
Prince; but that he should be freed as soon as they
came to land. So that they concluded it wholly
necessary to free the Prince from his irons, that he
might show himself to the rest; that they might
have an eye upon him, and that they could not fear
a single man.

This being resolved, to make the obligation the
greater, the captain himself went to Oroonoko;
where, after many compliments, and assurances of
what he had already promised, he receiving from
the Prince his parole, and his hand, for his good
behaviour, dismissed his irons, and brought him
to his own cabin; where, after having treated and
reposed him a while, (for he had neither eaten nor
slept in four days before) he besought him to visit
those obstinate people in chains, who refused all
manner of sustenance; and entreated him to oblige
them to eat, and assure them of their liberty the first
opportunity.

Oroonoko, who was too generous not to give credit to his words, showed himself to his people, who were transported with excess of joy at the sight of their darling Prince; falling at his feet, and kissing and embracing them ; believing, as some divine oracle, all he assured them. But he besought them to bear their chains with that bravery that became those whom he had seen act so nobly in arms; and that they could not give him greater proofs of their love and friendship, since it was all the security the captain (his friend) could have against the revenge, he said, they might possibly justly take for the injuries sustained by him.   And they all, with one accord, assured him, that they could not suffer enough, when it was for his repose and safety.

After this, they no longer refused to eat, but took what was brought them, and were pleased with their captivity, since by it they hoped to redeem the Prince, who, all the rest of the voyage, was treated with all the respect due to his birth, though nothing could divert his melancholy; and he would often sigh for Imoinda, and think this a punishment due to his misfortune, in having left that noble maid behind him, that fatal night, in the Otan, when he fled to the camp.

Possessed with a thousand thoughts of past joys with this fair young person, and a thousand griefs for her eternal loss, he endured a tedious voyage, and at last arrived at the mouth of the River of Surinam, a colony belonging to the King of England, and where they were to deliver some part of their slaves.   There the merchants and gentlemen of the country going on board, to demand those lots of slaves they had already agreed on ; and amongst those, the overseers of those plantations where I then chanced to be.   The captain, who had given the word, ordered his men to bring up those noble slaves in fetters, whom I have spoken of ; and having put them, some in one, and some in other lots, with women and children (which they call pickaninnies) they sold them off, as slaves to several merchants and gentlemen; not putting any two in one lot, because they would separate them far from each other; nor daring to trust them together, lest rage and courage should put them upon contriving some great action, to the ruin of the colony.

Oroonoko was first seized on, and sold to our overseer, who had the first lot, with seventeen more of all sorts and sizes, but not one of quality with him. When he saw this, he found what they meant; for, as I said, he understood English pretty well; and being wholly unarmed and defenceless, so as it was in vain to make any resistance, he only beheld the captain with a look all fierce and disdainful, upbraiding him with eyes that forced blushes on his guilty cheeks, he only cried in passing over the side of the ship: 'Farewell, sir, 'tis worth my sufferings to gain so true a knowledge, both of you, and of your gods, by whom you swear.' And desiring those that held him to forbear their pains, and telling them he would make no resistance, he cried, 'Come, my fellow-slaves, let us descend, and see if we can meet with more honour and honesty in the next world we shall touch upon.' So he nimbly leapt into the boat, and showing no more concern, suffered himself to be rowed up the river, with his seventeen companions.

The gentleman that bought him was a young Cornish gentleman, whose name was Trefry; a man of great wit, and fine learning, and was carried into those parts by the Lord ——, Governor, to manage all his affairs. He reflecting on the last words of Oroonoko to the captain, and beholding the richness of his vest, no sooner came into the boat, but he fixed his eyes on him; and finding something so extraordinary in his face, his shape and mien, a greatness of look, and haughtiness in his air, and finding he spoke English, had a great mind to be inquiring into his quality and fortune; which, though Oroonoko endeavoured to hide, by only confessing he was above the rank of common slaves, Trefry soon found he was yet something greater than he confessed; and from that moment began to conceive so vast an esteem for him, that he ever after loved him as his dearest brother, and showed him all the civilities due to so great a man.

Trefry was a very good mathematician, and a linguist; could speak French and Spanish; and in the three days they remained in the boat, (for so long were they going from the ship to the plantation) he entertained Oroonoko so agreeably with his art and discourse, that he was no less pleased with Trefry, than he was with the Prince; and he thought himself, at least, fortunate in this, that since he was a slave, as long as he would suffer himself to remain so, he had a man of so excellent wit and parts for a master. So that before they had finished their voyage up the river, he made no scruple of declaring to Trefry all his fortunes, and most part of what I have here re-lated, and put himself wholly into the hands of his new friend, who he found resented all the injuries were done him, and was charmed with all the great-nesses of his actions; which were recited with that modesty, and delicate sense, as wholly vanquished him, and subdued him to his interest. And he promised him, on his word and honour, he would find the means to reconduct him to his own country again; assuring him, he had a perfect abhorrence of so dishonourable an action; and that he would sooner have died, than have been the author of such a perfidy. He found the Prince was very much concerned to know what became of his friends, and how they took their slavery; and Trefry promised to take care about the inquiring after their condition, and that he should have an account of them.

Though, as Oroonoko afterwards said, he had little reason to credit the words of a *Backearary;* yet he knew not why, but he saw a kind of sincerity, and awful truth in the face of Trefry; he saw honesty in his eyes, and he found him wise and witty enough to understand honour : for it was one of his maxims, *A man of wit could not be a knave or villain.*

In their passage up the river, they put in at several houses for refreshment ; and ever when they landed, numbers of people would flock to behold this man : not but their eyes were daily entertained with the sight of slaves ; but the fame of Oroonoko was gone before him, and all people were in admiration of his beauty. Besides, he had a rich habit on, in which he was taken, so different from the rest, and which the captain could not strip him of, because he was forced to surprise his person in the minute he sold him. When he found his habit made him liable, as he thought, to be gazed at the more, he begged Trefry to give him something more befitting a slave, which he did, and took off his robes : nevertheless, he shone through all, and his osenbrigs (a sort of brown Holland suit he had on) could not conceal the graces of his looks and mien ; and he had no less admirers than when he had his dazzling habit on. The Royal Youth appeared in spite of the slave, and people could not help treating him after a different manner, without designing it. As soon as they approached him, they venerated and esteemed him ; his eyes insensibly commanded respect, and his behaviour insinuated it into every soul. So that there was nothing talked of but this young and gallant slave, even by those who yet knew not that he was a prince.

I ought to tell you that the Christians never buy any slaves but they give them some name of their own, their native ones being likely very barbarous, and hard to pronounce ; so that Mr. Trefry gave Oroonoko that of Cæsar ; which name will live in that country as long as that (scarce more) glorious one of the great Roman : for it is most evident he wanted no part of the personal courage of that Cæsar, and acted things as memorable, had they been done in some part of the world replenished with people and historians, that might have given him his due. But his misfortune was, to fall in an obscure world, that afforded only a female pen to celebrate his fame; though I doubt not but it had lived from others' endeavours, if the Dutch, who immediately after his time took that country, had not killed, banished and dispersed all those that were capable of giving the world this great man's life, much better than I have done. And Mr. Trefry, who designed it, died before he began it, and bemoaned himself for not having undertaken it in time.

For the future therefore I must call Oroonoko Cæsar; since by that name only he was known in our western world, and by that name he was received on shore at Parham House, where he was destined a slave. But if the king himself (God bless him) had come ashore there could not have been greater expectation by all the whole plantation, and those neighbouring ones, than was on ours at that time: and he was received more like a governor than a slave: notwithstanding, as the custom was, they assigned him his portion of land, his house and his business up in the plantation. But as it was more for form, than any design to put him to his task, he endured no more of the slave but the name, and remained some days in the house, receiving all visits that were made him, without stirring towards that part of the plantation where the negroes were.

At last, he would needs go view his land, his house, and the business assigned him. But he no sooner came to the houses of the slaves, which are like a little town by itself, the negroes all having left work, but they all came forth to behold him, and found he was that Prince who had, at several times, sold most of them to these parts; and from a veneration they pay to great men, especially if they know them, and from the surprise and awe they had at the sight of him, they all cast themselves at his feet, crying out, in their language, 'Live, O King! Long live, O

King!' and kissing his feet, paid him even divine
homage.

Several English gentlemen were with him, and
what Mr. Trefry had told them was here confirmed;
of which he himself before had no other witness than
Cæsar himself. But he was infinitely glad to find his
grandeur confirmed by the adoration of all the slaves.

Cæsar, troubled with their over-joy, and over-
ceremony, besought them to rise, and to receive him
as their fellow-slave; assuring them he was no better.
At which they set up with one accord a most terrible
and hideous mourning and condoling, which he and
the English had much ado to appease: but at last
they prevailed with them, and they prepared all their
barbarous music, and every one killed and dressed
something of his own stock (for every family has
their land apart, on which, at their leisure times, they
breed all eatable things) and clubbing it together,
made a most magnificent supper, inviting their
Grandee Captain, their *Prince*, to honour it with his
presence; which he did, and several English with
him, where they all waited on him, some playing,
others dancing before him all the time, according to
the manners of their several nations, and with unwearied industry endeavouring to please and delight
him.

While they sat at meat, Mr. Trefry told Cæsar,
that most of these young slaves were undone in love
with a fine she-slave, whom they had had about six
months on their land; the Prince, who never heard
the name of love without a sigh, nor any mention of
it without the curiosity of examining further into
that tale, which of all discourses was most agreeable
to him, asked, how they came to be so unhappy, as
to be all undone for one fair slave? Trefry, who was
naturally amorous, and delighted to talk of love as
well as anybody, proceeded to tell him, they had the
most charming black that ever was beheld on their
plantation, about fifteen or sixteen years old, as he

guessed; that for his part he had done nothing but sigh for her ever since she came; and that all the white beauties he had seen, never charmed him so absolutely as this fine creature had done; and that no man, of any nation, ever beheld her, that did not fall in love with her; and that she had all the slaves perpetually at her feet; and the whole country resounded with the fame of Clemene, for so (said he) we have christened her: but she denies us all with such a noble disdain, that 'tis a miracle to see, that she who can give such eternal desires, should herself be all ice and unconcern. She is adorned with the most graceful modesty that ever beautified youth; the softest sigher——that, if she were capable of love, one would swear she languished for some absent happy man; and so retired, as if she feared a rape even from the God of Day, or that the breezes would steal kisses from her delicate mouth. Her task of work, some sighing lover every day makes it his petition to perform for her; which she accepts blushing, and with reluctancy, for fear he will ask her a look for a recompense, which he dares not presume to hope: so great an awe she strikes into the hearts of her admirers. 'I do not wonder,' replied the Prince, 'that Clemene should refuse slaves, being, as you say, so beautiful; but wonder how she escapes those that can entertain her as you can do; or why, being your slave, you do not oblige her to yield?' 'I confess,' said Trefry, 'when I have, against her will, entertained her with love so long, as to be transported with my passion even above decency, I have been ready to make use of those advantages of strength and force nature has given me. But, oh! she disarms me with that modesty and weeping, so tender and so moving, that I retire, and thank my stars she overcame me.' The company laughed at his civility to a slave, and Cæsar only applauded the nobleness of his passion and nature, since that slave might be noble, or, what was better, have true notions of honour and virtue in her. Thus passed they this night, after having received from the slaves all imaginable respect and obedience.

The next day, Trefry asked Cæsar to walk when the heat was allayed, and designedly carried him by the cottage of the fair slave; and told him she whom he spoke of last night lived there retired: 'But,' says he, 'I would not wish you to approach; for I am sure you will be in love as soon as you behold her.' Cæsar assured him, he was proof against all the charms of that sex; and that if he imagined his heart could be so perfidious to love again after Imoinda, he believed he should tear it from his bosom. They had no sooner spoken, but a little shock-dog, that Clemene had presented her, which she took great delight in, ran out; and she, not knowing anybody was there, ran to get it in again, and bolted out on those who were just speaking of her: when seeing them, she would have run in again, but Trefry caught her by the hand, and cried, 'Clemene, however you fly a lover, you ought to pay some respect to this stranger,' pointing to Cæsar. But she, as if she had resolved never to raise her eyes to the face of a man again, bent them the more to the earth, when he spoke, and gave the Prince the leisure to look the more at her. There needed no long gazing, or consideration, to examine who this fair creature was; he soon saw Imoinda all over her; in a minute he saw her face, her shape, her air, her modesty, and all that called forth his soul with joy at his eyes, and left his body destitute of almost life: it stood without motion, and for a minute knew not that it had a being; and, I believe, he had never come to himself, so oppressed he was with over-joy, if he had not met with this allay, that he perceived Imoinda fall dead in the hands of Trefry. This awakened him, and he ran to her aid, and caught her in his arms, where by degrees she came to herself; and it is needless to tell with what transports, what ecstasies of joy, they both a while beheld each other, without speaking; then snatched each other to their arms; then gazed again, as if they still doubted whether they possessed the blessing they grasped: but when they recovered their speech, it is not to be imagined what tender things they expressed to each other; wondering what strange fate had brought them again together. They soon informed each other of their fortunes, and equally bewailed their fate; but at the same time they mutually protested, that even fetters and slavery were soft and easy, and would be supported with joy and pleasure, while they could be so happy to possess each other, and to be able to make good their vows. Cæsar swore he disdained the empire of the world, while he could behold his Imoinda; and she despised grandeur and pomp, those vanities of her sex, when she could gaze on Oroonoko. He adored the very cottage where she resided, and said, That little inch of the world would give him more happiness than all the universe could do; and she vowed it was a palace, while adorned with the presence of Oroonoko.

Trefry was infinitely pleased with this novel, and found this Clemene was the fair mistress of whom Cæsar had before spoke; and was not a little satisfied, that heaven was so kind to the Prince as to sweeten his misfortunes by so lucky an accident; and leaving the lovers to themselves, was impatient to come down to Parham House (which was on the same plantation) to give me an account of what had happened. I was as impatient to make these lovers a visit, having already made a friendship with Cæsar, and from his own mouth learned what I have related; which was confirmed by his Frenchman, who was set on shore to seek his fortune, and of whom they could not make a slave, because a Christian; and he came daily to Parham Hill to see and pay his respects to his pupil Prince. So that concerning and interesting myself in all that related to Cæsar, whom I had assured of liberty as soon as the Governor arrived, I hasted presently to the place where these lovers were, and was infinitely glad to find this beautiful young slave (who had already gained all our esteems, for her modesty and extraordinary prettiness) to be the same I had heard Cæsar speak so much of. One may imagine then we paid her a treble respect; and though from her being carved in fine flowers and birds all over her body, we took her to be of quality before, yet when we knew Clemene was Imoinda, we could not enough admire her.

I had forgot to tell you, that those who are nobly born of that country, are so delicately cut and raised all over the fore-part of the trunk of their bodies, that it looks as if it were japanned, the works being raised like high point round the edges of the flowers. Some are only carved with a little flower, or bird, at the sides of the temples, as was Cæsar; and those who are so carved over the body, resemble our ancient Picts that are figured in the chronicles, but these carvings are more delicate.

From that happy day Cæsar took Clemene for his wife, to the general joy of all people; and there was as much magnificence as the country could afford at the celebration of this wedding: and in a very short time after she conceived with child, which made Cæsar even adore her, knowing he was the last of his great race. This new accident made him more impatient of liberty, and he was every day treating with Trefry for his and Clemene's liberty, and offered either gold, or a vast quantity of slaves, which should be paid before they let him go, provided he could have any security that he should go when his ransom was paid. They fed him from day to day with promises, and delayed him till the Lord-Governor should come; so that he began to suspect them of falsehood, and that they would delay him till the time of his wife's delivery, and make a slave of the child too; for all the breed is theirs to whom the

parents belong. This thought made him very uneasy, and his sullenness gave them some jealousies
of him ; so that I was obliged, by some persons who
feared a mutiny (which is very fatal sometimes in
those colonies that abound so with slaves, that they
exceed the whites in vast numbers), to discourse with
Cæsar, and to give him all the satisfaction I possibly
could. They knew he and Clemene were scarce an
hour in a day from my lodgings; that they ate with
me, and that I obliged them in all things I was
capable. I entertained them with the lives of the
Romans, and great men, which charmed him to my
company ; and her, with teaching her all the pretty
works that I was mistress of, and telling her stories
of nuns, and endeavouring to bring her to the knowledge of the true God. But of all discourses, Cæsar
liked that the worst, and would never be reconciled
to our notions of the trinity, of which he ever made
a jest; it was a riddle he said would turn his brain
to conceive, and one could not make him understand
what faith was. However, these conversations failed
not altogether so well to divert him, that he liked the
company of us women much above the men, for he
could not drink, and he is but an ill companion in
that country that cannot. So that obliging him to
love us very well, we had all the liberty of speech
with him, especially myself, whom he called his *Great
Mistress ;* and indeed my word would go a great way
with him. For these reasons I had opportunity to
take notice of him, that he was not well pleased of
late, as he used to be; was more retired and thought-
ful ; and told him, I took it ill he should suspect we
would break our words with him, and not permit both
him and Clemene to return to his own kingdom,
which was not so long a way, but when he was once
on his voyage he would quickly arrive there. He
made me some answers that showed a doubt in him,
which made me ask, what advantage it would be to
doubt ? It would but give us a fear of him, and

possibly compel us to treat him so as I should be very loth to behold; that is, it might occasion his confinement. Perhaps this was not so luckily spoke of me, for I perceived he resented that word, which I strove to soften again in vain : however, he assured me, that whatsoever resolutions he should take, he would act nothing upon the white people ; and as for myself, and those upon that plantation where he was, he would sooner forfeit his eternal liberty, and life itself, than lift his hand against his greatest enemy on that place. He besought me to suffer no fears upon his account, for he could do nothing that honour should not dictate; but he accused himself for having suffered slavery so long ; yet he charged that weakness on love alone, who was capable of making him neglect even glory itself; and, for which, now he reproaches himself every moment of the day. Much more to this effect he spoke, with an air impatient enough to make me know he would not be long in bondage ; and though he suffered only the name of a slave, and had nothing of the toil and labour of one, yet that was sufficient to render him uneasy ; and he had been too long idle, who used to be always in action, and in arms. He had a spirit all rough and fierce, and that could not be tamed to lazy rest : and though all endeavours were used to exercise himself in such actions and sports as this world afforded, as running, wrestling, pitching the bar, hunting and fishing, chasing and killing tigers of a monstrous size, which this continent affords in abundance; and wonderful snakes, such as Alexander is reported to have encountered at the river of Amazons, and which Cæsar took great delight to overcome; yet these were not actions great enough for his large soul, which was still panting after more renowned actions.

Before I parted that day with him, I got, with much ado, a promise from him to rest yet a little longer with patience, and wait the coming of the

Lord-Governor, who was every day expected on our shore. He assured me he would, and this promise he desired me to know was given perfectly in complaisance to me, in whom he had an entire confidence.

After this, I neither thought it convenient to trust him much out of our view, nor did the country, who feared him; but with one accord it was advised to treat him fairly, and oblige him to remain within such a compass, and that he should be permitted, as seldom as could be, to go up to the plantations of the negroes; or, if he did, to be accompanied by some that should be rather, in appearance, attendants than spies. This care was for some time taken, and Cæsar looked upon it as a mark of extraordinary respect, and was glad his discontent had obliged them to be more observant to him; he received new assurance from the overseer, which was confirmed to him by the opinion of all the gentlemen of the country, who made their court to him. During this time that we had his company more frequently than hitherto we had had, it may not be unpleasant to relate to you the diversions we entertained him with, or rather he us.

My stay was to be short in that country; because my father died at sea, and never arrived to possess the honour designed him, (which was Lieutenant-General of six-and-thirty islands, besides the continent of Surinam) nor the advantages he hoped to reap by them: so that, though we were obliged to continue on our voyage, we did not intend to stay upon the place. Though, in a word, I must say thus much of it; that certainly had his late Majesty, of sacred memory, but seen and known what a vast and charming world he had been master of in that continent, he would never have parted so easily with it to the Dutch. It is a continent, whose vast extent was never yet known, and may contain more noble earth than all the universe beside; for, they say, it reaches from east to west one way as far as China,

and another to Peru. It affords all things both for
beauty and use; it is there eternal spring, always the
very months of April, May, and June; the shades are
perpetual, the trees bearing at once all degrees of
leaves, and fruit, from blooming buds to ripe autumn:
groves of oranges, lemons, citrons, figs, nutmegs, and
noble aromatics, continually bearing their fragrances:
the trees appearing all like nosegays, adorned with
flowers of different kinds; some are all white, some
purple, some scarlet, some blue, some yellow; bearing
at the same time ripe fruit, and blooming young, or
producing every day new. The very wood of all
these trees has an intrinsic value, above common
timber; for they are, when cut, of different colours,
glorious to behold, and bear a price considerable, to
inlay withal. Besides this, they yield rich balm, and
gums; so that we make our candles of such an
aromatic substance, as does not only give a sufficient
light, but as they burn, they cast their perfumes all
about. Cedar is the common firing, and all the houses
are built with it. The very meat we eat, when set on
the table, if it be native, I mean of the country, perfumes the whole room; especially a little beast called
an Armadillo, a thing which I can liken to nothing
so well as a rhinoceros; it is all in white armour,
so jointed, that it moves as well in it, as if it had
nothing on. This beast is about the bigness of a pig
of six weeks old. But it were endless to give an
account of all the divers wonderful and strange things
that country affords, and which he took a great
delight to go in search of; though those adventures
are oftentimes fatal, and at least dangerous. But
while we had Cæsar in our company on these designs,
we feared no harm, nor suffered any.

As soon as I came into the country, the best house
in it was presented me, called St. John's Hill. It
stood on a vast rock of white marble, at the foot of
which the river ran a vast depth down, and not to be
descended on that side; the little waves still dashing

and washing the foot of this rock, made the softest murmurs and purlings in the world; and the opposite bank was adorned with such vast quantities of different flowers eternally blowing, and every day and hour new, fenced behind them with lofty trees of a thousand rare forms and colours, that the prospect was the most ravishing that fancy can create. On the edge of this white rock, towards the river, was a walk, or grove, of orange and lemon trees, about half the length of the Mall here, whose flowery and fruit-bearing branches met at the top, and hindered the sun, whose rays are very fierce there, from entering a beam into the grove; and the cool air that came from the river made it not only fit to entertain people in, at all the hottest hours of the day, but refresh the sweet blossoms, and made it always sweet and charming; and sure, the whole globe of the world cannot show so delightful a place as this grove was: not all the gardens of boasted Italy can produce a shade to outvie this, which nature has joined with art to render so exceeding fine; and it is a marvel to see how such vast trees, as big as English oaks, could take footing on so solid a rock, and in so little earth as covered that rock. But all things by nature there are rare, delightful, and wonderful. But to our sports.

Sometimes we would go surprising, and in search of young tigers in their dens, watching when the old ones went forth to forage for prey: and oftentimes we have been in great danger, and have fled apace for our lives, when surprised by the dams. But once, above all other times, we went on this design, and Cæsar was with us; who had no sooner stolen a young tiger from her nest, but going off, we encountered the dam, bearing a buttock of a cow, which she had torn off with her mighty paw, and going with it towards her den. We had only four women, Cæsar, and an English gentleman, brother to Harry Martin the great Oliverian; we found there was no escaping this enraged and ravenous beast. However, we women

fled as fast as we could from it ; but our heels had
not saved our lives, if Cæsar had not laid down her
cub, when he found the tiger quit her prey to make
the more speed towards him; and taking Mr. Martin's
sword, desired him to stand aside, or follow the ladies.
He obeyed him; and Cæsar met this monstrous beast
of mighty size, and vast limbs, who came with open
jaws upon him ; and fixing his awful stern eyes full
upon those of the beast, and putting himself into
a very steady and good aiming posture of defence,
ran his sword quite through his breast, down to his
very heart, home to the hilt of the sword. The dying
beast stretched forth her paw, and going to grasp his
thigh, surprised with death in that very moment, did
him no other harm than fixing her long nails in his
flesh very deep, feebly wounded him, but could not
grasp the flesh to tear off any. When he had done
this, he halloaed us to return ; which, after some
assurance of his victory, we did, and found him
lugging out the sword from the bosom of the tiger,
who was laid in her blood on the ground. He took
up the cub, and with an unconcern that had nothing
of the joy or gladness of victory, he came and laid
the whelp at my feet. We all extremely wondered
at his daring, and at the bigness of the beast, which
was about the height of a heifer, but of mighty
great and strong limbs.

Another time, being in the woods, he killed a tiger,
that had long infested that part, and borne away
abundance of sheep and oxen, and other things, that
were for the support of those to whom they belonged.
Abundance of people assailed this beast, some affirm-
ing they had shot her with several bullets quite
through the body at several times ; and some swearing they shot her through the very heart ; and they
believed she was a devil, rather than a mortal thing.
Cæsar had often said, he had a mind to encounter
this monster, and spoke with several gentlemen who
had attempted her ; one crying, I shot her with so

many poisoned arrows, another with his gun in this
part of her, and another in that ; so that he remark-
ing all the places where she was shot, fancied still he
should overcome her, by giving her another sort of
a wound than any had yet done ; and one day said
(at the table) 'What trophies and garlands, ladies,
will you make me, if I bring you home the heart of
this ravenous beast that eats up all your lambs and
pigs ?' We all promised he should be rewarded at
our hands. So taking a bow, which he chose out
of a great many, he went up into the wood, with two
gentlemen, where he imagined this devourer to be.
They had not passed very far into it when they heard
her voice, growling and grumbling, as if she were
pleased with something she was doing. When they
came in view, they found her nuzzling in the belly
of a new ravished sheep, which she had torn open ;
and seeing herself approached, she took fast hold
of her prey with her fore-paws, and set a very fierce
raging look on Cæsar, without offering to approach
him, for fear at the same time of losing what she
had in possession. So that Cæsar remained a good
while, only taking aim, and getting an opportunity
to shoot her where he designed. It was some time
before he could accomplish it ; and to wound her,
and not kill her, would but have enraged her the
more, and endangered him. He had a quiver of
arrows at his side, so that if one failed, he could be
supplied. At last, retiring a little, he gave her
opportunity to eat, for he found she was ravenous,
and fell to as soon as she saw him retire, being
more eager of her prey, than of doing new mischiefs ; when he going softly to one side of her, and
hiding his person behind certain herbage, that grew
high and thick, he took so good aim that, as he
intended he shot her just into the eye, and the
arrow was sent with so good a will, and so sure
a hand, that it stuck in her brain, and made her
caper, and become mad for a moment or two ; but

being seconded by another arrow, she fell dead upon the prey. Cæsar cut her open with a knife, to see where those wounds were that had been reported to him, and why she did not die of them. But I shall now relate a thing that, possibly, will find no credit among men; because it is a notion commonly received with us, that nothing can receive a wound in the heart, and live. But when the heart of this courageous animal was taken out, there were seven bullets of lead in it, the wound seamed up with great scars, and she lived with the bullets a great while, for it was long since they were shot. This heart the conqueror brought up to us, and it was a very great curiosity, which all the country came to see; and which gave Cæsar occasion of many fine discourses of accidents in war, and strange escapes.

At other times he would go a-fishing; and discoursing on that diversion, he found we had in that country a very strange fish, called a Numb-Eel, (an eel of which I have eaten) that while it is alive, it has a quality so cold, that those who are angling, though with a line of ever so great a length, with a rod at the end of it, it shall in the same minute the bait is touched by this eel, seize him or her that holds the rod with a numbness, that shall deprive them of sense for a while; and some have fallen into the water, and others dropped, as dead, on the banks of the rivers where they stood, as soon as this fish touches the bait. Cæsar used to laugh at this, and believed it impossible a man could lose his force at the touch of a fish; and could not understand that philosophy, that a cold quality should be of that nature; however, he had a great curiosity to try whether it would have the same effect on him it had on others, and often tried, but in vain. At last, the sought-for fish came to the bait, as he stood angling on the bank; and instead of throwing away the rod, or giving it a sudden twitch out of the water, whereby he might have caught both the eel, and have dismissed the rod, before it could have too much power over him; for experiment-sake, he grasped it but the harder, and fainting, fell into the river; and being still possessed of the rod, the tide carried him, senseless as he was, a great way, till an Indian boat took him up; and perceived when they touched him, a numbness seize them, and by that knew the rod was in his hand; which with a paddle, (that is a short oar) they struck away, and snatched it into the boat, eel and all. If Cæsar was almost dead, with the effect of this fish, he was more so with that of the water, where he had remained the space of going a league, and they found they had much ado to bring him back to life; but at last they did, and brought him home, where he was in a few hours well recovered and refreshed, and not a little ashamed to find he should be overcome by an eel, and that all the people, who heard his defiance, would laugh at him. But we cheered him up; and he being convinced, we had the eel at supper, which was a quarter of an ell about, and most delicate meat; and was of the more value, since it cost so dear as almost the life of so gallant a man.

About this time we were in many mortal fears, about some disputes the English had with the Indians; so that we could scarce trust ourselves, without great numbers, to go to any Indian towns, or place where they abode, for fear they should fall upon us, as they did immediately after my coming away; and the place being in the possession of the Dutch, they used them not so civilly as the English; so that they cut in pieces all they could take, getting into houses, and hanging up the mother, and all her children about her; and cut a footman I left behind me, all in joints, and nailed him to trees.

This feud began while I was there: so that I lost half the satisfaction I proposed, in not seeing and visiting the Indian towns. But one day, bemoaning of our misfortunes on this account, Cæsar told us, we need not fear, for if we had a mind to go, he would undertake to be our guard. Some would, but most would not venture. About eighteen of us resolved, and took barge, and after eight days, arrived near an Indian town. But approaching it, the hearts of some of our company failed; and they would not venture on shore; so we polled, who would, and who would not. For my part, I said, if Cæsar would, I would go. He resolved; so did my brother, and my woman, a maid of good courage. Now none of us speaking the language of the people, and imagining we should have a half diversion in gazing only; and not knowing what they said, we took a fisherman that lived at the mouth of the river, who had been a long inhabitant there, and obliged him to go with us. But because he was known to the Indians as trading among them, and being, by long living there, become a perfect Indian in colour, we, who had a mind to surprise them, by making them see something they never had seen (that is, white people), resolved only myself, my brother and woman should go. So Cæsar, the fisherman, and the rest, hiding behind some thick reeds and flowers that grew in the banks, let us pass on towards the town, which was on the bank of the river all along. A little distant from the houses, or huts, we saw some dancing, others busied in fetching and carrying of water from the river. They had no sooner spied us, but they set up a loud cry, that frighted us at first; we thought it had been for those that should kill us, but it seems it was of wonder and amazement. They were all naked; and we were dressed, so as is most commode for the hot countries, very glittering and rich; so that we appeared extremely fine; my own hair was cut short, and I had a taffety cap, with black feathers on my head; my brother was in a stuff-suit, with silver loops and buttons, and abundance of green ribbon. This was all infinitely surprising to them : and because we saw them stand still till we approached them, we took heart and advanced, came up to them, and offered them our hands ; which they took, and looked on us round about, calling still for more company; who came swarming out, all wondering, and crying out *Tepeeme;* taking their hair up in their hands, and spreading it wide to those they called out to ; as if they would say (as indeed it signified) *Numberless Wonders,* or not to be recounted, no more than to number the hair of their heads. By degrees they grew more bold, and from gazing upon us round, they touched us, laying their hands upon all the features of our faces, feeling our breasts and arms, taking up one petticoat, then wondering to see another; admiring our shoes and stockings, but more our garters, which we gave them, and they tied about their legs, being laced with silver lace at the ends; for they much esteem any shining things. In fine, we suffered them to survey us as they pleased, and we thought they never would have done admiring us. When Cæsar, and the rest, saw we were received with such wonder, they came up to us; and finding the Indian trader whom they knew, (for it is by these fishermen, called Indian traders, we hold a commerce with them ; for they love not to go far from home, and we never go to them) when they saw him therefore, they set up a new joy, and cried in their language, 'Oh, here's our Tiguamy, and we shall know whether these things can speak.' So advancing to him, some of them gave him their hands, and cried, ' Amora Tiguamy '; which is as much as, *How do you do?* or, *Welcome, friend ;* and all, with one din, began to gabble to him, and asked, if we had sense and wit ? If we could talk of affairs of life and war, as they could do? If we could hunt, swim, and do a thousand things they use? He answered them, We could. Then they invited us into their houses, and dressed venison and buffalo for us ; and going out, gathered

a leaf of a tree, called a *Sarumbo* leaf, of six yards
long, and spread it on the ground for a table-cloth ;
and cutting another in pieces instead of plates, set us
on little low Indian stools, which they cut out of one
entire piece of wood, and paint in a sort of Japan-
work. They serve every one their mess on these pieces
of leaves ; and it was very good, but too high-seasoned
with pepper. When we had eaten, my brother and I
took out our flutes, and played to them, which gave
them new wonder ; and I soon perceived, by an
admiration that is natural to these people, and by the
extreme ignorance and simplicity of them, it were not
difficult to establish any unknown or extravagant
religion among them, and to impose any notions
or fictions upon them. For seeing a kinsman of mine
set some paper on fire with a burning-glass, a trick
they had never before seen, they were like to have
adored him for a god, and begged he would give
them the characters or figures of his name, that they
might oppose it against winds and storms : which he
did, and they held it up in those seasons, and fancied
it had a charm to conquer them, and kept it like a
holy relic. They are very superstitious, and called
him the Great Peeie, that is, *Prophet*. They showed
us their Indian Peeie, a youth of about sixteen years
old, as handsome as nature could make a man.
They consecrate a beautiful youth from his infancy,
and all arts are used to complete him in the finest
manner, both in beauty and shape. He is bred to all
the little arts and cunning they are capable of ; to all
the legerdemain tricks and sleight of hand whereby
he imposes on the rabble, and is both a doctor in
physic and divinity : and by these tricks makes the
sick believe he sometimes eases their pains, by drawing from the afflicted part little serpents, or odd flies,
or worms, or any strange thing : and though they
have besides undoubted good remedies for almost all
their diseases, they cure the patient more by fancy
than by medicines, and make themselves feared,

loved, and reverenced. This young Peeie had a very young wife, who seeing my brother kiss her, came running and kissed me. After this they kissed one another, and made it a great jest, it being so novel; and new admiration and laughing went round the multitude, that they never will forget that ceremony, never before used or known. Cæsar had a mind to see and talk with their war-captains, and we were conducted to one of their houses, where we beheld several of the great captains, who had been at council. But so frightful a vision it was to see them, no fancy can create; no sad dreams can represent so dreadful a spectacle. For my part, I took them for hobgoblins, or fiends, rather than men. But however their shapes appeared, their souls were very humane and noble; but some wanted their noses, some their lips, some both noses and lips, some their ears, and others cut through each cheek, with long slashes, through which their teeth appeared. They had several other formidable wounds and scars, or rather dismemberings. They had *Comitias*, or little aprons before them, and girdles of cotton, with their knives naked stuck in it; a bow at their back, and a quiver of arrows on their thighs; and most had feathers on their heads of divers colours. They cried 'Amora Tiguamy' to us at our entrance, and were pleased we said as much to them. They seated us, and gave us drink of the best sort, and wondered as much as the others had done before to see us. Cæsar was marvelling as much at their faces, wondering how they should be all so wounded in war; he was impatient to know how they all came by those frightful marks of rage or malice, rather than wounds got in noble battle. They told us by our interpreter, that when any war was waging, two men, chosen out by some old captain whose fighting was past, and who could only teach the theory of war, were to stand in competition for the generalship, or great war-captain; and being brought before the old judges, now past labour, they are asked, what they dare do to show they are worthy to lead an army? When he who is first asked, making no reply, cuts off his nose, and throws it contemptibly on the ground; and the other does something to himself that he thinks surpasses him, and perhaps deprives himself of lips and an eye. So they slash on till one gives out, and many have died in this debate. And it is by a passive valour they show and prove their activity; a sort of courage too brutal to be applauded by our black hero; nevertheless, he expressed his esteem of them.

In this voyage Cæsar begat so good an understanding between the Indians and the English, that there were no more fears or heart-burnings during our stay, but we had a perfect, open, and free trade with them. Many things remarkable, and worthy reciting, we met with in this short voyage; because Cæsar made it his business to search out and provide for our entertainment, especially to please his dearly adored Imoinda, who was a sharer in all our adventures; we being resolved to make her chains as easy as we could, and to compliment the Prince in that manner that most obliged him.

As we were coming up again, we met with some Indians of strange aspects; that is, of a larger size, and other sort of features than those of our country. Our Indian slaves, that rowed us, asked them some questions; but they could not understand us, but showed us a long cotton string, with several knots on it, and told us, they had been coming from the mountains so many moons as there were knots: they were habited in skins of a strange beast, and brought along with them bags of gold-dust; which, as well as they could give us to understand, came streaming in little small channels down the high mountains, when the rains fell; and offered to be the convoy to anybody, or persons, that would go to the mountains. We carried these men up to Parham, where they were kept till the Lord-Governor came. And because all

the country was mad to be going on this golden
adventure, the Governor, by his letters, commanded
(for they sent some of the gold to him) that a guard
should be set at the mouth of the river of Amazons
(a river so called, almost as broad as the river of
Thames) and prohibited all people from going up that
river, it conducting to those mountains of gold.   But
we going off for England before the project was
further prosecuted, and the Governor being drowned
in a hurricane, either the design died, or the Dutch
have the advantage of it.   And it is to be bemoaned
what his Majesty lost, by losing that part of America.

Though this digression is a little from my story,
however, since it contains some proofs of the curiosity
and daring of this great man, I was content to omit
nothing of his character.

It was thus for some time we diverted him ; but
now Imoinda began to show she was with child, and
did nothing but sigh and weep for the captivity of
her lord, herself, and the infant yet unborn ; and
believed, if it were so hard to gain the liberty of two,
it would be more difficult to get that for three.   Her
griefs were so many darts in the great heart of Cæsar,
and taking his opportunity, one Sunday, when all
the whites were overtaken in drink, as there were
abundance of several trades, and slaves for four
years, that inhabited among the negro houses ; and
Sunday being their day of debauch, (otherwise they
were a sort of spies upon Cæsar) he went, pretending
out of goodness to them, to feast among them, and
sent all his music, and ordered a great treat for the
whole gang, about three hundred negroes, and about
a hundred and fifty were able to bear arms, such
as they had, which were sufficient to do execution,
with spirits accordingly.   For the English had none
but rusty swords, that no strength could draw from
a scabbard ; except the people of particular quality,
who took care to oil them, and keep them in good
order.   The guns also, unless here and there one,

or those newly carried from England, would do no
good or harm ; for it is the nature of that country to
rust and eat up iron, or any metals but gold and
silver.   And they are very expert at the bow, which
the negroes and Indians are perfect masters of.

Cæsar, having singled out these men from the
women and children, made a harangue to them
of the miseries and ignominies of slavery; counting
up all their toils and sufferings, under such loads,
burdens and drudgeries, as were fitter for beasts than
men ; senseless brutes, than human souls.   He told
them, it was not for days, months or years, but for
eternity ; there was no end to be of their misfortunes.
They suffered not like men, who might find a glory
and fortitude in oppression ; but like dogs, that loved
the whip and bell, and fawned the more they were
beaten ; that they had lost the divine quality of men,
and were become insensible asses, fit only to bear :
nay, worse ; an ass, or dog, or horse, having done
his duty, could lie down in retreat, and rise to work
again, and while he did his duty, endured no stripes ;
but men, villainous, senseless men, such as they, toiled
on all the tedious week till Black Friday ; and then,
whether they worked or not, whether they were faulty
or meriting, they, promiscuously, the innocent with
the guilty, suffered the infamous whip, the sordid
stripes, from their fellow-slaves, till their blood
trickled from all parts of their body ; blood, whose
every drop ought to be revenged with a life of some
of those tyrants that impose it.   'And why,' said he,
'my dear friends and fellow-sufferers, should we be
slaves to an unknown people?   Have they vanquished
us nobly in fight?   Have they won us in honourable
battle?   And are we by the chance of war become
their slaves?   This would not anger a noble heart ;
this would not animate a soldier's soul.   No, but we
are bought and sold like apes or monkeys, to be
the sport of women, fools and cowards; and the
support of rogues and runagates, that have aban-

doned their own countries for rapine, murders, theft and villainies. Do you not hear every day how they upbraid each other with infamy of life, below the wildest savages? And shall we render obedience to such a degenerate race, who have no one human virtue left, to distingush them from the vilest creatures? Will you, I say, suffer the lash from such hands?' They all replied with one accord, 'No, no, no; Cæsar has spoke like a great captain, like a great king.'

After this he would have proceeded, but was interrupted by a tall negro, of some more quality than the rest, his name was Tuscan; who bowing at the feet of Cæsar, cried, 'My lord, we have listened with joy and attention to what you have said; and, were we only men, would follow so great a leader through the world. But O! consider we are husbands and parents too, and have things more dear to us than life; our wives and children, unfit for travel in those unpassable woods, mountains and bogs. We have not only difficult lands to overcome, but rivers to wade, and mountains to encounter; ravenous beasts of prey.'

To this Cæsar replied, that honour was the first principle in nature, that was to be obeyed; but as no man would pretend to that, without all the acts of virtue, compassion, charity, love, justice and reason, he found it not inconsistent with that, to take equal care of their wives and children as they would of themselves; and that he did not design, when he led them to freedom, and glorious liberty, that they should leave that better part of themselves to perish by the hand of the tyrant's whip. But if there were a woman among them so degenerate from love and virtue, to choose slavery before the pursuit of her husband, and with the hazard of her life, to share with him in his fortunes; that such a one ought to be abandoned, and left as a prey to the common enemy.

To which they all agreed—and bowed. After this, he spoke of the impassable woods and rivers; and convinced them, the more danger the more glory. He told them, that he had heard of one Hannibal, a great captain, had cut his way through mountains of solid rocks; and should a few shrubs oppose them, which they could fire before them? No, it was a trifling excuse to men resolved to die, or overcome. As for bogs, they are with a little labour filled and hardened; and the rivers could be no obstacle, since they swam by nature, at least by custom, from the first hour of their birth. That when the children were weary, they must carry them by turns, and the woods and their own industry would afford them food. To this they all assented with joy.

Tuscan then demanded, what he would do. He said he would travel towards the sea, plant a new colony, and defend it by their valour; and when they could find a ship, either driven by stress of weather, or guided by providence that way, they would seize it, and make it a prize, till it had transported them to their own countries: at least they should be made free in his kingdom, and be esteemed as his fellow-sufferers, and men that had the courage and the bravery to attempt, at least, for liberty; and if they died in the attempt, it would be more brave, than to live in perpetual slavery.

They bowed and kissed his feet at this resolution, and with one accord vowed to follow him to death; and that night was appointed to begin their march. They made it known to their wives, and directed them to tie their hammocks about their shoulders, and under their arms, like a scarf, and to lead their children that could go, and carry those that could not. The wives, who pay an entire obedience to their husbands, obeyed, and stayed for them where they were appointed. The men stayed but to furnish themselves with what defensive arms they could get; and all met at the rendezvous, where Cæsar

F

made a new encouraging speech to them and led them out.

But as they could not march far that night, on Monday early, when the overseers went to call them all together, to go to work, they were extremely surprised, to find not one upon the place, but all fled with what baggage they had. You may imagine this news was not only suddenly spread all over the plantation, but soon reached the neighbouring ones; and we had by noon about six hundred men, they call the Militia of the country, that came to assist us in the pursuit of the fugitives. But never did one see so comical an army march forth to war. The men of any fashion would not concern themselves, though it were almost the common cause; for such revoltings are very ill examples, and have very fatal consequences oftentimes, in many colonies. But they had a respect for Cæsar, and all hands were against the Parhamites (as they called those of Parham Plantation) because they did not in the first place love the Lord-Governor; and secondly, they would have it, that Cæsar was ill-used, and baffled with: and it is not impossible but some of the best in the country was of his council in this flight, and depriving us of all the slaves; so that they of the better sort would not meddle in the matter. The Deputy-Governor, of whom I have had no great occasion to speak, and who was the most fawning fair-tongued fellow in the world, and one that pretended the most friendship to Cæsar, was now the only violent man against him; and though he had nothing, and so need fear nothing, yet talked and looked bigger than any man. He was a fellow, whose character is not fit to be mentioned with the worst of the slaves. This fellow would lead his army forth to meet Cæsar, or rather to pursue him. Most of their arms were of those sort of cruel whips they call *Cat with nine tails;* some had rusty useless guns for show; others old basket-hilts, whose blades had never seen the light in this age; and others had long staffs and clubs. Mr. Trefry went along, rather to be a mediator than a conqueror in such a battle; for he foresaw and knew, if by fighting they put the negroes into despair, they were a sort of sullen fellows, that would drown or kill themselves before they would yield; and he advised that fair means was best. But Byam was one that abounded in his own wit, and would take his own measures.

It was not hard to find these fugitives; for as they fled, they were forced to fire and cut the woods before them; so that night or day they pursued them by the light they made, and by the path they had cleared. But as soon as Cæsar found he was pursued, he put himself in a posture of defence, placing all the women and children in the rear; and himself, with Tuscan by his side, or next to him, all promising to die or conquer. Encouraged thus, they never stood to parley, but fell on pell-mell upon the English, and killed some, and wounded a great many; they having recourse to their whips, as the best of their weapons. And as they observed no order, they perplexed the enemy so sorely, with lashing them in the eyes; and the women and children seeing their husbands so treated, being of fearful and cowardly dispositions, and hearing the English cry out, ' Yield, and live! Yield, and be pardoned!' they all ran in amongst their husbands and fathers, and hung about them, crying out, ' Yield! Yield! and leave Cæsar to their revenge,' that by degrees the slaves abandoned Cæsar, and left him only Tuscan and his heroic Imoinda, who grown as big as she was, did nevertheless press near her lord, having a bow and a quiver full of poisoned arrows, which she managed with such dexterity, that she wounded several, and shot the Governor into the shoulder; of which wound he had liked to have died, but that an Indian woman, his mistress, sucked the wound, and cleansed it from the venom. But however, he stirred not from the place till he had parleyed with Cæsar, who he found was resolved to die fighting, and would not be taken ; no more would Tuscan or Imoinda.   But he, more thirsting after revenge of another sort, than that of depriving him of life, now made use of all his art of talking and dissembling, and besought Cæsar to yield himself upon terms which he himself should propose, and should be sacredly assented to, and kept by him.   He told him, it was not that he any longer feared him, or could believe the force of two men, and a young heroine, could overthrow all them, and with all the slaves now on their side also ; but it was the vast esteem he had for his person, the desire he had to serve so gallant a man, and to hinder himself from the reproach hereafter, of having been the occasion of the death of a Prince, whose valour and magnanimity deserved the empire of the world.   He protested to him, he looked upon his action as gallant and brave, however tending to the prejudice of his lord and master, who would by it have lost so considerable a number of slaves ; that this flight of his should be looked on as a heat of youth, and a rashness of a too forward courage, and an unconsidered impatience of liberty, and no more ; and that he laboured in vain to accomplish that which they would effectually perform as soon as any ship arrived that would touch on his coast : ' So that if you will be pleased,' continued he, ' to surrender yourself, all imaginable respect shall be paid you ; and yourself, your wife and child, if it be born here, shall depart free out of our land.'   But Cæsar would hear of no composition ; though Byam urged, if he pursued and went on in his design, he would inevitably perish, either by great snakes, wild beasts or hunger ; and he ought to have regard to his wife, whose condition required ease, and not the fatigues of tedious travel, where she could not be secured from being devoured.   But Cæsar told him there was no faith in the white men, or the gods they adored ; who instructed them in principles so false, that honest men

could not live amongst them; though no people professed so much, none performed so little : that he knew
what he had to do when he dealt with men of honour;
but with them a man ought to be eternally on his
guard, and never to eat and drink with Christians,
without his weapon of defence in his hand ; and, for
his own security, never to credit one word they spoke.
As for the rashness and inconsiderateness of his
action, he would confess the Governor is in the right;
and that he was ashamed of what he had done, in
endeavouring to make those free, who were by
nature slaves, poor wretched rogues, fit to be used as
Christians' tools; dogs, treacherous and cowardly, fit
for such masters; and they wanted only but to be
whipped into the knowledge of the Christian gods, to
be the vilest of all creeping things; to learn to worship such deities as had not power to make them just,
brave, or honest.   In fine, after a thousand things of
this nature, not fit here to be recited, he told Byam
he had rather die than live upon the same earth with
such dogs.   But Trefry and Byam pleaded and protested together so much, that Trefry believing the
Governor to mean what he said, and speaking very
cordially himself, generously put himself into Cæsar's
hands, and took him aside, and persuaded him, even
with tears, to live, by surrendering himself, and to
name his conditions.   Cæsar was overcome by his wit
and reasons, and in consideration of Imoinda ; and
demanding what he desired, and that it should be
ratified by their hands in writing, because he had
perceived that was the common way of contract
between man and man amongst the whites ; all this
was performed, and Tuscan's pardon was put in, and
they surrendered to the Governor, who walked peace-
ably down into the plantation with them, after giving
order to bury their dead.   Cæsar was very much
toiled with the bustle of the day, for he had fought
like a fury ; and what mischief was done, he and
Tuscan performed alone; and gave their enemies a

fatal proof, that they durst do anything, and feared no mortal force.

But they were no sooner arrived at the place where all the slaves receive their punishments of whipping, but they laid hands on Cæsar and Tuscan, faint with heat and toil; and surprising them, bound them to two several stakes, and whipped them in a most deplorable and inhuman manner, rending the very flesh from their bones, especially Cæsar, who was not perceived to make any moan or to alter his face, only to roll his eyes on the faithless Governor, and those he believed guilty, with fierceness and indignation; and to complete his rage, he saw every one of those slaves who but a few days before adored him as something more than mortal, now had a whip to give him some lashes, while he strove not to break his fetters; though if he had, it were impossible: but he pronounced a woe and revenge from his eyes, that darted fire, which was at once both awful and terrible to behold.

When they thought they were sufficiently revenged on him, they untied him, almost fainting with loss of blood from a thousand wounds all over his body, from which they had rent his clothes, and led him bleeding and naked as he was, and loaded him all over with irons; and then rubbed his wounds, to complete their cruelty, with Indian pepper, which had like to have made him raving mad; and, in this condition made him so fast to the ground, that he could not stir, if his pains and wounds would have given him leave. They spared Imoinda, and did not let her see this barbarity committed towards her lord, but carried her down to Parham, and shut her up; which was not in kindness to her, but for fear she should die with the sight, or miscarry, and then they should lose a young slave, and perhaps the mother.

You must know, that when the news was brought on Monday morning, that Cæsar had betaken himself to the woods, and carried with him all the negroes, we were possessed with extreme fear, which no per-

suasions could dissipate, that he would secure himself
till night, and then would come down and cut all our
throats. This apprehension made all the females of
us fly down the river, to be secured; and while we
were away, they acted this cruelty; for I suppose I
had authority and interest enough there, had I suspected any such thing, to have prevented it: but we
had not gone many leagues, but the news overtook
us, that Cæsar was taken and whipped like a common
slave. We met on the river with Colonel Martin, a
man of great gallantry, wit, and goodness, and whom
I have celebrated in a character of my new comedy,
by his own name, in memory of so brave a man. He
was wise and eloquent, and, from the fineness of his
parts, bore a great sway over the hearts of all the
colony. He was a friend to Cæsar, and resented this
false dealing with him very much. We carried him
back to Parham, thinking to have made an accommodation; when he came, the first news we heard,
was, that the Governor was dead of a wound Imoinda
had given him; but it was not so well. But it seems,
he would have the pleasure of beholding the revenge
he took on Cæsar; and before the cruel ceremony
was finished, he dropped down; and then they perceived the wound he had on his shoulder was by a
venomed arrow, which, as I said, his Indian mistress
healed, by sucking the wound.

We were no sooner arrived, but we went up to the
plantation to see Cæsar; whom we found in a very
miserable and inexpressible condition; and I have a
thousand times admired how he lived in so much
tormenting pain. We said all things to him, that
trouble, pity and good-nature could suggest, protesting our innocency of the fact, and our abhorrence of
such cruelties; making a thousand professions and
services to him, and begging as many pardons for the
offenders, till we said so much, that he believed we
had no hand in his ill-treatment; but told us, he
could never pardon Byam; as for Trefry, he con-

fessed he saw his grief and sorrow for his suffering, which he could not hinder, but was like to have been beaten down by the very slaves, for speaking in his defence. But for Byam, who was their leader, their head—and should, by his justice and honour, have been an example to them—for him, he wished to live to take a dire revenge of him ; and said, 'It had been well for him, if he had sacrificed me, instead of giving me the contemptible whip.' He refused to talk much ; but begging us to give him our hands, he took them, and protested never to lift up his to do us any harm. He had a great respect for Colonel Martin, and always took his counsel like that of a parent ; and assured him, he would obey him in anything, but his revenge on Byam : ' Therefore,' said he, ' for his own safety, let him speedily despatch me; for if I could despatch myself, I would not, till that justice were done to my injured person, and the contempt of a soldier. No, I would not kill myself, even after a whipping, but will be content to live with that infamy, and be pointed at by every grinning slave, till I have completed my revenge; and then you shall see, that Oroonoko scorns to live with the indignity that was put on Cæsar.' All we could do, could get no more words from him ; and we took care to have him put immediately into a healing bath, to rid him of his pepper, and ordered a chirurgeon to anoint him with healing balm, which he suffered, and in some time he began to be able to walk and eat. We failed not to visit him every day, and to that end had him brought to an apartment at Parham.

The Governor had no sooner recovered, and had heard of the menaces of Cæsar, but he called his Council, who (not to disgrace them, or burlesque the Government there) consisted of such notorious villains as Newgate never transported ; and, possibly, originally were such who understood neither the laws of God or man, and had no sort of principles to make them worthy the name of men ; but at the very council-table would contradict and fight with one another, and swear so bloodily, that it was terrible to hear and see them. (Some of them were afterwards hanged, when the Dutch took possession of the place, others sent off in chains.) But calling these special rulers of the nation together, and requiring their counsel in this weighty affair, they all concluded, that (damn them) it might be their own cases; and that Cæsar ought to be made an example to all the negroes, to fright them from daring to threaten their betters, their lords and masters; and at this rate no man was safe from his own slaves; and concluded, *nemine contradicente*, that Cæsar should be hanged.

Trefry then thought it time to use his authority, and told Byam, his command did not extend to his lord's plantation; and that Parham was as much exempt from the law as White Hall; and that they ought no more to touch the servants of the Lord —— (who there represented the King's person) than they could those about the King himself; and that Parham was a sanctuary; and though his lord were absent in person, his power was still in being there, which he had entrusted with him, as far as the dominions of his particular plantations reached, and all that belonged to it; the rest of the country, as Byam was lieutenant to his lord, he might exercise his tyranny upon. Trefry had others as powerful, or more, that interested themselves in Cæsar's life, and absolutely said, he should be defended. So turning the Governor, and his wise Council, out of doors, (for they sat at Parham House) we set a guard upon our lodging-place, and would admit none but those we called friends to us and Cæsar.

The Governor having remained wounded at Parham, till his recovery was completed, Cæsar did not know but he was still there, and indeed for the most part, his time was spent there: for he was one that loved to live at other people's expense, and if he were a day absent, he was ten present there; and used to

play, and walk, and hunt, and fish with Cæsar. So
that Cæsar did not at all doubt, if he once recovered
strength, but he should find an opportunity of being
revenged on him; though, after such a revenge, he
could not hope to live: for if he escaped the fury of
the English mobile, who perhaps would have been
glad of the occasion to have killed him, he was resolved not to survive his whipping; yet he had some
tender hours, a repenting softness, which he called his
fits of cowardice, wherein he struggled with love for
the victory of his heart, which took part with his
charming Imoinda there; but for the most part, his
time was passed in melancholy thoughts, and black
designs. He considered, if he should do this deed,
and die either in the attempt, or after it, he left his
lovely Imoinda a prey, or at best a slave to the enraged multitude; his great heart could not endure
that thought: 'Perhaps,' said he, 'she may be first
ravished by every brute; exposed first to their nasty
lusts, and then a shameful death.' No, he could not
live a moment under that apprehension, too insupportable to be borne.   These were his thoughts, and
his silent arguments with his heart, as he told us
afterwards. So that now resolving not only to kill
Byam, but all those he thought had enraged him;
pleasing his great heart with the fancied slaughter he
should make over the whole face of the plantation;
he first resolved on a deed (that however horrid it
first appeared to us all) when we had heard his
reasons, we thought it brave and just.   Being able to
walk, and, as he believed, fit for the execution of his
great design, he begged Trefry to trust him into the
air, believing a walk would do him good; which was
granted him; and taking Imoinda with him, as he
used to do in his more happy and calmer days, he led
her up into a wood, where (after with a thousand
sighs, and long gazing silently on her face, while tears
gushed, in spite of him, from his eyes) he told her his
design, first of killing her, and then his enemies, and

next himself, and the impossibility of escaping, and therefore he told her the necessity of dying. He found the heroic wife faster pleading for death, than he was to propose it, when she found his fixed resolution; and, on her knees, besought him not to leave her a prey to his enemies. He (grieved to death) yet pleased at her noble resolution, took her up, and embracing of her with all the passion and languishment of a dying lover, drew his knife to kill this treasure of his soul, this pleasure of his eyes; while tears trickled down his cheeks, hers were smiling with joy she should die by so noble a hand, and be sent into her own country (for that is their notion of the next world) by him she so tenderly loved, and so truly adored in this. For wives have a respect for their husbands equal to what any other people pay a deity; and when a man finds any occasion to quit his wife, if he love her, she dies by his hand; if not, he sells her, or suffers some other to kill her. It being thus, you may believe the deed was soon resolved on; and it is not to be doubted, but the parting, the eternal leave-taking of two such lovers, so greatly born, so sensible, so beautiful, so young, and so fond, must be very moving, as the relation of it was to me afterwards.

All that love could say in such cases, being ended, and all the intermitting irresolutions being adjusted, the lovely, young and adored victim lays herself down before the sacrificer; while he, with a hand resolved, and a heart-breaking within, gave the fatal stroke, first cutting her throat, and then severing her yet smiling face from that delicate body, pregnant as it was with the fruits of tenderest love. As soon as he had done, he laid the body decently on leaves and flowers, of which he made a bed, and concealed it under the same cover-lid of nature; only her face he left yet bare to look on. But when he found she was dead, and past all retrieve, never more to bless him with her eyes, and soft language, his grief swelled up to rage; he tore, he raved, he roared like some monster of the wood, calling on the loved name of Imoinda. A thousand times he turned the fatal knife that did the deed toward his own heart, with a resolution to go immediately after her; but dire revenge, which was now a thousand times more fierce in his soul than before, prevents him; and he would cry out, 'No, since I have sacrificed Imoinda to my revenge, shall I lose that glory which I have purchased so dear, as at the price of the fairest, dearest, softest creature that ever nature made? No, no!' Then at her name grief would get the ascendant of rage, and he would lie down by her side, and water her face with showers of tears, which never were wont to fall from those eyes; and however bent he was on his intended slaughter, he had not power to stir from the sight of this dear object, now more beloved, and more adored than ever.

He remained in this deplorable condition for two days, and never rose from the ground where he had made her sad sacrifice; at last rousing from her side, and accusing himself with living too long, now Imoinda was dead, and that the deaths of those barbarous enemies were deferred too long, he resolved now to finish the great work: but offering to rise, he found his strength so decayed, that he reeled to and fro, like boughs assailed by contrary winds; so that he was forced to lie down again, and try to summon all his courage to his aid. He found his brains turned round, and his eyes were dizzy, and objects appeared not the same to him they were wont to do; his breath was short, and all his limbs surprised with a faintness he had never felt before. He had not eaten in two days, which was one occasion of his feebleness, but excess of grief was the greatest; yet still he hoped he should recover vigour to act his design, and lay expecting it yet six days longer; still mourning over the dead idol of his heart, and striving every day to rise, but could not.

In all this time you may believe we were in no little affliction for Cæsar and his wife; some were of opinion he was escaped, never to return; others thought some accident had happened to him. But however, we failed not to send out a hundred people several ways, to search for him. A party of about forty went that way he took, among whom was Tuscan, who was perfectly reconciled to Byam. They had not gone very far into the wood, but they smelt an unusual smell, as of a dead body; for stinks must be very noisome, that can be distinguished among such a quantity of natural sweets, as every inch of that land produces: so that they concluded they should find him dead, or somebody that was so; they passed on towards it, as loathsome as it was, and made such rustling among the leaves that lie thick on the ground, by continual falling, that Cæsar heard he was approached; and though he had, during the space of these eight days, endeavoured to rise, but found he wanted strength, yet, looking up, and seeing his pursuers, he rose, and reeled to a neighbouring tree, against which he fixed his back; and being within a dozen yards of those that advanced and saw him, he called out to them, and bid them approach no nearer, if they would be safe. So that they stood still, and hardly believing their eyes, that would persuade them that it was Cæsar that spoke to them, so much he was altered; they asked him what he had done with his wife, for they smelt a stink that almost struck them dead? He, pointing to the dead body, sighing, cried, 'Behold her there.' They put off the flowers that covered her, with their sticks, and found she was killed, and cried out, 'Oh, monster! thou hast murdered thy wife.' Then asking him, why he did so cruel a deed? He replied, he had no leisure to answer impertinent questions: 'You may go back,' continued he, 'and tell the faithless Governor, he may thank fortune that I am breathing my last; and that my arm is too feeble to obey my heart, in what it

had designed him.' But his tongue faltering, and
trembling, he could scarce end what he was saying.
The English taking advantage by his weakness, cried,
'Let us take him alive by all means.' He heard
them; and, as if he had revived from a fainting, or
a dream, he cried out, 'No, gentlemen, you are
deceived; you will find no more Cæsars to be
whipped; no more find a faith in me. Feeble as you
think me, I have strength yet left to secure me from
a second indignity.' They swore all anew; and he
only shook his head, and beheld them with scorn.
Then they cried out, 'Who will venture on this single
man? Will nobody?' They stood all silent, while
Cæsar replied, 'Fatal will be the attempt of the first
adventurer, let him assure himself,' and, at that word,
held up his knife in a menacing posture. 'Look ye,
ye faithless crew,' said he, ''tis not life I seek, nor am
I afraid of dying,' and at that word, cut a piece of
flesh from his own throat, and threw it at them, 'yet
still I would live if I could, till I had perfected my
revenge. But, oh! it cannot be; I feel life gliding
from my eyes and heart; and if I make not haste,
I shall fall a victim to the shameful whip.' At that,
he ripped up his own belly, and took his bowels and
pulled them out, with what strength he could; while
some, on their knees imploring, besought him to hold
his hand. But when they saw him tottering, they
cried out, 'Will none venture on him?' A bold
Englishman cried, 'Yes, if he were the Devil,' (taking
courage when he saw him almost dead) and swearing
a horrid oath for his farewell to the world, he rushed
on him. Cæsar with his armed hand, met him so
fairly, as stuck him to the heart, and he fell dead
at his feet. Tuscan seeing that, cried out, 'I love
thee, O Cæsar! and therefore will not let thee die, if
possible'; and running to him, took him in his arms;
but, at the same time, warding a blow that Cæsar
made at his bosom, he received it quite through his
arm; and Cæsar having not strength to pluck the knife

forth, though he attempted it, Tuscan neither pulled
it out himself nor suffered it to be pulled out, but
came down with it sticking in his arm; and the
reason he gave for it, was, because the air should not
get into the wound. They put their hands across,
and carried Cæsar between six of them, fainting as he
was, and they thought dead, or just dying; and they
brought him to Parham, and laid him on a couch,
and had the chirurgeon immediately to him, who
dressed his wounds, and sewed up his belly, and used
means to bring him to life, which they effected. We
ran all to see him! and, if before we thought him
so beautiful a sight, he was now so altered, that
his face was like a death's-head blacked over, nothing
but teeth and eye-holes. For some days we suffered
nobody to speak to him, but caused cordials to be
poured down his throat; which sustained his life, and
in six or seven days he recovered his senses. For,
you must know, that wounds are almost to a miracle
cured in the Indies; unless wounds in the legs, which
they rarely ever cure.

When he was well enough to speak, we talked
to him, and asked him some questions about his wife,
and the reasons why he killed her; and he then told
us what I have related of that resolution, and of his
parting, and he besought us we would let him die,
and was extremely afflicted to think it was possible
he might live. He assured us, if we did not despatch
him, he would prove very fatal to a great many. We
said all we could to make him live, and gave him new
assurances; but he begged we would not think so
poorly of him, or of his love to Imoinda, to imagine
we could flatter him to life again. But the chirurgeon
assured him he could not live, and therefore he need
not fear. We were all (but Cæsar) afflicted at this
news, and the sight was ghastly. His discourse was
sad; and the earthy smell about him so strong, that
I was persuaded to leave the place for some time,
(being myself but sickly, and very apt to fall into fits

of dangerous illness upon any extraordinary melancholy). The servants, and Trefry, and the chirurgeons, promised all to take what possible care they could of the life of Cæsar; and I, taking boat, went with other company to Colonel Martin's, about three days' journey down the river. But I was no sooner gone, than the Governor taking Trefry, about some pretended earnest business, a day's journey up the river, having communicated his design to one Banister, a wild Irishman, one of the Council, a fellow of absolute barbarity, and fit to execute any villainy, but rich; he came up to Parham, and forcibly took Cæsar, and had him carried to the same post where he was whipped; and causing him to be tied to it, and a great fire made before him, he told him he should die like a dog, as he was. Cæsar replied, This was the first piece of bravery that ever Banister did, and he never spoke sense till he pronounced that word; and if he would keep it, he would declare, in the other world, that he was the only man, of all the whites, that ever he heard speak truth. And turning to the men that had bound him, he said, 'My friends, am I to die, or to be whipt?' And they cried, 'Whipt! no, you shall not escape so well.' And then he replied, smiling, 'A blessing on thee'; and assured them they need not tie him, for he would stand fixed like a rock, and endure death so as should encourage them to die: 'But if you whip me,' said he, 'be sure you tie me fast.'

He had learned to take tobacco; and when he was assured he should die, he desired they would give him a pipe in his mouth, ready lighted; which they did. And the executioner came, and first cut off his members, and threw them into the fire; after that, with an ill-favoured knife, they cut off his ears and his nose, and burned them; he still smoked on, as if nothing had touched him; then they hacked off one of his arms, and still he bore up and held his pipe; but at the cutting off the other arm, his head sunk, and his pipe dropped, and he gave up the ghost, without a groan, or a reproach. My mother and sister were by him all the while, but not suffered to save him ; so rude and wild were the rabble, and so inhuman were the justices who stood by to see the execution, who after paid dear enough for their insolence. They cut Cæsar into quarters, and sent them to several of the chief plantations : one quarter was sent to Colonel Martin ; who refused it, and swore, he had rather see the quarters of Banister, and the Governor himself, than those of Cæsar, on his plantations ; and that he could govern his negroes, without terrifying and grieving them with frightful spectacles of a mangled king.

Thus died this great man, worthy of a better fate, and a more sublime wit than mine to write his praise. Yet, I hope, the reputation of my pen is considerable enough to make his glorious name to survive to all ages, with that of the brave, the beautiful and the constant Imoinda.

G

THE FAIR JILT

OR THE AMOURS OF PRINCE TARQUIN
AND MIRANDA

As love is the most noble and divine passion of the
soul, so it is that to which we may justly attribute
all the real satisfactions of life; and without it man
is unfinished and unhappy.

There are a thousand things to be said of the
advantages this generous passion brings to those,
whose hearts are capable of receiving its soft impressions; for it is not every one that can be sensible of
its tender touches. How many examples, from history and observation, could I give of its wondrous
power; nay, even to a degree of transmigration!
How many idiots has it made wise! How many
fools eloquent! How many home-bred squires
accomplished! How many cowards brave! And
there is no sort of species of mankind on whom it
cannot work some change and miracle, if it be a
noble well-grounded passion, except on the fop in
fashion, the hardened incorrigible fop; so often
wounded, but never reclaimed. For still, by a dire
mistake, conducted by vast opiniatrety, and a greater
portion of self-love, than the rest of the race of man,
he believes that affectation in his mien and dress,
that mathematical movement, that formality in every
action, that a face managed with care, and softened
into ridicule, the languishing turn, the toss, and the
back-shake of the periwig, is the direct way to the

heart of the fine person he adores; and instead of
curing love in his soul, serves only to advance his
folly; and the more he is enamoured, the more
industriously he assumes (every hour) the coxcomb.
These are love's playthings, a sort of animals with
whom he sports; and whom he never wounds, but
when he is in good humour, and always shoots
laughing. It is the diversion of the little god, to see
what a fluttering and bustle one of these sparks, new-
wounded, makes; to what fantastic fooleries he has
recourse. The glass is every moment called to
counsel, the valet consulted and plagued for new
invention of dress, the footman and scrutore perpetually employed; billet-doux and madrigals take
up all his mornings, till playtime in dressing, till
night in gazing; still, like a sun-flower, turned towards the beams of the fair eyes of his Cælia, ad-
justing himself in the most amorous posture he can
assume, his hat under his arm, while the other hand
is put carelessly into his bosom, as if laid upon his
panting heart; his head a little bent to one side, supported with a world of cravat-string, which he takes
mighty care not to put into disorder; as one may
guess by a never-failing and horrid stiffness in his
neck; and if he had any occasion to look aside, his
whole body turns at the same time, for fear the
motion of the head alone should incommode the
cravat or periwig. And sometimes the glove is well
managed, and the white hand displayed. Thus, with
a thousand other little motions and formalities, all in
the common place or road of foppery, he takes
infinite pains to show himself to the pit and boxes,
a most accomplished ass. This is he, of all human
kind, on whom love can do no miracles, and who can
nowhere, and upon no occasion, quit one grain of his
refined foppery, unless in a duel, or a battle, if ever
his stars should be so severe and ill-mannered, to
reduce him to the necessity of either. Fear then
would ruffle that fine form he had so long preserved

in nicest order, with grief considering, that an unlucky chance-wound in his face, if such a dire misfortune should befall him, would spoil the sale of it
for ever.

Perhaps it will be urged, that since no metamor-
phosis can be made in a fop by love, you must consider him one of those that only talks of love, and
thinks himself that happy thing, a lover; and wanting fine sense enough for the real passion, believes
what he feels to be it.   There are in the quiver of the
god a great many different darts; some that wound
for a day, and others for a year; they are all fine,
painted, glittering darts, and show as well as those
made of the noblest metal; but the wounds they
make reach the desire only, and are cured by possess-
ing, while the short-lived passion betrays the cheat.
But it is that refined and illustrious passion of the
soul whose aim is virtue, and whose end is honour,
that has the power of changing nature, and is capable
of performing all those heroic things, of which history is full.

How far distant passions may be from one another,
I shall be able to make appear in these following
rules.   I'll prove to you the strong effects of love in
some unguarded and ungoverned hearts; where it
rages beyond the inspirations of 'a God all soft and
gentle,' and reigns more like 'a Fury from Hell.'

I do not pretend here to entertain you with a
feigned story, or anything pieced together with romantic accidents; but every circumstance, to a tittle,
is truth.   To a great part of the main I myself was
an eye-witness; and what I did not see, I was confirmed of by actors in the intrigue, holy men, of the
order of St. Francis.   But for the sake of some of her
relations, I shall give my Fair Jilt a feigned name,
that of Miranda; but my hero must retain his own, it
being too illustrious to be concealed.

You are to understand, that in all the Catholic
countries, where Holy Orders are established, there

are abundance of differing kinds of religious, both of men and women. Amongst the women, there are those we call Nuns, that make solemn vows of perpetual chastity; there are others who make but a simple vow, as for five or ten years, or more or less; and that time expired, they may contract anew for longer time, or marry, or dispose of themselves as they shall see good; and these are ordinarily called Galloping Nuns. Of these there are several Orders; as Canonesses, Begines, Quests, Swart-Sisters, and Jesuitesses, with several others I have forgot. Of those of the Begines was our fair votress.

These Orders are taken up by the best persons of the town, young maids of fortune, who live together, not inclosed, but in palaces that will hold about fifteen hundred or two thousand of these *filles devotes ;* where they have a regulated government, under a sort of Abbess, or Prioress, or rather a *Governante.* They are obliged to a method of devotion, and are under a sort of obedience. They wear a habit much like our widows of quality in England, only without a bando; and their veil is of a thicker crape than what we have here, through which one cannot see the face; for when they go abroad, they cover themselves all over with it; but they put them up in the churches, and lay them by in the houses. Every one of these has a confessor, who is to them a sort of steward. For, you must know, they that go into these places, have the management of their own fortunes, and what their parents design them. Without the advice of this confessor, they act nothing, nor admit of a lover that he shall not approve; at least, this method ought to be taken, and is by almost all of them; though Miranda thought her wit above it, as her spirit was.

But as these women are, as I said, of the best quality, and live with the reputation of being retired from the world a little more than ordinary, and because there is a sort of difficulty to approach them, they are the people the most courted, and liable to

the greatest temptations ; for as difficult as it seems
to be, they receive visits from all the men of the best
quality, especially strangers.   All the men of wit and
conversation meet at the apartments of these fair
filles devotes, where all manner of gallantries are
performed, while all the study of these maids is
to accomplish themselves for these noble conversations.   They receive presents, balls, serenades, and
billets.   All the news, wit, verses, songs, novels, music,
gaming, and all fine diversion, is in their apartments,
they themselves being of the best quality and fortune.
So that to manage these gallantries, there is no sort
of female arts they are not practised in, no intrigue
they are ignorant of, and no management of which
they are not capable.

Of this happy number was the fair Miranda, whose
parents being dead, and a vast estate divided between
herself and a young sister, (who lived with an unmarried old uncle, whose estate afterwards was all
divided between them) she put herself into this unin-
closed religious house ; but her beauty, which had all
the charms that ever nature gave, became the envy of
the whole sisterhood.   She was tall, and admirably
shaped ; she had a bright hair, and hazel eyes, all full
of love and sweetness.   No art could make a face so
fair as hers by nature, which every feature adorned
with a grace that imagination cannot reach.   Every
look, every motion charmed, and her black dress
showed the lustre of her face and neck.   She had an
air, though gay as so much youth could inspire, yet
so modest, so nobly reserved, without formality, or
stiffness, that one who looked on her would have
imagined her soul the twin-angel of her body ; and
both together made her appear something divine.   To
this she had a great deal of wit, read much, and
retained all that served her purpose.   She sang
delicately, and danced well, and played on the lute to
a miracle.   She spoke several languages naturally; for,
being co-heiress to so great a fortune, she was bred

with the nicest care, in all the finest manners of education; and was now arrived to her eighteenth year.

It were needless to tell you how great a noise the
fame of this young beauty, with so considerable a
fortune, made in the world. I may say, the world,
rather than confine her fame to the scanty limits of a
town; it reached to many others. And there was
not a man of any quality that came to Antwerp, or
passed through the city, but made it his business to
see the lovely Miranda, who was universally adored.
Her youth and beauty, her shape, and majesty of
mien, and air of greatness, charmed all her beholders;
and thousands of people were dying by her eyes,
while she was vain enough to glory in her conquests,
and make it her business to wound. She loved
nothing so much as to behold sighing slaves at her
feet, of the greatest quality; and treated them all with
an affability that gave them hope. Continual music,
as soon as it was dark, and songs of dying lovers,
were sung under her windows; and she might well
have made herself a great fortune (if she had not been
so already) by the rich presents that were hourly
made her; and everybody daily expected when she
would make some one happy, by suffering herself to
be conquered by love and honour, by the assiduities
and vows of some one of her adorers. But Miranda
accepted their presents, heard their vows with pleasure, and willingly admitted all their soft addresses;
but would not yield her heart, or give away that
lovely person to the possession of one, who could
please itself with so many. She was naturally amorous, but extremely inconstant. She loved one for his
wit, another for his face, and a third for his mien;
but above all, she admired quality. Quality alone
had the power to attach her entirely; yet not to one
man, but that virtue was still admired by her in all.
Wherever she found that, she loved, or at least acted
the lover with such art, that (deceiving well) she failed
not to complete her conquest; and yet she never

durst trust her fickle humour with marriage. She
knew the strength of her own heart, and that it could
not suffer itself to be confined to one man, and wisely
avoided those inquietudes, and that uneasiness of life
she was sure to find in that married state, which
would, against her nature, oblige her to the embraces
of one, whose humour was, to love all the young and
the gay. But Love, who had hitherto only played with
her heart, and given it nought but pleasing wanton
wounds, such as afforded only soft joys, and not pains,
resolved, either out of revenge to those numbers she
had abandoned, and who had sighed so long in vain, or
to try what power he had upon so fickle a heart, to send
an arrow dipped in the most tormenting flames that
rage in hearts most sensible. He struck it home and
deep, with all the malice of an angry god.

There was a church belonging to the Cordeliers,
whither Miranda often repaired to her devotion ; and
being there one day, accompanied with a young sister
of the Order, after the Mass was ended, as it is the
custom, some one of the Fathers goes about the
church with a box for contribution, or charity-money.
It happened that day, that a young Father, newly
initiated, carried the box about, which, in his turn, he
brought to Miranda. She had no sooner cast her
eyes on this young friar but her face was overspread
with blushes of surprise. She beheld him steadfastly,
and saw in his face all the charms of youth, wit, and
beauty ; he wanted no one grace that could form him
for love, he appeared all that is adorable to the fair
sex, nor could the misshapen habit hide from her the
lovely shape it endeavoured to cover, nor those
delicate hands that approached her too near with the
box. Besides the beauty of his face and shape, he
had an air altogether great, in spite of his professed
poverty, it betrayed the man of quality ; and that
thought weighed greatly with Miranda. But love,
who did not design she should now feel any sort of
those easy flames, with which she had heretofore

burnt, made her soon lay all those considerations aside, which used to invite her to love, and now loved she knew not why.

She gazed upon him, while he bowed before her, and waited for her charity, till she perceived the lovely friar to blush, and cast his eyes to the ground. This awakened her shame, and she put her hand into her pocket, and was a good while in searching for her purse, as if she thought of nothing less than what she was about; at last she drew it out, and gave him a pistole; but with so much deliberation and leisure, as easily betrayed the satisfaction she took in looking on him; while the good man, having received her bounty, after a very low obeisance, proceeded to the rest; and Miranda casting after him a look all languishing, as long as he remained in the church, departed with a sigh as soon as she saw him go out, and returned to her apartment without speaking one word all the way to the young *fille devote* who attended her; so absolutely was her soul employed with this young holy man. Cornelia (so was this maid called who was with her) perceiving she was so silent, who used to be all wit and good humour, and observing her little disorder at the sight of the young father, though she was far from imagining it to be love, took an occasion, when she was come home, to speak of him. 'Madam,' said she, 'did you not observe that fine young Cordelier, who brought the box?' At a question that named that object of her thoughts, Miranda blushed; and she finding she did so, redoubled her confusion, and she had scarce courage enough to say, 'Yes, I did observe him.' And then, forcing herself to smile a little, continued, 'And I wondered to see so jolly a young friar of an Order so severe and mortified.' 'Madam', replied Cornelia, 'when you know his story, you will not wonder.' Miranda, who was impatient to know all that concerned her new conqueror, obliged her to tell his story; and Cornelia obeyed, and proceeded.

THE STORY OF PRINCE HENRICK

'You must know, Madam, that this young holy man is a Prince of Germany, of the House of ——, whose fate it was to fall most passionately in love with a fair young lady, who loved him with an ardour equal to what he vowed her. Sure of her heart, and wanting only the approbation of her parents, and his own, which her quality did not suffer him to despair of, he boasted of his happiness to a young Prince, his elder brother, a youth amorous and fierce, impatient of joys, and sensible of beauty, taking fire with all fair eyes. He was his father's darling, and delight of his fond mother; and, by an ascendant over both their hearts, ruled their wills.

'This young Prince no sooner saw, but loved the fair mistress of his brother; and with an authority of a sovereign, rather than the advice of a friend, warned his brother Henrick (this now young friar) to approach no more this lady, whom he had seen; and, seeing, loved.

'In vain the poor surprised Prince pleads his right of love, his exchange of vows, and assurance of a heart that could never be but for himself. In vain he urges his nearness of blood, his friendship, his passion, or his life, which so entirely depended on the possession of the charming maid. All his pleading served but to blow his brother's flame; and the more he implores, the more the other burns; and while Henrick follows him, on his knees, with humble submissions, the other flies from him in rages of transported love; nor could his tears, that pursued his brother's steps, move him to pity. Hot-headed, vain-conceited of his beauty, and greater quality, as elder brother, he doubts not of success, and resolved to sacrifice all to the violence of his new-born passion.

'In short, he speaks of his design to his mother, who promised him her assistance; and accordingly

proposing it first to the Prince her husband, urging
the languishment of her son, she soon wrought so on
him, that a match being concluded between the
parents of this young beauty and Henrick's brother,
the hour was appointed before she knew of the sacrifice she was to be made. And while this was in
agitation, Henrick was sent on some great affairs, up
into Germany, far out of the way; not but his boding
heart, with perpetual sighs and throbs, eternally foretold him his fate.

'All the letters he wrote were intercepted, as well
as those she wrote to him. She finds herself every
day perplexed with the addresses of the Prince she
hated; he was ever sighing at her feet. In vain
were all her reproaches, and all her coldness, he was
on the surer side; for what he found love would not
do, force of parents would.

'She complains, in her heart, of young Henrick, from
whom she could never receive one letter; and at last
could not forbear bursting into tears, in spite of all her
force, and feigned courage, when, on a day, the Prince
told her, that Henrick was withdrawn to give him
time to court her; to whom he said, he confessed he
had made some vows, but did repent of them, knowing
himself too young to make them good : that it was for
that reason he brought him first to see her; and for
that reason, that after that he never saw her more, nor
so much as took leave of her; when, indeed, his
death lay upon the next visit, his brother having
sworn to murder him; and to that end, put a guard
upon him, till he was sent into Germany.

'All this he uttered with so many passionate as-
severations, vows, and seeming pity for her being so
inhumanly abandoned, that she almost gave credit to
all he had said, and had much ado to keep herself
within the bounds of moderation and silent grief. Her
heart was breaking, her eyes languished, and her
cheeks grew pale, and she had like to have fallen dead
into the treacherous arms of him that had reduced

her to this discovery ; but she did what she could to
assume her courage, and to show as little resentment
as possible for a heart, like hers, oppressed with love,
and now abandoned by the dear subject of its joys and
pains.

'But, Madam, not to tire you with this adventure,
the day arrived wherein our still weeping fair unfortunate was to be sacrificed to the capriciousness
of love; and she was carried to Court by her parents,
without knowing to what end, where she was even
compelled to marry the Prince.

'Henrick, who all this while knew no more of his
unhappiness, than what his fears suggested, returns,
and passes even to the presence of his father, before
he knew anything of his fortune; where he beheld
his mistress and his brother, with his father, in such
a familiarity, as he no longer doubted his destiny.
It is hard to judge, whether the lady, or himself, was
most surprised; she was all pale and unmovable in
her chair, and Henrick fixed like a statue; at last
grief and rage took place of amazement, and he
could not forbear crying out, 'Ah, traitor! Is it
thus you have treated a friend and brother? And
you, O perjured charmer! Is it thus you have
rewarded all my vows?' He could say no more;
but reeling against the door, had fallen in a swoon
upon the floor, had not his page caught him in his
arms, who was entering with him. The good old
Prince, the father, who knew not what all this meant,
was soon informed by the young weeping Princess;
who, in relating the story of her amour with Henrick,
told her tale in so moving a manner, as brought tears
to the old man's eyes, and rage to those of her
husband; he immediately grew jealous to the last
degree. He finds himself in possession ('tis true)
of the beauty he adored, but the beauty adoring
another; a Prince young and charming as the light,
soft, witty, and raging with an equal passion. He
finds this dreaded rival in the same house with him,

with an authority equal to his own; and fancies, where two hearts are so entirely agreed, and have so good an understanding, it would not be impossible to find opportunities to satisfy and ease that mutual flame, that burned so equally in both; he therefore resolved to send him out of the world, and to establish his own repose by a deed, wicked, cruel, and unnatural, to have him assassinated the first opportunity he could find. This resolution set him a little at ease, and he strove to dissemble kindness to Henrick, with all the art he was capable of, suffering him to come often to the apartment of the Princess, and to entertain her oftentimes with discourse, when he was not near enough to hear what he spoke; but still watching their eyes, he found those of Henrick full of tears, ready to flow, but restrained, looking all dying, and yet reproaching, while those of the Princess were ever bent to the earth, and she as much as possible, shunning his conversation. Yet this did not satisfy the jealous husband; it was not her complaisance that could appease him; he found her heart was panting within, whenever Henrick approached her, and every visit more and more confirmed his death.

'The father often found the disorders of the sons; the softness and address of the one gave him as much fear, as the angry blushings, the fierce looks, and broken replies of the other, whenever he beheld Henrick approach his wife; so that the father, fearing some ill consequence of this, besought Henrick to withdraw to some other country, or travel into Italy, he being now of an age that required a view of the world. He told his father that he would obey his commands, though he was certain, that moment he was to be separated from the sight of the fair Princess, his sister, would be the last of his life; and, in fine, made so pitiful a story of his suffering love, as almost moved the old Prince to compassionate him so far, as to permit him to stay; but he saw inevitable

danger in that, and therefore bid him prepare for his
journey.

'That which passed between the father and Henrick, being a secret, none talked of his departing
from Court; so that the design the brother had went
on; and making a hunting-match one day, where
most young people of quality were, he ordered some
whom he had hired to follow his brother, so as if he
chanced to go out of the way, to despatch him; and
accordingly, fortune gave them an opportunity; for
he lagged behind the company, and turned aside into
a pleasant thicket of hazels, where alighting, he walked
on foot in the most pleasant part of it, full of thought,
how to divide his soul between love and obedience.
He was sensible that he ought not to stay; that he
was but an affliction to the young Princess, whose
honour could never permit her to ease any part of
his flame; nor was he so vicious to entertain a thought
that should stain her virtue. He beheld her now as
his brother's wife, and that secured his flame from all
loose desires, if her native modesty had not been
sufficient of itself to have done it, as well as that
profound respect he paid her; and he considered,
in obeying his father, he left her at ease, and his
brother freed of a thousand fears; he went to seek
a cure, which if he could not find, at last he could
but die; and so he must, even at her feet. However,
that it was more noble to seek a remedy for his
disease, than expect a certain death by staying.
After a thousand reflections on his hard fate, and
bemoaning himself, and blaming his cruel stars, that
had doomed him to die so young, after an infinity
of sighs and tears, resolvings and unresolvings, he,
on the sudden, was interrupted by the trampling of
some horses he heard, and their rushing through the
boughs, and saw four men make towards him. He
had not time to mount, being walked some paces
from his horse. One of the men advanced, and cried,
'Prince, you must die.' 'I do believe thee,' replied

Henrick, 'but not by a hand so base as thine,' and at the same time drawing his sword, ran him into the groin. When the fellow found himself so wounded, he wheeled off and cried, 'Thou art a prophet, and hast rewarded my treachery with death.' The rest came up, and one shot at the Prince, and shot him in the shoulder ; the other two hastily laying hold (but too late) on the hand of the murderer, cried, 'Hold, traitor ; we relent, and he shall not die.' He replied, ''Tis too late, he is shot ; and see, he lies dead. Let us provide for ourselves, and tell the Prince, we have done the work ; for you are as guilty as I am.' At that they all fled, and left the Prince lying under a tree, weltering in his blood.

'About the evening, the forester going his walks, saw the horse richly caparisoned, without a rider, at the entrance of the wood ; and going farther, to see if he could find its owner, found there the Prince almost dead ; he immediately mounts him on the horse, and himself behind, bore him up, and carried him to the lodge; where he had only one old man, his father, well skilled in surgery, and a boy. They put him to bed ; and the old forester, with what art he had, dressed his wound, and in the morning sent for an abler surgeon, to whom the Prince enjoined secrecy, because he knew him. The man was faithful, and the Prince in time was recovered of his wound ; and as soon as he was well, he came for Flanders, in the habit of a pilgrim, and after some time took the Order of St. Francis, none knowing what became of him, till he was professed ; and then he wrote his own story to the Prince his father, to his mistress, and his ungrateful brother. The young Princess did not long survive his loss, she languished from the moment of his departure ; and he had this to confirm his devout life, to know she died for him.

'My brother, Madam, was an officer under the Prince his father, and knew his story perfectly well; from whose mouth I had it.

What!' replied Miranda then, 'is Father Henrick a man of quality?' 'Yes, Madam,' said Cornelia, 'and has changed his name to Francisco.' But Miranda, fearing to betray the sentiments of her heart, by asking any more questions about him, turned the discourse; and some persons of quality came in to visit her (for her apartment was about six o'clock, like the presence-chamber of a queen, always filled with the greatest people). There meet all the *beaux esprits*, and all the beauties. But it was visible Miranda was not so gay as she used to be; but pensive, and answering *mal à propos* to all that was said to her. She was a thousand times going to speak, against her will, something of the charming friar, who was never from her thoughts; and she imagined, if he could inspire love in a coarse, grey, ill-made habit, a shorn crown, a hair-cord about his waist, bare-legged, in sandals instead of shoes; what must he do, when looking back on time, she beholds him in a prospect of glory, with all that youth, and illustrious beauty, set off by the advantage of dress and equipage? She frames an idea of him all gay and splendid, and looks on his present habit as some disguise proper for the stealths of love; some feigned put-on shape, with the more security to approach a mistress, and make himself happy; and that the robe laid by, she has the lover in his proper beauty, the same he would have been, if any other habit (though ever so rich) were put off. In the bed, the silent gloomy night, and the soft embraces of her arms, he loses all the friar, and assumes all the prince; and that awful reverence, due alone to his holy habit, he exchanges for a thousand dalliances, for which his youth was made: for love, for tender embraces, and all the happiness of life. Some moments she fancies him a lover, and that the fair object that takes up all his heart, has left no room for her there; but that was a thought that did not long perplex her, and which, almost as soon as born, she turned to her advantage. She beholds him a

H

lover, and therefore finds he has a heart sensible and tender; he had youth to be fired, as well as to inspire; he was far from the loved object, and totally without hope; and she reasonably considered, that flame would of itself soon die, that had only despair to feed on. She beheld her own charms; and experience, as well as her glass, told her, they never failed of conquest, especially where they designed it. And she believed Henrick would be glad, at least, to quench that flame in himself, by an amour with her, which was kindled by the young Princess of —— his sister.

These, and a thousand other self-flatteries, all vain and indiscreet, took up her waking nights, and now more retired days; while love, to make her truly wretched, suffered her to soothe herself with fond imaginations; not so much as permitting her reason to plead one moment to save her from undoing. She would not suffer it to tell her, he had taken Holy Orders, made sacred and solemn vows of everlasting chastity, that it was impossible he could marry her, or lay before her any argument that might prevent her ruin; but love, mad malicious love, was always called to counsel, and like easy monarchs, she had no ears, but for flatterers.

Well then, she is resolved to love, without considering to what end, and what must be the consequence of such an amour. She now missed no day of being at that little church, where she had the happiness, or rather the misfortune (so love ordained) to see this ravisher of her heart and soul; and every day she took new fire from his lovely eyes. Unawares, unknown, and unwillingly, he gave her wounds, and the difficulty of her cure made her rage the more. She burned, she languished, and died for the young innocent, who knew not he was the author of so much mischief.

Now she resolves a thousand ways in her tortured mind, to let him know her anguish, and at last pitched upon that of writing to him soft billets, which she had

learned the art of doing ; or if she had not, she had
now fire enough to inspire her with all that could
charm and move. These she delivered to a young
wench, who waited on her, and whom she had entirely
subdued to her interest, to give to a certain lay-
brother of the Order, who was a very simple harmless
wretch, and who served in the kitchen, in the nature
of a cook, in the monastery of Cordeliers. She gave
him gold to secure his faith and service ; and not
knowing from whence they came (with so good
credentials) he undertook to deliver the letters to
Father Francisco ; which letters were all afterwards,
as you shall hear, produced in open court. These
letters failed not to come every day ; and the sense of
the first was, to tell him, that a very beautiful young
lady, of a great fortune, was in love with him, without
naming her ; but it came as from a third person, to
let him know the secret, that she desired he would
let her know whether she might hope any return from
him ; assuring him, he needed but only see the fair
languisher, to confess himself her slave.

This letter being delivered him, he read by himself,
and was surprised to receive words of this nature,
being so great a stranger in that place ; and could
not imagine, or would not give himself the trouble of
guessing who this should be, because he never designed to make returns.

The next day, Miranda, finding no advantage from
her messenger of love, in the evening sends another
(impatient of delay) confessing that she who suffered
the shame of writing and imploring, was the person
herself who adored him. It was there her raging
love made her say all things that discovered the
nature of its flame, and propose to flee with him to
any part of the world, if he would quit the convent ;
that she had a fortune considerable enough to make
him happy ; and that his youth and quality were not
given him to so unprofitable an end as to lose themselves in a convent, where poverty and ease was all

the business. In fine, she leaves nothing unurged that might debauch and invite him; not forgetting to send him her own character of beauty, and left him to judge of her wit and spirit by her writing, and her love by the extremity of passion she professed. To all which the lovely friar made no return, as believing a gentle capitulation or exhortation to her would but inflame her the more, and give new occasions for her continuing to write. All her reasonings, false and vicious, he despised, pitied the error of her love, and was proof against all she could plead. Yet notwithstanding his silence, which left her in doubt, and more tormented her, she ceased not to pursue him with her letters, varying her style; sometimes all wanton, loose and raving; sometimes feigning a virgin-modesty all over, accusing herself, blaming her conduct, and sighing her destiny, as one compelled to the shameful discovery by the austerity of his vow and habit, asking his pity and forgiveness; urging him in charity to use his fatherly care to persuade and reason with her wild desires, and by his counsel drive the god from her heart, whose tyranny was worse than that of a fiend; and he did not know what his pious advice might do. But still she writes in vain, in vain she varies her style, by a cunning, peculiar to a maid possessed with such a sort of passion.

This cold neglect was still oil to the burning lamp, and she tries yet more arts, which for want of right thinking were as fruitless. She has recourse to presents; her letters came loaded with rings of great price, and jewels, which fops of quality had given her. Many of this sort he received, before he knew where to return them, or how; and on this occasion alone he sent her a letter, and restored her trifles, as he called them. But his habit having not made him forget his quality and education, he wrote to her with all the profound respect imaginable; believing by her presents, and the liberality with which she parted with them, that she was of quality. But the whole

letter, as he told me afterwards, was to persuade her
from the honour she did him, by loving him; urging
a thousand reasons, solid and pious, and assuring her,
he had wholly devoted the rest of his days to heaven,
and had no need of those gay trifles she had sent
him, which were only fit to adorn ladies so fair as
herself, and who had business with this glittering
world, which he disdained, and had for ever abandoned. He sent her a thousand blessings, and told
her, she should be ever in his prayers, though not in
his heart, as she desired. And abundance of goodness more he expressed, and counsel he gave her,
which had the same effect with his silence; it made
her love but the more, and the more impatient she
grew. She now had a new occasion to write, she now
is charmed with his wit; this was the new subject.
She rallies his resolution, and endeavours to recall
him to the world, by all the arguments that human
invention is capable of.

But when she had above four months languished
thus in vain, not missing one day, wherein she went
not to see him, without discovering herself to him;
she resolved, as her last effort, to show her person,
and see what that, assisted by her tears, and soft
words from her mouth, could do, to prevail upon him.

It happened to be on the eve of that day when she
was to receive the Sacrament, that she, covering herself with her veil, came to vespers, purposing to make
choice of the conquering friar for her confessor.

She approached him; and as she did so, she
trembled with love. At last she cried, 'Father, my
confessor is gone for some time from the town, and
I am obliged to-morrow to receive, and beg you will
be pleased to take my confession.'

He could not refuse her; and led her into the
sacristy, where there is a confession-chair, in which
he seated himself; and on one side of him she
kneeled down, over against a little altar, where the
priests' robes lie, on which were placed some lighted

wax-candles, that made the little place very light and splendid, which shone full upon Miranda.

After the little preparation usual in confession, she turned up her veil, and discovered to his view the most wondrous object of beauty he had ever seen, dressed in all the glory of a young bride ; her hair and stomacher full of diamonds, that gave a lustre all dazzling to her brighter face and eyes. He was surprised at her amazing beauty, and questioned whether he saw a woman, or an angel at his feet. Her hands, which were elevated, as if in prayer, seemed to be formed of polished alabaster ; and he confessed, he had never seen anything in nature so perfect, and so admirable.

He had some pain to compose himself to hear her confession, and was obliged to turn away his eyes, that his mind might not be perplexed with an object so diverting ; when Miranda, opening the finest mouth in the world, and discovering new charms, began her confession.

'Holy father,' said she, 'amongst the number of my vile offences, that which afflicts me to the greatest degree, is, that I am in love. Not,' continued she, 'that I believe simple and virtuous love a sin, when it is placed on an object proper and suitable ; but, my dear father,' said she, and wept, 'I love with a violence which cannot be contained within the bounds of reason, moderation, or virtue. I love a man whom I cannot possess without a crime, and a man who cannot make me happy without being perjured.' 'Is he married?' replied the father. 'No,' answered Miranda. 'Are you so?' continued he. 'Neither,' said she. 'Is he too near allied to you?' said Francisco, 'a brother, or relation?' 'Neither of these,' said she. 'He is unenjoyed, unpromised ; and so am I. Nothing opposes our happiness, or makes my love a vice, but you——'Tis you deny me life : 'tis you that forbid my flame : 'tis you will have me die, and seek my remedy in my grave, when I complain of tortures, wounds, and flames. O cruel charmer! 'tis for you I languish; and here, at your feet, implore that pity, which all my addresses have failed of procuring me.'

With that, perceiving he was about to rise from his seat, she held him by his habit, and vowed she would in that posture follow him, wherever he flew from her. She elevated her voice so loud, he was afraid she might be heard, and therefore suffered her to force him into his chair again; where being seated, he began, in the most passionate terms imaginable, to dissuade her; but finding she the more persisted in eagerness of passion, he used all the tender assurances that he could force from himself, that he would have for her all the respect, esteem, and friendship that he was capable of paying; that he had a real compassion for her: and at last she prevailed so far with him, by her sighs and tears, as to own he had a tenderness for her, and that he could not behold so many charms, without being sensibly touched by them, and finding all those effects, that a maid so fair and young causes in the souls of men of youth and sense. But that, as he was assured, he could never be so happy to marry her, and as certain he could not grant anything but honourable passion, he humbly besought her not to expect more from him than such. And then began to tell her how short life was, and transitory its joys; how soon she would grow weary of vice, and how often change to find real repose in it, but never arrive to it. He made an end, by new assurance of his eternal friendship, but utterly forbad her to hope.

Behold her now denied, refused and defeated, with all her pleading youth, beauty, tears, and knees, imploring, as she lay, holding fast his scapular, and embracing his feet. What shall she do? She swells with pride, love, indignation and desire; her burning heart is bursting with despair, her eyes grow fierce, and from grief she rises to a storm; and in her agony of passion, with looks all disdainful, haughty, and full of rage, she began to revile him, as the poorest of animals; tells him his soul was dwindled to the meanness of his habit, and his vows of poverty, were suited to his degenerate mind. 'And,' said she, 'since all my nobler ways have failed me; and that, for a little hypocritical devotion, you resolve to lose the greatest blessings of life, and to sacrifice me to your religious pride and vanity, I will either force you to abandon that dull dissimulation, or you shall die, to prove your sanctity real. Therefore answer me immediately, answer my flame, my raging fire, which your eyes have kindled; or here, in this very moment, I will ruin thee; and make no scruple of revenging the pains I suffer, by that which shall take away your life and honour.'

The trembling young man, who, all this while, with extreme anguish of mind, and fear of the dire result, had listened to her ravings, full of dread, demanded what she would have him do? When she replied, 'Do what thy youth and beauty were ordained to do: this place is private, a sacred silence reigns here, and no one dares to pry into the secrets of this holy place. We are as secure from fears of interruption, as in deserts uninhabited, or caves forsaken by wild beasts. The tapers too shall veil their lights, and only that glimmering lamp shall be witness of our dear stealths of love. Come to my arms, my trembling, longing arms : and curse the folly of thy bigotry, that has made thee so long lose a blessing, for which so many princes sigh in vain.'

At these words she rose from his feet, and snatching him in her arms, he could not defend himself from receiving a thousand kisses from the lovely mouth of the charming wanton ; after which, she ran herself, and in an instant put out the candles. But he cried to her, 'In vain, O too indiscreet fair one, in vain you put out the light! for Heaven still has eyes, and will look down upon my broken vows. I own your power, I own I have all the sense in the world of

your charming touches ; I am frail flesh and blood,
but——yet——yet I can resist; and I prefer my
vows to all your powerful temptations. I will be deaf
and blind, and guard my heart with walls of ice, and
make you know, that when the flames of true devotion are kindled in a heart, it puts out all other fires ;
which are as ineffectual, as candles lighted in the face
of the sun. Go, vain wanton, and repent, and mortify
that blood which has so shamefully betrayed thee,
and which will one day ruin both thy soul and body.'

At these words, Miranda, more enraged, the nearer
she imagined herself to happiness, made no reply; but
throwing herself, in that instant, into the confessing-
chair, and violently pulling the young friar into her
lap, she elevated her voice to such a degree, in crying
out, 'Help, help! A rape! Help, help!' that she
was heard all over the church, which was full of
people at the evening's devotion ; who flocked about
the door of the sacristy, which was shut with a spring-
lock on the inside, but they durst not open the door.

It is easily to be imagined in what condition our
young friar was, at this last devilish stratagem of his
wicked mistress. He strove to break from those
arms that held him so fast; and his bustling to get
away, and hers to retain him, disordered her hair and
habit to such a degree, as gave the more credit to her
false accusation.

The fathers had a door on the other side, by which
they usually entered, to dress in this little room ; and
at the report that was in an instant made them, they
hasted thither, and found Miranda and the good
Father very indecently struggling ; which they mis-
interpreted, as Miranda desired ; who, all in tears,
immediately threw herself at the feet of the Provincial, who was one of those that entered ; and
cried, 'O holy father! revenge an innocent maid,
undone and lost to fame and honour, by that vile
monster, born of goats, nursed by tigers, and bred up
on savage mountains, where humanity and religion

are strangers. For, O holy father, could it have entered into the heart of man, to have done so barbarous and horrid a deed, as to attempt the virgin-honour of an unspotted maid, and one of my degree, even in the moment of my confession, in that holy time, when I was prostrate before him and heaven, confessing those sins that pressed my tender conscience, even then to load my soul with the blackest of infamies, to add to my number a weight that must sink me to hell? Alas! under the security of his innocent looks, his holy habit, and his awful function, I was led into this room to make my confession; where, he locking the door, I had no sooner began, but he gazing on me, took fire at my fatal beauty; and starting up, put out the candles and caught me in his arms; and raising me from the pavement, set me in the confession-chair; and then—— Oh, spare me the rest.'

With that a shower of tears burst from her fair dissembling eyes, and sobs so naturally acted, and so well managed, as left no doubt upon the good men, but all she had spoken was truth.

'At first,' proceeded she, 'I was unwilling to bring so great a scandal on his Order, as to cry out; but struggled as long as I had breath; pleaded the heinousness of the crime, urging my quality, and the danger of the attempt. But he, deaf as the winds, and ruffling as a storm, pursued his wild design with so much force and insolence, as I at last, unable to resist, was wholly vanquished, robbed of my native purity. With what life and breath I had, I called for assistance, both from men and heaven; but oh, alas! your succours came too late. You find me here a wretched, undone, and ravished maid. Revenge me, fathers; revenge me on the perfidious hypocrite, or else give me a death that may secure your cruelty and injustice from ever being proclaimed over the world; or my tongue will be eternally reproaching you, and cursing the wicked author of my infamy.'

She ended as she began, with a thousand sighs and tears ; and received from the Provincial all assurances of revenge.

The innocent betrayed victim, all the while she was speaking, heard her with an astonishment that may easily be imagined ; yet showed no extravagant signs of it, as those would do, who feign it, to be thought innocent ; but being really so, he bore with a humble, modest, and blushing countenance, all her accusations ; which silent shame they mistook for evident signs of his guilt.

When the Provincial demanded, with an unwonted severity in his eyes and voice, what he could answer for himself? calling him profaner of his sacred vows, and infamy to the Holy Order ; the injured, but innocently accused, only replied : ' May Heaven forgive that bad woman, and bring her to repentance ! ' For his part, he was not so much in love with life, as to use many arguments to justify his innocence ; unless it were to free that Order from a scandal, of which he had the honour to be professed. But as for himself, life or death were things indifferent to him, who heartily despised the world.

He said no more, and suffered himself to be led before the magistrate ; who committed him to prison, upon the accusation of this implacable beauty ; who, with so much feigned sorrow, prosecuted the matter, even to his trial and condemnation ; where he refused to make any great defence for himself. But being daily visited by all the religious, both of his own and other Orders, they obliged him (some of them knowing the austerity of his life, others his cause of griefs that first brought him into Orders, and others pretending a nearer knowledge, even of his soul itself) to stand upon his justification, and discover what he knew of that wicked woman ; whose life had not been so exemplary for virtue, not to have given the world a thousand suspicions of her lewdness and prostitutions.

The daily importunities of these fathers made
him produce her letters. But as he had all the gown-
men on his side, she had all the hats and feathers on
hers; all the men of quality taking her part, and all
the church-men his. They heard his daily protestations and vows, but not a word of what passed at
confession was yet discovered. He held that as a
secret sacred on his part; and what was said in
nature of a confession, was not to be revealed, though
his life depended on the discovery. But as to the
letters, they were forced from him, and exposed;
however, matters were carried with so high a hand
against him, that they served for no proof at all of
his innocence, and he was at last condemned to be
burned at the market-place.

After his sentence was passed, the whole body of
priests made their addresses to the Marquis Castel
Roderigo, the then Governor of Flanders, for a reprieve; which, after much ado, was granted him for
some weeks, but with an absolute denial of pardon.
So prevailing were the young cavaliers of his Court,
who were all adorers of this fair jilt.

About this time, while the poor innocent young
Henrick was thus languishing in prison, in a dark
and dismal dungeon, and Miranda, cured of her love,
was triumphing in her revenge, expecting and daily
giving new conquests: and who, by this time, had re-
assumed all her wonted gaiety; there was a great
noise about the town, that a Prince of mighty name,
and famed for all the excellences of his sex, was
arrived; a Prince young, and gloriously attended,
called Prince Tarquin.

We had often heard of this great man, and that
he was making his travels in France and Germany.
And we had also heard, that some years before, he
being about eighteen years of age, in the time when
our King Charles, of blessed memory, was in Brussels,
in the last year of his banishment, that all on a-sudden,
this young man rose up upon them like the sun all

glorious and dazzling, demanding place of all the
princes in that Court. And when his pretence was
demanded, he owned himself Prince Tarquin, of the
race of the last Kings of Rome, made good his title,
and took his place accordingly. After that he
travelled for about six years up and down the world,
and then arrived at Antwerp, about the time of my
being sent thither by King Charles.

Perhaps there could be nothing seen so magnificent
as this Prince. He was, as I said, extremely handsome, from head to foot exactly formed, and he
wanted nothing that might adorn that native beauty
to the best advantage. His parts were suitable to
the rest. He had an accomplishment fit for a Prince,
an air haughty, but a carriage affable, easy in conversation, and very entertaining, liberal and good-
natured, brave and inoffensive. I have seen him pass
the streets with twelve footmen, and four pages ; the
pages all in green velvet coats laced with gold, and
white velvet tunics ; the men in cloth, richly laced
with gold ; his coaches, and all other officers suitable
to a great man.

He was all the discourse of the town ; some laughing at his title, others reverencing it. Some cried
that he was an impostor ; others, that he had made
his title as plain, as if Tarquin had reigned but a
year ago. Some made friendships with him, others
would have nothing to say to him. But all wondered
where his revenue was, that supported this grandeur ;
and believed, though he could make his descent from
the Roman kings very well out, that he could not
lay so good a claim to the Roman land. Thus everybody meddled with what they had nothing to do ;
and, as in other places, thought themselves on the
surer side, if, in these doubtful cases, they imagined
the worst.

But the men might be of what opinion they pleased
concerning him ; the ladies were all agreed that he
was a prince, and a young handsome prince, and a

prince not to be resisted. He had all their wishes, all their eyes, and all their hearts. They now dressed only for him ; and what church he graced, was sure, that day, to have the beauties, and all that thought themselves so.

You may believe, our amorous Miranda was not the least conquest he made. She no sooner heard of him, which was as soon as he arrived, but she fell in love with his very name. 'Jesu! A young King of Rome!' Oh, it was so novel, that she doted on the title ; and had not cared whether the rest had been man or monkey almost. She was resolved to be the Lucretia that this young Tarquin should ravish.

To this end, she was no sooner up the next day, but she sent him a *billet doux*, assuring him how much she admired his fame ; and that being a stranger in the town, she begged the honour of introducing him to all the *belle* conversations, etc., which he took for the invitation of some coquette, who had interest in fair ladies ; and civilly returned her an answer, that he would wait on her. She had him that day watched to church ; and impatient to see what she heard so many people flock to see, she went also to the same church ; those sanctified abodes being too often profaned by such devotees, whose business is to ogle and ensnare.

But what a noise and humming was heard all over the church, when Tarquin entered ! His grace, his mien, his fashion, his beauty, his dress, and his equipage, surprised all that were present. And by the good management and care of Miranda, she got to kneel at the side of the altar, just over against the Prince, so that, if he would, he could not avoid looking full upon her. She had turned up her veil, and all her face and shape appeared such, and so enchanting, as I have described ; and her beauty heightened with blushes, and her eyes full of spirit and fire, with joy, to find the young Roman monarch so charming, she

appeared like something more than mortal, and compelled his eyes to a fixed gazing on her face ; she
never glanced his way, but she met them ; and then
would feign so modest a shame, and cast her eyes
downwards with such inviting art, that he was wholly
ravished and charmed, and she overjoyed to find he
was so.

The ceremony being ended, he sent a page to
follow that lady home, himself pursuing her to the
door of the church, where he took some holy water,
and threw upon her, and made her a profound reverence.   She forced an innocent look, and a modest
gratitude in her face, and bowed, and passed forward,
half assured of her conquest; leaving her, to go
home to his lodging, and impatiently wait the return
of his page.   And all the ladies who saw this first
beginning between the Prince and Miranda, began to
curse and envy her charms, who had deprived them
of half their hopes.

After this, I need not tell you, he made Miranda a
visit; and from that day never left her apartment, but
when he went home at nights, or unless he had
business; so entirely was he conquered by this fair
one.   But the Bishop, and several men of quality, in
Orders, that professed friendship to him, advised him
from her company ; and spoke several things to him,
that might (if love had not made him blind) have
reclaimed him from the pursuit of his ruin.   But
whatever they trusted him with, she had the art to
wind herself about his heart, and make him unravel
all his secrets; and then knew as well, by feigned
sighs and tears, to make him disbelieve all ; so that
he had no faith but for her ; and was wholly enchanted and bewitched by her.   At last, in spite of
all that would have opposed it, he married this
famous woman, possessed by so many great men and
strangers before, while all the world was pitying his
shame and misfortunes.

Being married, they took a great house; and as

she was indeed a great fortune, and now a great
princess, there was nothing wanting that was agreeable to their quality; all was splendid and magnificent.   But all this would not acquire them the
world's esteem; they had an abhorrence for her
former life, and despised her; and for his espousing
a woman so infamous, they despised him.   So that
though they admired, and gazed upon their equipage,
and glorious dress, they foresaw the ruin that attended
it, and paid her quality little respect.

She was no sooner married, but her uncle died;
and dividing his fortune between Miranda and her
sister, leaves the young heiress, and all her fortune,
entirely in the hands of the Princess.

We will call this sister Alcidiana; she was about
fourteen years of age, and now had chosen her
brother, the Prince, for her guardian.   If Alcidiana
were not altogether so great a beauty as her sister,
she had charms sufficient to procure her a great many
lovers, though her fortune had not been so considerable as it was; but with that addition, you may
believe, she wanted no courtships from those of the
best quality; though everybody deplored her being
under the tutorage of a lady so expert in all the vices
of her sex, and so cunning a manager of sin, as was
the Princess; who, on her part, failed not, by all the
caresses, and obliging endearments, to engage the
mind of this young maid, and to subdue her wholly
to her government.   All her senses were eternally
regaled with the most bewitching pleasures they were
capable of.   She saw nothing but glory and magnificence, heard nothing but music of the sweetest
sounds; the richest perfumes employed her smelling;
and all she ate and touched was delicate and inviting;
and being too young to consider how this state and
grandeur was to be continued, little imagined her
vast fortune was every day diminishing, towards its
needless support.

When the Princess went to church, she had her

gentleman bare before her, carrying a great velvet
cushion, with great golden tassels, for her to kneel
on, and her train borne up a most prodigious length,
led by a gentleman usher, bare; followed by innumerable footmen, pages, and women. And in this
state she would walk in the streets, as in those
countries it is the fashion for the great ladies to do,
who are well; and in her train two or three coaches,
and perhaps a rich velvet chair embroidered, would
follow in state.

It was thus for some time they lived, and the
Princess was daily pressed by young sighing lovers,
for her consent to marry Alcidiana; but she had still
one art or other to put them off, and so continually
broke all the great matches that were proposed to
her, notwithstanding their kindred and other friends
had industriously endeavoured to make several great
matches for her; but the Princess was still positive
in her denial, and one way or other broke all. At
last it happened, there was one proposed, yet more
advantageous, a young count, with whom the young
maid grew passionately in love, and besought her
sister to consent that she might have him, and got
the Prince to speak in her behalf; but he had no
sooner heard the secret reasons Miranda gave him,
but (entirely her slave) he changed his mind, and
suited it to hers, and she, as before, broke off that
amour: which so extremely incensed Alcidiana, that
she, taking an opportunity, got from her guard, and
ran away, putting herself into the hands of a wealthy
merchant, her kinsman, and one who bore the greatest
authority in the city; him she chose for her guardian,
resolving to be no longer a slave to the tyranny of
her sister. And so well she ordered matters, that she
writ to this young cavalier, her last lover, and retrieved him; who came back to Antwerp again, to
renew his courtship.

Both parties being agreed, it was no hard matter
to persuade all but the Princess. But though she

I

opposed it, it was resolved on, and the day appointed for marriage, and the portion demanded ; demanded only, but never to be paid, the best part of it being spent. However, she put them off from day to day, by a thousand frivolous delays ; and when she saw they would have recourse to force, and that all her magnificence would be at an end, if the law should prevail against her ; and that without this sister's fortune, she could not long support her grandeur ; she bethought herself of a means to make it all her own, by getting her sister made away ; but she being out of her tuition, she was not able to accomplish so great a deed of darkness. But since it was resolved it must be done, she contrives a thousand stratagems ; and at last pitches upon an effectual one.

She had a page called Van Brune, a youth of great address and wit, and one she had long managed for her purpose. This youth was about seventeen years of age, and extremely beautiful ; and in the time when Alcidiana lived with the Princess, she was a little in love with this handsome boy ; but it was checked in its infancy, and never grew up to a flame. Nevertheless, Alcidiana retained still a sort of tenderness for him, while he burned in good earnest with love for the Princess.

The Princess one day ordering this page to wait on her in her closet, she shut the door ; and after a thousand questions of what he would undertake to serve her, the amorous boy finding himself alone, and caressed by the fair person he adored, with joyful blushes that beautified his face, told her ' There was nothing upon earth he would not do, to obey her least commands.' She grew more familiar with him, to oblige him ; and seeing love dance in his eyes, of which she was so good a judge, she treated him more like a lover, than a servant ; till at last the ravished youth, wholly transported out of himself, fell at her feet, and impatiently implored to receive her commands quickly, that he might fly to execute

them; for he was not able to bear her charming
words, looks, and touches, and retain his duty. At
this she smiled, and told him, the work was of such
a nature, as would mortify all flames about him; and
he would have more need of rage, envy, and malice,
than the aids of a passion so soft as what she now
found him capable of. He assured her, he would
stick at nothing, though even against his nature,
to recompense for the boldness he now, through his
indiscretion, had discovered. She smiling, told him,
he had committed no fault; and that possibly, the
pay he should receive for the service she required at
his hands, should be—what he most wished for in the
world. At this he bowed to the earth; and kissing
her feet, bade her command. And then she boldly
told him, it was to kill her sister Alcidiana. The
youth, without so much as starting or pausing upon
the matter, told her, it should be done; and bowing
low, immediately went out of the closet. She called
him back, and would have given him some instruction; but he refused it, and said, 'The action and the
contrivance should be all his own.' And offering to
go again, she again recalled him; putting into his
hand a purse of a hundred pistoles, which he took,
and with a low bow departed.

He no sooner left her presence, but he goes directly,
and buys a dose of poison, and went immediately to
the house where Alcidiana lived; where desiring to
be brought to her presence, he fell a-weeping; and
told her, his lady had fallen out with him, and dismissed him her service; and since from a child he
had been brought up in the family, he humbly
besought Alcidiana to receive him into hers, she
being in a few days to be married. There needed not
much entreaty to a thing that pleased her so well,
and she immediately received him to pension. And
he waited some days on her, before he could get an
opportunity to administer his devilish potion. But
one night, when she drank wine with roasted apples,

which was usual with her; instead of sugar, or with the sugar, the baneful drug was mixed, and she drank it down.

About this time, there was a great talk of this page's coming from one sister, to go to the other. And Prince Tarquin, who was ignorant of the design from the beginning to the end, hearing some men of quality at his table speaking of Van Brune's change of place (the Princess then keeping her chamber upon some trifling indisposition), he answered, 'That surely they were mistaken, that he was not dismissed from the Princess's service': and calling some of his servants, he asked for Van Brune; and whether anything had happened between her Highness and him, that had occasioned his being turned off. They all seemed ignorant of this matter; and those who had spoken of it, began to fancy there was some juggle in the case, which time would bring to light.

The ensuing day it was all about the town, that Alcidiana was poisoned; and though not dead, yet very near it; and that the doctors said, she had taken mercury. So that there was never so formidable a sight as this fair young creature; her head and body swollen, her eyes starting out, her face black, and all deformed. So that diligent search was made, who it should be that did this; who gave her drink and meat. The cook and butler were examined, the footmen called to account; but all concluded, she received nothing but from the hand of her new page, since he came into her service. He was examined, and showed a thousand guilty looks. And the apothecary, then attending among the doctors, proved he had bought mercury of him three or four days before; which he could not deny; and making many excuses for his buying it, betrayed him the more; so ill he chanced to dissemble. He was immediately sent to be examined by the Margrave or Justice, who made his *Mittimus*, and sent him to prison.

It is easy to imagine, in what fears and confusion the Princess was at this news. She took her chamber upon it, more to hide her guilty face, than for any indisposition. And the doctors applied such remedies to Alcidiana, such antidotes against the poison, that in a short time she recovered ; but lost the finest hair in the world, and the complexion of her face ever after.

It was not long before the trials for criminals came on ; and the day being arrived, Van Brune was tried the first of all ; everybody having already read his destiny, according as they wished it; and none would believe, but just indeed as it was. So that for the revenge they hoped to see fall upon the Princess, every one wished he might find no mercy, that she might share of his shame and misery.

The sessions-house was filled that day with all the ladies, and chief of the town, to hear the result of his trial; and the sad youth was brought, loaded with chains, and pale as death ; where every circumstance being sufficiently proved against him, and he making but a weak defence for himself, he was convicted, and sent back to prison, to receive his sentence of death on the morrow ; where he owned all, and who set him on to do it. He owned it was not reward of gain he did it for, but hope he should command at his pleasure the possession of his mistress, the Princess, who should deny him nothing, after having entrusted him with so great a secret ; and that besides, she had elevated him with the promise of that glorious reward, and had dazzled his young heart with so charming a prospect, that blind and mad with joy, he rushed forward to gain the desired prize, and thought on nothing but his coming happiness. That he saw too late the follies of his presumptuous flame, and cursed the deluding flatteries of the fair hypocrite, who had soothed him to his undoing. That he was a miserable victim to her wickedness; and hoped he should warn all young

He was dressed all in mourning, and very fine linen, bare-headed, with his own hair, the fairest that could be seen, hanging all in curls on his back and shoulders, very long. He had a prayer-book of black velvet in his hand, and behaved himself with much penitence and devotion.

When he came under the gibbet, he seeing his mistress in that condition, showed an infinite concern, and his fair face was covered over with blushes; and falling at her feet, he humbly asked her pardon for having been the occasion of so great an infamy to her, by a weak confession, which the fears of youth, and hopes of life, had obliged him to make, so greatly to her dishonour; for indeed he wanted that manly strength, to bear the efforts of dying, as he ought, in silence, rather than of committing so great a crime against his duty, and honour itself; and that he could not die in peace, unless she would forgive him. The Princess only nodded her head, and cried, 'I do.'

And after having spoken a little to his father-confessor, who was with him, he cheerfully mounted the ladder, and in sight of the Princess he was turned off, while a loud cry was heard through all the market-place, especially from the fair sex; he hanged there till the time the Princess was to depart; and then she was put into a rich embroidered chair, and carried away, Tarquin going into his, for he had all that time stood supporting the Princess under the gallows, and was very weary. She was sent back, till her release-ment came, which was that night about seven o'clock; and then she was conducted to her own house in great state, with a dozen white wax flambeaux about her chair.

If the guardian of Alcidiana, and her friends, before were impatient of having the portion out of the hands of these extravagants, it is not to be imagined but they were now much more so; and the next day they sent an officer, according to law, to demand it, or to summon the Prince to give reasons why he would not pay it. The officer received for answer, that the money should be called in, and paid in such a time, setting a certain time, which I have not been so curious as to retain, or put in my journal-observations; but I am sure it was not long, as may be easily imagined, for they every moment suspected the Prince would pack up, and be gone, some time or other, on the sudden; and for that reason they would not trust him without bail, or two officers to remain in his house, to watch that nothing should be removed or touched. As for bail, or security, he could give none; every one slunk their heads out of the collar, when it came to that. So that he was obliged, at his own expense, to maintain officers in his house.

The Princess finding herself reduced to the last extremity, and that she must either produce the value of a hundred thousand crowns, or see the Prince her husband lodged for ever in a prison, and all their glory vanish; and that it was impossible to fly, since guarded; she had recourse to an extremity, worse than the affair of Van Brune. And in order to this, she first puts on a world of sorrow and concern, for what she feared might arrive to the Prince. And indeed, if ever she shed tears which she did not dissemble, it was upon this occasion. But here she almost over-acted. She stirred not from her bed, and refused to eat, or sleep, or see the light; so that the day being shut out of her chamber, she lived by wax-lights, and refused all comfort and consolation.

The Prince, all raving with love, tender compassion and grief, never stirred from her bedside, nor ceased to implore, that she would suffer herself to live. But she, who was not now so passionately in love with Tarquin, as she was with the Prince; nor so fond of the man as his titles, and of glory, foresaw the total ruin of the last, if not prevented by avoiding the payment of this great sum; which could not otherwise be, than by the death of Alcidiana. And therefore, without ceasing, she wept, and cried out, 'She could

not live, unless Alcidiana died. This Alcidiana,'
continued she, 'who has been the author of my
shame; who has exposed me under a gibbet, in the
public market-place! Oh! I am deaf to all reason,
blind to natural affection. I renounce her, I hate her
as my mortal foe, my stop to glory, and the finisher
of my days, ere half my race of life be run.'

Then throwing her false, but snowy charming arms
about the neck of her heart-breaking lord and lover,
who lay sighing, and listening by her side, he was
charmed and bewitched into saying all things that
appeased her; and lastly, told her, 'Alcidiana should
be no longer any obstacle to her repose; but that, if
she would look up, and cast her eyes of sweetness
and love upon him, as heretofore; forget her sorrow,
and redeem her lost health; he would take what
measures she should propose to despatch this fatal
stop to her happiness, out of the way.'

These words failed not to make her caress him in
the most endearing manner that love and flattery
could invent; and she kissed him to an oath, a solemn
oath, to perform what he had promised; and he
vowed liberally. And she assumed in an instant her
good-humour, and suffered a supper to be prepared,
and did eat; which in many days before she had not
done. So obstinate and powerful was she in dissembling well.

The next thing to be considered was, which way
this deed was to be done; for they doubted not, but
when it was done all the world would lay it upon the
Princess, as done by her command. But she urged,
suspicion was no proof; and that they never put to
death any one, but when they had great and certain
evidence who were the offenders. She was sure of
her own constancy, that racks and tortures should
never get the secret from her breast; and if he were
as confident on his part, there was no danger. Yet
this preparation she made towards laying the fact on
others, that she caused several letters to be wrote

from Germany, as from the relations of Van Brune, who threatened Alcidiana with death, for depriving their kinsman (who was a gentleman) of his life, though he had not taken away hers. And it was the report of the town, how this young maid was threatened. And indeed, the death of the page had so afflicted a great many, that Alcidiana had procured herself abundance of enemies upon that account, because she might have saved him if she had pleased; but, on the contrary, she was a spectator, and in full health and vigour, at his execution. And people were not so much concerned for her at this report, as they would have been.

The Prince, who now had, by reasoning the matter soberly with Miranda, found it absolutely necessary to despatch Alcidiana, resolved himself, and with his own hand, to execute it; not daring to trust any of his most favourite servants, though he had many, who possibly would have obeyed him; for they loved him as he deserved, and so would all the world, had he not been so purely deluded by this fair enchantress. He therefore, as I said, resolved to keep this great secret to himself; and taking a pistol, charged well with two bullets, he watched an opportunity to shoot her as she should go out or into her house, or coach, some evening.

To this end he waited several nights near her lodgings, but still, either she went not out, or when she returned, she was so guarded with friends, her lover, and flambeaux, that he could not aim at her without endangering the life of some other. But one night above the rest, upon a Sunday, when he knew she would be at the theatre, for she never missed that day seeing the play, he waited at the corner of the Stadt House, near the theatre, with his cloak cast over his face, and a black periwig, all alone, with his pistol ready cocked; and remained not very long but he saw her kinsman's coach come along; it was almost dark, day was just shutting up her beauties, and left

such a light to govern the world, as served only just
to distinguish one object from another, and a convenient help to mischief. He saw alight out of the
coach only one young lady, the lover, and then the
destined victim ; which he (drawing near) knew rather
by her tongue than shape. The lady ran into the
play-house, and left Alcidiana to be conducted by
her lover into it, who led her to the door, and went to
give some order to the coachman ; so that the lover
was about twenty yards from Alcidiana ; when she
stood the fairest mark in the world, on the threshold
of the entrance of the theatre, there being many
coaches about the door, so that hers could not come
so near. Tarquin was resolved not to lose so fair an
opportunity, and advanced, but went behind the
coaches ; and when he came over against the door,
through a great booted velvet coach, that stood
between him and her, he shot ; and she having the
train of her gown and petticoat on her arm, in great
quantity, he missed her body, and shot through her
clothes, between her arm and her body. She, frightened to find something hit her, and to see the smoke,
and hear the report of the pistol ; running in, cried, ' I
am shot, I am dead.'

This noise quickly alarmed her lover ; and all the
coachmen and footmen immediately ran, some one
way, and some another. One of them seeing a man
haste away in a cloak ; he being a lusty bold German,
stopped him ; and drawing upon him, bid him stand,
and deliver his pistol, or he would run him through.

Tarquin being surprised at the boldness of this
fellow to demand his pistol, as if he positively knew
him to be the murderer (for so he thought himself,
since he believed Alcidiana dead), had so much
presence of mind as to consider, if he suffered himself
to be taken, he should poorly die a public death ; and
therefore resolved upon one mischief more, to secure
himself from the first. And in the moment that the
German bade him deliver his pistol, he cried, ' Though

I have no pistol to deliver, I have a sword to chastise
thy insolence.' And throwing off his cloak, and
flinging his pistol from him, he drew, and wounded,
and disarmed the fellow.

This noise of swords brought everybody to the
place; and immediately the bruit ran, ' The murderer
was taken, the murderer was taken.' Yet none knew
which was he, nor as yet so much as the cause of the
quarrel between the two fighting men ; for it was now
darker than before. But at the noise of the murderer
being taken, the lover of Alcidiana, who by this time
found his lady unhurt, all but the trains of her gown
and petticoat, came running to the place, just as
Tarquin had disarmed the German, and was ready to
kill him ; when laying hold of his arm, they arrested
the stroke, and redeemed the footman.

They then demanded who this stranger was, at
whose mercy the fellow lay ; but the Prince, who now
found himself venturing for his last stake, made no
reply ; but with two swords in his hands went to fight
his way through the rabble. And though there were
above a hundred persons, some with swords, others
with long whips (as coachmen), so invincible was the
courage of this poor unfortunate gentleman at that
time, that all these were not able to seize him ; but he
made his way through the ring that encompassed him,
and ran away ; but was, however, so closely pursued,
the company still gathering as they ran, that toiled
with fighting, oppressed with guilt, and fear of being
taken, he grew fainter and fainter, and suffered himself, at last, to yield to his pursuers, who soon found
him to be Prince Tarquin in disguise. And they
carried him directly to prison, being Sunday, to wait
the coming day, to go before a magistrate.

In an hour's time the whole fatal adventure was
carried all over the city, and every one knew that
Tarquin was the intended murderer of Alcidiana ;
and not one but had a real sorrow and compassion
for him. They heard how bravely he had defended

himself, how many he had wounded before he could be taken, and what numbers he had fought through. And even those that saw his valour and bravery, and who had assisted at his being seized, now repented from the bottom of their hearts their having any hand in the ruin of so gallant a man ; especially since they knew the lady was not hurt. A thousand addresses were made to her not to prosecute him ; but her lover, a hot-headed fellow, more fierce than brave, would by no means be pacified, but vowed to pursue him to the scaffold.

The Monday came, and the Prince being examined, confessed the matter of fact, since there was no harm done ; believing a generous confession the best of his game. But he was sent back to closer imprisonment, loaded with irons, to expect the next sessions. All his household goods were seized, and all they could find, for the use of Alcidiana. And the Princess, all in rage, tearing her hair, was carried to the same prison, to behold the cruel effects of her hellish designs.

One need not tell here how sad and horrid this meeting appeared between her lord and her. Let it suffice, it was the most melancholy and mortifying object that ever eyes beheld. On Miranda's part, it was sometimes all rage and fire, and sometimes all tears and groans ; but still it was sad love, and mournful tenderness on his. Nor could all his sufferings, and the prospect of death itself, drive from his soul one spark of that fire the obstinate god had fatally kindled there. And in the midst of all his sighs, he would recall himself, and cry, ' I have Miranda still.'

He was eternally visited by his friends and acquaintance ; and this last action of bravery had got him more than all his former conduct had lost. The fathers were perpetually with him ; and all joined with one common voice in this, that he ought to abandon a woman so wicked as the Princess ; and that however fate dealt with him, he could not show himself a true penitent, while he laid the author of so much evil in his bosom : that heaven would never bless him, till he had renounced her : and on such conditions he would find those that would employ their utmost interest to save his life, who else would not stir in this affair.   But he was so deaf to all, that he could not so much as dissemble a repentance of having married her.

He lay a long time in prison, and all that time the poor Father Francisco remained there also.   And the good fathers who daily visited these two amorous prisoners, the Prince and Princess ; and who found, by the management of matters, it would go very hard with Tarquin, entertained them often with holy matters relating to the life to come ; from which, before his trial, he gathered what his stars had appointed, and that he was destined to die.

This gave an unspeakable torment to the now repenting beauty, who had reduced him to it ; and she began to appear with a more solid grief : which being perceived by the good fathers, they resolved to attack her on the yielding side ; and after some discourse upon the judgment for sin, they came to reflect on the business of Father Francisco ; and told her, she had never thriven since her accusing of that father, and laid it very home to her conscience ; assuring her that they would do their utmost in her service, if she would confess that secret sin to all the world, so that she might atone for the crime, by the saving that good man.   At first she seemed inclined to yield ; but shame of being her own detector, in so vile a matter, recalled her goodness, and she faintly persisted in it.

At the end of six months, Prince Tarquin was called to his trial ; where I will pass over the circumstances, which are only what is usual in such criminal cases, and tell you, that he being found guilty of the intent of killing Alcidiana, was condemned to lose his head in the market-place, and the Princess to be banished her country.

After sentence pronounced, to the real grief of all the spectators, he was carried back to prison. And now the fathers attack her anew; and she, whose griefs daily increased, with a languishment that brought her very near her grave, at last confessed all her life, all the lewdness of her practices with several princes and great men, besides her lusts with people that served her, and others in mean capacity: and lastly, the whole truth of the young friar; and how she had drawn the page, and the Prince her husband, to this designed murder of her sister. This she signed with her hand, in the presence of the Prince, her husband, and several holy men who were present. Which being signified to the magistrates, the friar was immediately delivered from his irons (where he had languished more than two whole years) in great triumph, with much honour, and lives a most exemplary pious life, as he did before; for he is now living in Antwerp.

After the condemnation of these two unfortunate persons, who begot such different sentiments in the minds of the people (the Prince, all the compassion and pity imaginable; and the Princess, all the contempt and despite); they languished almost six months longer in prison: so great an interest there was made, in order to the saving his life, by all the men of the robe. On the other side, the Princes, and great men of all nations, who were at the Court of Brussels, who bore a secret revenge in their hearts against a man who had, as they pretended, set up a false title, only to take place of them; who indeed was but a merchant's son of Holland, as they said; so incensed them against him, that they were too hard at Court for the church-men. However, this dispute gave the Prince his life some months longer than was expected; which gave him also some hope, that a reprieve for ninety years would have been granted, as was desired. Nay, Father Francisco so interested himself in this concern, that he writ to his father, and several princes of Germany, with whom the Marquis Castel Roderigo was well acquainted, to intercede with him for the saving of Tarquin; since it was more by his persuasions, than those of all who attacked her, that made Miranda confess the truth of her affair with him. But at the end of six months, when all applications were found fruitless and vain, the Prince received news, that in two days he was to die, as his sentence had been before pronounced, and for which he prepared himself with all cheerfulness.

On the following Friday, as soon as it was light, all people of any condition came to take their leaves of him; and none departed with dry eyes, or hearts unconcerned to the last degree. For Tarquin, when he found his fate inevitable bore it with a fortitude that showed no signs of regret; but addressed himself to all about him with the same cheerful, modest, and great air, he was wont to do in his most flourishing fortune. His valet was dressing him all the morning, so many interruptions they had by visitors; and he was all in mourning, and so were all his followers; for even to the last he kept up his grandeur, to the amazement of all people. And indeed, he was so passionately beloved by them, that those he had dismissed, served him voluntarily, and would not be persuaded to abandon him while he lived.

The Princess was also dressed in mourning, and her two women; and notwithstanding the unheard-of lewdness and villainies she had confessed of herself, the Prince still adored her; for she had still those charms that made him first do so; nor, to his last moment, could he be brought to wish, that he had never seen her; but on the contrary, as a man yet vainly proud of his fetters, he said, 'All the satisfaction this short moment of life could afford him, was, that he died in endeavouring to serve Miranda, his adorable Princess.'

K

After he had taken leave of all, who thought it necessary to leave him to himself for some time, he retired with his confessor; where they were about an hour in prayer, all the ceremonies of devotion that were fit to be done, being already passed. At last the bell tolled, and he was to take leave of the Princess, as his last work of life, and the most hard he had to accomplish. He threw himself at her feet, and gazing on her as she sat more dead than alive, overwhelmed with silent grief, they both remained some moments speechless; and then, as if one rising tide of tears had supplied both their eyes, it burst out in streams at the same instant: and when his sighs gave way, he uttered a thousand farewells, so soft, so passionate, and moving, that all who were by were extremely touched with it, and said, that nothing could be seen more deplorable and melancholy. A thousand times they bade farewell, and still some tender look, or word, would prevent his going; then embrace, and bid farewell again. A thousand times she asked his pardon for being the occasion of that fatal separation; a thousand times assuring him, she would follow him, for she could not live without him. And Heaven knows when their soft and sad caresses would have ended, had not the officers assured him it was time to mount the scaffold. At which words the Princess fell fainting in the arms of her women, and they led Tarquin out of prison.

When he came to the market-place, whither he walked on foot, followed by his own domestics, and some bearing a black velvet coffin with silver hinges; the headsman before him with his fatal scimitar drawn, his confessor by his side, and many gentlemen and church-men, with Father Francisco attending him, the people showering millions of blessings on him, and beholding him with weeping eyes, he mounted the scaffold; which was strown with some sawdust, about the place where he was to kneel, to receive the blood. For they behead people kneeling, and with the back-stroke of a scimitar; and not lying on a block, and with an axe, as we in England. The scaffold had a low rail about it, that everybody might more conveniently see. This was hung with black, and all that state that such a death could have, was here in most decent order.

He did not say much upon the scaffold. The sum of what he said to his friends was, to be kind, and take care of the poor penitent his wife, To others, recommending his honest and generous servants, whose fidelity was so well known and commended, that they were soon promised preferment. He was some time in prayer, and a very short time in speaking to his confessor; then he turned to the headsman, and desired him to do his office well, and gave him twenty louis d'ors; and undressing himself with the help of his valet and page, he pulled off his coat, and had underneath a white satin waistcoat. He took off his periwig, and put on a white satin cap, with a holland one done with point under it, which he pulled over his eyes; then took a cheerful leave of all, and kneeled down, and said, 'When he lifted up his hands the third time, the headsman should do his office.' Which accordingly was done, and the headsman gave him his last stroke, and the Prince fell on the scaffold. The people with one common voice, as if it had been but one entire one, prayed for his soul; and murmurs of sighs were heard from the whole multitude, who scrambled for some of the bloody sawdust, to keep for his memory.

The headsman going to take up the head, as the manner is, to show it to the people, he found he had not struck it off, and that the body stirred; with that he stepped to an engine, which they always carry with them, to force those who may be refractory; thinking, as he said, to have twisted the head from the shoulders, conceiving it to hang but by a small matter of flesh. Though it was an odd shift of the fellow's, yet it was done, and the best shift he could suddenly propose. The Margrave, and another officer, old men, were on the scaffold, with some of the Prince's friends and servants; who seeing the headsman put the engine about the neck of the Prince, began to call out, and the people made a great noise. The Prince, who found himself yet alive; or rather, who was past thinking but had some sense of feeling left, when the headsman took him up, and set his back against the rail, and clapped the engine about his neck, got his two thumbs between the rope and his neck, feeling himself pressed there; and struggling between life and death, and bending himself over the rail backward, while the headsman pulled forward, he threw himself quite over the rail, by chance, and not design, and fell upon the heads and shoulders of the people, who were crying out with amazing shouts of joy. The headsman leaped after him, but the rabble had liked to have pulled him to pieces. All the city was in an uproar, but none knew what the matter was, but those who bore the body of the Prince, whom they found yet living; but how, or by what strange miracle preserved, they knew not, nor did examine; but with one accord, as if the whole crowd had been one body, and had but one motion, they bore the Prince on their heads about a hundred yards from the scaffold, where there is a monastery of Jesuits; and there they secured him. All this was done, his beheading, his falling, and his being secured, almost in a moment's time; the people rejoicing, as at some extraordinary victory won. One of the officers being, as I said, an old timorous man, was so frightened at the accident, the bustle, the noise, and the confusion, of which he was wholly ignorant, that he died with amazement and fear; and the other was fain to be let blood.

The officers of justice went to demand the prisoner, but they demanded in vain; the Jesuits had now a right to protect him, and would do so. All his overjoyed friends went to see in what condition he

was, and all of quality found admittance. They saw
him in bed, going to be dressed by the most skilful
surgeons, who yet could not assure him of life. They
desired nobody should speak to him, or ask him any
questions. They found that the headsman had
struck him too low, and had cut him into the
shoulder-bone. A very great wound, you may be
sure; for the sword, in such executions, carries an
extreme force. However, so great care was taken on
all sides, and so greatly the fathers were concerned
for him, that they found an amendment, and hopes
of a good effect of their incomparable charity and
goodness.

At last, when he was permitted to speak, the first
news he asked was after the Princess. And his
friends were very much afflicted to find, that all his
loss of blood had not quenched that flame, nor let
out that which made him still love that bad woman.
He was solicited daily to think no more of her. And
all her crimes are laid so open to him, and so shamefully represented; and on the other side, his virtues
so admired; and which, they said, would have been
eternally celebrated, but for his folly with this
infamous creature; that at last, by assuring him of
all their assistance if he abandoned her; and to renounce him, and deliver him up, if he did not; they
wrought so far upon him, as to promise he would
suffer her to go alone into banishment, and would
not follow her, or live with her any more. But alas!
this was but his gratitude that compelled this complaisance, for in his heart he resolved never to abandon her; nor was he able to live, and think of doing
it. However, his reason assured him, he could not
do a deed more justifiable, and one that would regain
his fame sooner.

His friends asked him some questions concerning
his escape; and since he was not beheaded, but only
wounded, why he did not immediately rise up. But
he replied, he was so absolutely prepossessed, that at

the third lifting up his hands he should receive the stroke of death, that at the same instant the sword touched him, he had no sense; nay, not even of pain, so absolutely dead he was with imagination; and knew not that he stirred, as the headsman found he did; nor did he remember anything, from the lifting up of his hands, to his fall; and then awakened, as out of a dream, or rather a moment's sleep without dream, he found he lived, and wondered what was arrived to him, or how he came to live; having not, as yet, any sense of his wound, though so terrible an one.

After this, Alcidiana, who was extremely afflicted for having been the prosecutor of this great man; who, bating this last design against her, which she knew was at the instigation of her sister, had obliged her with all the civility imaginable; now sought all means possible of getting his pardon, and that of her sister; though of a hundred thousand crowns, which she should have paid her, she could get but ten thousand; which was from the sale of her rich beds, and some other furniture. So that the young Count, who before should have married her, now went off for want of fortune; and a young merchant (perhaps the best of the two) was the man to whom she was destined.

At last, by great intercession, both their pardons were obtained; and the Prince, who would be no more seen in a place that had proved every way so fatal to him, left Flanders, promising never to live with the fair hypocrite more; but ere he departed, he wrote her a letter, wherein he ordered her, in a little time, to follow him into Holland; and left a bill of exchange with one of his trusty servants, whom he had left to wait upon her, for money for her accommodation; so that she was now reduced to one woman, one page, and this gentleman. The Prince, in this time of his imprisonment, had several bills of great sums from his father, who was exceeding rich, and this all the children he had in the world, and whom he tenderly loved.

As soon as Miranda was come into Holland, she was welcomed with all imaginable respect and endearment by the old father; who was imposed upon so, as that he knew not she was the fatal occasion of all these disasters to his son; but rather looked on her as a woman, who had brought him a hundred and fifty thousand crowns, which his misfortunes had consumed. But, above all, she was received by Tarquin with a joy unspeakable; who, after some time, to redeem his credit, and gain himself a new fame, put himself into the French army, where he did wonders; and after three campaigns, his father dying, he returned home, and retired to a country-house: where, with his Princess, he lived as a private gentleman, in all the tranquillity of a man of good fortune. They say Miranda has been very penitent for her life past, and gives Heaven the glory for having given her these afflictions that have reclaimed her, and brought her to as perfect a state of happiness, as this troublesome world can afford.

Since I began this relation, I heard that Prince Tarquin died about three-quarters of a year ago.

THE NUN

OR THE PERJURED BEAUTY

A TRUE NOVEL

DON HENRIQUE was a person of great birth, of a great estate, of a bravery equal to either, of a most generous education, but of more passion than reason. He was besides of an opener and freer temper than generally his countrymen are (I mean, the Spaniards) and always engaged in some love-intrigue or other.

One night as he was retreating from one of those engagements, Don Sebastian, whose sister he had abused with a promise of marriage, set upon him at the corner of a street, in Madrid, and by the help of three of his friends, designed to have despatched him on a doubtful embassy to the Almighty Monarch. But he received their first instructions with better address than they expected, and dismissed his envoy first, killing one of Don Sebastian's friends. Which so enraged the injured brother, that his strength and resolution seemed to be redoubled, and so animated his two surviving companions, that (doubtless) they had gained a dishonourable victory, had not Don Antonio accidentally come in to the rescue; who after a short dispute, killed one of the two who attacked him only; whilst Don Henrique, with the greatest difficulty, defended his life, for some moments, against Sebastian, whose rage deprived him of strength, and gave his adversary the unwished advantage of his seeming death, though not without bequeathing some bloody legacies to Don Henrique. Antonio had received but one slight wound in the left arm, and his surviving antagonist none; who however thought it not advisable to begin a fresh dispute against two, of whose courage he had but too fatal a proof, though one of them was sufficiently disabled. The conquerors on the other side, politicly retreated, and quitting the field to the conquered, left the living to bury the dead, if he could, or thought convenient.

As they were marching off, Don Antonio, who all this while knew not whose life he had so happily preserved, told his companion in arms, that he thought it indispensably necessary that he should quarter with him that night for his further preservation. To which he prudently consented, and went, with no little uneasiness, to his lodgings; where he surprised Antonio with the sight of his dearest friend. For they had certainly the nearest sympathy in all their thoughts, that ever made two brave men unhappy. And, undoubtedly, nothing but death, or more fatal love, could have divided them. However, at present, they were united and secure.

In the meantime, Don Sebastian's friend was just going to call help to carry off the bodies, as the ——— came by; who seeing three men lie dead, seized the fourth: who as he was about to justify himself, by discovering one of the authors of so much bloodshed, was interrupted by a groan from his supposed dead friend Don Sebastian; whom, after a brief account of some part of the matter, and a knowledge of his quality, they took up, and carried to his house; where, within a few days he was recovered past the fear of death. All this while Henrique and Antonio durst not appear, so much as by night; nor could be found, though diligent and daily search was made after the first; but upon Don Sebastian's recovery, the search ceasing, they took the advantage of the night, and, in disguise, retreated to Seville. It was there they thought themselves most secure, where indeed they were in the

greatest danger; for though (haply) they might there
have escaped the murderous attempt of Don Sebastian and his friends, yet they could not there avoid
the malicious influence of their stars.

This city gave birth to Antonio, and to the cause
of his greatest misfortunes, as well as of his death.
Dona Ardelia was born there, a miracle of beauty and
falsehood. It was more than a year since Don Antonio
had first seen and loved her. For it was impossible
any man should do one without the other. He had
had the unkind opportunity of speaking and convey-
ing a billet to her at church; and to his greater misfortune, the next time he found her there, he met with
too kind a return both from her eyes and from her
hand, which privately slipped a paper into his; in
which he found abundantly more than he expected,
directing him in that, how he should proceed, in order
to carry her off from her father with the least danger
he could look for in such an attempt; since it would
have been vain and fruitless to have asked her of her
father, because their families had been at enmity for
several years; though Antonio was as well descended
as she, and had as ample a fortune; nor was his
person, according to his sex, any way inferior to hers;
and certainly, the beauties of his mind were more
excellent, especially if it be an excellence to be
constant.

He had made several attempts to take possession
of her, but all proved ineffectual; however, he had
the good fortune not to be known, though once or
twice he narrowly escaped with life, bearing off his
wounds with difficulty. (Alas, that the wounds of
love should cause those of hate!) Upon which she
was strictly confined to one room, whose only window
was towards the garden, and that too was grated with
iron; and, once a month, when she went to church,
she was constantly and carefully attended by her
father, and a mother-in-law, worse than a *Duegna*.
Under this miserable confinement Antonio under-

stood she still continued, at his return to Seville, with
Don Henrique, whom he acquainted with his invincible passion for her; lamenting the severity of
her present circumstances, that admitted of no
prospect of relief; which caused a generous concern
in Don Henrique, both for the sufferings of his friend,
and of the lady. He proposed several ways to Don
Antonio, for the release of the fair prisoner; but
none of them was thought practicable, or at least
likely to succeed. But Antonio, who (you may
believe) was then more nearly engaged, bethought
himself of an expedient that would undoubtedly
reward their endeavours. It was, that Don Henrique,
who was very well acquainted with Ardelia's father,
should make him a visit, with pretence of begging
his consent and admission to make his addresses to
his daughter; which, in all probability, he could not
refuse to Don Henrique's quality and estate; and
then this freedom of access to her would give him the
opportunity of delivering the lady to his friend. This
was thought so reasonable, that the very next day it
was put in practice; and with so good success, that
Don Henrique was received by the father of Ardelia
with the greatest and most respectful ceremony
imaginable. And when he made the proposal to him
of marrying his daughter, it was embraced with a
visible satisfaction and joy in the air of his face.
This their first conversation ended with all imaginable content on both sides; Don Henrique being
invited by the father to dinner the next day, when
Dona Ardelia was to be present; who, at that time,
was said to be indisposed, (as it is very probable she
was, with so close an imprisonment). Henrique returned to Antonio, and made him happy with the
account of his reception; which could not but have
terminated in the perfect felicity of Antonio, had his
fate been just to the merits of his love. The day
and hour came which brought Henrique, with a
private commission from his friend, to Ardelia. He

saw her; (ah! would he had only seen her veiled!)
and, with the first opportunity, gave her the letter,
which held so much love, and so much truth, as ought
to have preserved him in the empire of her heart. It
contained, besides, a discovery of his whole design
upon her father, for the completing of their happiness; which nothing then could obstruct but herself.
But Henrique had seen her; he had gazed, and
swallowed all her beauties at his eyes. How greedily
his soul drank the strong poison in! But yet his
honour and his friendship were strong as ever, and
bravely fought against the usurper love, and got a
noble victory; at least he thought and wished so.
With this, and a short answer to his letter, Henrique
returned to the longing Antonio; who, receiving the
paper with the greatest devotion, and kissing it with
the greatest zeal, opened and read these words to
himself:—

Don Antonio,
You have, at last, made use of the best and only
expedient for my enlargement; for which I thank you,
since I know it is purely the effect of your love. Your
agent has a mighty influence on my father: and you may
assure yourself, that as you have advised and desired me,
he shall have no less on me, who am
Yours entirely,
And only yours,
Ardelia.

Having respectfully and tenderly kissed the name,
he could not choose but show the billet to his friend;
who reading that part of it which concerned himself,
started and blushed: which Antonio observing, was
curious to know the cause of it. Henrique told him,
that he was surprised to find her express so little love,
after so long an absence. To which his friend replied
for her, that, doubtless, she had not time enough to
attempt so great a matter as a perfect account of her
love; and added, that it was confirmation enough to

him of its continuance, since she subscribed herself his entirely, and only his. How blind is love! Don Henrique knew how to make it bear another meaning; which, however, he had the discretion to conceal. Antonio, who was as real in his friendship, as constant in his love, asked him what he thought of her beauty? To which the other answered, that he thought it irresistible to any, but to a soul prepossessed, and nobly fortified with a perfect friendship: 'Such as is thine, my Henrique,' added Antonio; 'yet as sincere and perfect as that is, I know you must, nay, I know, you do love her.' 'As I ought to do,' replied Henrique. 'Yes, yes,' returned his friend, 'it must be so; otherwise the sympathy which unites our souls would be wanting, and consequently our friendship were in a state of imperfection.' 'How industriously you would argue me into a crime, that would tear and destroy the foundation of the strongest ties of truth and honour!' said Henrique. 'But,' he continued, 'I hope within a few days, to put it out of my power to be guilty of so great a sacrilege.' 'I can't determine,' said Antonio, 'if I knew that you loved one another, whether I could easier part with my friend, or my mistress.' 'Though what you say is highly generous,' replied Henrique, 'yet give me leave to urge, that it looks like a trial of friendship, and argues you inclinable to jealousy. But, pardon me, I know it to be sincerely meant by you; and must therefore own, that it is the best, because it is the noblest way of securing both your friend and mistress.' 'I need not make use of any arts to secure me of either,' replied Antonio, 'but expect to enjoy them both in a little time.'

Henrique, who was a little uneasy with a discourse of this nature, diverted it, by reflecting on what had passed at Madrid, between them two and Don Sebastian and his friends; which caused Antonio to bethink himself of the danger to which he exposed his friend, by appearing daily, though in disguise. For, doubtless, Don Sebastian would pursue his revenge to the utmost extremity. These thoughts put him upon desiring his friend, for his own sake, to hasten the performance of his attempt; and accordingly, each day Don Henrique brought Antonio nearer the hopes of happiness, while he himself was hourly sinking into the lowest state of misery. The last night before the day in which Antonio expected to be blessed in her love, Don Henrique had a long and fatal conference with her about her liberty. Being then with her alone in an arbour of the garden, which privilege he had had for some days; after a long silence, and observing Don Henrique in much disorder, by the motion of his eyes, which were sometimes steadfastly fixed on the ground, then lifted up to her or heaven, (for he could see nothing more beautiful on earth) she made use of the privilege of her sex, and began the discourse first, to this effect: 'Has anything happened, sir, since our retreat hither, to occasion that disorder which is but too visible in your face, and too dreadful in your continued silence? Speak, I beseech you, sir, and let me know if I have any way unhappily contributed to it!' 'No, madam,' replied he, 'my friendship is now likely to be the only cause of my greatest misery; for to-morrow I must be guilty of an unpardonable crime, in betraying the generous confidence which your noble father has placed in me. To-morrow,' added he, with a piteous sigh, 'I must deliver you into the hands of one whom your father hates even to death, instead of doing myself the honour of becoming his son-in-law within a few days more.—But—I will consider and remind myself, that I give you into the hands of my friend; of my friend, that loves you better than his life, which he has often exposed for your sake; and what is more than all, to my friend, whom you love more than any consideration on earth.' 'And must this be done?' she asked. 'Is it inevitable as fate?' 'Fixed as the laws of nature, madam,' replied he. 'Don't you find the

necessity of it, Ardelia?' continued he, by way of
question. 'Does not your love require it? Think,
you are going to your dear Antonio, who alone can
merit you, and whom only you can love.' 'Were
your last words true,' returned she, 'I should yet be
unhappy in the displeasure of a dear and tender
father, and infinitely more, in being the cause of your
infidelity to him. No, Don Henrique,' continued she,
'I could with greater satisfaction return to my miserable confinement, than by any means disturb the
peace of your mind, or occasion one moment's interruption of your quiet.' 'Would to Heaven you did
not,' sighed he to himself. Then addressing his words
more distinctly to her, cried he, 'Ah, cruel! ah,
unjust Ardelia! these words belong to none but
Antonio; why then would you endeavour to persuade me, that I do, or ever can merit the tenderness
of such an expression? Have a care!' pursued he,
'have a care, Ardelia! your outward beauties are too
powerful to be resisted; even your frowns have such
a sweetness that they attract the very soul that is not
strongly prepossessed with the noblest friendship,
and the highest principles of honour. Why then,
alas! did you add such sweet and charming accents?
Why——' 'Ah, Don Henrique!' she interrupted,
'why did you appear to me so charming in your
person, so great in your friendship, and so illustrious
in your reputation? Why did my father, ever since
your first visit, continually fill my ears and thoughts
with noble characters and glorious ideas, which yet
but imperfectly and faintly represent the inimitable
original! But (what is most severe and cruel) why,
Don Henrique, why will you defeat my father in his
ambition of your alliance, and me of those glorious
hopes with which you had blessed my soul, by casting me away from you to Antonio!' 'Ha,' cried he,
starting, 'what said you, madam! What did Ardelia
say? That I had blessed your soul with hopes!
That I would cast you away to Antonio! Can they

who safely arrive in their wished-for port, be said to be shipwrecked? Or, can an abject indigent wretch make a king? These are more than riddles, madam; and I must not think to expound them.' 'No,' said she, 'let it alone, Don Henrique; I'll ease you of that trouble, and tell you plainly that I love you.' 'Ah,' cried he, 'now all my fears are come upon me!' 'How!' asked she, 'were you afraid I should love you? Is my love so dreadful then?' 'Yes, when misplaced,' replied he; 'but it was your falsehood that I feared. Your love was what I would have sought with the utmost hazard of my life, nay, even of my future happiness, I fear, had you not been engaged; strongly obliged to love elsewhere, both by your own choice and vows, as well as by his dangerous services, and matchless constancy.' 'For which,' said she, 'I do not hate him, though his father killed my uncle. Nay, perhaps,' continued she, 'I have a friendship for him, but no more.' 'No more, said you, madam?' cried he; 'but tell me, did you never love him?' 'Indeed I did,' replied she; 'but the sight of you has better instructed me, both in my duty to my father, and in causing my passion for you, without whom I shall be eternally miserable. Ah, then pursue your honourable proposal, and make my father happy in my marriage!' 'It must not be,' returned Don Henrique, 'my honour, my friendship forbids it.' 'No,' she returned, 'your honour requires it; and if your friendship opposes your honour, it can have no sure and solid foundation.' 'Female sophistry,' cried Henrique: 'but you need no art nor artifice, Ardelia, to make me love you. Love you!' pursued he, 'by that bright sun, the light and heat of all the world, you are my only light and heat—— Oh, friendship! Sacred friendship, now assist me!' [Here for a time he paused, and then afresh proceeded thus,] 'You told me, or my ears deceived me, that you loved me, Ardelia.' 'I did,' she replied, 'and that I do love you, is as true as that I told you so.' ''Tis well; but

L

would it were not so!' 'Did ever man receive a
blessing thus?' 'Why, I could wish I did not love
you, Ardelia! But that were impossible——' 'At
least unjust,' interrupted she. 'Well then,' he went
on, 'to show you that I do sincerely consult your
particular happiness, without any regard to my own,
to-morrow I will give you to Don Antonio; and as a
proof of your love to me, I expect your ready consent
to it.' 'To let you see, Don Henrique, how perfectly
and tenderly I love you, I will be sacrificed to-morrow
to Don Antonio, and to your quiet.' 'Oh, strongest,
dearest obligation!' cried Henrique. 'To-morrow
then, as I have told your father, I am to bring you to
see the dearest friend I have on earth, who dares not
appear within this city for some unhappy reasons,
and therefore cannot be present at our nuptials; for
which cause, I could not but think it my duty to one
so nearly related to my soul, to make him happy in
the sight of my beautiful choice, ere yet she be my
bride.' 'I hope,' said she, 'my loving obedience may
merit your compassion; and that at last, ere the fire
is lighted that must consume the offering, I mean the
marriage-tapers' (alluding to the old Roman ceremony) 'that you or some other pitying angel, will
snatch me from the altar.' 'Ah, no more, Ardelia!
say no more,' cried he, 'we must be cruel, to be just
to ourselves.' [Here their discourse ended, and they
walked into the house, where they found the good old
gentleman and his lady, with whom he stayed till
about an hour after supper, when he returned to his
friend with joyful news, but a sorrowful heart.]

Antonio was all rapture with the thoughts of the
approaching day; which though it brought Don
Henrique and his dear Ardelia to him, about five
o'clock in the evening, yet at the same time brought
his last and greatest misfortune. He saw her then at
a she relation's of his, above three miles from Seville,
which was the place assigned for their fatal interview.
He saw her, I say; but ah! how strange! how altered

from the dear, kind Ardelia she was when last he left
her! 'Tis true, he flew to her with arms expanded,
and with so swift and eager a motion, that she could
not avoid, nor get loose from his embrace, till he had
kissed, and sighed, and dropped some tears, which all
the strength of his mind could not restrain; whether
they were the effects of joy, or whether (which rather
may be feared) they were the heat-drops which preceded and threatened the thunder and tempest that
should fall on his head, I cannot positively say; yet
all this she was then forced to endure, ere she had
liberty to speak, or indeed to breathe. But as soon as
she had freed herself from the loving circle that
should have been the dear and loved confinement or
centre of a faithful heart, she began to dart whole
showers of tortures on him from her eyes; which that
mouth that he had just before so tenderly and sacredly
kissed, seconded with whole volleys of deaths crammed
in every sentence, pointed with the keenest affliction
that ever pierced a soul. 'Antonio,' she began, 'you
have treated me now as if you were never like to see
me more: and would to Heaven you were not!'
'Ha!' cried he, starting and staring wildly on her,
'What said you, madam? What said you, my Ardelia?'
'If you like the repetition, take it!' replied she, un-
moved. 'Would to Heaven you were never like to
see me more!' 'Good! very good!' cried he, with
a sigh that threw him trembling into a chair behind
him, and gave her the opportunity of proceeding thus.
'Yet, Antonio, I must not have my wish; I must
continue with you, not out of choice, but by command, by the strictest and severest obligation that
ever bound humanity. Don Henrique, your friend,
commands it; Don Henrique, the dearest object of
my soul, enjoins it; Don Henrique, whose only aversion I am, will have it so.' 'Oh, do not wrong me,
madam!' cried Don Henrique. 'Lead me, lead me
a little more by the light of your discourse, I beseech
you,' said Don Antonio, 'that I may see your mean-

she swooned away in Don Antonio's arms; who, though he was happy that he had her fast there, yet was obliged to call in his cousin, and Ardelia's attendants, ere she could be perfectly recovered. In the meanwhile Don Henrique had not the power to go out of sight of the house, but wandered to and fro about it, distracted in his soul; and not being able longer to refrain her sight, her last words still resounding in his ears, he came again into the room where he left her with Don Antonio, just as she revived, and called him, exclaiming on his cruelty, in leaving her so soon. But when, turning her eyes towards the door, she saw him; oh! with what eager haste she flew to him! then clasped him round the waist, obliging him, with all the tender expressions that the soul of a lover, and a woman's too, is capable of uttering, not to leave her in the possession of Don Antonio. This so amazed her slighted lover, that he knew not, at first, how to proceed in this tormenting scene; but at last, summoning all his wonted resolution, and strength of mind, he told her, he would put her out of his power, if she would consent to retreat for some few hours to a nunnery that was not above half a mile distant from thence, till he had discoursed with his friend, Don Henrique, something more particularly than hitherto, about this matter. To which she readily agreed, upon the promise that Don Henrique made her, of seeing her with the first opportunity. They waited on her then to the convent, where she was kindly and respectfully received by the Lady Abbess; but it was not long before her grief renewing with greater violence, and more afflicting circumstances, had obliged them to stay with her till it was almost dark, when they once more begged the liberty of an hour's absence; and the better to palliate their design, Henrique told her, that he would make use of her father Don Richardo's coach, in which they came to Don Antonio's, for so small a time: which they did, leaving only Eleonora, her attendant, with her, without whom she had been at a loss, among so many fair strangers; strangers, I mean, to her unhappy circumstances. Whilst they were carried near a mile farther, where, just as it was dark, they lighted from the coach, Don Henrique ordering the servants not to stir thence till their return from their private walk, which was about a furlong, in a field that belonged to the convent. Here Don Antonio told Don Henrique, that he had not acted honourably; that he had betrayed him, and robbed him at once both of a friend and mistress. To which the other returned, that he understood his meaning, when he proposed a particular discourse about this affair, which he now perceived must end in blood. 'But you may remind yourself,' continued he, 'that I have kept my promise in delivering her to you.' 'Yes,' cried Antonio, 'after you had practised foully and basely on her.' 'Not at all!' returned Henrique. 'It was her fate that brought this mischief on her; for I urged the shame and scandal of inconstancy, but all in vain, to her.' 'But don't you love her, Henrique?' the other asked. 'Too well, and cannot live without her, though I fear I may feel the cursed effects of the same inconstancy. However, I had quitted her all to you, but you see how she resents it.' 'And you shall see, sir,' cried Antonio, drawing his sword in a rage, 'how I resent it.' Here, without more words, they fell to action; to bloody action. (Ah! how wretched are our sex, in being the unhappy occasion of so many fatal mischiefs, even between the dearest friends!) They fought on each side with the greatest animosity of rivals, forgetting all the sacred bonds of their former friendship; till Don Antonio fell, and said, dying, 'Forgive me, Henrique! I was to blame; I could not live without her: I fear she will betray thy life, which haste and preserve, for my sake——Let me not die all at once! Heaven pardon both of us! Farewell! Oh, haste!' 'Farewell!' returned Don Henrique, 'Farewell, thou

bravest, truest friend! Farewell, thou noblest part of
me! And farewell all the quiet of my soul.' Then
stooping, he kissed his cheek; but, rising, he found
he must retire in time, or else must perish through
loss of blood, for he had received two or three dangerous wounds, besides others of less consequence.
Wherefore, he made all the convenient haste he could
to the coach, into which, by the help of the footmen,
he got, and ordered them to drive him directly to
Don Richardo's with all imaginable speed; where he
arrived in little more than half an hour's time, and
was received by Ardelia's father with the greatest
confusion and amazement that is expressible, seeing
him returned without his daughter, and so desperately
wounded. Before he thought it convenient to ask
him any question more than to inquire of his
daughter's safety, to which he received a short but
satisfactory answer, Don Richardo sent for an eminent
and able surgeon, who probed and dressed Don
Henrique's wounds, who was immediately put to bed;
not without some despondency of his recovery: but
(thanks to his kind stars, and kinder constitution!) he
rested pretty well for some hours that night, and early
in the morning, Ardelia's father, who had scarce
taken any rest all that night, came to visit him, as
soon as he understood from the servants who watched
with him, that he was in a condition to suffer a short
discourse; which, you may be sure, was to learn the
circumstances of the past night's adventure; of which
Don Henrique gave him a perfect and pleasant account, since he heard that Don Antonio, his mortal
enemy, was killed; the assurance of whose death was
the more delightful to him, since, by this relation, he
found that Antonio was the man, whom his care of
his daughter had so often frustrated. Don Henrique
hardly made an end of his narration, ere a servant
came hastily to give Richardo notice, that the officers
were come to search for his son-in-law that should
have been; whom the old gentleman's wise pre-

caution had secured in a room so unsuspected, that they might as reasonably have imagined the entire walls of his house had a door made of stones, as that there should have been one to that close apartment. He went therefore boldly to the officers, and gave them all the keys of his house, with free liberty to examine every room and chamber; which they did, but to no purpose; and Don Henrique lay there undiscovered, till his cure was perfected.

In the meantime Ardelia, who that fatal night but too rightly guessed that the death of one or both her lovers was the cause that they did not return to their promise, the next day fell into a high fever, in which her father found her soon after he had cleared himself of those who come to search for a lover. The assurance which her father gave her of Henrique's life, seemed a little to revive her; but the severity of Antonio's fate was no way obliging to her, since she could not but retain the memory of his love and constancy; which added to her afflictions, and heightened her distemper, insomuch that Richardo was constrained to leave her under the care of the good Lady Abbess, and to the diligent attendance of Eleonora, not daring to hazard her life in a removal to his own house. All their care and diligence was however ineffectual; for she languished even to the least hope of recovery, till immediately after the first visit of Don Henrique, which was the first he made in a month's time, and that by night *incognito*, with her father, her distemper visibly retreated each day. Yet, when at last she enjoyed a perfect health of body, her mind grew sick, and she plunged into a deep melancholy; which made her entertain a positive resolution of taking the veil at the end of her novitiate; which accordingly she did, notwithstanding all the entreaties, prayers, and tears both of her father and lover. But she soon repented her vow, and often wished that she might by any means see and speak to Don Henrique, by whose help she promised to herself a deliverance out of her voluntary imprisonment: nor were his wishes wanting to the same effect, though he was forced to fly into Italy, to avoid the prosecution of Antonio's friends. Thither she pursued him; nor could he any way shun her, unless he could have left his heart at a distance from his body; which made him take a fatal resolution of returning to Seville in disguise, where he wandered about the convent every night like a ghost (for indeed his soul was within, while his inanimate trunk was without) till at last he found means to convey a letter to her, which both surprised and delighted her. The messenger that brought it her was one of her mother-in-law's maids whom he had known before, and met accidentally one night as he was going his rounds, and she coming out from Ardelia; with her he prevailed, and with gold obliged her to secrecy and assistance: which proved so successful, that he understood from Ardelia her strong desire of liberty, and the continuance of her passion for him, together with the means and time most convenient and likely to succeed for her enlargement. The time was the fourteenth night following, at twelve o'clock, which just completed a month since his return thither; at which time they both promised themselves the greatest happiness on earth. But you may observe the justice of Heaven, in their disappointment.

Don Sebastian, who still pursued him with a most implacable hatred, had traced him even to Italy, and there narrowly missing him, posted after him to Toledo; so sure and secret was his intelligence! As soon as he arrived, he went directly to the convent where his sister Elvira had been one of the professed, ever since Don Henrique had forsaken her, and where Ardelia had taken her repented vow. Elvira had all along concealed the occasion of her coming thither from Ardelia; and though she was her only confidant, and knew the whole story of her misfortunes, and heard the name of Don Henrique repeated a hundred times a day, whom still she loved most perfectly, yet never gave her beautiful rival any cause of suspicion that she loved him, either by words or looks. Nay more, when she understood that Don Henrique came to the convent with Ardelia and Antonio, and at other times with her father; yet she had so great a command of herself, as to refrain seeing him, or to be seen by him; nor ever intended to have spoken or writ to him, had not her brother Don Sebastian put her upon the cruel necessity of doing the last; who coming to visit his sister (as I have said before) found her with Dona Ardelia, whom he never remembered to have seen, nor who ever had seen him but twice, and that was about six years before, when she was but ten years of age, when she fell passionately in love with him, and continued her passion till about the fourteenth year of her empire, when unfortunate Antonio first began his court to her. Don Sebastian was really a very desirable person, being at that time very beautiful, his age not exceeding six-and-twenty, of a sweet conversation, very brave, but revengeful and irreconcilable (like most of his countrymen) and of an honourable family. At the sight of him Ardelia felt her former passion renew; which proceeded and continued with such violence, that it utterly defaced the ideas of Antonio and Henrique. (No wonder that she who could resolve to forsake her God for man, should quit one lover for another.) In short, she then only wished that he might love her equally, and then she doubted not of contriving the means of their happiness betwixt them. She had her wish, and more, if possible; for he loved her beyond the thought of any other present or future blessing, and failed not to let her know it, at the second interview; when he received the greatest pleasure he could have wished, next to the joys of a bridal bed. For she confessed her love to him, and presently put him upon thinking on the means of her escape; but not finding his designs so likely to succeed, as those measures she had sent to Don Henrique, she communicates the very same to Don Sebastian, and agreed with him to make use of them on that very night, wherein she had obliged Don Henrique to attempt her deliverance. The hour indeed was different, being determined to be at eleven. Elvira, who was present at the conference, took the hint; and not being willing to disoblige a brother who had so hazarded his life in vindication of her, either does not, or would not seem to oppose his inclinations at that time. However, when he retired with her to talk more particularly of his intended revenge on Don Henrique, who he told her lay somewhere absconded in Toledo, and whom he had resolved, as he assured her, to sacrifice to her injured honour, and his resentments; she opposed that his vindictive resolution with all the forcible arguments in a virtuous and pious lady's capacity, but in vain: so that immediately, upon his retreat from the convent, she took the opportunity of writing to Don Henrique as follows, the fatal hour not being then seven nights distant.

DON HENRIQUE,

My brother is now in town, in pursuit of your life; nay more, of your mistress, who has consented to make her escape from the convent, at the same place of it, and by the same means on which she had agreed to give herself entirely to you, but the hour is eleven. I know, Henrique, your Ardelia is dearer to you than your life: but your life, your dear life, is more desired than anything in this world, by

Your injured and forsaken

ELVIRA.

This she delivered to Richardo's servant, whom Henrique had gained that night, as soon as she came to visit Ardelia, at her usual hour, just as she went out of the cloister.

Don Henrique was not a little surprised with this

billet ; however, he could hardly resolve to forbear
his accustomed visits to Ardelia, at first.   But upon
more mature consideration, he only chose to converse
with her by letters, which still pressed her to be
mindful of her promise, and of the hour, not taking
notice of any caution that he had received of her
treachery.   To which she still returned in words
that might assure him of her constancy.

The dreadful hour wanted not a quarter of being
perfect, when Don Henrique came ; and having fixed
his rope-ladder to that part of the garden-wall, where
he was expected, Ardelia, who had not stirred from
that very place for a quarter of an hour before,
prepared to ascend by it ; which she did, as soon as
his servant had returned and fixed it on the inner side
of the wall : on the top of which, at a little distance,
she found another fastened, for her to descend on the
outside, whilst Don Henrique eagerly waited to
receive her.   She came at last, and flew into his
arms ; which made Henrique cry out in a rapture,
'Am I at last once more happy in having my Ardelia
in my possession!'   She, who knew his voice, and
now found she was betrayed, but knew not by whom,
shrieked out, ' I am ruined! help! help! Loose me,
I charge you, Henrique! Loose me !'   At that very
moment, and at those very words, came Sebastian,
attended by only one servant ; and hearing Henrique
reply, ' Not all the powers of hell shall snatch you
from me,' drawing his sword, without one word, made
a furious pass at him.   But his rage and haste mis-
guided his arm, for his sword went quite through
Ardelia's body, who only said, ' Ah, wretched maid !'
and dropped from Henrique's arms, who then was
obliged to quit her, to preserve his own life, if possible : however he had not had so much time as
to draw, had not Sebastian been amazed at this
dreadful mistake of his sword ; but presently recol-
lecting himself, he flew with redoubled rage to attack
Henrique ; and his servant had seconded him, had

not Henrique's, who was now descended, otherwise
diverted him. They fought with the greatest animosity on both sides, and with equal advantage ; for
they both fell together : 'Ah, my Ardelia, I come to
thee now !' Sebastian groaned out. 'Twas this unlucky
arm, which now embraces thee, that killed thee.'
' Just Heaven !' she sighed out, ' Oh, yet have mercy !'
[Here they both died.] ' Amen,' cried Henrique,
dying, ' I want it most——Oh, Antonio ! Oh ! Elvira !
Ah, there's the weight that sinks me down. And yet
I wish forgiveness. Once more, sweet Heaven, have
mercy !' He could not outlive that last word ; which
was echoed by Elvira, who all this while stood weeping, and calling out for help, as she stood close to the
wall in the garden.

This alarmed the rest of the sisters, who rising,
caused the bell to be rung out, as upon dangerous
occasions it used to be ; which raised the neighbour-
hood, who came time enough to remove the dead
bodies of the two rivals, and of the late fallen angel
Ardelia. The injured and neglected Elvira, whose
piety designed quite contrary effects, was immediately
seized with a violent fever, which, as it was violent,
did not last long : for she died within four-and-twenty
hours, with all the happy symptoms of a departing
saint.

THE HISTORY OF
AGNES DE CASTRO

THOUGH love, all soft and flattering, promises nothing but pleasures; yet its consequences are often sad and fatal. It is not enough to be in love, to be happy; since Fortune, who is capricious, and takes delight to trouble the repose of the most elevated and virtuous, has very little respect for passionate and tender hearts, when she designs to produce strange adventures.

Many examples of past ages render this maxim certain; but the reign of Don Alphonso IV., King of Portugal, furnishes us with one, the most extraordinary that history can produce.

He was the son of that Don Denis, who was so successful in all his undertakings, that it was said of him, that he was capable of performing whatever he designed, (and of Isabella, a Princess of eminent virtue) who when he came to inherit a flourishing and tranquil State, endeavoured to establish peace and plenty in abundance in his kingdom.

And to advance this his design, he agreed on a marriage between his son Don Pedro (then about eight years of age) and Bianca, daughter of Don Pedro, King of Castile; and whom the young Prince married when he arrived to his sixteenth year.

Bianca brought nothing to Coimbra but infirmities and very few charms. Don Pedro, who was full of sweetness and generosity, lived nevertheless very well

with her; but those distempers of the Princess de-
generating into the palsy, she made it her request
to retire, and at her intercession the Pope broke the
marriage, and the melancholy Princess concealed her
languishment in a solitary retreat: and Don Pedro,
for whom they had provided another match, married
Constantia Manuel, daughter of Don John Manuel,
a prince of the blood of Castile, and famous for the
enmity he had to his king.

Constantia was promised to the King of Castile;
but that King not keeping his word, they made no
difficulty of bestowing her on a young Prince, who
was one day to reign over a number of fine provinces.
He was but five-and-twenty years of age, and the man
of all Spain that had the best fashion and grace: and
with the most advantageous qualities of the body he
.possessed those of the soul, and showed himself
worthy in all things of the crown that was destined
for him.

The Princess Constantia had beauty, wit, and
generosity, in as great a measure as it was possible
for a woman to be possessed with; her merit alone
ought to have attached Don Pedro eternally to her;
and certainly he had for her an esteem, mixed with so
great a respect, as might very well pass for love with
those that were not of a nice and curious observation:
but alas! his real care was reserved for another
beauty.

Constantia brought into the world, the first year
after her marriage, a son, who was called Don Louis:
but it scarce saw the light, and died almost as soon as
born. The loss of this little Prince sensibly touched
her, but the coldness she observed in the Prince her
husband, went yet nearer her heart; for she had
given herself absolutely up to her duty, and had made
her tenderness for him her only concern: but puissant
glory, which tied her so entirely to the interest of the
Prince of Portugal, opened her eyes upon his actions,
where she observed nothing in his caresses and civili-

ties that was natural, or could satisfy her delicate
heart.

At first she fancied herself deceived, but time
having confirmed her in what she feared, she sighed
in secret; yet had that consideration for the Prince,
as not to let him see her disorder : and which nevertheless she could not conceal from Agnes de Castro,
who lived with her, rather as a companion, than a
maid of honour, and whom her friendship made her
infinitely distinguish from the rest.

This maid, so dear to the Princess, very well
merited the preference her mistress gave her; she
was beautiful to excess, wise, discreet, witty, and had
more tenderness for Constantia than she had for
herself, having quitted her family, which was illustrious, to give herself wholly to the service of the
Princess, and to follow her into Portugal. It was
into the bosom of this maid, that the Princess un-
laded her first moans ; and the charming Agnes
forgot nothing that might give ease to her afflicted
heart.

Nor was Constantia the only person who complained of Don Pedro before his divorce from
Bianca, he had expressed some care and tenderness
for Elvira Gonzales, sister to Don Alvaro Gonzales,
favourite to the King of Portugal; and this amusement in the young years of the Prince, had made
a deep impression on Elvira, who flattered her ambition with the infirmities of Bianca. She saw, with
a secret rage, Constantia take her place, who was
possessed with such charms, that quite divested her
of all hopes.

Her jealousy left her not idle, she examined all the
actions of the Prince, and easily discovered the little
regard he had for the Princess ; but this brought him
not back to her. And it was upon very good grounds
that she suspected him to be in love with some other
person, and possessed with a new passion ; and which
she promised herself, she would destroy as soon as

M

she could find it out.   She had a spirit altogether
proper for bold and hazardous enterprises ; and the
credit of her brother gave her so much vanity, as
all the indifference of the Prince was not capable
of humbling.

The Prince languished, and concealed the cause with
so much care, that it was impossible for any to find it
out.   No public pleasures were agreeable to him, and
all conversations were tedious ; and it was solitude
alone that was able to give him any ease.

This change surprised all the world.   The King,
who loved his son very tenderly, earnestly pressed
him to know the reason of his melancholy ; but the
Prince made no answer, but only this, that it was the
effect of his temper.

But time ran on, and the Princess was brought to
bed of a second son, who lived, and was called Fernando.   Don Pedro forced himself a little to take
part in the public joy, so that they believed his
humour was changing ; but this appearance of a calm
endured not long, and he fell back again into his
black melancholy.

The artful Elvira was incessantly agitating in
searching out the knowledge of this secret.   Chance
wrought for her ; and, as she was walking, full of
indignation and anger, in the garden of the palace of
Coimbra, she found the Prince of Portugal sleeping
in an obscure grotto.

Her fury could not contain itself at the sight of
this loved object, she rolled her eyes upon him, and
perceived, in spite of sleep, that some tears escaped
his eyes ; the flame which burnt yet in her heart,
soon grew soft and tender there : but oh ! she heard
him sigh, and after that utter these words, 'Yes,
divine Agnes, I will sooner die than let you know it.
Constantia shall have nothing to reproach me with.'
Elvira was enraged at this discourse, which represented to her immediately, the same moment, Agnes
de Castro with all her charms ; and not at all doubt-

ing, but it was she who possessed the heart of Don Pedro, she found in her soul more hatred for this fair rival, than tenderness for him.

The grotto was not a fit place to make reflections in, or to form designs. Perhaps her first transports would have made her waken him, if she had not perceived a paper lying under his hand, which she softly seized on; and that she might not be surprised in the reading it, she went out of the garden with as much haste as confusion.

When she was retired to her apartment, she opened the paper, trembling, and found in it these verses, writ by the hand of Don Pedro; and which, in appearance, he had newly then composed.

> In vain, oh! sacred honour, you debate
>   The mighty business in my heart:
> Love! charming love! rules all my fate;
>   Interest and glory claim no part.
> The god, sure of his victory, triumphs there,
>   And will have nothing in his empire share.
>
> In vain, oh! sacred duty, you oppose;
>   In vain, your nuptial tie you plead:
> Those forced devoirs Love overthrows,
>   And breaks the vows he never made.
> Fixing his fatal arrows everywhere,
>   I burn and languish in a soft despair.
>
> Fair Princess, you to whom my faith is due;
>   Pardon the destiny that drags me on:
> 'Tis not my fault my heart's untrue,
>   I am compelled to be undone.
> My life is yours, I gave it with my hand,
>   But my fidelity I can't command.

Elvira did not only know the writing of Don Pedro, but she knew also that he could write verses. And seeing the sad part which Constantia had in these which were now fallen into her hands, she made no scruple of resolving to let the Princess see them: but that she might not be suspected, she took care not to appear in this business herself; and since it was not enough for Constantia to know that the

Prince did not love her, but that she must know also that he was a slave to Agnes de Castro, Elvira caused these few verses to be written in an unknown hand, under those writ by the Prince.

> Sleep betrayed th' unhappy lover,
> While tears were streaming from his eyes;
> His heedless tongue without disguise,
> The secret did discover:
> The language of his heart declare,
> That *Agnes'* image triumphs there.

Elvira regarded neither exactness nor grace in these lines: and if they had but the effect she designed, she wished no more.

Her impatience could not wait till the next day to expose them: she therefore went immediately to the lodgings of the Princess, who was then walking in the garden of the palace; and passing without resistance, even to her cabinet, she put the paper into a book, in which the Princess used to read, and went out again unseen, and satisfied with her good fortune.

As soon as Constantia was returned, she entered into her cabinet, and saw the book open, and the verses lying in it, which were to cost her so dear: she soon knew the hand of the Prince which was so familiar to her; and besides the information of what she had always feared, she understood it was Agnes de Castro (whose friendship alone was able to comfort her in her misfortunes) who was the fatal cause of it: she read over the paper a hundred times, desiring to give her eyes and reason the lie; but finding but too plainly she was not deceived, she found her soul possessed with more grief than anger: when she considered, as much in love as the Prince was, he had kept his torment secret. After having made her moan, without condemning him, the tenderness she had for him, made her shed a torrent of tears, and inspired her with a resolution of concealing her resentment.

She would certainly have done it by a virtue extraordinary, if the Prince, who missing his verses when

he waked, and fearing they might fall into indiscreet
hands, had not entered the palace, all troubled with
his loss ; and hastily going into Constantia's apartment, saw her fair eyes all wet with tears, and at the
same instant cast his own on the unhappy verses that
had escaped from his soul, and now lay before the
Princess.

He immediately turned pale at this sight, and
appeared so moved, that the generous Princess felt
more pain than he did : 'Madam,' said he (infinitely
alarmed), 'from whom had you that paper?' 'It cannot come but from the hand of some person,' answered
Constantia, ' who is an enemy both to your repose and
mine. It is the work, sir, of your own hand ; and
doubtless the sentiment of your heart. But be not
surprised, and do not fear ; for if my tenderness should
make it pass for a crime in you, the same tenderness
which nothing is able to alter, shall hinder me from
complaining.'

The moderation and calmness of Constantia, served
only to render the Prince more ashamed and confused.
'How generous are ·you, madam,' pursued he, 'and
how unfortunate am I!' Some tears accompanied
his words, and the Princess, who loved him with
extreme ardour, was so sensibly touched, that it was
a good while before she could utter a word. Constantia
then broke silence, and showing him what Elvira had
caused to be written, 'You are betrayed, sir,' added
she, 'you have been heard speak, and your secret is
known.' It was at this very moment that all the
forces of the Prince abandoned him; and his condition
was really worthy compassion : he could not pardon
himself the involuntary crime he had committed, in
exposing of the lovely and the innocent Agnes. And
though he was convinced of the virtue and goodness
of Constantia, the apprehensions that he had, that
this modest and prudent maid might suffer by his
conduct, carried him beyond all consideration.

The Princess, who heedfully surveyed him, saw so

many marks of despair in his face and eyes, that she
was afraid of the consequences; and holding out her
hand, in a very obliging manner to him, she said,
'I promise you, sir, I will never more complain of
you, and that Agnes shall always be very dear to me;
you shall never hear me make you any reproaches:
and since I cannot possess your heart, I will content
myself with endeavouring to render myself worthy
of it.' Don Pedro, more confused and dejected than
before he had been, bent one of his knees at the feet
of Constantia, and with respect kissed that fair kind
hand she had given him, and perhaps forgot Agnes for
a moment.

But love soon put a stop to all the little advances
of Hymen; the fatal star that presided over the
destiny of Don Pedro had not yet vented its malignity;
and one moment's sight of Agnes gave new force to
his passion.

The wishes and desires of this charming maid had
no part in this victory; her eyes were just, though
penetrating, and they searched not in those of the
Prince, what they had a desire to discover to her.

As she was never far from Constantia, Don Pedro
was no sooner gone out of the closet, but Agnes
entered; and finding the Princess all pale and languishing in her chair, she doubted not but there was some
sufficient cause for her affliction: she put herself in
the same posture the Prince had been in before, and
expressing an inquietude, full of concern: 'Madam,'
said she, 'by all your goodness, conceal not from me
the cause of your trouble.' 'Alas, Agnes,' replied the
Princess, 'what would you know? And what should
I tell you? The Prince, the Prince, my dearest maid,
is in love; the hand that he gave me, was not a present
of his heart; and for the advantage of this alliance,
I must become the victim of it.' 'What! the Prince
in love!' replied Agnes, with an astonishment mixed
with indignation. 'What beauty can dispute the
empire over a heart so much your due? Alas, madam,

all the respect I owe him, cannot hinder me from murmuring against him.' 'Accuse him of nothing,' interrupted Constantia, 'he does what he can; and I am more obliged to him for desiring to be faithful, than if I possessed his real tenderness. It is not enough to fight, but to overcome; and the Prince does more in the condition wherein he is, than I ought reasonably to hope for. In fine, he is my husband, and an agreeable one; to whom nothing is wanting, but what I cannot inspire; that is, a passion which would have made me but too happy.' 'Ah! madam,' cried out Agnes, transported with her tenderness for the Princess, 'he is a blind and stupid Prince, who knows not the precious advantages he possesses.' 'He must surely know something,' replied the Princess modestly. 'But, madam,' replied Agnes, 'is there anything, not only in Portugal, but in all Spain, that can compare with you? And, without considering the charming qualities of your person, can we enough admire those of your soul?' 'My dear Agnes,' interrupted Constantia, sighing, 'she who robs me of my husband's heart, has but too many charms to plead his excuse; since it is thou, child, whom fortune makes use of, to give me the killing blow. Yes, Agnes, the Prince loves thee; and the merit I know thou art possessed of, puts bounds to my complaints, without suffering me to have the least resentment.'

The delicate Agnes little expected to hear what the Princess told her. Thunder would have less surprised, and less oppressed her. She remained a long time without speaking; but at last, fixing her looks all frightful on Constantia, 'What say you, madam?' cried she, 'and what thoughts have you of me? What, that I should betray you? And coming hither only full of ardour to be the repose of your life, do I bring a fatal poison to afflict it? What detestation must I have for the beauty they find in me, without aspiring to make it appear? And how ought I to

curse the unfortunate day, on which I first saw the
Prince? But, madam, it cannot be me whom Heaven
has chosen to torment you, and to destroy all your
tranquillity. No, it cannot be so much my enemy, to
put me to so great a trial. And if I were that odious
person, there is no punishment, to which I would not
condemn myself. It is Elvira, madam, the Prince
loves, and loved before his marriage with you, and
also before his divorce from Bianca; and somebody
has made an indiscreet report to you of this intrigue
of his youth. But, madam, what was in the time of
Bianca, is nothing to you.' 'It is certain that Don
Pedro loves you,' answered the Princess, 'and I have
vanity enough to believe, that none besides yourself
could have disputed his heart with me. But the secret
is discovered, and Don Pedro has not disowned it.'
'What,' interrupted Agnes, more surprised than ever,
'is it then from himself you have learned his weakness?' The Princess then showed her the verses, and
there was never any despair like to hers.

While they were both thus sadly employed, both
sighing, and both weeping, the impatient Elvira, who
was willing to learn the effect of her malice, returned
to the apartment of the Princess, where she freely
entered; even to the cabinet where these unhappy
persons were: who all afflicted and troubled as they
were, blushed at her approach, whose company they
did not desire. She had the pleasure to see Constantia
hide from her the paper which had been the cause of
all their trouble, and which the Princess had never
seen, but for her spite and revenge; and to observe
also in the eyes of the Princess, and those of Agnes,
an immoderate grief. She stayed in the cabinet as
long as it was necessary to be assured, that she had
succeeded in her design; but the Princess, who did
not desire such a witness of the disorder in which she
then was, prayed to be left alone. Elvira then went
out of the cabinet, and Agnes de Castro withdrew at
the same time.

It was in her own chamber, that Agnes examining more freely this adventure, found it as cruel as death. She loved Constantia sincerely, and had not till then anything more than an esteem, mixed with admiration, for the Prince of Portugal; which indeed, none could refuse to so many fine qualities. And looking on herself as the most unfortunate of her sex, as being the cause of all the sufferings of the Princess, to whom she was obliged for the greatest bounties, she spent the whole night in tears and complaints, sufficient to have revenged Constantia for all the griefs she made her suffer.

The Prince, on his side, was in no great tranquillity; the generosity of his Princess increased his remorse, without diminishing his love: he feared, and with reason, that those who were the occasion of Constantia's seeing those verses, should discover his passion to the King, from whom he hoped for no indulgence: and he would most willingly have given his life, to have been free from this extremity.

In the meantime the afflicted Princess languished in a most deplorable sadness: she found nothing in those who were the cause of her misfortunes, but things fitter to move her tenderness than her anger. It was in vain that jealousy strove to combat the inclination she had to love her fair rival; nor was there any occasion of making the Prince less dear to her: and she felt neither hatred, nor so much as indifference for innocent Agnes.

While these three disconsolate persons abandoned themselves to their melancholy, Elvira, not to leave her vengeance imperfect, studied in what manner she might bring it to the height of its effects. Her brother, on whom she depended, showed her a great deal of friendship, and judging rightly that the love of Don Pedro to Agnes de Castro would not be approved by the King, she acquainted Don Alvaro her brother with it, who was not ignorant of the passion the Prince had once protested to have for his

sister. He found himself very much interested in
this news, from a second passion he had for Agnes ;
which the business of his fortune had hitherto hindered him from discovering. And he expected a
great many favours from the King, that might render
the effort of his heart the more considerable.

He hid not from his sister this one thing, which he
found difficult to conceal; so that she was now possessed with a double grief, to find Agnes sovereign of
all the hearts to which she had a pretension.

Don Alvaro was one of those ambitious men, that
are fierce without moderation, and proud without
generosity ; of a melancholy, cloudy humour, of a
cruel inclination, and to effect his ends, found nothing
difficult or unlawful. Naturally he loved not the
Prince, who, on all accounts, ought to have held the
first rank in the heart of the King, which should
have set bounds to the favour of Don Alvaro ; who
when he knew the Prince was his rival, his jealousy
increased his hate of him : and he conjured Elvira
to employ all her care, to oppose an engagement that
could not but be destructive to them both ; she
promised him, and he not very well satisfied, relied
on her promise.

Don Alvaro, who had too lively a representation
within himself, of the beauties and grace of the
Prince of Portugal, thought of nothing, but how to
combat his merits, he himself not being handsome, or
well made. His fashion was as disagreeable as his
humour, and Don Pedro had all the advantages that
one man may possibly have over another. In fine, all
that Don Alvaro wanted, adorned the Prince : but as
he was the husband of Constantia, and depended upon
an absolute father, and that Don Alvaro was free,
and master of a good fortune, he thought himself
more assured of Agnes, and fixed his hopes on that
thought.

He knew very well, that the passion of Don Pedro
could not but inspire a violent anger in the soul of

the King. Industrious in doing ill, his first business
was to carry this unwelcome news to him. After he
had given time to his grief, and had composed himself
to his desire, he then besought the King to interest
himself in his amorous affair, and to be the protector
of his person.

Though Don Alvaro had no other merit to recom-
mend him to the King, than a continual and blind
obedience to all his commands ; yet he had favoured
him with several testimonies of his vast bounty ; and
considering the height to which the King's liberality
had raised him, there were few ladies that would have
refused his alliance. The King assured him of the
continuation of his friendship and favour, and promised
him, if he had any authority, he would give him the
charming Agnes.

Don Alvaro, perfectly skilful in managing his
master, answered the King's last bounty with a profound submission. He had yet never told Agnes
what he felt for her ; but he thought now he might
make a public declaration of it, and sought all means
to do it.

The gallantry which Coimbra seemed to have forgotten, began now to be awakened. The King to
please Don Alvaro, under pretence of diverting Constantia, ordered some public sports, and commanded
that everything should be magnificent.

Since the adventure of the verses, Don Pedro
endeavoured to lay a constraint on himself, and to
appear less troubled ; but in his heart he suffered
always alike : and it was not but with great uneasiness he prepared himself for the tournament. And
since he could not appear with the colours of Agnes,
he took those of his wife, without device, or any
great magnificence.

Don Alvaro adorned himself with the liveries of
Agnes de Castro ; and this fair maid, who had yet
found no consolation from what the Princess had told
her, had this new cause of being displeased.

Don Pedro appeared in the list with an admirable grace; and Don Alvaro, who looked on this day as his own, appeared there all shining with gold, mixed with stones of blue, which were the colours of Agnes; and there were embroidered all over his equipage, flaming hearts of gold on blue velvet, and nets for the snares of love, with abundance of double *A's;* his device was a love coming out of a cloud, with these verses written underneath:

> Love from a cloud breaks like the god of day,
> And to the world his glories does display;
> To gaze on charming eyes, and make them know,
> What to soft hearts, and to his power they owe.

The pride of Don Alvaro was soon humbled at the feet of the Prince of Portugal, who threw him against the ground with twenty others, and carried alone the glory of the day. There was in the evening a noble assembly at Constantia's, where Agnes would not have been, unless expressly commanded by the Princess. She appeared there all negligent and careless in her dress, but yet she appeared all beautiful and charming. She saw, with disdain, her name, and her colours, worn by Don Alvaro, at a public triumph; and if her heart was capable of any tender motions, it was not for such a man as he for whom her delicacy destined them. She looked on him with a contempt, which did not hinder him from pressing so near, that there was a necessity for her to hear what he had to declare to her.

She treated him not uncivilly, but her coldness would have rebated the courage of any but Alvaro. 'Madam,' said he (when he could be heard of none but herself), 'I have hitherto concealed the passion you have inspired me with, fearing it should displease you; but it has committed a violence on my respect; and I could no longer conceal it from you.' 'I never reflected on your actions,' answered Agnes with all the indifference of which she was capable, 'and if you think you offend me, you are in the wrong to make me perceive it.' 'This coldness is but an ill omen for me,' replied Don Alvaro, 'and if you have not found me out to be your lover to-day, I fear you will never approve my passion.'

'Oh! what a time have you chosen to make it appear to me?' pursued Agnes. 'Is it so great an honour for me, that you must take such care to show it to the world? And do you think that I am so desirous of glory, that I must aspire to it by your actions? If I must, you have very ill maintained it in the tournament; and if it be that vanity that you depend upon, you will make no great progress on a soul that is not fond of shame. If you were possessed of all the advantages, which the Prince has this day carried away, you yet ought to consider what you are going about; and it is not a maid like me, who is touched with enterprises, without respect or permission.'

The favourite of the King was too proud to hear Agnes, without indignation: but as he was willing to conceal it, and not offend her, he made not his resentment appear; and considering the observation she made on the triumphs of Don Pedro (which increased his jealousies), 'If I have not overcome at the tournament,' replied he, 'I am not the less in love for being vanquished, nor less capable of success on occasion.'

They were interrupted here, but from that day, Don Alvaro, who had opened the first difficulties, kept no more his wonted distance, but perpetually persecuted Agnes; yet, though he were protected by the King, that inspired in her never the more consideration for him. Don Pedro was always ignorant by what means the verses he had lost in the garden, fell into the hands of Constantia. As the Princess appeared to him indulgent, he was only concerned for Agnes; and the love of Don Alvaro, which was then so well known, increased the pain: and had he been possessed of the authority, he would not have

suffered her to have been exposed to the persecutions
of so unworthy a rival. He was also afraid of the
King's being advertised of his passion, but he thought
not at all of Elvira, nor apprehended any malice from
her resentment.

While she burned with a desire of destroying
Agnes, against whom she vented all her venom, she
was never weary of making new reports to her brother,
assuring him, that though they could not prove that
Agnes made any returns to the tenderness of the
Prince, yet that was the cause of Constantia's grief:
and, that if this Princess should die of it, Don Pedro
might marry Agnes. In fine, she so incensed the
jealous Don Alvaro's jealousy, that he could not
hinder himself from running immediately to the King,
with the discovery of all he knew, and all he guessed,
and who, he had the pleasure to find, was infinitely
enraged at the news. 'My dear Alvaro,' said the
King, 'you shall instantly marry this dangerous
beauty: and let possession assure your repose and
mine. If I have protected you on other occasions,
judge what a service of so great an importance for
me, would make me undertake; and without any
reserve, the forces of this State are in your power, and
almost anything that I can give shall be assured you,
so you render yourself master of the destiny of
Agnes.'

Don Alvaro pleased, and vain with his master's
bounty, made use of all the authority he gave him.
He passionately loved Agnes, and would not, on the
sudden, make use of violence; but resolved with
himself to employ all possible means to win her
fairly; yet if that failed, to have recourse to force, if
she continued always insensible.

While Agnes de Castro (importuned by his assiduities, despairing at the grief of Constantia, and perhaps
made tender by those she had caused in the Prince of
Portugal) took a resolution worthy of her virtue; yet,
amiable as Don Pedro was, she found nothing in him,

but his being husband to Constantia, that was dear to
her. And, far from encouraging the power she had
got over his heart, she thought of nothing but removing from Coimbra. The passion of Don Alvaro,
which she had no inclination to favour, served her as
a pretext; and pressed with the fear of causing, in
the end, a cruel divorce between the Prince and his
Princess, she went to find Constantia, with a trouble,
which all her care was not able to hide from her.

The Princess easily found it out; and their common misfortunes having not changed their friendship,
'What ails you, Agnes?' said the Princess to her, in
a soft tone, and with her ordinary sweetness. 'And
what new misfortune causes that sadness in thy
looks?' 'Madam,' replied Agnes, shedding a rivulet
of tears, 'the obligations and ties I have to you, put
me upon a cruel trial. I had bounded the felicity of
my life in hope of passing it near your Highness, yet
I must carry to some other part of the world this
unlucky face of mine, which renders me nothing but
ill offices. And it is to obtain that liberty, that I am
come to throw myself at your feet; looking upon you
as my sovereign.'

Constantia was so surprised and touched with the
proposition of Agnes, that she lost her speech for
some moments. Tears, which were sincere, expressed her first sentiments: and after having shed
abundance, to give a new mark of her tenderness to
the fair afflicted Agnes, she with a sad and melancholy
look, fixed her eyes upon her, and holding out her
hand to her, in a most obliging manner, sighing, cried,
'You will then, my dear Agnes, leave me; and expose
me to the griefs of seeing you no more?' 'Alas,
madam,' interrupted this lovely maid, 'hide from the
unhappy Agnes a bounty which does but increase her
misfortunes. It is not I, madam, that would leave
you; it is my duty, and my reason that orders my
fate. And those days which I shall pass far from
you, promise me nothing to oblige me to this design,

if I did not see myself absolutely forced to it. I am not ignorant of what passes at Coimbra; and I shall be an accomplice of the injustice there committed, if I should stay there any longer.' 'Ah, I know your virtue,' cried Constantia, 'and you may remain here in all safety, while I am your protectress; and let what will happen, I will accuse you of nothing.' 'There's no answering for what's to come,' replied Agnes, sadly, 'and I shall be sufficiently guilty, if my presence cause sentiments, which cannot be innocent. Besides, madam, the importunities of Don Alvaro are insupportable to me; and though I find nothing but aversion to him, since the King protects his insolence, and he's in a condition of undertaking anything, my flight is absolutely necessary. But, madam, though he has nothing but what seems odious to me; I call Heaven to witness, that if I could cure the Prince by marrying Don Alvaro, I would not consider of it a moment; and finding in my punishment the consolation of sacrificing myself to my Princess, I would support it without murmuring. But if I were the wife of Don Alvaro, Don Pedro would always look upon me with the same eyes. So that I find nothing more reasonable for me, than to hide myself in some corner of the world; where, though I shall most certainly live without pleasure, yet I shall preserve the repose of my dearest mistress.' 'All the reason you find in this design,' answered the Princess, 'cannot oblige me to approve of your absence. Will it restore me the heart of Don Pedro? And will he not fly away with you? His grief is mine, and my life is tied to his; do not make him despair then, if you love me. I know you, I tell you so once more; and let your power be ever so great over the heart of the Prince, I will not suffer you to abandon us.'

Though Agnes thought she had perfectly known Constantia, yet she did not expect to find so entire a virtue in her, which made her think herself more happy, and the Prince more criminal. 'Oh, wisdom!

Oh, bounty without example!' cried she. 'Why is it, that the cruel destinies do not give you all you deserve? You are the disposer of my actions,' continued she, in kissing the hand of Constantia, 'I'll do nothing but what you'll have me. But consider, and weigh well the reasons that ought to counsel you in the measures you oblige me to take.'

Don Pedro, who had not seen the Princess all that day, came in then, and finding them both extremely troubled, with a fierce impatience, demanded the cause: 'Sir,' answered Constantia, 'Agnes too wise, and too scrupulous, fears the effects of her beauty, and will live no longer at Coimbra; and it was on this subject (which cannot be agreeable to me) that she asked my advice.' The Prince grew pale at this discourse, and snatching the words from her mouth (with more concern than possessed either of them) cried with a voice very feeble, 'Agnes cannot fail, if she follow your counsel, madam: and I leave you full liberty to give it her.' He then immediately went out, and the Princess, whose heart he perfectly possessed, not being able to hide her displeasure, said, 'My dear Agnes, if my satisfaction did not only depend on your conversation, I should desire it of you, for Don Pedro's sake; it is the only advantage that his unfortunate love can hope. And would not the world have reason to call me barbarous, if I contribute to deprive him of that?' 'But the sight of me will prove a poison to him,' replied Agnes. 'And what should I do, my Princess, if after the reserve he has hitherto kept, his mouth should add anything to the torments I have already felt, by speaking to me of his flame?' 'You would hear him sure, without causing him to despair,' replied Constantia, 'and I should put this obligation to the account of the rest you have done.' 'Would you then have me expect those events which I fear, madam?' replied Agnes. Well—I will obey, but just Heaven,' pursued she, 'if they prove fatal, do not punish an innocent heart for

N

it.' Thus this conversation ended. Agnes withdrew
into her chamber, but it was not to be more at ease.

What Don Pedro had learned of the design of
Agnes, caused a cruel agitation in his soul; he wished
he had never loved her, and desired a thousand times
to die. But it was not for him to make vows against
a thing which fate had designed him; and whatever
resolutions he made, to bear the absence of Agnes,
his tenderness had not force enough to consent to it.

After having, for a long time, combated with himself, he determined to do what was impossible for him
to let Agnes do. His courage reproached him with
the idleness, in which he passed the most youthful and
vigorous part of his days: and making it appear to
the King, that his allies, and even the Prince Don
John Emanuel, his father-in-law, had concerns in the
world which demanded his presence on the frontiers,
he easily obtained liberty to make this journey, to
which the Princess would put no obstacle.

Agnes saw him part without any concern, but it
was not upon the account of any aversion she had to
him. Don Alvaro began then to make his importunity
an open persecution; he forgot nothing that might
touch the insensible Agnes, and made use, a long
time, only of the arms of love. But seeing that this
submission and respect was to no purpose, he formed
strange designs.

As the King had a deference for all his counsels,
it was not difficult to inspire him with what he had
a mind to. He complained of the ungrateful Agnes,
and forgot nothing that might make him perceive
that she was not cruel to him on his account, but
from the too much sensibility she had for the Prince.
The King, who was extremely angry at this, reiterated
all the promises he had made him.

The King had not yet spoken to Agnes in favour
of Don Alvaro; and not doubting but his approbation
would surmount all obstacles, he took an occasion to
entertain her with it. And removing some distance

from those who might hear him, 'I thought Don Alvaro had merit enough,' said he to her, 'to have obtained a little share in your esteem; and I could not imagine there would have been any necessity of my soliciting it for him: I know you are very charming, but he has nothing that renders him unworthy of you; and when you shall reflect on the choice my friendship has made of him from among all the great men of my Court, you will do him at the same time justice. His fortune is none of the meanest, since he has me for his protector. He is nobly born, a man of honour and courage; he adores you, and it seems to me that all these reasons are sufficient to vanquish your pride.'

The heart of Agnes was so little disposed to give itself to Don Alvaro, that all the King of Portugal had said had no effect on her in his favour. 'If Don Alvaro, sir,' answered she, 'were without merit, he possesses advantages enough in the bounty your Majesty is pleased to honour him with, to make him master of all things. It is not that I find any defect in him that I answer not his desires. But, sir, by what obstinate power would you that I should love, if Heaven has not given me a soul that is tender? And why should you pretend that I should submit to him, when nothing is dearer to me than my liberty?' 'You are not so free, nor so insensible, as you say,' answered the King, blushing with anger; 'and if your heart were exempt from all sorts of affection, he might expect a more reasonable return than what he finds. But imprudent maid, conducted by an ill fate,' added he in fury, 'what pretensions have you to Don Pedro? Hitherto I have hid the chagrin, which his weakness and yours give me; but it was not the less violent for being hid. And since you oblige me to speak out, I must tell you, that if my son were not already married to Constantia, he should never be your husband; renounce then those vain ideas, which will cure him, and justify you.'

The courageous Agnes was scarce mistress of the

first transports, at a discourse so full of contempt;
but calling her virtue to the aid of her anger, she
recovered herself by the assistance of reason.   And
considering the outrage she received, not as coming
from a great King, but a man blinded and possessed
by Don Alvaro, she thought him not worthy of her
resentment; her fair eyes animated themselves with
so shining a vivacity, they answered for the purity of
her sentiments; and fixing them steadfastly on the
King, 'If the Prince Don Pedro have weaknesses,'
replied she, with an air disdainful, 'he never communicated them to me; and I am certain, I never
contributed wilfully to them.   But to let you see how
little I regard your defiance, and to put my glory in
safety, I will live far from you, and all that belongs to
you.   Yes, sir, I will quit Coimbra with pleasure; and
for this man, who is so dear to you,' answered she
with a noble pride and fierceness, of which the King
felt all the force, 'for this favourite, so worthy to
possess the most tender affections of a great prince,
I assure you, that into whatever part of the world
fortune conducts me, I will not carry away the least
remembrance of him.'   At these words she made
a profound reverence, and made such haste from his
presence, that he could not oppose her going if he
would.

The King was now more strongly convinced than
ever, that she favoured the passion of Don Pedro, and
immediately went to Constantia, to inspire her with
the same thought; but she was not capable of receiving such impressions, and following her own natural
inclinations, she generously defended the virtue of his
actions.   The King, angry to see her so well in-
tentioned to her rival, whom he would have had her
hate, reproached her with the sweetness of her temper,
and went thence to mix his anger with Don Alvaro's
rage, who was totally confounded when he saw the
negotiation of his master had taken no effect.   'The
haughty maid braves me then, sir,' said he to the

King, 'and despises the honour which your bounty offered her! Why cannot I resist so fatal a passion? But I must love her, in spite of myself; and if this flame consume me, I can find no way to extinguish it.' 'What can I further do for you?' replied the King. 'Alas, sir,' answered Don Alvaro, 'I must do by force, what I cannot otherwise hope from the proud and cruel Agnes.' 'Well, then,' added the King, 'since it is not fit for me to authorise publicly a violence in the midst of my kingdom, choose those of my subjects whom you think most capable of serving you, and take away by force the beauty that charms you ; and if she do not yield to your love, put that power you are master of into execution, to oblige her to marry you.'

Don Alvaro, ravished with this proposition, which at the same time flattered both his love and his anger, cast himself at the feet of the King, and renewed his acknowledgments by fresh protestations, and thought of nothing but employing his unjust authority against Agnes.

Don Pedro had been about three months absent, when Alvaro undertook what the King counselled him to ; though the moderation was known to him, yet he feared his presence, and would not attend the return of a rival, with whom he would avoid all disputes.

One night when the said Agnes, full of her ordinary inquietudes, in vain expected the god of sleep, she heard a noise, and after saw some men unknown enter her chamber, whose measures being well consulted, they carried her out of the palace, and putting her in a close coach, forced her out of Coimbra, without being hindered by any obstacle. She knew not of whom to complain, nor whom to suspect. Don Alvaro seemed too puissant to seek his satisfaction this way; and she accused not the Prince of this attempt, of whom she had so favourable an opinion ; whatever she could think or say, she could not hinder

her ill fortune. They hurried her on with diligence,
and before it was day, were a considerable way off
from the town.

As soon as day began to break, she surveyed those
that encompassed her, without so much as knowing
one of them ; and seeing that her cries and prayers
were all in vain with these deaf ravishers, she satisfied
herself with imploring the protection of Heaven, and
abandoned herself to its conduct.

While she sat thus overwhelmed with grief, uncer-
tain of her destiny, she saw a body of horse advance
towards the troop which conducted her. The ravishers
did not shun them, thinking it to be Don Alvaro : but
when he approached more near, they found it was the
Prince of Portugal who was at the head of them, and
who, without foreseeing the occasion that would offer
itself of serving Agnes, was returning to Coimbra full
of her idea, after having performed what he ought in
this expedition.

Agnes, who did not expect him, changed now her
opinion, and thought that it was the Prince that had
caused her to be stolen away. 'Oh, sir !' said she to
him, having still the same thought, 'is it you that
have torn me from the Princess ? And could so cruel
a blow come from a hand that is so dear to her ?
What will you do with an unfortunate creature who
desires nothing but death ? And why will you obscure the glory of your life, by an artifice unworthy
of you ?' This language astonished the Prince no
less than the sight of Agnes had done ; he found by
what she had said, that she was taken away by force ;
and immediately passing to the height of rage, he
made her understand by one only look, that he was
not the base author of her trouble. 'I tear you from
Constantia, whose only pleasure you are !' replied he.
'What opinion have you of Don Pedro ? No, madam,
though you see me here, I am altogether innocent of
the violence that has been done you ; and there is
nothing I will refuse to hinder it.' He then turned

himself to behold the ravishers, but his presence
had already scattered them; he ordered some of his
men to pursue them, and to seize some of them,
that he might know what authority it was that set
them at work.

During this, Agnes was no less confused than
before; she admired the conduct of her destiny, that
brought the Prince at a time when he was so necessary
to her. Her inclinations to do him justice soon repaired the offence her suspicions had caused; she was
glad to have escaped a misfortune, which appeared
certain to her: but this was not a sincere joy, when
she considered that her lover was her deliverer, and
a lover worthy of all her acknowledgments, but who
owed his heart to the most amiable Princess in the
world.

While the Prince's men were pursuing the ravishers
of Agnes, he was left almost alone with her; and
though he had always resolved to shun being so, yet
his constancy was not proof against so fair an occasion: 'Madam,' said he to her, 'is it possible that
men born amongst those that obey us, should be
capable of offending you? I never thought myself
destined to revenge such an offence; but since Heaven
has permitted you to receive it, I will either perish or
make them repent it.' 'Sir,' replied Agnes, more
concerned at this discourse than at the enterprise of
Don Alvaro, 'those who are wanting in their respect
to the Princess and you, are not obliged to have any
for me. I do not in the least doubt but Don Alvaro
was the undertaker of this enterprise; and I judged
what I ought to fear from him, by what his importunities have already made me suffer. He is sure of the
King's protection, and he will make him an accomplice
in his crime: but, sir, Heaven conducted you hither
happily for me, and I am indebted to you for the
liberty I have of serving the Princess yet longer.'
'You will do for Constantia,' replied the Prince,
'what 'tis impossible not to do for you; your good-

ness attaches you to her, and my destiny engages me
to you for ever.'

The modest Agnes, who feared this discourse as
much as the misfortune she had newly shunned,
answered nothing but by downcast eyes; and the
Prince, who knew the trouble she was in, left her to go
to speak to his men, who brought back one of those
that belonged to Don Alvaro, by whose confession he
found the truth. He pardoned him, thinking not fit
to punish him, who obeyed a man whom the weakness
of his father had rendered powerful.

Afterwards they conducted Agnes back to Coimbra,
where her adventure began to make a great noise.
The Princess was ready to die with despair, and at
first thought it was only a continuation of the design
this fair maid had of retiring; but some women that
served her having told the Princess, that she was
carried away by violence, Constantia made her
complaint to the King, who regarded her not at all.

'Madam,' said he to her, 'let this fatal plague
remove itself, who takes from you the heart of your
husband; and without afflicting yourself for her
absence, bless Heaven and me for it.'

The generous Princess took Agnes's part with a
great deal of courage, and was then disputing her
defence with the King, when Don Pedro arrived at
Coimbra.

The first object that met the Prince's eyes was
Don Alvaro, who was passing through one of the
courts of the palace, amidst a crowd of courtiers,
whom his favour with the King drew after him. This
sight made Don Pedro rage; but that of the Princess
and Agnes caused in Alvaro another sort of emotion.
He easily divined, that it was Don Pedro, who had
taken her from his men, and, if his fury had acted
what it would, it might have produced very sad
effects.

'Don Alvaro,' said the Prince to him, 'is it thus
you make use of the authority which the King my

father hath given you? Have you received employ-
ments and power from him, for no other end but to
do these base actions, and to commit rapes on ladies?
Are you ignorant how the Princess interests herself
in all that concerns this maid? And do you not
know the tender and affectionate esteem she has for
her?' 'No,' replied Don Alvaro, with an insolence
that had like to have put the Prince past all patience,
'I am not ignorant of it, nor of the interest your
heart takes in her.' 'Base and treacherous as thou
art,' replied the Prince, 'neither the favour which
thou hast so much abused, nor the insolence which
makes thee speak this, should hinder me from punish-
ing thee, wert thou worthy of my sword; but there
are other ways to humble thy pride, and 'tis not fit for
such an arm as mine to seek so base an employment
to punish such a slave as thou art.'

Don Pedro went away at these words, and left
Alvaro in a rage, which is not to be expressed;
despairing to see himself defeated in an enterprise
he thought so sure; and at the contempt the Prince
showed him, he promised himself to sacrifice all to his
revenge.

Though the King loved his son, he was so prepossessed against his passion, that he could not pardon
him what he had done, and condemned him as much
for this last act of justice, in delivering Agnes, as if it
had been the greatest of crimes.

Elvira, whom the sweetness of hope flattered some
moments, saw the return of Agnes with a sensible
displeasure, which suffered her to think of nothing
but irritating her brother.

In fine, the Prince saw the King, but instead of
being received by him with a joy due to the success
of his journey, he appeared all sullen and out of
humour. After having paid him his first respects,
and given him an exact account of what he had done,
he spoke to him about the violence committed against
the person of Agnes de Castro, and complained to

him of it in the name of the Princess, and of his own.
'You ought to be silent in this affair,' replied the
King; 'and the motive which makes you speak is so
shameful for you, that I sigh and blush at it.   What
is it to you, if this maid, whose presence is troublesome to me, be removed hence, since 'tis I that desire
it?' 'But, sir,' interrupted the Prince, 'what necessity
is there of employing force, artifice, and the night, when
the least of your orders had been sufficient?   Agnes
would willingly have obeyed you; and if she continue
at Coimbra, it is perhaps against her will : but be it
as it will, sir, Constantia is offended, and if it were
not for fear of displeasing you (the only thing that
retains me), the ravisher should not have gone un-
punished.'   'How happy are you,' replied the King,
smiling with disdain, 'in making use of the name of
Constantia to uphold the interest of your heart! You
think I am ignorant of it, and that this unhappy
Princess looks on the injury you do her with indifference.   Never speak to me more of Agnes' (with
a tone very severe). 'Content yourself, that I pardon
what's passed, and think maturely of the considerations I have for Don Alvaro, when you would design
anything against him.'   'Yes, sir,' replied the Prince
with fierceness, 'I will speak to you no more of
Agnes ; but Constantia and I will never suffer, that
she should be any more exposed to the insolence of
your favourite.'   The King had like to have broke
out into a rage at this discourse ; but he had yet
a rest of prudence left that hindered him.   'Retire,'
said he to Don Pedro, 'and go make reflections on
what my power can do, and what you owe me.'

During this conversation, Agnes was receiving from
the Princess, and from all the ladies of the Court,
great expressions of joy and friendship.   Constantia
saw again her husband, with a great deal of satisfaction ; and far from being sorry at what he had
lately done for Agnes, she privately returned him
thanks for it, and still was the same towards him, not-

was both surprised and troubled. The Prince had the
same destiny, and was astonished at an order which
ought to have excepted him.

The next day Constantia appeared, but so altered,
that it was not difficult to imagine what she had
suffered. Agnes was the most impatient to approach
her, and the Princess could not forbear weeping.
They were both silent for some time, and Constantia
attributed this silence of Agnes to some remorse
which she felt: and this unhappy maid being able to
hold no longer, 'Is it possible, madam,' said she,
'that two days should have taken from me all the
goodness you had for me? What have I done? And
for what do you punish me?' The Princess regarded
her with a languishing look, and returned her no
answer but sighs. Agnes, offended with this reserve,
went out with very great dissatisfaction and anger;
which contributed to her being thought criminal.
The Prince came in immediately after, and found
Constantia more disordered than usual, and conjured
her in a most obliging manner to take care of her
health. 'The greatest good for me,' said she, 'is not
the continuation of my life; I should have more care
of it if I loved you less: but——' She could not
proceed; and the Prince, excessively afflicted at her
trouble, sighed sadly, without making her any answer,
which redoubled her grief. Spite then began to mix
itself; and all things persuading the Princess that
they made a sacrifice of her, she would enter into no
explanation with her husband, but suffered him to go
away without saying anything to him.

Nothing is more capable of troubling our reason,
and consuming our health, than secret notions of
jealousy in solitude.

Constantia, who used to open her heart freely to
Agnes, now believing she had deceived her, abandoned
herself so absolutely to grief, that she was ready to
sink under it; she immediately fell sick with the
violence of it, and all the Court was concerned at

this misfortune. Don Pedro was truly afflicted at it, but Agnes more than all the world beside. Constantia's coldness towards her, made her continually sigh ; and her distemper created merely by fancy, caused her to reflect on everything that offered itself to her memory : so that at last she began even to fear herself, and to reproach herself for what the Princess suffered.

But the distemper began to be such that they feared Constantia's death, and she herself began to feel the approaches of it. This thought did not at all disquiet her : she looked on death as the only relief from all her torments ; and regarded the despair of all that approached her without the least concern.

The King, who loved her tenderly, and who knew her virtue, was infinitely moved at the extremity she was in. And Don Alvaro, who lost not the least occasion of making him understand that it was jealousy which was the cause of Constantia's dis-temper, did but too much incense him against criminals, worthy of compassion. The King was not of a temper to conceal his anger long : 'You give fine examples,' said he to the Prince, 'and such as will render your memory illustrious ! The death of Constantia (of which you only are to be accused) is the unhappy fruit of your guilty passion. Fear Heaven after this : and behold yourself as a monster that does not deserve to see the light. If the interest you have in my blood did not plead for you, what ought you not to fear from my just resentment ? But what must not imprudent Agnes, to whom nothing ties me, expect from my hands ? If Constantia dies, she, who has the boldness, in my Court, to cherish a foolish flame by vain hopes, and make us lose the most amiable Princess, whom thou art not worthy to possess, shall feel the effects of her indiscretion.'

Don Pedro knew very well, that Constantia was not ignorant of his sentiments for Agnes ; but he knew also with what moderation she received it. He was very sensible of the King's reproaches ; but as his fault was not voluntary, and that a commanding power, a fatal star, had forced him to love in spite of himself, he appeared afflicted and confused: 'You condemn me, sir,' answered he, 'without having well examined me ; and if my contentions were known to you, perhaps you would not find me so criminal. I would take the Princess for my judge, who you say I sacrifice, if she were in a condition to be consulted. If I am guilty of any weakness, her justice never reproached me for it; and my tongue never informed Agnes of it. But suppose I have committed any fault, why would you punish an innocent lady, who perhaps condemns me for it as much as you?' 'Ah, villain!' interrupted the King, 'she has but too much favoured you. You would not have loved thus long, had she not made you some returns.' 'Sir,' replied the Prince, pierced with grief for the outrage that was committed against Agnes, 'you offend a virtue, than which nothing can be purer; and those expressions which break from your choler, are not worthy of you. Agnes never granted me any favours; I never asked any of her ; and I protest to Heaven, I never thought of anything contrary to the duty I owe Constantia.'

As they thus argued, one of the Princess's women came all in tears to acquaint Don Pedro, that the Princess was in the last extremities of life : 'Go see thy fatal work,' said the King, 'and expect from a too-long patient father the usage thou deservest.'

The Prince ran to Constantia, whom he found dying, and Agnes in a swoon, in the arms of some of the ladies. What caused this double calamity, was, that Agnes, who could suffer no longer the indifference of the Princess, had conjured her to tell her what was her crime, and either to take her life from her, or restore her to her friendship.

Constantia, who found she must die, could no longer keep her secret affliction from Agnes ; and after some words, which were a preparation to the sad explanation, she showed her that fatal billet, which Elvira

had caused to be written : 'Ah, madam!' cried out
the fair Agnes, after having read it, 'ah, madam!
how many cruel inquietudes had you spared me, had
you opened your heart to me with your wonted
bounty! 'Tis easy to see that this letter is counter-
feit, and that I have enemies without compassion.
Could you believe the Prince so imprudent, to make
use of any other hand but his own, on an occasion like
this? And do you believe me so simple to keep
about me this testimony of my shame, with so little
precaution? You are neither betrayed by your husband nor me ; I attest Heaven, and those efforts I
have made to leave Coimbra. Alas, my dear Princess!
how little have you known her, whom you have so
much honoured! Do not believe that when I have
justified myself, I will have any more communication
with the world. No, no ; there will be no retreat far
enough from hence for me. I will take care to hide
this unlucky face, where it shall be sure to do no more
harm.'

The Princess touched at this discourse, and the
tears of Agnes, pressed her hand, which she held in
hers ; and fixing looks upon her capable of moving
pity in the most insensible souls,' If I have committed
any offence, my dear Agnes,' answered she, 'death,
which I expect in a moment, shall revenge it. I ought
also to protest to you, that I have not ceased loving
you, and that I believe everything you have said,
giving you back my most tender affections.'

It was at this time that the grief, which equally
oppressed them, put the Princess into such an extremity, that they sent for the Prince. He came, and
found himself almost without life or motion at this
sight. And what secret motive soever might call him
to the aid of Agnes, it was to Constantia he ran.
The Princess, who finding her last moments drawing
on, by a cold sweat that covered her all over ; and
finding she had no more business with life, and causing
those persons she most suspected to retire, 'Sir,' said

she to Don Pedro, 'if I abandon life without regret,
it is not without trouble that I part with you.   But,
Prince, we must vanquish when we come to die ; and
I will forget myself wholly, to think of nothing but
of you.   I have no reproaches to make against you,
knowing that 'tis inclination that disposes hearts, and
not reason.   Agnes is beautiful enough to inspire the
most ardent passion, and virtuous enough to deserve
the first fortunes in the world.   I ask her, once more,
pardon for the injustice I have done her, and recom-
mend her to you, as a person most dear to me.
Promise me, my dear Prince, before I expire, to give
her my place in your throne : it cannot be better
filled : you cannot choose a Princess more perfect for
your people, nor a better mother for our little children.
And you, my dear and faithful Agnes,' pursued she,
'listen not to a virtue too scrupulous, that may make
any opposition to the Prince of Portugal.   Refuse
him not a heart of which he is worthy ; and give him
that friendship which you had for me, with that which
is due to his merit.   Take care of my little Fernando,
and the two young Princesses : let them find me in
you, and speak to them sometimes of me.   Adieu, live
both of you happy, and receive my last embraces.'

The afflicted Agnes, who had recovered a little her
forces, lost them again a second time ; her weakness
was followed with convulsions so vehement, that they
were afraid of her life ; but Don Pedro never removed
from Constantia : 'What, madam,' said he, 'you will
leave me then ; and you think 'tis for my good?   Alas,
Constantia ! if my heart has committed an outrage
against you, your virtue has sufficiently revenged you
on me in spite of you.   Can you think me so barbarous?'   As he was going on, he saw death shut the
eyes of the most generous Princess for ever ; and he
was within a very little of following her.

But what loads of grief did this bring upon Agnes,
when she found in that interval, wherein life and
death were struggling in her soul, that Constantia

o

was newly expired! She would then have taken away her own life, and have let her despair fully appear.

At the noise of the death of the Princess, the town and the palace were all in tears. Elvira, who saw then Don Pedro free to engage himself, repented of having contributed to the death of Constantia; and thinking herself the cause of it, promised in her griefs never to pardon herself.

She had need of being guarded several days together; during which time she failed not incessantly to weep. And the Prince gave all those days to deepest mourning. But when the first emotions were past, those of his love made him feel that he was still the same.

He was a long time without seeing Agnes; but this absence of his served only to make her appear the more charming when he did see her.

Don Alvaro, who was afraid of the liberty of the Prince, made new efforts to move Agnes de Castro, who was now become insensible to everything but grief. Elvira, who was willing to make the best of the design she had begun, consulted all her woman's arts, and the delicacy of her wit, to revive the flames with which the Prince once burnt for her. But his constancy was bounded, and it was Agnes alone that was to reign over his heart. She had taken a firm resolution, since the death of Constantia, to pass the rest of her days in a solitary retreat. In spite of the precaution she took to hide this design, the Prince was informed of it, and did all he was able to dispose his constancy and fortitude to it. He thought himself stronger than he really was; but after he had well consulted his heart, he found but too well how necessary the presence of Agnes was to him. 'Madam,' said he to her one day, with a heart big, and his eyes in tears, 'which action of my life has made you determine my death? Though I never told you how much I loved you, yet I am persuaded you are not ignorant of it. I was constrained to be silent during some years for your sake, for Constantia's, and my own; but 'tis not possible for me to put this force upon my heart for ever: I must once at least tell you how it languishes. Receive then the assurances of a passion, full of respect and ardour, with an offer of my fortune, which I wish not better, but for your advantage.'

Agnes answered not immediately to these words, but with abundance of tears; which having wiped away, and beholding Don Pedro with an air which made him easily comprehend she did not agree with his desires, 'If I were capable of the weakness with which you'd inspire me, you'd be obliged to punish me for it. What!' said she, 'Constantia is scarce buried, and you would have me offend her! No, my Prince,' added she with more softness, 'no, no, she whom you have heaped so many favours on, will not call down the anger of Heaven, and the contempt of men upon her, by an action so perfidious. Be not obstinate then in a design in which I will never show you favour. You owe to Constantia, after her death, a fidelity that may justify you: and I, to repair the ills I have made her suffer, ought to shun all converse with you.' 'Go, madam,' replied the Prince, growing pale, 'go, and expect the news of my death; in that part of the world, whither your cruelty shall lead you, the news shall follow close after; you shall quickly hear of it: and I will go seek it in those wars which reign among my neighbours.'

These words made the fair Agnes de Castro perceive that her innocency was not so great as she imagined, and that her heart interested itself in the preservation of Don Pedro: 'You ought, sir, to preserve your life,' replied Agnes, 'for the sake of the little Prince and Princesses, which Constantia has left you. Would you abandon their youth,' continued she, with a tender tone, 'to the cruelty of Don Alvaro? Live! sir, live! and let the unhappy Agnes be the only sacrifice.' 'Alas, cruel maid!' interrupted Don Pedro, 'why do you command me to live, if I cannot

live with you? Is it an effect of your hatred?' 'No,
sir,' replied Agnes, 'I do not hate you; and I wish to
God that I could be able to defend myself against the
weakness with which I find myself possessed. Oblige
me to say no more, sir: you see my blushes, interpret
them as you please: but consider yet, that the less
aversion I find I have to you, the more culpable I am;
and that I ought no more to see, or speak to you. In
fine, sir, if you oppose my retreat, I declare to you,
that Don Alvaro, as odious as he is to me, shall serve
for a defence against you; and that I will sooner consent to marry a man I abhor, than to favour a passion
that cost Constantia her life.' 'Well then, Agnes,' replied the Prince, with looks all languishing and dying,
'follow the motions which barbarous virtue inspires
you with; take these measures you judge necessary
against an unfortunate lover, and enjoy the glory of
having cruelly refused me.'

At these words he went away; and troubled as
Agnes was, she would not stay him. Her courage
combated with her grief, and she thought now, more
than ever, of departing.

It was difficult for her to go out of Coimbra; and not
to defer what appeared to her so necessary, she went
immediately to the apartment of the King, notwithstanding the interest of Don Alvaro. The King received her with a countenance severe, not being able
to consent to what she demanded: 'You shall not go
hence,' said he, 'and if you are wise, you shall enjoy
here with Don Alvaro both my friendship and my
favour.' 'I have taken another resolution,' answered
Agnes, 'and the world has no part in it.' 'You will
accept Don Pedro,' replied the King, 'his fortune is
sufficient to satisfy an ambitious maid: but you will
not succeed Constantia, who loved you so tenderly;
and Spain has Princesses enough to fill up part of the
throne which I shall leave him.' 'Sir,' replied Agnes,
piqued at this discourse, 'if I had a disposition to love,
and a design to marry, perhaps the Prince might be

the only person on whom I would fix it. And you know, if my ancestors did not possess crowns, yet they were worthy to wear them. But let it be how it will, I am resolved to depart, and to remain no longer a slave in a place to which I came free.'

This bold answer, which showed the character of Agnes, angered and astonished the King. 'You shall go when we think fit,' replied he, 'and without being a slave at Coimbra, you shall attend our order.'

Agnes saw she must stay, and was so grieved at it, that she kept her chamber several days, without daring to inform herself of the Prince; and this retirement spared her the affliction of being visited by Don Alvaro.

During this, Don Pedro fell sick, and was in so great danger, that there was a general apprehension of his death. Agnes did not in the least doubt, but it was an effect of his discontent: she thought at first she had strength and resolution enough to see him die, rather than to favour him; but had she reflected a little, she had soon been convinced to the contrary. She found not in her heart that cruel constancy she thought there so well established. She felt pains and inquietude, shed tears, made wishes; and, in fine, discovered that she loved.

It was impossible to see the heir of the crown, a Prince that deserved so well, even at the point of death, without a general affliction. The people who loved him, passed whole days at the palace gate to hear news of him. The Court was all overwhelmed with grief.

Don Alvaro knew very well how to conceal a malicious joy, under an appearance of sadness. Elvira, full of tenderness, and perhaps of remorse, suffered also on her side. The King, although he condemned the love of his son, yet still had a tenderness for him, and could not resolve to lose him. Agnes de Castro, who knew the cause of his distemper, expected the end of it with strange anxieties.

In fine, after a month had passed away in fears, they
began to have a little hopes of his recovery. The
Prince and Don Alvaro were the only persons that
were not glad of it: but Agnes rejoiced enough for
all the rest.

Don Pedro, seeing that he must live whether he
would or no, thought of nothing but passing his days
in melancholy and discontent. As soon as he was in
a condition to walk, he sought out the most solitary
places, and gained so much upon his own weakness,
to go everywhere, where Agnes was not; but her idea
followed him always, and his memory, faithful to
represent her to him with all her charms, rendered
her always dangerous.

One day, when they had carried him into the
garden, he sought out a labyrinth which was at the
farthest part of it, to hide his melancholy, during
some hours; there he found the sad Agnes, whom
grief, little different from his, had brought thither;
the sight of her whom he expected not, made him
tremble. She saw by his pale and meagre face the
remains of his distemper; his eyes full of languishment troubled her, and though her desire was so great
to have fled from him, an unknown power stopped
her, and it was impossible for her to go.

After some moments of silence, which many sighs
interrupted, Don Pedro raised himself from the place
where his weakness had forced him to sit; he made
Agnes see, as he approached her, the sad marks of
his sufferings: and not content with the pity he saw
in her eyes, 'You have resolved my death then, cruel
Agnes,' said he, 'my desire was the same with yours;
but Heaven has thought fit to reserve me for other
misfortunes, and I see you again, as unhappy, but
more in love than ever.'

There was no need of these words to move Agnes
to compassion, the languishment of the Prince spoke
enough: and the heart of this fair maid was but too
much disposed to yield itself. She thought then that

Constantia ought to be satisfied ; love, which combated for Don Pedro, triumphed over friendship, and
found that happy moment, for which the Prince of
Portugal had so long sighed.

'Do not reproach me, for that which has cost me
more than you, sir,' replied she, 'and do not accuse
a heart, which is neither ungrateful nor barbarous :
and I must tell you, that I love you. But now I have
made you that confession, what is it farther that you
require of me ?' Don Pedro, who expected not a
change so favourable, felt a double satisfaction ; and
falling at the feet of Agnes, he expressed more by the
silence his passion created, than he could have done
by the most eloquent words.

After having known all his good fortune, he then
consulted with the amiable Agnes, what was to be
feared from the King ; they concluded that the cruel
billet, which so troubled the last days of Constantia,
could come from none but Elvira and Don Alvaro.
The Prince, who knew that his father had searched
already an alliance for him, and was resolved on his
favourite's marrying Agnes, conjured her so tenderly
to prevent these persecutions, by consenting to a
secret marriage, that, after having a long time considered, she at last consented. 'I will do what you
will have me,' said she, 'though I presage nothing but
fatal events from it ; all my blood turns to ice, when
I think of this marriage, and the image of Constantia
seems to hinder me from doing it.'

The amorous Prince surmounted all her scruples,
and separated himself from Agnes, with a satisfaction
which soon redoubled his forces ; he saw her afterward with the pleasure of a mystery. And the day
of their union being arrived, Don Gill, Bishop of
Guarda, performed the ceremony of the marriage, in
the presence of several witnesses, faithful to Don
Pedro, who saw him possessor of all the charms of
the fair Agnes.

She lived not the more peaceable for belonging to

the Prince of Portugal; her enemies, who continually persecuted her, left her not without troubles: and the King, whom her refusal enraged, laid his absolute commands on her to marry Don Alvaro, with threats to force her to it, if she continued rebellious.

The Prince took loudly her part; and this, joined to the refusal he made of marrying the Princess of Aragon, caused suspicions of the truth in the King his father. He was seconded by those that were too much interested, not to unriddle this secret. Don Alvaro and his sister acted with so much care, gave so many gifts, and made so many promises, that they discovered the secret engagements of Don Pedro and Agnes.

The King wanted but little of breaking out into all the rage and fury so great a disappointment could inspire him with, against the Princess. Don Alvaro, whose love was changed into the most violent hatred, appeased the first transports of the King, by making him comprehend, that if they could break the marriage of them, that would not be a sufficient revenge; and so poisoned the soul of the King, to consent to the death of Agnes.

The barbarous Don Alvaro offered his arm for this terrible execution, and his rage was security for the sacrifice.

The King, who thought the glory of his family disgraced by this alliance, and his own in particular in the procedure of his son, gave full power to this murderer, to make the innocent Agnes a victim to his rage.

It was not easy to execute this horrid design. Though the Prince saw Agnes but in secret, yet all his cares were still awake for her, and he was married to her above a year, before Don Alvaro could find out an opportunity so long sought for.

The Prince diverted himself but little, and very rarely went far from Coimbra; but on a day, an unfortunate day, and marked out by Heaven for an unheard-of and horrid assassination, he made a party

to hunt at a fine house, which the King of Portugal
had near the city.

Agnes loved everything that gave the Prince satisfaction; but a secret trouble made her apprehend
some misfortune in this unhappy journey. 'Sir,' said
she to him, alarmed, without knowing the reason why,
'I tremble, seeing you to-day as it were designed the
last of my life. Preserve yourself, my dear Prince;
and though the exercise you take be not very dangerous, beware of the least hazards, and bring me
back all that I trust with you.' Don Pedro, who had
never found her so handsome and so charming before,
embraced her several times, and went out of the
palace with his followers, with a design not to return
till the next day.

He was no sooner gone, but the cruel Don Alvaro
prepared himself for the execution he had resolved
on; he thought it of that importance, that it required
more hands than his own, and so chose for his companions Don Lopez Pacheo, and Pedro Cuello, two
monsters like himself, whose cruelty he was assured
of by the presents he had made them.

They waited the coming of the night, and the
lovely Agnes was in her first sleep, which was the
last of her life, when these assassins approached her
bed. Nothing made resistance to Don Alvaro, who
could do everything, and whom the blackest furies
introduced to Agnes; she wakened, and opening her
curtains, saw, by the candle burning in her chamber,
the poniard with which Don Alvaro was armed; he
having his face not covered, she easily knew him, and
forgetting herself, to think of nothing but the Prince:
'Just Heaven,' said she, lifting up her fine eyes, 'if
you will revenge Constantia, satisfy yourself with my
blood only, and spare that of Don Pedro.' The
barbarous man that heard her, gave her not time to
say more; and finding he could never (by all he could
do by love) touch the heart of the fair Agnes, he
pierced it with his poniard: his accomplices gave her

several wounds, though there was no necessity of so many to put an end to an innocent life.

What a sad spectacle was this for those who approached her bed the next day! And what dismal news was this to the unfortunate Prince of Portugal! He returned to Coimbra at the first report of this adventure, and saw what had certainly cost him his life, if men could die of grief. After having a thousand times embraced the bloody body of Agnes, and said all that a just despair could inspire him with, he ran like a madman into the palace, demanding the murderers of his wife, of things that could not hear him. In fine, he saw the King, and without observing any respect, he gave a loose to his resentment: after having railed a long time, overwhelmed with grief, he fell into a swoon, which continued all that day. They carried him into his apartment: and the King, believing that his misfortune would prove his cure, repented not of what he had permitted.

Don Alvaro, and the two other assassins, quitted Coimbra. This absence of theirs made them appear guilty of the crime; for which the afflicted Prince vowed a speedy vengeance to the ghost of his lovely Agnes, resolving to pursue them to the uttermost part of the universe. He got a considerable number of men together, sufficient to have made resistance, even to the King of Portugal himself, if he should yet take the part of the murderers: with these he ravaged the whole country, as far as the Duero Waters, and carried on a war, even till the death of the King, continually mixing tears with blood, which he gave to the revenge of his dearest Agnes.

Such was the deplorable end of the unfortunate love of Don Pedro of Portugal, and of the fair Agnes de Castro, whose remembrance he faithfully preserved in his heart, even upon the throne, to which he mounted, by the right of his birth, after the death of the King.

THE LOVER'S WATCH

OR THE ART OF MAKING LOVE

THE ARGUMENT

IT is in the most happy and august Court of the best and greatest monarch of the world, that Damon, a young nobleman, whom we will render under that name, languishes for a maid of quality, who will give us leave to call her Iris.

Their births are equally illustrious; they are both rich, and both young; their beauty such as I do not too nicely particularise, lest I should discover (which I am not permitted to do) who these charming lovers are. Let it suffice, that Iris is the most fair and accomplished person that ever adorned a Court; and that Damon is only worthy of the glory of her favour; for he has all that can render him lovely in the fair eyes of the amiable Iris. Nor is he master of those superficial beauties alone, that please at first sight; he can charm the soul with a thousand arts of wit and gallantry. And, in a word, I may say, without flattering either, that there is no one beauty, no one grace, no perfection of mind and body, that wants to complete a victory on both sides.

The agreement of age, fortunes, quality and humours in these two fair lovers, made the impatient Damon hope, that nothing would oppose his passion; and if he saw himself every hour languishing for the adorable maid, he did not however despair. And if Iris sighed, it was not for fear of being one day more happy.

In the midst of the tranquillity of these two lovers, Iris was obliged to go into the country for some months, whither it was impossible for Damon to wait on her, he being obliged to attend the King his master; and being the most amorous of his sex, suffered with extreme impatience the absence of his mistress. Nevertheless, he failed not to send to her every day, and gave up all his melancholy hours to thinking, sighing, and writing to her the softest letters that love could inspire. So that Iris even blessed that absence that gave her so tender and convincing proofs of his passion; and found this dear way of conversing, even recompensed all her sighs for his absence.

After a little intercourse of this kind, Damon bethought himself to ask Iris a discretion which he had won of her before she left the town; and in a billet-doux to that purpose, pressed her very earnestly for it. Iris being infinitely pleased with his importunity, suffered him to ask it often; and he never failed of doing so.

But as I do not here design to relate the adventures of these two amiable persons, nor give you all the billet-douxs that passed between them; you shall here find nothing but the watch this charming maid sent her impatient lover.

IRIS TO DAMON

IT must be confessed, Damon, that you are the most importuning man in the world. Your billets have a hundred times demanded a discretion, which you won of me; and tell me, will you not wait my return to be paid? You are either a very faithless creditor, or believe me very unjust, that you dun with such impatience. But to let you see that I am a maid of honour, and value my word, I will acquit myself of this obligation I have to you, and send you a watch of my fashion ; perhaps you never saw any so good. It is not one of those that have always something to be mended in it : but one that is without fault, very just and good, and will remain so as long as you continue to love me : but, Damon, know, that the very minute you cease to do so, the string will break, and it will go no more. 'Tis only useful in my absence, and when I return 'twill change its motion : and though I have set it but for the springtime, it will serve you the whole year round : and it will be necessary only that you alter the business of the hours (which my cupid, in the middle of my watch, points you out) according to the length of the days and nights. Nor is the dart of that little god directed to those hours, so much to inform you how they pass, as how you ought to pass them ; how you ought to employ those of your absence from Iris. 'Tis there you shall find the whole business of a lover, from his mistress ; for I have designed it a rule to all your actions. The consideration of the workman ought to make you set a value upon the work : and though it be not an accomplished and perfect piece ; yet, Damon, you ought to be grateful and esteem it, since I have made it for you alone. But however I may boast of the design, I know, as well as I believe you love me, that you will not suffer me to have the glory of it wholly, but will say in your heart :

> That Love, the great instructor of the mind,
>   That forms anew, and fashions every soul,
> Refines the gross defects of human kind ;
>   Humbles the proud and vain, inspires the dull ;
> Gives cowards noble heat in fight,
> And teaches feeble women how to write :
> That doth the universe command,
> Does from my Iris' heart direct her hand.

I give you the liberty to say this to your heart, if you please : and that you may know with what justice you do so, I will confess in my turn.

THE CONFESSION

That Love's my conduct where I go,
And Love instructs me all I do.
Prudence no longer is my guide,
Nor take I counsel of my pride.
In vain does honour now invade,
In vain does reason take my part,
If against Love it do persuade,
If it rebel against my heart.
If the soft evening do invite,
And I incline to take the air,
The birds, the spring, the flow'rs no more delight :
'Tis Love makes all the pleasure there :
Love, which about me still I bear ;
I'm charm'd with what I thither bring,
And add a softness to the spring.
If for devotion I design,
Love meets me, even at the shrine ;
In all my worship claims a part,
And robs even Heaven of my heart :
All day does counsel and control,
And all the night employs my soul.
No wonder then if all you think be true,
That Love's concerned in all I do for you.

And, Damon, you know that Love is no ill master ; and I must say, with a blush, that he has found me no unapt scholar ; and he instructs too agreeably not to succeed in all he undertakes.

Who can resist his soft commands?
When he resolves, what God withstands?

But I ought to explain to you my watch : the naked cupid which you will find in the middle of it, with his wings clipped, to show you he is fixed and constant, and will not fly away, points you out with his arrow the four-and-twenty hours that compose the day and the night : over every hour you will find written what you ought to do, during its course ; and every half-hour is marked with a sigh, since the quality of a lover is, to sigh day and night : sighs are the children of lovers, that are born every hour. And that my watch may always be just, Love himself ought to conduct it ; and your heart should keep time with the movement :

> My present's delicate and new,
> If by your heart the motion's set ;
> According as that's false or true,
> You'll find my Watch will answer it.

Every hour is tedious to a lover, separated from his mistress : and to show you how good I am, I will have my watch instruct you, to pass some of them without inquietude ; that the force of your imagination may sometimes charm the trouble you have for my absence :

> Perhaps I am mistaken here,
> My heart may too much credit give :
> But, Damon, you can charm my fear,
> And soon my error undeceive.

But I will not disturb my repose at this time with a jealousy, which I hope is altogether frivolous and vain ; but begin to instruct you in the mysteries of my watch. Cast then your eyes upon the eighth hour in the morning, which is the hour I would have you begin to wake : you will find there written :

EIGHT O'CLOCK

AGREEABLE REVERIE

Do not rise yet ; you may find thoughts agreeable enough, when you awake, to entertain you longer in bed. And 'tis in that hour you ought to recollect all the dreams you had in the night. If you had dreamed anything to my advantage, confirm yourself in that thought ; but if to my disadvantage, renounce it, and disown the injurious dream. It is in this hour also that I give you leave to reflect on all that I have ever said and done, that has been most obliging to you, and that gives you the most tender sentiments.

THE REFLECTIONS

Remember, Damon, while your mind
   Reflects on things that charm and please,
You give me proofs that you are kind,
   And set my doubting soul at ease :
For when your heart receives with joy
   The thoughts of favours which I give,
My smiles in vain I not employ,
   And on the square we love and live.

Think then on all I ever did,
   That e'er was charming, e'er was dear ;
Let nothing from that soul be hid,
   Whose griefs and joys I feel and share.
All that your love and faith have sought,
All that your vows and sighs have bought,
Now render present to your thought.

And for what's to come, I give you leave, Damon, to flatter yourself and to expect, I shall still pursue those methods, whose remembrance charms so well. But, if it be possible, conceive these kind thoughts between sleeping and waking, that all my too forward complaisance, my goodness, and my tenderness, which I confess to have for you, may pass for half dreams : for it is most certain

That though the favours of the fair
Are ever to the lover dear ;
Yet, lest he should reproach that easy flame,
That buys its satisfaction with its shame ;
She ought but rarely to confess
How much she finds of tenderness ;
Nicely to guard the yielding part,
And hide the hard-kept secret in her heart.

For, let me tell you, Damon, though the passion of a
woman of honour be ever so innocent, and the lover
ever so discreet and honest; her heart feels I know
not what of reproach within, at the reflection of any
favours she has allowed him.   For my part, I never
call to mind the least soft or kind word I have
spoken to Damon, without finding at the same
instant my face covered over with blushes, and my
heart with sensible pain.   I sigh at the remembrance
of every touch I have stolen from his hand, and have
upbraided my soul, which confesses so much guilty
love, as that secret desire of touching him made
appear.   I am angry at the discovery, though I am
pleased at the same time with the satisfaction I take
in doing so ; and ever disordered at the remembrance
of such arguments of too much love.   And these un-
quiet sentiments alone are sufficient to persuade me,
that our sex cannot be reserved too much.   And I
have often, on these occasions, said to myself:

THE RESERVE

Though Damon every virtue have,
    With all that pleases in his form,
That can adorn the just and brave,
    That can the coldest bosom warm ;
Though wit and honour there abound,
    Yet the pursuer's ne'er pursued,
And when my weakness he has found,
    His love will sink to gratitude :
While on the asking part he lives,
'Tis she th' obliger is who gives.

And he that at one throw the stake has won
Gives over play, since all the stock is gone.
And what dull gamester ventures certain store
With losers who can set no more ?

P

NINE O'CLOCK

DESIGN TO PLEASE NOBODY

I should continue to accuse you of that vice I have often done, that of laziness, if you remained past this hour in bed : it is time for you to rise ; my watch tells you it is nine o'clock. Remember that I am absent, therefore do not take too much pains in dressing yourself, and setting your person off.

THE QUESTION

Tell me ! What can he design,
Who in his mistress' absence will be fine?
   Why does he cock, and comb, and dress?
Why is his cravat string in print?
   What does th' embroidered coat confess?
   Why to the glass this long address,
If there be nothing in 't?
If no new conquest is design'd,
If no new beauty fill his mind?
Let fools and fops, whose talents lie
   In being neat, in being spruce,
Be dressed in vain, and tawdery ;
   With men of sense, 'tis out of use :
The only folly that distinction sets
Between the noisy fluttering fools and wits.
Remember, *Iris* is away ;
   And sighing to your valet cry,
Spare your perfumes and care to-day,
I have no business to be gay,
   Since Iris is not by.
I'll be all negligent in dress,
   And scarce set off for complaisance :
Put me on nothing that may please,
   But only such as may give no offence.

Say to yourself, as you are dressing, ' Would it please Heaven, that I might see Iris to-day ! But oh ! it is impossible : therefore all that I shall see will

be but indifferent objects, since it is Iris only that
I wish to see.'   And sighing, whisper to yourself:

THE SIGH

Ah! charming object of my wishing thought!
    Ah! soft idea of a distant bliss!
That only art in dreams and fancy brought,
    That give short intervals of happiness.
But when I waking find thou absent art,
    And with thee, all that I adore,
What pains, what anguish fills my heart!
    What sadness seizes me all o'er!
All entertainments I neglect,
    Since Iris is no longer there:
Beauty scarce claims my bare respect,
    Since in the throng I find not her.
Ah then! how vain it were to dress, and show;
Since all I wish to please, is absent now!

It is with these thoughts, Damon, that your mind
ought to be employed, during your time of dressing.
And you are too knowing in love, to be ignorant

That when a lover ceases to be blest
    With the object he desires,
Ah! how indifferent are the rest!
    How soon their conversation tires!
Though they a thousand arts to please invent,
Their charms are dull, their wit impertinent.

TEN O'CLOCK

READING OF LETTERS

My cupid points you now the hour in which you
ought to retire into your cabinet, having already passed
an hour in dressing: and for a lover, who is sure not
to appear before his mistress, even that hour is too
much to be so employed. But I will think, you
thought of nothing less than dressing while you were

about it. Lose then no more minutes, but open your escritoire, and read over some of those billets you have received from me. Oh! what pleasures a lover feels about his heart, in reading those from a mistress he entirely loves!

THE JOY

Who, but a lover, can express
The joys, the pants, the tenderness,
That the soft amorous soul invades,
While the dear billet-doux he reads?
Raptures divine the heart o'erflow,
Which he that loves not cannot know.

A thousand tremblings, thousand fears,
The short-breathed sighs, the joyful tears!
The transport, where the love's confessed;
The change, where coldness is expressed;
The diff'ring flames the lover burns,
As those are shy, or kind, by turns.

However you find them, Damon, construe them all to my advantage: possibly, some of them have an air of coldness, something different from that softness they are usually too amply filled with; but where you find they have, believe there, that the sense of honour, and my sex's modesty, guided my hand a little against the inclinations of my heart; and that it was as a kind of an atonement, I believed I ought to make, for something I feared I had said too kind, and too obliging before. But wherever you find that stop, that check in my career of love, you will be sure to find something that follows it to favour you, and deny that unwilling imposition upon my heart; which, lest you should mistake, love shows himself in smiles again, and flatters more agreeably, disdaining the tyranny of honour and rigid custom, that imposition upon our sex; and will, in spite of me, let you see he reigns absolutely in my soul.

The reading my billet-doux may detain you an hour: I have had so much goodness to write you enough to entertain you so long at least, and sometimes reproach myself for it; but, contrary to all my scruples, I find myself disposed to give you those frequent marks of my tenderness. If yours be so great as you express it, you ought to kiss my letters a thousand times; you ought to read them with attention, and weigh every word, and value every line. A lover may receive a thousand endearing words from a mistress, more easily than a billet. One says a great many kind things of course to a lover, which one is not willing to write, or to give testified under one's hand, signed and sealed. But when once a lover has brought his mistress to that degree of love, he ought to assure himself, she loves not at the common rate.

LOVE'S WITNESS

Slight unpremeditated words are borne
  By every common wind into the air ;
Carelessly uttered, die as soon as born,
  And in one instant give both hope and fear :
Breathing all contraries with the same wind,
According to the caprice of the mind.

But billet-doux are constant witnesses,
  Substantial records to eternity ;
Just evidence, who the truth confess,
  On which the lover safely may rely ;
They're serious thoughts, digested and resolved ;
And last when words are into clouds devolved.

I will not doubt, but you give credit to all that is kind in my letters; and I will believe, you find a satisfaction in the entertainment they give you, and that the hour of reading them is not disagreeable to you. I could wish, your pleasure might be extreme, even to the degree of suffering the thought of my absence not to diminish any part of it. And I could wish too, at the end of your reading, you would sigh with pleasure, and say to yourself:

THE TRANSPORT

O Iris ! While you thus can charm,
While at this distance you can wound and warm ;
My absent torments I will bless and bear,
That give me such dear proofs how kind you are.
Present, the valued store was only seen,
Now I am rifling the bright mass within.

Every dear, past, and happy day,
When languishing at Iris' feet I lay ;
When all my prayers and all my tears could move
No more than her permission, I should love :
Vain with my glorious destiny,
I thought, beyond, scarce any Heaven could be.

But, charming maid, now I am taught,
That absence has a thousand joys to give,
On which the lovers present never thought,
That recompense the hours we grieve.
Rather by absence let me be undone,
Than forfeit all the pleasures that has won.

With this little rapture, I wish you would finish
the reading my letters, shut your escritoire, and quit
your cabinet ; for my love leads to eleven o'clock.

ELEVEN O'CLOCK

THE HOUR TO WRITE IN

If my watch did not inform you it is now time to
write, I believe, Damon, your heart would, and tell
you also that I should take it kindly, if you would
employ a whole hour that way ; and that you should
never lose an occasion of writing to me, since you
are assured of the welcome I give your letters.
Perhaps you will say, an hour is too much, and that
it is not the mode to write long letters. I grant you,
Damon, when we write those indifferent ones of
gallantry in course, or necessary compliment ; the
handsome comprising of which in the fewest words,

renders them the most agreeable : but in love we have a thousand foolish things to say, that of themselves bear no great sound, but have a mighty sense in love ; for there is a peculiar eloquence natural alone to a lover, and to be understood by no other creature. To those, words have a thousand graces and sweetnesses ; which, to the unconcerned, appear meanness, and easy sense, at the best. But, Damon, you and I are none of those ill judges of the beauties of love ; we can penetrate beyond the vulgar, and perceive the fine soul in every line, through all the humble dress of phrase ; when possibly they who think they discern it best in florid language, do not see it at all. Love was not born or bred in courts, but cottages ; and, nursed in groves and shades, smiles on the plains, and wantons in the streams ; all unadored and harmless. Therefore, Damon, do not consult your wit in this affair, but love alone ; speak all that he and nature taught you, and let the fine things you learn in schools alone. Make use of those flowers you have gathered there, when you conversed with statesmen and the gown. Let Iris possess your heart in all its simple innocence, that is the best eloquence to her that loves : and that is my instruction to a lover that would succeed in his amours ; for I have a heart very difficult to please, and this is the nearest way to it.

ADVICE TO LOVERS

Lovers, if you would gain the heart
    Of Damon, learn to win the prize ;
He'll show you all its tend'rest part,
    And where its greatest danger lies ;
The magazine of its disdain,
Where honour, feebly guarded, does remain.

If present, do but little say ;
    Enough the silent lover speaks :
But wait, and sigh, and gaze all day ;
    Such rhetoric more than language takes.
For words the dullest way do move ;
And uttered more to show your wit than love.

Let your eyes tell her of your heart ;
   Its story is, for words, too delicate.
Souls thus exchange, and thus impart,
   And all their secrets can relate.
A tear, a broken sigh, she'll understand ;
Or the soft trembling pressings of the hand.

Or if your pain must be in words exprest,
   Let them fall gently, unassured, and slow ;
And where they fail, your looks may tell the rest :
   Thus Damon spoke, and I was conquered so.
The witty talker has mistook his art ;
The modest lover only charms the heart.

Thus, while all day you gazing sit,
   And fear to speak, and fear your fate,
You more advantages by silence get,
   Than the gay forward youth with all his prate.
Let him be silent here ; but when away,
Whatever love can dictate, let him say.

There let the bashful soul unveil,
   And give a loose to love and truth ;
Let him improve the amorous tale,
   With all the force of words, and fire of youth ;
There all, and anything let him express ;
Too long he cannot write, too much confess.

O Damon! How well have you made me understand this soft pleasure! You know my tenderness too well, not to be sensible how I am charmed with your agreeable long letters.

THE INVENTION

Ah ! he who first found out the way
Souls to each other to convey,
Without dull speaking, sure must be,
Something above humanity.
Let the fond world in vain dispute,
And the first sacred mystery impute
Of letters to the learned brood,
And of the glory cheat a god :
'Twas Love alone that first the art essayed,
And Psyche was the first fair yielding maid,
That was by the dear billet-doux betrayed.

It is an art too ingenious to have been found out by man, and too necessary to lovers, not to have been invented by the god of love himself. But, Damon, I do not pretend to exact from you those letters of gallantry, which, I have told you, are filled with nothing but fine thoughts, and writ with all the arts of wit and subtilty : I would have yours still all tender unaffected love, words unchosen, thoughts unstudied, and love unfeigned. I had rather find more softness than wit in your passion ; more of nature than of art ; more of the lover than the poet.

Nor would I have you write any of those little short letters, that are read over in a minute ; in love, long letters bring a long pleasure : do not trouble yourself to make them fine, or write a great deal of wit and sense in a few lines ; that is the notion of a witty billet, in any affair but that of love. And have a care rather to avoid these graces to a mistress ; and assure yourself, dear Damon, that what pleases the soul pleases the eye, and the largeness or bulk of your letter shall never offend me ; and that I only am displeased when I find them small. A letter is ever the best and most powerful agent to a mistress, it almost always persuades, it is always renewing little impressions, that possibly otherwise absence would deface. Make use then, Damon, of your time while it is given you, and thank me that I permit you to write to me. Perhaps I shall not always continue in the humour of suffering you to do so ; and it may so happen, by some turn of chance and fortune, that you may be deprived, at the same time, both of my presence, and of the means of sending to me. I will believe that such an accident would be a great misfortune to you, for I have often heard you say, that ' To make the most happy lover suffer martyrdom, one need only forbid him seeing, speaking and writing to the object he loves.' Take all the advantages then you can, you cannot give me too often marks too powerful of your passion : write therefore during this hour, every day. I give you leave to believe, that while you do so, you are serving me the most obligingly and agreeably you can, while absent; and that you are giving me a remedy against all grief, uneasiness, melancholy, and despair; nay, if you exceed your hour, you need not be ashamed. The time you employ in this kind devoir, is the time that I shall be grateful for, and no doubt will recompense it. You ought not however to neglect heaven for me; I will give you time for your devotion, for my watch tells you it is time to go to the temple.

TWELVE O'CLOCK

INDISPENSABLE DUTY

There are certain duties which one ought never to neglect: that of adoring the gods is of this nature; and which we ought to pay, from the bottom of our hearts: and that, Damon, is the only time I will dispense with your not thinking on me. But I would not have you go to one of those temples, where the celebrated beauties, and those that make a profession of gallantry, go; and who come thither only to see, and be seen; and whither they repair, more to show their beauty and dress, than to honour the gods. If you will take my advice, and oblige my wish, you shall go to those that are least frequented, and you shall appear there like a man that has a perfect veneration for all things sacred.

THE INSTRUCTION

Damon, if your heart and flame,
You wish, should always be the same,
Do not give it leave to rove,
    Nor expose it to new harms:
Ere you think on't, you may love,
    If you gaze on beauty's charms:
If with me you would not part,
Turn your eyes into your heart.

If you find a new desire
In your easy soul take fire,
From the tempting ruin fly ;
    Think it faithless, think it base:
Fancy soon will fade and die,
    If you wisely cease to gaze.
Lovers should have honour too,
Or they pay but half Love's due.

Do not to the temple go,
With design to gaze or show :
Whate'er thoughts you have abroad,
    Though you can deceive elsewhere,
There's no feigning with your God ;
    Souls should be all perfect there.
The heart that's to the altar brought,
Only heaven should fill its thought.

Do not your sober thoughts perplex,
By gazing on the ogling sex :
Or if beauty call your eyes,
    Do not on the object dwell ;
Guard your heart from the surprise,
    By thinking Iris doth excel.
Above all earthly things I'd be,
Damon, most beloved by thee ;
And only heaven must rival me.

ONE O'CLOCK

FORCED ENTERTAINMENT

I perceive it will be very difficult to you to quit the temple, without being surrounded with compliments from people of ceremony, friends, and newsmongers, and several of those sorts of persons, who afflict and busy themselves, and rejoice at a hundred things they have no interest in ; coquettes and politicians, who make it the business of their whole lives, to gather all the news of the town ; adding or diminishing according to the stock of their wit and invention, and spreading it all abroad to the believing fools and gossips ; and perplexing everybody with a hundred

ridiculous novels, which they pass off for wit and
entertainment. Or else some of those recounters of
adventures, that are always telling of intrigues, and
that make a secret to a hundred people of a thousand
foolish things they have heard: like a certain pert
and impertinent lady of the town, whose youth and
beauty being past, set up for wit, to uphold a feeble
empire over hearts; and whose character is this:

THE COQUETTE

Milanda, who had never been
Esteem'd a beauty at fifteen,
Always amorous was, and kind :
   To every swain she lent an ear ;
Free as air, but false as wind ;
   Yet none complained she was severe.
She eased more than she made complain .
Was always singing, pert, and vain.

Where'er the throng was, she was seen,
And swept the youths along the green
With equal grace she flattered all ;
   And fondly proud of all address,
Her smiles invite, her eyes do call,
   And her vain heart her looks confess.
She rallies this, to that she bowed,
Was talking ever, laughing loud.

On every side she makes advance,
And everywhere a confidence ;
She tells for secrets all she knows,
   And all to know she does pretend :
Beauty in maids she treats as foes :
   But every handsome youth as friend.

Scandal still passes off for truth ;
And noise and nonsense, wit and youth.
Coquette all o'er, and every part,
Yet wanting beauty, even of art ;
Herds with the ugly, and the old ;
   And plays the critic on the rest :
Of men, the bashful, and the bold,
   Either, and all, by turns, likes best :
Even now, though youth be languished, she
Sets up for love and gallantry.

This sort of creature, Damon, is very dangerous; not
that I fear you will squander away a heart upon her,
but your hours; for, in spite of you, she'll detain you
with a thousand impertinences, and eternal tattle.
She passes for a judging wit; and there is nothing
so troublesome as such a pretender. She, perhaps,
may get some knowledge of our correspondence;
and then, no doubt, will improve it to my disadvantage. Possibly she may rail at me; that is her
fashion by the way of friendly speaking; and an
awkward commendation, the most effectual way of
defaming and traducing. Perhaps she tells you, in
a cold tone, that you are a happy man to be beloved
by me: that Iris indeed is handsome, and she wonders she has no more lovers; but the men are not
of her mind; if they were, you should have more
rivals. She commends my face, but that I have blue
eyes, and it is a pity my complexion is no better:
my shape but too much inclining to fat.   Cries—she
would charm infinitely with her wit, but that she
knows too well she is mistress of it.   And concludes,
——but altogether she is well enough.   Thus she
runs on without giving you leave to edge in a word
in my defence; and ever and anon crying up her
own conduct and management: tells you how she is
oppressed with lovers, and fatigued with addresses;
and recommending herself, at every turn, with a per-
ceivable cunning.   And all the while is jilting you
of your good opinion; which she would buy at the
price of anybody's repose, or her own fame, though but
for the vanity of adding to the number of her lovers.
When she sees a new spark, the first thing she does,
she inquires into his estate; if she finds it such as
may (if the coxcomb be well managed) supply her
vanity, she makes advances to him, and applies
herself to all those little arts, she usually makes use
of to gain her fools; and according to his humour
dresses and affects her own.   But, Damon, since
I point to no particular person in this character, I will

not name who you should avoid ; but all of this sort
I conjure you, wheresoever you find them.   But if
unlucky chance throw you in their way, hear all they
say, without credit or regard, as far as decency will
suffer you ; hear them without approving their foppery ; and hear them without giving them cause to
censure you.   But it is so much lost time to listen to
all the novels this sort of people will perplex you
with ; whose business is to be idle, and who even
tire themselves with their own impertinences.   And
be assured after all there is nothing they can tell
you that is worth your knowing.   And Damon, a
perfect lover never asks any news but of the maid
he loves.

THE INQUIRY

Damon, if your love be true
    To the heart that you possess,
Tell me what you have to do
    Where you have no tenderness?
Her affairs who cares to learn,
For whom he has not some concern?

    If a lover fain would know
    If the object loved be true,
    Let her but industrious be
    To watch his curiosity ;
Though ne'er so cold his questions seem,
They come from warmer thoughts within.

    When I hear a swain inquire
        What gay Melinda does to live,
    I conclude there is some fire
        In a heart inquisitive ;
Or 'tis, at least, the bill that's set
To show, the heart is to be let.

TWO O'CLOCK

DINNER-TIME

Leave all those fond entertainments or you will disoblige me, and make dinner wait for you; for my cupid tells you it is that hour. Love does not pretend to make you lose that; nor is it my province to order you your diet. Here I give you a perfect liberty to do what you please; and possibly, it is the only hour in the whole four-and-twenty that I will absolutely resign you, or dispense with your even so much as thinking on me. It is true, in seating yourself at table, I would not have you placed over against a very beautiful object; for in such a one there are a thousand little graces in speaking, looking, and laughing, that fail not to charm, if one gives way to the eyes, to gaze and wander that way; in which, perhaps, in spite of you, you will find a pleasure. And while you do so, though without design or concern, you give the fair charmer a sort of vanity in believing you have placed yourself there, only for the advantage of looking on her; and she assumes a hundred little graces and affectations which are not natural to her, to complete a conquest, which she believes so well begun already. She softens her eyes, and sweetens her mouth; and in fine, puts on another air than when she had no design, and when you did not, by your continual looking on her, rouse her vanity, and increase her easy opinion of her own charms. Perhaps she knows I have some interest in your heart, and prides herself, at least, with believing she has attracted the eyes of my lover, if not his heart; and thinks it easy to vanquish the whole, if she pleases; and triumphs over me in her secret imaginations. Remember, Damon, that while you act thus in the company and conversation of other beauties, every look or word you give in favour of

them, is an indignity to my reputation ; and which
you cannot suffer if you love me truly, and with
honour : and assure yourself, so much vanity as you
inspire in her, so much fame you rob me of ; for
whatever praises you give another beauty, so much
you take away from mine.   Therefore, if you dine
in company, do as others do : be generally civil, not
applying yourself by words or looks to any particular person : be as gay as you please ; talk and
laugh with all, for this is not the hour for chagrin.

THE PERMISSION

My Damon, though I stint your love,
    I will not stint your appetite ;
That I would have you still improve,
    By every new and fresh delight.
Feast till Apollo hides his head,
Or drink the amorous god to Thetis' bed.

Be like yourself : all witty, gay !
    And o'er the bottle bless the board ;
The listening round will, all the day,
    Be charmed, and pleased with every word.
Though Venus' son inspire your wit,
'Tis the Silenian god best utters it.

Here talk of everything but me,
    Since ev'rything you say with grace :
If not disposed your humour be,
    And you'd this hour in silence pass ;
Since something must the subject prove
Of Damon's thoughts, let it be me and Love.

But, Damon, this enfranchised hour,
    No bounds, or laws, will I impose ;
But leave it wholly in your power,
    What humour to refuse or choose :
I rules prescribe but to your flame ;
For I, your mistress, not physician, am

THREE O'CLOCK

VISITS TO FRIENDS

Damon, my watch is juster than you imagine; it would not have you live retired and solitary, but permits you to go and make visits. I am not one of those that believe love and friendship cannot find a place in one and the same heart. And that man would be very unhappy, who, as soon as he had a mistress, should be obliged to renounce the society of his friends. I must confess I would not that you should have so much concern for them, as you have for me; for I have heard a sort of a proverb that says 'He cannot be very fervent in love, who is not a little cold in friendship.' You are not ignorant, that when Love establishes himself in a heart, he reigns a tyrant there, and will not suffer even friendship, if it pretend to share his empire there.

CUPID

Love is a god, whose charming sway
Both heaven, and earth, and seas obey;
A power that will not mingled be
With any dull equality.
Since first from heaven, which gave him birth,
He ruled the empire of the earth;
Jealous of sov'reign power he rules,
And will be absolute in souls.

I should be very angry if you had any of those friendships which one ought to desire in a mistress only; for many times it happens that you have sentiments a little too tender for those amiable persons; and many times love and friendship are so confounded together, that one cannot easily discern one from the other. I have seen a man flatter himself with an opinion, that he had but an esteem for a woman, when by some turn of fortune in her life,

Q

as marrying, or receiving the addresses of men, he has found by spite and jealousies within, that that was love, which he before took for complaisance or friendship. Therefore have a care, for such amities are dangerous : not but that a lover may have fair and generous female friends, whom he ought to visit; and perhaps I should esteem you less, if I did not believe you were valued by such, if I were perfectly assured they were friends and not lovers. But have a care you hide not a mistress under this veil, or that you gain not a lover by this pretence : for you may begin with friendship, and end with love ; and I should be equally afflicted should you give it or receive it. And though you charge our sex with all the vanity, yet I often find nature to have given you as large a portion of that common crime, which you would shuffle off, as ashamed to own; and are as fond and vain of the imagination of a conquest, as any coquette of us all : though at the same time you despise the victim, you think it adds a trophy to your fame. And I have seen a man dress and trick, and adjust his looks and mien to make a visit to a woman he loved not, nor ever could love, as for those he made to his mistress ; and only for the vanity of making a conquest upon a heart, even unworthy of the little pains he has taken about it. And what is this but buying vanity at the expense of ease ; and with fatigue to purchase the name of a conceited fop, besides that of a dishonest man ? For he who takes pains to make himself beloved, only to please his curious humour, though he should say nothing that tends to it, more than by his looks, his sighs, and now and then breaking into praises and commendations of the object; by the care he takes, to appear well dressed before her, and in good order, he lies in his looks, he deceives with his mien and fashion, and cheats with every motion, and every grace he puts on. He cozens when he sings or dances ; he dissembles when he sighs : and everything he does that wilfully gains upon her, is malice prepense, baseness, and art below a man of sense or virtue: and yet these arts, these cozenages, are the common practices of the town. What is this but that damnable vice, of which they so reproach our sex; that of jilting for hearts? And it is in vain that my lover, after such foul play, shall think to appease me, with saying 'He did it to try how easy he could conquer, and of how great force his charms were; and why should I be angry if all the town loved him, since he loved none but Iris?' Oh foolish pleasure! How little sense goes to the making of such a happiness! And how little love must he have for one particular person, who would wish to inspire it into all the world, and yet himself pretend to be insensible! But this, Damon, is rather what is but too much practised by your sex, than any guilt I charge on you: though vanity be an ingredient that nature very seldom omits in the composition of either sex; and you may be allowed a tincture of it at least. And, perhaps, I am not wholly exempt from this leaven in my nature, but accuse myself sometimes of finding a secret joy of being adored, though I even hate my worshipper. But if any such pleasure touch my heart, I find it at the same time blushing in my cheeks with a guilty shame, which soon checks the petty triumphs; and I have a virtue at soberer thoughts, that I find surmounts my weakness and indiscretion; and I hope Damon finds the same: for, should he have any of those attachments, I should have no pity for him.

THE EXAMPLE

Damon, if you'd have me true,
  Be you my precedent and guide:
Example sooner we pursue,
  Than the dull dictates of our pride.
Precepts of virtue are too weak an aim:
'Tis demonstration that can best reclaim.

Show me the path you'd have me go ;
  With such a guide I cannot stray :
What you approve, whate'er you do,
  It is but just I bend the way.
If true, my honour favours your design ;
If false, revenge is the result of mine.

A lover true, a maid sincere,
  Are to be prized as things divine :
'Tis justice makes the blessing dear,
  Justice of love without design.
And she that reigns not in a heart alone,
Is never safe, or easy, on her throne.

FOUR O'CLOCK

GENERAL CONVERSATION

In this visiting-hour, many people will happen to meet at one and the same time together, in a place : and as you make not visits to friends, to be silent, you ought to enter into conversation with them; but those conversations ought to be general, and of general things : for there is no necessity of making your friend the confidant of your amours. It would infinitely displease me, to hear you have revealed to them all that I have reposed in you; though secrets ever so trivial, yet since uttered between lovers, they deserve to be prized at a higher rate. For what can show a heart more indifferent and indiscreet, than to declare in any fashion, or with mirth, or joy, the tender things a mistress says to her lover ; and which possibly, related at second hand, bear not the same sense, because they have not the same sound and air they had originally, when they came from the soft heart of her, who sighed them first to her lavish lover? Perhaps they are told again with mirth, or joy, unbecoming their character and business ; and then they lose their graces: (for love is the most solemn thing in nature, and the most unsuiting with gaiety). Perhaps the soft expressions suit not so

well the harsher voice of the masculine lover, whose
accents were not formed for so much tenderness; at
least, not of that sort: for words that have the same
meaning, are altered from their sense by the least
tone or accent of the voice; and those proper and
fitted to my soul, are not possibly so to yours,
though both have the same efficacy upon us; yours
upon my heart, as mine upon yours: and both will
be misunderstood by the unjudging world. Besides
this, there is a holiness in love that is true, that ought
not to be profaned. And as the poet truly says, at
the latter end of an ode, of which I will recite the
whole:

THE INVITATION

Amynta, fear not to confess
The charming secret of thy tenderness:
   That which a lover can't conceal,
   That which, to me, thou shouldst reveal;
And is but what thy lovely eyes express.
   Come, whisper to my panting heart,
That heaves and meets thy voice half-way;
   That guesses what thou wouldst impart,
And languishes for what thou hast to say.
Confirm my trembling doubt, and make me know,
Whence all these blessings, and these sighings flow.

Why dost thou scruple to unfold
A mystery that does my life concern?
   If thou ne'er speakest, it will be told;
For lovers all things can discern.
From every look, from every bashful grace,
That still succeed each other in thy face,
I shall the dear transporting secret learn:
   But 'tis a pleasure not to be exprest,
   To hear it by the voice confest,
   When soft sighs breathe it on my panting breast.

All calm and silent is the grove,
Whose shading boughs resist the day;
   Here thou may'st blush, and talk of love,
While only winds, unheeding, stay,
That will not bear the sound away:
   While I with solemn awful joy,
   All my attentive faculties employ;

Listening to every valued word ;
And in my soul the secret treasure hoard :
  There like some mystery divine,
  The wondrous knowledge I'll enshrine.
Love can his joys no longer call his own,
That the dear secret's kept unknown.

There is nothing more true than those two last lines : and that love ceases to be a pleasure, when it ceases to be a secret, and one you ought to keep sacred. For the world, which never makes a right judgment of things, will misinterpret love, as they do religion ; everyone judging it, according to the notion he hath of it, or the talent of his sense. Love (as a great Duke said) is like apparitions ; everyone talks of them, but few have seen them. Everybody thinks himself capable of understanding love, and that he is a master in the art of it ; when there is nothing so nice, or difficult, to be rightly comprehended ; and indeed cannot be, but to a soul very delicate. Nor will he make himself known to the vulgar : there must be an uncommon fineness in the mind that contains him ; the rest he only visits in as many disguises as there are dispositions and natures, where he makes but a short stay, and is gone. He can fit himself to all hearts, being the greatest flatterer in the world : and he possesses everyone with a confidence, that they are in the number of his elect ; and they think they know him perfectly, when nothing but the spirits refined possess him in his excellency. From this difference of love, in different souls, proceed those odd fantastic maxims, which so many hold of so different kinds. And this makes the most innocent pleasures pass oftentimes for crimes, with the unjudging crowd, who call themselves lovers. And you will have your passion censured by as many as you shall discover it to, and as many several ways. I advise you therefore, Damon, to make no confidants of your amours ; and believe, that silence has, with me, the most powerful charm.

'Tis also in these conversations, that those indiscreetly civil persons often are, who think to oblige a good man, by letting him know he is beloved by someone or other; and making him understand how many good qualities he is master of, to render him agreeable to the fair sex, if he would but advance where love and good fortune call; and that a too constant lover loses a great part of his time, which might be managed to more advantage, since youth hath so short a race to run. This, and a thousand the like indecent complaisances, give him a vanity that suits not with that discretion, which has hitherto acquired him so good a reputation. I would not have you, Damon, act on these occasions, as many of the easy sparks have done before you, who receive such weakness and flattery for truth; and passing it off with a smile, suffer them to advance in folly, till they have gained a credit with them, and they believe all they hear; telling them they do so, by consenting gestures, silence, or open approbation. For my part, I should not condemn a lover that should answer a sort of civil brokers for love, somewhat briskly; and by giving them to understand they are already engaged, or directing them to fools, that will possibly hearken to them, and credit such stuff, shame them out of a folly so infamous and disingenuous. In such a case only I am willing you should own your passion; not that you need tell the object which has charmed you. And you may say, you are already a lover, without saying you are beloved. For so long as you appear to have a heart unengaged, you are exposed to all the little arts and addresses of this sort of obliging procurers of love, and give way to the hope they have of making you their proselyte. For your own reputation then, and my ease and honour, shun such conversations; for they are neither creditable to you, nor pleasing to me. And believe me, Damon, a true lover has no curiosity, but what concerns his mistress.

FIVE O'CLOCK

DANGEROUS VISITS

I foresee, or fear, that these busy impertinent friends will oblige you to visit some ladies of their acquaintance, or yours; my watch does not forbid you. Yet I must tell you, I apprehend danger in such visits; and I fear, you will have need of all your care and precaution, in these encounters, that you may give me no cause to suspect you. Perhaps you will argue, that civility obliges you to it. If I were assured there would no other design be carried on, I should believe it were to advance an enormous prudence too far, to forbid you. Only keep yourself upon your guard; for the business of most part of the fair sex, is, to seek only the conquest of hearts. All their civilities are but so many interests; and they do nothing without design. And in such conversations there is always a *Je ne sais quoi*, that is feared, especially when beauty is accompanied with youth and gaiety; and which they assume upon all occasions that may serve their turn. And I confess it is not an easy matter to be just in these hours and conversations : the most certain way of being so, is to imagine I read all your thoughts, observe all your looks, and hear all your words.

THE CAUTION

My Damon, if your heart be kind,
  Do not too long with beauty stay ;
For there are certain moments when the mind
  Is hurried by the force of charms away.
In fate a minute critical there lies,
That waits on Love, and takes you by surprise.

> A lover pleased with constancy,
> Lives still as if the maid he loved were by:
>   As if his actions were in view,
>   As if his steps she did pursue;
>   Or that his very soul she knew.
> Take heed; for though I am not present there,
> My Love, my genius waits you everywhere.

I am very much pleased with the remedy, you say, you make use of to defend yourself from the attacks that beauty gives your heart; which in one of your billets, you said was this, or to this purpose:

THE CHARM FOR CONSTANCY

> Iris, to keep my soul entire and true,
> It thinks, each moment of the day, on you.
>   And when a charming face I see,
>   That does all other eyes incline,
>   It has no influence on me:
>   I think it ev'n deformed to thine.
> My eyes, my soul, and sense, regardless move
> To all, but the dear object of my love.

But, Damon, I know all lovers are naturally flatterers, though they do not think so themselves; because everyone makes a sense of beauty according to his own fancy. But perhaps you will say in your own defence, that it is not flattery to say an unbeautiful woman is beautiful, if he that says so believes she is so. I should be content to acquit you of the first, provided you allow me the last: and if I appear charming in Damon's eyes, I am not fond of the approbation of any other. It is enough the world thinks me not altogether disagreeable, to justify his choice; but let your good opinion give what increase it pleases to my beauty, though your approbation give me a pleasure, it shall not a vanity; and I am contented that Damon should think me a beauty, without my believing I am one. It is not to draw new assurances, and new vows from you, that I speak this; though tales of love are the only ones we desire to hear often told, and which never tire the hearers if addressed to themselves. But it is not to this end I now seem to doubt what you say to my advantage: no, my heart knows no disguise, nor can dissemble one thought of it to Damon; it is all sincere, and honest as his wish. Therefore it tells you, it does not credit everything you say; though I believe you say abundance of truths in a great part of my character. But when you advance to that, which my own sense, my judgment, or my glass cannot persuade me to believe, you must give me leave either to believe you think me vain enough to credit you, or pleased that your sentiments and mine are differing in this point. But I doubt I may rather reply in some verses, a friend of yours and mine sent to a person she thought had but indifferent sentiments for her; yet, who nevertheless flattered her, because he imagined she had a very great esteem for him. She is a woman that, you know, naturally hates flattery: on the other side she was extremely dissatisfied, and uneasy at his opinion of his being more in her favour than she desired he should believe. So that one night having left her full of pride and anger, she next morning sent him these verses, instead of a billet-doux.

THE DEFIANCE

By Heaven 'tis false, I am not vain;
    And rather would the subject be
Of your indifference, or disdain,
    Than wit or raillery.

Take back the trifling praise you give,
    And pass it on some easier fool,
Who may the injuring wit believe,
    That turns her into ridicule.

Tell her, she's witty, fair and gay,
    With all the charms that can subdue:
Perhaps she'll credit what you say;
    But curse me if I do.

If your diversion you design,
  On my good-nature you have prest:
Or if you do intend it mine,
  You have mistook the jest.

Philander, fly that guilty art:
  Your charming facile wit will find,
It cannot play on any heart,
  That is sincere and kind.

For wit with softness to reside,
  Good-nature is with pity stored;
But flattery's the result of pride,
  And fawns to be adored.

Nay, even when you smile and bow,
  'Tis to be rendered more complete:
Your wit, with ev'ry grace you show,
  Is but a popular cheat.

Laugh on, and call me coxcomb—do;
  And, your opinion to improve,
Think, all you think of me is true;
  And to confirm it, swear I love.

Then, while you wreck my soul with pain,
  And of a cruel conquest boast,
'Tis you, Philander, that are vain,
  And witty at my cost.

Possibly, the angry Amynta, when she writ these
verses, was more offended, that he believed himself
beloved, than that he flattered; though she would
seem to make that a great part of the quarrel, and
cause of her resentment. For we are often in a
humour to seem more modest in that point, than
naturally we are; being too apt to have a favourable
opinion of ourselves: and it is rather the effects of
a fear that we are flattered, than our own ill opinion
of the beauty flattered; and that the praiser thinks
not so well of it, as we do ourselves, or at least we
wish he should. Not but there are grains of allow-
ance for the temper of him that speaks. One man's
humour is to talk much; and he may be permitted
to enlarge upon the praise he gives the person he

pretends to, without being accused of much guilt. Another hates to be wordy; from such a one, I have known one soft expression, one tender thing, go as far as whole days' everlasting protestations urged with vows, and mighty eloquence. And both the one and the other, indeed, must be allowed in good manners, to stretch the compliment beyond the bounds of nice truth: and we must not wonder to hear a man call a woman a beauty, when she is not ugly; or another a great wit, if she have but common-sense above the vulgar; well bred, when well dressed; and good-natured, when civil. And as I should be very ridiculous, if I took all you said for absolute truth; so I should be very unjust, not to allow you very sincere in almost all you said besides; and those things, the most material to love, honour, and friendship. And for the rest, Damon, be it true or false, this believe, you speak with such a grace, that I cannot choose but credit you; and find an infinite pleasure in that faith, because I love you. And if I cannot find the cheat, I am contented you should deceive me on, because you do it so agreeably.

SIX O'CLOCK

WALK WITHOUT DESIGN

You yet have time to walk; and my watch foresaw you could not refuse your friends. You must to the Park, or to the Mall; for the season is fair and inviting, and all the young beauties love those places too well, not to be there. It is there that a thousand intrigues are carried on, and as many more designed. It is there that everyone is set out for conquest; and who aim at nothing less than hearts. Guard yours well, my Damon; and be not always admiring what you see. Do not, in passing by, sigh them silent

praises. Suffer not so much as a guilty wish to
approach your thoughts, nor a heedful glance to steal
from your fine eyes: those are regards you ought
only to have for her you love. But oh! above all,
have a care of what you say. You are not reproach-
able, if you should remain silent all the time of your
walk; nor would those that know you believe it the
effects of dulness, but melancholy. And if any of
your friends ask you why you are so, I will give
you leave to sigh, and say:

THE MALCONTENT

Ah! wonder not if I appear
Regardless of the pleasures here;
Or that my thoughts are thus confined
To the just limits of my mind.
My eyes take no delight to rove
O'er all the smiling charmers of the grove,
Since she is absent whom they love.

Ask me not, Why the flow'ry spring,
Or the gay little birds that sing,
Or the young streams no more delight,
Or shades and arbours can't invite?
Why the soft murmurs of the wind,
Within the thick-grown groves confined,
No more my soul transport, or cheer;
Since all that's charming—Iris, is not here;
Nothing seems glorious, nothing fair.

Then suffer me to wander thus,
With downcast eyes, and arms across:
Let beauty unregarded go;
The trees and flowers unheeded strow;
Let purling streams neglected glide;
With all the spring's adorning pride.
'Tis Iris only soul can give
To the dull shades, and plains, and make them thrive;
Nature and my last joys retrieve.

I do not, for all this, wholly confine your eyes:
you may look indifferently on all, but with a particular regard on none. You may praise all the

beauties in general, but no single one too much. I
will not exact from you neither an entire silence.
There are a thousand civilities you ought to pay to
all your friends and acquaintance; and while I
caution you of actions, that may get you the reputation of a lover of some of the fair that haunt those
places, I would not have you, by an unnecessary and
uncomplaisant sullenness, gain that of a person too
negligent or morose. I would have you remiss in
no one punctilio of good manners. I would have
you very just, and pay all you owe; but in these
affairs be not over generous, and give away too much.
In fine, you may look, speak, and walk; but, Damon,
do it all without design : and while you do so, remember that Iris sent you this advice.

THE WARNING

Take heed, my Damon, in the grove,
Where beauties with design do walk ;
Take heed, my Damon, how you look and talk,
    For there are ambuscades of love.
The very winds that softly blow,
    Will help betray your easy heart ;
And all the flowers that blushing grow,
The shades about, and rivulets below,
    Will take the victor's part.

Remember, Damon, all thy safety lies
In the just conduct of your eyes.
The heart, by nature good and brave,
Is to those treacherous guards a slave.
    If they let in the fair destructive foe,
Scarce honour can defend her noble seat :
    Ev'n she will be corrupted too,
Or driven to a retreat.
The soul is but the cully to the sight,
And must be pleased in what that takes delight.

Therefore examine yourself well; and conduct your
eyes, during this walk, like a lover that seeks nothing:
and do not stay too long in these places.

SEVEN O'CLOCK

VOLUNTARY RETREAT

It is time to be weary, it is night: take leave of your friends and retire home. It is in this retreat that you ought to recollect in your thoughts all the actions of the day, and all those things that you ought to give me an account of, in your letter. You cannot hide the least secret from me, without treason against sacred love. For all the world agrees that confidence is one of the greatest proofs of the passion of love; and that lover who refuses his confidence to the person he loves, is to be suspected to love but very indifferently, and to think very poorly of the sense and generosity of his mistress. But that you may acquit yourself like a man, and a lover of honour, and leave me no doubt upon my soul; think of all you have done this day, that I may have all the story of it in your next letter to me: but deal faithfully, and neither add nor diminish in your relation; the truth and sincerity of your confession will atone even for little faults that you shall commit against me, in some of those things you shall tell me. For if you have failed in any point or circumstance of love, I had much rather hear it from you than another: for it is a sort of repentance to accuse yourself; and would be a crime unpardonable, if you suffer me to hear it from any other: and be assured, while you confess it, I shall be indulgent enough to forgive you. The noblest quality of man is sincerity; and, Damon, one ought to have as much of it in love, as in any other business of one's life, notwithstanding the most part of men make no account of it there; but will believe there ought to be double-dealing,

and an art practised in love as well as in war.   But,
oh! beware of that notion.

SINCERITY

Sincerity! thou greatest good!
 Thou virtue which so many boast!
And art so nicely understood!
 And often in the searching lost!
For when we do approach thee near,
 The fine idea framed of thee,
Appears not now so charming fair
 As the most useful flattery.
Thou hast no glitt'ring to invite;
Nor takest the lover at first sight.

The modest virtue shuns the crowd,
 And lives, like Vestals, in a cell;
In cities 'twill not be allowed,
 Nor takes delight in Courts to dwell;
'Tis nonsense with the man of wit;
 And ev'n a scandal to the great:
For all the young, and fair, unfit;
 And scorned by wiser fops of state.
A virtue yet was never known
To the false trader, or the falser gown.

And, Damon, though thy noble blood
 Be most illustrious, and refined;
Though ev'ry grace and ev'ry good
 Adorn thy person and thy mind:
Yet, if this virtue shine not there,
 This God-like virtue, which alone,
Wert thou less witty, brave, or fair,
 Would for all these, less prized, atone;
My tender folly I'd control,
And scorn the conquest of thy soul.

EIGHT O'CLOCK

IMPATIENT DEMANDS

After you have sufficiently collected yourself of all the past actions of the day, call your page into your cabinet, or him whom you trusted with your last letter to me; where you ought to inquire of him a thousand things, and all of me. Ask impatiently, and be angry if he answers not your curiosity soon enough. Think that he has a dreaming in his voice, in these moments more than at other times; and reproach him with dulness: for 'tis most certain that when one loves tenderly, we would know in a minute, what cannot be related in an hour. Ask him, How I did? How I received his letter? And if he examined the air of my face, when I took it? If I blushed or looked pale? If my hand trembled, or I spoke to him with short interrupting sighs? If I asked him any questions about you, while I was opening the seal? Or if I could not well speak, and was silent? If I read it attentively, and with joy? And all this, before you open the answer I have sent you by him: which, because you are impatient to read, you, with the more haste and earnestness, demand all you expect from him; and that you may the better know what humour I was in, when I writ that to you. For, oh! a lover has a thousand little fears, and dreads, he knows not why. In fine, make him recount to you all that passed, while he was with me; and then you ought to read that which I have sent, that you may inform yourself of all that passes in my heart: for you may assure yourself, all that I say to you that way proceeds from thence.

R

THE ASSURANCE

How shall a lover come to know,
Whether he's beloved or no?
What dear things must she impart,
To assure him of her heart?
Is it when her blushes rise;
And she languish in her eyes;
Tremble when he does approach;
Look pale, and faint at ev'ry touch?

Is it, when a thousand ways
She does his wit and beauty praise;
Or she venture to explain,
In less moving words, a pain;
Though so indiscreet she grows,
To confirm it with her vows?

These some short-lived passion moves,
While the object's by she loves;
While the gay and sudden fire
Kindles by some fond desire:
And a coldness will ensue,
When the lover's out of view.
Then she reflects with scandal o'er
The easy scene that passed before:
Then, with blushes, would recall
The unconsidering criminal;
In which a thousand faults she'll find,
And chide the errors of her mind.
Such fickle weight is found in words,
As no substantial faith affords:
Deceived and baffled all may be,
Who trust that frail security.

But a well-digested flame,
That will always be the same;
And that does from merit grow,
Established by our reason too;
By a better way will prove,
'Tis th' unerring fire of love.
Lasting records it will give:
And, that all she says may live;
Sacred and authentic stand,
Her heart confirms it by her hand.
If this, a maid, well-born, allow;
Damon, believe her just and true.

NINE O'CLOCK

MELANCHOLY REFLECTIONS

You will not have much trouble to explain what my watch designs here. There can be no thought more afflicting, than that of the absence of a mistress: and which the sighings of the heart will soon make you find. Ten thousand fears oppress him; he is jealous of everybody, and envies those eyes and ears that are charmed by being near the object adored. He grows impatient, and makes a thousand resolutions, and as soon abandons them all. He gives himself wholly up to the torment of uncertainty; and by degrees, from one cruel thought to another, winds himself up to insupportable chagrin. Take this hour then, to think on your misfortunes, which cannot be small to a soul that is wholly sensible of love. And everyone knows, that a lover, deprived of the object of his heart, is deprived of all the world, and inconsolable: for though one wishes without ceasing for the dear charmer one loves, and though you speak of her every minute; though you are writing to her every day, and though you are infinitely pleased with the dear and tender answer; yet, to speak sincerely, it must be confessed, that the felicity of a true lover is to be always near his mistress. And you may tell me, O Damon! what you please; and say that absence inspires the flame, which perpetual presence would satiate. I love too well to be of that mind, and when I am, I shall believe my passion is declining. I know not whether it advances your love; but surely it must ruin your repose: and it is possible to be, at once, an absent lover, and happy too. For my part, I can meet with nothing that can please in the absence of Damon; but on the contrary I see all things with disgust. I will flatter myself, that it is so with you; and that the least evils appear great misfortunes; and that all those who speak to you of anything but of what you love, increase your pain, by a new remembrance of her absence. I will believe that these are your sentiments, when you are assured not to see me in some weeks; and if your heart do not betray your words, all those days will be tedious to you. I would not, however, have your melancholy too extreme; and to lessen it, you may persuade yourself, that I partake it with you: for, I remember, in your last you told me, you would wish we should be both grieved at the same time, and both at the same time pleased; and I believe I love too well not to obey you.

LOVE SECURED

Love, of all joys, the sweetest is,
  The most substantial happiness;
The softest blessing life can crave,
The noblest passion souls can have.
Yet, if no interruption were,
  No difficulties came between,
'Twould not be rendered half so dear:
  The sky is gayest when small clouds are seen.
The sweetest flower, the blushing rose,
Amidst the thorns securest grows.
If love were one continued joy,
How soon the happiness would cloy!
The wiser god did this foresee;
  And to preserve the bliss entire,
Mixed it with doubt and jealousy,
  Those necessary fuels to the fire;
Sustained the fleeting pleasures with new fears;
With little quarrels, sighs and tears;
  With absence, that tormenting smart,
That makes a minute seem a day,
  A day a year to the impatient heart,
That languishes in the delay,
But cannot sigh the tender pain away;
That still returns, and with a greater force,
Through every vein it takes its grateful course.
  But whatsoe'er the lover does sustain,
Though he still sigh, complain, and fear;
  It cannot be a mortal pain,
When two do the affliction bear.

TEN O'CLOCK

REFLECTIONS

After the afflicting thoughts of my absence, make some reflections on your happiness. Think it a blessing to be permitted to love me; think it so, because I permit it to you alone, and never could be drawn to allow it any other. The first thing you ought to consider, is, that at length I have suffered myself to be overcome, to quit that nicety that is natural to me, and receive your addresses; nay, thought them agreeable: and that I have at last confessed, the present of your heart is very dear to me. It is true, I did not accept of it the first time it was offered me, nor before you had told me a thousand times, that you could not escape expiring, if I did not give you leave to sigh for me, and gaze upon me; and that there was an absolute necessity for me, either to give you leave to love, or die. And all those rigours my severity has made you suffer, ought now to be recounted to your memory, as subjects of pleasure; and you ought to esteem and judge of the price of my affections, by the difficulties you found in being able to touch my heart. Not but you have charms that can conquer at first sight; and you ought not to have valued me less, if I had been more easily gained. But it is enough to please you, to think and know I am gained; no matter when and how. When, after a thousand cares and inquietudes, that which we wish for succeeds to our desires, the remembrance of those pains and pleasures we encountered in arriving at it, gives us a new joy.

Remember also, Damon, that I have preferred you before all those that have been thought worthy of my esteem; and that I have shut my eyes to all their pleading merits, and could survey none but yours.

Consider then, that you had not only the happiness to please me, but that you only found out the way of doing it, and I had the goodness at last to tell you so, contrary to all the delicacy and niceness of my soul, contrary to my prudence, and all those scruples, you know, are natural to my humour.

My tenderness proceeded further, and I gave you innocent marks of my new-born passion, on all occasions that presented themselves. For, after that from my eyes and tongue you knew the sentiments of my heart, I confirmed that truth to you by my letters. Confess, Damon, that if you make these reflections, you will not pass this hour very disagreeably.

BEGINNING LOVE

As free as wanton winds I lived,
  That unconcerned do play :
No broken faith, no fate I grieved ;
  No fortune gave me joy.
A dull content crowned all my hours,
  My heart no sighs opprest ;
I called in vain on no deaf powers,
  To ease a tortured breast.

The sighing swains regardless pined,
  And strove in vain to please :
With pain I civilly was kind,
  But could afford no ease.
Though wit and beauty did abound,
  The charm was wanting still,
That could inspire the tender wound,
  Or bend my careless will.

Till in my heart a kindling flame
  Your softer sighs had blown ;
Which I, with striving, love and shame,
  Too sensibly did own.
Whate'er the god before could plead ;
  Whate'er the youth's desert ;
The feeble siege in vain was laid
  Against my stubborn heart.

At first my sighs and blushes spoke,
    Just when your sighs would rise ;
And when you gazed, I wished to look,
    But durst not meet your eyes.
I trembled when my hand you pressed,
    Nor could my guilt control ;
But love prevailed, and I confessed
    The secrets of my soul.

And when upon the giving part,
    My present to avow,
By all the ways confirmed my heart,
    That honour would allow ;
Too mean was all that I could say,
    Too poorly understood :
I gave my soul the noblest way,
    My letters made it good.

You may believe I did not easily, nor suddenly,
bring my heart to this condescension ; but I loved,
and all things in Damon were capable of making me
resolve so to do. I could not think it a crime, where
every grace, and every virtue justified my choice.
And when once one is assured of this, we find not
much difficulty in owning that passion which will so
well commend one's judgment ; and there is no
obstacle that love does not surmount. I confessed
my weakness a thousand ways, before I told it you ;
and I remember all those things with pleasure, but
yet I remember them also with shame.

ELEVEN O'CLOCK

SUPPER

I will believe, Damon, that you have been so well
entertained during this hour, and have found so much
sweetness in these thoughts, that if one did not tell
you that supper waits, you would lose yourself in
reflections so pleasing, many more minutes. But you
must go where you are expected ; perhaps, among

the fair, the young, the gay; but do not abandon
your heart to too much joy, though you have so
much reason to be contented: but the greatest
pleasures are always imperfect, if the object beloved
do not partake of it. For this reason be cheerful
and merry with reserve: do not talk too much, I
know you do not love it; and if you do it, it will be
the effect of too much complaisance, or with some
design of pleasing too well; for you know your own
charming power, and how agreeable your wit and
conversation are to all the world.   Remember, I am
covetous of every word you speak, that is not
addressed to me, and envy the happy listener, if I
am not by.   And I may reply to you as Amynta did
to Philander, when he charged her of loving a talker:
and because, perhaps, you have not heard it, I will,
to divert you, send it to you; and at the same time
assure you, Damon, that your more noble quality, of
speaking little, has reduced me to a perfect abhorrence
of those wordy sparks, that value themselves upon
their ready and much talking upon every trivial
subject, and who have so good an opinion of their
talent that way, they will let nobody edge in a word,
or a reply; but will make all the conversation themselves, that they may pass for very entertaining
persons, and pure company.   But the verses:

THE REFORMATION

Philander, since you'll have it so,
   I grant I was impertinent;
And, till this moment, did not know,
   Through all my life what 'twas I meant.
Your kind opinion was the flattering glass,
In which my mind found how deformed it was.

In your clear sense, which knows no art,
   I saw the errors of my soul;
And all the foibles of my heart
   With one reflection you control.
Kind as a god, and gently you chastise:
By what you hate, you teach me to be wise.

Impertinence, my sex's shame,
  That has so long my life pursued,
You with such modesty reclaim,
  As all the women has subdued.
To so divine a power what must I owe,
That renders me so like the perfect You?

That conversable thing I hate,
  Already, with a just disdain,
That prides himself upon his prate,
  And is, of words, that nonsense, vain :
When in your few appears such excellence,
As have reproached, and charmed me into sense.

For ever may I listening sit,
  Though but each hour a word be born ;
I would attend thy coming wit,
  And bless what can so well inform.
Let the dull world henceforth to words be damned ;
I'm into nobler sense than talking shamed.

I believe you are so good a lover, as to be of my opinion; and that you will neither force yourself against nature, nor find much occasion to lavish out those excellent things that must proceed from you, whenever you speak. If all women were like me, I should have more reason to fear your silence than your talk : for you have a thousand ways to charm without speaking, and those which to me show a great deal more concern. But, Damon, you know the greatest part of my sex judge the fine gentleman by the volubility of his tongue, by his dexterity in repartee, and cry ' Oh ! he never wants fine things to say : he's eternally talking the most surprising things.' But, Damon, you are well assured, I hope, that Iris is none of these coquettes : at least, if she had any spark of it once in her nature, she is by the excellency of your contrary temper taught to know, and scorn the folly. And take heed your conduct never gives me cause to suspect you have deceived me in your temper.

TWELVE O'CLOCK

COMPLAISANCE

Nevertheless, Damon, civility requires a little complaisance after supper; and I am assured, you can
never want that, though I confess, you are not accused
of too general a complaisance, and do not often make
use of it to those persons you have an indifference
for: though one is not the less esteemable for having
more of this than one ought; and though an excess
of it be a fault, it is a very excusable one. Have
therefore some for those with whom you are: you
may laugh with them, drink with them, dance or
sing with them; yet think of me. You may discourse
of a thousand indifferent things with them, and at
the same time still think of me. If the subject be
any beautiful lady, whom they praise, either for her
person, wit, or virtue, you may apply it to me: and
if you dare not say it aloud, at least, let your heart
answer in this language:

> Yes, the fair object, whom you praise,
> Can give us love a thousand ways;
> Her wit and beauty charming are;
> But still my Iris is more fair.

Nobody ever spoke before me of a faithful lover,
but still I sighed, and thought of Damon: and ever
when they tell me tales of love, any soft pleasing
intercourses of an amour; oh! with what pleasures
do I listen! and with pleasure answer them, either
with my eyes, or tongue:

> That lover may his Sylvia warm,
> But cannot, like my Damon, charm.

If I have not all these excellent qualities you meet
with in those beautiful people, I am however very

glad that love prepossesses your heart to my advantage: and I need not tell you, Damon, that a true lover ought to persuade himself, that all other objects ought to give place to her, for whom his heart sighs. But see, my Cupid tells you it is one o'clock, and that you ought not to be longer from your apartment; where, while you are undressing, I will give you leave to say to yourself:

THE REGRET

Alas! and must the sun decline,
   Before it have informed my eyes
Of all that's glorious, all that's fine,
   Of all I sigh for, all I prize?
How joyful were those happy days,
When Iris spread her charming rays,
Did my unwearied heart inspire
With never-ceasing awful fire,
And ev'ry minute gave me new desire!
But now, alas! all dead and pale,
   Like flow'rs that wither in the shade:
Where no kind sunbeams can prevail,
   To raise its cold and fading head,
   I sink into my useless bed.
I grasp the senseless pillow as I lie;
A thousand times, in vain, I sighing cry,
Ah! would to heaven my Iris were as nigh.

ONE O'CLOCK

IMPOSSIBILITY TO SLEEP

You have been up long enough; and Cupid, who takes care of your health, tells you, it is time for you to go to bed. Perhaps you may not sleep as soon as you are laid, and possibly you may pass an hour in bed, before you shut your eyes. In this impossibility of sleeping, I think it very proper for you to imagine what I am doing where I am. Let your fancy take a little journey then, invisible, to observe my actions

and my conduct. You will find me sitting alone in
my cabinet (for I am one that do not love to go to
bed early) and will find me very uneasy and pensive,
pleased with none of those things that so well entertain others. I shun all conversation, as far as civility
will allow, and find no satisfaction like being alone,
where my soul may, without interruption, converse
with Damon. I sigh, and sometimes you will see
my cheeks wet with tears, that insensibly glide down
at a thousand thoughts that present themselves soft
and afflicting. I partake of all your inquietude.
On other things I think with indifference, if ever my
thoughts do stray from the more agreeable object.
I find, however, a little sweetness in this thought,
that, during my absence, your heart thinks of me,
when mine sighs for you. Perhaps I am mistaken,
and that at the same time that you are the entertainment of all my thoughts, I am no more in yours ;
and perhaps you are thinking of those things that
immortalise the young and brave, either by those
glories the Muses flatter you with, or that of Bellona,
and the god of war ; and serving now a monarch,
whose glorious acts in arms has outgone all the
feigned and real heroes of any age, who has, himself,
outdone whatever history can produce of great and
brave, and set so illustrious an example to the under-
world, that it is not impossible, as much a lover as
you are, but you are thinking now how to render
yourself worthy the glory of such a god-like master,
by projecting a thousand things of gallantry and
danger. And though I confess, such thoughts are
proper for your youth, your quality, and the place
you have the honour to hold under our sovereign,
yet let me tell you, Damon, you will not be without
inquietude, if you think of either being a delicate
poet, or a brave warrior ; for love will still interrupt
your glory, however you may think to divert him
either by writing or fighting. And you ought to
remember these verses :

LOVE AND GLORY

Beneath the kind protecting laurel's shade,
For sighing lovers, and for warriors made,
The soft Adonis, and rough Mars were laid.

Both were designed to take their rest ;
But Love the gentle boy opprest,
And false alarms shook the stern hero's breast.

This thinks to soften all his toils of war,
In the dear arms of the obliging fair ;
And that, by hunting, to divert his care.

All day, o'er hills and plains, wild beasts he chased,
Swift as the flying winds, his eager haste ;
In vain, the god of Love pursues as fast.

But oh ! no sports, no toils, divertive prove,
The evening still returns him to the grove,
To sigh and languish for the Queen of Love :

Where elegies and sonnets he does frame,
And to the listening echoes sighs her name,
And on the trees carves records of his flame.

The warrior in the dusty camp all day
With rattling drums and trumpets, does essay
To fright the tender flatt'ring god away.

But still, alas, in vain : whate'er delight,
What cares he takes the wanton boy to fright,
Love still revenges it at night.

'Tis then he haunts the royal tent,
The sleeping hours in sighs are spent,
And all his resolutions does prevent.

In all his pains, Love mixed his smart ;
In every wound he feels a dart ;
And the soft god is trembling in his heart.

Then he retires to shady groves,
And there, in vain, he seeks repose,
And strives to fly from what he cannot lose.

While thus he lay, Bellona came,
And with a gen'rous fierce disdain,
Upbraids him with his feeble flame.

Arise, the world's great terror, and their care;
Behold the glitt'ring host from far,
That waits the conduct of the god of war.

Beneath these glorious laurels, which were made
To crown the noble victor's head,
Why thus supinely art thou laid?

Why on that face, where awful terror grew,
Thy sun-parched cheeks why do I view
The shining tracks of falling tears bedew?

What god has wrought these universal harms?
What fatal nymph, what fatal charms,
Has made the hero deaf to war's alarms?

Now let the conqu'ring ensigns up be furled:
Learn to be gay, be soft, and curled;
And idle, lose the empire of the world.

In fond effeminate delights go on;
Lose all the glories you have won:
Bravely resolve to love, and be undone.

'Tis thus the martial virgin pleads;
Thus she the am'rous god persuades
To fly from Venus, and the flow'ry meads.

You see here that poets and warriors are oftentimes in affliction, even under the shades of their
protecting laurels; and let the nymphs and virgins
sing what they please to their memory, under the
myrtles, and on flowery beds, they are much better
days than in the campaign. Nor do the crowns of
glory surpass those of love: the first is but an
empty name, which is now kept and lost with hazard;
but love more nobly employs a brave soul, and all
his pleasures are solid and lasting; and when one has
a worthy object of one's flame, glory accompanies
love too. But go to sleep, the hour is come; though
it is now that your soul ought to be entertained in
dreams.

TWO O'CLOCK

CONVERSATION IN DREAMS

I doubt not but you will think it very bold and arbitrary, that my watch should pretend to rule even your sleeping hours, and that my cupid should govern your very dreams ; which are but thoughts disordered, in which reason has no part ; chimeras of the imagination, and no more. But though my watch does not pretend to counsel unreasonable, yet you must allow it here, if not to pass the bounds, at least to advance to the utmost limits of it. I am assured, that after having thought so much of me in the day, you will think of me also in the night. And the first dream my watch permits you to make, is to think you are in conversation with me.

Imagine, Damon, that you are talking to me of your passion, with all the transport of a lover, and that I hear you with satisfaction ; that all my looks and blushes, while you are speaking, give you new hopes and assurances ; that you are not indifferent to me ; and that I give you a thousand testimonies of my tenderness, all innocent and obliging.

While you are saying all that love can dictate, all that wit and good manners can invent, and all that I wish to hear from Damon, believe in this dream, all flattering and dear, that after having showed me the ardour of your flame, I confess to you the bottom of my heart, and all the loving secrets there ; that I give you sigh for sigh, tenderness for tenderness, heart for heart, and pleasure for pleasure. And I would have your sense of this dream so perfect, and your joy so entire, that if it happen you should awake with the satisfaction of this dream, you should find your heart still panting with the soft pleasure of the dear deceiving transport, and you should be ready to cry out :

> Ah ! how sweet it is to dream,
> When charming Iris is the theme !

For such, I wish, my Damon, your sleeping and your waking thoughts should render me to your heart.

THREE O'CLOCK

CAPRICIOUS SUFFERING IN DREAMS

It is but just to mix a little chagrin with these pleasures, a little bitter with your sweet ; you may be cloyed with too long an imagination of my favours : and I will have your fancy in dreams represent me to it, as the most capricious maid in the world. I know, here you will accuse my watch, and blame me with unnecessary cruelty, as you will call it : but lovers have their little ends, their little advantages, to pursue by methods wholly unaccountable to all, but that heart which contrives them. And as good a lover as I believe you, you will not enter into my design at first sight ; and though, on reasonable thoughts, you will be satisfied with this conduct of mine, at its first approach you will be ready to cry out :

THE REQUEST

> Oh Iris ! let my sleeping hours be fraught
> With joys, which you deny my waking thought.
> Is't not enough you absent are ?
>   Is't not enough I sigh all day,
> And languish out my life in care,
>   To ev'ry passion made a prey ?
> I burn with love, and soft desire ;
>   I rave with jealousy and fear :
> All day, for ease, my soul I tire ;
> In vain I search it ev'rywhere :
> It dwells not with the witty or the fair.

It is not in the camp or court,
In business, music, or in sport ;
The plays, the Park, the Mall afford
No more than the dull basset-board.
The beauties in the drawing-room,
With all their sweetness, all their bloom,
No more my faithful eyes invite,
    Nor rob my Iris of a sigh or glance,
Unless soft thoughts of her incite
    A smile, or trivial complaisance.
Then since my days so anxious prove,
    Ah, cruel tyrant ! give
A little loose to joys in love,
    And let your Damon live.

Let him in dreams be happy made,
    And let his sleep some bliss provide :
The nicest maid may yield in night's dark shade,
    What she so long by daylight had denied.
There let me think you present are,
And court my pillow for my fair.
There let me find you kind, and that you give
All that a man of honour dares receive.
And may my eyes eternal watches keep,
Rather than want that pleasure when I sleep.

Some such complaint as this I know you will
make ; but, Damon, if the little quarrels of lovers
render the reconciling moments so infinitely charming, you must needs allow, that these little chagrins
in capricious dreams must awaken you to more joy to
find them but dreams, than if you had met with no
disorder there. It is for this reason that I would have
you suffer a little pain for a coming pleasure ; nor,
indeed, is it possible for you to escape the dreams my
cupid points you out. You shall dream that I have
a thousand foibles, something of the lightness of my
sex ; that my soul is employed in a thousand vanities ;
that (proud and fond of lovers) I make advances for
the glory of a slave, without any other interest or design
than that of being adored. I will give you leave to
think my heart fickle, and that, far from resigning it
to anyone, I lend it only for a day, or an hour, and

S

take it back at pleasure; that I am a very coquette, even to impertinence.

All this I give you leave to think, and to offend me: but it is in sleep only that I permit it; for I would never pardon you the least offence of this nature, if in any other kind than in a dream. Nor is it enough affliction to you, to imagine me thus idly vain; but you are to pass on to a hundred more capricious humours: as that I exact of you a hundred unjust things; that I pretend you should break off with all your friends, and for the future have none at all; that I will myself do those things, which I violently condemn in you; and that I will have for others, as well as you, that tender friendship that resembles love, or rather love which people call friendship; and that I will not, after all, have you dare complain of me.

In fine, be as ingenious as you please to torment yourself; and believe, that I am become unjust, ungrateful, and insensible. But were I so indeed, O Damon! consider your awaking heart, and tell me, would your love stand the proof of all these faults in me? But know, that I would have you believe I have none of these weaknesses, though I am not wholly without faults, but those will be excusable to a lover; and this notion I have of a perfect one:

> Whate'er fantastic humours rule the fair,
> She's still the lover's dotage, and his care.

FOUR O'CLOCK

JEALOUSY IN DREAMS

Do not think, Damon, to wake yet; for I design you shall yet suffer a little more: jealousy must now possess you, that tyrant over the heart, that compels your very reason, and seduces all your good-nature. And in this dream you must believe that in sleeping, which you could not do me the injustice to do when awake. And here you must explain all my actions to the utmost disadvantage: nay, I will wish, that the force of this jealousy may be so extreme, that it may make you languish in grief, and be overcome with anger.

You shall now imagine, that one of your rivals is with me, interrupting all you say, or hindering all you would say; that I have no attention to what you say aloud to me, but that I incline mine ear to hearken to all that he whispers to me. You shall repine, that he pursues me everywhere, and is eternally at your heels if you approach me; that I caress him with sweetness in my eyes, and that vanity in my heart, that possesses the humours of almost all the fair; that is, to believe it greatly for my glory to have abundance of rivals for my lovers. I know you love me too well not to be extremely uneasy in the company of a rival, and to have one perpetually near me; for let him be beloved or not by the mistress, it must be confessed, a rival is a very troublesome person. But, to afflict you to the utmost, I will have you imagine that my eyes approve of all his thoughts; that they flatter him with hopes; and that I have taken away my heart from you, to make a present of it to this more lucky man. You shall suffer, while possessed with this dream, all that a cruel jealousy can make a tender soul suffer.

THE TORMENT

O jealousy! thou passion most ingrate!
Tormenting as despair, envious as hate!
Spiteful as witchcraft, which th' Invoker harms;
Worse than the wretch that suffers by its charms.
Thou subtile poison in the fancy bred,
Diffused through every vein, the heart and head,
And over all, like wild contagion spread,
Thou, whose sole property is to destroy,
Thou opposite to good, antipathy to joy;
Whose attributes are cruel rage and fire,
Reason debauched, false sense, and mad desire.

In fine, it is a passion that ruffles all the senses, and disorders the whole frame of nature. It makes one hear and see what was never spoken, and what never was in view. It is the bane of health and beauty, an unmannerly intruder; and an evil of life worse than death. She is a very cruel tyrant in the heart; she possesses and pierces it with infinite unquiets; and we may lay it down as a certain maxim—

> She that would rack a lover's heart
> To the extent of cruelty,
> Must his tranquillity pervert
> To the most torturing jealousy.

I speak too sensibly of this passion, not to have loved well enough to have been touched with it. And you shall be this unhappy lover, Damon, during this dream, in which nothing shall present itself to your tumultuous thoughts, that shall not bring its pain. You shall here pass and repass a hundred designs, that shall confound one another. In fine, Damon, anger, hatred, and revenge, shall surround your heart.

> There they shall all together reign
> With mighty force, with mighty pain;
> In spite of reason, in contempt of love:
> Sometimes by turns, sometimes united move.

FIVE O'CLOCK

QUARRELS IN DREAMS

I perceive you are not able to suffer all this injustice, nor can I permit it any longer: and though you commit no crime yourself, yet you believe in this dream, that I complain of the injuries you do my fame; and that I am extremely angry with a jealousy so prejudicial to my honour. Upon this belief you accuse me of weakness; you resolve to see me no more, and are making a thousand feeble vows against love. You esteem me as a false one, and resolve to cease loving the vain coquette, and will say to me, as a certain friend of yours said to his false mistress:

THE INCONSTANT

Though, Sylvia, you are very fair,
    Yet disagreeable to me ;
And since you so inconstant are,
    Your beauty's damned with levity.
Your wit, your most offensive arms,
For want of judgment, wants its charms.

To every lover that is new,
    All new and charming you surprise ;
But when your fickle mind they view,
    They shun the danger of your eyes.
Should you a miracle of beauty show,
Yet you're inconstant, and will still be so.

It is thus you will think of me : and in fine, Damon, during this dream, we are in perpetual state of war.

Thus both resolve to break their chain,
And think to do't without much pain,
But oh ! alas ! we strive in vain.

For lovers, of themselves, can nothing do ;
There must be the consent of two :
You give it me, and I must give it you.

And if we shall never be free, till we acquit one another, this tie between you and I, Damon, is likely to last as long as we live ; therefore in vain you endeavour, but can never attain your end ; and in conclusion you will say, in thinking of me :

Oh ! how at ease my heart would live,
Could I renounce this fugitive ;
This dear, but false, attracting maid
That has her vows and faith betrayed !
Reason would have it so, but love
Dares not the dang'rous trial prove.

Do not be angry then, for this afflicting hour is drawing to an end, and you ought not to despair of coming into my absolute favour again :

> Then do not let your murm'ring heart,
> Against my int'rest, take your part.
> The feud was raised by dreams, all false and vain,
> And the next sleep shall reconcile again.

SIX O'CLOCK

ACCOMMODATION IN DREAMS

Though the angry lovers force themselves, all they can, to chase away the troublesome tenderness of the heart, in the height of their quarrels, love sees all their sufferings, pities and redresses them. And when we begin to cool, and a soft repentance follows the chagrin of the love-quarrel, it is then that love takes the advantage of both hearts, and renews the charming friendship more forcibly than ever, puts a stop to all our feuds, and renders the peace-making minutes the most dear and tender part of our life. How pleasing it is to see your rage dissolve! How sweet, how soft is every word that pleads for pardon at my feet! It is there that you tell me, your very sufferings are overpaid, when I but assure you from my eyes, that I will forget your crime. And your imagination shall here present me the most sensible of your past pain, that you can wish; and that all my anger being banished, I give you a thousand marks of my faith and gratitude; and lastly, to crown all, that we again make new vows to one another of inviolable peace :

> After these debates of love,
> Lovers thousand pleasures prove,
> Which they ever think to taste,
> Though oftentimes they do not last.

Enjoy then all the pleasures that a heart that is very amorous, and very tender, can enjoy. Think no more on those inquietudes that you have suffered; bless Love for his favours, and thank me for my graces: and resolve to endure anything, rather than enter upon any new quarrels. And however dear the reconciling moments are, there proceeds a great deal of evil from these little frequent quarrels; and I think the best counsel we can follow, is to avoid them as near as we can. And if we cannot, but that, in spite of love and good understanding, they should break out, we ought to make as speedy peace as possible; for it is not good to grate the heart too long, lest it grow hardened insensibly, and lose its native temper. A few quarrels there must be in love: love cannot support itself without them: and, besides the joy of an accommodation, love becomes by it more strongly united, and more charming. Therefore let the lover receive this as a certain receipt against declining love:

LOVE RECONCILED

He that would have the passion be
    Entire between the am'rous pair,
Let not the little feuds of jealousy
    Be carried on to a despair:
That palls the pleasure he would raise;
The fire that he would blow, allays.

When understandings false arise,
    When misinterpreted your thought,
If false conjectures of your smiles and eyes
    Be up to baneful quarrels wrought;
Let love the kind occasion take,
And straight accommodations make.

The sullen lover, long unkind,
    Ill-natured, hard to reconcile,
Loses the heart he had inclined;
    Love cannot undergo long toil;
He's soft and sweet, not born to bear
The rough fatigues of painful war.

SEVEN O'CLOCK

DIVERS DREAMS

Behold, Damon, the last hour of your sleep, and of my watch. She leaves you at liberty now, and you may choose your dreams : trust them to your imagination, give a loose to fancy, and let it rove at will, provided, Damon, it be always guided by a respectful love. For thus far I pretend to give bounds to your imagination, and will not have it pass beyond them. Take heed, in sleeping, you give no ear to a flattering cupid, that will favour your slumbering minutes with lies too pleasing and vain : you are discreet enough when you are awake ; will you not be so in dreams?

Damon, awake ; my watch's course is done : after this, you cannot be ignorant of what you ought to do during my absence. I did not believe it necessary to caution you about balls and comedies ; you know, a lover deprived of his mistress, goes seldom there. But if you cannot handsomely avoid these diversions, I am not so unjust a mistress, to be angry with you for it, go, if civility, or other duties oblige you. I will only forbid you, in consideration of me, not to be too much satisfied with those pleasures ; but see them so, as the world may have reason to say, you do not seek them, you do not make a business or pleasure of them ; and that it is complaisance, and not inclination, that carries you thither. Seem rather negligent than concerned at anything there ; and let every part of you say, Iris is not here.

I say nothing to you neither of your duty elsewhere ; I am satisfied you know it too well ; and have too great a veneration for your glorious master, to neglect any part of that for even love itself. And I very well know how much you love to be eternally near his illustrious person ; and that you scarce prefer your mistress before him, in point of love : in all things else, I give him leave to take place of Iris in the noble heart of Damon.

I am satisfied you pass your time well now at Windsor, for you adore that place; and it is not, indeed, without great reason; for it is most certainly now rendered the most glorious palace in the Christian world. And had our late gracious sovereign, of blessed memory, had no other miracles and wonders of his life and reign to have immortalised his fame (of which there shall remain a thousand to posterity) this noble structure alone, this building (almost divine) would have eternised the great name of glorious Charles II. till the world moulder again to its old confusion, its first chaos. And the painting of the famous Varrio, and noble carvings of the inimitable Gibbon, shall never die, but remain to tell succeeding ages, that all arts and learning were not confined to ancient Rome and Greece, but that England, too, could boast its mightiest share. Nor is the inside of this magnificent structure, immortalised with so many eternal images of the illustrious Charles and Catharine, more to be admired than the wondrous prospects without. The stupendous height, on which the famous pile is built, renders the fields, and flowery meadows below, the woods, the thickets, and the winding streams, the most delightful object that ever nature produced. Beyond all these, and far below, in an inviting vale, the venerable college, an old, but noble building, raises itself, in the midst of all the beauties of nature, high-grown trees, fruitful plains, purling rivulets, and spacious gardens, adorned with all variety of sweets that can delight the senses.

At farther distance yet, on an ascent almost as high as that to the royal structure, you may behold the famous and noble Clifdon rise, a palace erected by the illustrious Duke of Buckingham, who will leave this wondrous piece of architecture, to inform the future world of the greatness and delicacy of his mind; it being for its situation, its prospects, and its marvellous contrivances, one of the finest villas of the world; at least, were it finished as begun; and would sufficiently declare the magnificent soul of the hero that caused it to be built, and contrived all its fineness. And this makes up not the least part of the beautiful prospect from the Palace Royal, while on the other side lies spread a fruitful and delightful park and forest well stored with deer, and all that makes the prospect charming; fine walks, groves, distant valleys, downs, and hills, and all that nature could invent, to furnish out a quiet soft retreat for the most fair and most charming of queens, and the most heroic, good, and just of kings. And these groves alone are fit and worthy to divert such earthly gods.

Nor can heaven, nature, or human art contrive an addition to this earthly paradise, unless those great inventors of the age, Sir Samuel Moreland, or Sir Robert Gordon, could by the power of engines, convey the water so into the park and Castle, as to furnish it with delightful fountains, both useful and beautiful. These are only wanting, to render the place all perfection, and without exception.

This, Damon, is a long digression from the business of my heart; but, you know I am so in love with that charming Court, that when you gave me an occasion, by your being there now, only to name the place, I could not forbear transgressing a little, in favour of its wondrous beauty; and the rather, because I would, in recounting it, give you to understand how many fine objects there are, besides the ladies that adorn it, to employ your vacant moments in; and I hope you will, without my instructions, pass a great part of your idle time in surveying these prospects, and give that admiration you should pay to living beauty, to those more venerable monuments of everlasting fame.

Neither need I, Damon, assign you your waiting times: your honour, duty, love, and obedience, will instruct you when to be near the person of the King; and, I believe, you will omit no part of that devoir.

You ought to establish your fortune and your glory: for I am not of the mind of those critical lovers, who believe it a very hard matter to reconcile love and interest, to adore a mistress, and serve a master at the same time. And I have heard those, who on this subject, say, 'Let a man be never so careful in these double duties, it is ten to one but he loses his fortune or his mistress.' These are errors that I condemn: and I know that love and ambition are not incompatible, but that a brave man may preserve all his duties to his sovereign, and his passion and his respect for his mistress. And this is my notion of it:

LOVE AND AMBITION

The nobler lover, who would prove
    Uncommon in address,
Let him Ambition join with Love;
    With Glory, Tenderness:
But let the virtues so be mixt,
    That when to Love he goes,
Ambition may not come betwixt,
    Nor Love his power oppose.
The vacant hours from softer sport,
Let him give up to interest and the court.

'Tis Honour shall his business be,
    And Love his noblest play:
Those two should never disagree,
    For both make either gay.
Love without Honour were too mean
    For any gallant heart;
And Honour singly, but a dream,
    Where Love must have no part.
A flame like this you cannot fear,
Where Glory claims an equal share.

Such a passion, Damon, can never make you quit any part of your duty to your Prince. And the monarch you serve is so gallant a master, that the inclination you have to his person obliges you to serve him, as much as your duty; for Damon's loyal soul loves the man, and adores the monarch: for he is certainly all that compels both, by a charming force and goodness, from all mankind.

THE KING

Darling of Mars ! Bellona's care !
The second deity of war !
Delight of heaven, and joy of earth !
Born for great and wondrous things,
Destined at his auspicious birth
T' outdo the numerous race of long-past kings.

Best representative of heaven,
To whom its chiefest attributes are given !
Great, pious, steadfast, just, and brave !
To vengeance slow, but swift to save !
Dispensing mercy all abroad !
Soft and forgiving as a god !

Thou saving angel who preserv'st the land
From the just rage of the avenging hand ;
Stopt the dire plague, that o'er the earth was hurled,
And sheathing thy almighty sword,
Calmed the wild fears of a distracted world,
(As heaven first made it) with a sacred word !

But I will stop the low flight of my humble Muse, who when she is upon the wing, on this glorious subject, knows no bounds. And all the world has agreed to say so much of the virtues and wonders of this great monarch, that they have left me nothing new to say; though indeed he every day gives us new themes of his growing greatness, and we see nothing that equals him in our age. Oh ! how happy are we to obey his laws ; for he is the greatest of kings, and the best of men.

You will be very unjust, Damon, if you do not confess I have acquitted myself like a maid of honour, of all the obligations I owe you, upon the account of the discretion I lost to you. If it be not valuable enough, I am generous enough to make it good : and since I am so willing to be just, you ought to esteem me, and to make it your chiefest care to preserve me yours; for I believe I shall deserve it, and wish you should believe so too.   Remember me, write to me, and observe punctually all the motions of my watch: the more you regard it, the better you will like it; and whatever you think of it at first sight, it is no ill present.   The invention is soft and gallant; and Germany, so celebrated for rare watches, can produce nothing to equal this.

> Damon, my watch is just and new;
> And all a lover ought to do,
> My cupid faithfully will show.
> And ev'ry hour he renders there,
> Except *l'heure du Bergère.*

THE CASE
FOR THE WATCH

DAMON TO IRIS

Expect not, O charming Iris! that I should choose words to thank you in; (words, that least part of love, and least the business of the lover) but will say all, and everything that a tender heart can dictate, to make an acknowledgment for so dear and precious a present as this of your charming watch: while all I can say will but too dully express my sense of gratitude, my joy, and the pleasure I receive in the mighty favour. I confess the present too rich, too gay, and too magnificent for my expectation: and though my love and faith deserve it, yet my humbler hope never durst carry me to a wish of so great a bliss, so great an acknowledgment from the maid I adore. The materials are glorious, the work delicate, and the movement just, and even gives rules to my heart, who shall observe very exactly all that the cupid remarks to me; even to the minutes, which I will point with sighs, though I am obliged to them there but every half hour.

You tell me, fair Iris, that I ought to preserve it tenderly, and yet you have sent it me without a case. But that I may obey you justly, and keep it dear to me, as long as I live, I will give it a case of my fashion: it shall be delicate, and suitable to the fine present, of such materials too. But because I would have it perfect, I will consult your admirable wit and invention in an affair of so curious a consequence.

THE FIGURE OF THE CASE

I design to give it the figure of the heart. Does not your watch, Iris, rule the heart? It was your heart that contrived it, and it was your heart you consulted in all the management of it; and it was your heart that brought it to so fine a conclusion. The heart never acts without reason, and all the heart projects, it performs with pleasure.

Your watch, my lovely maid, has explained to me a world of rich secrets of love: and where should thoughts so sacred be stored, but in the heart, where all the secrets of the soul are treasured up, and of which only Love alone can take a view? It is thence he take his sighs and tears, and all his little flatteries and arts to please; all his fine thoughts, and all his mighty raptures; nothing is so proper as the heart to preserve it, nothing so worthy as the heart to contain it; and it concerns my interest too much, not to be infinitely careful of so dear a treasure. And believe me, charming Iris, I will never part with it.

THE VOTARY

Fair goddess of my just desire,
Inspirer of my softest fire !
Since you, from out the num'rous throng
That to your altars do belong,
To me the sacred myst'ry have revealed,
From all my rival-worshippers concealed ;
And taught my soul with heav'nly fire,
Refined it from its grosser sense,
And wrought it to a higher excellence ;
It can no more return to earth,
Like things that thence receive their birth :
But still aspiring, upward move,
And teach the world new flights of love ;
New arts of secrecy shall learn,
And render youth discreet in love's concern.

> In his soft heart, to hide the charming things
>   A mistress whispers to his ear ;
>   And ev'ry tender sigh she brings,
>   Mix with his soul, and hide it there.
> To bear himself so well in company,
>   That if his mistress present be,
>   It may be thought by all the fair,
>   Each in his heart does claim a share,
>   And all are more beloved than she.
> But when with the dear maid apart,
>   Then at her feet the lover lies ;
> Opens his soul, shows all his heart,
>   While joy is dancing in his eyes.
> Then all that honour may, or take, or give,
>   They both distribute, both receive.
> A looker-on would spoil a lover's joy ;
> For love's a game where only two can play.
>   And 'tis the hardest of love's mysteries,
> To feign love where it is not, hide it where it is.

After having told you, my lovely Iris, that I design to put your watch into a heart, I ought to show you the ornaments of the case.   I do intend to have them crowned ciphers : I do not mean those crowns of vanity, which are put indifferently on all sorts of ciphers ; no, I must have such as may distinguish mine from the rest, and may be true emblems of what I would represent.   My four ciphers therefore shall be crowned with these four wreaths of olive, laurel, myrtle, and roses : and the letters that begin the names of Iris and Damon shall compose the ciphers ; though I must intermix some other letters that bear another sense, and have another signification.

THE FIRST CIPHER

The first cipher is composed of an I and a D, which are joined by an L and an E ; which signifies Love Extreme.   And it is but just, O adorable Iris ! that love should be mixed with our ciphers, and that love alone should be the union of them.

T

Love ought alone the mystic knot to tie ;
Love, that great master of all arts :
And this dear cipher is to let you see,
Love unites names as well as hearts.

Without this charming union, our souls could not communicate those invisible sweetnesses, which complete the felicity of lovers, and which the most tender and passionate expressions are too feeble to make us comprehend. But, my adorable Iris, I am contented with the vast pleasure I feel in loving well, without the care of expressing it well; if you will imagine my pleasure, without expressing it. For I confess, it would be no joy to me to adore you, if you did not perfectly believe I did adore you. Nay, though you loved me, if you had no faith in me, I should languish and love in as much pain, as if you scorned ; and at the same time believe I died for you. For surely, Iris, it is a greater pleasure to please than to be pleased ; and the glorious power of giving, is infinitely a greater satisfaction, than that of receiving : there is so great and god-like a quality in it. I would have your belief therefore equal to my passion, extreme ; as indeed all love should be, or it cannot bear that divine name : it can pass but for an indifferent affection. And these ciphers ought to make the world find all the noble force of delicate passion : for, O my Iris! what would love signify, if we did not love fervently? Sisters and brothers love; friends and relations have affections : but where the souls are joined, which are filled with eternal soft wishes, oh! there is some excess of pleasure, which cannot be expressed!

Your looks, your dear obliging words, and your charming letters, have sufficiently persuaded me of your tenderness; and you might surely see the excess of my passion by my cares, my sighs, and entire resignation to your will. I never think of Iris, but my heart feels double flames, and pants and heaves with double sighs ; and whose force makes its ardours known, by a thousand transports. And they are very much to blame, to give the name of love to feeble easy passions. Such transitory tranquil inclinations are at best but well-wishers to love; and a heart that has such heats as those, ought not to put itself into the rank of those nobler victims that are offered at the shrine of Love. But our souls, Iris, burn with a more glorious flame, that lights and conducts us beyond a possibility of losing one another. It is this that flatters all my hopes; it is this alone makes me believe myself worthy of Iris: and let her judge of its violence, by the greatness of its splendour.

Does not a passion of this nature, so true, so ardent, deserve to be crowned? And will you wonder to see, over this cipher, a wreath of myrtles, those boughs so sacred to the Queen of Love, and so worshipped by lovers? It is with these soft wreaths, that those are crowned, who understand how to love well and faithfully.

> The smiles, the graces, and the sports,
> That in the secret groves maintain their courts,
>   Are with these myrtles crowned :
> Thither the nymphs their garlands bring ;
> Their beauties, and their praises sing,
>   While echoes do the songs resound.
>
> Love, though a god, with myrtle wreaths
>   Does his soft temples bind ;
> More valued are those consecrated leaves,
>   Than the bright wealth in Eastern rocks confined:
> And crowns of glory less ambition move,
> Than those more sacred diadems of love.

THE SECOND CIPHER

Is crowned with olives; and I add to the two letters of our names an R and L, for Reciprocal Love. Every time that I have given you, O lovely Iris, testimonies of my passion, I have been so blest, as to receive some from your bounty; and you have been pleased to flatter me with a belief, that I was not indifferent to you. I dare therefore say, that being honoured with the glory of your tenderness and care, I ought, as a trophy of my illustrious conquest, to adorn the watch with a cipher that is so advantageous to me. Ought I not to esteem myself the most fortunate and happy of mankind, to have exchanged my heart with so charming and admirable a person as Iris? Ah! how sweet, how precious is the change; and how vast a glory arrives to me from it! Oh! you must not wonder if my soul abandons itself to a thousand ecstasies! In the merchandise of hearts, oh, how dear it is to receive as much as one gives; and barter heart for heart! Oh! I would not receive mine again, for all the crowns the universe contains! Nor ought you, my adorable, make any vows or wishes, ever to retrieve yours; or show the least repentance for the blessing you have given me. The exchange we made, was confirmed by a noble faith; and you ought to believe, you have bestowed it well, since you are paid for it a heart that is so conformable to yours, so true, so just, and so full of adoration. And nothing can be the just recompense of love, but love: and to enjoy the true felicity of it, our hearts ought to keep an equal motion; and, like the scales of justice, always hang even.

It is the property of reciprocal love, to make the heart feel the delicacy of love, and to give the lover all the ease and softness he can reasonably hope. Such a love renders all things advantageous and prosperous: such a love triumphs over all other pleasures. And I put a crown of olives over the cipher of reciprocal love, to make known, that two hearts, where love is justly equal, enjoy a peace that nothing can disturb.

Olives are never fading seen ;
But always flourishing, and green.
　The emblem 'tis of Love and Peace ;
　For Love that's true, will never cease :
　And Peace does pleasure still increase.
Joy to the world, the peace of kings imparts ;
And peace in love distributes it to hearts.

THE THIRD CIPHER

The C and L, which are joined to the letters of our
names in this cipher crowned with laurel, explains a
Constant Love.   It will not, my fair Iris, suffice, that
my love is extreme, my passion violent, and my
wishes fervent, or that our loves are reciprocal ; but
they ought also to be constant : for in love, the
imagination is oftener carried to those things that may
arrive, and which we wish for, than to things that
time has robbed us of.   And in those agreeable
thoughts of joys to come, the heart takes more delight
to wander, than in all those that are past ; though
the remembrance of them be very dear, and very
charming.   We should be both unjust, if we were not
persuaded we are possessed with a virtue, the use of
which is so admirable as that of constancy.   Our
loves are not of that sort that can finish, or have an
end ; but such a passion, so perfect, and so constant,
that it will be a precedent for future ages, to love perfectly ; and when they would express an extreme
passion, they will say 'They loved, as Damon did the
charming Iris.'   And he that knows the glory of
constant love, will despise those fading passions,
those little amusements, that serve for a day.   What
pleasure or dependence can one have in a love of that
sort ?   What concern ?   What raptures can such an
amour produce in a soul ?   And what satisfaction can
one promise one's self in playing with a false
gamester ; who though you are aware of him, in spite
of all your precaution, puts the false dice upon you,
and wins all ?

Those eyes that can no better conquest make,
    Let them ne'er look abroad :
Such, but the empty name of lovers take,
    And so profane the god.
Better they never should pretend,
Than, ere begun, to make an end.

Of that fond flame what shall we say,
That's born and languished in a day ?
Such short-lived blessings cannot bring
The pleasure of an envying.
Who is't will celebrate that flame,
That's damned to such a scanty fame ?
While constant love the nymphs and swains
Still sacred make, in lasting strains
And cheerful lays throughout the plains.
A constant love knows no decay ;
But still advancing ev'ry day,
Will last as long as life can stay,
With ev'ry look and smile improves,
With the same ardour always moves,
With such as Damon charming Iris loves !

Constant love finds itself impossible to be shaken; it resists the attacks of envy, and a thousand accidents that endeavour to change it. Nothing can disoblige it but a known falseness, or contempt : nothing can remove it ; though for a short moment it may lie sullen and resenting, it recovers, and returns with greater force and joy. I therefore, with very good reason, crown this cipher of constant love with a wreath of laurel ; since such love always triumphs over time and fortune, though it be not her property to besiege : for she cannot overcome, but in defending herself ; but the victories she gains are nevertheless glorious.

For far less conquest, we have known
The victor wear the laurel crown.
The triumph with more pride let him receive ;
While those of love, at least, more pleasures give.

THE FOURTH CIPHER

Perhaps, my lovely maid, you will not find out
what I mean by the S and the L, in this last cipher,
that is crowned with roses. I will therefore tell you,
I mean Secret Love. There are very few people who
know the nature of that pleasure, which so divine a
love creates : and let me say what I will of it, they
must feel it themselves, who would rightly understand
it, and all its ravishing sweets. But this there is a
great deal of reason to believe, that the secrecy in
love doubles the pleasures of it. And I am so absolutely persuaded of this, that I believe all those
favours that are not kept secret, are dull and pallid,
very insipid and tasteless pleasures : and let the
favours be ever so innocent that a lover receives from
a mistress, she ought to value them, set a price upon
them, and make the lover pay dear ; while he receives
them with difficulty, and sometimes with hazard. A
lover that is not secret, but suffers every one to count
his sighs, has at most but a feeble passion, such as
produces sudden and transitory desires which die as
soon as born. A true love has not this character ; for
whensoever it is made public, it ceases to be a pleasure,
and is only the result of vanity. Not that I expect
our loves should always remain a secret. No, I should
never, at that rate, arrive to a blessing, which, above
all the glories of the earth, I aspire to ; but even then
there are a thousand joys, a thousand pleasures that
I shall be as careful to conceal from the foolish world,
as if the whole preservation of that pleasure depended
on my silence ; as indeed it does in a great measure.

To this cipher I put a crown of roses, which are
not flowers of a very lasting date. And it is to let
you see, that it is impossible love can be long hid.
We see every day, with what fine dissimulation and
pains, people conceal a thousand hates and malices,
disgusts, disobligations, and resentments, without

being able to conceal the least part of their love : but reputation has an odour as well as roses ; and a lover ought to esteem that as the dearest and tenderest thing : not only that of his own, which is, indeed, the least part ; but that of his mistress, more valuable to him than life. He ought to endeavour to give people no occasion to make false judgments of his actions, or to give their censures ; which most certainly are never in the favour of the fair person : for likely, those false censurers are of the busy female sex, the coquettes of that number ; whose little spites and railleries, joined to that fancied wit they boast of, set them at odds with all the beautiful and innocent. And how very little of that kind serves to give the world a faith, when a thousand virtues, told of the same persons, by more credible witnesses and judges, shall pass unregarded ! so willing and inclined is all the world to credit the ill, and condemn the good ! And yet, oh ! what pity it is we are compelled to live in pain, to oblige this foolish scandalous world ! And though we know each other's virtue and honour, we are obliged to observe that caution (to humour the talking town) which takes away so great a part of the pleasure of life.   It is therefore that among those roses, you will find some thorns ; by which you may imagine, that in love, precaution is necessary to its secrecy.   And we must restrain ourselves, upon a thousand occasions, with so much care, that, O Iris ! it is impossible to be discreet, without pain ; but it is a pain that creates a thousand pleasures.

> Where should a lover hide his joys,
> Free from malice, free from noise ;
>   Where no envy can intrude ;
>   Where no busy rival's spy,
>   Made, by disappointment, rude,
>   May inform his jealousy ?
> The heart will the best refuge prove ;
> Which nature meant the cabinet of love.
> What would a lover not endure,
> His mistress' fame and honour to secure ?

Iris, the care we take to be discreet,
Is the dear toil that makes the pleasure sweet :
The thorn that does the wealth inclose,
That with less saucy freedom we may touch the rose.

THE CLASP OF THE WATCH

Ah, charming Iris! Ah, my lovely maid! it is now, in a more peculiar manner, that I require your aid in the finishing of my design, and completing the whole piece to the utmost perfection ; and without your aid it cannot be performed. It is about the clasp of the watch ; a material in all appearance, the most trivial of any part of it. But that it may be safe for ever, I design it the image, or figure of two hands ; that fair one of the adorable Iris, joined to mine; with this motto, "Inviolable Faith." For in this case, this heart ought to be shut up by this eternal clasp. Oh! there is nothing so necessary as this! Nothing can secure love, but faith.

That virtue ought to be a guard to all the heart thinks, and all the mouth utters : nor can love say he triumphs without it. And when that remains not in the heart, all the rest deserves no regard. Oh! I have not loved so ill to leave one doubt upon your soul. Why then, will you want that faith, O unkind charmer, that my passion and my services so justly merit ?

When two hearts entirely love,
And in one sphere of honour move,
Each maintains the other's fire,
With a faith that is entire.
For, what heedless youth bestows,
On a faithless maid, his vows?
Faith without love, bears Virtue's price ;
But love without her mixture, is a vice.
Love, like religion, still should be,
In the foundation firm and true ;
In points of faith should still agree,
Though innovations vain and new,
Love's little quarrels, may arise ;
In foundations still they're just and wise.

> Then, charming maid, be sure of this ;
>   Allow me faith, as well as love :
> Since that alone affords no bliss,
>   Unless your faith your love improve.
> Either resolve to let me die
> By fairer play, your cruelty ;
> Than not your love with faith impart,
> And with your vows to give your heart.
> In mad despair I'd rather fall,
> Than lose my glorious hopes of conquering all.

So certain it is, that love without faith, is of no value.

In fine, my adorable Iris, this case shall be, as near as I can, like those delicate ones of filigrain work, which do not hinder the sight from taking a view of all within : you may therefore see, through this heart, all your watch. Nor is my desire of preserving this inestimable piece more, than to make it the whole rule of my life and actions. And my chiefest design in these ciphers, is to comprehend in them the principal virtues that are most necessary to love. Do not we know that reciprocal love is justice? Constant love, fortitude? Secret love, prudence? Though it is true that extreme love, that is, excess of love, in one sense, appears not to be temperance ; yet you must know, my Iris, that in matters of love, excess is a virtue, and that all other degrees of love are worthy scorn alone. It is this alone that can make good the glorious title : it is this alone that can bear the name of love ; and this alone that renders the lovers truly happy, in spite of all the storms of fate, and shocks of fortune. This is an antidote against all other griefs : this bears up the soul in all calamity ; and is the very heaven of life, the last refuge of all worldly pain and care, and may well bear the title of divine.

THE ART OF LOVING WELL

That Love may all perfection be,
Sweet, charming to the last degree,
The heart, where the bright flames do dwell,
In faith and softness should excel :
Excess of love should fill each vein,
And all its sacred rites maintain.

The tend'rest thoughts heav'n can inspire,
Should be the fuel to its fire :
And that, like incense, burn as pure ;
Or that in urns should still endure.
No fond desire should fill the soul,
But such as honour may control.

Jealousy I will allow :
Not the amorous winds that blow,
Should wanton in my Iris' hair,
Or ravish kisses from my fair.
Not the flowers that grow beneath,
Should borrow sweetness of her breath.

If her bird she do caress,
How I grudge its happiness,
When upon her snowy hand
The wanton does triumphing stand !
Or upon her breast she skips,
And lays her beak to Iris' lips !
Fainting at my ravished joy,
I could the innocent destroy.

If I can no bliss afford
To a little harmless bird,
Tell me, O thou dear-loved maid !
What reason could my rage persuade,
If a rival should invade ?

If thy charming eyes should dart
Looks that sally from the heart ;
If you sent a smile, or glance,
To another though by chance ;
Still thou giv'st what's not thy own,
They belong to me alone.

All submission I would pay :
Man was born the fair t' obey.
Your very look I'd understand,
And thence receive your least command :
Never your justice will dispute ;
But like a lover execute.

I would no usurper be,
But in claiming sacred thee.
I would have all, and every part ;
No thought would hide within thy heart.
Mine a cabinet was made,
Where Iris' secrets should be laid.

In the rest, without control,
She should triumph o'er the soul !
Prostrate at her feet I'd lie,
Despising power and liberty ;
Glorying more by love to fall,
Than rule the universal ball.

Hear me, O you saucy youth !
And from my maxims learn this truth :
Would you great and powerful prove ?
Be a humble slave to love.
'Tis nobler far a joy to give,
Than any blessing to receive.

THE LADY'S LOOKING-GLASS
TO DRESS HERSELF BY

OR THE ART OF CHARMING

HOW long, O charming Iris! shall I speak in vain
of your adorable beauty? You have been just, and
believe I love you with a passion perfectly tender and
extreme, and yet you will not allow your charms to
be infinite. You must either accuse my flames to be
unreasonable, and that my eyes and heart are false
judges of wit and beauty; or allow that you are the
most perfect of your sex. But instead of that, you
always accuse me of flattery, when I speak of your
infinite merit; and when I refer you to your glass,
you tell me, that flatters as well as Damon: though
one would imagine, that should be a good witness for
the truth of what I say, and undeceive you of the
opinion of my injustice. Look —— and confirm yourself, that nothing can equal your perfections. All the
world says it, and you must doubt it no longer. O,
Iris! will you dispute against the whole world?

But since you have so long distrusted your own
glass, I have here presented you with one, which
I know is very true; and having been made for you
only, can serve only you. All other glasses present
all objects, but this reflects only Iris: whenever you
consult it, it will convince you; and tell you how
much right I have done you, when I told you, you
were the fairest person that ever nature made. When

other beauties look into it, it will speak to all the fair ones : but let them do what they will, it will say nothing to their advantage.

Iris, to spare what you call flattery,
   Consult your glass each hour of the day :
'Twill tell you where your charms and beauties lie,
   And where your little wanton graces play :
Where love does revel in your face and eyes ;
What look invites your slaves, and what denies.

Where all the loves adorn you with such care,
   Where dress your smiles, where arm your lovely eyes ;
Where deck the flowing tresses of your hair :
   How cause your snowy breasts to fall and rise.
How this severe glance makes a lover die ;
How that, more soft, gives immortality.

Where you shall see what 'tis enslaves the soul ;
   Where ev'ry feature, ev'ry look combines :
When the adorning air, o'er all the whole,
   To so much wit, and so nice virtue joins.
Where the *belle taille*, and motion still afford
Graces to be eternally adored.

But I will be silent now, and let your glass speak.

THE LADY'S LOOKING-GLASS

Damon (O charming Iris !) has given me to you, that you may sometimes give yourself the trouble, and me the honour of consulting me in the great and weighty affairs of beauty. I am, my adorable mistress ! a faithful glass; and you ought to believe all I say to you.

THE SHAPE OF IRIS

I must begin with your shape, and tell you without flattery, it is the finest in the world, and gives love and admiration to all that see you. Pray observe how free and easy it is, without constraint, stiffness, or affectation : those mistaken graces of the fantastic, and the formal, who give themselves pain to show their will to please, and whose dressing makes the greatest part of their fineness, when they are more obliged to the tailor than to nature; who add or diminish, as occasion serves, to form a grace, where heaven never gave it. And while they remain on this wreck of pride, they are eternally uneasy, without pleasing anybody. Iris, I have seen a woman of your acquaintance, who, having a greater opinion of her own person than anybody else, has screwed her body into so fine a form (as she calls it) that she dares no more stir a hand, lift up an arm, or turn her head aside, than if, for the sin of such a disorder, she were to be turned into a pillar of salt; the less stiff and fixed statue of the two. Nay, she dares not speak or smile, lest she should put her face out of that order she had set it in her glass, when she last looked on herself: and is all over such a Lady Nice (excepting in her conversation) that ever made a ridiculous figure. And there are many ladies more, but too much tainted with that nauseous formality, that old-fashioned vice. But Iris, the charming, the all-perfect Iris, has nothing in her whole form that is not free, natural and easy; and whose every motion cannot but please extremely; and which has not given Damon a thousand rivals.

> Damon, the young, the am'rous, and the true,
> Who sighs incessantly for you ;
> Whose whole delight, now you are gone,
> Is to retire to shades alone,
> And to the echoes make his moan.
> By purling streams the wishing youth is laid,
> Still sighing Iris ! lovely charming maid !
> See, in thy absence, how thy lover dies !
> While to his sighs the echo still replies.
>
> Then with a stream he holds discourse :
> O thou that bend'st thy liquid force
> To lovely Thames ! upon whose shore
> The maid resides whom I adore !
> My tears of love upon thy surface bear :
> And if upon thy banks thou seest my fair :
> In all thy softest murmurs sing,
> From Damon I this present bring ;

My ev'ry curl contains a tear !
Then at her feet thy tribute pay :
But haste, O happy stream ! away ;
Lest charmed too much, thou shouldst for ever stay.
And thou, O gentle, murm'ring breeze !
That plays in air, and wantons with the trees ;
On thy young wings, where gilded sunbeams play,
To Iris my soft sighs convey,
Still as they rise, each minute of the day :
But whisper gently in her ear ;
Let not the ruder winds thy message hear,
Nor ruffle one dear curl of her bright hair.
Oh ! touch her cheeks with sacred reverence,
   And stay not gazing on her lovely eyes !
But if thou bear'st her rosy breath from thence,
'Tis incense of that excellence,
   That as thou mount'st, 'twill perfume all the skies.

IRIS'S COMPLEXION

Say what you will, I am confident, if you will confess your heart, you are, every time you view yourself in me, surprised at the beauty of your complexion ; and will secretly own, you never saw anything so fair. I am not the first glass, by a thousand, that has assured you of this. If you will not believe me, ask Damon ; he tells it you every day, but that truth from him offends you : and because he loves too much, you think his judgment too little ; and since this is so perfect, that must be defective. But it is most certain your complexion is infinitely fine, your skin soft and smooth as polished wax, or ivory, extremely white and clear; though if anybody speaks but of your beauty, an agreeable blush casts itself all over your face, and gives you a thousand new graces.

And then two flowers newly born,
   Shine in your heav'nly face ;
The rose that blushes in the morn,
   Usurps the lily's place :
Sometimes the lily does prevail,
And makes the gen'rous crimson pale.

IRIS'S HAIR

Oh, the beautiful hair of Iris! it seems as if nature had crowned you with a great quantity of lovely fair brown hair, to make us know that you were born to rule, and to repair the faults of fortune that has not given you a diadem. And do not bewail the want of that (so much your merit's due) since heaven has so gloriously recompensed you with what gains more admiring slaves.

> Heav'n for sovereignty has made your form :
> And you were more than for dull empire born ;
> O'er hearts your kingdom shall extend,
> Your vast dominion know no end.
> Thither the Loves and Graces shall resort ;
> To Iris make their homage, and their court.
> No envious star, no common fate,
> Did on my Iris' birthday wait ;
> But all was happy, all was delicate.
> Here fortune would inconstant be in vain :
> Iris, and love, eternally shall reign.

Love does not make less use of your hair for new conquests, than of all the rest of your beauties that adorn you. If he takes our hearts with your fine eyes, it ties them fast with your hair; and if it weaves a chain, it is not easily broken. It is not of those sorts of hair, whose harshness discovers ill-nature ; nor of those whose softness shows us the weakness of the mind ; not that either of these arguments are without exception. But it is such as bears the character of a perfect mind, and a delicate wit ; and for its colour, the most faithful, discreet, and beautiful in the world ; such as shows a complexion and constitution, neither so cold to be insensible, nor so hot to have too much fire : that is, neither too white, nor too black ; but such a mixture of the two colours, as makes it the most agreeable in the world.

U

'Tis that which leads those captivated hearts,
　That bleeding at your feet do lie ;
'Tis that the obstinate converts,
　That dare the power of love deny :
'Tis that which Damon so admires ;
Damon, who often tells you so.
If from your eyes Love takes his fires,
　'Tis with your hair he strings his bow :
Which touching but the feathered dart,
It never missed the destined heart.

IRIS'S EYES

I believe, my fair mistress, I shall dazzle you with
the lustre of your own eyes. They are the finest blue
in the world : they have all the sweetness that ever
charmed the heart, with a certain languishment that's
irresistible ; and never any looked on them, that did
not sigh after them.   Believe me, Iris, they carry unavoidable darts and fires ; and whoever expose themselves to their dangers, pay for their imprudence.

Cold as my solid crystal is,
　Hard and impenetrable too ;
Yet I am sensible of bliss,
　When your charming eyes I view·
Even by me their flames are felt ; .
And at each glance I fear to melt.

Ah, how pleasant are my days !
　How my glorious fate I bless !
Mortals never knew my joys,
　Nor monarch guessed my happiness.
Every look that's soft and gay,
Iris gives me every day.

Spite of her virtue and her pride,
　Every morning I am blest
With what to Damon is denied ;
　To view her when she is undrest.
All her heaven of beauty's shown
To triumphing me—alone.

songs, that the Graces themselves have not more than
Iris.   And one may truly say, that you alone know
how to join the ornaments and dress with beauty;
and you are still adorned, as if that shape and air
had a peculiar art to make all things appear gay and
fine.   Oh! how well dressed you are!   How everything becomes you!   Never singular, never gaudy;
but always suiting with your quality.

> Oh ! how that negligence becomes your air !
> That careless flowing of your hair,
> That plays about with wanton grace,
> With evrey motion of your face :
> Disdaining all that dull formality,
> That dares not move the lip, or eye,
> But at some fancied grace's cost ;
> And think, with it, at least, a lover lost.
> But the unlucky minute to reclaim,
> And ease the coquette of her pain,
> The pocket-glass adjusts the face again :
> Resets the mouth, and languishes the eyes ;
> And thinks, the spark that ogles that way—dies.
>
> Of Iris learn, O ye mistaken fair !
> To dress your face, your smiles, your air :
> Let easy nature all the business do,
> She can the softer graces show ;
> Which art but turns to ridicule,
> And where there's none serves but to show the fool.
>
> In Iris you all graces find ;
> Charms without art, a motion unconfined ;
> Without constraint, she smiles, she looks, she talks ;
> And without affectation, moves and walks.
> Beauties so perfect ne'er were seen :
> O ye mistaken fair !   Dress ye by Iris' mien.

THE DISCRETION OF IRIS

But, O Iris ! the beauties of the body are imperfect,
if the beauties of the soul do not advance themselves
to an equal height.   But, O Iris ! what mortal is
there so damned to malice, that does not, with adoration, confess, that you, O charming maid, have an

that are not your adorers. Damon therefore is excusable, if he be not contented with your noble friendship alone ; for he is the most tender of that number.

> No ! give me all, th' impatient lover cries ;
>   Without your soul I cannot live :
> Dull friendship cannot mine suffice,
>   That dies for all you have to give.
> The smiles, the vows, the heart must all be mine ;
> I cannot spare one thought, or wish of thine.
>
> I sigh, I languish all the day ;
>   Each minute ushers in my groans :
> To ev'ry god in vain I pray ;
>   In ev'ry grove repeat my moans.
> Still Iris' charms are all my sorrows' themes !
> They pain me waking, and they rack in dreams.
>
> Return, fair Iris ! Oh, return !
>   Lest sighing long your slave destroys.
> I wish, I rave, I faint, I burn ;
>   Restore me quickly all my joys :
> Your mercy else will come too late ;
> Distance in love more cruel is than hate.

THE WIT OF IRIS

You are deceived in me, fair Iris, if you take me for one of those ordinary glasses, that represent the beauty only of the body ; I remark to you also the beauties of the soul. And all about you declares yours the finest that ever was formed ; that you have a wit that surprises, and is always new. It is none of those that loses its lustre when one considers it ; the more we examine yours, the more adorable we find it. You say nothing that is not at once agreeable and solid ; it is always quick and ready, without impertinence, that little vanity of the fair : who, when they know they have wit, rarely manage it so, as not to abound in talking ; and think, that all they say must please, because luckily they sometimes chance to do so. But Iris never speaks, but it is of use ; and gives a pleasure to all that hear her. She has the perfect air of penetrating, even the most secret thoughts. How often have you known, without being told, all that has passed in Damon's heart! For all great wits are prophets too.

Tell me ; oh, tell me ! charming prophetess ;
For you alone can tell my love's success.
   The lines in my dejected face,
I fear, will lead you to no kind result :
   It is your own that you must trace ;
Those of your heart you must consult.
   'Tis there my fortune I must learn,
   And all that Damon does concern.

I tell you that I love a maid,
   As bright as heav'n, of angel-hue ;
The softest nature ever made,
   Whom I with sighs and vows pursue.
Oh, tell me, charming prophetess !
Shall I this lovely maid possess ?

A thousand rivals do obstruct my way ;
   A thousand fears they do create :
They throng about her all the day,
   Whilst I at awful distance wait.
Say, will the lovely maid so fickle prove,
To give my rivals hope, as well as love ?

She has a thousand charms of wit,
   With all the beauty heav'n e'er gave :
Oh ! let her not make use of it,
   To flatter me into the slave.
Oh ! tell me truth, to ease my pain ;
Say rather, I shall die by her disdain.

THE MODESTY OF IRIS

I perceive, fair Iris, you have a mind to tell me, I have entertained you too long with a discourse on yourself. I know your modesty makes this declaration an offence, and you suffer me, with pain, to unveil those treasures you would hide. Your modesty, that so commendable a virtue in the fair, and so peculiar to you, is here a little too severe. Did I flatter you, you should blush : did I seek, by praising you, to show an art of speaking finely, you might chide. But, O Iris, I say nothing but such plain truths, as all the world can witness are so : and so far I am from flattery, that I seek no ornament of words. Why do you take such care to conceal your virtues? They have too much lustre, not to be seen, in spite of all your modesty : your wit, your youth, and reason, oppose themselves against this dull obstructer of our happiness. Abate, O Iris, a little of this virtue, since you have so many others to defend yourself against the attacks of your adorers. You yourself have the least opinion of your own charms : and being the only person in the world, that is not in love with them, you hate to pass whole hours before your looking-glass; and to pass your time, like most of the idle fair, in dressing, and setting off those beauties, which need so little art. You, more wise, disdain to give those hours to the fatigue of dressing, which you know so well how to employ a thousand ways. The Muses have blessed you, above your sex ; and you know how to gain a conquest with your pen, more absolutely than all the industrious fair, who trust to dress and equipage.

I have a thousand things to tell you more, but willingly resign my place to Damon, that faithful lover; he will speak more ardently than I : for let a glass use all its force, yet, when it speaks its best, it speaks but coldly.

If my glass, O charming Iris, have the good fortune (which I could never entirely boast) to be believed, it will serve at least to convince you I have not been so guilty of flattery, as I have a thousand times been charged. Since then my passion is equal to your beauty (without comparison, or end), believe, O lovely maid! how I sigh in your absence ; and be persuaded to lessen my pain, and restore me to my joys; for there is no torment so great, as the absence of a lover from his mistress; of which this is the idea.

THE EFFECTS OF ABSENCE FROM WHAT WE LOVE

Thou one continued sigh ! all over pain !
Eternal wish ! but wish, alas, in vain !
Thou languishing, impatient hoper on ;
A busy toiler, and yet still undone !
A breaking glimpse of distant day,
Enticing on, and leading more astray !
Thou joy in prospect, future bliss extreme ;
Never to be possessed, but in a dream !
Thou fab'lous goddess, which the ravished boy
In happy slumbers proudly did enjoy ;
But waking, found an airy cloud he prest ;
His arms came empty to his panting breast.
Thou shade, that only haunt'st the soul by night ;
And when thou shouldst in form thou fly'st the sight :
Thou false idea of the thinking brain,
That labours for the charming form in vain :
Which if by chance it catch, thou'rt lost again.

THE LUCKY MISTAKE

A NEW NOVEL

THE river Loire has on its delightful banks abundance of handsome, beautiful, and rich towns and villages, to which the noble stream adds no small graces and advantages, blessing their fields with plenty, and their eyes with a thousand diversions. In one of these happily situated towns, called Orleans, where abundance of people of the best quality and condition reside, there was a rich nobleman, now retired from the busy Court, where in his youth he had been bred, wearied with the toils of ceremony and noise, to enjoy that perfect tranquillity of life, which is nowhere to be found but in retreat, a faithful friend, and a good library ; and, as the admirable Horace says, in a little house and a large garden. Count Bellyaurd, for so was this nobleman called, was of this opinion ; and the rather, because he had one only son, called Rinaldo, now grown to the age of fifteen, who having all the excellent qualities and graces of youth by nature, he would bring him up in all virtues and noble sciences, which he believed the gaiety and lustre of the Court might divert. He therefore in his retirement spared no cost to those that could instruct and accomplish him ; and he had the best tutors and masters that could be purchased at Court : Bellyaurd making far less account of riches than of fine parts. He found his son capable of all impressions, having a wit suitable to his delicate person, so that he was the sole joy of his life, and the darling of his eyes.

In the very next house, which joined close to that of Bellyaurd's, there lived another Count, who had in his youth been banished the Court of France for some misunderstandings in some high affairs wherein he was concerned. His name was De Pais, a man of great birth, but of no fortune; or at least one not suitable to the grandeur of his origin. And as it is most natural for great souls to be most proud (if I may call a handsome disdain by that vulgar name) when they are most depressed; so De Pais was more retired, more estranged from his neighbours, and kept a greater distance, than if he had enjoyed all he had lost at Court; and took more solemnity and state upon him, because he would not be subject to the reproaches of the world, by making himself familiar with it. So that he rarely visited; and, contrary to the custom of those in France, who are easy of access, and free of conversation, he kept his family retired so close, that it was rare to see any of them; and when they went abroad, which was but seldom, they wanted nothing as to outward appearance, that was fit for his quality, and what was much above his condition.

This old Count had two only daughters, of exceeding beauty, who gave the generous father ten thousand torments, as often as he beheld them, when he considered their extreme beauty, their fine wit, their innocence, modesty, and above all their birth; and that he had not a fortune to marry them according to their quality; and below it, he had rather see them laid in their silent graves, than consent to it: for he scorned the world should see him forced by his poverty to commit an action below his dignity.

There lived in a neighbouring town, a certain nobleman, friend to De Pais, called Count Vernole, a man of about forty years of age, of low stature, complexion very black and swarthy, lean, lame, ex-

tremely proud and haughty ; extracted of a descent
from the blood-royal; not extremely brave, but very
glorious : he had no very great estate, but was in
election of a greater, and of an addition of honour
from the King, his father having done most worthy
services against the Huguenots, and by the high favour
of Cardinal Mazarin, was represented to his Majesty,
as a man related to the Crown, of great name, but
small estate : so that there were now nothing but
great expectations and preparations in the family of
Count Vernole to go to the Court, to which he daily
hoped an invitation or command.

Vernole's fortune being hitherto something akin to
that of De Pais, there was a greater correspondence
between these two gentlemen, than they had with
any other persons; they accounting themselves above
the rest of the world, believed none so proper and fit
for their conversation, as that of each other; so that
there was a very particular intimacy between them.
Whenever they went abroad, they clubbed their train,
to make one great show ; and were always together,
bemoaning each other's fortune, and that from so
high a descent, as one from monarchs by the mother's
side, and the other from dukes of the father's side,
they were reduced by fate to the degree of private
gentlemen.   They would often consult how to
manage affairs most to advantage, and often De Pais
would ask counsel of Vernole, how best he should
dispose of his daughters, which now were about their
ninth year the eldest, and eighth the youngest.
Vernole had often seen those two buds of beauty,
and already saw opening in Atlante's face and mind
(for that was the name of the eldest, and Charlot the
youngest) a glory of wit and beauty, which could not
but one day display itself, with dazzling lustre, to the
wondering world.

Vernole was a great virtuoso, of a humour nice,
delicate, critical, and opinionative : he had nothing
of the French mien in him, but all the gravity of the

x

don. His ill-favoured person, and his low estate, put him out of humour with the world; and because that should not upbraid or reproach his follies and defects, he was sure to be beforehand with that, and to be always satiric upon it; and loved to live and act contrary to the custom and usage of all mankind besides.

He was infinitely delighted to find a man of his own humour in De Pais, or at least a man that would be persuaded to like his so well, to live up to it; and it was no little joy and satisfaction to him to find, that he kept his daughters in that severity, which was wholly agreeable to him, and so contrary to the manner and fashion of the French quality; who allow all freedoms, which to Vernole's rigid nature, seemed as so many steps to vice, and in his opinion, the ruiner of all virtue and honour in womankind. De Pais was extremely glad his conduct was so well interpreted, which was no other in him than a proud frugality; who, because they could not appear in so much gallantry as their quality required, kept them retired, and unseen to all, but his particular friends, of whom Vernole was the chief.

Vernole never appeared before Atlante (which was seldom) but he assumed a gravity and respect fit to have entertained a maid of twenty, or rather a matron of much greater years and judgment. His discourses were always of matters of state or philosophy; and sometimes when De Pais would (laughing) say 'He might as well entertain Atlante with Greek and Hebrew,' he would reply gravely, 'You are mistaken, sir, I find the seeds of great and profound matter in the soul of this young maid, which ought to be nourished now while she is young, and they will grow up to very great perfection: I find Atlante capable of the noble virtues of the mind, and am infinitely mistaken in my observations, and art of physiognomy, if Atlante be not born for greater things than her fortune does now promise. She will be very considerable in the world (believe me), and this will arrive to her perfectly from the force of her charms.' De Pais was extremely overjoyed to hear such good prophesied of Atlante, and from that time set a sort of an esteem upon her, which he did not on Charlot his younger; whom, by the persuasions of Vernole, he resolved to put in a monastery, that what he had might descend to Atlante: not but he confessed Charlot had beauty extremely attractive, and a wit that promised much, when it should be cultivated by years and experience; and would show itself with great advantage and lustre in a monastery. All this pleased De Pais very well, who was easily persuaded, since he had not a fortune to marry her well in the world.

As yet Vernole had never spoken to Atlante of love, nor did his gravity think it prudence to discover his heart to so young a maid; he waited her more sensible years, when he could hope to have some return. And all he expected from this her tender age, was by his daily converse with her, and the presents he made her suitable to her years, to ingratiate himself insensibly into her friendship and esteem, since she was not yet capable of love; but even in that he mistook his aim, for every day he grew more and more disagreeable to Atlante, and would have been her absolute aversion, had she known she had every day entertained a lover; but as she grew in years and sense, he seemed the more despicable in her eyes as to his person; yet as she had respect to his parts and qualities, she paid him all the complaisance she could, and which was due to him, and so must be confessed. Though he had a stiff formality in all he said and did, yet he had wit and learning, and was a great philosopher. As much of his learning as Atlante was capable of attaining to, he made her mistress of, and that was no small portion; for all his discourse was fine and easily comprehended, his notions of philosophy fit for ladies; and he took greater pains with

Atlante, than any master would have done with a scholar. So that it was most certain, he added very great accomplishment to her natural wit: and the more, because she took a great delight in philosophy; which very often made her impatient of his coming, especially when she had many questions to ask him concerning it, and she would often receive him with a pleasure in her face, which he did not fail to interpret to his own advantage, being very apt to flatter himself. Her sister Charlot would often ask her, 'How she could give whole afternoons to so disagreeable a man. What is it,' said she, 'that charms you so? his tawny leather-face, his extraordinary high nose, his wide mouth and eyebrows, that hang lowering over his eyes, his lean carcase, and his lame and halting hips?' But Atlante would discreetly reply, 'If I must grant all you say of Count Vernole to be true, yet he has a wit and learning that will atone sufficiently for all those faults you mention. A fine soul is infinitely to be preferred to a fine body; this decays, but that is eternal; and age that ruins one, refines the other.' Though possibly Atlante thought as ill of the Count as her sister, yet in respect to him, she would not own it.

Atlante was now arrived to her thirteenth year, when her beauty, which every day increased, became the discourse of the whole town, which had already gained her as many lovers as had beheld her; for none saw her without languishing for her, or at least, but what were in very great admiration of her. Everybody talked of the young Atlante, and all the noblemen, who had sons (knowing the smallness of her fortune, and the lustre of her beauty), would send them, for fear of their being charmed with her beauty, either to some other part of the world, or exhorted them, by way of precaution, to keep out of her sight. Old Bellyaurd was one of those wise parents; and timely prevention, as he thought, of Rinaldo's falling in love with Atlante, perhaps was the occasion of his

being so. He had before heard of Atlante, and of
her beauty, yet it had made no impressions on his
heart; but his father no sooner forbid him loving,
than he felt a new desire tormenting him, of seeing
this lovely and dangerous young person. He wonders
at his unaccountable pain, which daily solicits him
within, to go where he may behold this beauty; of
whom he frames a thousand ideas, all such as were
most agreeable to him; but then upbraids his fancy
for not forming her half so delicate as she was; and
longs yet more to see her, to know how near she
approaches to the picture he has drawn of her in his
mind: and though he knew she lived the next house
to him, yet he knew also she was kept within like a
vowed nun, or with the severity of a Spaniard. And
though he had a chamber, which had a jutting window, that looked just upon the door of Monsieur
De Pais, and that he would watch many hours at a
time, in hope to see them go out, yet he could never
get a glimpse of her; yet he heard she often frequented the Church of Our Lady. Thither then
young Rinaldo resolved to go, and did so two or
three mornings; in which time, to his unspeakable
grief, he saw no beauty appear that charmed him;
and yet he fancied that Atlante was there, and that
he had seen her; that some one of those young ladies
that he saw in the church was she, though he had nobody to inquire of, and that she was not so fair as the
world reported; for which he would often sigh. as if
he had lost some great expectation However, he
ceased not to frequent this church, and one day saw
a young beauty, who at first glimpse made his heart
leap to his mouth, and fall a-trembling again into its
wonted place; for it immediately told him, that that
young maid was Atlante: she was with her sister
Charlot, who was very handsome, but not comparable
to Atlante. He fixed his eyes upon her as she kneeled
at the altar; he never moved from that charming face
as long as she remained there; he forgot all devotion,

but what he paid to her; he adored her, he burnt and languished already for her, and found he must possess Atlante or die. Often as he gazed upon her, he saw her fair eyes lifted up towards his, where they often met; which she perceiving, would cast hers down into her bosom, or on her book, and blush as if she had done a fault. Charlot perceived all the motions of Rinaldo, how he folded his arms, how he sighed and gazed on her sister; she took notice of his clothes, his garniture, and every particular of his dress, as young girls do; and seeing him so very handsome, and so much better dressed than all the young cavaliers that were in the church, she was very much pleased with him; and could not forbear saying, in a low voice, to Atlante, 'Look, look, my sister, what a pretty monsieur yonder is! see how fine his face is, how delicate his hair, how gallant his dress! and do but look how he gazes on you!' This would make Atlante blush anew, who durst not raise her eyes for fear she should encounter his. While he had the pleasure to imagine they were talking of him, and he saw in the pretty face of Charlot, that what she said was not to his disadvantage, and by the blushes of Atlante, that she was not displeased with what was spoken to her; he perceived the young one impor-tunate with her; and Atlante jogging her with her elbow, as much as to say, 'Hold your peace': all this he made a kind interpretation of, and was transported with joy at the good omens. He was willing to flatter his new flame, and to compliment his young desire with a little hope; but the divine ceremony ceasing, Atlante left the church, and it being very fair weather, she walked home. Rinaldo, who saw her going, felt all the agonies of a lover, who parts with all that can make him happy; and seeing only Atlante attended with her sister, and a footman following with their books, he was a thousand times about to speak to them; but he no sooner advanced a step or two towards them to that purpose (for he

followed them) but his heart failed, and a certain awe
and reverence, or rather the fears and tremblings of a
lover, prevented him.   But when he considered, that
possibly he might never have so favourable an opportunity again, he resolved anew, and called up so
much courage to his heart, as to speak to Atlante;
but before he did so, Charlot looking behind her, saw
Rinaldo very near to them, and cried out with a voice
of joy, 'O sister, sister! look where the handsome
monsieur is, just behind us! sure he is somebody of
quality, for see he has two footmen that follow him,
in just such liveries, and so rich as those of our
neighbour Monsieur Bellyaurd.'   At this Atlante
could not forbear, but before she was aware of it,
turned her head, and looked on Rinaldo; which
encouraged him to advance, and putting off his hat,
which he clapped under his arm, with a low bow, said,
'Ladies, you are slenderly attended, and so many
accidents arrive to the fair in the rude streets, that I
humbly implore you will permit me, whose duty it is
as a neighbour, to wait on you to your door.'   'Sir,'
said Atlante, blushing, 'we fear no insolence, and
need no protector; or if we did, we should not be so
rude to take you out of your way, to serve us.'
'Madam,' said he, 'my way lies yours.   I live at the
next door, and am son to Bellyaurd, your neighbour.
But, madam,' added he, 'if I were to go all my life
out of the way, to do you service, I should take it for
the greatest happiness that could arrive to me; but,
madam, sure a man can never be out of his way, who
has the honour of so charming company.'   Atlante
made no reply to this, but blushed and bowed.   But
Charlot said, 'Nay, sir, if you are our neighbour, we
will give you leave to conduct us home; but pray,
sir, how came you to know we are your neighbours?
for we never saw you before, to our knowledge.'   'My
pretty miss,' replied Rinaldo, 'I knew it from that
transcendent beauty that appeared in your faces, and
fine shapes; for I have heard, there was no beauty in

the world like that of Atlante's; and I no sooner
saw her, but my heart told me it was she.' 'Heart!'
said Charlot, laughing, 'why, do hearts speak?'
'The most intelligible of anything,' Rinaldo replied,
'when it is tenderly touched, when it is charmed and
transported.' At these words he sighed, and Atlante,
to his extreme satisfaction, blushed. 'Touched,
charmed, and transported,' said Charlot, 'what's that?
And how do you do to have it be all these things?
For I would give anything in the world to have my
heart speak.' 'Oh!' said Rinaldo, 'your heart is too
young, it is not yet arrived to the years of speaking;
about thirteen or fourteen, it may possibly be saying
a thousand soft things to you; but it must be first inspired by some noble object, whose idea it must
retain.' 'What,' replied this pretty prattler, 'I'll
warrant I must be in love?' 'Yes,' said Rinaldo,
'most passionately, or you will have but little conversation with your heart.' 'Oh!' replied she, 'I am
afraid the pleasure of such a conversation will not
make me amends for the pain that love will give
me.' 'That,' said Rinaldo, 'is according as the object
is kind, and as you hope; if he love, and you hope,
you will have double pleasure: and in this, how
great an advantage have fair ladies above us men!
It is almost impossible for you to love in vain, you
have your choice of a thousand hearts, which you
have subdued, and may not only choose your slaves,
but be assured of them; without speaking, you are
beloved, it need not cost you a sigh or a tear. But
unhappy man is often destined to give his heart,
where it is not regarded, to sigh, to weep, and
languish, without any hope of pity.' 'You speak so
feelingly, sir,' said Charlot, 'that I am afraid this is
your case.' 'Yes, madam,' replied Rinaldo, sighing,
'I am that unhappy man.' 'Indeed it is pity,' said
she. Pray, how long have you been so?' 'Ever
since I heard of the charming Atlante,' replied he,
sighing again. 'I adored her character; but now I

have seen her, I die for her.' 'For me, sir!' said
Atlante, who had not yet spoken, 'this is the common
compliment of all the young men, who pretend to be
lovers; and if one should pity all those sighers, we
should have but very little left for ourselves.' 'I
believe,' said Rinaldo, 'there are none that tell you
so, who do not mean as they say: yet among all
those adorers, and those who say they will die for
you, you will find none will be so good as their words
but Rinaldo.' 'Perhaps,' said Atlante, 'of all those
who tell me of dying, there are none that tell me of
it with so little reason as Rinaldo, if that be your
name, sir.' 'Madam, it is,' said he, 'and who am
transported with an unspeakable joy, to hear those
last words from your fair mouth: and let me, O lovely
Atlante! assure you, that what I have said, are not
words of course, but proceed from a heart that has
vowed itself eternally yours, even before I had the
happiness to behold this divine person; but now
that my eyes have made good all my heart before
imagined, and did but hope, I swear, I will die a
thousand deaths, rather than violate what I have said
to you; that I adore you; that my soul and all my
faculties are charmed with your beauty and innocence,
and that my life and fortune, not inconsiderable, shall
be laid at your feet.' This he spoke with a fervency
of passion, that left her no doubt of what he had
said; yet she blushed for shame, and was a little
angry at herself, for suffering him to say so much to
her, the very first time she saw him, and accused herself for giving him any encouragement. And in this
confusion she replied, 'Sir, you have said too much
to be believed; and I cannot imagine so short an
acquaintance can make so considerable an impression; of which confession I accuse myself much
more than you, in that I did not only hearken to
what you said, without forbidding you to entertain
me at that rate, but for unheedily speaking something, that has encouraged this boldness: for so I

must call it, in a man so great a stranger to me.'
'Madam,' said he, 'if I have offended by the sudden-
ness of my presumptuous discovery, I beseech you to
consider my reasons for it, the few opportunities I am
like to have, and the impossibility of waiting on you,
both from the severity of your father and mine ; who,
ere I saw you, warned me of my fate, as if he foresaw
I should fall in love, as soon as I should chance to
see you; and for that reason has kept me closer
to my studies, than hitherto I have been.   And from
that time I began to feel a flame, which was kindled
by report alone, and the description my father gave
of your wondrous and dangerous beauty.   Therefore,
madam, I have not suddenly told you of my passion.
I have been long your lover, and have long languished
without telling of my pain ; and you ought to pardon
it now, since it is done with all the respect and
religious awe, that it is possible for a heart to deliver
and unload itself in.   Therefore, madam, if you have
by chance uttered anything, that I have taken advantage or hope from, I assure you it is so small, that
you have no reason to repent it ; but rather, if you
would have me live, send me not from you, without a
confirmation of that little hope.   See, madam,' said
he, more earnestly and trembling, 'see we are almost
arrived at our homes, send me not to mine in a
despair that I cannot support with life ; but tell me, I
shall be blessed with your sight, sometimes in your
balcony, which is very near to a jutting window in
our house, from whence I have sent many a longing
look towards yours, in hope to have seen my soul's
tormentor.'   'I shall be very unwilling,' said she, 'to
enter into an intrigue of love or friendship with a
man, whose parents will be averse to my happiness,
and possibly mine as refractory, though they cannot
but know such an alliance would be very considerable,
my fortune not being suitable to yours : I tell you
this, that you may withdraw in time from an engagement, in which I find there will be a great many

obstacles.' 'Oh! madam,' replied Rinaldo, sighing, 'if my person be not disagreeable to you, you will have no occasion to fear the rest; it is that I dread, and that which is all my fear.' He, sighing, beheld her with a languishing look, that told her, he expected her answer; when she replied, 'Sir, if that will be satisfaction enough for you at this time, I do assure you, I have no aversion for your person, in which I find more to be valued, than in any I have yet seen; and if what you say be real, and proceed from a heart truly affected, I find, in spite of me, you will oblige me to give you hope.'

They were come so near their own houses, that he had not time to return her any answer; but with a low bow he acknowledged her bounty, and expressed the joy her last words had given him, by a look that made her understand he was charmed and pleased: and she bowing to him with an air of satisfaction in her face, he was well assured, there was nothing to be seen so lovely as she then appeared, and left her to go into her own house. But till she was out of sight, he had not power to stir, and then sighing, retired to his own apartment, to think over all that had passed between them. He found nothing but what gave him a thousand joys, in all she had said; and he blessed this happy day, and wondered how his stars came so kind, to make him in one hour at once see Atlante, and have the happiness to know from her mouth, that he was not disagreeable to her. Yet with this satisfaction, he had a thousand thoughts mixed which were tormenting, and those were the fear of their parents; he foresaw from what his father had said to him already, that it would be difficult to draw him to a consent of his marriage with Atlante. These joys and fears were his companions all the night, in which he took but little rest. Nor was Atlante without her inquietudes. She found Rinaldo more in her thoughts than she wished, and a sudden change of humour, that made her know something was the

matter with her more than usual ; she calls to mind
Rinaldo's speaking of the conversation with his
heart, and found hers would be tattling to her, if she
would give way to it ; and yet the more she strove to
avoid it, the more it importuned her, and in spite of
all her resistance, would tell her, that Rinaldo had
a thousand charms.   It tells her, that he loves and
adores her, and that she would be the most cruel of
her sex, should she not be sensible of his passion.
She finds a thousand graces in his person and conversation, and as many advantages in his fortune, which
was one of the most considerable in all those parts ;
for his estate exceeded that of the most noble men in
Orleans, and she imagines she should be the most fortunate of all womankind in such a match.   With these
thoughts she employed all the hours of the night ;
so that she lay so long in bed the next day, that
Count Vernole, who had invited himself to dinner,
came before she had quitted her chamber, and she
was forced to say, she had not been well.   He had
brought her a very fine book, newly come out, of
delicate philosophy, fit for the study of ladies.   But
he appeared so disagreeable to that heart, wholly
taken up with a new and fine object, that she could
now hardly pay him that civility she was wont to do ;
while on the other side that little state and pride
Atlante assumed, made her appear the more charming
to him : so that if Atlante had no mind to begin
a new lesson of philosophy, while she fancied her
thoughts were much better employed, the Count
every moment expressing his tenderness and passion,
had as little an inclination to instruct her, as she had
to be instructed.   Love had taught her a new lesson,
and he would fain teach her a new lesson of love, but
fears it will be a diminishing his gravity and grandeur,
to open the secrets of his heart to so young a maid.
He therefore thinks it more agreeable to his quality
and years, being about forty, to use her father's
authority in this affair, and that it was sufficient for

him to declare himself to Monsieur De Pais, who he knew would be proud of the honour he did him. Some time passed, before he could be persuaded even to declare himself to her father. He fancies the little coldness and pride he saw in Atlante's face, which was not usual, proceeded from some discovery of passion, which his eyes had made, or now and then a sigh, that unawares broke forth; and accuses himself of a levity below his quality, and the dignity of his wit and gravity; and therefore assumes a more rigid and formal behaviour than he was wont, which rendered him yet more disagreeable than before ; and it was with greater pain than ever, she gave him that respect which was due to his quality.

Rinaldo, after a restless night, was up very early in the morning ; and though he was not certain of seeing his adorable Atlante, he dressed himself with all that care, as if he had been to have waited on her, and got himself into the window, that overlooked Monsieur De Pais's balcony, where he had not remained long, before he saw the pretty Charlot come into it, not with any design of seeing Rinaldo, but to look and gaze about her a little. Rinaldo saw her, and made her a very low reverence, and found some disordered joy on the sight of even Charlot, since she was sister to Atlante. He called to her (for the window was so near her, he could easily he heard by her), and told her 'He was infinitely indebted to her bounty, for giving him an opportunity yesterday of falling on that discourse, which had made him the happiest man in the world.' He said, 'If she had not by her agreeable conversation encouraged him, and drawn him from one word to another, he should never have had the confidence to have told Atlante, how much he adored her.' 'I am very glad,' replied Charlot, 'that I was the occasion of the beginning of an amour which was displeasing to neither one nor the other; for I assure you for your comfort, my sister nothing but thinks on you : we lie together, and you have taught

her already to sigh so, that I could not sleep for her.'
At this his face was covered all over with a rising joy,
which his heart could not contain : and after some
discourse, in which this innocent girl discovered more
than Atlante wished she should, he besought her to
become his advocate; and she had no brother, to give
him leave to assume that honour, and call her sister.
Thus, by degrees, he flattered her into a consent of
carrying a letter from him to Atlante; which she,
who believed all as innocent as herself, and being not
forbid to do so, immediately consented to ; when he
took his pen and ink, that stood in the window, with
paper, and wrote Atlante this following letter :—

RINALDO TO ATLANTE

If my fate be so severe, as to deny me the happiness
of sighing out my pain and passion daily at your feet, if
there be any faith in the hope you were pleased to give me
(as it were a sin to doubt), O charming Atlante ! suffer me
not to languish, both without beholding you, and without
the blessing of now and then a billet, in answer to those
that shall daily assure you of my eternal faith and vow ; it
is all I ask, till fortune, and our affairs, shall allow me the
unspeakable satisfaction of claiming you : yet if your charity
can sometimes afford me a sight of you, either from your
balcony in the evening, or at a church in the morning, it
would save me from that despair and torment, which must
possess a heart so unassured, as that of your eternal adorer,

RIN. BELLYAURD.

He having writ and sealed this, tossed it into the
balcony to Charlot, having first looked about to see if
none perceived them. She put it in her bosom, and
ran in to her sister, whom by chance she found alone;
Vernole having taken De Pais into the garden, to
discourse him concerning the sending Charlot to the
monastery, which work he desired to see performed,
before he declared his intentions to Atlante : for
among all his other good qualities, he was very

avaricious; and as fair as Atlante was, he thought
she would be much fairer with the addition of
Charlot's portion. This affair of his with Monsieur
De Pais, gave Charlot an opportunity of delivering
her letter to her sister; who no sooner drew it from
her bosom, but Atlante's face was covered over with
blushes. For she imagined from whence it came, and
had a secret joy in that imagination, though she
thought she must put on the severity and niceness
of a virgin, who would not be thought to have surrendered her heart with so small an assault, and the
first too. So she demanded from whence Charlot
had that letter; who replied with joy, 'From the
fine young gentleman, our neighbour.' At which
Atlante assumed all the gravity she could, to chide
her sister; who replied, 'Well, sister, had you this day
seen him, you would not have been angry to have
received a letter from him; he looked so handsome,
and was so richly dressed, ten times finer than he was
yesterday; and I promised him you should read it:
therefore, pray let me keep my word with him; and
not only so, but carry him an answer.' 'Well,' said
Atlante, 'to save your credit with Monsieur Rinaldo,
I will read it.' Which she did, and finished with
a sigh. While she was reading, Charlot ran into the
garden, to see if they were not likely to be surprised;
and finding the Count and her father set in an arbour,
in deep discourse, she brought pen, ink, and paper to
her sister, and told her, she might write without the
fear of being disturbed: and urged her so long to what
was enough her inclination, that she at last obtained
this answer :—

ATLANTE TO RINALDO

Charlot, your little importunate advocate, has at last subdued me to a consent of returning you this. She has put
me on an affair with which I am wholly unacquainted; and
you ought to take this very kindly from me, since it is the
very first time I ever wrote to one of your sex, though perhaps I might with less danger have done it to any other man.

I tremble while I write, since I dread a correspondence of
this nature, which may insensibly draw us into an incon-
venience, and engage me beyond the limits of that nicety
I ought to preserve. For this way we venture to say a
thousand little kind things, which in conversation we dare
not do : for now none can see us blush. I am sensible
I shall this way put myself too soon into your power; and
though you have abundance of merit, I ought to be
ashamed of confessing, I am but too sensible of it——
But hold—I shall discover for your repose (which I would
preserve) too much of the heart of   ATLANTE.

She gave this letter to Charlot; who immediately
ran into the balcony with it, where she still found
Rinaldo in a melancholy posture, leaning his head on
his hand. She showed him the letter, but was afraid
to toss it to him, for fear it might fall to the ground;
so he ran and fetched a long cane, which he cleft at
one end, and held it while she put the letter into the
cleft, and stayed not to hear what he said to it. But
never was man so transported with joy, as he was at
the reading of this letter; it gives him new wounds;
for to the generous, nothing obliges love so much as
love: though it is now too much the nature of that
inconstant sex, to cease to love as soon as they are
sure of the conquest. But it was far different with
our cavalier; he was the more inflamed, by imagining
he had made some impressions on the heart of
Atlante, and kindled some sparks there, that in time
might increase to something more; so that he now
resolves to die hers: and considering all the obstacles
that may possibly hinder his happiness, he found
none but his father's obstinacy, perhaps occasioned
by the meanness of Atlante's fortune. To this he
urged again, that he was his only son, and a son
whom he loved equal to his own life; and that
certainly, as soon as he should behold him dying
for Atlante, which if he were forced to quit her he
must be, he then believed the tenderness of so fond
a parent would break forth into pity, and plead

within for his consent. These were the thoughts that
flattered this young lover all the day; and whether
he were riding the great horse, or at his study of
philosophy, or mathematics, singing, dancing, or
whatsoever other exercise his tutors ordered, his
thoughts were continually on Atlante. And now
he profited no more, whatever he seemed to do;
every day he failed not to write to her by the
hand of the kind Charlot; who, young as she was,
had conceived a great friendship for Rinaldo, and
failed not to fetch her letters, and bring him answers,
such as he wished to receive. But all this did not
satisfy our impatient lover; absence killed, and he
was no longer able to support himself, without a sight
of this adorable maid. He therefore implores, she
will give him that satisfaction: and she at last grants
it, with a better will than he imagined. The next
day was the appointed time, when she would, under
pretence of going to church, give him an assignation.
And because all public places were dangerous, and
might make a great noise, and they had no private
place to trust to, Rinaldo, under pretence of going up
the river in his pleasure-boat, which he often did, sent
to have it made ready by the next day at ten of the
clock. This was accordingly done, and he gave
Atlante notice of his design of going an hour or two
on the river in his boat, which lay near to such
a place, not far from the church. She and Charlot
came thither: and because they durst not come out
without a footman or two, they taking one, sent him
with a 'How-do-ye' to some young ladies, and told
him, he should find them at church. So getting rid
of their spy, they hastened to the river-side, and
found a boat and Rinaldo, waiting to carry them on
board his little vessel, which was richly adorned, and
a very handsome collation ready for them, of cold
meats, salads and sweetmeats.

As soon as they were come into the pleasure-boat,
unseen of any, he kneeled at the feet of Atlante, and

Y

there uttered so many passionate and tender things to her, with a voice so trembling and soft, with eyes so languishing, and a fervency and a fire so sincere, that her young heart, wholly incapable of artifice, could no longer resist such language, and such looks of love. She grows tender, and he perceives it in her fine eyes, who could not dissemble; he reads her heart in her looks, and found it yielding apace; and therefore assaults it anew, with fresh forces of sighs and tears. He implores she would assure him of her heart, which she could no other way do, than by yielding to marry him. He would carry her to the next village, there consummate that happiness, without which he was able to live no longer; for he had a thousand fears, that some other lover was, or would suddenly be provided for her; and therefore he would make sure of her while he had this opportunity: and to that end, he answered all the objections she could make to the contrary. But ever, when he named marriage, she trembled, with fear of doing something that she fancied she ought not to do without the consent of her father. She was sensible of the advantage, but had been so used to a strict obedience, that she could not without horror think of violating it; and therefore besought him, as he valued her repose, not to urge her to that. And told him further, that if he feared any rival, she would give him what other assurance and satisfaction he pleased, but that of marriage; which she could not consent to, till she knew such an alliance would not be fatal to him: for she feared, as passionately as he loved her, when he should find she had occasioned him the loss of his fortune, or his father's affection, he would grow to hate her. Though he answered to this all that a fond lover could urge, yet she was resolved, and he forced to content himself with obliging her by his prayers and protestations, his sighs and tears, to a contract, which they solemnly made each other, vowing on either side, they would never marry any other. This being solemnly concluded, he assumed a look more gay and contented than before : he presented her a very rich ring, which she durst not put on her finger, but hid it in her bosom. And beholding each other now as man and wife, she suffered him all the decent freedoms he could wish to take; so that the hours of this voyage seemed the most soft and charming of his life : and doubtless they were so; every touch of Atlante transported him, every look pierced his soul, and he was all raptures of joy, when he considered this charming lovely maid was his own.

Charlot all this while was gazing above - deck, admiring the motion of the little vessel, and how easily the wind and tide bore her up the river. She had never been in anything of this kind before, and was very well pleased and entertained, when Rinaldo called her down to tea; where they enjoyed themselves, as well as was possible: and Charlot was wondering to see such a content in their eyes.

But now they thought it was high time for them to return; they fancy the footman missing them at church, would go home and alarm their father, and the Knight of the Ill-favoured Countenance, as Charlot called Count Vernole, whose severity put their father on a greater restriction of them, than naturally he would do of himself. At the name of this Count, Rinaldo changed colour, fearing he might be some rival; and asked Atlante, if this Vernole was akin to her? She answered no; but was a very great friend to her father, and one who from their infancy had had a particular concern for their breeding, and was her master for philosophy. 'Ah!' replied Rinaldo, sighing, 'this man's concern must proceed from something more than friendship for her father'; and therefore conjured her to tell him, whether he was not a lover. 'A lover!' replied Atlante, 'I assure you, he is a perfect antidote against that passion.' And though she suffered his ugly presence now, she should loathe and hate him, should he but name love to her.

She said 'she believed she need not fear any such persecution, since he was a man who was not at all amorous ; that he had too much of the satire in his humour, to harbour any softness there : and nature had formed his body to his mind, wholly unfit for love. And that he might set his heart absolutely at rest, she assured him her father had never yet proposed any marriage to her, though many advantageous ones were offered him every day.

The sails being turned to carry them back from whence they came ; after having discoursed of a thousand things, and all of love, and contrivance to carry on their mutual design, they with sighs parted ; Rinaldo staying behind in the pleasure-boat, and they going ashore in the wherry that attended : after which he cast many an amorous and sad look, and perhaps was answered by those of Atlante.

It was past church-time two or three hours, when they arrived at home, wholly unprepared with an excuse, so absolutely was Atlante's soul possessed with softer business. The first person they met was the footman, who opened the door, and began to cry out how long he had waited in the church, and how in vain ; without giving them time to reply. De Pais came towards them, and with a frowning look demanded where they had been. Atlante, who was not accustomed to excuses and untruth, was a while at a stand ; when Charlot with a voice of joy cried out, 'O sir ! we have been aboard of a fine little ship. At this Atlante blushed, fearing she would tell the truth. But she proceeded on, and said, that they had not been above a quarter of an hour at church, when the Lady ——, with some other ladies and cavaliers, were going out of the church, and that spying them, they would needs have them go with them. 'My sister, sir,' continued she, 'was very loth to go, for fear you should be angry ; but my Lady —— was so importunate with her on one side, and I on the other, because I never saw a little ship in my life, that at last we prevailed with her; therefore, good sir, be not angry.' He promised them he was not. And when they came in, they found Count Vernole, who had been inspiring De Pais with severity, and counselled him to chide the young ladies, for being too long absent, under pretence of going to their devotion. Nor was it enough for him to set the father on, but himself with a gravity, where concern and malice were both apparent, reproached Atlante with levity; and told her he believed she had some other motive than the invitation of a lady, to go on ship-board; and that she had too many lovers, not to make them doubt that this was a designed thing; and that she had heard love from someone, for whom it was designed. To this she made but a short reply, that if it was so, she had no reason to conceal it, since she had sense enough to look after herself; and if anybody had made love to her, he might be assured, it was someone whose quality and merit deserved to be heard: and with a look of scorn, she passed on to another room, and left him silently raging within with jealousy: which, if before she tormented him, this declaration increased it to a pitch not to be concealed. And this day he said so much to the father, that he resolved forthwith to send Charlot to a nunnery: and accordingly the next day he bid her prepare to go. Charlot, who was not yet arrived to the years of distinction, did not much regret it; and having no trouble but leaving her sister, she prepared to go to a nunnery, not many streets from that where she dwelt. The Lady Abbess was her father's kinswoman, and had treated her very well, as often as she came to visit her: so that with satisfaction enough, she was condemned to a monastic life, and was now going for her probation-year. Atlante was troubled at her departure, because she had nobody to bring and to carry letters between Rinaldo and she: however, she took her leave of her, and promised to come and see her as often as she should be permitted to go abroad; for she feared now some constraint extraordinary would be put upon her: and so it happened.

Atlante's chamber was that to which the balcony belonged; and though she durst not appear there in the daytime, she could in the night, and that way give her lover as many hours of conversation as she pleased, without being perceived. But how to give Rinaldo notice of this, she could not tell; who not knowing Charlot was gone to a monastery, waited many days at his window to see her: at last, they neither of them knowing who to trust with any message, one day, when he was, as usual, upon his watch, he saw Atlante step into the balcony, who having a letter, in which she had put a piece of lead, she tossed it into his window, whose casement was open, and ran in again unperceived by any but himself. The paper contained only this:—

My chamber is that which looks into the balcony; from whence, though I cannot converse with you in the day, I can at night, when I am retired to go to bed: therefore be at your window. Farewell.

There needed no more to make him a diligent watcher: and accordingly she was no sooner retired to her chamber, but she would come into the balcony, where she failed not to see him attending at his window. This happy contrivance was thus carried on for many nights, where they entertained one another with all the endearment that two hearts could dictate, who were perfectly united and assured of each other; and this pleasing conversation would often last till day appeared, and forced them to part.

But old Bellyaurd perceiving his son frequent that chamber more than usual, fancied something extraordinary must be the cause of it; and one night asking for his son, his valet told him, he was gone into the Great Chamber, so this was called. Bellyaurd asked the valet what he did there; he told him he could not tell; for often he had lighted him thither, and that his master would take the candle from him at the chamber-door, and suffer him to go no farther. Though the old gentleman could not imagine what affairs he could have alone every night in that chamber, he had a curiosity to see: and one unlucky night, putting off his shoes, he came to the door of the chamber, which was open; he entered softly, and saw the candle set in the chimney, and his son at a great open bay-window. He stopped awhile to wait when he would turn, but finding him unmovable, he advanced something farther, and at last heard the soft dialogue of love between him and Atlante, whom he knew to be she, by his often calling her by her name in their discourse. He heard enough to confirm him how matters went; and unseen as he came, he returned, full of indignation, and thought how to prevent so great an evil, as this passion of his son might produce. At first he thought to round him severely in the ear about it, and upbraid him for doing the only thing he had thought fit to forbid him; but then he thought that would but terrify him for a while, and he would return again, where he had so great an inclination, if he were near her; he therefore resolves to send him to Paris, that by absence he might forget the young beauty that had charmed his youth. Therefore, without letting Rinaldo know the reason, and without taking notice that he knew anything of his amour, he came to him one day, and told him, all the masters he had for the improving him in noble sciences were very dull, or very remiss; and that he resolved he should go for a year or two to the Academy at Paris. To this the son made a thousand evasions; but the father was positive, and not to be persuaded by all his reasons: and finding he should absolutely displease him if he refused to go, and not daring to tell him the dear cause of his desire to remain at Orleans, he therefore, with a breaking heart, consents to go, nay, resolves it, though

it should be his death.   But alas! he considers that
this parting will not only prove the greatest torment
upon earth to him, but that Atlante will share in his
misfortunes also.   This thought gives him a double
torment, and yet he finds no way to evade it.

The night that finished this fatal day, he goes
again to his wonted station, the window; where he
had not sighed very long, but he saw Atlante enter
the balcony: he was not able a great while to speak
to her, or to utter one word.   The night was light
enough to see him at the wonted place; and she
admires at his silence, and demands the reason in
such obliging terms as adds to his grief; and he, with
a deep sigh, replied, 'Urge me not, my fair Atlante,
to speak, lest by obeying you I give you more cause
of grief than my silence is capable of doing': and
then sighing again, he held his peace, and gave her
leave to ask the cause of these last words.   But when
he made no reply but by sighing, she imagined it
much worse than indeed it was; and with a trembling
and fainting voice, she cried, 'Oh! Rinaldo, give me
leave to divine that cruel news you are so unwilling
to tell me: is it that,' added she, 'you are destined to
some more fortunate maid than Atlante?'   At this
tears stopped her speech, and she could utter no
more.   'No, my dearest charmer,' replied Rinaldo,
elevating his voice, 'if that were all, you should see
with what fortitude I would die, rather than obey any
such commands.   I am vowed yours to the last
moment of my life; and will be yours in spite of all
the opposition in the world: that cruelty I could
evade, but cannot this that threatens me.'   'Ah!'
cried Atlante, 'let Fate do her worst, so she still continue Rinaldo mine, and keep that faith he hath
sworn to me entire.   What can she do beside, that
can afflict me?'   'She can separate me,' cried he,
'for some time from Atlante.'   'Oh!' replied she,
'all misfortunes fall so below that which I first
imagined, that methinks I do not resent this, as I

should otherwise have done ; but I know, when I
have a little more considered it, I shall even die with
the grief of it, absence being so greater an enemy to
love, and making us soon forget the object beloved.
This, though I never experienced, I have heard, and
fear it may be my fate.' He then convinced her
fears with a thousand new vows, and a thousand imprecations of constancy. She then asked him if
their loves were discovered, that he was with such
haste to depart? He told her nothing of that was
the cause ; and he could almost wish it were discovered, since he could resolutely then refuse to go
but it was only to cultivate his mind more effectually
than he could do here ; it was the care of his father
to accomplish him the more ; and therefore he could
not contradict it. 'But,' said he, 'I am not sent where
seas shall part us, nor vast distances of earth, but to
Paris,' from whence he might come in two days to see
her again ; and that he would expect from that
balcony, that had given him so many happy moments,
many more when he should come to see her. He besought her to send him away with all the satisfaction
she could, which she could no otherwise do, than by
giving him new assurances that she would never give
away that right he had in her to any other lover.
She vows this with innumerable tears ; and is almost
angry with him for questioning her faith. He tells
her he has but one night more to stay, and his grief
would be unspeakable, if he should not be able to
take a better leave of her, than at a window ; and
that, if she would give him leave, he would by a rope
or two, tied together, so as it may serve for steps,
ascend her balcony ; he not having time to provide a
ladder of ropes. She tells him she has so great a
confidence in his virtue and love, that she will refuse
him nothing, though it would be a very bold venture
for a maid, to trust herself with a passionate young
man, in silence of night : and though she did not
extort a vow from him to secure her, she expected

he would have a care of her honour. He swore to
her, his love was too religious for so base an attempt.
There needed not many vows to confirm her faith;
and it was agreed on between them, that he should
come the next night into her chamber.

It happened that night, as it often did, that Count
Vernole lay with Monsieur De Pais, which was in a
ground-room, just under that of Atlante's. As soon as
she knew all were in bed, she gave the word to Rinaldo,
who was attending with the impatience of a passionate
lover below, under the window; and who no sooner
heard the balcony open, but he ascended with some
difficulty, and entered the chamber, where he found
Atlante trembling with joy and fear. He throws himself at her feet, as unable to speak as she; who
nothing but blushed and bent down her eyes, hardly
daring to glance them towards the dear object of her
desires, the lord of all her vows. She was ashamed
to see a man in her chamber, where yet none had
ever been alone, and by night too. He saw her fear,
and felt her trembling; and after a thousand sighs of
love had made way for speech, he besought her to
fear nothing from him, for his flame was too sacred,
and his passion too holy to offer anything but what
honour with love might afford him. At last he
brought her to some courage, and the roses of her
fair cheeks assumed their wonted colour, not blushing
too red, nor languishing too pale. But when the
conversation began between them, it was the softest
in the world: they said all that parting lovers could
say; all that wit and tenderness could express. They
exchanged their vows anew; and to confirm his, he
tied a bracelet of diamonds about her arm, and she
returned him one of her hair, which he had long
begged, and she had on purpose made, which clasped
together with diamonds; this she put about his arm,
and he swore to carry it to his grave. The night was
far spent in tender vows, soft sighs and tears on both
sides, and it was high time to part: but, as if death

had been to have arrived to them in that minute, they
both lingered away the time, like lovers who had forgot themselves; and the day was near approaching
when he bid farewell, which he repeated very often:
for still he was interrupted by some commanding softness from Atlante, and then lost all his power of
going; till she, more courageous and careful of his
interest and her own fame, forced him from her: and
it was happy she did, for he was no sooner got over
the balcony, and she had flung him down his rope,
and shut the door, but Vernole, whom love and contrivance kept waking, fancied several times he heard
a noise in Atlante's chamber.   And whether in passing over the balcony, Rinaldo made any noise or not,
or whether it was still his jealous fancy, he came up in
his night-gown, with a pistol in his hand.   Atlante
was not so much lost in grief, though she were all in
tears, but she heard a man come up, and imagined
it had been her father, she not knowing of Count
Vernole's lying in the house that night; if she had,
she possibly had taken more care to have been silent:
but whoever it was, she could not get to bed soon
enough, and therefore turned herself to her dressing-
table, where a candle stood, and where lay a book
open of the story of Ariadne and Theseus.   The
Count turning the latch, entered halting into her
chamber in his night-gown clapped close about him,
which betrayed an ill-favoured shape, his night-cap
on, without a periwig, which discovered all his lean
withered jaws, his pale face, and his eyes staring: and
made altogether so dreadful a figure, that Atlante,
who no more dreamt of him than of a devil, had
possibly have rather seen the last.   She gave a great
shriek, which frightened Vernole; so both stood for a
while staring on each other, till both were recollected.
He told her the care of her honour had brought him
thither; and then rolling his small eyes round the
chamber, to see if he could discover anybody, he
proceeded, and cried, 'Madam, if I had no other

motive than your being up at this time of night, or
rather of day, I could easily guess how you have been
entertained.' 'What insolence is this,' said she, all in
a rage, 'when to cover your boldness of approaching
my chamber at this hour, you would question how
I have been entertained! Either explain yourself, or
quit my chamber; for I am not used to see such
terrible objects here.' 'Possibly those you do see,'
said the Count, 'are indeed more agreeable, but I am
afraid have not that regard to your honour as I have':
and at that word he stepped to the balcony, opened it,
and looked out; but seeing nobody, he shut it to
again. This enraged Atlante beyond all patience;
and snatching the pistol out of his hand, she told him
he deserved to have it aimed at his head, for having
the impudence to question her honour, or her conduct;
and commanded him to avoid her chamber as he
loved his life, which she believed he was fonder of
than of her honour. She speaking this in a tone
wholly transported with rage, and at the same time
holding the pistol towards him made him tremble
with fear; and he now found, whether she were guilty
or not, it was his turn to beg pardon. For you must
know, however it came to pass that his jealousy made
him come up in that fierce posture, at other times
Vernole was the most tame and passive man in the
world, and one who was afraid of his own shadow in
the night. He had a natural aversion for danger, and
thought it below a man of wit, or common-sense, to be
guilty of that brutal thing, called courage or fighting.
His philosophy told him, 'It was safe sleeping in
a whole skin'; and possibly he apprehended as much
danger from this virago, as ever he did from his own
sex. He therefore fell on his knees, and besought
her to hold her fair hand, and not to suffer that,
which was the greatest mark of his respect, to be the
cause of her hate or indignation. The pitiful faces
he made, and the signs of mortal fear in him, had
almost made her laugh, at least it allayed her anger;

and she bid him rise and play the fool hereafter somewhere else, and not in her presence. Yet for once
she would deign to give him this satisfaction, that she
was got into a book, which had many moving stories
very well written; and that she found herself so well
entertained, she had forgotten how the night passed.
He most humbly thanked her for this satisfaction,
and retired, perhaps not so well satisfied as he pretended.

After this, he appeared more submissive and respectful towards Atlante; and she carried herself
more reserved and haughty towards him; which was
one reason, he would not yet discover his passion.

Thus the time ran on at Orleans, while Rinaldo
found himself daily languishing at Paris. He was
indeed in the best academy in the city, amongst
a number of brave and noble youths, where all things
that could accomplish them, were to be learned by
those that had any genius; but Rinaldo had other
thoughts, and other business: his time was wholly
passed in the most solitary parts of the garden, by
the melancholy fountains, and in the most gloomy
shades, where he could with most liberty breathe out
his passion and his griefs. He was past the tutorage
of a boy; and his masters could not upbraid him, but
found he had some secret cause of grief, which made
him not mind those exercises, which were the delight
of the rest; so that nothing being able to divert his
melancholy, which daily increased upon him, he
feared it would bring him into a fever, if he did not
give himself the satisfaction of seeing Atlante. He
had no sooner thought of this, but he was impatient
to put it in execution; he resolved to go (having very
good horses) without acquainting any of his servants
with it. He got a very handsome and light ladder of
ropes made, which he carried under his coat, and
away he rode for Orleans, stayed at a little village, till
the darkness of the night might favour his design.
And then walking about Atlante's lodgings, till he

saw a light in her chamber, and then making that noise on his sword, as was agreed between them, he was heard by his adorable Atlante, and suffered to mount her chamber, where he would stay till almost break of day, and then return to the village, and take horse, and away for Paris again. This, once in a month, was his exercise, without which he could not live; so that his whole year was passed in riding between Orleans and Paris, between excess of grief, and excess of joy by turns.

It was now that Atlante, arrived to her fifteenth year, shone out with a lustre of beauty greater than ever; and in this year, in the absence of Rinaldo, had carried herself with that severity of life, without the youthful desire of going abroad, or desiring any diversion, but what she found in her own retired thoughts, that Vernole, wholly unable longer to conceal his passion, resolved to make a publication of it, first to the father, and then to the lovely daughter, of whom he had some hope, because she had carried herself very well towards him for this year past; which she would never have done, if she had imagined he would ever have been her lover. She had seen no signs of any such misfortune towards her in these many years he had conversed with her, and she had no cause to fear him. When one day her father taking her into the garden, told her what honour and happiness was in store for her; and that now the glory of his fallen family would rise again, since she had a lover of an illustrious blood, allied to monarchs; and one whose fortune was newly increased to a very considerable degree, answerable to his birth. She changed colour at this discourse, imagining but too well who this illustrious lover was; when De Pais proceeded and told her, 'indeed his person was not the most agreeable that ever was seen: but he married her to glory and fortune, not the man: 'And a woman,' says he, 'ought to look no further.'

She needed not any more to inform her who this

intended husband was; and therefore, bursting forth
into tears, she throws herself at his feet, imploring
him not to use the authority of a father, to force her
to a thing so contrary to her inclination: assuring
him, she could not consent to any such thing; and
that she would rather die than yield. She urged
many arguments for this her disobedience; but none
would pass for current with the old gentleman, whose
pride had flattered him with hopes of so considerable
a son-in-law. He was very much surprised at Atlante's
refusing what he believed she would receive with joy;
and finding that no arguments on his side could draw
hers to an obedient consent, he grew to such a rage,
as very rarely possessed him: vowing, if she did not
conform her will to his, he would abandon her to all
the cruelty of contempt and poverty. So that at last
she was forced to return him this answer, 'That she
would strive all she could with her heart; but she
verily believed she should never bring it to consent
to a marriage with Monsieur the Count.' The father
continued threatening her, and gave her some days to
consider of it: so leaving her in tears, he returned to
his chamber, to consider what answer he should give
Count Vernole, who he knew would be impatient to
learn what success he had, and what himself was to
hope. De Pais, after some consideration, resolved
to tell him, she received the offer very well, but that
he must expect a little maiden-nicety in the case: and
accordingly did tell him so; and he was not at all
doubtful of his good fortune.

But Atlante, who resolved to die a thousand deaths
rather than break her solemn vows to Rinaldo, or to
marry the Count, cast about how she should avoid
it with the least hazard of her father's rage. She
found Rinaldo the better and the more advantageous
match of the two, could they but get his father's consent. He was beautiful and young; his title was
equal to that of Vernole, when his father should die;
and his estate exceeded his: yet she dares not make

a discovery, for fear she should injure her lover; who at this time, though she knew it not, lay sick of a fever, while she was wondering that he came not as he used to do. However, she resolved to send him a letter, and acquaint him with the misfortune; which she did in these terms:—

ATLANTE TO RINALDO

My father's authority would force me to violate my sacred vows to you, and give them to the Count Vernole, whom I mortally hate, yet could wish him the greatest monarch in the world, that I might show you I could even then despise him for your sake. My father is already too much enraged by my denial, to hear reason from me, if I should confess to him my vows to you: so that I see nothing but a prospect of death before me; for assure yourself, my Rinaldo, I will die rather than consent to marry any other. Therefore come, my Rinaldo, and come quickly, to see my funeral, instead of those nuptials they vainly expect from your faithful   ATLANTE.

This letter Rinaldo received; and there needed no more to make him fly to Orleans. This raised him soon from his bed of sickness, and getting immediately to horse, he arrived at his father's house; who did not so much admire to see him, because he heard he was sick of a fever, and gave him leave to return, if he pleased. He went directly to his father's house, because he knew somewhat of the business, he was resolved to make his passion known, as soon as he had seen Atlante, from whom he was to take all his measures. He therefore failed not, when all were in bed, to rise and go from his chamber into the street; where finding a light in Atlante's chamber, for she every night expected him, he made the usual sign, and she went into the balcony; and he having no conveniency of mounting up into it, they discoursed, and said all they had to say. From thence she tells him of the Count's passion, of her father's resolution, and that her own was rather to die his, than live for anybody else. And at last, as their refuge, they resolved to discover the whole matter : she to her father, and he to his, to see what accommodation they could make; if not, to die together. They parted at this resolve, for she would permit him no longer to stay in the street after such a sickness ; so he went home to bed, but not to sleep.

The next day, at dinner, Monsieur Bellyaurd believing his son absolutely cured, by absence, of his passion ; and speaking of all the news in the town, among the rest, told him he was come in good time to dance at the wedding of Count Vernole with Atlante, the match being agreed on. ' No, sir,' replied Rinaldo, ' I shall never dance at the marriage of Count Vernole with Atlante ; and you will see in Monsieur De Pais's house a funeral sooner than a wedding.' And thereupon he told his father all his passion for that lovely maid ; and assured him, if he would not see him laid in his grave, he must consent to this match. Bellyaurd rose in a fury, and told him he had rather see him in his grave, than in the arms of Atlante : ' Not,' continued he, ' so much for any dislike I have to the young lady, or the smallness of her fortune; but because I have so long warned you from such a passion, and have with such care endeavoured by your absence to prevent it.' He traversed the room very fast, still protesting against this alliance : and was deaf to all Rinaldo could say. On the other side the day being come, wherein Atlante was to give her final answer to her father concerning her marriage with Count Vernole ; she assumed all the courage and resolution she could, to withstand the storm that threatened a denial. And her father came to her, and demanding her answer, she told him she could not be the wife of Vernole, since she was wife to Rinaldo, only son to Bellyaurd. If her father stormed before, he grew like a man distracted at her confession ; and Vernole hearing them loud, ran to the chamber to

z

learn the cause; where just as he entered he found De Pais's sword drawn, and ready to kill his daughter, who lay all in tears at his feet. He withheld his hand; and asking the cause of his rage, he was told all that Atlante had confessed; which put Vernole quite beside all his gravity, and made him discover the infirmity of anger, which he used to say ought to be dissembled by all wise men. So that De Pais forgot his own to appease his, but it was in vain, for he went out of the house, vowing revenge to Rinaldo. And to that end, being not very well assured of his own courage, as I said before, and being of the opinion, that no man ought to expose his life to him who has injured him; he hired Swiss and Spanish soldiers to attend him in the nature of footmen; and watched several nights about Bellyaurd's door, and that of De Pais's, believing he should some time or other see him under the window of Atlante, or perhaps mounting into it: for now he no longer doubted but this happy lover was he, whom he fancied he heard go from the balcony that night he came up with his pistol; and being more a Spaniard than a Frenchman in his nature, he resolved to take him any way unguarded or unarmed, if he came in his way.

Atlante, who heard his threatenings when he went from her in a rage, feared his cowardice might put him on some base action, to deprive Rinaldo of his life; and therefore thought it not safe to suffer him to come to her by night, as he had before done; but sent him word in a note, that he should forbear her window, for Vernole had sworn his death. This note came, unseen by his father, to his hands: but this could not hinder him from coming to her window, which he did as soon as it was dark: he came thither, only attended with his valet, and two footmen; for now he cared not who knew the secret. He had no sooner made the sign, but he found himself encompassed with Vernole's bravos; and himself standing at a distance cried out 'That is he.' With that they all drew on both sides, and Rinaldo received a wound in his arm. Atlante heard this, and ran crying out 'That Rinaldo pressed by numbers, would be killed.' De Pais, who was reading in his closet, took his sword, and ran out; and, contrary to all expectation, seeing Rinaldo fighting with his back to the door, pulled him into the house, and fought himself with the bravos: who being very much wounded by Rinaldo, gave ground, and sheered off; and De Pais, putting up old Bilbo into the scabbard, went into his house, where he found Rinaldo almost fainting with loss of blood, and Atlante, with her maids binding up his wound; to whom De Pais said, 'This charity, Atlante, very well becomes you, and is what I can allow you; and I could wish you had no other motive for this action.' Rinaldo by degrees recovered of his fainting, and as well as his weakness would permit him, he got up and made a low reverence to De Pais, telling him he had now a double obligation to pay him all the respect in the world; first, for his being the father of Atlante; and secondly, for being the preserver of his life: two ties that should eternally oblige him to love and honour him, as his own parent. De Pais replied, he had done nothing but what common humanity compelled him to do. But if he would make good that respect he professed towards him, it must be in quitting all hopes of Atlante, whom he had destined to another, or an eternal enclosure in a monastery. He had another daughter, whom if he would think worthy of his regard, he should take his alliance as a very great honour; but his word and reputation, nay his vows were passed, to give Atlante to Count Vernole. Rinaldo, who before he spoke took measure from Atlante's eyes, which told him her heart was his, returned this answer to De Pais, 'That he was infinitely glad to find by the generosity of his offer, that he had no aversion against his being his son-in-law; and that, next to Atlante, the greatest happiness he could wish would be his receiving Charlot from his hand; but that he could not think of quitting Atlante, how necessary soever it would be, for glory, and his—(the further) repose.' De Pais would not let him at this time argue the matter further, seeing he was ill, and had need of looking after; he therefore begged he would for his health's sake retire to his own house, whither he himself conducted him, and left him to the care of his men, who were escaped the fray; and returning to his own chamber, he found Atlante retired, and so he went to bed full of thoughts. This night had increased his esteem for Rinaldo, and lessened it for Count Vernole; but his word and honour being passed, he could not break it, neither with safety nor honour: for he knew the haughty resenting nature of the Count, and he feared some danger might arrive to the brave Rinaldo, which troubled him very much. At last he resolved, that neither might take anything ill at his hands, to lose Atlante, and send her to the monastery where her sister was, and compel her to be a nun. This he thought would prevent mischief on both sides; and accordingly, the next day (having in the morning sent word to the Lady Abbess what he would have done), he carries Atlante, under pretence of visiting her sister (which they often did), to the monastery, where she was no sooner come, but she was led into the enclosure. Her father had rather sacrifice her, than she should be the cause of the murder of two such noble men as Vernole and Rinaldo.

The noise of Atlante being enclosed, was soon spread all over the busy town, and Rinaldo was not the last to whom the news arrived. He was for a few days confined to his chamber; where, when alone, he raved like a man distracted. But his wounds had so incensed his father against Atlante, that he swore he would see his son die of them, rather than suffer him to marry Atlante; and was extremely overjoyed to find she was condemned for ever, to the monastery. So that the son thought it the wisest course, and most for the advantage of his love, to say nothing to contradict his father; but being almost assured Atlante would never consent to be shut up in a cloister, and abandon him, he flattered himself with hope, that he should steal her from thence, and marry her in spite of all opposition. This he was impatient to put in practice. He believed, if he were not permitted to see Atlante, he had still a kind advocate in Charlot, who was now arrived to her thirteenth year, and infinitely advanced in wit and beauty. Rinaldo therefore often goes to the monastery, surrounding it, to see what possibility there was of accomplishing his design; if he could get her consent, he finds it not impossible, and goes to visit Charlot; who had command not to see him, or speak to him. This was a cruelty he looked not for, and which gave him an unspeakable trouble, and without her aid it was wholly impossible to give Atlante any account of his design. In this perplexity he remained many days, in which he languished almost to death; he was distracted with thought, and continually hovering about the nunnery walls, in hope, at some time or other, to see or hear from that lovely maid, who alone could make his happiness. In these traverses he often met Vernole, who had liberty to see her when he pleased. If it happened that they chanced to meet in the day-time, though Vernole was attended with an equipage of ruffians, and Rinaldo but only with a couple of footmen, he could perceive Vernole shun him, grow pale, and almost tremble with fear sometimes, and get to the other side of the street; and if he did not, Rinaldo having a mortal hate to him, would often bear up so close to him, that he would jostle him against the wall, which Vernole would patiently put up, and pass on; so that he could never be provoked to fight by daylight, how solitary soever the place was where they met. But if they chanced to meet at night, they were certain of a skirmish, in which he would have no part himself; so that Rinaldo was often like to be assassinated, but still came off with some slight wound. This continued so long, and made so great a noise in the town, that the two old gentlemen were mightily alarmed by it; and Count Bellyaurd came to De Pais, one day, to discourse with him of this affair; and Bellyaurd, for the preservation of his son, was almost consenting, since there was no remedy, that he should marry Atlante. De Pais confessed the honour he proffered him, and how troubled he was, that his word was already passed to his friend, the Count Vernole, whom he said she should marry, or remain for ever a nun; but if Rinaldo could displace his love from Atlante, and place it on Charlot, he should gladly consent to the match. Bellyaurd, who would now do anything for the repose of his son, though he believed this exchange would not pass, yet resolved to propose it, since by marrying him he took him out of the danger of Vernole's assassinates, who would never leave him till they had despatched him, should he marry Atlante.

While Rinaldo was contriving a thousand ways to come to speak to, or send billets to Atlante, none of which could succeed without the aid of Charlot, his father came and proposed this agreement between De Pais and himself, to his son. At first Rinaldo received it with a changed countenance, and a breaking heart; but swiftly turning from thought to thought, he conceived this the only way to come at Charlot, and so consequently at Atlante: he therefore, after some dissembled regret, consents, with a sad put-on look: and Charlot had notice given her to see and entertain Rinaldo. As yet they had not told her the reason; which her father would tell her, when he came to visit her, he said. Rinaldo overjoyed at this contrivance, and his own dissimulation, goes to the monastery, and visits Charlot; where he ought to have said something of this proposition:

but wholly bent upon other thoughts, he solicits her to convey some letters, and presents to Atlante; which she readily did, to the unspeakable joy of the poor distressed. Sometimes he would talk to Charlot of her own affairs; asking her, if she resolved to become a nun. To which she would sigh, and say, if she must, it would be extremely against her inclinations; and, if it pleased her father, she had rather begin the world with any tolerable match.

Things passed thus for some days, in which our lovers were happy, and Vernole assured he should have Atlante. But at last De Pais came to visit Charlot, who asked her, if she had seen Rinaldo. She answered, she had. 'And how does he entertain you?' replied De Pais. 'Have you received him as a husband? and has he behaved himself like one?' At this a sudden joy seized the heart of Charlot; and loth to confess what she had done for him to her sister, she hung down her blushing face to study for an answer. De Pais continued, and told her the agreement between Bellyaurd and him, for the saving of bloodshed.

She, who blessed the cause, whatever it was, having always a great friendship and tenderness for Rinaldo, gave her father a thousand thanks for his care; and assured him, since she was commanded by him, she would receive him as her husband.

And the next day, when Rinaldo came to visit her, as he used to do, and bringing a letter with him, wherein he proposed the sight of Atlante; he found a coldness in Charlot, as soon as he told her his design, and desired her to carry the letter. He asked the reason of this change: she tells him she was informed of the agreement between their two fathers, and that she looked upon herself as his wife, and would act no more as a confidante; that she had ever a violent inclination of friendship for him, which she would soon improve into something more soft.

He could not deny the agreement, nor his promise;

but it was in vain to tell her, he did it only to get a correspondence with Atlante. She is obstinate, and he as pressing, with all the tenderness of persuasion. He vows he can never be any but Atlante's, and she may see him die, but never break his vows. She urges her claim in vain, so that at last she was overcome, and promised she would carry the letter; which was to have her make her escape that night. He waits at the gate for her answer, and Charlot returns with one that pleased him very well; which was, that night her sister would make her escape, and that he must stand in such a place of the nunnery wall, and she would come out to him.

After this she upbraids him with his false promise to her, and of her goodness to serve him after such a disappointment. He receives her reproaches with a thousand sighs, and bemoans her misfortune in not being capable of more than friendship for her; and vows, that next Atlante, he esteems her of all womankind. She seems to be obliged by this, and assured him, she would hasten the flight of Atlante; and taking leave, he went home to order a coach, and some servants to assist him.

In the meantime Count Vernole came to visit Atlante; but she refused to be seen by him: and all he could do there that afternoon, was entertaining Charlot at the grate; to whom he spoke a great many fine things, both of her improved beauty and wit; and how happy Rinaldo would be in so fair a bride. She received this with all the civility that was due to his quality; and their discourse being at an end, he took his leave, it being towards the evening.

Rinaldo, wholly impatient, came betimes to the corner of the dead wall, where he was appointed to stand, having ordered his footmen and coach to come to him as soon as it was dark. While he was there walking up and down, Vernole came by the end of the wall to go home: and looking about, he saw, at the other end, Rinaldo walking, whose back was towards him, but he knew him well; and though he feared and dreaded his business there, he durst not encounter him, they being both attended but by one footman apiece. But Vernole's jealousy and indignation were so high, that he resolved to fetch his bravos to his aid, and come and assault him : for he knew he waited there for some message from Atlante.

In the meantime it grew dark, and Rinaldo's coach came with another footman; which were hardly arrived, when Vernole, with his assistants, came to the corner of the wall, and screening themselves a little behind it, near to the place where Rinaldo stood, who waited now close to a little door, out of which the gardeners used to throw the weeds and dirt, Vernole could perceive anon the door to open, and a woman come out of it, calling Rinaldo by his name, who stepped up to her, and caught her in his arms with signs of infinite joy. Vernole being now all rage, cried to his assassinates, 'Fall on, and kill the ravisher.' And immediately they all fell on. Rinaldo, who had only his two footmen on his side, was forced to let go the lady; who would have run into the garden again, but the door fell to and locked: so that while Rinaldo was fighting, and beaten back by the bravos, one of which he laid dead at his feet, Vernole came to the frightened lady, and taking her by the hand, cried, 'Come, my fair fugitive, you must go along with me.' She, wholly scared out of her senses, was willing to go anywhere out of the terror she heard so near her, and without reply, gave herself into his hand, who carried her directly to her father's house; where she was no sooner come, but he told her father all that had passed, and how she was running away with Rinaldo, but that his good fortune brought him just in the lucky minute. Her father turning to reproach her, found by the light of a candle that this was Charlot, and not Atlante, whom Vernole had brought home.

At which Vernole was extremely astonished. Her father demanded of her why she was running away with a man, who was designed her by consent? 'Yes,' said Charlot, 'you had his consent, sir, and that of his father; but I was far from getting it: I found he resolved to die rather than quit Atlante; and promising him my assistance in his amour, since he could never be mine, he got me to carry a letter to Atlante; which was, to desire her to fly away with him. Instead of carrying her this letter, I told her, he was designed for me, and had cancelled all his vows to her. She swooned at this news; and being recovered a little, I left her in the hands of the nuns, to persuade her to live; which she resolves not to do without Rinaldo. Though they pressed me, yet I resolved to pursue my design, which was to tell Rinaldo she would obey his kind summons. He waited for her; but I put myself into his hands in lieu of Atlante; and had not the Count received me, we had been married by this time, by some false light that could not have discovered me. But I am satisfied, if I had, he would never have lived with me longer than the cheat had been undiscovered; for I find them both resolved to die, rather than change. And for my part, sir, I was not so much in love with Rinaldo, as I was out of love with the nunnery; and took any opportunity to quit a life absolutely contrary to my humour.' She spoke this with a gaiety so brisk, and an air so agreeable, that Vernole found it touched his heart; and the rather because he found Atlante would never be his; or if she were, he should be still in danger from the resentment of Rinaldo: he therefore bowing to Charlot, and taking her by the hand, cried, 'Madam, since Fortune has disposed you thus luckily for me, in my possession, I humbly implore you would consent she should make me entirely happy, and give me the prize for which I fought, and have conquered with my sword.' 'My lord,' replied Charlot, with a modest air, 'I am super-

stitious enough to believe, since Fortune, so contrary
to all our designs, has given me into your hands,
that she from the beginning destined me to the
honour, which, with my father's consent, I shall
receive as becomes me.' De Pais transported with
joy, to find all things would be so well brought
about, it being all one to him, whether Charlot or
Atlante gave him Count Vernole for his son-in-law,
readily consented ; and immediately a priest was sent
for, and they were that night married. And it being
now not above seven o'clock, many of their friends
were invited, the music sent for, and as good a supper
as so short a time would provide, was made ready.

All this was performed in as short a time as
Rinaldo was fighting ; and having killed one, and
wounded the rest, they all fled before his conquering
sword, which was never drawn with so good a will.
When he came where his coach stood, just against
the back-garden door, he looked for his mistress : but
the coachman told him, he was no sooner engaged,
but a man came, and with a thousand reproaches on
her levity, bore her off.

This made our young lover rave ; and he is satisfied
she is in the hands of his rival, and that he had been
fighting, and shedding his blood, only to secure her
flight with him. He lost all patience, and it was with
much ado his servants persuaded him to return ;
telling him in their opinion, she was more likely to
get out of the hands of his rival, and come to him,
than when she was in the monastery.

He suffers himself to go into his coach and be
carried home ; but he was no sooner alighted, than he
heard music and noise at De Pais's house. He saw
coaches surround his door, and pages and footmen,
with flambeaux. The sight and noise of joy made
him ready to sink at the door ; and sending his footmen to learn the cause of this triumph, the pages that
waited told him, that Count Vernole was this night
married to Monsieur De Pais's daughter. He needed

no more to deprive him of all sense; and staggering against his coach, he was caught by his footmen and carried into his house, and to his chamber, where they put him to bed, all senseless as he was, and had much ado to recover him to life. He asked for his father, with a faint voice, for he desired to see him before he died. It was told him he was gone to Count Vernole's wedding, where there was a perfect peace agreed on between them, and all their animosities laid aside. At this news Rinaldo fainted again; and his servants called his father home, and told him in what condition they had brought home their master, recounting to him all that was past. He hastened to Rinaldo, whom he found just recovered of his swooning; who, putting his hand out to his father, all cold and trembling, cried, 'Well, sir, now you are satisfied, since you have seen Atlante married to Count Vernole. I hope now you will give your unfortunate son leave to die; as you wished he should, rather than give him to the arms of Atlante.' Here his speech failed, and he fell again into a fit of swooning. His father ready to die with fear of his son's death, kneeled down by his bedside; and after having recovered a little, he said, 'My dear son, I have been indeed at the wedding of Count Vernole, but it is not Atlante to whom he is married, but Charlot; who was the person you were bearing from the monastery, instead of Atlante, who is still reserved for you, and she is dying till she hear you are reserved for her. Therefore, as you regard her life, make much of your own, and make yourself fit to receive her; for her father and I have agreed to the marriage already.' And without giving him leave to think, he called to one of his gentlemen, and sent him to the monastery, with this news to Atlante. Rinaldo bowed himself as low as he could in his bed, and kissed the hand of his father, with tears of joy. But his weakness continued all the next day; and they were fain to bring Atlante to him, to confirm his happiness.

It must only be guessed by lovers, the perfect joy these two received in the sight of each other. Bellyaurd received her as his daughter; and the next day made her so, with very great solemnity, at which were Vernole and Charlot. Between Rinaldo and him was concluded a perfect peace, and all thought themselves happy in this double union thousand pounds in money and jewels; which obliged him to get himself dubbed, that she might not descend to an inferior quality. When he was in town, he lived—let me see! in the Strand; or, as near as I can remember, somewhere about Charing Cross; where, first of all Mr. Would-be King, a gentleman of a large estate in houses, land and money, of a haughty, extravagant and profuse humour, very fond of every new face, had the misfortune to fall passionately in love with Philibella, who then lived with her uncle.

This Mr. Would-be it seems had often been told, when he was yet a stripling, either by one of his nurses, or his own grandmother, or by some other gipsy, that he should infallibly be what his surname implied, a king, by Providence or chance, ere he died, or never. This glorious prophecy had so great an influence on all his thoughts and actions, that he distributed and dispersed his wealth sometimes so largely, that one would have thought he had undoubtedly been king of some part of the Indies; to see a present made to-day of a diamond ring, worth two or three hundred pounds, to Madam Flippant; to-morrow, a large chest of the finest china to my Lady Fleece-well; and next day, perhaps, a rich necklace of large Oriental pearl, with a locket to it of sapphires, emeralds, rubies, etc., to pretty Miss Ogle-me, for an amorous glance, for a smile, and (it may be, though but rarely) for the mighty blessing of one single kiss. But such were his largesses, not to reckon his treats, his balls, and serenades besides, though at the same time he had married a virtuous lady, and of good quality. But her relation to him (it may be feared) made her very disagreeable: for a man of his humour and estate can no more be satisfied with one woman, than with one dish of meat; and to say truth, it is something unmodish. However, he might have died a pure celibate, and altogether unexpert of women, had his good or bad hopes only terminated in Sir Philip's niece. But the brave and haughty Mr. Would-be was not to be baulked by appearances of virtue, which he thought all womankind only did affect; besides, he promised himself the victory over any lady whom he attempted, by the force of his damned money, though her virtue were ever so real and strict.

With Philibella he found another pretty young creature, very like her, who had been a quondam mistress to Sir Philip. He, with young Goodland, was then diverting his mistress and niece at a game at cards, when Would-be came to visit him; he found them very merry, with a flask or two of claret before them, and oranges roasting by a large fire, for it was Christmas-time. The Lady Friendly understanding that this extraordinary man was with Sir Philip in the parlour, came in to them, to make the number of both sexes equal, as well as in hopes to make up a purse of guineas towards the purchase of some new fine business that she had in her head, from his accustomed design of losing at play to her. Indeed, she had part of her wish, for she got twenty guineas of him; Philibella ten; and Lucy, Sir Philip's quondam, five. Not but that Would-be intended better fortune to the young ones, than he did to Sir Philip's lady; but her ladyship was utterly unwilling to give him over to their management, though at the last, when they were all tired with the cards, after Would-be had said as many obliging things as his present genius would give him leave, to Philibella and Lucy, especially to the first, not forgetting his *baisemains* to the Lady Friendly, he bid the Knight and Goodland adieu; but with a promise of repeating his visit at six o'clock in the evening on twelfth-day, to renew the famous and ancient solemnity of choosing king and queen; to which Sir Philip before invited him, with a design yet unknown to you, I hope.

As soon as he was gone, everyone made their remarks on him, but with very little or no difference in all their figures of him. In short, all mankind, had they ever known him, would have universally

2 A

agreed in this his character, that he was an original; since nothing in humanity was ever so vain, so haughty, so profuse, so fond, and so ridiculously ambitious, as Mr. Would-be King. They laughed and talked about an hour longer, and then young Goodland was obliged to see Lucy home in his coach; though he had rather have sat up all night in the same house with Philibella, I fancy, of whom he took but an unwilling leave; which was visible enough to everyone there, since they were all acquainted with his passion for my fair friend.

About twelve o'clock on the day prefixed, young Goodland came to dine with Sir Philip, whom he found just returned from Court, in a very good humour. On the sight of Valentine, the Knight ran to him, and embracing him, told him, that he had prevented his wishes, in coming thither before he sent for him, as he had just then designed. The other returned, that he therefore hoped he might be of some service to him, by so happy a prevention of his intended kindness. 'No doubt,' replied Sir Philip, 'the kindness, I hope, will be to us both; I am assured it will, if you will act according to my measures.' 'I desire no better prescriptions for my happiness,' returned Valentine, 'than what you shall please to set down to me: but is it necessary or convenient that I should know them first?' 'It is,' answered Sir Philip, 'let us sit, and you shall understand them. I am very sensible,' continued he, 'of your sincere and honourable affection and pretension to my niece, who, perhaps, is as dear to me as my own child could be, had I one; nor am I ignorant how averse Sir George your father is to your marriage with her, insomuch that I am confident he would disinherit you immediately upon it, merely for want of a fortune somewhat proportionable to your estate: but I have now contrived the means to add two or three thousand pounds to the five hundred I have designed to give with her; I mean, if you marry her, Val, not other-

wise; for I will not labour so for any other man.'
'What inviolable obligations you put upon me!'
cried Goodland. 'No return, by way of compliments,
good Val,' said the Knight. "Had I not engaged to
my wife, before marriage, that I would not dispose of
any part of what she brought me, without her consent, I would certainly make Philibella's fortune
answerable to your estate. And besides, my wife is
not yet full eight-and-twenty, and we may therefore
expect children of our own, which hinders me from
proposing anything more for the advantage of my
niece. But now to my instructions; King will be
here this evening without fail, and, at some time
or other to-night, will show the haughtiness of his
temper to you, I doubt not, since you are in a manner
a stranger to him. Be sure therefore you seem to
quarrel with him before you part, but suffer as much
as you can first from his tongue; for I know he will
give you occasions enough to exercise your passive
valour. I must appear his friend, and you must retire
home, if you please, for this night, but let me see you
as early as your convenience will permit to-morrow:
my late friend Lucy must be my niece too. Observe
this, and leave the rest to me.' 'I shall most punctually,
and will in all things be directed by you,' said Valentine. 'I had forgot to tell you,' said Friendly, 'that
I have so ordered matters, that he must be king
to-night, and Lucy queen, by the lots in the cake.'
'By all means,' returned Goodland; 'it must be
Majesty.'

Exactly at six o'clock came Would-be in his coach-
and-six, and found Sir Philip, and his lady, Goodland,
Philibella, and Lucy ready to receive him; Lucy as
fine as a duchess, and almost as beautiful as she was
before her fall. All things were in ample order for his
entertainment. They played till supper was served
in, which was between eight and nine. The treat was
very seasonable and splendid. Just as the second
course was set on the table, they were all on a sudden

surprised, except Would-be, with a flourish of violins, and other instruments, which proceeded to entertain them with the best and newest airs in the last new plays, being then in the year 1683. The ladies were curious to know to whom they owed the cheerful part of their entertainment : on which he called out, ' Hey! Tom Farmer! Aleworth! Eccles! Hall! and the rest of you! Here's a health to these ladies, and all this honourable company.' They bowed ; he drank, and commanded another glass to be filled, into which he put something yet better than the wine, I mean, ten guineas. ' Here, Farmer,' said he then, ' this for you and your friends.' We humbly thank the honourable Mr. Would-be King. They all returned, and struck up with more sprightliness than before. For gold and wine, doubtless, are the best rosin for musicians.

After supper they took a hearty glass or two to the King, Queen, Duke, etc. And then the mighty cake, teeming with the fate of this extraordinary personage, was brought in, the musicians playing an overture at the entrance of the Alimental Oracle; which was then cut and consulted, and the royal bean and pea fell to those to whom Sir Philip had designed them. It was then the Knight began a merry bumper, with three huzzas, and ' Long live King Would-be!' to Goodland, who echoed and pledged him, putting the glass about to the harmonious attendants ; while the ladies drank their own quantities among themselves, to his aforesaid Majesty. Then of course you may believe Queen Lucy's health went merrily round, with the same ceremony. After which he saluted his royal consort, and condescended to do the same honour to the two other ladies.

Then they fell a-dancing, like lightning ; I mean, they moved as swift, and made almost as little noise ; but his Majesty was soon weary of that ; for he longed to be making love both to Philibella and Lucy, who (believe me) that night might well enough have passed for a queen.

They fell then to questions and commands; to cross purposes: 'I think a thought, what is it like?' etc. In all which, his Would-be Majesty took the opportunity of showing the excellence of his parts, as, How fit he was to govern! How dexterous at mining and countermining! and, how he could reconcile the most contrary and distant thoughts! The music, at last, good as it was, grew troublesome and too loud; which made him dismiss them. And then he began to this effect, addressing himself to Philibella: 'Madam, had fortune been just, and were it possible that the world should be governed and influenced by two suns, undoubtedly we had all been subjects to you, from this night's chance, as well as to that lady, who indeed alone can equal you in the empire of beauty, which yet you share with her Majesty here present, who only could dispute it with you, and is only superior to you in title.' 'My wife is infinitely obliged to your Majesty,' interrupted Sir Philip, 'who in my opinion, has greater charms, and more than both of them together.' 'You ought to think so, Sir Philip,' returned the new dubbed King, 'however you should not so liberally have expressed yourself, in opposition and derogation to Majesty. Let me tell you it is a saucy boldness that thus has loosed your tongue! What think you, young kinsman and counsellor?' said he to Goodland. 'With all respect due to your sacred title,' returned Valentine, rising and bowing, 'Sir Philip spoke as became a truly affectionate husband; and it had been presumption in him, unpardonable, to have seemed to prefer her Majesty, or that other sweet lady, in his thoughts, since your Majesty has been pleased to say so much and so particularly of their merits. It would appear as if he durst lift up his eyes, with thoughts too near the heaven you only would enjoy.' 'And only can deserve, you should have added,' said King, no longer Would-be. 'How! may it please your Majesty,' cried Friendly, 'both my nieces! though you deserve

ten thousand more, and better, would your Majesty
enjoy them both?' 'Are they then both your nieces?'
asked Chance's King. 'Yes, both, sir,' returned the
Knight, 'her Majesty's the eldest, and in that Fortune
has shown some justice.' 'So she has,' replied the
titular monarch. 'My lot is fair,' pursued he, 'though
I can be blessed but with one.

> Let Majesty with Majesty be joined,
> To get and leave a race of kings behind.

'Come, madam,' continued he, kissing Lucy, 'this, as
an earnest of our future endeavours.' 'I fear,' returned the pretty Queen, 'your Majesty will forget
the unhappy Statira, when you return to the embraces
of your dear and beautiful Roxana.' 'There is none
beautiful but you,' replied the titular King, 'unless
this lady, to whom I yet could pay my vows most
zealously, were it not that fortune has thus pre-
engaged me. But, madam,' continued he, 'to show
that still you hold our royal favour, and that, next to
our royal consort, we esteem you, we greet you thus'
(kissing Philibella), 'and as a signal of our continued
love, wear this rich diamond' (here he put a diamond
ring on her finger, worth three hundred pounds).
'Your Majesty,' pursued he to Lucy, 'may please to
wear this necklace, with this locket of emeralds.'
'Your Majesty is bounteous as a god!' said Valentine.
'Art thou in want, young spark?' asked the King of
Bantam; 'I'll give thee an estate shall make thee
merit the mistress of thy vows, be she who she will.'
'That is my other niece, sir,' cried Friendly. 'How!
how! presumptuous youth! How are thy eyes and
thoughts exalted? ha!' 'To bliss your Majesty must
never hope for,' replied Goodland. 'How now! thou
creature of the basest mould! Not hope for what
thou dost aspire to!' 'Mock-King; thou canst not,
darest not, shalt not hope it,' returned Valentine in
a heat. 'Hold, Val,' cried Sir Philip, 'you grow
warm, forget your duty to their Majesties, and abuse

It was then about the hour that Sir Philip's (and, it may be, other ladies) began to yawn and stretch; when the spirits refreshed, trolled about, and tickled the blood with desires of action; which made Majesty and Worship think of a retreat to bed : where in less than half an hour, or before ever he could say his prayers, I'm sure the first fell fast asleep; but the last, perhaps, paid his accustomed devotion, ere he began his progress to the shadow of death. However, he waked earlier than his cully Majesty, and got up to receive young Goodland, who came according to his word, with the first opportunity. Sir Philip received him with more than usual joy, though not with greater kindness, and let him know every syllable and accident that had passed between them till they went to bed : which you may believe was not a little pleasantly surprising to Valentine, who began then to have some assurance of his happiness with Phili-bella. His friend told him, that he must now be reconciled to his Mock-Majesty, though with some difficulty; and so taking one hearty glass apiece, he left Valentine in the parlour to carry the ungrateful news of his visit to him that morning. King —— was in an odd sort of taking, when he heard that Valentine was below; and had been, as Sir Philip informed Majesty, at Majesty's palace, to inquire for him there. But when he told him, that he had already schooled him on his own behalf for the affront done in his house, and that he believed he could bring his Majesty off without any loss of present honour, his countenance visibly discovered his past fear, and present satisfaction; which was much increased too, when Friendly showing him his bond for the money he won of him at play, let him know, that if he paid three thousand guineas to Philibella, he would im-mediately deliver him up his bond, and not expect the two hundred guineas overplus. His Majesty of Bantam was then in so good a humour, that he could have made love to Sir Philip; nay, I believe he could have kissed Valentine, instead of seeming angry. Down they came, and saluted like gentlemen: but after the greeting was over, Goodland began to talk something of affront, satisfaction, honour, etc., when immediately Friendly interposed, and after a little seeming uneasiness and reluctancy, reconciled the hot and choleric youth to the cold phlegmatic King.

Peace was no sooner proclaimed, than the King of Bantam took his rival and late antagonist with him in his own coach, not excluding Sir Philip by any means, to Locket's, where they dined.   Thence he would have them to Court with him, where the met the Lady Flippant, the Lady Harpy, the Lady Crocodile, Madam Tattlemore, Miss Medler, Mrs. Gingerly, a rich grocer's wife, and some others, besides knights and gentlemen of as good humours as the ladies; all whom he invited to a ball at his own house, the night following; his own lady being then in the country.   Madam Tattlemore, I think, was the first he spoke to in Court, and whom first he surprised with the happy news of his advancement to the title of King of Bantam.   How wondrous hasty was she to be gone, as soon as she heard it!   It was not in her power, because not in her nature, to stay long enough to take a civil leave of the company; but away she flew, big with the empty title of a fantastic King, proclaiming it to every one of her acquaintance, as she passed through every room, till she came to the presence-chamber, where she only whispered it; but her whispers made above half the honourable company quit the presence of the King of Great Britain, to go make their court to his Majesty of Bantam: some cried 'God bless your Majesty!'   Some 'Long live the King of Bantam!'   Others, 'All hail to your Sacred Majesty!'   In short, he was congratulated on all sides.   Indeed I don't hear that his Majesty King Charles II. ever sent an ambassador to compliment him; though possibly, he saluted him by his title the first time he saw him afterwards: for, you know, he is a wonderful good-natured and well-bred gentle-man.

After he thought the Court of England was universally acquainted with his mighty honour, he was pleased to think fit to retire to his own more private palace, with Sir Philip and Goodland, whom he entertained that night very handsomely, till about seven o'clock; when they went together to the play, which was that night, *A King and no King*. His attendant-friends could not forbear smiling, to think how aptly the title of the play suited his circumstances. Nor could he choose but take notice of it behind the scenes, between jest and earnest; telling the players how kind Fortune had been the night past, in disposing the bean to him; and justifying what one of her prophetesses had foretold some years since. 'I shall now no more regard,' said he, 'that old doating fellow Pythagoras's saying, *Abstineto a fabis*, that is,' added he, by way of construction, "Abstain from beans": for I find the excellence of them in cakes and dishes; from the first, they inspire the soul with mighty thoughts; and from the last our bodies receive a strong and wholesome nourishment.' 'That is,' said a wag among those sharp youths, I think it was my friend the Count, 'these puff you up in mind, sir, those in body.' They had some further discourse among the nymphs of the stage, ere they went into the pit; where Sir Philip spread the news of his friend's accession to the title, though not yet to the throne of Bantam; upon which he was there again complimented on that occasion. Several of the ladies and gentlemen who saluted him, he invited to the next night's ball at his palace.

The play done, they took each of them a bottle at the 'Rose,' and parted till seven the night following; which came not sooner than desired: for he had taken such care, that all things were in readiness before eight, only he was not to expect the music till the end of the play. About nine, Sir Philip, his

Lady, Goodland, Philibella, and Lucy came.   Sir
Philip returned him *Rabelais*, which he had borrowed
of him, wherein the Knight had written, in an old
odd sort of a character, this prophecy of his own
making ; with which he surprised the Majesty of
Bantam, who vowed he had never taken notice of it
before ; but he said, he perceived it had been long
written, by the character ; and here it follows, as near
as I can remember :—

> When M. D. C. come L. before,
> Three XXX's, two II's and one I. more ;
> Then K I N G, though now but name to thee,
> Shall both thy name and title be.

They had hardly made an end of reading it, ere
the whole company, and more than he had invited,
came in, and were received with a great deal of
formality and magnificence.   Lucy was there attended
as his Queen; and Philibella, as the Princess her
sister.   They danced then till they were weary ; and
afterwards retired to another large room, where they
found the tables spread and furnished with all the
most seasonable cold meat ; which was succeeded by
the choicest fruits, and the richest dessert of sweetmeats that luxury could think on, or at least that
this town could afford.   The wines were almost
excellent in their kind ; and their spirits flew about
through every corner of the house.   There was scarce
a spark sober in the whole company, with drinking
repeated glasses to the health of the King of Bantam,
and his Royal Consort, with the Princess Philibella's,
who sat together under a royal canopy of state,
his Majesty between the two beautiful sisters : only
Friendly and Goodland wisely managed that part of
the engagement where they were concerned, and preserved themselves from the heat of the debauch.
Between three and four most of them began to
draw off, laden with fruit and sweetmeats, and rich
favours composed of yellow, green, red and white,

the colours of his new Majesty of Bantam. Before
five they were left to themselves; when the Lady
Friendly was discomposed, for want of sleep, and her
usual cordial, which obliged Sir Philip to wait on her
home, with his two nieces. But his Majesty would
by no means part with Goodland; whom, before nine
that morning, he made as drunk as a lord, and by
consequence, one of his peers; for Majesty was then,
indeed, as great as an Emperor. He fancied himself
Alexander, and young Valentine his Hephestion;
and did so be-buss him, that the young gentleman
feared he was fallen into the hands of an Italian.
However, by the kind persuasions of his condescend-
ing and dissembling Majesty, he ventured to go into
bed with him; where King Would-be fell asleep hand-
over-head: and not long after, Goodland, his new-made
peer, followed him to the cool retreats of Morpheus.

About three the next afternoon they both waked,
as by consent, and called to dress. And after that
business was over, I think they swallowed each of
them a pint of old hock, with a little sugar, by the
way of healing. Their coaches were got ready in
the meantime; but the peer was forced to accept of
the honour of being carried in his Majesty's to Sir
Philip's, whom they found just risen from dinner,
with Philadelphia and his two nieces. They sat
down, and asked for something to relish a glass of
wine, and Sir Philip ordered a cold chine to be set
before them, of which they ate about an ounce
apiece; but they drank more by half, I daresay.

After their little repast, Friendly called the Would-
be-Monarch aside, and told him, that he would have
him go to the play that night, which was 'The
London-Cuckolds'; promising to meet him there in
less than half an hour after his departure: telling him
withal, that he would surprise him with a much
better entertainment than the stage afforded. Majesty
took the hint, imagining, and that rightly, that the
Knight had some intrigue in his head, for the promo-

tion of the Commonwealth of Cuckoldom. In order therefore to his advice, he took his leave about a quarter of an hour after.

When he was gone, Sir Philip thus bespoke his pretended niece: 'Madam, I hope your Majesty will not refuse me the honour of waiting on you to a place where you will meet with better entertainment than your Majesty can expect from the best comedy in Christendom. Val,' continued he, 'you must go with us, to secure me against the jealousy of my wife.' 'That, indeed,' returned his lady, 'is very material; and you are mightily concerned not to give me occasion, I must own.' 'You see I am now,' replied he: 'But —— come! on with hoods and scarf!' pursued he, to Lucy. Then addressing himself again to his lady: 'Madam,' said he, 'we'll wait on you.' In less time than I could have drunk a bottle to my share, the coach was got ready, and on they drove to the play-house. 'By the way,' said Friendly to Val, 'your Honour, noble peer, must be set down at Long's; for only Lucy and I must be seen to his Majesty of Bantam. And now, I doubt not, you understand what you must trust to.'—'To be robbed of her Majesty's company, I warrant,' returned the other, 'for these long three hours.' 'Why,' cried Lucy, 'you don't mean, I hope, to leave me with his Majesty of Bantam?' 'It is for thy good, child! It is for thy good,' returned Friendly. To the 'Rose' they got then; where Goodland alighted, and expected Sir Philip; who led Lucy into the King's box, to his new Majesty; where, after the first scene, he left them together. The overjoyed fantastic monarch would fain have said some fine obliging things to the Knight, as he was going out; but Friendly's haste prevented them, who went directly to Valentine, took one glass, called a reckoning, mounted his chariot, and away home they came: where I believe he was welcome to his lady; for I never heard anything to the contrary.

In the meantime, his Majesty had not the patience
to stay out half the play, at which he was saluted by
above twenty gentlemen and ladies by his new and
mighty title: but out he led Miss Majesty ere the
third act was half done; pretending, that it was so
damned a bawdy play, that he knew her modesty had
been already but too much offended at it; so into his
coach he got her. When they were seated, she told
him she would go to no place with him, but to the
lodgings her mother had taken for her, when she first
came to town, and which still she kept. 'Your mother,
madam,' cried he, 'why, is Sir Philip's sister living
then?' 'His brother's widow is, sir,' she replied. 'Is
she there?' he asked. 'No, sir,' she returned; 'she
is in the country.' 'Oh, then we will go thither to
choose.' The coachman was then ordered to drive
to Jermain Street; where, when he came in to the
lodgings, he found them very rich and modishly
furnished. He presently called one of his slaves, and
whispered him to get three or four pretty dishes for
supper; and then getting a pen, ink and paper wrote
a note to C——d the goldsmith with Temple Bar, for
five hundred guineas; which Watchful brought him,
in less than an hour's time, when they were just in the
height of supper; Lucy having invited her landlady,
for the better colour of the matter. His Bantamite
Majesty took the gold from his slave, and threw it by
him in the window, that Lucy might take notice of it
(which you may assure yourself she did, and after
supper winked on the goodly matron of the house to
retire, which she immediately obeyed). Then his
Majesty began his court very earnestly and hotly,
throwing the naked guineas into her lap; which she
seemed to refuse with much disdain; but upon his
repeated promises, confirmed by unheard-of oaths
and imprecations, that he would give her sister three
thousand guineas to her portion, she began by degrees
to mollify, and let the gold lie quietly in her lap.
And the next night, after he had drawn notes on two

2 B

or three of his bankers, for the payment of three thousand guineas to Sir Philip, or order, and received his own bond, made for what he had lost at play, from Friendly, she made no great difficulty to admit his Majesty to her bed. Where I think fit to leave them for the present; for (perhaps) they had some private business.

The next morning before the titular King was (I won't say up, or stirring, but) out of bed, young Goodland and Philibella were privately married; the bills being all accepted and paid in two days' time. As soon as ever the fantastic monarch could find in his heart to divorce himself from the dear and charming embraces of his beautiful bedfellow, he came flying to Sir Philip, with all the haste that imagination big with pleasure could inspire him with, to discharge itself to a supposed friend. The Knight told him, that he was really much troubled to find that his niece had yielded so soon and easily to him; however, he wished him joy: to which the other returned, that he could never want it, whilst he had the command of so much beauty, and that without the ungrateful obligations of matrimony, which certainly are the most nauseous, hateful, pernicious and destructive of love imaginable. 'Think you so, sir?' asked the Knight; 'we shall hear what a friend of mine will say on such an occasion, to-morrow about this time: but I beseech your Majesty to conceal your sentiments of it to him, lest you make him as uneasy as you seem to be in that circumstance.' 'Be assured I will,' returned the other: 'but when shall I see the sweet, the dear, the blooming, the charming Philibella?' 'She will be with us at dinner.' 'Where's her Majesty?' asked Sir Philip. 'Had you inquired before, she had been here; for, look, she comes!' Friendly seems to regard her with a kind of displeasure, and whispered Majesty, that he should express no particular symptoms of familiarity with Lucy in his house, at any time, especially when

Goodland was there, as then he was above with his lady and Philibella, who came down presently after to dinner.

About four o'clock, as his Majesty had intrigued with her, Lucy took a hackney-coach, and went to her lodgings; whither, about an hour after, he followed her. Next morning, at nine, he came to Friendly's, who carried him up to see his new-married friend. But (O damnation to thoughts!) what torments did he feel, when he saw young Goodland and Philibella in bed together; the last of which returned him humble and hearty thanks for her portion and husband, as the first did for his wife. He shook his head at Sir Philip, and without speaking one word, left them, and hurried to Lucy, to lament the ill-treatment he had met with from Friendly. They cooed and billed as long as he was able; she (sweet hypocrite) seeming to bemoan his misfortunes; which he took so kindly, that when he left her, which was about three in the afternoon, he caused a scrivener to draw up an instrument, wherein he settled a hundred pounds a year on Lucy for her life, and gave her a hundred guineas more against her lying-in: (for she told him, and indeed it was true, that she was with child, and knew herself to be so from a very good reason), and indeed she was so by the Friendly Knight. When he returned to her, he threw the obliging instrument into her lap (it seems, he had a particular kindness for that place); then called for wine, and something to eat; for he had not drunk a pint to his share all the day (though he had plied it at the chocolate house). The landlady, who was invited to sup with them, bid them good-night, about eleven: when they went to bed, and partly slept till about six; when they were entertained by some gentlemen of their acquaintance, who played and sang very finely, by way of epithalamium, these words and more:—

> Joy to great Bantam !
> Live long, love and wanton !
> And thy Royal Consort !
> For both are of one sort, etc.

The rest I have forgot. He took some offence at the words; but more at the visit that Sir Philip, and Goodland, made him, about an hour after, who found him in bed with his Royal Consort; and after having wished them joy, and thrown their Majesties' own shoes and stockings at their head, retired. This gave Monarch in Fancy so great a caution, that he took his Royal Consort into the country (but above forty miles off the place where his own lady was), where, in less than eight months, she was delivered of a princely babe, who was christened by the heathenish name of Hayoumorecake Bantam, while her Majesty lay in like a pretty Queen.

THE ADVENTURE OF
THE BLACK LADY

ABOUT the beginning of last June (as near as I can remember) Bellamora came to town from Hampshire, and was obliged to lodge the first night at the same inn where the stage-coach set up. The next day she took coach for Covent Garden, where she thought to find Madam Brightly, a relation of hers, with whom she designed to continue for about half a year un-discovered, if possible, by her friends in the country : and ordered therefore her trunk, with her clothes, and most of her money and jewels, to be brought after her to Madam Brightly's by a strange porter, whom she spoke to in the street as she was taking coach ; being utterly unacquainted with the neat practices of this fine city. When she came to Bridges Street, where indeed her cousin had lodged near three or four years since, she was strangely surprised that she could not learn anything of her ; no, nor so much as meet with any one that had ever heard of her cousin's name. Till, at last, describing Madam Brightly to one of the housekeepers in that place, he told her, that there was such a kind of lady, whom he had sometimes seen there about a year and a half ago ; but that he believed she was married and removed towards Soho. In this perplexity she quite forgot her trunk and money, etc., and wandered in her hackney-coach all over St. Anne's parish ; inquiring for Madam Brightly, still describing her person, but in vain; for no soul could give her any tale or tidings of such a lady. After she had thus fruitlessly rambled, till she, the coachman, and the very horses were even tired, by good fortune for her, she happened on a private house, where lived a good, discreet, ancient gentlewoman, who was fallen to decay, and forced to let lodgings for the best part of her livelihood. From whom she understood, that there was such a kind of lady who had lain there somewhat more than a twelvemonth, being near three months after she was married; but that she was now gone abroad with the gentleman her husband, either to the play, or to take the fresh air; and she believed would not return till night. This discourse of the good gentlewoman's so elevated Bellamora's drooping spirits, that after she had begged the liberty of staying there till they came home, she discharged the coachman in all haste, still forgetting her trunk, and the more valuable furniture of it.

When they were alone, Bellamora desired she might be permitted the freedom to send for a pint of sack; which, with some little difficulty, was at last allowed her. They began then to chat for a matter of half an hour of things indifferent: and at length the ancient gentlewoman asked the fair innocent (I must not say foolish) one, of what country, and what her name was: to both which she answered directly and truly, though it might have proved not discreetly. She then inquired of Bellamora if her parents were living, and the occasion of her coming to town. The fair unthinking creature replied, that her father and mother were both dead; and that she had escaped from her uncle, under the pretence of making a visit to a young lady, her cousin, who was lately married, and lived above twenty miles from her uncle's, in the road to London, and that the cause of her quitting the country, was to avoid the hated importunities of a gentleman, whose pretended love to her she feared had been her eternal ruin. At which she wept and sighed most extravagantly. The discreet gentle-woman endeavoured to comfort her by all the softest and most powerful arguments in her capacity; promising her all the friendly assistance that she could expect from her, during Bellamora's stay in town: which she did with so much earnestness, and visible integrity, that the pretty innocent creature was going to make her a full and real discovery of her imaginary insupportable misfortunes; and (doubtless) had done it, had she not been prevented by the return of the lady, whom she hoped to have found her Cousin Brightly. The gentleman her husband just saw her within doors, and ordered the coach to drive to some of his bottle-companions; which gave the women the better opportunity of entertaining one another, which happened to be with some surprise on all sides. As the lady was going up into her apart-ment, the gentlewoman of the house told her there was a young lady in the parlour, who came out of the country that very day on purpose to visit her. The lady stepped immediately to see who it was, and Bella-mora approaching to receive her hoped-for cousin, stopped on the sudden just as she came to her; and sighed out aloud, 'Ah, madam! I am lost; it is not your ladyship I seek.' 'No, madam,' returned the other, 'I am apt to think you did not intend me this honour. But you are as welcome to me, as you could be to the dearest of your acquaintance: have you for-gotten me, Madam Bellamora?' continued she. That name startled the other: however, it was with a kind of joy. 'Alas! madam,' replied the young one, 'I now remember that I have been so happy to have seen you; but where and when, my memory cannot tell me.' 'It is indeed some years since,' returned the lady, 'but of that another time. Meanwhile, if you are unprovided of a lodging, I dare undertake, you shall be welcome to this gentlewoman.' The un-fortunate returned her thanks; and whilst a chamber was preparing for her, the lady entertained her in her

own. About ten o'clock they parted, Bellamora being
conducted to her lodging by the mistress of the house,
who then left her to take what rest she could amidst
her so many misfortunes; returning to the other lady,
who desired her to search into the cause of Bellamora's retreat to town.

The next morning the good gentlewoman of the
house coming up to her, found Bellamora almost
drowned in tears, which by many kind and sweet
words she at last stopped; and asking whence so
great signs of sorrow should proceed, vowed a most
profound secrecy if she would discover to her their
occasion; which, after some little reluctancy, she did,
in this manner.

'I was courted,' said she, 'above three years ago,
when my mother was yet living, by one Mr. Fondlove,
a gentleman of good estate, and true worth; and one
who, I dare believe, did then really love me. He
continued his passion for me, with all the earnest and
honest solicitations imaginable, till some months before my mother's death; who, at that time, was most
desirous to see me disposed of in marriage to another
gentleman, of much better estate than Mr. Fondlove;
but one whose person and humour did by no means
hit with my inclinations. And this gave Fondlove
the unhappy advantage over me. For, finding me
one day all alone in my chamber, and lying on my
bed, in as mournful and wretched a condition to my
then foolish apprehension, as now I am, he urged his
passion with such violence, and accursed success for
me, with reiterated promises of marriage, whensoever
I pleased to challenge them, which he bound with the
most sacred oaths, and most dreadful execrations:
that partly with my aversion to the other, and partly
with my inclinations to pity him, I ruined myself.'
Here she relapsed into a greater extravagance of grief
than before; which was so extreme that it did not
continue long. When therefore she was pretty well
come to herself, the ancient gentlewoman asked her,

why she imagined herself ruined. To which she answered, 'I am great with child by him, madam, and wonder you did not perceive it last night. Alas! I have not a month to go: I am ashamed, ruined, and damned, I fear, for ever lost.' 'Oh! fie, madam, think not so,' said the other, 'for the gentleman may yet prove true, and marry you.' 'Ay, madam,' replied Bellamora, 'I doubt not that he would marry me; for soon after my mother's death, when I came to be at my own disposal, which happened about two months after, he offered, nay most earnestly solicited me to it, which still he perseveres to do.' 'This is strange!' returned the other, 'and it appears to me to be your own fault, that you are yet miserable. Why did you not, or why will you not consent to your own happiness?' 'Alas!' cried Bellamora, 'it is the only thing I dread in this world: for, I am certain, he can never love me after. Besides, ever since I have abhorred the sight of him: and this is the only cause that obliges me to forsake my uncle, and all my friends and relations in the country, hoping in this populous and public place to be most private, especially, madam, in your house, and in your fidelity and discretion.' 'Of the last you may assure yourself, madam,' said the other: 'but what provision have you made for the reception of the young stranger that you carry about you?' 'Ah, madam!' cried Bellamora, 'you have brought to my mind another misfortune.' Then she acquainted her with the supposed loss of her money and jewels, telling her withal, that she had but three guineas and some silver left, and the rings she wore, in her present possession. The good gentlewoman of the house told her, she would send to inquire at the inn where she lay the first night she came to town; for haply, they might give some account of the porter to whom she had entrusted her trunk; and withal repeated her promise of all the help in her power, and for that time left her much more composed than she found her. The good

gentlewoman went directly to the other lady, her
lodger, to whom she recounted Bellamora's mournful
confession; at which the lady appeared mightily
concerned: and at last she told her landlady, that she
would take care that Bellamora should lie in according to her quality: 'for,' added she, 'the child, it
seems, is my own brother's.'

As soon as she had dined, she went to the Exchange, and bought child-bed linen; but desired that
Bellamora might not have the least notice of it. And
at her return despatched a letter to her brother Fondlove in Hampshire, with an account of every particular;
which soon brought him up to town, without satisfying
any of his or her friends with the reason of his sudden
departure. Meanwhile, the good gentlewoman of the
house had sent to the Star Inn on Fish Street Hill,
to demand the trunk, which she rightly supposed to
have been carried back thither: for by good luck, it
was a fellow that plied thereabouts, who brought it to
Bellamora's lodgings that very night, but unknown
to her. Fondlove no sooner got to London, but he
posts to his sister's lodgings, where he was advised
not to be seen of Bellamora till they had worked
farther upon her, which the landlady began in this
manner. She told her that her things were mis-
carried, and she feared lost; that she had but a little
money herself, and if the Overseers of the Poor
(justly so called from their overlooking them) should
have the least suspicion of a strange and unmarried
person, who was entertained in her house big with
child, and so near her time as Bellamora was, she
should be troubled, if they could not give security to
the parish of twenty or thirty pounds, that they
should not suffer by her, which she could not; or
otherwise she must be sent to the house of correction,
and her child to a parish nurse. This discourse, one
may imagine, was very dreadful to a person of her
youth, beauty, education, family and estate: however,
she resolutely protested, that she had rather undergo

all this, than be exposed to the scorn of her friends and relations in the country. The other told her then, that she must write down to her uncle a farewell letter, as if she were just going aboard the packet-boat for Holland, that he might not send to inquire for her in town, when he should understand she was not at her new-married cousin's in the country; which accordingly she did, keeping herself close prisoner to her chamber; where she was daily visited by Fond-love's sister and the landlady, but by no soul else, the first dissembling the knowledge she had of her mis-fortunes. Thus she continued for above three weeks, not a servant being suffered to enter her chamber, so much as to make her bed, lest they should take notice of her great belly: but for all this caution, the secret had taken wind, by the means of an attendant of the other lady below, who had overheard her speaking of it to her husband. This soon got out of doors, and spread abroad, till it reached the long ears of the wolves of the parish, who next day designed to pay her a visit. But Fondlove, by good providence, pre-vented it; who, the night before, was ushered into Bellamora's chamber by his sister, his brother-in-law, and the landlady. At the sight of him she had like to have swooned away: but he taking her in his arms, began again, as he was wont to do, with tears in his eyes, to beg that she would marry him ere she was delivered; if not for his, nor her own, yet for the child's sake, which she hourly expected; that it might not be born out of wedlock, and so be made incapable of inheriting either of their estates; with a great many more pressing arguments on all sides. To which at last she consented; and an honest officious gentleman, whom they had before provided, was called up, who made an end of the dispute. So to bed they went together that night; next day to the Exchange, for several pretty businesses that ladies in her con-dition want. Whilst they were abroad, came the vermin of the parish (I mean the Overseers of the

Poor, who eat the bread from them), to search for a young black-haired lady (for so was Bellamora) who was either brought to bed, or just ready to lie down. The landlady showed them all the rooms in the house, but no such lady could be found. At last she bethought herself, and led them into her parlour, where she opened a little closet door, and showed them a black cat that had just kittened: assuring them, that she should never trouble the parish as long as she had rats or mice in the house; and so dismissed them like loggerheads as they came.

FINIS